MOTHER — *of* — DEATH & DAWN

THE WAR OF LOST HEARTS: VOL. III

CARISSA BROADBENT

For you.
I did this last time, but I cannot imagine dedicating this book to anyone else. Thank you for following Tisaanah and Max on their journeys, and for giving me the ability to take this journey of my own.

PROLOGUE

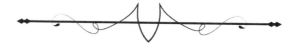

Tell me, little butterfly, what would you do for love?

The woman knows the tower, now.

She knows every angle of its imposing shape as it rises from the surf. She knows the way the whorls carved into its surface feel beneath her palms. She knows how the bone-white stone looks smeared with her blood. She knows its scent, acrid and stagnant, like death itself.

She knows everything, except for how to break it.

This place has taken something from her, you see. Taken the most precious thing.

Tell me, little butterfly, what would you do to get him back?

Anything. Everything.

The first time she tries, it is an act of pure desperation. She has conquered cities and defeated armies. She has ended wars. Surely she is powerful enough to do this.

Now she does not need to conquer a city, just a single prison.

She does not need to free a civilization. Just one person.

The stone strikes her down like a palm to a fly. Minutes, and she is crashing back into the surf, pulled out again by friends who barely manage to escape with their lives.

But the woman knows nothing if not how to fail.

So she tries again, again, again. She collects another scar, another night of an aching heart, and a little more of her dies. She gets up and goes again.

The last night is stormy and dark—the sort of night yanked from horror stories. Her friends beg her not to go. *Wait one more day*, they say. *If the guards don't kill you then the storm will.*

What's one more day, they say, *after all of this?*

What's one more day? She would have laughed if she wasn't choking back sheer rage. One more day is twenty-four hours— one thousand four hundred and forty minutes—eighty-six thousand seconds of torture for the man trapped within those walls.

The storm is a monster. It is so dark she can barely see, the white tower of Ilyzath lit only in garish blue-white flashes as lightning cracks the night. Rain shreds the air like silver blades. As always, she makes it to the prison. And as always—faster than they once did—the eyeless guards are upon her in seconds.

She fights back. But there are many of them, and only one of her. Her head smashes against the ground.

CRACK.

The sky splits open, just as her skin does, just as her heart does.

She rises to her feet. Blood is in her eyes, staining the world crimson.

And there, in that moment of desperation, she feels a sliver of the magic that had so evaded her for these last weeks—a flicker of a familiar soul, contorted in pain and buried within layers of stone.

He is so, so close.

It cuts something primal loose in her.

The next time a blade opens her flesh, she doesn't feel it. She fights back like an animal. These are not people before her—they are obstacles. Obstacles keeping her away from her most precious person, obstacles who dared deny her broken heart every time she came here, fighting for the queen that had put a dagger in her back.

She becomes nothing but the desire to burn down the world that did this to him.

CRACK.

Lightning illuminates flashes of blood, of opened bodies, of rotting flesh. Flashes of her own seeping wounds.

She fights and fights and fights as tears stream down her cheeks.

Tell me, little butterfly, what would you do for love?

PART ONE:
LOST

CHAPTER ONE

TISAANAH

He liked me.

But then, of course he did. I anticipated his every need, every discomfort, every desire. I never stopped listening. Never stopped watching. When I danced, I counted every footfall.

Months had passed and my magic remained, for the most part, painfully out of reach. Once, I had easily drawn from its deepest levels, making me a force of nature. Now, ever since the collapse at the Scar, I struggled to even use it at all. But I had learned that I didn't need it to be the perfect slave. I had gotten so good at being exactly what men wanted me to be.

Lord Farimov smiled at me. It would have been a pleasant smile in any other context. He was not an unattractive man, with grey-streaked, sandy hair and a warm face. Perhaps if I was someone else—a different "someone else" than the someone I pretended to be now—I might have thought he was kind.

But I was not another someone. I was a slave. And Farimov perhaps seemed kind, but it was the sort of kindness that one bestowed upon a sweet dog. Even the kindest people corrected undesirable behavior in dogs. I never needed to be corrected, and that was why his smile was so pleasant as I placed the plate of berries at the table.

"Good, Roza," he said.

Roza. My name, as it had been for the last two weeks. I gave him a demure nod as I straightened, pushing a sheet of smooth chestnut hair behind my ear. I caught a glimpse of myself in the mirror in the movement.

The face that stared back at me was unfamiliar, though if I looked closely, I could find traces of the one I had worn my entire life. No Fragmented skin, just smooth sandy tan. No silver hair, just deep chestnut. No scars. A slightly wider mouth, narrower nose, softer brow. Me, but... not. The only thing that remained was the eyes. One silver, one green. Eyes, Ishqa had said, were impossible to hide with any illusion, even with the advanced Fey potions he had taken from Ela'Dar.

But no illusion was perfect, and no illusion could last forever. I had been wearing this one for too long. Every time I looked at myself, I half expected to see my own Fragmented skin.

I was supposed to be out of here days ago. But each time the Fey's visit to their Threllian allies was delayed, I thought to myself, *I've stayed too long to give up now.* I decided that the illusion would just need to hold up a little bit longer.

I had spent weeks here, monitoring the rhythm of the household, waiting for this meeting.

Farimov frowned down at the berries. The feast was something to behold—flowers and fruits and meats and cheeses. Maids flurried about the room, adjusting each detail of the display.

"Do you think that Fey even like fruit?" he mused, to no one in particular. "I heard once that they only eat living flesh. Perhaps I should have gotten something... alive."

I imagined Ishqa chomping down on live creatures and almost laughed. *Ishqa,* who barely managed to hide his disgust at the very thought of eating something that had once been moving.

"How could they not be impressed?" I said. "It is magnificent. And so clever, to showcase the best of every region of the

Threllian empire. A brilliant idea, and a feast worthy of royalty, my Lord."

Farimov puffed slightly with pride. He liked that I noticed what he had done with the menu. Impossible not to. *"The best of every region of the Threllian empire"* really meant *"the best of all Threll has stolen from the nations they conquered."* Nyzrenese blood apricots were right there in the middle of the table, next to a vase of Deralin cerulean blue blossoms.

My gaze lingered on the flowers a little too long. An unwelcome image flashed through my mind—Max holding those very flowers as the two of us sat alone at night in the Threllian plains. The night I kissed him for the first time. The night I let myself fall.

And now he was—

"My Lord." A nervous-looking maid appeared at the door. "The Fey emissaries have arrived."

———————

I HADN'T SEEN these Fey before. After months of war, one might think that I would have encountered more of them, but the Threllians and their slaves were far more common foes than the Fey. The two women were strangely, ethereally beautiful—as the Fey, I'd learned, usually were. One had dark hair that seemed to flash blue when the light hit it the right way, blunt to her shoulders. The other was taller, with sleek blond hair that reached her waist, sharp cheekbones, and a piercing stare of gold that triggered a wave of recognition.

Sometimes, I almost found it amusing to watch the dynamics between the Threllians and the Fey. The Threllian Lords were just so desperate to be seen as powerful—they loved the fact that the Fey came out of hundreds of years of hiding only to immediately propose an alliance. What was better validation of their egos than a race of near-immortals choosing them as their sole human partners? So foolish. Ishqa had told me plenty about the Fey king and his desire to destroy humanity. Sooner or later, once the Threllians outlived their usefulness to him, they would meet an end, too. But in the meantime, the Threllians would provide the scale and numbers that the Fey lacked, and they would stumble and blush over their Fey allies.

Farimov smiled and began to launch into a flowery greeting, but the blond Fey cut him off.

"This is my second, Nessiath Vareid." She gestured to her dark-haired companion, then bowed her own head. "I am General Iajqa Sai'Ess. King Caduan has sent us. Forgive us if we have little time for pleasantries."

Sai'Ess.

I kept my expression very still as I poured iced teas at the table.

No wonder she looked so familiar — she was a relative of Ishqa's. A sister? A cousin?

Another couple followed them into the room — a tall man with sharp dark eyes and fair hair neatly slicked back, and a petite woman with enormous blue eyes and golden curls who looked like she could be a porcelain doll. They wore fine silk clothes. All white, of course. One glance told me they were Threllian power.

Farimov's smile faded, eyes widening.

"Lord and Lady Zorokov. What a... surprise."

I nearly dropped the pitcher. I was not prepared for the unwelcome deluge of memories.

The smell of rotting flesh. The sight of a box of severed hands at my doorstep. The sound of the death screams the monster bearing it had given me.

The Zorokov family, the monster had whispered, *does not like being lied to.*

The Zorokovs had murdered hundreds of slaves. And all because of me.

I righted the pitcher quickly, my knuckles so tight around the handle that they were white. No one noticed my fumble except for Lady Zorokov, whose doe-like stare fell to me.

"Goodness. Are you alright?"

If I didn't know better, I might mistake that for genuine concern.

"Yes, my lady," I murmured. "My greatest apologies."

She cocked her head and smiled.

"Oh, look at that. You do have the most beautiful eyes, don't you?"

I lowered my gaze immediately. "Thank you, my lady."

There were no fewer than eight freshly sharpened dinner knives at the table right now. My fingers itched for them. Seconds, and I could kill them both. I didn't even need my magic to do it.

"A welcome surprise, of course." Lord Farimov was in the process of quickly correcting his less-than-overjoyed reaction. "It is always a pleasure to receive a visit from you."

"A discovery like this deserves to be seen firsthand," Lord Zorokov said.

Farimov put his shock away for good and grinned. "Wonderful. There is more than enough food! Come, sit, eat, and we shall—"

"We have no time for such comforts, I fear," Iajqa said. "King Caduan is quite impatient. Given the acceleration of Aran aggression, you must understand that time is of the essence."

"But what a shame to—"

"Our *deepest* apologies, Lord Farimov," the dark-haired Fey—Nessiath—said, not looking particularly apologetic at all.

Farimov sighed, failing to hide his disappointment. "Very well. Of course I understand." He gestured to one of the slaves, who crossed the room and returned with a polished mahogany box with a gold latch. It was modestly sized, smaller in length and width than the dinner plate Farimov moved aside to place it on the table. The carvings on its surface had been partially eaten by time, despite its obvious, careful restoration.

Utter silence. The breath seemed to have left everyone in the room at once.

"This is it?" Iajqa said, quietly.

"It is. My collections of artifacts are quite extensive, you see. It took months of searching to locate this. But alas…"

He unclasped the box and opened it.

There, in a bed of black silk, sat a glass orb. Mist swirled within it like storm clouds, subtle and yet eerily unsettling. The hairs stood on the back of my neck, a strange sensation nagging deep inside of me. It was the sort of gut feeling I hadn't gotten in months—not since my magic eluded me after the Aran war.

"So this is the thing that King Caduan lays so many hopes upon," Lord Zorokov murmured, transfixed.

Iajqa said nothing. She reached out to touch the orb, and sparks and clouds collected under the glass beneath her fingertips.

I tried not to let my interest show, turning away as I swallowed my uncertainty. This thing did not look like a weapon. A magical curiosity, perhaps, but not a weapon.

The two Fey exchanged an unimpressed glance that seemed to betray the same thought.

"I—I have others, too," Farimov said, sensing their disappointment. "Many other artifacts. Some of the greatest treasures in all of Threll! Perhaps they, too, are of value to your king?"

And at this moment, I felt a telltale burning at my fingertips.

A pit of dread grew in my stomach. I casually glanced down to see a flicker at the tips of my fingers. Smooth skin and my Fragmented Valtain skin shuddered alternately in and out of view.

Shit. *Shit*. Not now. It was the worst possible timing for the illusion to start falling away. Hands would be easy enough to hide, but I had maybe half an hour before the disguise disintegrated completely—less than that before it became obvious that something was not right about my appearance.

I clasped my hands behind my back and donned my most charming voice.

"Lord Farimov owns the rarest collection of artifacts in Threll," I said. "Many were even recovered from the same tombs as this one."

Farimov beamed. He was so, so eager to show off his trea-
sure that his pride outweighed any displeasure at a slave
speaking out of turn. And just as I knew it would, this statement
caught the Feys' attention.

"Very well," Iajqa said. "We shall see them."

"A gift to you," Farimov said, leading them out the door.
"Anything you please."

The minute the footsteps softened down the hall, I crossed
the room and opened the box.

The other slave—Melina, I thought her name was—lurched
forward, eyes wide. "But—"

"Sh." I gave her a look, sharp enough to make her mouth
snap closed, and opened the box.

Our spies had heard so many stories about this—this artifact
that Caduan Iero, the mad Fey king, was so desperate for. We
didn't know what it was or what it did. Even the Fey's Threllian
allies, it seemed, did not know that. But the fact alone that it
was so desperately sought after was enough to make Ishqa
adamant that it could not fall into the hands of the Fey or the
Threllians.

Whatever it was, we had theorized, I might be able to make
use of it, given my connection to the deep magics that Caduan
manipulated. A stretch, considering that over these last months I
could barely use any magic at all.

And this, selfishly, was my only thought as I looked down at
this magical trinket.

I had dreamed of something powerful enough to break down
the walls of an ancient prison and tear down one of the greatest
militaries in the world. I had dreamed of something powerful
enough to bring the one most important person in the universe
back to me.

This glass orb did not look like such a thing.

"Roza..." Melina whispered, nervously. I ignored her as I
reached out to touch the sphere—

The next thing I knew, my back slammed against the floor.
My breath hit me like a stone crashing down on my chest. And

my skin was *burning, burning, burning,* so intensely that I had to bite down hard to keep from letting out a cry.

My skin. My *hand.*

"Roza!" Melina fell to her knees beside me.

Long seconds, and the pain subsided to a tolerable throb. I forced my eyes open and bit back a gasp.

Gold covered my fingertips, reaching down over my palm in organic shapes that looked like the veins of a leaf. The strokes were slightly raised, and my skin clung to the edges, irritated where the gold met my flesh.

This wasn't *on* me. This was *in* me.

I lifted my eyes to the box on the table. It was now empty.

Oh, gods.

I looked at the gold spreading across my palm with renewed horror. This thing—this *was* the artifact.

Melina made a strangled sound of panic and suddenly pulled away from me.

It took me a moment to realize why. I had been so preoccupied with the gold that I hadn't realized what it was covering: my skin. My normal, *Fragmented* skin. The illusion was gone.

Melina turned to the door, presumably to get help. I moved faster. I leapt to my feet, grabbed her, and pressed my hand to her mouth.

"Don't move," I hissed. "I am one of you."

Her back was against me, my arm firmly around her shoulders to keep her from moving. I could not see her face, but I felt her trembling.

"I am Tisaanah Vytezic," I whispered. "Do you know that name?"

A pause. Then a small nod.

"I need you to tell me how we can get out of here, Melina. Fast. Quietly."

She jumped a little. I knew why—the "we."

That one word made life much more difficult, especially since I barely knew this girl. But I couldn't leave her alone here to face the consequences of my escape.

Slowly, I removed my hand from her mouth, though I didn't release her just yet—just in case.

"We can't," she whispered. "There's too many people here now, in the middle of the day."

"There has to be something."

"Can't you just… use magic?"

I almost laughed. I knew what she was thinking: *This girl has ended wars, and she can't get herself out of this stupid house?*

I spent a lot of time lately thinking about my magic and all the things it couldn't do.

"No," I said. "Not here. There are too many wards."

Farimov's estate, like those of many of the Threllian Lords, had been protected with many, many Stratagram wards since the beginning of the war—protection against magic wielding rebel slaves like myself, and against Nura's armies.

I tried not to think about the fact that if I still had Reshaye, I could tear through those wards easily. If I still harbored a connection to deep magic…

I shook the thought away. Unhelpful.

I reached into my pocket and folded my fingers around the gold feather there. Ishqa was not prepared for me now. Under the original plan, I was to call for him at night, when I could make it past the strongest of the wards, and he would fly me out of the estate. This escape would be much more difficult now, in the middle of the day.

Still, he was our best chance of making it out of here alive.

I pulled out the feather and dipped it into the candle flame. Ishqa would feel its call, but I had no idea where he was right now, or even if he would be able to get to us in time.

"The servants' tunnels," I said. "Will they get us out of the house?"

"They aren't really tunnels. More like… a basement. And they don't go as far as the estate walls."

"They just need to take us outside."

The feather was now a dusting of ash, which I hastily brushed under the table runner.

Weapon. I needed a weapon. A decorative saber hung on the wall, which I yanked free as quietly as I could. It was a gaudy thing, the hilt covered in impractical rubies. The blade was dull. It was clearly never intended to be used for actual combat, but if I stabbed someone with it hard enough, it would do some damage.

"Let's go." I was already at the door before I realized that Melina was not with me. I turned to see her standing still, eyes wide, lips parted but releasing no words.

She looked so utterly terrified. Is that how I had looked, I wondered, when Serel put me on that horse and told me to go find a new life?

I never would have said it aloud, but back then, I had been so frightened of leaving everything I had ever known. I dealt with it by drowning myself in my obsession with the future I swore I'd create. But...

Uninvited, the memory settled over me. The snap of a fire in cool night air. A familiar scent of ash and lilac. A little sarcastic laugh. A smile that started on the left side first.

Home. I had never thought I would find a home.

Even if it had been a temporary one.

My chest ached, and my stance softened. I returned to Melina, taking her hand in a firm, comforting grasp.

"There are lots of people like you," I said, quietly. "Like us. If we make it out of here today, you'll be amazed at what freedom can be."

She gave me a weak smile and swallowed hard.

"This way."

CHAPTER TWO

MAX

It's not all that hard to keep yourself sane, so long as you're flexible with your definition of the term.

It's just a matter of finding one solid thing—one constant. Numbers were perfect in theory, at least in the beginning. Three always came after two always came after one. It never changed. And yet, when you have nothing in your life but those numbers, it's so easy for them to unravel before you. Does three *really* come after two? Does one thousand seven hundred and six *actually* follow one thousand seven hundred and five?

This was the problem with the numbers. They were too intangible. That was why, I think, I started with the drawing.

I say *the drawing* because there was only one. Three shapes, always in the same arrangement. And I say *"I think"* because I couldn't recall when I started drawing them, or why. Only that it was the only thing my hands felt right doing.

Maybe the shapes meant something in a dream, once. Maybe they meant something in a memory. Both were equally hazy, now.

Now, I lay on my stomach, left hand flat against the cold ivory stone of the floor. Everything in here was the same—ivory floor, walls, ceilings. Ilyzath was a dead place. Everything was empty. The air was eerily silent, Ilyzath's magic choking back every sound. The walls were bare save for the carvings etched into them—no windows, not even a door. When people did come here, the opening simply stepped out of the stone, and it was gone again as soon as they were.

The white was torturous, so bright and dark at once that it seemed to burn my eyes, but it was preferable to the alternative.

My other hand clutched a little piece of metal, just sharp enough to etch into the stone. I knew Ilyzath well enough by now to know that the moment I took my eyes away from this drawing, it would be gone when I looked at this spot next. Ilyzath had a way of erasing any mark its prisoners tried to make on the world.

Maybe it was my petty act of defiance, then.

The drawing was the same every time. A cluster of three shapes, always in the same arrangement—one lopsided circle to the left, another slightly lower to its right, and a third, longer shape beneath the first, the three of them together forming a triangular formation of patches.

In the beginning, I would wonder what they were. Now I figured it didn't even matter.

The air shifted, and I froze.

I knew this feeling by now. A pit formed in my stomach and I dutifully ignored it, my eyes trained on the markings I etched into the floor, even as the room darkened.

I would not look.

I would not *fucking* look.

Sweat prickled at the back of my neck. A red cast suffused the room. The snap of flames grew unnaturally loud.

"Max."

I knew that voice. I knew it even though, still, I didn't understand who it belonged to. And yet, the sound of it still made my eyes snap up, no matter how many times I told them not to.

The sight of her was just as horrifying as it always was.

The girl was perhaps eleven or twelve. She had long, sleek

18

black hair and a demeanor that seemed so familiar in more ways than one. Also, most notably, she was on fire.

Sometimes, she was weeping as she crawled across the ground to me. Sometimes, she was furious, trying to strike me. Today, she just stood there, almost serene, as chunks of flesh melted off her face.

She looked sad.

"Why did you do this to me?" she asked. "Why would you of all people do this to me? Those were my last thoughts, you know. It hurt worse than any of this."

She gestured, weakly, to her burning body.

And there was something there, just for a moment, some shard of a memory that kicked me in the gut. Gone before I could wrap my fingers around it.

Or maybe… maybe I stopped myself before I let myself remember.

I looked away.

"You're not real," I muttered.

"Yes, I am."

"Nothing in this place is real. You're just another nightmare."

The stench of burning flesh now seared my nostrils. I forced my eyes back to the ground. As I suspected, the marks I had etched into it minutes ago were now gone.

Oh well.

I started again—always, the same three shapes, again, again, again.

Still, out of the corner of my eye, I could see the markings on Ilyzath's walls shifting, as if all to orient themselves towards me.

Ah, you think this is a nightmare?

It wasn't quite a voice. Ilyzath spoke in a million blended inconsequential sounds, creaks and wind and groans of stone bleeding into something like words.

I didn't answer. Sure, I'd talk to my hallucinations, but I generally tried not to speak to the prison itself. A man had to draw a line somewhere.

What makes you think, Maxantarius, that nightmares are not real? Perhaps it is all real, and that is the greatest nightmare of all.

My jaw tightened, and my hand paused its familiar path. I wouldn't admit it — not even silently to myself — but that thought struck a nerve.

There was, after all, so much I didn't know about my own past.

The time before I came to Ilyzath was a blur, like a hundred colors of paint all running together in the same soupy sewer water. Every so often I'd grasp glimpses of images, memories, sensations — sometimes the smell of flowers and a certain shade of green were seared into my head, vivid enough to almost lead me to the memories they kept, always just out of reach. Sometimes they were darker, ash and moans and the feel of my hands around blood-slicked, unforgiving metal. Burning and burning and burning.

I squeezed my eyes shut.

Only a nightmare, Max. Pull yourself together.

The burning girl was still standing there.

I would not look.

"Max —" she said again, but then the sound of grinding stone cut her short.

All at once, the shadows and the glow of the fire disappeared. I looked up to see that a door had opened in my cell, two eyeless, black-clad soldiers standing there, spears in hand.

"Get up," the blond one said. "The Queen needs to see you again."

I was already rising to my feet. Honestly, I'd take the Queen's torture over Ilyzath's any day.

And today, at least, I had a plan.

***

THINGS HAD GOTTEN WORSE.

Ara was at war. When I was in Ilyzath, I understood this only distantly — nothing penetrated Ilyzath's walls, and that, I supposed, included horrific warfare. But every time the Queen had me brought to the mainland, its marks were visible everywhere.

This time, it was worse than I'd ever seen it. The Syrizen and I walked down cobblestone paths. The Palace loomed to the left, silent and mournful. Two of its knifelike peaks had been snapped off since the last time I was here. Ahead, the Towers loomed. The upper windows of the silver one had all shattered, leaving a fragile-looking silver skeleton to be devoured by the clouds.

Around us, groups of exhausted soldiers gathered in clusters. I slowed my steps, watching them. One of the groups parted just enough for me to see between them—at the monstrous carcass seeping blood on the ground.

Ascended above.

The sight of the thing, even lifeless, made a shiver pass over me. It was perhaps two or three times the size of the soldiers that surrounded it, its form comprised of darkness and too-long limbs. I stared at it, but the boundaries of its shape never quite came into focus, like my mind couldn't decide where it ended and its shadow began.

I've seen that thing before.

The thought popped into my mind without warning. Like most of my thoughts these days, it was unhelpful.

One of the soldiers looked up and met my stare. His eyes went wide before he turned to mutter frantically to his companions.

A sharp nudge jolted me from my thoughts. I nearly stumbled. My ankles were bound, just loosely enough to allow me to walk. My wrists, too tight to let them move at all.

"Let's get this over with, Max," the blond Syrizen, who gripped my right arm, muttered. "No time to linger."

"How many were there?" I asked. "Those creatures. There must have been many of them. More than this." I nodded to the field, where the soldiers gathered around the carcasses. "Sent by the Fey, right? How far did they get? Did they make it to the top of the Towers?"

The guard didn't answer, but her lips pressed together in a way that confirmed my suspicions.

"And that was what," I went on, "a few hours ago, by the looks of things?"

Again, no answer.

I didn't need one. I knew I was right.

Less than a full day after some of the worst attacks yet, and the Queen was pulling me out. She was doing it now, in daylight —rare that happened, and only recently. At first, it had just been a few scattered outings, always at night, always when there weren't many people around. I hadn't figured out why. Only now did that piece click into place, as I watched the soldiers around us all look up to stare at me.

These people knew who I was. Not that I had a clue why.

And for whatever reason, the Queen would prefer that they didn't think about me. Again, not that I had a clue why.

You killed hundreds of innocent people, a voice whispered in the back of my mind. *Isn't that reason enough for infamy?*

An expression I couldn't read passed over the guard's face. "Here's hoping that the Queen is right and you're our damned savior," she muttered, pushing me forward. "Let's go."

CHAPTER THREE

TISAANAH

Melina was right. These weren't exactly tunnels, just hallways that happened to be underground, and they were far from private. We passed too many other people to make me comfortable as we hurried down hall after hall together. Most were other slaves, which was our only saving grace. Perhaps some recognized me—I was, after all, unusual looking—but thankfully, no one stopped us. The further away we moved from the heart of the estate, the quieter the halls grew.

We stopped when we came to a juncture. "That way goes out to the stables," Melina said, then pointed in the other direction. "And that one goes to the fields."

"Which is farthest from the main house?"

She paused. "Probably—"

My heart stopped.

"Sh."

She gave me a curious look, but I grabbed her arm and pulled both of us against the wall. "*Sh*," I said again.

There it was—quiet, but if I strained my ears I could hear the voices above.

"...have gone too far... still can catch them... I've ordered every guard in the house—yes, *every* guard, I assure you..."

I resisted the urge to hiss a curse.

Melina's eyes shot to me, wide with terror. "Do you have any idea how many guards are in this place? They'll know we went here—"

"We don't have time to be scared," I said, firmly. "Only to act. Which way, Melina?"

Her eyes darted between the two halls, then she pointed. "To the fields."

We flew.

The glances we had earned from those we passed now turned to outright stares. I kept my hand firmly around Melina's wrist, urging her forward even when fear began to falter her steps.

"Focus," I murmured to her. "We are so close—"

We rounded a corner, and she stopped short, sending both of us stumbling.

Ahead of us was a short staircase and a door with sunlight spilling beneath it. Standing before it was a young man in a guard's uniform. He looked to be about Melina's age, perhaps in his late teens. Tousled dark hair fell over his forehead, low enough to frame the surprise in his eyes when he saw us.

"*Melina?*"

"Markus!"

Melina had gone completely still. Both of the names came in little breaths that carried too many shades to count.

A knot of unease formed in my stomach as I watched the two of them—watched the way they looked at each other. Like teenagers in love.

Gods, was there anything more unpredictably dangerous than teenagers in love?

Markus stood between us and freedom. He frowned. My stare fell to his hand, which rested at the hilt of his sword.

"You're the one they're looking for?" His gaze flicked to me, and something shifted in it.

"We need to get out, Markus," Melina said, her voice small. "You can come with us, you can…"

"Get out?" His brow knotted.

I was getting a terrible feeling about this.

"Come with us." She took a step forward, hand slightly outstretched. "You can come. They'll never find you. They'll never know."

I saw it, in that moment, in the nearly invisible hardening of the muscles around his eyes. He would never do it.

Because this young man was not a slave. He was a hired guard, paid, albeit meagerly, for his services. Perhaps he liked Melina. Perhaps he even loved her, or thought he did.

But the minute Melina used the word "we," used it to make him one of us, he was gone.

She kept walking forward. "Markus, please…"

The moment she touched him, he grabbed her.

But I was ready. I moved just as fast as he did.

Whatever apology he muttered was dampened by the sound of her body slamming against the wall as he tried to restrain her.

And then by the sound of steel against steel, as I lunged for him with my stolen sword. He blocked me, but it was distracted, clumsy. I was a better swordsman, and I seized upon his inexperience.

Melina let out a strangled cry. Blood spattered over me.

Markus slumped to the ground, clutching a wound on his throat, life already leaving his eyes.

The hallway was silent but for the sounds of activity above us and the pounding of blood in my ears. Melina pressed herself to the wall, her hand to her mouth, shaking.

My heart ached with pity for her. "We need to go."

"I—I—"

I took her arm, gently but firmly. "I'm sorry, but we need to go, Melina."

She loosened a long breath, tore her eyes away from him, and turned to the door. Together, we stepped over the body of her lover and took our next steps to freedom.

IT WAS A BEAUTIFUL DAY OUTSIDE. When we ran through the door, we were met with a stunning view—the fields of crops, wheat and fruits and leafy greens, in perfect rows like streaks of paint. The sky, pink-blue, and empty. Together, Melina and I ran.

We'd make it past the crops, and then hopefully Ishqa would get here in—

Melina's arm was roughly yanked from my grasp. Her rough cry split the air. Someone tried to grab me, but I struck wildly with my sword and slipped their grip, backing against the wall of a grain silo.

Before me, a guard held Melina. And beside him was Lady and Lord Zorokov, surrounded by three other guards.

I was careful not to look panicked, even though my heartbeat was out of control. We had been too loud in the tunnels. We had let too many people see us. We had been too slow. Or perhaps we had just been unlucky.

Lady Zorokov smiled at me. "I think I know you, don't I? Tisaanah Vytezic! Such a pleasure to finally meet the legend."

I could not take my eyes off Melina. I dropped my sword. Raised my palms.

"I'm unarmed," I said. "Let her go."

Lord Zorokov snorted. "Surely you cannot expect us to fall for that."

Still, they didn't move for me yet. I'd earned quite a reputation for collapsing Esmaris Mikov's estate, and for my acts during the Aran civil war. They probably thought I had enough powerful magic within me to destroy this entire city with a flick of my fingers.

If only they knew how useless I really was right now.

Come on, Ishqa. Hurry.

Movement from the left—the two Fey, cornering me from another angle. "The artifact," Iajqa said, coldly. "Where is it?"

"I don't have it."

My palm still burned with my lie. I prayed they would not look too closely at it.

Still, no one moved. They were afraid of me, I realized—even the Fey.

Melina let out a little sound of pain, blood now dripping down the flesh of her throat.

"She tried to stop me," I said. "She has nothing to do with it." I just needed time.

Hurry, Ishqa. Please, please hurry.

Lord Zorokov gave me a slow smile. "Shall we give you her foot this time? I think you already have plenty of hands."

The surge of fury made it difficult to speak.

"I'm not here to play games," I said, as calmly as I could manage. "Let her go, and I will consider returning to you what I've—"

The dark-haired Fey uttered an unfamiliar word beneath her breath, one that sounded like a curse. "*That* is it," she breathed. "You *do* have it."

She was looking at my hand—at the strange gold now covering it.

Shit.

"That's ridiculous—" I started, but the words barely made it out of my mouth.

"We aren't here to play games, either, little slave," Zorokov snarled, and I had no time to react before Melina's throat was open, and her body was falling to the ground in a bloody heap.

And then another guard was on me. Two. Three.

"Take her hand," someone shouted, and pain exploded at my wrist, so intense that for a moment everything else fell away.

I clawed my way back to consciousness. Clawed my way to my magic.

Do this, Tisaanah. You'll die here if you don't.

I summoned every scrap of magic in me, every remaining little fragment of it. *Forced* it through my veins through sheer will. *Gods*, it hurt, like the magic was burning me from the inside out.

The guards holding me let out shouts of pain, pulling away

rot-covered hands. My own right hand was useless—they had cut so deep that I glimpsed bone. When I grabbed my sword from the ground, I had to wield it left-handed.

Everything faded into a frantic smear of images. The guard falling, face black with rot. My sword plunging through another's chest.

Something strange happened as I fought. Other images careened through me—not of my own desperate battle, but of other people that I knew were far away from here. As if, for split seconds, I was looking through someone else's eyes.

First, I saw a copper-haired man with concerned green eyes, gazing at me. A beautiful room full of greenery and refracted sunlight. Utter, all-consuming *hatred*.

Gone. And then another image: a white room. Carvings on the ground, the same shapes over and over. Exhaustion. Fear. Looking down at hands that I knew very well by now, and the Stratagrams that inked the arms attached to them.

My heart stopped. I faltered. The image disappeared.

Max.

That was him. I saw him. I felt him. I *was* him.

This realization struck me so hard that I faltered, mid-movement. A guard struck me. My back hit the ground.

No. Go back. Go back.

I tried to reach back out to my magic, but it was out of reach. The magic surrounding my sword fell away, leaving only pitiful steel that one of the guards knocked from my grasp easily.

Iajqa stalked towards me, gaze fixed upon my hand. "Take it," she commanded.

The guard raised his sword. I tried to dodge, tried to roll away, but another man gripped my shoulders and pressed my wrist to the ground.

But just as that blade was about to come down, a streak of gold hit the earth, knocking my captor away. I blinked, and before me I saw nothing but wings spread out beneath the blazing sunset light, shielding me.

I let out a breath of relief.

Ishqa glanced over his shoulder at me, looking annoyed. "This was not the plan."

"Later," I rasped, and scrambled to my feet. His arms were around me, ready to fly us away, when a voice shouted, "Ishqa!"

Ishqa's head snapped towards the blond Fey, and he went still.

"Iajqa," he said, sounding as if he didn't know he was speaking aloud.

She approached, her brows drawn together. "Come back," she said. "The king would take you back. Your son is not well, he—"

"*Ishqa*," I hissed. We didn't have time for this.

My prompt seemed to snap Ishqa out of some trance, because in one breathless movement we launched into the sky. I clung to him embarrassingly tightly and watched the spectators—the slaves, the guards, the Fey, the Zorokovs—grow smaller and smaller beneath us. Melina's body was a little, broken heap, surrounded by crimson.

"Will she follow us?" I asked.

"No. Her flying is weak now. She knows she cannot catch us."

My stomach dropped as he dove, picking up speed. The estate was far behind us now, and we soared over miles of crops. He eyed my hand, which I cradled carefully. "You are injured."

"It's nothing," I lied.

"This was not the plan."

No. No, it certainly was not.

"The wind is loud," I said, straining my voice. "We'll talk later."

Another stupid, transparent lie. But Ishqa allowed me the mercy. We did not speak again.

CHAPTER FOUR

AEFE

E very time I closed my eyes, I saw white. White isn't even a color, merely the absence of one. Above all, white is empty.

I hated white, and yet it followed me everywhere. Everything was empty, now. There was nothing in my head but my own thoughts. Nothing in my lungs but my own breath. There was only one heartbeat throbbing beneath my skin. My body was cavernous, lonely. Now everything I wished to escape merely echoed, louder than ever.

There was nothing so terrible as to be so alone.

That aloneness consumed me in my dreams. I had forgotten what it was to dream—how overwhelming they are, when you were forced to bear the brunt of them alone. Most of the time, my dreams were the worst moments of my past.

But rarely—very rarely—they instead brought me shards of connection.

I always knew when it was them—Tisaanah and Maxantarius. You know the shape of someone's mind when you have lived inside of it for so long.

I knew Tisaanah's shrewd determination and the vulnerable heart beneath it, and so I knew it was her when I saw flashes of a slender body falling, a throat opening, the feeling of sadness as the wind rushed around me.

I knew Maxantarius's sharp mind, and so I knew it was him when I saw a white ceiling covered in circular marks, felt overwhelming pain, felt myself being swept away by a terrible force.

For one beautiful moment, I was not alone. I tried to cling to that moment of connection to them, but my past took me anyway.

My dreams brought me to another familiar place. I was in a strange circular building of stone, surrounded by humans. I was falling to the ground, my muscles suddenly useless. I was screaming Ishqa's name and watching him turn away. A gust of wind fanned out his golden hair as he left me here. Left me alone to half a millennium of torture.

I woke up screaming.

The figure beneath me let out a mangled cry. I barely heard it. My fingers found my attacker's throat. Limbs flailed. A strike hit my cheek, and I snarled, returning it in kind.

For the first time in days, I felt mercifully powerful. I loved anger. Anger was red and black, screams and shouts. The opposite of emptiness. The opposite of *white and white and white.*

It was Ishqa's face hidden under that mass of fair hair. Ishqa, who had betrayed me. Ishqa, who had ruined me.

I grabbed a dinner knife from the tray, raised it, and—

"Aefe!"

The shout made me freeze.

I hated the name. I was not Aefe.

Someone yanked me backwards. I flailed out, teeth bared, knife swinging. I struck something.

"Stop. *Stop.*"

The tighter the hold became, the more I thrashed. A hand gripped my wrist, twisted, and the blade went clattering away. I didn't care—I fought just as hard, with my teeth, my fingernails—

Until my back slammed against the ground.

The world slowed. My breath heaved.

Caduan leaned over me, his hands pressed to my shoulders. Violet slashed his left cheek, the blood threatening to drip on my face. His eyes, bright like the sun through leaves, grabbed my attention and refused to relinquish it. They were solid. Real.

My breath slowed.

"She tried to kill me!" the maid shrieked, across the room. Low murmurs joined her. Footsteps. Others were here.

Caduan did not look away. I did not understand faces and all the wordless things they said. Most of the time I did not try. And yet, in his eyes, I saw something that made me want to squirm away. I welcomed a strike or a shout. Caduan's piercing observation was more frightening than any of those cruelties.

"Let me go," I snarled.

"I will if you allow me to." His voice lowered. "It was only a dream."

My face snapped back towards him, anger flaring.

How *dare* he say those words.

"No," I hissed. "It was *real* for so many days."

Something shifted in Caduan's eyes. "Not anymore. You are safe."

You are safe, Tisaanah used to whisper to me, in the mind we shared—a mind that now belonged to no one but me.

"I am not *safe*!"

"Aefe—"

"Do not call me that. I am Reshaye."

"You are more than this," he murmured.

"Let me go!"

At last, he obeyed. I scrambled away from him, pressing myself to the corner, my eyes darting around the room.

My bedchamber was large, with tall ceilings that let in fractured light through warped glass. Some said it was beautiful. Servants commented on the fact that I had been given a prime location, on the top floor of the castle. They said it with an odd tone, as if there was something strange about it.

I didn't care. I felt nothing when I looked at this place. Beautiful things were abstract shapes meant for a different soul.

Now, half a dozen people clustered in this room, looking at me. Two of Caduan's advisors helped the blond maid from the floor and a guard led her away.

I disliked the way they were looking at me.

"She shouldn't have been here," Caduan said to them, quietly but firmly. "No one is supposed to wake her. And I specified no blondes."

The two advisors looked at each other. One was a woman, short and delicate with cropped gold-copper hair—Luia, the Chief of Military. The other a dark-haired man with broad shoulders and a strong jaw—Vythian, the Chief of Coin, though he looked better suited to the fighting ring than a coin room.

"My King..." Luia said, quietly.

"Not now." Caduan turned to me. I stared at the ground, but I felt the searching weight of his stare bearing into me. "I'll be back soon, Aefe. Rest."

Rest. I hated rest.

The three of them left, leaving only me. For a moment I stood there, breath still heaving. Then I crossed the room and pressed myself to the door.

Beyond it, I heard the whispers.

"...allow this to go on." Luia's voice.

"It has only been a few months." Caduan's.

"You made a considerable investment in her," Vythian said. "Time is not in our favor."

"You need to ask her," Luia hissed. "We need her. After last night, it's clearer than ever. We can't win a war like this."

A beat of silence. I could imagine a withering stare. "We will not win it with her, either. Not yet. She isn't ready."

Yet.

The word formed a hot ball of anger in my stomach. Anger and—hurt?

I did not know why it surprised me. It shouldn't. It was all anyone had ever wanted to do to me. What use was I, after all, but to be a weapon?

Two footsteps, as if he started to walk away. I pressed closer to the door, ears straining.

"When *will* she be ready, then?" Luia's words came sharper, louder. "When the Aran queen cements her human alliances and sends half a million men to our doorstep? Or perhaps after she perfects her experiments and—"

"Enough." Caduan spoke quietly, but the word sliced through the air, demanding silence. "Do you understand what she has gone through? Do you understand what they did to her? Five hundred years of torture. They took everything from her. Her name, her body. Everything. All so she could become their weapon. Their desires were more important than her soul." His voice drew closer, low, simmering. "And *what*," he breathed, "are you now asking me to do? Do you want me to make that decision again? Become just as monstrous as the humans?"

Several long seconds.

"Of course not, my King," Luia said, finally.

A low murmur of agreement from Vythian.

Caduan's voice faded down the hall as he said, "Don't propose such a thing again."

HOURS PASSED. I lay on the floor and looked up at the stars through the glass ceiling. Had I liked looking at the sky, once? Now it just made me feel small and lonely. When I was with Tisaanah and Maxantarius, my world was swaddled tightly around me. I was nestled securely in the thoughts and mind of another. Even when I was confined, I was not alone.

Not like now.

Once the quiet crept in, I was desperate to distract myself. I closed my eyes and tried to seize upon that moment of connection I had felt earlier that day. Strange, how the brush of intimacy made my loneliness sharper than ever. I reached for them, but felt nothing but my own mind.

I was there, lying in the middle of the floor with my eyes closed, when Caduan returned.

"You should try the bed," he said. "It's very comfortable."

I did not look at him. "I did try. I don't like it."

"Why?"

"It is..." Too much. Too many different textures touching me. Too soft. Too smothering.

I gave up on trying to find words, instead pressing my palms flat to the floor. "This is better."

"Alright." He leaned over me and looked down. Now he wore a simple white shirt and breeches, plain even by the standards of peasantry. For some reason, I liked this, as if there was something about his current appearance that was disarming.

I swiftly drowned that thought beneath my anger. He was simply using me. I was a tool to him. He brought me back to life for his own selfish purposes.

No better than any of them.

"Come with me, Aefe." He held out his hand.

I did not move. "Stop calling me that. It is not my name."

"It was once. Would you like to choose another one?"

My teeth ground. He didn't understand. Names were for living things. I was not one of them.

"Come," he said again.

"Where?"

"Let's do something different. I want to show you something." When I stared blankly at him, he said, "Unless you would prefer to sit in this room, alone."

Silence. I closed my eyes again. Caduan let out a long, slow breath.

"Very well," he said, softly, and began to walk away. "Then sit in this room, alone."

Alone.

The word twisted a knife in me. I did not want to go with Caduan. And yet, the idea of lying here in my own loneliness for hours more seemed... seemed like agony.

"Wait." I opened my eyes and sat up. "I will go."

CHAPTER FIVE

MAX

I was taken into the Towers and all the way down to the bottom floor, several levels beneath the earth. I was always brought to the same set of rooms—messy chambers clearly used for research and experimentation, packed with overflowing bookcases and desks and exam tables. When I first started coming here, they were relatively neat, but with every visit their atmosphere grew more frenetic, like the desperation of Ara as a country was seeping into the walls.

When I arrived, the Queen leaned over a cluttered desk, her palms braced at its edge. She wore a white military jacket and slim matching pants. Her silver hair, normally bound in braids, was loose over her shoulders, only the top of it pulled back. The crown was tangled within it, so hopelessly knotted there that she probably couldn't remove it even if she wanted to.

She straightened. Her face was hard. Dark circles surrounded her eyes, and blood soiled her throat and hands, as if she had changed her clothing but hadn't had time to bathe.

I knew her. Once I'd even known her well. I was certain of this. The memories were gone, but the imprints they left behind remained. Every time I looked at her, I was furious for reasons I didn't understand.

Then again, I had more than enough reason to hate her for the memories I did have.

"What is this?" She held up a piece of parchment, which bore, scribbled in ink, the same three shapes I always drew. The last time I'd been here, I had scratched them onto a scrap of paper in my delirium, half-out-of-my-mind in the aftermath of the Queen's experiments.

I said nothing.

"Is it a map?" she asked.

"It must be." Another voice came from the opposite side of the room, and I stiffened. A thin, elderly Valtain man rose and gave me a manic, chilling grin. "Perhaps some piece of knowledge he stole from his Fey possessor. Wouldn't that be interesting?"

Vardir. I hated him, too.

"I'm surprised," I said.

The Queen cocked an eyebrow. "Surprised."

"I'm surprised that you're willing to make it so obvious how desperate you are. Pulling me out here in broad daylight, when you haven't even had time to wash the blood off yourself. Things are that bad?" I lifted my chin towards the door at the other end of the room. "How many dead volunteers are in there, today?"

She held my stare for a second too long, then looked away. "I need no moralizing from you. War criminals don't get to lecture me for the measures I take to save my people."

Fire. Screams. A city of bodies so burnt that families buried only bones and ash.

The onslaught of images, as they always did, left me slightly sickened. I had to fight hard to remain stoic.

Ilyzath's whisper again echoed through my thoughts: *Perhaps it is all real, and that is the greatest nightmare of all.*

In rare times—in moments like this—I was grateful for my broken mind. Maybe some things were better left forgotten.

The Queen turned to Vardir, her arms crossed over her chest.

"This needs to work," she hissed. "Do whatever you need to do. We're out of time."

Vardir looked irritated. "It's not *my* fault that *he's* so much more useless than he was last time."

"Enough of the excuses," the Queen said. "Go."

The door at the back of the room opened. The guards took hold of my arms, but I stood of my own accord.

The chamber was circular and white, with a second door at the opposite side. It was a small space, with white walls, a white floor, a white ceiling. As we entered, two other guards were disappearing through the second door, carrying a lifeless body. I glimpsed dangling feet covered in black veins just before it slammed closed.

To the left was a wide window that could be used to observe what happened within—magically reinforced, I had learned, during one of my many attempts at rebellion. Still, I'd nearly killed the person trying to hold me down by flinging them against it, and even though the glass hadn't broken, it had been very satisfying.

I wasn't rebellious today.

Instead, I went to the table at the center of the room and obediently lay down on it, blinking up at the ceiling. Stratagrams adorned it in garish crimson paint.

Hands held down my wrists, strapping them to the table, palm up. Vardir's assistant today was a Valtain woman, but Vardir did the work. I didn't even need to see the needles to know what was coming next. I was prepared for the pain.

"There's no more room," the woman muttered. "He has so many already..."

"There's room," Vardir said, cheerfully, before starting in on the tattoos on my palms.

I realized, as I had countless times now, that preparation didn't mean much. The agony overtook me anyway. These weren't normal tattoos. The ink marked every layer of my skin, seared there by magic.

The myriad of Stratagrams tattooed across my body cut me

off from my power. Every time I managed to slip through, another tattoo would be added, closing each loophole. I wasn't sure what I'd done to deserve these ones, but I'd learned that the Queen was very afraid of whatever might happen if I gained even a fraction of control over my own magic.

That was the only conclusion I could make, anyway. The reactions of others told me it was highly unusual for someone to have *so many* shackles inked into their body.

Eventually, Vardir finished his work. Even when the needles were gone, I was left dazed and numb in the aftershock of it.

Vardir patted my shoulder. "Excellent work. Now, the real fun."

"Great," I gritted out.

I heard the doors close. The room went dark.

Vardir's assistant stood at my head, her hands resting on the table on either side of me. "What do I —"

"Just don't let him die," Vardir said.

Well, that inspired confidence. I focused intently on my breathing.

I had done some variation of this countless times since my imprisonment, though it changed a little with each test. I didn't understand what they were trying to do, exactly. But I could string together some assumptions based on what I *did* know.

I knew that the Queen wanted a weapon powerful enough to win her war. I knew that somehow, they expected to get one from me. And now, I knew that desperation was driving them to rush — to be sloppy. To take risks.

It was only recently that I realized their experiments were largely out of their control. And what was out of their control might, just *might*, be within mine.

And this time —

No time to brace myself. Nothing existed anymore but the pain.

I gritted my teeth, tried to ground myself in the cadence of my breath, in the metal against my skin. But so quickly, those markers of the world fell away. A fire had started in my blood and had nowhere to go, so it consumed me instead.

The white walls dissolved. In their place were an onslaught of fragmented moments.

I saw a beautiful house with gold columns and a lion at its gates. My hand pressed to the door, but someone whispered in my ear, *You don't want to go back there again.*

Now, a blanket of flowers surrounding a little stone cabin. Someone calling for me—an accented voice, breaking my name into two melodic syllables. I knew that voice. I had heard it many times, at the edges of dreams and memories I couldn't grasp.

I tried to turn, but the image evaporated.

And then I was in a white room, white and white and white.

And then I was on a battlefield, watching my weapon skewer a teenage boy.

And then I was in a dark place, with a warm glow radiating from the walls. Braided white hair fell around my face. The Queen leaned over me, her mouth twisted into a sneer. *"You should have killed me."*

The world dissolved. Again, again, again.

Through the pain and disorientation, I tried to anchor myself.

You have a plan, I reminded myself. Yes, the Stratagram tattoos cut me off from my magic. But they were opening a door for me, using me as a vessel for a magic even they didn't seem to understand.

Surely, I could use that somehow.

Magic was rushing around me, sweeping me up like floodwaters. With great effort, I stabilized myself. Tried to reverse the power. Tried to capture what surged through me.

And for the briefest moment, *I fucking had it.*

The magic no longer carried me away. I was *channeling* it. It took every bit of strength in me—my physical body, surely, had to be dying. Nothing but death could be this painful.

Still. For one moment, one beautiful fucking moment, it was right there.

But then—

I felt something strange, something that distracted me. Another presence. Someone I knew, someone I knew well. I caught a flash of cold air, warm blood. Of someone falling to the ground, a sword hacking through their throat.

Utter, deep sadness. Sadness and *fury*.

And familiarity. Bone-deep, soul-shaking familiarity. *I know you.*

It struck me so hard that it made my heart stop.

The moment of distraction was too much. I lost control. The pent-up energy burst all at once. The pain pulled the flesh from my bones.

What a way to die, I thought, grumpily.

My consciousness faded.

───────◆───────

"Max."

May-oocks.

That voice again.

My vision was blurry. For a moment I could make out sweeps of color—white skin and tan, one splash of green, one of silver.

"*Max.*" Sharper this time.

I blinked. The figure was gone. Instead, the Queen leaned over me. When my eyes opened, her shoulders lowered in a breath of relief.

"Good," she muttered. "Here. Drink."

I struggled to push myself to my elbows and tried very hard not to vomit. She held out a cup that I pointedly did not take.

She rolled her eyes. "What? You think it's poisoned? It isn't."

"I'm perplexed by your sudden concern for my well-being."

"You're too valuable to let die. Drink the damned water." She shoved the glass into my hands, whirling around to give Vardir a withering look. "That was unacceptable."

"It was a theory," Vardir said.

"It was a failure, and you nearly killed him."

41

He looked annoyed. "It was almost a success, and it wasn't *my* fault that it wasn't."

"Oh? Whose fault is it, then?"

Vardir gave me a bone-chilling smile. Ascended above, I *hated* that man. "Maxantarius's, of course."

The Queen scoffed.

"So much within him has been locked away," he went on. "We cannot access what he can't even access himself."

I looked down at my arms—at the tattoos covering them. I had to admit, a part of me would have found it darkly funny if they had sabotaged their own efforts.

The Queen followed my stare.

"We need our precautions," she said, "when dealing with a dangerous criminal."

Dangerous criminal. She made me sound so vicious.

Vardir laughed. "No, no, I am not talking about the Strata-gram tattoos. I'm talking about something deeper. His magic is built upon his past. And now, his mind is not—"

"Enough." The Queen spoke too quickly, glancing at me and then immediately looking away, as if she hadn't intended to.

I let out a raspy laugh. "What, do you want me to leave so you can talk about me in private?"

The Queen didn't dignify this with an answer. She stood and turned away. "Vardir, you and I will have a discussion later about your failures. Syrizen, take Maxantarius back to Ilyzath."

WHATEVER VARDIR HAD DONE to me didn't wear off right away. It took effort to stand up straight, at first. My wrists and ankles were bound, and I was again led out of the Towers. It was late afternoon now, and much colder and greyer. I wondered how long I had been unconscious. Maybe longer than I'd thought.

I couldn't stop thinking about what I had seen.

Most of what I saw during Vardir's experiments faded quickly, like dreams that dissolved upon waking. But whatever I had seen—had felt—when I tried to reach for control stuck with me. That sense of familiarity... It was so intangible and yet... it was the only real thing I had experienced in a very long time.

I wasn't even sure I cared that it had disrupted my plan. There would be another experiment. Another chance. I would try again. I carefully ignored the nagging question that triggered: *Then what?*

We were halfway to the docks when Vivian, one of my two Syrizen guards, stopped short, her face to the horizon.

"What?" the other said.

"Do you feel that, Merah?"

Merah frowned and shook her head. "No."

But the hair prickled at the back of my neck. Something shivered in the air, like the suspended tension before a lightning strike.

The three of us stood in silence for a moment. The soldiers still hurried about, continuing their clean-up. Birds sang. The breeze rustled the leaves.

Vivian turned away. "I just thought—"

The words became a wet crunch.

Vivian was no longer standing there.

She was in two pieces, clutched in the grasp of a creature of shadow, her head dangling from one spindly-fingered hand, and her body from the other.

As if they had just stepped from the air, the monsters were everywhere.

CHAPTER SIX

TISAANAH

I was confused about the bowl of raspberries.

"Where did those come from?" I asked Sammerin when we entered the tent. He shrugged, said he had no idea, and mentioned that berries were the last thing I should be concerned about when my hand was hanging from a few threads of flesh.

The two of us sat at the table now, Sammerin painstakingly reconnecting every piece of severed bone and muscle. It hurt horrifically. Even after all this time, I still found it stomach-turning to watch him work. So instead, I watched the raspberries, frowning. A single fly circled them lazily. They seeped red onto the white cloth beneath them.

It was hard to get raspberries out here. This encampment was so far east that the rolling plains of native Nyzerene started to wither into desert. It was a temporary base, as the rebel leadership—me, Serel, Filias, Riasha, and our closest teams of spies and diplomats—mapped our next steps in our war for freedom against the Threllians and the Fey.

My head hurt. I blinked and saw Melina's small body falling to the ground.

I pushed away the thought, burying it instead beneath a thousand other worries.

"Any news from Orasiev?" I asked. "Shirav? Malakahn?"

"Not as far as I've heard. Not that that means anything."

I chewed my lip. I just needed something to think about. And I wanted to know that Orasiev was alright. Remarkably, we were actually starting to win this thing, and victory felt more precarious than loss ever did.

I hadn't fully realized the spark I was igniting by killing the Mikov family, nor the flames that we were fanning by returning to Threll. Slaves across the country had begun to realize how much power they held, and how much more possibility lay beyond their lives. The city of Orasiev was the first—a lesser estate overthrown by a successful slave rebellion. We took Shirav next, and then Malakahn, and finally, Exendriff. Four cities that belonged—truly belonged—to once-dead civilizations. Yes, they were small ones, spread across the outskirts of the Threllian empire. But they were *ours*. We had fought and bled for them.

For the first few weeks in Orasiev, I woke up every morning certain that Threllian Lords would be at our gates by sundown, ready to tear us to the ground. Miraculously, it did not happen.

These were strange times. The entire world, it seemed, was at war. The Fey—and by extension, their Threllian allies—were locked in a bloodthirsty conflict with Ara. This played out both across the sea and in Ara's Threllian territory, which Nura had slowly but surely expanded from what was once the Mikov estate over recent months.

A thousand knives were poised at our backs—Nura's, the Fey's, the Threllians'. And yet, perhaps because everyone was so distracted by all the other people they had to go kill, our infant nation still stood.

Still, at least once a week I dreamed of fire consuming the tentative freedom my people and I had created, just as it had once consumed a stone cabin and sprawling garden that I thought of as—

I hissed in a breath as pain shot up my arm.

"Sorry," Sammerin murmured. "Reattaching nerves."

I made the mistake of glancing at my wrist and immediately regretted it.

Sammerin frowned down at my hand, examining, not for the first time, the strange mark. The gold had formed an intricate pattern, like spiderwebs that started at my fingertips and twined down the front of my palm. It ended near my wrist, the metallic streaks dwindling and disappearing. The marks felt different than my flesh—harder, and colder, like metal—but I could still open and close my hand normally.

"And Ishqa had no ideas as to what this could be?"

"He said he will look closer when he returns."

He'd barely had time to glance at it before dumping me on the ground and flying away again. Apparently, he had somewhere very important to be that I had disrupted with my butchering of our plans. We were all used to it. Ishqa came and went as he pleased, often disappearing for days or weeks on end without a word. Not that any of us could complain. Our mysterious Fey ally, and the information that he brought us, had been key to so many of our victories against the Threl- lians. Ishqa viewed the Fey as our ultimate adversary, and every blow to the Threllian empire weakened them by extension.

"Hm." Sammerin looked concerned. But then again, he always looked concerned, these days.

My other hand curled into a fist of frustration.

"Whatever this thing is, I don't think it's a weapon," I said. "At least not one that is powerful enough."

Powerful enough to break into Ilyzath.

I didn't need to say that part aloud—not to Sammerin. He knew that Max's imprisonment dominated my every thought. These last few months had been a brutal balancing act. The rebellion needed me. I gave them every part of myself that I could offer. I gave them my steadfast leadership, my scraps of magic, my dreams for the future, my plans, my diplomacy.

But there was so much I couldn't give them, because half my heart was trapped in a prison hundreds of miles away.

Sammerin's deep brown eyes flicked up to me with wry amusement. "You say that," he said, "but we both know that you'll try, anyway."

I chuckled.

He was right. In here, with Sammerin, I could speak my doubts. But out there, I would keep them locked away. I would relentlessly learn about this thing that had attached itself to me, and I would tell myself and everyone else that I would use it to free Max, and I would refuse to accept any alternative.

I did not dignify uncertainty aloud.

"You're right," I said.

"I always am."

"And I have always known it."

"Smart woman. Certainly too smart for Max."

The sound of his name sucked all the air out of the room. Sammerin's smile faded. He didn't meet my eyes.

I frowned. There was something odd about that expression.

But before I could say anything, the door to the tent opened, and Serel and Filias entered.

"Whew, that looks better than it did an hour ago," Serel said in Thereni, brightly. He kissed the top of my head. "Good. That must've hurt."

"Glad you got out safe." Filias peered at my hand. "So. This is it."

I nodded. I had told Serel and Riasha about the artifact when I had arrived back at camp.

"Ishqa will help us learn more about it once he returns," I said. "Surely it's powerful, if the Fey are so desperate for it. It will be valuable for the rebellion. And to use against Ilyzath."

I had done exactly what Sammerin knew I would. Confidence, after all, was my only defense.

But Serel and Filias were oddly silent. They exchanged a long, meaningful look. They had been giving each other a lot of those looks, lately—like they had a language all their own. Serel hadn't talked to me about it yet, but the attraction between them was obvious.

This, though... this was not lovestruck gazing.

I glanced between them. "What?"

Serel sat in the chair across from me, his blue eyes deep with concern.

"There's something that we need to talk to you about."

A pit formed in my stomach.

"It's been five months," Filias said. He stood awkwardly, his hands bracing on the back of Serel's chair. "Three since the night you almost—"

"—Since we started sending battalions to Ilyzath," Serel cut in, a little too sharply, shooting Filias a disapproving stare.

My mouth had gone dry. I nodded.

I had personally gone to Ilyzath many times at first, desperate to find a way to penetrate its walls. But after one horrible failure that ended with Serel fishing my limp body out of the sea, I agreed that we would send teams of soldiers there instead, freeing me to do work for the rebellion that only I could do.

Even that... I didn't like it, even if I knew they were right.

"The eleventh group just returned to Orasiev," Serel said.

My heart leapt, even though I knew—I *knew*, from Serel's expression, that it was not good news.

"And?"

Sammerin reconnected another nerve. I barely felt it.

Serel's face was grim. He shook his head.

"Jaklin Atrivas died last night," Filias said. "The Ilyzath guards killed him, and the rest of the team couldn't save him."

My heart crashed to the floor.

I knew Jaklin. He was one of our best warriors, and a good leader. He'd been critical to the successful takeover of Orasiev. He had two young children.

I closed my eyes and saw Melina's lifeless body.

"What a loss," I murmured. "Give his family anything they

need. Food. Money. Give them—give them a pension. I'll find a way to pay for it personally."

Serel and Filias exchanged another glance. Filias's face was hard, and Serel's eyes big and gentle.

"They have never managed to make it past the outer walls, Tisaanah," Filias said. "Not once."

"I have managed to make it through," I said. "I can go with them again next—"

"We have only made it this far in the rebellion because of you. Don't think we don't know that." Serel gave me a weak smile. "There are so many things that only you can do. You're our greatest advantage."

"I can't keep throwing away good people and good soldiers on an impossible mission," Filias said. "Not now, when we need them more than ever to defend the rebellion. I'm sorry, Tisaanah. I'm—" He looked so deeply uncomfortable. "I'm sorry."

I flinched—as if I'd been struck by a devastating blow.

Do not lose control. Do not fall apart. Look forward.

"I understand," I said, tightly. "Then I'll go alone, again. By myself. No one to risk but me."

"That's a death wish. You barely even have—" Serel stopped himself before saying it: *You barely even have magic.* "You can't survive that."

"I've done it before."

He reached out and took my hand before I could pull it away. "I thought we lost you the last time, Tisaanah," he murmured. "I don't want to lose you."

Serel looked at me with such unending love. And yet, in this moment, I resented him for it.

I don't care, I wanted to say. *I'd rather die trying to save him than stop.*

"I'm willing to take the risk."

Filias and Serel exchanged another look—gods, I wished they would stop doing that.

"This is bigger than you," Filias said. "You know so much. If Nura captured you—"

The anger—the sheer *rage*—hit me like a wave.

He thought I was a liability.

He was telling me that he was going to leave my lover in prison, and was forbidding me from getting him out myself because he thought I—*I*, who had sacrificed *everything*, sacrificed far too much—was a gods-damned liability.

I jolted to my feet, yanking my hand away from Serel's grasp.

"I won't leave him there. I agreed to help you. I agreed to start going on missions here. But I have always made it clear from the beginning that I *will not leave him there*."

"I know, Tisaanah—" Serel started, but I cut him off.

"Did you know that he was the only one who helped me get you out? The *only one*? None of us would be here now if it wasn't for him. Every single one of us owes him our lives."

"It wasn't the decision we wanted to make," said Filias, a little gruffly.

I took in several long breaths, struggling to control my emotions.

I turned to Sammerin. "Do you understand this?" I asked, in Aran.

He gave a small nod, and something about the look on his face made me feel as if the floor had opened beneath me.

"You already knew," I murmured.

He winced. "I tried to talk them out of it."

I have one excellent friend who's far better than I deserve, Max had told me, once. *And if Sammerin were ever in that position, I would never allow him to stay there.*

The sound that escaped my lips was a strangled, sad excuse for a laugh. "He would have died before he let you remain in that place. And now you are giving up on him, too? You're his *brother*."

Sammerin looked as if I had struck him. "Never, Tisaanah. Never."

"I don't like it, either," Filias said. "I really don't. But we have all lost people. We have all left people behind. And we can't lose more of them just to get one back. We just... we just can't."

50

Serel half-rose, reaching for me. "I'm so sorry, Tisaanah."

My eyes fell to those gods-damned raspberries.

Now I understood. *We're so very sorry, Tisaanah. Here, have some raspberries.*

In that moment, I hated—truly *hated*—every single one of them.

"I need to be alone," I said. "Please."

They didn't argue with me. I didn't see whatever pitying looks they might have given me as they left. The minute they were gone, I picked up the bowl of raspberries and hurled it against the table. The clay shattered just as my composure did. The berries were overripe. They hit the wood in a crimson smear, spattering my face like blood.

CHAPTER SEVEN

AEFE

I hated walking through Ela'Dar. Perhaps to some it was a pleasing place. The city consisted of intricate copper structures and lush greenery, punctuated with windows of multicolored glass and inhabited by elegant Fey clad in flowing silks. But I noted these things only in passing. All I saw was how its people looked at me.

Caduan drew attention wherever he went. He rarely dressed differently than the people he ruled, and usually did not wear a crown. Nevertheless, everyone knew him, greeted him, and bowed their heads. And then, inevitably, their gaze would fall to me. I did not know how to read those stares, and I hated that most of all. Was it disgust? Curiosity? Hatred? Perhaps it didn't matter. I did not want to be looked at. I did not want to be seen.

Today, thankfully, Caduan did not take me through the main streets of the city. Instead, we walked behind the castle, taking rocky side paths that led through lush forests of deep green. All of Ela'Dar, despite its considerable size and density, was intertwined with nature—the northern half of the city built into the cliffs of the mountainside, and the southern half embracing the woods. The castle sat between them, overlooking both the mountains and the forest.

We walked through the trees in silence until we reached a small stone building. Inside, there was a sand floor, and large windows, and weapons—swords, axes, spears—lining the walls.

I stopped short. Caduan kept walking.

"What is this?"

"It's a training ring. The guards use it at times, but today, no one else will be here."

"Why did you bring me here?"

"Once, a very long time ago, you taught me almost everything I know today about combat."

"That wasn't me."

"Maybe not in some ways." He went to the opposite side of the ring and knelt beside a crate, retrieving something wrapped in dark fabric. He returned to me, placed the items on the ground, and unwrapped them.

My breath caught for reasons I did not understand.

Two blades lay in the sand. They were identical, long for daggers but short for swords, with a slight curve to them. They were made of a sleek black steel.

The sight of them stirred a strange sensation within me.

"Do you recognize these?" Caduan asked.

"No." Half a lie.

"You used to wield them. Not these exact ones, but blades just like these."

"I told you that was not me."

"I understand." The corner of his mouth lifted. "Fair enough. But perhaps you might enjoy doing something physical."

I didn't move.

"Or not," Caduan said, lifting one shoulder. "If you would prefer to return to your room."

I did not want to return to my room. I did not want to walk back through Ela'Dar. I wondered if perhaps Caduan knew that.

I picked up the blades.

As my hands closed around their hilts, instant familiarity

shook me. The sensation was so intense that the hairs rose on the back of my neck. For a moment, I was holding these very weapons, so long ago, in a city made of black stone. For one split second, I regained some grasp of who I once had been.

And then, seconds later, it was drowned beneath a thousand other memories. Memories of a thousand other weapons in a hundred other bodies, weapons that I had been forced to wield—forced to *be*—in so many other lives.

I needed to move. I needed anger. Anger was real.

Caduan had been watching me carefully. When I struck, he was prepared. His sword was already out, ready to block me—which he did easily. Not that it was difficult. My attacks were sloppy, half-hearted. I barely knew how to control a body by myself anymore.

And yet, there was something breathlessly satisfying in the clash of metal against metal, in the strain of my muscles. The way my emotion *went* somewhere.

Caduan looked oddly pleased.

"I knew you would remember," he said.

Clash. Our weapons struck.

"Even back then," he went on, "I don't think it was the violence that you enjoyed. It was the physicality of it."

With every lunge, my heart beat faster, my rage burning hotter, like I had opened up a passage I didn't know how to close again.

Why was he talking about what I used to be? Why was he reminding me of everything that had been taken away from me? Didn't he see that I could never be that person again? That I couldn't reclaim her, even if I tried? Why would he shove my face into everything I couldn't be, like a boot grinding my cheek into the mud?

A particularly vicious strike left our faces inches apart, our weapons vibrating between us.

"Why did you bring me back?" The words tore from my throat without my permission.

"Because you deserved a life."

"You cannot lie to me."

I drew back and struck again. Faster. *Harder.* He stumbled slightly in order to block in time.

His lip curled. "Because what they did to you was an injustice."

Injustice? *Injustice?* My fury ran so hot that I stumbled, waiting a fraction too long, and Caduan managed to push me back.

Clang! Our weapons crashed between us. Hot sweat soaked my clothing. It felt invigorating, marking the boundaries of my body—burning muscles, panting breath. My strikes were wild, breathless. I pushed Caduan back in several vicious slashes. He could barely keep up. He fell against the wall.

"Do I frighten you?" I panted.

Clatter, as his sword fell to the floor.

And then the world stopped as it was just me and him, my blade pressed to the underside of his chin. The warmth of his own exertion warmed the space between us. His stare seemed brighter, furious. What was the meaning of that expression?

"Yes," he said, breath heavy. "You frighten me. But not in the way you think you do."

You should be terrified of me.

"You brought me back to use me." I hurled the words faster, harder, than any of my strikes. "You brought me back to make me your weapon."

"That is not true."

"*Do not lie to me!* You pretend to be better than them. Pretend that you have such noble causes. But you have done the same thing *they* always have."

"Aefe—"

"Why did you not just let me die? *I just wanted to die!*"

And there it was. That stare of pity. Of compassion.

A trickle of violet blood rolled down the smooth pale column of his throat. How easy it would be, to kill him. I had once found such power in such things. I could kill him here, take my revenge, take the uncomfortable look from his eyes. I could kill him and throw myself from the tallest tower of the castle, shatter my fragile, lonely, useless body upon the mountain stones.

And I would be free.

Is that freedom? another voice whispered.

A warm hand closed around mine—around the hilt of the blade. My wrist trembled.

"Kill me," Caduan said, softly. "If that's what you want, then do it."

Do it. Do it. Do it.

My teeth clenched so hard my jaw shook.

At last, I yanked my weapon away. And then I turned, looked him straight in the eye, and said, "I hate you."

His hand went to his throat, touching the wound. He took two steps forward, his lips parted, and then a voice shouted from the door.

"My King."

A guard stood there, looking panicked.

"Come. Quickly."

CHAPTER EIGHT

AEFE

The messenger led us to Caduan's private wing of the castle. The double doors were closed. Some awareness lingering beneath my fragile mortal senses shuddered as we approached— something that nagged at fragments of old memories.

I hesitated, and Caduan noticed. He paused, his hand on the door.

"I can have someone return you to your room," he said.

I wasn't sure why this felt like an insult. "I do not want to return to my room."

"You do not want to see what is in here, either."

I knew that he was likely right. Whatever I felt emanating from within reminded me far too much of the nightmares that plagued me at night. And yet... it called to me, too.

"I will stay," I said.

I thought Caduan might argue with me. But instead he gave me a long stare that I could not decipher and said nothing more before opening the door.

I had never seen this room before. It was circular, with many windows and few decorations. The floor was white marble. The combination of the waning sunlight spilling through the window and the gleaming bright tile made the pools of violet blood seem to glow.

There was so much blood.

All of it dripped from a single table at the center of the room. Upon it lay a Fey man, a once-white sheet pulled up to his neck. Luia, Vythian, two healers, and a soldier surrounded him. A nauseating wave rolled over me, as if something in the air itself was rotten.

Caduan's face was grim. He approached the table and pulled back the sheet. Luia let out a shocked curse.

A massive, savage gash ran from the man's navel all the way up to the base of his throat. Someone had stitched the wound, but the blood still pooled and dripped from it. Black and purple mottled the flesh around it. Dark veins spread beneath the Fey's skin, reaching out over the golden skin of his chest and abdomen, almost to his shoulders.

The man was weeping. When the sheet moved over him, he let out a wordless cry, body lurching. The healers held him down.

I couldn't move.

The strange sensation I felt in the air grew thicker. My stomach threatened to empty. My ears filled with a high-pitched scream, though I recognized what I was hearing was not a "sound"—it was not coming from the disfigured man's twisted lips, but somewhere deeper.

"How did he make the journey back alive?" Caduan muttered.

"We made sure that he lived," the soldier said. She was covered in violet, her face pale. "You needed to see firsthand what the humans are doing, my King. What they are doing to those of us they capture."

"He was recovered from Ara?"

"By the shades. Yes. He was a soldier assigned to send a message to our Threllian allies in the south. Shortly after his assignment, he disappeared."

"He went too close to Ara's Threllian outposts," Luia said.

"We did not think we'd recover him, but..." The soldier's eyes fell to the man on the table, and words seemed to escape her.

Luia's lip curled with hatred. "That Aran bitch is a vile beast. Who knows how long she had kept him alive like this? All for her twisted experiments."

Caduan leaned over the figure, solemn.

"He won't live."

A new voice came from behind us.

I turned and went still.

For a moment I was looking at another person, one that I knew long ago. A man with golden hair who I hated so much it burned me alive. The man who had betrayed me.

The past and the present collided, until I realized...

No—no, it wasn't him.

This was a different man. His eyes were a bit larger, features sharper, and his hair shorter, skimming his shoulders. And one of his wings—silvery-gold—was hacked off at the joint, leaving a ragged edge.

Still, I stiffened, and out of the corner of my eye I noticed Caduan flick a vigilant glance to me.

The man approached, a lopsided smile at his lips. It struck me as a deeply unhappy expression.

"Apparently I'm late. I apologize if I missed the message."

"You don't need to be here, Meajqa," Caduan said.

"I'm your second. I should be here."

Meajqa stood beside the table, and the smile faded as he watched the man writhe.

"It was cruel to keep him alive long enough to bring him back," he said, quietly, as if to himself.

"It was their duty to see if he could be saved," Luia replied, but the healer gave her a pitying look.

Even I knew it. There was no saving this person. His soul stank of rot.

Caduan leaned over the man.

"Look at me, friend."

The man's eyes opened slowly, as if he had to fight for it.

"Ela'Dar is deeply in your debt," Caduan said. "I will never forget the contributions that you have made to our home. Our people are safer because of you. Do you understand?"

The man nodded, a minuscule movement.

Caduan's voice was firm, gentle. "You are going to die. But do not fear death. Death is a door, and though none of us can follow you through it today, you will cross its threshold knowing that the mark you have left behind will be a worthy one. This is not an end."

The man's trembling had subsided. Even the agony that I had sensed in the world beneath seemed to still, as if soothed by Caduan's words.

"Do not be afraid," Caduan said, again, quietly.

The man swallowed. Nodded. Tears rolled down blood-stained cheeks.

"Are you prepared?"

Again, the man nodded.

Caduan bowed his head. "Thank you." He brought his hands to the man's temples.

The man's body jolted violently, and his limbs suddenly went slack.

Meajqa turned away.

Several seconds of silence passed. Caduan straightened. He did not look away from the corpse on the table, and he did not wipe the blood off his fingertips.

"Make sure his family are provided for. Tell them that he was killed in battle. There's no benefit in them knowing how he suffered."

"Perhaps the people of Ela'Dar should know," Luia said. "If they truly understand what the humans are capable of, they'll be clamoring to take up arms against them."

"The last thing we need is for individuals to make rash, stupid mistakes out of anger."

"She will not stop doing this, Caduan. She will not stop taking Fey from our southern reaches. And the rest of her people are no better. Humans have done nothing but destroy. Even the Threllians do such horrific things to their own. Yet we just lie here in bed with snakes. With every passing day, that bitch gets closer to doing something that could be catastrophic to all of us. What happens when *this* no longer fails?"

She thrust her palm to the table. Already, the corpse looked… odd, formless, like it was beginning to break down.

"Letting a hundred thousand Fey die on a battlefield will not change any of this," Caduan said.

"We don't need to let a hundred thousand Fey die," Luia shot back. "Not if you stop refusing to utilize all of the power that we have in our possession."

Caduan looked at me, and then looked away, as if he didn't intend to allow himself to do so. The others were not as subtle.

Many people here treated me as if I was stupid. But I was not stupid. I understood exactly what Luia was saying. A snarl tugged at my lip without my permission. I hated how this mortal face did that—moved on its own.

"Everyone talks about her, and yet no one asks her." Meajqa's smile had returned. I met his stare even though the familiar shade of his gold eyes speared me with unwelcome memories. "You and I have lived the worst of them, Aefe. If you had the opportunity to punish them for what they did to you, wouldn't you want to take it? We deserve our vengeance. Just as those who never made it out of their grasp do."

Vengeance. The word awoke something in me, like a scent from an old memory.

"This is not about vengeance," Caduan said, coldly.

I nearly laughed. How could he say such a thing? I understood little about mortal ways. I could not read the expressions on their faces or the inflections in their voices. But I understood vengeance, understood how hunger for it devoured all else, and I saw that hunger shining in Caduan's eyes every time he looked at me.

Everyone wanted revenge.

Tisaanah had desired it to sear her mark into a world that

refused to acknowledge her. Maxantarius had clawed for it as a means of obtaining the power he so desperately craved. The ones who came before had begged for it, too, even if those memories had long ago withered.

As Reshaye, I was nothing but wrath and desire rushing through another being's veins. And now there was no one here but me, and that left only flesh, blood, and fury.

At least Meajqa seemed to see that in me. Perhaps because he saw it in himself, too.

"They will be punished." Caduan's words were quiet but full of promise. "By the time we are finished with them, the human race will be nothing but the scars they left behind. Question my methods, but do not question that."

He wasn't looking at Meajqa. He was looking only at me.

Footsteps rushed into the room, shattering the tense silence. A messenger leaned against the doorframe, panting.

Caduan's face fell, as if already bracing for bad news. "What is it?"

"The wayfinder," the messenger said. "It has been stolen."

The room collectively muttered curses.

"How?" Luia barked. "How did we let that happen?"

"Who took it?" Caduan said. I watched his fingers curl. His face and voice were calm, but his knuckles were white.

"The humans," the messenger said.

"*Which* humans?"

"The Threllians must have double-crossed us," Luia muttered, but Caduan shot her a warning glance that made her go quiet.

"It was not the Threllians," the messenger said. "It was the rebel slaves. Tisaanah Vytezic."

I stopped breathing. The sound of Tisaanah's name shook me. There was still a part of me that felt like a part of her. I craved the rare moments I felt close to her, and yet, the thought of her brought with it a wave of hurt, too. She was one more person who had abandoned me.

Every line of Caduan's body tensed. He reminded me of an

animal cringing in pain, trying not to let their discomfort show to predators.

"Humans absolutely cannot hold that power," Luia said. "If they get their hands on what it leads to—"

"I know." A muscle fluttered in Caduan's jaw. "I know."

"What is it?"

Even I surprised myself with the question. Everyone looked at me as if they didn't realize I could speak.

"A key," Luia said, at last. "A key that leads to manifestations of magic even more powerful than you."

More powerful than me? I wanted to correct her—*perhaps once I was powerful, but now I am nothing.*

"Was she alone?" Meajqa asked, in an odd, flat tone. The messenger seemed unsure if he should answer.

"No. Your father helped her escape."

Meajqa's lips went thin. He went to the window, his back to the rest of the room, and said nothing more.

Luia turned to Caduan. "It is one thing for the rebels to have it. That's bad enough. But if the Arans capture Vytezic and come into possession of it..."

"I may be able to track the key. Imperfectly, but... there must be..." Caduan's voice trailed off, as if it couldn't keep up with his thoughts.

The words were on the tip of my tongue—*I could find it.* I had *felt* Tisaanah, after all. I knew that I could follow the thread that connected me to her, if I wanted to.

But I said nothing.

Caduan turned to the messenger. "Send word to General Sai'Ess. I will get them information about the key's location as soon as possible. Tell them to do whatever they must to get it back."

"And the Arans?" Luia motioned to the dead body on the table.

Caduan flinched, the motion there and gone in less than a second.

"I will send shades."

"We don't have more."

"I can make more."

"My King—"

Caduan was already striding across the room. "You can protest later. I have work to do."

CHAPTER NINE

MAX

Vivian was no longer human, just a mangled mass of meat and black leather.

The thing that held her was a twisted nightmare of flesh and shadow, every part of it wrong in some skin-crawling way. Its fingers were too long and too human, with too many joints that bent in too many different directions. It was tall enough to cast a shadow over us. Most horrifyingly, it had *no face*—what should have been features was instead a blur of nothingness.

It was the kind of horrifying that sent every primal animal intuition in me screaming, *Either kill that thing IMMEDIATELY or get as far away from it as you possibly can.*

Chaos erupted around us—soldiers springing into action as more of those things appeared across the cliff line, walking out of nothingness. They were everywhere at once.

The creature dropped Vivian and went for me.

I barely evaded the creature's grasp. The restraints binding my ankles shortened what needed to be a long stride. I stumbled. Hit the ground hard. Rolled.

A sickening crunch filled my ears. Excruciating pain tore through my foot.

Fuck.

Clawed fingers locked around my ankle. The creature leaned over me and a burning smell filled my nostrils. Its face, a strange void of shadow, lowered close to mine. That darkness gave way to a hundred other images—a little girl's face, surrounded by fire. A teenage boy wearing broken glasses.

I needed to look away. I knew that I needed to look away, but I couldn't, I—

A voice that was everywhere and nowhere at once whispered, *I know you. I know you. I know you.*

Wake up, Max!

I was jolted from my trance. On instinct, I tried to use magic, and was rewarded with only a burst of burning pain beneath my skin. The Stratagrams—*fuck*.

I looked around, eyes landing on Vivian's discarded spear. If I could just—

Merah let out a roar as her weapon impaled that faceless head. The creature shrieked.

My ankle was free. I had only seconds. Gritting my teeth against the pain, I dove for the spear. The creature had turned on Merah now—*Ascended above, that spear through its head hadn't been enough to kill it?*—encircling her with claws.

My bound wrists made wielding a weapon clumsy. But the movements came easily. My body knew what to do, even if my mind no longer did.

With all my strength, I buried the spear beneath the monster's raised arms—into, I hoped, its heart. The hit met less resistance than I would have expected, as if its flesh was already half decomposed.

The creature let out a bone-rattling howl and dropped Merah, whirling to me.

It was sheer luck that I managed to keep my grip on the spear's handle, yanking it from the monster's flesh. That I was able to move fast enough as it dove for me—

—And that the creature leapt at just the right angle for the point to go plunging through its throat, tilted up, tip protruding from the back of its skull.

The monster slumped. I didn't know if it was dead, or if I had only seconds before it would come for me again. I whirled to Merah, who limped towards me. *"Unchain me,"* I demanded.

"I can't do that. You know I can't."

"For fuck's sake, either you unchain me or you'll need to explain to the Queen how I ended up dead," I spat.

After a moment of hesitation, Merah cursed and knelt beside me. She released the restraints around my wrists, then ankles. As soon as they were free, I stood, ignoring the pain that snaked up my left leg.

I muttered a thank you and pulled the spear from the creature's body with a sickening wet *pop*. "Let's—"

A smear of black.

Blood spattered my face, and Merah was just… gone. I dropped to the ground, rolled, barely dodged another set of claws. The creature that grabbed her was even larger than the first one. It crushed her in its hands like she was nothing. Her blood rained down over my face. I leapt to my feet even though my injured leg screamed at me for it—tried to drive my weapon into its guts, but the monster scuttled away into the chaos before I could stop, Merah nothing but tatters in its grasp.

The whole thing took seconds, and I was left there alone, in an eerie moment of stillness among a maelstrom. I looked down at my unbound wrists, unbound ankles. Then to my dead guards. And then I looked to the docks, not so very far—to all the boats left abandoned by fleeing fishermen.

This was my opportunity. All I had to do was fight my way to the shore. And then go…

…somewhere.

But somewhere that was, at least, *not* Ilyzath. That was good enough for me.

I grabbed the spear and turned to take one more look at the chaos around me. Dozens of these monsters dotted the shore, and they ripped apart Ara's military as if they were rag dolls. Now I saw why the Queen was so desperate.

I started to move, but I only made it halfway across the field when I froze.

My eyes landed on a blond boy in a military uniform locked in a fight he was losing. He held a bloody sword in one hand, and magic glowed in the other. Neither was enough.

The world stopped.

The boy was in the opposite direction of the docks. And yet, I was moving before I realized it. I crossed the battlefield in a wild sprint, the pain of my ankle a distant thrum.

The creature had the boy in his grasp by the time I reached him.

In moments, he would be dead. I could not let that happen. *I would not let that happen.*

I plunged my spear into the creature's throat—and fire tore up its length.

The creature let out a high-pitched, bodiless shriek. It moved for me. I danced backwards. Dodged. Seized the opening it afforded me.

I couldn't see through the flames. But I was fighting based on something deeper than sight now, something more like intuition. I didn't know how I had called my magic to me. Didn't care at this point. I drove my spear between its ribs, deep into its core. Fire roared from my fingertips and through the veins of the spear.

The creature's shriek became an echo. Its body ruptured, moving in a thousand different directions at once, as if the boundaries between its form and the air had been disrupted. Licks of flame tore through its shadowy insides.

I held on for as long as I could, until I couldn't maintain the connection to my magic any longer. Then I withdrew the spear and fell back, just in time for the creature to release a final wail and collapse. The flames fell away. My breaths came in ragged, aching gasps.

I turned around. The boy was on the ground, staring up at

me with big blue eyes through tendrils of fair hair. Ascended above, he was young. Too young to be wearing a military uniform.

Certainly too young to die here.

I knelt beside him. There was so much blood that at first, I couldn't see the wound. Closer examination revealed a slash that cut across the boy's entire abdomen.

Fatal, maybe. Unless he got to a healer fast.

I looked around to see only a mass of violence and chaos. No one was coming for him out here. But…

My gaze lifted towards the Towers. There was lots of death between us and there, yes, but the boy would certainly die if he stayed here.

I ripped my shirt off over my head.

"What's your name?" I asked the boy.

A wrinkle of confusion deepened over his brows, which framed terrified blue eyes. "Wh-what?"

"Name?" I asked again.

Finally, he rasped out, "Moth."

A flicker of recognition passed through me, gone before I could look too closely at it.

"What kind of a name is that?" I asked, giving him just enough time to look indignant before I pulled the shirt around his wound, tight.

He let out a wordless grunt of pain. Beads of sweat broke out over his face.

"Sorry," I said. "I can't let you bleed to death before we get where we're going."

Ascended, it was odd, the way the boy stared at me.

"You aren't going to die today, Moth," I said. "We'll get you to the Towers and get you to a healer there. But you can't walk. So… I won't lie, this is going to hurt."

He swallowed and gave me a grim nod.

Brave kid, I thought, with an odd sense of pride.

"Ready?"

I didn't wait for an answer. I picked up the boy and hoisted him over my back. Fuck, I was out of shape. I felt his body go rigid with pain, but to his credit, he didn't make a sound. And then I ran, bobbing and weaving through dying men and attacking creatures.

I didn't believe in miracles, but if I did, the fact that we made it the other side alive would qualify.

Once we made it to the Towers, I gently let him down and grabbed the nearest person I could find wearing a healer's patch.

"He needs help," I barked. "*Right now.*"

The man nodded, a little frantic, and hurried away.

But before I could turn, the boy grabbed my wrist, stopping me.

"Max," he rasped out.

I blinked in surprise. *He knew me—?*

"Find Tisaanah," he choked out. "Alright? She's looking for you."

Tisaanah. Something inside of me rattled at the name.

"I don't—"

"*Listen,*" he said, face blotchy with exertion. His grip was shockingly firm. "They... all remember you. They'd all still... follow you. Alright? Understand?"

I wasn't sure that I did. But I nodded all the same as the boy's grasp slipped away and his eyelids fluttered.

"Get yourself patched up, Moth," I said. "You've got a lot of life left to live."

By the time I stood, the boy was no longer conscious, and a healer crouched beside him.

The violence had gotten worse even in those few minutes, as the monsters seemed to push towards the Towers. More of them now poured from the cliffs, decimating groups of soldiers.

A streak of shadow had swept from the far entrance of the Tower of Midnight—the Queen—surrounded by darkness that eerily resembled wings, wielding two long knives. She cut through the fighting like a meteor slicing through the sky.

Maybe I could still get away. Maybe. I could barely see the

shore. But what did I have to lose? Death might be preferable to returning to Ilyzath.

I fought, moving fast. I didn't even try to kill anymore, only defend myself enough to slip by. Out of the corner of my eye, I saw the Queen's head turn—saw her gaze land on me. Her course changed, the path of her destruction coming closer.

My steps faltered. That was a moment of distraction I couldn't afford. Pain tore through my leg—the same one that had already been injured. I was looking at the grey sky.

And then I was looking at a faceless beast.

Fuck.

I recovered fast. But now, once again, my attempt at using magic rewarded me only with terrible pain, and no fire. A strike to its throat had the creature stumbling but quickly righting itself.

I began to roll out of the way and—

The creature's clawed hand came crashing down on my leg, digging deeper into the flesh. Then the other pinned my shoulder. It leaned over me, its face coming close to mine, as if... curious.

We have been looking for you, the wind seemed to whisper.

I angled my spear and, with all the strength my injured left arm would allow, thrust it through the creature's body. It met no resistance, flying through its shadowy flesh as if it were nothing but fog.

I almost laughed. Ascended above. To think I was so fucking close.

The creature had no face, and yet, I could have sworn that it smiled. It leaned in closer.

And—

It screamed, releasing me. It reared up so fast that at first my addled mind couldn't put together what I was seeing.

A sword.

A massive sword, piercing through the creature's body, the black-blood-soaked tip protruding from its navel.

The creature flailed as the sword hoisted up in one powerful movement, gutting the beast—nearly cutting it in half.

Everything was blurry shapes, now. I was losing so much blood.

The creature fell, and a man kicked it off of his sword. Then he approached me. The bloody sunset silhouetted him, but I could make out a dark, critical stare, a set jaw, long black hair bound in a braid over one shoulder.

It's funny how I had spent so much time trying to remember people and failing. And yet, this man's name came to me easily, like a flame illuminating a darkened room.

I heard the Queen's voice gasp behind me, "What are you doing here?"

Brayan's gaze snapped up, hard and cold.

"Why," he hissed, "is my brother imprisoned in fucking Ilyzath?"

My vision went dark.

CHAPTER TEN

MAX

I was in a garden. Flowers sprawled over the landscape like an
untamed beast. The air was bright but cool with encroaching
autumn. I sat cross-legged in the grass.

Someone was beside me. Close—close enough that I was
acutely aware of their presence. They drew Stratagrams in the
dirt. The person did not speak, but I knew they were frustrated.
Each mark produced either a tiny result, or no result at all.

"We can try something else," I said.

No answer. My companion just kept on drawing. I watched
their hands, pale skin spotted with tan. I knew they would not
listen, would not stop, and felt an odd swell of pride at this.

Still, I didn't look at the person who sat beside me.

I didn't look because I couldn't bring myself to. Because I
knew that I might notice too much about the shade of their eyes
or curve of their mouth, and feel something that I wasn't
prepared to feel.

So I just stared at the dirt, pulling dead weeds from the earth.

But avoiding it didn't save me. Despite the pungent flowers,
it was this other sweet, citrus scent that consumed me. Despite

the cold air, it was the warmth of this other body that devoured me.

"Max."

May-ooks.

And then I woke.

———————

A VALTAIN WOMAN leaned over me. She had a round, pretty face and curly white hair, and frowned with concentration. My eyes snapped open, and I sat up so fast that I nearly smashed her forehead with my own.

Fuck.

Ascended fucking above.

I fucking *remembered.*

Not everything, but—but more than I did before, all hinged upon a single sentence. It looped through my mind over and over again: *Brayan is here.*

Brayan is here.

Brayan is here.

Brayan. I knew who that was. My older brother. And with that memory, fifteen years came roaring back to me at once.

If I remembered my brother, that meant I remembered my parents. My siblings—Atraclius, Kira, Marisca, Shailia, Variaslus.

If I remembered my brother, that meant I remembered our home, Korvius. It meant I remembered leaving to join the Orders. I remembered endless long nights and early mornings of training, always failing to meet his expectations.

It meant I remembered the Queen. The Queen—*Nura.*

Holy fucking hell.

It's a strange sensation, for half your life to suddenly come slamming back onto you like a million-pound weight. It was like I had been standing in a dark room all along, and the light had suddenly flipped on. Yet, it was a flickering light, one that obscured the questions I needed to answer the most. So much was still missing.

I remembered Brayan, and my family, but I didn't know what had happened to them… even though I knew… I knew, somehow, that they were gone, the ache of their absence throbbing in my chest at the thought of them.

I remembered joining the Orders, and I knew it had changed my life, but I didn't know how.

All of that was shrouded in the shadows still left behind the light.

"What's wrong with him?"

"For fuck's sake, aren't you supposed to *do* something?"

The voices sounded very far away.

"Breathe, Max. *Breathe.*"

I became aware of hands on my shoulders, of magic reaching towards my mind. I didn't like *that* sensation one fucking bit.

"Get the hell *out of my head*," I snapped, yanking away from the healer's touch. The Valtain woman stepped back fast, clearly afraid of me.

Only now did I take stock of my surroundings.

I was in the Towers. But I wasn't in the basement, where Nura usually took me for experimentation. The floor-to-ceiling windows revealed a churning surf and a sunrise-drenched sky. Standing in front of that window was the Queen, her white suit blood spattered, crown tangled even more viciously in her hair. She looked so wildly different from my memories of her as a scrawny preteen.

And beside her was my brother.

The sight of him alone was so disorienting that a headache immediately began pulsing behind my temples. The present and my patchwork understanding of the past collided, making my stomach churn.

In my memories of Brayan, he was a young military champion—in his twenties and the prime of his career. For so much of my life, I cared about nothing more than I cared about what he thought of me.

The man who stood before me now looked like a different person.

He, like Nura, was drenched in blood. A wound across his cheek seeped red. His hair was still long, as I remembered it, bound over one shoulder in a braid that now had a few strands of silver mixed in with the black. He wore a long burgundy jacket that seemed vaguely military in style, though I didn't think it was from Ara.

When I was younger, I had admired the way Brayan managed to embody that mix of savagery and elegance so coveted by the military—cold and animalistic on the battlefield, then proper enough to wash the blood off his hands and guide noble ladies around a ballroom. Now, he seemed... different. Like the balance had been disrupted.

He surveyed me with a dark-eyed, sharp stare.

When was the last time I had seen Brayan? I racked my brain. Memory beyond my teenage years dissolved into nothingness. I had the overwhelming sense that I hadn't seen Brayan in a very long time. That he hadn't seen *me* in a very long time.

Why?

I opened my mouth and wasn't sure what would come out. It turned out to be, "Good to see you, Brayan."

Nura's eyebrows arched slightly. "You recognize him?"

If Nura's surprise meant anything to Brayan, he didn't show it. He just stared at me in silence.

"He'll live?" Nura said to the healer, and the woman nodded. "He'll live."

"Good. Call the Syrizen. We'll get him out of here."

Finally, Brayan spoke. "Absolutely not."

He didn't look at me, only the Queen.

"We have had this discussion, Brayan."

"We have not, Nura. Not to my satisfaction."

"I can't do anything about his sentence."

Brayan's face hardened. "That's a lie."

"Brayan—"

"What he did at Sarlazai made him a hero. He ended the Great Ryvenai War that day."

"And he also—"

"It is unacceptable for him to be imprisoned for those actions."

"It wasn't my ruling."

I scoffed. "Bullshit."

I remembered little about my trial. But I understood that I was in Ilyzath because Nura wanted me to be there. This fact, too, now hit me with a strange new discomfort. What happened? How did we get here?

Brayan barely gave me a passing glance.

"Bullshit indeed," he said.

Nura's face went cold and hard. "Let's talk about this later. We have a lot to catch up on."

But Brayan said, calmly, "We'll talk about it now, and he is not leaving this room until we do."

I had never seen the Queen give anyone so much patience before. A muscle feathered in her throat. But when she looked back to Brayan, something changed in her face—she looked younger.

Those new, old memories nagged at me. Nura looking up at Brayan when we were children. She had always adored him. It was odd to recognize that perhaps a part of her still did, even all these years later.

She turned to the healer, who looked deeply fraught by being caught in the middle of this discussion.

"Go. Get the Syrizen to escort Maxantarius back to Ilyzath."

"But—"

"*Go*, Willa."

The healer couldn't leave fast enough. Nura turned to the window, her back to us both.

"I'm happy to see you, Brayan. I've missed you. I'm grateful that you fought with us today. Now you've seen how bad things have gotten, and there's no one I'd rather have at my back for this war. But—"

"What a tremendous disrespect." Brayan's voice sliced through hers, cold and lethal. "This is how you thank my parents for treating you like one of their own children? You throw their son in Ilyzath?"

Every muscle of Nura's body went tense. I could see it even in her back. When she looked over her shoulder at him, all remaining vestiges of warmth were gone.

"*My Queen*," she hissed. "Address me by my title. And *no one* interrupts me, Brayan. Not even you. When I saw you, I thought that…"

Her voice faltered, and in that moment a realization snapped into place.

This wasn't anger. This was hurt. She had truly been excited to see Brayan, and, beyond all reason, had allowed herself to believe that he would help her. Was that how desperate she was for a friend?

Now, she seemed to be cursing herself for her own foolishness.

The door opened, and the Syrizen arrived.

"He is not leaving this room, Nura," Brayan said, firmly. He took two steps back, subtlety putting himself between me and the door.

I blinked, stunned. Was Brayan about to get into a fucking *fight* for me?

There was a long, awkward silence. Ice hardened Nura's features.

"Or what, Brayan?" she said, voice deadly calm. She nodded to Brayan's sword. "Will you use that to murder soldiers from your home country? The people you swore on your life to serve?"

Brayan's jaw was tight. He didn't need to reply. We all knew the answer. He was nothing if not loyal to Ara. He would never raise a blade against the people who had once been his brothers and sisters in arms.

And in this moment, I was glad for it.

Because it didn't matter how strong of a warrior Brayan was —if he did, they would kill him. And that was something my remaining scraps of sanity couldn't withstand.

So when Nura said to the Syrizen, "Take Maxantarius back to Ilyzath," I let them take me without argument. Nura turned to the window and didn't look at any of us as I was led away again, my brother staring after me.

———————————

THE BATTLE HAD TAKEN its toll on Ara. The Towers still stood, but I looked back to see that more windows had been destroyed near the top of the Tower of Midnight. The field leading to the shore was littered with corpses. The Syrizen who led me away were in particularly bad moods. I hadn't seen these two before. One of them moved oddly—in tentative, lurching movements, as if always half-afraid she'd run into something—and her eye scars were red and angry. I guessed she was maybe eighteen years old. Maybe.

She was new. I wondered how many they were forcing through training before they were ready.

Hummingbird. The word popped into my head without warning, another shard of a useless memory. Slang. They used to call Syrizen that, because they moved in blurs with their spears drawn like a hummingbird's beak, each strike covering the front of their uniforms with blood.

As I watched this teenage girl stumble around, the nickname now seemed so fucking cruel. Hummingbirds were tiny, fragile creatures, and this one clearly couldn't fly. She'd get crushed the next time one of those Fey monsters turned up on Ara's shores. I felt so bad for her that I didn't even fight her as she led me to the shore, then Stratagrammed me back to prison.

Ilyzath, as always, welcomed me with open arms. It was oddly quiet today. No hallucinations, no whispers. I lay down in the middle of the floor. All my limbs felt heavy. My wounds had been healed, but my body still protested every movement. And my head—my head was killing me, like each new invading memory was a pickaxe slamming into my skull.

I was angry for reasons I didn't understand. Angry on behalf of all the deaths I had witnessed today. Angry at the Queen for sending me here. Angry at myself on behalf of everyone I couldn't save—myself included. And I was even angry at Brayan for... reasons that completely evaded me.

I wasn't sure how long I lay there before I heard the familiar sound of shifting stone.

"Hello, Max."

"Why are you here?" I asked, not moving.

No answer. Finally, I sat up. Nura stood against the wall, her arms crossed over her chest.

"Why are you here?" I repeated.

"You were injured badly. I wanted to make sure you didn't die on me. You're an important asset."

I gave her a look that told her I knew she was lying.

"You recognized Brayan," she said.

"I did."

"So you remember..."

"Enough."

A lie. It wasn't enough. But it was somewhat telling how discomfitted Nura looked at that response. There was much in our past, it seemed, that she didn't want me to remember.

I laughed. "I see. You don't like that I remember who you used to be."

Her face barely moved, but I knew I was right.

"Don't be so full of yourself," she said. "You hate who you used to be so much that you purged it from your own mind. I look my past in the eye."

"You aren't even looking *me* in the eye."

She did, defiantly, as if meeting a challenge.

"Is Brayan gone?" I asked.

"No. He isn't happy about... your position, of course, but he agreed to stay and fight for his country. As I knew he would."

It seemed about right. I could barely string my newly recovered memories together, but even the ones that were smashed into pieces had one thing in common: that Brayan was excellent at fighting wars, and he loved nothing more.

"Terrific," I said. "A great boon for the Aran military."

"It is."

A long pause. We looked at each other.

"There was a boy in the attack earlier," I said, at last. "Blond. A Solarie. Military. He was injured, but I got him to a healer. His name was Moth."

She frowned. "Moth," she repeated, an odd tone to her voice.

"Ridiculous name. I just…" I cleared my throat. "Do you know if he lived?"

"No. I don't know."

"He was too young to be out there."

"I guarantee there are younger buttoning up their uniforms right now."

"And does that feel right to you?"

She laughed, rough and ugly. "No, of course not, Max. None of this feels right. Thousands of Arans have died since this war began, Max. *Thousands*. And the damned Fey king hasn't even shown his face here yet. He hasn't even exhausted a *fraction* of what he's capable of. You think I don't feel the weight of that?"

She curled her hand into a fist and then pressed it to her chest, over her heart, as if for emphasis.

Thousands. I had been able to paint the broad strokes of how bad it was based on the scenes I saw beyond the Tower in the rare times that Nura pulled me out of Ilyzath in daylight. I saw the devastation today. Those monsters tore our soldiers apart like paper. Hell, they had nearly done the same to me.

The truth was, I believed her. It justified nothing, but I believed her.

Finally, I said, "Why are you here?"

She drew in a long breath, then let it out slow.

"I am here," she said, "because I need you to understand how much we need you."

"Why me?"

This was the thing I never could understand.

Countless times now, Nura had pulled me out of Ilyzath to be the subject of Vardir's machinations. Their escalating desperation was enough to tell me that they needed me. But I didn't understand why. Why was I so important? What did I have that any other Wielder didn't?

This was the puzzle piece I couldn't snap into place.

Nura gave me a look that held many words she wouldn't say. "Soon, Vardir will have a revised process to test on you," she said. "I come here on my hands and knees, Max, asking you to help us."

"What makes you think that I can?" I said. "It's not as if I'm making Vardir's experiments fail by choice."

I refrained from adding that I definitely would if I could.

"You remembered Brayan."

"What does that have to do with anything?"

Nura's lips pressed together, and she hesitated before answering, as if reluctant to reveal her hand.

"Vardir believes that we can't tap into your power because you have blocked it within yourself," she said. "Your own connection to it is severed."

"That's rich, considering that you're the reason why I got this way."

"I won't defend what I've done to you, Max. I'm not ashamed of it, but I won't defend it. Yes, perhaps I'm the reason why you were sentenced to Ilyzath. But whatever happened to the inside of your mind? That part had nothing to do with me."

She began to turn away.

"Nura."

She stopped.

Maybe this was a question better left unasked. I didn't even know how to phrase it. I settled on, "What happened? With us?"

She was silent for a long moment, her back to me.

"I loved your family," she said. "No matter what I did to you. No matter what I've had to do since. I loved them."

And before I could say anything more, the wall parted, and she was gone.

CHAPTER ELEVEN

AEFE

I dreamed of a city in the forest. I tread suspended paths near the tops of the trees, which cradled ramshackle wooden buildings. I looked back to see Caduan there, walking behind me. He looked different than he does now —younger. He gave me a small smile, which I returned without thinking.

A blur, and then we were in a crowded room with raucous Fey gathered around tables and benches, clutching mugs of mead. My senses were dull, clouded by many glasses of wine. Caduan's were too, his words slightly slurred. We were arguing.

Suddenly the window shattered.

Suddenly we were falling.

Suddenly there was fire everywhere.

We were on the ground. Caduan did not move. I bent down and bit his wrist, drinking his blood—and life blossomed in me, in him, a thread connecting us and making us both more powerful.

Humans everywhere. Pain in my abdomen. I was pinned to the wall, a spear impaling me.

Caduan's magic clustered around him as he fought his way to me.

This is a memory, I realized. A long-ago memory.

Everything froze, like time held its breath.

I observed the scene around me, the fire paralyzed mid-stroke, the *white-haired human's wide-eyed face, the smoke hanging motionless in the air. I lingered on Caduan. His face at first seemed calm, focused... but those eyes, and the way they looked at me... maybe back then I didn't know how to recognize such hidden wrath. But I knew how to see it now.*

My chest tightened. I reached out, as if to touch him, and—

The world split in two. Something in the magic beneath me tore apart —tore apart in a way that was deeply wrong. Like a wound ripping through the center of my soul.

The memory was gone. This was no longer the past. This was the present.

I was now three different places at once.

My room, in Ela'Dar.

A cell of white stone, panic filling me, death surrounding me. I knew these eyes. These were Maxantarius's.

A tent of blue cloth, staring up at the sky. Grief ate me alive, but I would not show it. I swallowed it deep. I knew this soul. This was Tisaanah's.

For a moment and an age, I felt them so vividly, like their hands were interlocked with mine.

And then the roar of this terrible, broken magic took me away.

———————

I STUMBLED ACROSS MY ROOM. The buzzing still filled my ears, my skin covered in goosebumps.

That was not a dream. That was not a memory. Something was happening *now*. And whatever it was still persisted, beckoning to me.

I went to the door and sagged against it. For a moment I looked at my hand on the knob.

Caduan always told me that I could leave as I pleased, but I never wanted to go anywhere. I hated this room, but at least it was safe, far away from the judging eyes. Even now, a part of me hesitated—longing to stay tucked away here.

And yet... the call was too strong.

I opened the door.

I DIDN'T KNOW how I knew where to go. I just did.

I walked through the empty halls of the castle, then down, down, down staircase after staircase. I found myself wandering out into the cold night air, treading barefoot through the forest. I passed the building where Caduan had taken me before, and kept going.

My steps were graceless and uneven for reasons that had nothing to do with my cut-up bare feet. The tear in the magic below left me off-kilter. Whatever it was... it was wrong. Dangerous. And, in equal measure, enticing, pulling me ever forward.

I came to another small, stone building. The door opened easily at my touch. Orange light warmed my face. The floor was rusted, dark metal, with carvings etched into it that spiraled towards its center, illuminated with a faint, throbbing glow. At its center was a large, circular table that continued the same patterns. The light emanated from an orb at its center, so bright that for a moment it overwhelmed my eyes and drowned out the shadows.

The glow faded slightly. My vision adjusted to the darkness, and what I saw within it made me gasp and stumble against the brick.

The room was lined with creatures—creatures made of shadow, standing perfectly still against the walls, faces yawning pits of emptiness. They were silent. One by one, they stepped backwards, simply disappearing into the dusk.

They were... strange beasts. Unnatural. They should not exist.

"Aefe?"

The voice made me jolt.

My eyes fell to the opposite wall. I had been so distracted that I hadn't even noticed him—Caduan, sagging against the table's edge, as if the stone was the only thing keeping him standing.

"What are you doing here?" he asked.

"I—"

Words were gummy in my mouth. The strange buzzing sensation was starting to fade, but only barely. I could not take my eyes from those creatures.

Caduan followed my gaze. "Don't worry. The shades are harmless to you, and they will be gone soon."

His voice sounded strange. His lashes fluttered, like he didn't have the strength to keep his eyes focused on me.

I approached him slowly.

"What is wrong with you?"

"You shouldn't be here."

"What is this? What was—I felt something so *strange*. Something deep, something—" I didn't know how to describe it. I looked to the table at the center of the room, and the glow at its center.

Hello, lost child, it seemed to whisper.

I shuddered.

An expression I could not decipher flickered across Caduan's face. He looked around the room as if he was realizing all over again where we were. "You shouldn't be here," he said again. "I was working."

"Working?"

He lifted his gaze to me, and I recoiled from it.

"Stop."

"What?"

Looking at me that way.

He straightened, limbs carefully rearranging.

"I'm done," he said. "Come. Walk back with me."

He took two steps closer, but he was wobbling on his feet.

"Something is wrong with you," I said, sharply. I did not know why it bothered me so much.

"Just tired. I promise." Then he held out his arm. "Walk with me."

———————

Up close, even in the night, Caduan's green eyes seemed so eerily bright—like there was some light inside of him that crept out through his irises. Or perhaps they appeared that way because the darkness around them was now so pronounced.

I remembered little from my former life. But in this moment, I remembered feeling stripped bare beneath a stare just like this one.

I pulled my hand away from those thoughts. It was easier not to remember.

I did not think that Caduan would be able to walk, but he did, though he moved slowly and steadied himself against trees with every few steps.

For a long time, we walked in silence. It was a strange game. We both watched each other so closely, and pretended not to.

"You were creating... things," I said, at last. "For the war."

"Shades. Yes."

"Because of what Luia said to you today?"

Caduan's lips thinned. "Because we needed more forces to send to Ara, and I would rather sacrifice shades that feel nothing than Fey."

"The man we saw today," I said. "The Aran queen has done that to many others."

His gaze darkened. "I know."

"It is not *just her*. So many of them are like that. They are terrible."

"I know."

I knew it because I had been one of them. Hundreds of years and I became nothing but pain and want and a gaping hole—a desire for love, for power, for safety, a hunger that never ended. Now the wound they had left inside of me consumed everything.

The words ground through my clenched teeth before I realized I was speaking.

"And yet you left me there."

He stopped walking and turned to me. The movement was sharp, almost angry, and for a moment I was gleeful to see it —*yes, fight me. Give me something bloody. Give me something that hurts.*

But when a cloud fell away from the moon, the cold light across his face revealed only sadness.

"I thought you were dead. I thought…" A hard swallow. "Do you remember Niraja?"

Niraja. A beautiful city of flowers and stone. Laughing children. A strange kind of hope. And —

Blood and broken glass on the floor. Dead bodies. A terrible feeling of guilt, of betrayal.

And then, one image that was so clear it left me shaken:

The image of Caduan, clutching his abdomen, falling backwards over the rail.

It was the clearest memory I'd had in a long time. I did not, could not, answer.

We resumed walking. We were nearly at the castle doors.

"The city was destroyed," he said, quietly. "So many people died there that night. I awoke at the edge of the river. Both of my legs were broken. I would have died too, if… Ishqa had not returned."

The sound of his name made me stiffen.

"He pulled me from the ruins and took me back to the House of Wayward Winds." Caduan's voice was tight as a drawn bowstring. "He told me that we were the only ones to survive. He told me that the humans killed you."

I wish they had.

Death was like a lost lover. We circled each other. I craved more with every brush of its touch. All I wanted was for it to take me to its bed and never let me leave.

I tried to imagine the world I had lived in, so many years ago. I tried to imagine what it had been like to be *Aefe*.

"What was I like?" I whispered.

And there was no hesitation as he answered, "You were exceptional."

We reached the door. He leaned heavily against the stone wall of the castle. "You were like no one I had ever met. Passionate and driven and honest the way so few Fey were, in those days. Because of you, I saw the potential in the new world the Fey could build. But with you gone... everything that I feared would happen came to pass. The House of Wayward Winds and the House of Obsidian went to war, provoked by your father's foolish actions, and that war nearly led to our extinction."

My father. I remembered nothing of him but a shadow and a lingering sense of grief, like a reaching hand that was always empty.

"And this is why you brought me back," I said. "Because I have the power you need to win your wars, now."

"It isn't that simple, Aefe."

"Do not patronize me. I know what it is to be used."

"You *only* know what it is to be used, and that makes me angrier than I can ever express." We reached the door, and he held it open for me. When it closed behind us, the darkness of the empty hallway swallowed us both.

"Ishqa stood beside me for hundreds of years," Caduan said. "He became a close friend and a trusted advisor. But when he told me the truth of what he had done to you—the truth of what *they* had done to you..." He heaved himself upright and paused, his back to me. I watched the line of his shoulders rise and fall and thought of what it had been like to feel someone else's breath running through me.

"Then why would you bring me back, if not to make me your weapon?" I asked.

He was quiet for such a long time that I thought perhaps he hadn't heard me.

"Five hundred years is a very long time," he said, at last. "One hundred and eighty thousand days, and I thought of you in every one."

My throat grew tight for reasons I did not understand.

"The woman you knew then was not me."

"She was not. And she was." Slowly, he straightened, turned, and gave me the weak ghost of a smile.

"Goodnight, Aefe. Thank you for passing the time with me."

He still looked unwell. He was pale, and the darkness

surrounding his eyes seemed even more pronounced than before. A strange feeling stirred in my chest, a feeling that made me want to thrust out my arm to steady him.

He set off down the hall, his hand braced against the stone.

His words echoed: *You only know what it is to be used.* The gaping wound the humans left within me throbbed.

A part of me loved them. A part of me mourned them. And a part of me hated them, for using me, for abandoning me.

"Wait," I said.

He stopped short. Perhaps I imagined the surprise in his expression as he turned.

"Yes?"

"I know where she is. Tisaanah. Sometimes I… I dream it. I feel her."

A wrinkle formed between his brows. I imagined judgement in it.

"I don't know how else to describe it," I said, somewhat helplessly.

"I understand perfectly what you mean." He started towards me, and I closed the gap between us. His fingers lifted to my temple. I felt a strange tug, as if he was reaching through me to the threads that connected me to deeper layers of my magic — the layer that I shared with them.

He withdrew his hand. I tried to understand his expression and failed.

"Thank you," he said, after a long silence.

I nodded. A part of me was… glad. Proud of myself.

I watched him. And he was almost at the end of the hall when I said, without fully intending to, "Goodnight."

Perhaps I imagined the brief pause, as if in surprise. But he did not look back as he disappeared around the corner.

CHAPTER TWELVE

TISAANAH

I dealt with unpleasant emotions the same way I always did: burying myself in work. At least there was never a shortage of people who needed my attention, plans that needed my eyes, problems that needed my brain. Filias, Serel, and Sammerin didn't even try to approach me. Riasha came to me under the guise of work, but she watched me with concern that had nothing to do with trade strategies.

"We'll find another way to free him, child," she said, quietly, unprompted. "I promise."

I had to clench my jaw so hard that it trembled to keep from saying something I'd regret.

"We have work to do," I said, after a long silence, and Riasha nodded, and we didn't speak of it again.

It was dark by the time she left, and by then, my mind was useless. The walls of my tent suffocated me. My rage had begun to fade, replaced with an even more unpleasant hopelessness.

Finally, I rose and went out into the night. Most people had retreated to their tents. I passed Serel's, illuminated from within with warm flickering lantern lights. I could make out two silhouettes within. The shapes were distorted by their embrace, but I knew what I was seeing. I'd recognize Serel's form anywhere, and Filias's, tall and lean, was easy to identify.

I turned away. A terrible, acrid feeling stirred in my stomach.

Of course it's easy to make this choice when he still has someone to go back to every night. He doesn't know how it feels. Why should he care?

My own bitterness shocked me the minute the thought flitted through my mind, and I immediately hated myself for it. Serel deserved happiness. And Filias, however we sometimes disagreed, was a good man.

This isn't who you are, Tisaanah, I told myself.

But sometimes it was so damned hard to be kind.

I tucked my hands into my pockets and kept walking. There was a little ridge at the edge of the encampment, which had become one of my favorite places to sit alone at night. But as I approached, I realized someone had already beaten me there.

I hesitated, then approached.

I sat beside Sammerin, who was smoking a pipe and scratching little ink drawings into a beaten-up notebook. We sat in silence for a few long seconds.

Sammerin spoke first. "I never intended to give up on him."

"I know. I shouldn't have said that."

"No. It was justified." He let out a long breath and set down his notebook. "I fought against that decision, Tisaanah. At least, as hard as I could, considering the language barrier. But I made my position very clear."

"I know," I said, quietly.

"I wanted to have another option by the time you returned. Another path forward." A humorless smile twisted the corner of his mouth. "The cruel thing is, I have never been a good idea person. Back in our military days, that was him."

It didn't matter if Sammerin was an "idea person" or not. I had been racking my brain for hours, and I was beginning to think that we had simply run out of options.

I would never, ever say that aloud.

"The thing is..." A long puff of smoke. "I may not agree with their decision, but I do understand why they're making it. Perhaps if I were them, I would make the same one."

I fought the urge to argue with him—*never*, I wanted to say. And yet... I thought of Jaklin's children, both under ten. Thought of Melina's dead body.

"It makes me sick, Sammerin. It actually *hurts* to think of him suffering in that place. I can't just... give up."

"I know. But you're only one person."

Despite myself, I choked a bitter laugh. "People are always telling me that. I don't understand why."

Sammerin gave me a deadpan look out of the corner of his eye and released a long exhale of smoke. "I wonder indeed."

It felt good to laugh, even half-heartedly. But my smile faded fast. And it was the first time I had ever given voice to this confession—this precious, shameful secret—when I said, "Before the Arch Commandant fight, he asked me if I ever thought about what it would be like to stay with him forever."

I could still remember it so clearly—*What if it wasn't just two weeks? What if this was our lives?*

He had said it the way someone spoke of a dream, with all the vulnerability and joy of giving life to something precious. He had handed me his heart.

And what did I give him in return?

My eyes burned. "And I said *nothing*. I didn't answer him. Because I was afraid."

Because I was too cowardly to let myself believe in a future. Too terrified of my own selfishness. Too overwhelmed by how much I wanted him and the dream he offered.

Shame curled in my stomach.

"What if he's in that place, alone, and he thinks that I have abandoned him?"

What if he didn't know that I was here, loving him so much I couldn't breathe, couldn't think, couldn't live?

"He doesn't think that."

"How can you know?"

"When Max believes in something, he gives it his whole self.

It's his greatest strength and greatest weakness. And you, Tisaanah, were the first thing he had believed in for a long, long time. It takes more than four walls to break that kind of faith."

He said it so matter-of-factly, like it was nothing more and nothing less than the truth.

My composure threatened to unravel. Like I had so many times, I collected myself, closing away my pain like a wound that had been stitched up too many times. The stitches would break again later, in private. They'd hold long enough until then.

I gave Sammerin a sidelong glance.

"How are you, Sammerin?"

One eyebrow twitched. "I am utterly fantastic."

Sammerin's sarcasm was like expensive whiskey. Subtle and refined, but plenty potent.

I leaned my head against his shoulder. The position gave me a better view of the notebook in his lap. He had been drawing a little Aran townhouse with a sign over the door, upon which Sammerin had scratched, *Esrin & Imat.*

It was his practice.

"I'm just tired," he said, softly, after a moment. "We've been fighting for a long time. Traveling for a long time."

I recognized the emotion in his voice. I had felt it myself, many times.

My people were fighting to reclaim their homes, while Sammerin had been wrenched away from his. The others liked him well enough, but he struggled with the language. And Sammerin's life here, like all of ours, had become a monotonous string of battles and broken bodies and camps moved late in the night.

"You miss your home," I murmured.

"I left a lot behind. My patients, my practice. Family."

A pang of guilt twinged in my chest. "We will make sure you return."

He gave me a small smile—the sort of smile that said he appreciated the sentiment, but didn't entirely believe me.

But it would need to be true, I decided. I wouldn't accept any alternative.

"It just takes time," I said. "A wise man once told me that creating is harder than destroying."

The corner of Sammerin's mouth lifted, recognizing his own words echoed back to him.

"I suppose," he said, "it will be worth it."

Gods, I hoped so. I hoped so.

———————————

I WAS ACCUSTOMED, by now, to strange dreams. But this was not a dream. It started as one, and ended as one. Whatever happened between was a cataclysm.

One moment, I was in a field of flowers watching a familiar left-skewed smile—a dream, of course—and the next, the entire world was falling apart, as if sight and sound and touch and smell and the invisible forces that held all of those things together were being ripped apart from the inside out. Somewhere far away, yes, but physical distance meant nothing here. The pain was immeasurable.

A thousand different moments collided.

Suddenly I was in a beautiful, unfamiliar room that I hated, looking up at the ceiling, gasping for breath.

Suddenly I was trapped between four white carved walls, beating at them with my fists, fire in my veins with nowhere to go.

That moment of connection existed only for seconds—less, even, and yet it made everything else stop. That was Max. I'd know his presence anywhere, even by a few fractured seconds through his eyes.

I needed to go back. Needed to reach him. I tried to harness this overwhelming flood of magic, tried to channel it, but there was no structure to it, no reason. It was a putrid flood that went in every direction at once. A fundamental shift in the world.

I screamed his name, but I had no voice, no words. Whatever wound was being ripped into the deep layers of this world tore wider. I was swept away.

"TISAANAH."

I didn't want to wake up. Didn't want to relinquish my dream.

Was it a dream? It had felt so real. I reached out for my magic again, feeling for those roots that connected me to the world beneath—feeling for him.

Nothing.

"*Tisaanah.*"

My eyes snapped open and I jerked away. Ishqa slowly came into focus. It was dark. A single lantern lit my tent.

It took me a moment to collect myself. "You're late," I said.

"I apologize."

I sat up as he approached my bedroll. With the flickering light of the single flame falling across him, illuminating his gold hair and gold eyes while the rest of him fell into shadow, he at first looked like some sort of apparition rather than a living being.

And yet, as he came closer, he seemed... oddly human. I blinked the sleep from my eyes. "Are you alright?"

"Why do you ask?"

"You seem..." *Sad.* "Tired."

Only the corner of his mouth moved. "It has been a long hundred years."

Was that a...joke?

My head hurt so, so much. I rubbed my temples. Everything felt as if it was tilting. When I rose, I half expected to tip over.

"Where were you?" I asked.

"You are not alright." He rarely asked questions. He mostly made statements.

"I had... a strange dream."

"A dream."

I heard what he really meant in the tone of his voice. What he was really asking.

"You must be careful," he said. "You do not know whether

the king is still able to take advantage of your use of deep magic. And we can't risk—"

"I know."

I spoke more harshly than I intended, mostly because I hated that Ishqa was right. I knew how dangerous it was. I was there when it happened to Max—when Max drew deep from his magic during his fight with Nura, and the Fey king seized upon that passageway. I was the one who had cut that connection out of him at Max's desperate request... even though I knew it could destroy so much of his mind.

The memory alone made me ill.

"It wasn't like that," I said. "It was... I don't know how to describe it. A shattering."

Anyone else might have acted like I was being nonsensical, and I wouldn't have blamed them for it. But Ishqa just seemed concerned.

"Did you feel anything else?"

I wasn't sure why I hesitated to say it. "A bit. A strange place I did not recognize. And..."

"Him."

I nodded.

Ishqa looked uneasy. "We need to be careful."

"I can't turn away from any chance at learning more. Not if we're to win this war."

He gave me a long, piercing look. "I may seem old and inhuman to you," he said. "But I understand why you are doing this, and I understand that it has nothing to do with the war. I know what it is to mourn someone. But—"

I didn't want to have *this* conversation again.

"You didn't answer my question," I said, tightly. "Where did you go?"

"That is irrelevant."

"Did you go to see your son?"

A single muscle twitched in Ishqa's throat, the only movement in a marble-still expression. "No."

I rose, stepped closer to him—close enough to see all the little imperfections in his face that distance and the darkness had shrouded. A faint wrinkle at the corner of his eyes, a scar at the angle of his chin, a few strands of that sleek golden hair that whispered silver. How easy it was for his kind to hide the painful markers of a life of mistakes, the wounds of the past carefully stitched up and tucked away beneath layers of elegant stillness. Humans just bled our pain all over everything, denying it with our last breath while crimson seeped between our fingers.

That's how I'd felt, these last few months. Like I was bleeding out.

"These people have given you their trust, Ishqa," I said. "And they don't trust easily. You've earned it. We're grateful for all that you've done for us. But..."

The "but" escaped my lips without my permission, my voice trailing off. I still felt something, whenever I looked at Ishqa—something with a razored edge.

Ishqa said, quietly, "But there are still pieces of her hatred for me in you."

Her. It. Reshaye. Aefe.

I didn't answer.

"It was my greatest mistake," he said. "I can say this a million times over, and it would not be enough. Perhaps the loss of my son is punishment for what I did then."

A single crack in his calm expression revealed a hint of pain. Such a human, recognizable thing.

He spoke as if his son was dead. He wasn't—though he had been close to it, in Nura's captivity. He had been rescued by the Fey king's forces and remained loyal to King Caduan. Ishqa rarely spoke of it. Only now did I glimpse what he must be feeling, knowing that his son probably thought he was a traitor. To him, his son was just as unreachable as Max was in Ilyzath.

Pity knotted in my chest.

"Perhaps our attachments are inconvenient," I said, quietly, "but what are we doing any of this for, if not for them?"

Ishqa looked as if he would respond, and then thought better of it. He put out his hand.

"Show me."

I obeyed. He cradled my palm, frowning down at the swirls of gold. They looked even more otherworldly now, with the lantern light streaking the metal bands like little rivers of fire over my skin. The burning had dulled to a faint ache. Otherwise, they didn't feel like much of anything.

"Tell me again what happened," he said.

I did, describing the orb that Farimov had presented to the Fey, and what it had done when I tried to touch it.

Ishqa was silent. My palm tingled as his magic reached for mine, as if testing the thing on my skin.

Then suddenly, he dropped my hand and straightened. His eyes leapt to mine, and I saw something very strange on Ishqa's face — *panic*.

"We need to leave," he said.

"Why?" I asked. "What did you —"

That was when the screaming started.

CHAPTER THIRTEEN

MAX

Time did not flow the same way in Ilyzath. Seconds stretched to months and the months compressed to seconds. I wasn't sure if this was a dream, or one of Ilyzath's tricks.

The shift happened all at once, as if something intrinsic to the world tore painfully apart, like flesh parted by a too-dull blade.

The next thing I knew, I was being dragged down, down, down, falling through the floor and through the earth and into something that felt deeper, rawer than all of it.

I felt the cold spray of sea salt on my face. The overwhelming sensation that I was being watched.

I felt a presence that I knew—a stranger that I knew, soul-deep— envelop me, the familiarity of it jarring, like something I had forgotten I was looking for had drawn close enough to touch.

They called my name.

I reached out for them, and then I was somewhere else entirely.

And then I felt another presence, someone encased in stone, someone looking down over a beautiful city in the mountains. That, too, lasted only for seconds.

The heat, the pain, tore me up. I felt burning, like flames were eating me alive.

I felt everything shattering.

An intangible understanding snapped into place: something is wrong.

Something is breaking.

This is dangerous.

The flames consumed me.

———————

I WAS on my feet before I even realized I had moved. Blood pounded in my ears, driven by sheer panic.

There were so many things I didn't understand. But when I opened my eyes, two certainties stood clear in my mind, the sharpest things I had felt in months.

One. Something cataclysmic had just happened. I didn't have the vocabulary to explain what it was, or even how I knew it. I felt it in a sense deeper than sight or sound, like an earthquake shaking the basest parts of me, leaving irreparable damage.

Two. Someone was looking for me. Someone important. I felt a connection to them like a rope knotted around my throat, pulling closer.

My hands met the wall before the act was a conscious decision.

Let me out.

A frantic attempt to use my magic resulted only blisters bubbling under my fingertips—my magic redirected by the Stratagrams inked over me. I barely felt the burns.

I NEED TO GET OUT.

Ilyzath's voice never sounded like words, exactly. Just a collection of sounds. Now, it enveloped me in creaks and groans. The carvings on the wall shuddered.

You feel this change, too. How strange. And yet, perhaps it is unsurprising, that a fly can sense the tremors of an incoming storm.

I pressed my palms to the wall, my breath heaving and heart pounding. The carvings shuddered just as frantically. I had never seen them do that before.

"What is that?" I rasped out. "What just happened?"

The groans of stone sounded like laughter or sobs. *It was the beginning of an end, brought upon by mortal hubris. Hands reaching into forces that should not be wielded, and thinning boundaries that should not be torn.*

"I don't understand."

No. Of course you do not.

The thread of connection to that strange, familiar soul was beginning to fade, like the blurry afterimage of a dream, and that thought devastated me.

I attempted another burst of magic and was again rewarded only with more burns over my hands. I didn't stop.

You cannot break these walls. Surely you are not so foolish to think you can. You belong here. Ilyzath's shadows caressed my face. *Why do you so wish to leave, my ashen son?*

"Because..." I didn't know how to describe it, the intensity of the sudden need. It was like I had been alerted to a lost piece of myself, somewhere far beyond this place.

The walls creaked in something akin to a chuckle, hearing my unspoken response. Ilyzath, after all, heard everything.

I, too, have lost pieces of myself. But like my loss, yours, too, is inevitable.

Another failed attempt at shattering those walls. Another burst of pain.

"Nothing is inevitable," I muttered.

The connection was almost gone.

I could have sworn Ilyzath laughed.

For an age of your people, I am here. Suns rise and set, and I am here. Empires fall, and I am here. Long before the sunrise or the stars or the shape of the Aran seas coastline. Long before these walls and long after mortals destroy this world. I will feel it fall around my feet, and I will watch. That is inevitability.

I scoffed. Fuck that.

I kept trying anyway. "That's what we do," I muttered, mostly to myself, panting with the exertion of my next blow. "Fight the inevitable. Even when it makes us fucking idiots."

A strange pause in the air, as if all Ilyzath's whispers ceased at once. It was so dark now that with every attempt at my magic, a red glow sparked over my face.

Hmmm.

I went still. A strange realization rocked through me.

All this time, I had been here, locked up in Ilyzath's box of horrors. I'd listened to its whispers, cowered at its visions. But never once had it occurred to me to wonder what it *was*—wonder if it was alive enough to *want.*

Not until now.

Someone I knew once had taught me that there was nothing more useful than understanding the hidden needs and wants of others. And now, in some strange element of the air, I felt it in Ilyzath. Want. Desire. Grief, and fear.

"You want something. I can help you."

A shudder of laughter. *Does a mountain need the help of an insect?*

"A mountain can't move. An insect can." I pressed my palms to the stone. "You want something. I can feel it. You need to stand here. But I can go, if you let me."

There was a long pause, and I prepared myself to resume my desperate clawing at the walls, because surely that made a hell of a lot more sense than trying to negotiate with a fucking prison.

But then the words whispered, *I will make a bargain with you, Maxantarius Farlione.*

I stopped. This had to be another hallucination. Another trick.

I will allow you to fight inevitability. I will give you your chance to repair the damage that is being wrought upon the underlayers of this world. You will fail, but I will allow you to try. The carvings collected around my palms, like ants circling a carcass. *But I ask for two conditions. You must bring a piece of me with you, and you must return when I call.*

My brow knitted. "Repair the damage? I don't understand. What does that mean?"

But there were no more words, no sounds. Only a silent, unspoken demand: *Yes or no?*

Maybe I should have been more discerning. Maybe I should have thought harder. But I wasn't thinking about the risks. I was thinking only about the pain that screamed in a world far beneath this one, an indescribable call that I felt like I had to answer, and a thread that pulled me towards someone else that needed me very much.

"Fine," I said. "You have a deal."

Pain ripped through my hand, worse than the fresh burns. I hissed a curse and leapt away from the wall. When I looked down, a black-and-blue mark adorned my left palm. The overlapping symbols resembled the ones marked into Ilyzath's walls, arranged in a diamond shape, and it seemed to shimmer slightly, as if shards of silver were buried within the ink.

"What is—?"

I looked up, and a doorway now stood before me.

You may leave, Ilyzath said. *No one will stop you.*

I THOUGHT it was a trick even after I reached the doors. But Ilyzath spoke the truth. There wasn't another soul in the white halls. Not prisoners, not guards, and not even a whisper from Ilyzath itself. I didn't think I even knew how to leave my room. I tracked the turns every time I was taken from my cell, but I knew they changed every time. Yet, minutes later I found myself at a large set of silver double doors. They opened as I approached, revealing the sea, dim beneath the waning light of dusk.

I can't fucking believe this is happening, I thought, as I stepped beyond them to freedom. A wall of cold, moist air enveloped me.

I drew in a sharp breath.

In the distance, I could see the shape of the Aran skyline, silhouetted by the sunset. Plumes of smoke pumped into the air, thick enough to see even from this distance. The Fey must have launched another attack—a bad one, by the looks of it.

It was so shocking that it took a moment for the truth to set in: that I was here, outside of Ilyzath's walls, without a shred of iron on me. *Free.*

No—not yet. Not quite. I needed to get off this island. I reached for my magic, only to be barred by the tangled mess of Stratagrams. I couldn't use a Stratagram of my own to leave, not with my magic locked away.

I needed a boat.

I needed —

"*Max*? How did you… Why…"

I turned and froze.

I was so accustomed to Ilyzath's visions that it took me a moment to determine whether the person who stood before me was real.

Brayan stared me down, sword clutched in his hands. His hair whipped violently in the wind, as did the cloak over his shoulders, red and black streaking against the broken sky. He now wore an Aran military uniform.

Figures that he would have joined them. Just as Nura said.

He looked at me like he wasn't sure if I was real, either.

I had no weapons. No magic. Even with it, I had barely ever been able to win a fight against my brother. Without it, I didn't even have a chance.

"I won't go back," I said.

He approached me, and I tensed.

"Brayan, I swear to the Ascended if—"

"Shut up." He raised a finger, pointing. There, where Ilyzath's entrance dropped off into the churning sea, was a little boat. "Let's go."

I didn't know what to say to that. The very thought of the Brayan I had known betraying the uniform he wore was incomprehensible.

He took another step forward, annoyed. "What the hell are you waiting for? Move, before the Syrizen find you."

I had no interest in arguing, even if nothing in the world made sense anymore. I was in a haze as I followed Brayan to the boat. We pushed away from Ilyzath. I watched it grow smaller, from a wall of white to a pillar to a shape barely visible through red-drenched mist.

"They'll come for us," I said softly, to myself, as we pushed away.

But they didn't.

No one did.

CHAPTER FOURTEEN

TISAANAH

The village was already burning.

My tent was on the far north side of our encampment, slightly offset from the rest. By the time Ishqa and I crested the hill, the night sky was lit up with the bloody glow of flames. How did this happen so fast?

Ishqa's stride didn't even slow as he drew his sword. I did the same, with considerably less grace.

Serel. Sammerin. I needed to find them.

"How?" I choked out. "How did they find us?"

Ishqa gave a pointed look to my hand. That alone was enough to make the pit in my stomach drop further. "They can *track* this?"

"I do not know. Maybe. If—"

Ishqa stopped short. I had to stop myself from stumbling into him. When I lifted my gaze to follow his, I felt sick. The soldiers were on horseback, silhouetted into four legged beasts through the thick black smoke and red glow of the flames. Human? Fey? I couldn't tell from this distance. Leading them down the main stretch of the encampment was the dark-haired Fey from earlier that day.

They were going through each tent methodically, ripping people from each before setting them aflame. In the distance, I heard my name on the lips of shouted orders.

"They're looking for—"

"You," Ishqa finished. "For *that*."

I grabbed his arm, wrenched him towards me. It must have looked comical—he was so much larger than me that it was like trying to drag a stone statue. "You need to tell me what this is."

"That is… a complicated question that I do not have time to answer. But we absolutely cannot, under any circumstances, allow them to take it. You need to leave here. Right now. We can be miles away by the time they realize you are gone."

He put out his hand for me, clearly intending to fly us both away, but I shook my head.

"Leave and let them burn this place to the ground? I won't do that."

"This is important, Tisaanah—"

Important, he says, as if my people were not.

Down the hill, I heard more shouts. Through the smoke I could make out a familiar tall, lanky form standing down the Fey, sword drawn. Filias, looking as if he was ready to take down the army himself.

He didn't even especially like me, but he was prepared to die for me.

No. No, leaving now was out of the question. If I was going to leave, I was going to make sure the Fey saw me do it—I was going to give them something to chase and give my friends time to escape.

I was out in the street, in full view of the attackers, by the time Ishqa even saw me moving. I heard him call my name, horrified, and ignored it.

The Fey woman smiled.

"How lovely to see you again so soon."

I stopped several paces short of her. The smoke was so thick it burned my eyes, the sky now red, the air dense. I could see little but the fire and the silhouettes moving within it.

Sammerin knelt next to an injured woman, his head turning to look at me.

Don't move, Sammerin. Not yet.

"Call off your men," I said.

"The Threllians are my allies, not my subordinates," the Fey woman said. "And they have been looking for your friends for a very long time. I cannot guarantee they will listen."

I tracked movement out of the corners of my vision. Soldiers, approaching me through the smoke. I nearly flinched as one of them lurched for me, only for them to stop short, neck snapping at an unnatural angle.

But I could also hear movement behind me—fragments of what I prayed was Riasha's voice.

I just needed to buy enough time for them to escape. The woods were not far from here. Thick enough for them to get lost in, I hoped. I understood one thing as truth. If I didn't do something, if I simply hid and ran into the night like Ishqa wanted me to, everyone here would die.

I took one step forward, and the Fey woman tensed. She was watching the distance between us so closely. I pretended not to notice.

"I understand," I said. "But if you can't make me that promise, then I won't go with you."

I pushed a strand of rebellious hair from my eyes—deliberately letting the movement linger, showing off my left hand and the gold that wrapped around it. The Fey watched me the way a hawk watched a fish circling beneath the water.

"As you wish," she said, at last, and murmured something in a language I couldn't understand to the Fey soldier at her side, who gave me a wary stare before riding off into the red mist.

I refused to show my breath of relief. I readied myself. Took a step forward.

And then a force hit me so hard that all the air was knocked out of my lungs.

I hit the ground. A body—no, two—were on top of me, one wrenching my arm behind my back, one yanking my head back by my hair. A splitting pain cut through me. *Pop*, as my shoulder left its socket.

I managed to press my hands together just enough—just enough to draw the final line of the Stratagram I had been inking onto my palm in blood.

… And nothing happened.

Shit.

My magic had become a volatile, unpredictable thing, never with me when I needed it most. And right now, I needed it to take me away from here.

Sour breath warmed my ear, my cheek. A Threllian soldier.

"What?" he breathed. "Your magic tricks fail you, slave?"

"Not all of them," I replied.

He screamed loud enough to drown out everything else as I pushed my blade from my sleeve, lodging it in his considerable gut. I seized the moment of freedom, rolling over and jamming my blade through the throat of the other soldier who reached for me. Shouts filled my ears, coming from all directions.

There were too many of them. I needed to Stratagram away —show them that I'd left, give them another target far away from here.

To my left, one of the men stopped short, his body lurching oddly. He clutched his chest, falling to his knees. His companion turned, only to suddenly jerk, his neck snapping is if twisted by invisible hands.

I whirled to see Sammerin rushing towards me.

"Don't let her go!" a voice screamed. The Fey woman charged for me.

Sammerin grabbed me split seconds before she did. I caught his eyes, dark and determined, and understood what he was about to do.

If I'd had time to speak, I would have asked him if he was sure. Coming with me meant being pursued. It meant one more step away from the peaceful life in Ara he so missed.

And yet, I could've sworn I saw him nod—nod, as he

wrapped me in his arms and drew a Stratagram over a scorched piece of parchment.

The Fey soldier's hands grabbed my elbow, nearly yanking me away from him.

The world fell away, and we were gone.

CHAPTER FIFTEEN

AEFE

I did not return to my room that night. My soul was restless. So when Caduan left, instead of going up the stairs to my chamber, I went down until there was nowhere else for me to go.

A faint, sour stench that was oddly familiar permeated my nostrils. There was a low buzz in the air—voices.

I followed the sound to an open arched door. Within it, bodies hunched over haphazardly placed little tables, clutching delicate glasses or large stone cups. It reminded me of memories that I could not place.

I entered the room. I barely received so much as a glance from the other people here. I liked that. I used to spend time in a place like this, I thought. I used to feel safe there. Safety now seemed so foreign that even the ghost of it was intoxicating.

"Aefe?"

The sound of the name shattered that thought.

My eyes settled on him across the room. The memory cut close to the bone—myself, screaming, *"You cannot leave me here!"*

No.

Not him, not Ishqa. A different face.

Meajqa smiled at me, lifting a glass of red liquid. Two raven-haired Fey women sat beside him, but he whispered something to them, and they shot me curious looks before relinquishing their seats.

"What a surprise to see you here," he said, gesturing to the newly empty bench beside him. "Join me! You look like you need a drink."

He grinned, but it was not a happy expression. It reminded me of grimaces of exertion from training soldiers. I wondered if perhaps Meajqa was putting just as much effort into this, even if he tried to hide it.

My instinct was to back away, one awkward half-step. But then another murky memory flitted through me, a memory of wine over my tongue and all the things it could wash away.

So I took the glass from Meajqa's outstretched hand and slid into the seat beside him. He let out an amused huff of surprise when my first sip was instead a series of gulps, mouthful after mouthful of the bitter liquid burning my throat. "I was right, you *did* need a drink," he said. I set down the empty glass and he promptly refilled it.

This is good.

Everything that was too loud and too big and too harsh about this world, this empty body, was a bit duller. Easier. I no longer felt as unsettled by what I had just witnessed.

I liked this.

"What has you in such dire need of wine?" Meajqa asked, then chuckled and shook his head. "That's a ridiculous question, isn't it?"

I did not know what he meant. Instead of answering, I just stared at him. He was dressed differently than he had been in Caduan's meeting. Or... no, his clothing was the same, just looser and disheveled. His shirt was unbuttoned, the wrinkled dark blue fabric now falling open past his sternum to reveal smooth scar-nicked skin. A strip of blue fabric, which before had been neatly draped over his shoulder, now fell haphazardly over his arm. One wing was tucked behind him, arranged to avoid the back of his chair. The color of his feathers was especially entrancing here in the darkness, with so many twinkling lights to reflect—with every shift, they could be silver, or copper, or bright gold.

It was so beautiful it seemed garish compared to his other side.

The stump was close enough to touch. Where silver-gold feathers would have spread into a majestic wing, they were instead interrupted by a vicious wound, the feathers failing to hide darkened, gnarled flesh. The shape of the bone jutted a few inches beyond the rest, as if whoever responsible had difficulty making the cut there.

"You seem to admire my best feature," Meajqa said.

My gaze flicked back to his face. The smile had not faded.

"I'm not offended," he added. "Everyone loves to stare."

"She did that to you."

"She?"

"The Aran queen."

It seemed strange to refer to her that way when I knew her not by syllables on a tongue, but by the way her jagged mind felt sawing into mine.

A barely-there twitch in that smile. "She did. Though she had some help with the harder parts."

"Why do you not hide it?" Most of his kind, I had noticed, did not keep their wings visible unless they were being used.

"Why should I?"

"A question is not an answer."

His eyebrows rose. "It is not," he agreed. "The unpleasant truth is that I can't. I can no longer shift."

He said it as if this was an amusing anecdote. But I knew that if I was within his mind, I would feel pain here—hot and sharp like blistering skin. I was so certain of it that for a moment, I could feel it myself.

"Why?" I asked.

"There are many unpleasant side effects to her magical experimentations."

"Experimentations," I repeated, thinking of a room of white

and white and white. For the first time, Meajqa's smile started to fade, his eyes going far away.

"I'm not afraid or ashamed to talk about what she did," he said. "She clearly knew nothing about us, at least at first. She was just testing, I think. Trying to understand what she could do with us. Our blood. Our bodies. Our skin—or wings." An ugly curl to his lip. "You might wonder how she was able to do that, when we are so much stronger than humans, physically."

I was not wondering this. I knew the answer all too well. But I said nothing. Perhaps Meajqa preferred to repeat this answer.

"Her own magic was powerful as it was," he went on. "It grasps the mind. And they had other methods... I couldn't move. I couldn't do anything, but I was conscious for all of it." He leaned close enough that I could smell the wine on his breath. "Months. Do you understand that sort of helplessness?"

Months. I had lived it for centuries. I almost laughed, but it seemed cruel to belittle his pain.

"I know what it is to be helpless," I said. "Locked in a place where you see nothing and feel everything. Humans are greedy creatures. They only know how to take. For five hundred years I did not even understand how much they stole."

My body, my past, my name, my face. My soul.

"Five hundred years," Meajqa repeated, softly. "I heard stories of... you. What you were."

"I became nothing. A tool to be used by them. Even my emotions were no longer my own, only mirrors to theirs."

His solemn expression enhanced an already-unpleasant resemblance. His gold eyes flicked to mine, and I looked away.

"I make you uncomfortable," he murmured. "Why?"

"You are Ishqa's son."

It was the first time I had ever said Ishqa's name aloud. In my mind, he was shades of betrayal and anger, not a person.

"I am, unfortunately. The king told me what he did to you. As Ela'Dar's head diplomat, I needed to be aware. Especially after my father's... departure. His actions..." His voice grew a shade too serious. "I wish I could apologize to you for my bloodline's betrayal. I know that I can't, but I wish I could."

His words were meaningless. I knew this. And yet, I found a strange kinship in Meajqa's sorrow. It was messy and raw, like my own.

"And now he is helping the humans, despite everything." He let out a rough laugh, took another drink of wine, and set the glass down hard. "Good riddance. We're better off without him. He may be willing to abandon his people to go help the humans, but we have a king who embodies loyalty to his own. To Caduan, we are not disposable. One has to admire that, even when it makes matters of diplomacy difficult." His gaze grew thoughtful. "And I have never seen my king so committed to anything as he is to this. He will burn them all to the ground in the name of a single Fey life."

The hair prickled at the back of my neck. Meajqa's long silence, and his stare, cut through me.

"He is doing this for you, Aefe," he said.

"He only brought me here because he wants my help."

"No. Maybe that's what he wants us to think. Caduan is a private person. No one knows how he managed to bring you back. Nor will I ask. I am no talented magician—such things are beyond me. But there are things I do know. I know hearts and minds, and I know the king's as well as any other. Humans hurt Fey one too many times. Again and again, he saw it happen. Thus, he calculated an inarguable equation. He will remove the future possibility. This is the decision his mind made, and he made it for all of us. But his heart?"

One hundred and eighty thousand days, and I thought of you in every one.

My own heart—strange thing—was suddenly very loud, as if pounding against the insides of my ribs.

Meajqa leaned closer. "His heart is what truly lit the fires of war, and the fire burns because of you. The decision was for all of us, yes. But the vengeance? The vengeance is for *you*."

FOR DAYS, I did not see Caduan. I stayed in my room, pacing. Every day, a maid would come and tell me that I could leave if I wished. Every day, I declined. On the third, I asked about Caduan. The maid gave me a strange look.

"The king is not well." was all she would say.

For days I sat there. Sleeping. Sitting. Dreaming of the inside of others' skins. Dreaming of past nightmares. Dreaming of white and white and white. Every day, when the maid came, I would ask about Caduan. Every day, I received the same answer.

I didn't know why I cared so much.

But on the sixth day, after the maid's footsteps disappeared down the hall, I stood and went to the door.

PEOPLE KEPT LOOKING at me and I decided not to care.

I had never been to Caduan's quarters before, but I knew it was at the highest point of the castle, and I knew it was not far from my own. So I walked, bare feet treading over the marble tile of the halls and then the cold copper of the stairwells, up and up. The stairs curved, following hammered-glass windows. Once I reached the top, I paused. Ela'Dar spread out beneath me, the city crawling over the forest-covered mountains as if it had grown alongside nature itself.

I remembered what it once had felt like to stand at the top of black cliffs and see my entire world stretching to the horizon.

Caduan had built a majestic kingdom. But five hundred years had taught me that there was little that could not be torn apart. Once, I had taken comfort in the certainty of destruction. But now, I was dizzy at the thought. I wondered what Caduan felt when he saw this view. Did he feel pride at what he had created? Or fear at the possibility of watching it crumble?

My ears pricked at the faint echo of a familiar voice. Behind me, a narrow hallway led to a door that was slightly ajar.

I approached it, peering through. There was a small room within, chairs and couches arranged around its center. Bookshelves lined the walls, plants spilling over their edges and winding across the shelves. In one chair sat Caduan, somewhat sprawled, his clothing simple and hair messy. His gaze flicked to me the minute I approached the door, and he straightened, a certain spark lighting up his expression. He looked... pleased to see me.

For a moment, I thought, without meaning to, *It is good that I came here.*

"Aefe," he said. "Come in."

I obeyed. But when I pushed the door open and stepped inside, I realized that Caduan wasn't alone. Luia, Meajqa, and Vythian were there, too. They gave me greetings I didn't return, except for a small smile to Meajqa that I couldn't help. Then I looked between them, to the table at the center of the room and the map spread across it, adorned with red marks.

I went still. A terrible feeling rose in my stomach.

"Excellent timing," Vythian said. "We were just discussing you."

Five words, and the air in the room suddenly went cold. Caduan gave Vythian a sharp look that seemed to imply many things. I could not read the muscles on Caduan's face, but I understood enough. I knew what it was to have my name on the lips of men looking at maps with red marks on them.

Already, I felt foolish.

"What does that mean?" I said, my voice hard.

Caduan's glare to Vythian withered as he looked to me. "Nothing important. We can discuss it later."

The anger took my breath away. My muscles were trembling, my jaw tight, my body betraying all the signs of my rage. Where that warmth had once glimmered in my chest, now there was a sharp ache, like a knife between my ribs.

"You can not lie to me," I hissed.

The remnants of Caduan's smile disappeared. He turned to Luia, Vythian, and Meajqa. "Go. Leave us alone."

There were murmurs of protest, ceased by Caduan's command, "*Go!*"

After a moment of hesitation, they shuffled from the room. I could feel them staring at me—could feel, in particular, Meajqa's curious, pitying gaze—but I didn't break my own from Caduan.

The door closed. His exhaustion did nothing to dull the striking green of his eyes, and I wished now, more than ever, that I knew how to read what lay in their depths.

"You've heard of Tisaanah Vytezic and the artifact that she now possesses," Caduan said.

The sound of Tisaanah's name brought me back to uncomfortable places. I didn't answer.

"The wayfinder that she has," he went on, "provides a means to discover, and perhaps even use, deep pools of magic called Lejaras. They are deeper and more powerful than any other magic that has been seen in many, many hundreds of years. For a long time, I thought they were a myth. So did most others. But the rumors have persisted for centuries. The humans who destroyed my own House were doing it because they believed one such pool existed there." His face hardened, and he went silent for a moment before continuing.

"Even one of the Lejaras can be devastating. All three used together can reshape reality itself. They are dangerous to wield, and it can only be done in specific locations that can channel such forces. But if the humans were to do such a thing, and find such a place, it would be devastating. They would be able to destroy all of us." He stood, heavily, as if it took him great effort. I took a step back.

"You know better than anyone," he said, "how terrible it would be if they came into that kind of power."

I did know. I knew intimately what humans did with unbridled destructive power, because I was the power, and it was my hands that drew the blood of their own peoples.

Still, I did not speak.

"Aefe," Caduan said, my name like a caress—too gentle for the anger I felt. "I didn't want this to be you. But we need to find these magics. We need to leverage them before the humans do. Trust me when I say I have tried all other ways. But you are the only key we have." He took one small step closer, and again, I stepped back. "You, Aefe. I need you."

Three words that landed like a strike.

I need you.

I had heard those words before, whispered or begged in the minds of the humans who held me. *I need you,* they would plead, before they unleashed me to inflict death upon their own. *I need you,* they would croon, before they betrayed me.

And here he was—Caduan, another one attempting to wield me, saying it again. *I need you.*

I want what you can give me.

Be my weapon.

The hurt spilled through me like acid.

"No," I said. "No, I will not do it."

I cannot do it. Not this. Not again.

Caduan looked pained.

"This cannot be a request, Aefe," he said, gently. "Not this time. I tried to find every other option."

My blood pooled in half-moons in my palms as my fingernails cut into my skin.

"I told you, *no.*"

"You don't have a choice."

Choice. *Choice!* I hated that word, hated it the way I hated dreams that never materialized.

"I have *never* had a choice. I have been given the choice to be —to be *more* than this. I will not be your weapon. Not again. *Never.*"

I did not realize I was shouting until my throat began to ache, my voice growing hoarse.

My hand closed around a quill sitting on the desk beside me. Distantly, I heard a loud slam as the door flung open, smashing against the wall. Luia ran into the room, her sword drawn.

Caduan shouted—*"Luia, stand down!"*—in the same moment that the quill went hurtling directly towards his emerald eyes.

He grabbed it from the air before it made contact, fist white-knuckled around the golden pen.

"One hundred and eighty thousand days I have been at the mercy of human kings," I snarled. "And if you think you are any better than any of them, you are a *fool*."

Still, Caduan met my stare. Calm. Affectionate, even.

Perhaps in another life I would have killed him—killed him for making me feel so ashamed, so betrayed, so abandoned. But today, I turned on my heel, pushing past Vythian and through the door. "Let her go," I heard Caduan's voice say.

"Aefe—" Meajqa murmured as I passed him, softer than the others, but I ignored him, too.

I walked down endless stairs, out the door of the castle. I walked through Ela'Dar's streets, and I did not even care about the stares.

I kept walking and walking and walking, until I was no longer in Ela'Dar at all.

CHAPTER SIXTEEN

MAX

It was a long time before either of us said anything—so long that the sound of Brayan's voice jolted me more than the spray of seawater.

How long had I just been staring out at the horizon? There was nothing but the sea around us, Ilyzath's shape long ago consumed by the misty sky. Blue-grey stretched out in all directions.

"What?"

"How did you get out?" Brayan repeated.

I honestly did not know how to answer that question.

I will let you go if you take a piece of me with you.

The memory was like a fever dream. I still struggled to wrap my mind around what had just occurred. None of the pieces fit together right.

I told him the truth, the story in its bizarre entirety, partly out of curiosity to see if it would seem as fucking outlandish out loud as it did in my head. The answer, it turned out, was very much yes.

When I finished, Brayan looked like he was more certain

than ever that I'd completely lost my mind, and I didn't blame him for it one bit.

"I know it sounds…" I settled on, "Strange."

"It does," he agreed.

But Ilyzath itself was strange. No one knew exactly how it worked. It was widely regarded to be one of the oldest magical locations in the world—older than Ara itself by millennia.

I looked down at the mark Ilyzath had given me. It was a circle of symbols, unintelligible, spiraling in tighter towards my palm. The flesh was slightly raised and red, as if angry.

Then I looked up at Brayan.

"Why were you there?" I asked. "Just… waiting at Ilyzath?"

He gave me a long, cold stare, not answering. It was the same sort of look he used to give me when I was a child. He had the same dark eyes as our mother, nearly black, and every time he'd looked at me, I'd felt like there were limitless judgements and demands hiding in that darkness.

"Why wouldn't I be there?" he said. "I've been there every day."

I blinked. "You—what?"

He looked to the horizon and avoided eye contact. "We need to think about where—"

"Brayan, answer the Ascended-damned question."

"You haven't changed," he remarked, and just as I was about to spit a curse and give up, he added, "I answered your question. I was at Ilyzath because I have been there every day. I was trying to see you. Not that the Syrizen would allow it."

Many, many unbelievable things had happened over these last few months. And yet, it was *this* that seemed so ridiculous that I let out a snort of laughter before I could stop myself.

His stare darkened. "What about that is funny?"

"I just…" I pinched the bridge of my nose. "Brayan Farlione, renowned general, loyal Aran, golden child of the Ryvenai upper class, just *broke me out of prison*."

"I didn't break you out. You were already out. I just had the boat."

He said this very, very seriously, and in that moment, it was the most hilarious thing I'd ever heard in my sorry life.

Maybe I was just going insane.

Going? No, actually, that ship had likely long ago sailed.

Brayan watched me, unamused. Long seconds passed. The sound of the sea lapping against the boat became deafening long after my laughter subsided, fading into awkward silence.

There were too many words to say. Too many questions to ask. Any normal person would have asked them. We were stranded on a boat with nothing else to talk about.

But no. That was a renowned Farlione trait, after all: ignoring the things that dangled right in front of our faces. And honestly? I was grateful for it, right now.

"So." I cleared my throat. "Now what?"

"We go to Besrith."

"Is that home? For you?"

"Home?" He gave me an odd look. "It's… where I've been living for the last few years. It's quiet there, and remote. They don't have diplomatic relationships with Ara. It will be hard for Nura to get to you there."

It still was fucking incredible that I was listening to Brayan outline the best way to evade the Aran government.

I glanced down at the boat carrying us—barely more than a rowboat. "I hate to shatter your hopes and dreams, Brayan, but there's no way this boat is making it to—"

"Not in this," he grumbled—in a tone that added an unspoken *obviously*. "We're going to Sarilla first. Then catch a charter ship to Threll and travel north from there. You can help us move faster then, can't you? With… magic and such."

His voice always took on an odd tone when referencing my magic. Like the entire concept made him slightly uncomfortable.

I shook my head.

"I can't. She… they took away as much of it as they could." The sleeves of my dirty white shirt were bunched up around my elbows, and my gaze trailed up my forearms—at all the Strata-grams now tattooed all over my skin. I was struck all over again by exactly how many of them there were, and a surge of anger overwhelmed me.

Up until this moment, I'd had to pour so much of my energy into keeping my life and my sanity. There had been nothing left for anger, so I'd locked it away. Now it hit me all at once, one pent-up wave powerful enough to break my ramshackle barriers.

Brayan made a noncommittal noise and turned away, as if he couldn't bear to look at me for too long. Fair. I hadn't had access to a mirror in months. I probably wouldn't want to look at me for too long, either.

"No matter," he said. "We'll still make it to Besrith."

I took him in, warily. He looked so different than the version of him that I remembered. I suppose that made sense. He had been—I racked my half-broken brain—what, in his mid-twenties, in those final fragmented shards of my memory? I remembered thinking of him as so powerful that he was ageless, the gulf separating us so much wider than a mere seven years. Now, he seemed... older.

I took in his clothing. A dark jacket with gold buttons across a double breast. An Aran military uniform. New.

"What about the uniform?" I asked.

"What about it?"

"Ara is at war."

He looked at me like I was an idiot. "So I've seen. And?"

"So why are you here with me instead of fighting it?"

"What kind of a question is that?"

"Isn't that your great love? Winning wars?"

Ascended above, did Brayan actually look *offended* by that? The last I remembered, he would have agreed with the assessment wholeheartedly. He had shaped his entire life around warfare, crafted himself into a tool to be wielded for a single purpose. He was, of course, exquisite at it. That's why military leaders spoke of Brayan with the same breathless admiration that one spoke of a rare, expensive sword. A kind of admiration laced with greed.

"I don't know what happened to Nura in the last ten years,"

he said, "but I know one thing beyond a doubt—what you did in Sarlazai made you a hero. The Ryvenai War ended because of you. You never should have been imprisoned for that."

A sour taste filled my mouth. I didn't know why.

But Brayan no longer seemed interested in talking. He turned, looking out at the horizon. "We should reach Sarilla in a few hours," he said, in the sort of tone that conveyed that he didn't expect to say another word until then. I didn't especially feel like arguing.

THERE WERE FAR TOO many eyes in Sarilla for my liking.

Sarilla was several hundred miles off the coast of Ara. It was largely used as farmland for large, luxurious operations owned by members of the upper-class. As a result, the island had only one major city, and even there, everyone would pay attention to a few strangers.

It was hot, but I still pulled the length of my sleeves down awkwardly as we stepped onto the docks. Right away, we were getting strange looks. We were unfamiliar here. We looked distinctly Ryvenai. Brayan was wearing a brand-new military uniform. And, of course, there were my tattoos.

"I'm not sure coming here was a good idea," I muttered to Brayan as we abandoned our boat and made our way onto the cobblestone streets. I took a fraction of a second to appreciate the way solid land felt beneath my feet—wonderful—and then a second more to appreciate that it *wasn't Ilyzath stone*—even more wonderful.

In any other context, it would have been borderline criminal not to spend at least a few minutes admiring how nauseatingly beautiful the island was. Lush foliage crawled over hills and valleys, all culminating in a single emerald mountain. Unlike Ara's mountains, which were rocky and jagged, this one was covered in greenery all the way up to its mist-cradled peak. Rocky shores stretched in one direction; in the other, a creamy sand beach. From our spot on the docks, we could see down to the west, where patches of farmland for massive plantation stretched out along the coast.

It was in this direction that Brayan walked, wordlessly, and I followed.

"We can't stay here long," I said. "Nura has probably sent out word already that I'm gone. It's just a matter of time before that call reaches here."

"The ship to Threll leaves at dawn." Brayan, too, was tracking all the people who tracked us—marking those who stopped to stare, and even more carefully observing those who didn't.

Dawn? Fifteen hours seemed like a hell of a long time to not be noticed here.

"We can't stay in town."

"No," Brayan agreed. "But I know somewhere we can go."

He said this so casually that I thought little more of it as he led us away from town, up the road, and through the rolling fields of a large farm. The main house was at the top of a hill, surrounded by fields of grazing cattle. The entrance was marked by a large, wrought-iron gate—majestic, for a farmhouse, and clearly belonging to someone with significant wealth.

Brayan strolled through the gates and up the path, then knocked on the door.

An attractive, fair-haired woman in a floral dress opened it. Her greeting stopped short halfway through. She stared at us with her brow knotted up, as if she couldn't quite believe what she was seeing.

I didn't quite believe what I was seeing, either. I had to bite back an, *Ascended above, Brayan, really?*

"Well," she said. "I can't say I predicted this turn to my day."

"It is lovely to see you again, Sella," Brayan said. So smoothly, as if there was nothing at all remarkable about showing up on the doorstep of your ex-fiancée, fugitive brother in tow.

CHAPTER SEVENTEEN

TISAANAH

W e landed in a forest, and I nearly toppled over. It had been a long time since I'd reacted so strongly to Stratagram travel, my stomach churning and the world spinning. Or maybe it was the smell of ash making me sick, or the remnants of my strange dream that still seemed to simmer in my veins.

I stumbled away from Sammerin's grasp, forcing my heartbeat to slow. I felt as if everything was running too hot.

Sammerin, too, was breathing heavily, leaning against a tree.

"Thank you," I managed.

"You looked like you needed help."

"How did you know? What I was trying to do?"

"You? Self-sacrifice? How would anyone guess."

I laughed, too shrilly. It wasn't funny, and I wasn't amused. I blinked and still saw the fire of the burning village, as if it was burned into my eyelids. A part of me screamed to go back, even though I knew it was the worst possible move.

"Where are we?" I asked.

"Somewhere south. I don't... know exactly where. I tried to fling us as far away as I could, but without a known target, I couldn't have gotten us more than a few miles away."

Gods. We were lucky we didn't wind up scattered into a hundred pieces. Stratagrams without a set destination were incredibly dangerous. Sammerin looked a little pale, as if he too was surprised we'd made it here—wherever *here* was—in one piece.

But the Fey saw me too. That was the most important thing. Hopefully they were searching for us now, instead of destroying the camp.

Sammerin's stare settled on my left hand. "Did Ishqa know what it is? Why they want it so much?"

"He did not get the chance to tell me."

But I needed that information desperately.

I reached into my pocket and closed my fingers around the single feather left in my pocket. Where was Ishqa right now? Was he helping to defend the village? Or did he leave it to burn while he came to find me?

The thought made it difficult to breathe.

Serel. Filias. Riasha. So many key members of rebellion leadership—so many of my friends. How many of them had been killed or captured?

I swallowed my panic.

"I can't go back. The Fey will keep trying to find me. Hopefully they already are, now that they know I left, instead of..."

I didn't want to give voice to my worst fears.

How much time did we have before I was found? What if the Fey *could* track the thing on my hand, as Ishqa seemed to suspect? It took them less than twenty-four hours to get to the village. But at least here, I was alone. We were surrounded by trees. Logistically, it would be harder to reach me.

I turned to Sammerin. He was buttoning his sleeve, looking so put-together I almost hated him for it.

"You can still leave," I said.

"Why would I do that?"

"Because half the Zorokovs' army, and the Fey, are probably on their way here."

He lifted one shoulder in a delicate shrug. "I have nowhere more interesting to be."

Maybe it was selfish of me to feel so relieved. And yet, to say that I was grateful to have Sammerin with me was an understatement.

I pulled the feather from my pocket.

"Alright," I said. "Then we walk. I call for Ishqa. And we hope he comes here with some answers before the Fey and the Zorokovs do."

―――――――――

IshQA DID, thankfully, reach us before the Zorokovs did. Sunrise was encroaching upon the night by then, the sky a mingling of dusky red with remnants of dark blue. When Ishqa arrived, he cut through that beautiful sun-stained sky like a streak of light, careening through the canopy of leaves in a flash of gold. Even at his most approachable, Ishqa never quite seemed human. But now, I wondered if perhaps ancient encounters between Fey and humans inspired the stories we told of gods and monsters. Ishqa, backlit by the sun, golden wings spread, looked like a god.

He pulled his wings in, surveyed us, and said, "It was foolish of you not to run when I told you to."

"The village," I said. "Did you stay to help? Did they…"

How could I even word the question?

Something softened in Ishqa's expression. "Many of your people were able to escape."

Many. Not *most.* Not *all.* I wasn't sure whether to be relieved.

"So long as you don't return to them, the Fey will let them go," he said. "You are far more important."

Ishqa had a strange way of comforting people. He reached into his robes and placed a glass vial in my hand. "Drink."

I blinked at the vial. It was perhaps the length of my palm, filled with a shimmery silver liquid.

"What is it?"

"It will help mask you—it—from them. Imperfectly, but we will need to settle for imperfection."

That was enough for me. I uncorked the vial and shot it back in one gulp, an act I immediately regretted. It felt like swallowing fire.

"I am not sure how humans will react to it," Ishqa said, somewhat thoughtfully. "It gives us terrible stomach cramps."

How nice. I tucked the vial away, then, yet again, thrust my hand out. "What is this, Ishqa?"

"It is a..." He paused, as if uncertain of which word to choose. "Wayfinder."

"A wayfinder?"

"A tool. A compass. A key that leads to other things."

"What other things?"

Ishqa was terrible at this. What was it about six-hundred-year life spans that made one so frustratingly bad at communication?

"You are aware of how magic works," he said. "That it is like rivers running beneath our world, different streams of different substances. Solarie magic, Valtain magic, and our Fey magic."

"And the deeper levels beneath them," I added.

Ishqa nodded.

"Yes. The deep magic that is still connected to you, even if that connection had been severed and stitched over. The very same magic that your lover drew from, that... Reshaye drew from."

He rarely spoke of Reshaye—of Aefe—by name. He never seemed to know which term to use.

"But," he went on, "magic is far more complicated than those four levels. None of us know how many different streams lurk beneath the surface of our world, or what they are capable of. Even the extensive modifications that humans and Fey have done to tap into deeper streams merely allow us to reach a fraction of what exists. And for many years—millennia—the Fey had no interest in learning more about those powers. The humans, at least, always strove to innovate. We... thought such things were blasphemous and unnatural. That is, until Caduan took power. He saw how we could use magical innovations to strengthen our civilization and help our people—end hunger, cure illness, even advance art and music."

Despite all that had happened, when Ishqa spoke of Caduan, there was a tinge of admiration to his voice.

"Five hundred years ago, when the humans were slaughtering our people, they were doing it because they were searching for power. Specifically, they were searching for mythical pools of deep magic—which we now know as Lejaras. They did not understand what, exactly, they were looking for, only that it was a power strong enough to win their own wars. And when they…" His voice stumbled. "…When they found another option, in Reshaye, they ceased their search. They had the power they needed. But that does not mean that the legends they were searching for did not exist. Caduan pursued knowledge relentlessly during his reign, and the Lejaras were no exception."

I pieced together what he was saying.

"And this thing," I said, "is a way to find these… these pools of magic."

"We believe so. Over these last few months, Caduan's drive for the pools was reinvigorated. While I was in Caduan's inner circle, we had not been able to locate them. But we knew that we could if we had *that*."

I looked at my hand. The mark didn't feel like a compass or a key. It just felt like some metal stuck to my skin.

"So now what do we do?"

"These powers cannot fall into Caduan's hands," Ishqa said. "Not under any circumstances. And while I may not know exactly what you hold, why it reacted to you as it has, or how we use it, I know that it's key to the Fey finding and harnessing these powers. Locating them before they do may be our only chance at defeating Caduan."

"You propose that we go use it ourselves. Just us." Sammerin looked unconvinced.

Ishqa gave him a cold stare. "Imagine what this war would be if either side came into possession of such power. Caduan, who wants nothing more than to wipe out your kind for good. Your human queen, who has already shown that she is willing to burn down the world to protect her country. Imagine what the world would be, if either of them—or worse, *both* of them—had the power to literally shape reality. We don't need to use it. Perhaps it would be better if we destroyed it, even. But we certainly need to keep it from them."

Sammerin was quiet, clearly unsettled by the future Ishqa painted. It unsettled me, too. I had seen what Nura was willing to do to win her wars. And though I did not know the Fey king beyond what Ishqa had told me, I had seen what he had done to Ara, had seen the monsters he created. I had *felt* his fury when I reached into Max's mind to sever the connection he had built there.

Ishqa was right. If either of them obtained that kind of devastating power, the world may very well end.

But that wasn't my first thought.

My first thought was of a stone prison off the Aran shores. I was thinking about walls I hadn't managed to break, no matter how hard I tried. And I was thinking of how much easier it might be if I had such a power.

I was so, so selfish—and I didn't even care.

You were the one that wanted to save the world. I just wanted to save you.

Max told me that, once. Now it seemed ironic. He had thought there was absolutely nothing that mattered to me more than my people, my goals, my duty.

He had been wrong. There was one thing more important.

"You're right," I said to Ishqa. "We cannot let Caduan or Nura find these powers. So I suppose we must do it ourselves."

Ishqa looked pleased with this reaction. If only he knew.

"The Fey will keep trying to hunt you," he said. "You understand that. It would be unwise to return to your people."

No. I wouldn't put them at risk. I thought of Serel and fought an overwhelming wave of sadness. The last time we talked, I had been so, so angry at him. The thought that it could be the last thing I ever said to him...

"You'll fly over them, though?" I said, my voice rougher than intended. "You'll find out if they are alright?"

"Yes," Ishqa said, solemnly. "I will."

I nodded and turned to Sammerin. "And are you sure you want to stay?"

"Of course," he said, as if it was a ridiculous question. Despite what we had just been told, he was remarkably calm. Right now, I found his stability the most comforting thing in the world, and I resisted the urge to embrace him.

I looked down at my hand and the rivulets of gold over it. Was it different than before? Had it spread? It was so hard to tell.

"I don't feel anything," I said. "If this is a... a compass of some kind, then I don't know how to use it."

"Nor do I," Ishqa said. "But I may know someone who does. We go north."

"North?"

"Closer to the Fey lands," Sammerin said. "Is that a good idea?"

"We don't have a choice," Ishqa replied. Then he turned, lifting his chin to the sky and raising a single finger. "North."

Nothing lay before us but a blanket of underbrush and forest. But nothing lay behind us, either. So I started walking. Sometimes there was nothing to do but put one foot in front of another.

CHAPTER EIGHTEEN

AEFE

I moved without thinking. Time and distance fell away, inconsequential compared to my wounded anger. When I found myself standing before a wall of black stone, I did not remember coming here.

The black stretched up to the misty sky. Carvings adorned its surface, flashing bright silver where the light struck them the right way. Windows and balconies interrupted the sheets of darkness. I knew somehow that once, long ago, they would have been lit with lanterns, bright and warm with the activity of the people who lived here.

No longer. The cliffs had partially shattered, sections of it ripped apart so its silhouette resembled a jagged mountain peak. Massive cracks stretched across its surface like lightning.

My head was now pounding. I remembered this place.

Once you felt belonging here. Thousands of other souls and you, connected to the same earth.

I had lived here. I was a ruler. A—a Teirness.

No. No you were not. You were tainted.

I remembered my father's hands around my throat. Remembered those stares of disapproval.

136

A part of me wanted to leave the past behind me, pull my hand away from the biting flame. Maybe it was easier not to remember what I had lost.

And yet, I found myself walking through the doors.

———————

ONCE THERE HAD BEEN lights in the black stone walls, like stars over the night sky. Now, they were dim and dusky. With every step through these halls, the past surrounded me.

I walked up and up through spiral staircases of mosaic glass, all the way to the private quarters of the royal family. The damage was worse up here. Some cracks in the ground were impassable. I barely noticed them. I saw only this place as it had existed half a millennium ago.

Here was the throne room where I would kneel before my own family, begging them to love me.

Here I saw the banquet hall where I would sit with the Blades, in the position I earned, not the one I was born into.

Here I saw my childhood bedroom, where my father tried to kill me. Where my mother, my poor, mad mother, saved my life.

And here…

I stopped at this door. It was closed, the mosaic tiles adorning it crooked and broken.

Orscheid. My lovely, beautiful, sweet sister, who was everything I was not, and who still loved me for all that I was.

I threw open the door. A bedchamber had been here, once. Now there was crumbling stone, shattered glass, the sun-bleached remains of a bed, and a chasm in the floor that revealed the distant forest, dizzyingly far below.

I could throw myself over it. Rot in the dust of my old home. The earth called to me, so far below.

You will never escape this place.

"I thought you might come here."

I had not heard Caduan approach.

"Orscheid," I choked out.

137

Silence. Perhaps I was growing better at understanding all the things living beings did not say. Because I knew, even in his wordlessness, that he did not want to give me an answer to the question I did not ask.

Gone. She was gone.

"Come back, Aefe," he said, softly. But I remained there, gripping the doorframe. Specks of silver fell to the abyss below —tears I didn't realize I was shedding.

No one could survive this. How could anyone, human or Fey, live this way? *Feeling* so much?

I just wanted to rest.

"Even then I was nothing," I said. "My father wanted to kill me because I did not deserve to live. I was nothing but what I stole from others."

"You *always* deserved to live," Caduan murmured.

When I was Reshaye, living a thousand lives inside a thousand strangers, I could dream that I was once something more. I was envious of the lives I invaded. I squeezed myself inside their minds and marveled at the depth of everything that thrived there.

I did not know what I was, but I could dream that perhaps once I'd had those things, too. Now, the truth came crashing down around me like these shattered cliffs. Even then, it had been the same.

"Aefe," he said, again. Was that fear I heard in his voice?

I turned away from the door, and, at last, I faced him.

"I need to know what happened here."

I thought he would argue with me. Instead, he said, "I will show you if you want to see. But know that it will be difficult."

The past was jagged glass. But I was drunk on the way it tore me up.

"Show me," I said, and Caduan gave me a strange look. This, I understood now, was tenderness.

"As you wish," he said.

WE WENT to what was once the throne room. It was badly damaged. The ceiling, once high and curved and etched with silver-dipped engravings, was torn up as if a beast with massive claws had shredded it to pieces. The floor was dust-coated and fissured. Upon the shattered dais stood two thrones. My father's, destroyed, the two halves of it caving in on each other. My mother's, bent and broken, the delicate silver warped nearly beyond recognition.

Orscheid's was simply gone.

Dried violet spilled over the dais steps in an elegant waterfall. I stared at it.

Death. This place reeked of death.

"I came here," Caduan said, "after I recovered from my injuries from Niraja. I came to speak to your father when I heard that he was about to launch a massive attack on the House of Wayward Winds. I knew, especially after seeing what happened to Niraja, that war between the two most powerful Fey houses would be catastrophic."

He opened his hand and revealed a mound of rose-colored powder. He blew into his palm, sending the powder scattering into the air in thick puffs of smoke. When it faded, I was in the past. The dais was intact. A younger version of Caduan stood at the center of the room, dressed in simpler, dirtier clothing. My father sat in his throne, my mother beside him on one side, and my sister on the other.

To see their faces made it difficult to breathe. The image was intangible, slightly blurry, and yet so real that I wanted to reach out and touch them.

The other Caduan, the younger one, did not kneel before my father. My father sneered at him, familiar hatred in his eyes. He rose to his feet.

"You come to a grieving family and disrespect us this way?"

"Do not insult me by implying I do not know grief." Caduan's voice was thick with anger. "It is only out of respect for Aefe that I come here at all. I come to appeal to you, one king to another.

Your desire for power has killed countless, but you can still stop. I beg you to, before your warmongering destroys all of us."

My father scoffed at him. Darkness bracketed his eyes. "Warmongering? I am fighting for my House. You should understand that, after I took in your people. I gave you your crown. I am avenging your people."

"You're sacrificing lives in search of more power for yourself. If you think no one sees that, you're more foolish than I thought you were."

Orscheid's eyes had gone wide. My mother, too, looked increasingly uncomfortable, shifting in her chair like a flighty bird desperate to take off.

I had never seen such fury on my father's face. For a moment, he was still—and then he crossed the dais steps in two strides and struck Caduan with enough force to send him to the ground.

Caduan recovered easily, coming to his feet with such grace that the fall seemed as if it could have been intentional. The only tell was his trembling right leg, which was visibly injured.

"You traitorous, ungrateful snake!" my father roared. "Who are you to challenge me? You don't even have a House to rule. I'll have you executed for treason, and your own people will not even mourn you."

Caduan was so deadly calm. His eyes slid to my mother, who sat quivering in her throne.

"Sareid," he said, addressing only her. "You could put a stop to all of this. Surely some part of you must know that."

No one ever spoke to my mother like that—with more sophistication than that of a small child. She wriggled in her seat, shaking her head.

"You understand this," Caduan said, firmly. "This house is yours, Sareid. *Yours.* You let your husband take your crown. Now you let him destroy your House. Stop him. I know you can."

My father whirled to her, teeth bared in a snarl, but I stood at just the right angle to see the glimmer of fear in his eyes.

"Do not address my wife so disrespectfully," he spat. "Blades! *Blades*!"

Guards in black Blades uniforms slipped from the shadows, approaching Caduan. But he stood his ground.

"Sareid," he said, voice harder. "*He killed Aefe*. Your husband killed your daughter."

My mother lurched to her feet, one ungraceful jolt, as if she had been struck. But she went no further—she did nothing more. The Blades surrounded Caduan, who ignored them.

"Please, Sareid. Act. You failed your daughter in her lifetime. Don't fail her now. Act, if not for her, then for the countless lives that will be lost if your husband's command is executed. But do it for her. She should be enough. *She should have been enough*."

I found myself holding my breath. Once, my mother protected me from him. And then she spent the rest of our lives offering me to him, feeding him all the power he desired.

I did not realize how much I wanted her to fight for me.

But she did not move. Instead, her wide eyes slipped to my father. She let out a whimper and reached for him, not in a strike, but in a caress.

I had never seen such hatred across Caduan's face. Such disgust.

"She deserved better," he snarled.

The Blades grabbed him and started to drag him away. But Caduan refused to move, his face calm but shoulders heaving. My father seized the sword from beside his throne and whirled to Caduan—

"Look away," Caduan whispered to me, urgently.

But how could I? How could I not watch?

Blood sprayed. The sun flashed against steel.

It was not Caduan who fell.

It was my father, as Orscheid leapt forward and cut his throat, wielding the little dagger I had given her long ago. Tears streamed down her face. "You *killed* her—" she choked out, her voice gurgling slightly.

And then, seconds later, she collapsed—as my father buried his sword through her delicate form in his final burst of strength.

I let out a strangled sound, stumbling forward. Caduan caught my arm. It was the only thing that kept me from falling through a crack in the floor.

In the past, Caduan broke free from the stunned Blades who held him and ran to Orscheid's side. My father died without a final word, hatred on his face. How easily he discarded his love even for his favorite, perfect daughter.

Orscheid was such a delicate creature. She fell like a handful of flower petals. My mother wept. Caduan tried to stop her bleeding, tried to mend the wound, silent in utter concentration. Her blood and my father's ran down the stairs together.

The image froze. Wavered. Faded.

"I tried to save her," Caduan murmured. His voice felt too real, too close, compared to the memory.

"Her life was worth too much to die alongside him." Why was my voice so strange? It cracked over the words. "Why would she—how could she—"

Orscheid didn't know how to fight, save for the few simple movements I had once taught her. Surprise alone allowed her to land her strike on my father, but she did not have the skill to evade his vengeful last act.

"You would have killed him," I whispered. "She did not need to...to..."

"I would have. I came here to do it."

Needless. So needless.

"And my... my mother?"

"She lives, though she does not know that you do. If you would like to see her, I—"

"No. Never." My eyes fell to my mother's face, contorted in agony, as she sank to her knees beside my sister. She had failed to fight for me. Failed to fight for Orscheid. I never wanted to see her again.

Slowly, the image of Caduan leaning over my dying sister faded, leaving nothing but a broken throne and dried blood.

"I was too late," Caduan said. "Your father's order had already been placed. He had launched his invasions against the House of Wayward Winds and their allies. The ensuing war destroyed all of the remaining Fey houses over the next two hundred years. For centuries, I regretted it. If I had gotten there two hours earlier, so much could have been different."

For a moment, I hated him for it, too.

"But there is only so much I can blame your father for what happened then. It was too easy to turn us against each other. One nudge, and we devoured ourselves. We weren't strong enough. I would often think of you and how different the world would have been if you had been allowed to assume your position. You would have been an incredible leader, Aefe."

I did not believe him. And yet, still, I could almost imagine myself differently, as seen through his eyes.

"I did not bring you here to use you," he murmured. "I did not bring you here to be a weapon. There were no lies in what you said to me yesterday. You never were given the opportunity to be more. And I have witnessed many injustices in six hundred years. But that, Aefe, is one of the greatest."

Injustice. Is that what it was? Could a single word encapsulate everything that had been taken from me, inflicted upon me, beaten into me?

Caduan put his hands over mine. I was shaking.

"Our people have managed to build something better than our forefathers. But it is delicate. I am fighting both to protect our home and to make it a stronger one than any civilization that came before it. I cannot think of anyone who deserves a hand in shaping that more than you. I am asking you—not forcing you— to help me. And I will not stop you if you want to walk away. I was wrong to say I would."

My throat was thick. I had to force the words out. "And once you find these—these magics, then what? What will you do?"

"Even one brings incredible power, though not without its dangers to the wielder. But all three unlocks unlimited possibility. If I were to find them, and find a place where I was capable of wielding them…" His throat bobbed. "I could build a new world for us. One free of the humans and their influence. A place where no one can be victimized by them ever again."

I thought of my sister's body, lying on those stairs—such needless death. I thought of Meajqa's broken smile and his missing wing. I thought of a room of white and white and white and all that had been inflicted upon me there.

I thought of the Queen of Ara, and how she was inflicting such pain upon so many other Fey, every day.

"If I help you," I choked out, "we will put an end to all of it. No one else will suffer like I have suffered."

"Yes."

My mind wandered elsewhere, to darker parts of my memory —to the minds I had shared. "Will we kill Tisaanah and Maxantarius?"

After a moment of hesitation, he said, "Perhaps. Yes."

I did not have a name for the feeling that answer brought me. Was that regret? Uncertainty?

They had abandoned you. Abused you. Used you for their own selfish needs.

But… there had been love in them, too. They had once shared my soul. Even now, I felt that there was a part of me left inside of them and a part of them left inside of me. How much was that worth, though, when weighed against the horrors I had endured? The things Meajqa had endured, and countless others?

It was easy to drown love beneath hatred.

"Will it mean killing the Queen of Ara?" I asked.

This time, there was no hesitation. "Yes."

I cast one final look at the wreckage around me, and the bloodstained dais.

I could not take revenge upon my father for what he stole from me. I could not take it from the hundreds or thousands of humans who had abused me over centuries. I could not scorch their bones.

But here, now, killing the Queen of Ara seemed like enough.

"Yes," I said.

One word. One word, and it tasted like blood. It tasted like vengeance.

CHAPTER NINETEEN

MAX

I was a little surprised that Sella didn't throw us back out into the street.

But no, she was a proper Aran lady. So instead, she invited us in, quickly arranged a guest room for us, gave us an opportunity to clean up, and informed us that dinner was starting shortly. She was polite, if a bit chilly and—understandably—confused as to why we were here.

I held my tongue until Brayan and I were left alone to clean up.

"This," I hissed, "was a terrible idea, Brayan."

"It was better than the alternative."

I wasn't sure if that was the case.

He shot me a frown. "Do you even remember Sella? What with your—"

"Of course I remember her."

Sella and Brayan were lovers for years. Even as a younger man, Brayan generally had only three affectations, and none of them were what I would describe as "warm." But still, everyone knew that he adored her. Hell, who wouldn't? She was kind, talented, beautiful, well-bred. My parents approved. She would be a perfect new Lady Farlione. All was well.

Except…

My brow knotted as I followed my broken trail of memory up until it faded. "Up until the end," I said. "I take it, then, that the wedding didn't happen."

He scowled and looked away. "No, the wedding did not happen."

"Why not?"

"Get dressed. Hide those tattoos," he said, and swung the door shut.

I did the best I could. I hadn't had access to a mirror since leaving Ilyzath—part of me wished that was still the case. No wonder Sella looked at us the way she did. Changing helped, marginally, as did shaving. I was careful to button the sleeves and collar to hide the Stratagram tattoos, though the edges of black circles still peeked past the cuffs and collar of the white shirt, and there was nothing to be done about the ones on my hands—nor the mark Ilyzath left on my palm.

Even that earned a disapproving look from Brayan, which I returned with a *"what do you expect me to do?"* shrug.

Still, I understood the concern. I tried to keep my hands out of sight at the dinner table, but I earned long, lingering stares from the cook as dinner was brought out.

I didn't like that look. Like he was trying to figure out how he knew my face.

There were few servants here for such a large house, but even a few were too many. Brayan and I exchanged a glance that silently confirmed we were thinking the same thing.

Sella, too, looked as if she understood the implications of prying eyes and quickly excused them, closing the door and leaving us in the dimly lit dining room in uncomfortable silence.

I started eating immediately. Ascended above, I had forgotten how good real food was. Good enough to make the palpable awkwardness of this dinner fade into the background. Food in

Ilyzath was something given to you just to keep you from death, and nothing more.

Brayan was, at last, the first to speak.

"Thank you for allowing us to stay," he said.

"Of course. I wouldn't turn away old friends. Even after so many years." Her voice was decidedly frosty as her gaze examined each of us.

"It is deeply appreciated, Sella," Brayan said, again. The softer cadence to his voice when he said her name made me stop chewing, one eyebrow twitching.

For a second there, I thought I still saw the infatuated teenager.

But immediately following the amusement was a sour note of unease. We were putting Sella at risk by coming here.

"We'll be leaving early tomorrow," Brayan said. "We will only bother you for a few more hours."

"I see," Sella said, taking a dainty bite of her dinner. "Then we'll waste no time on small talk."

Sella was a smart woman. The point to her voice said as much. She meant: *I won't ask you questions that I shouldn't know the answer to.*

Good.

Brayan looked up and down the table—there were enough chairs for several more people, but only three plates. "Will anyone else be joining us?"

Subtle, Brayan.

Sella gave a tight smile. "No, only me tonight."

Brayan looked as if he was trying very hard to have no reaction to this at all.

Dinner went quickly, with stilted, uncomfortable small talk that I barely listened to. I wasn't good at it before, and a broken mind and months of isolation and torture certainly hadn't improved my social skills.

When we were done, Sella rose from her seat. "We can go into the library for tea, if you would like some."

If I would like some.

I would *murder* someone for tea.

She led us to another large mahogany door and ushered us inside. The room was light-soaked, with large windows revealing the sun setting over the grazing fields and a hint of the distant ocean. Floor-to-ceiling bookcases lined the walls, with a few couches and armchairs arranged in the center of the room. In between them, a little girl was kneeling on the floor over a book.

The girl's head snapped up as we entered, and I almost let a *"fucking hell"* slip from between my teeth.

Brayan's eyes stared up at me on the face of a ten-year-old girl. Dark curls fell to her shoulders, framing a nearly black gaze and slightly sunburnt cheeks.

The resemblance left me stunned.

"I'm sorry," the girl said, pushing to her feet. "I didn't know you'd be coming here."

"Nothing you need to apologize for, sweetness," Sella said. "We'll just be a bit." She kissed the girl on the forehead. The girl continued to stare at us, curious, as Sella rested her hands on the child's shoulders.

Brayan looked—somehow—utterly neutral. Sella, too.

There was no way I could possibly be the only one to appreciate this situation for what it was.

Sella looked only at Brayan. "This is Adeline," she said, lightly.

Silence, for a moment too long. Brayan just stared at Sella, and then Adeline, saying nothing.

It was getting awkward, so I said, "It's lovely to meet you, Adeline," which snapped Brayan out of his trance.

"We apologize for displacing you," he said, politely. "Thank you for sharing your library."

"Oh, it's no trouble at all," said Adeline, with the charmingly precocious voice of a well-trained noble child.

Sella chuckled, kissed Adeline's head again, and sent her on her way. Adeline bid us a polite goodnight before disappearing up the stairs, leaving us in suffocating silence.

I shot Brayan a stare that he dutifully ignored.

"She seems polite," he said, at last.

She seems polite, he fucking says.

"She is." Sella smiled, faintly. "She's wonderful."

Brayan made a noncommittal noise.

"I have always told you exactly where I am, Brayan," Sella said. "If there is anything you want to know about my life, or my daughter, I would be happy to share it with you. I will be truthful."

Ascended fucking above. This was ridiculous.

Even I understood what was happening here. That she was daring him to ask her the obvious question.

There was a long silence.

And then Brayan said, "It's been a very long day. I think I'll excuse myself. Thank you."

<hr>

I CORNERED Brayan the moment the door was closed.

"Brayan, what the hell was that?"

"What do you mean?"

"*What do I mean?* That child—"

"I don't know what you're talking about," he snapped.

"Bullshit. You know what you saw."

He refused to look at me. "We're here because we have to be," he said. "One night, and Sella was kind enough to open her home to us. I won't thank her by asking invasive questions about her life."

I couldn't even believe what I was hearing.

"Sella was practically inviting you to ask, because—"

"I gave up my opportunity to have those kinds of questions."

He was very focused on the pamphlet of charter ship schedules. I let out a scoff.

Typical. It turned out ten years of memory loss meant nothing. Brayan hadn't gotten any less hardheaded. He hadn't gotten any better at seeing truths he didn't want to see.

"Brayan, if that child is your daughter, that fact doesn't change because you refuse to acknowledge it."

It had been so long since I'd seen this happen—since I'd seen how abruptly Brayan's perfect composure broke, like a snapped thread. One moment his back was to me, and the next, he whirled to me, every line of his form vibrating with anger.

"*You* do not get to lecture me about my responsibilities to my family. Is your mind too broken to even understand the hypocrisy of your bullshit?"

"I—"

"*Where the hell were you?*"

He took a step closer, pausing, as if he wanted me to actually answer the question.

Words escaped me. I didn't know what he was asking. "Where was—?"

"Yes, Max. *You. Where were you?* You didn't go to their funerals. Did you know that?"

My jaw snapped shut, words dying in my throat.

"Seven pyres, and me, and a thousand strangers asking me, 'Where is Maxantarius?' I made excuses for you. I told them you couldn't get back in time, that you were traveling with the military. You were the renowned hero, then, after Sarlazai. They believed me. But at night when I was by myself, I would try to figure out where you were. Write to all your commanders. Write to every Ascended-damned hospital in Ara." He scoffed. "Because I figured you had to be dying, right? You had to be dying to miss the funerals of our entire fucking family."

I couldn't speak, horrified with my past self.

No, I wanted to say. *You're wrong. I would never have done that.*

But I knew, of course, that he wasn't wrong. That he was the one looking for explanations I couldn't give him, and I was the one staring in frustration at a past that I no longer remembered, looking for those answers, too.

"You disappeared after that, and I searched for you for years. Years, Max, while I dealt with everything. All the responsibilities of being the new Lord Farlione. All the arrangements, the debts, the politics. I dealt with it alone, and then I would go search for you. *Fucking years.* And do you know where I finally found you?"

I didn't want to know. That door loomed there, in the back of my mind, whispering, *You don't want to go here again.*

Brayan's lip twisted into a sneer of disgust. "I found you in a Meriatan slum, so out of your mind on Seveseed that you didn't even know your own name, let alone mine. And here I thought I was my brother's rescuer. Here I thought something horrific must have happened to you to make you run away like that. But you had no interest in being anywhere but exactly where you were."

Brayan had his fair share of flaws, but he was not a liar. I knew that every word of this was true.

Shame simmered at the surface of my skin.

I wanted to believe there had to be some explanation. Some reason. Something I could tell him to make him understand—make *myself* understand.

But what excuses could I make for myself?

Brayan let out a low scoff and turned away. "A decade later, and a part of me still hoped I would get answers when I came back to Ara for you."

I shook my head. "I don't—"

"You don't remember. I know." Another scoff, this one more violent than the last. "I should have known it was a ridiculous thing to hope for."

"I would give you that, if I could," I said.

Was that true? If it was, why hadn't I done it in the last ten years?

Brayan and I had always had a... complicated relationship. Even with my incomplete memory, I understood that—I understood it the moment I saw his face. That past, even the past I didn't remember, tainted our every interaction. But I wouldn't have left him completely alone like that.

I wouldn't have.

Right?

The clock ticked, deafening.

"How did it happen?" I asked, quietly.

I didn't realize I was going to speak until the words were already leaving my lips. And in that same moment, the voice in my head again warned, *You do not want to open this door.*

He turned to the window, arms crossed over his chest.

"Ryvenai rebels," he said. "Angry about father's loyalist stance during the war. Perhaps angry because of… our positions in the military. They came to the house one night. Took their revenge. The war was practically over by then, after the crown's victory at Sarlazai. Pointless." His words were cold and tight. "Everyone had been dead for hours by the time they were found."

I was suddenly dizzy. I sat on the edge of the bed, steeling myself against an onslaught of horrible images.

It was strange to hear of something so intimate to my life as if it was something that happened to a stranger, as if being reminded in the first moments of the morning of something terrible that had happened the night before. Even now, even with my incomplete mind, the grief had always been there. Now, I had to brace myself against the sudden strength of it.

I took a moment to ruminate on this new puzzle piece. Killed by Ryvenai rebels. A meaningless, destructive revenge.

Something about the shape of its edges didn't seem to fit right, made a part of me think, *No, there is something else missing here.*

But you don't want to open that door.

"I wish I had been there," Brayan muttered, as if to himself, then let out a long breath and turned to me. I had glimpsed a rare moment of Brayan out of control. Now his careful composure clicked back into place, piece by piece—his shoulders lowering, back straightening, hands unclenching.

"That's enough of this," he said.

I wondered if he was talking to me or talking to himself.

I couldn't pretend that I wanted to continue the conversation. What would I say? I had no explanation for myself, and Brayan knew it, too. But though he carefully tucked away all that anger,

I looked down and saw a chasm between us so wide and deep that I felt like a fool for not noticing it before.

We left early in the morning, so early that Sella and her household weren't even awake yet. Brayan didn't say goodbye. But before we left, I scrawled a note on the library table.

Sella-

Thank you for everything.
We're glad life is treating you well.
If your daughter ever needs anything, know that she can come to me.

-Max

Maybe it was a stupid thing to do, given the circumstances. She seemed like she had everything here that one could want, and hopefully she would never be in a position where she needed help from a half-mad convict like myself.

But just in case. Just in case she ever found herself alone in the world. Everyone deserved, I figured, a thread back to their past.

Brayan and I didn't speak on the boat out to Threll. After last night, there wasn't much to say.

CHAPTER TWENTY

AEFE

The vase shattered against the wall. Caduan barely flinched, stepping slightly to the left to avoid the glass that now twinkled across half the floor.

My shoulders heaved, breath ragged, muscles shaking. I still was not accustomed to that, my body responding so physically to my frustrations.

"I can't," I gritted out.

"You can."

"I. Can't."

"How many times will we have this conversation?" Caduan nudged broken glass with his toe. "Soon I'll need to send someone to buy more vases."

I whirled to him, snarling. "You give me an impossible task."

"There is nothing impossible about it. Its possibilities are endless, actually."

I almost struck him. Perhaps then my magic would appear. My power had given Tisaanah the ability to wither flesh, Max the ability to reduce anything to ash. If I were to strike Caduan, perhaps a special gift that was only my own would appear. I imagined his too-calm face melting into a puddle of goo. This image brought me some brief comfort.

"Endless," I scoffed. "It's meaningless."

"That's not true."

It was true. For the last several days, ever since I tentatively agreed to help Caduan in his war, he brought me up to his chambers and tried to teach me how to use my magic.

That, at least, was what he claimed to be doing. In practice, he was putting an empty vase before me, and telling me to "create something."

Create something?

These instructions meant nothing to me. What was I to create? A butterfly? A flame? A snake?

"Any of those things would do," Caduan said, passively, when I asked.

But I could not create a butterfly without first molding Tisaanah's magic. I couldn't conjure a flame without Maxantarius's spark.

I asked for other suggestions. Caduan only said that he couldn't tell me what to create.

"Why not?" I had demanded.

He replied, "Because that wouldn't tell either of us anything worth knowing."

"You are not telling me anything worth knowing."

Caduan gave me a cryptic smile, and told me, more impatiently this time, to try again.

Days passed. The vase remained empty. Caduan's instructions grew more demanding. My vexation bubbled to the surface. Another vase shattered against the wall.

It had been five days. Five days of this. I was sick of it. A tight feeling now lived in my chest, and every time I looked at Caduan's disappointment, it grew more suffocating.

Enough. I agreed to try, but I hadn't known what I was agreeing to. I hadn't realized that trying something and failing— over and over again—made me feel just as helpless and trapped as I had in the room of white and white and white.

Useless. I was useless then, helpless, alone.

Just as I was now useless, helpless, alone.

That thought made my breath come faster, faster, faster. My hand closed around the water glass on the table. Lifted it.

Caduan cringed.

But instead of throwing the glass, at the last moment, I closed my hand around it, tight tight *tight*, until pain spasmed through my palm.

"This was a mistake. I don't have *anything*." The confession slipped from my tongue so easily. Unbidden, I remembered Tisaanah's steel mind, and the way she so carefully hid such insecurities from spoken words. I'd watched her tuck the thoughts away deep in the darkened crevices of her mind, the same ones that I had occupied.

I realized that I wasn't as strong as she was. Not in my magic, and not in my empty mind.

"You aren't trying," Caduan said.

I welcomed the flood of rage. Easier than hurt.

I whirled to him. Two strides and I was across the room, so close to his face. He didn't flinch.

"Not trying? For five days, you have remained in this room with me, and you tell me that *I am not trying?*"

A muscle twitched above Caduan's lip. "For five days I've watched you run in circles. I am helping you, Aefe."

I needed an outlet, needed something to shatter. I reached for another glass, but Caduan grabbed my wrist.

"You are better than this." His fingers tightened, hot against my skin.

"Then tell me what you want me to do."

"I want you to think. I want you to lean into the silence and find something there."

"Find what?"

"I can't tell you that."

His hand still clutched my wrist, tighter still, tight enough that it ached just slightly. I liked it—the constriction. It was the first thing in five days that felt even remotely familiar, like a tether when I had been floating at sea.

I leaned into it, my lips twisting into a sneer.

"What do you expect me to find there?" I hissed. "There is nothing inside of me but silence. I don't understand how anyone can live like this, in a world so empty. I need to feel… to feel…"

I stumbled. Words were too weak to describe what I meant, so I gave up.

"You would not understand it."

But Caduan's face had gone pensive. "Go on," he said, quietly.

"You would not understand." I tried to pull away, but his grip held firm.

"There's something there, Aefe. Do not back away. Go on. You say you can't make something out of nothing. Why?"

I hated him.

"I have seen what you can do," he pressed. "In all your forms, then and now."

"You don't know what it's like," I snapped. "I did great things, but only when I had something to… to become. A song to sing louder or…"

This did not make any sense to him.

"Go on, Aefe."

"When I was in them, I could take their magic and make it stronger. I knew I was powerful—infinitely powerful—but they gave me the material. Even so long ago, even as Aefe…"

My tongue ran over my teeth, the point of my canines. Not as sharp as they were long ago, in a different version of this body.

"Even as Aefe, I had no magic of my own, only the ability to take from others. And now, in this body, I am empty. What do you expect me to create? I need the magic of another. A power to amplify. I cannot make something from nothing."

"It isn't from nothing. It is from *you*."

I was so angry—how could he still not understand? "What am I, if not nothing?"

It was in the name I gave myself. Reshaye. No one. Nothing.

Caduan's lips went thin. In a movement so abrupt that it made me stumble, he wrenched me closer. He pressed my palm to him—down past the buttons of his loose shirt, against the smooth skin of his chest.

It was so unexpected that I tried to pull away, but his fingers tightened again.

"Listen," he demanded. "Stop fighting, and *listen*."

I wasn't sure why I obeyed. My breaths were still heaving, hard enough that at first I heard nothing but the rushing of my own blood in my ears.

"What do you feel?" Caduan asked.

"Nothing."

"Not true." His eyes met mine, spearing me. "What do you feel?"

Nothing, I still wanted to say. But then, I became aware of faint, faint movement beneath my fingertips—the thrum of warmth beneath his skin, a steady rhythm.

I became aware of the movement of his chest, rising and falling. Not just beneath my fingertips, but against my cheek, where his breath caressed my skin.

As soon as I noticed these things, they were everywhere.

The warmth of blood moving beneath his skin. The rhythm of his breathing. The minute vibrations of the muscles of his hand, still wrapped around my wrist. The sheer warmth of him, close enough to surround me like an embrace.

The sensation was like falling into something warm and familiar.

All this time, and I had felt so alone in this empty body. Perhaps my body was empty, but how had I not realized that being close to another could feel so similar to sharing one? I had been so certain that I could not understand this strange unspoken communication that I ignored these things. But now I wanted to bury myself in the minute movements of his flesh—in his breath, his heartbeat, in the low vibrations of his voice.

I did not realize that I had moved closer until he spoke, so quietly, and I felt it through my whole body.

"What do you feel?" he asked again.

"I feel... you."

I watched the muscle tighten at the corner of his upturned mouth, the flutter of pulse beneath his fair skin. I felt his breathing grow slightly more rapid, because I felt everything, now. His other hand had gone to rest at my back, a barely-there touch that sent ripples up my spine. For a moment I thought he would pull me closer, and I welcomed it, because I was nothing now but the desire to lose myself in the body of another.

But he did not. The touch remained light, gentle.

"You think you are alone, Aefe, in this body. But there is life everywhere. In blood and flesh. In breath. In a heartbeat." His thumb gently caressed the back of my hand, where he still pressed my palm over his heart, and my breath shuddered.

"Tell me," he murmured, "is this empty?"

"No."

I struggled to speak.

He pulled away slightly, and a small wordless sound of protest left my lips. But he still cradled my back, still gripped my wrist. He removed my hand from his chest and then pressed it to my own, so we now stood face to face, my palm to my heart.

"Tell me what you feel," he whispered.

At first, nothing. My own body seemed lackluster compared to everything I felt in his.

But then...

A steady beat, rushing a bit too fast. The inflation and deflation of my breath, the rhythm of my lungs. Warmth. Growth.

"A body is an incredible thing." He was close enough that his words rustled my hair. "There is life in every fiber of you. You are always moving, growing and changing. You are never stagnant. You are never silent." He pulled away just enough to look at me, his green eyes brighter than I had ever seen them. His fingers folded into mine, still pressed over my heartbeat—his other hand rose to take mine, opening it between us.

"You are not nothing, Aefe. You are a miracle. Now create something."

It was so easy, now. How had I not seen it?

I was full of it, teeming with it, this magic that I could manipulate just as I had once manipulated others'. I was made of it.

I simply had to sculpt it.

My skin tingled. I couldn't bring myself to look away from Caduan's eyes. Seconds passed, and his gaze lowered. A smile bloomed over his face.

"Look," he murmured.

I didn't want to. I wanted to watch that smile.

But finally, I looked down. There, cradled in my palm, was a tiny, black rosebud, fresh leaves still unfurling.

Strange. In the past, I had leveled cities and destroyed entire armies. But none of those things had ever brought me the pride of this single, tiny flower. Something created only by me. Something *alive*.

"Perfect."

And when I glanced up at Caduan, he was not looking at the flower — he was looking at me.

———————————

I DID NOT MAKE another flower that afternoon. I managed a few tiny leaves, and a single unopened bud. I didn't care. I felt euphoric. I could have continued all night. Though Caduan urged me to be patient, I couldn't stop myself, grinning with increasing glee with every leaf that sprouted in my palm.

How had I never known how good it felt to create things?

Caduan grew tired quickly. Soon he watched me from an armchair, then with one hand propping up his chin, and finally, I turned around to show him my latest creation to see him slumped over, asleep.

It was not late. I was not tired. But I watched him for a moment, then sat in the chair beside him. Practicing by myself did not seem as appealing.

I watched the rise and fall of his breaths, admiring, without anyone to make me self-conscious, all of these staggeringly beautiful, newly noticed things. He didn't wake; he barely even moved. When my own exhaustion set in, hours later, I reached across the table to rest my hand on his, my thumb over the inside of his wrist. The beat of his pulse lulled me to sleep.

"My king."

I blinked blearily. Luia leaned over Caduan. Dawn light spilled over his face, and mine. Our hands were still tangled between the two chairs.

"My king," Luia said, louder, a shaper note to her voice. She gripped his shoulders. "My king, wake up—"

His eyes opened, slowly.

Luia immediately released him, letting out a breath of relief. She barely looked at me.

"I'm…" Caduan rubbed his head, then glanced at me. "I apologize. I was more tired than I realized."

I rubbed sleep from my eyes.

"I apologize for waking you so early," Luia said. "It is our Threllian allies. They have asked urgently to speak with you. Meajqa has been handling them, but they're pressing. We will continue to work with them, but we wanted to make you aware—"

"I can meet with them."

Luia's eyebrows rose. "You are under no obligation to give them a personal meeting."

"Meajqa shouldn't travel to Threll, and if he insists, he certainly shouldn't go alone."

"I can go, or we can send—"

"No. I will go. I have been too far away from these matters." His eyes, still tired, flicked to me. "Aefe will come with me."

Luia's face twisted up. "What?"

What?

My first impulse was to refuse. The Aefe of before would have refused. But I stopped myself before the rejection left my lips.

I am different than I thought I was, I reminded myself. When I agreed, Caduan's smile flitted across his face like that early-morning sun.

CHAPTER TWENTY-ONE

MAX

"We shouldn't stay here."

I drew the back of my hand across my forehead, squinting towards the horizon. I was not made for this. I'd even take the swampy humidity of Ara's summer over this heat so intense it threatened to cook you on the street.

Our boat had landed in central Threll, in a city I couldn't pronounce the name of. Threllian architecture was beautiful, all crafted from white stone, so when you stood at the coast and looked up, the view that greeted you looked like a painting of various gleaming ivory strokes laid beneath striking blue. It was late in the day. The blue was starting to tinge pink.

Sunsets are beautiful in Threll, I thought, which surprised myself. I didn't realize I had been to Threll.

"We won't," Brayan said. "Threll is a mess right now. The less time we spend here, the better. We're lucky our boat didn't get shot to the bottom of the sea."

"Would the Fey or Threllians bother with a civilian ship?"

"Everyone wants to kill everyone here right now," Brayan said. "Rebels, too, fighting against the Threllians. It reminds me of the Threllian wars fifteen years ago. Everyone fighting everyone. But… at least that means everyone out here is so confused they shouldn't be looking too hard for us."

I pieced together the fragments of memories I did have. Nura had a presence in Threll—I had heard her discussing that with Vardir many times. The Fey did as well, via their Threllian allies, which was why Threll was never on my list of *"places to go if I manage to escape."*

I nodded to a stable up ahead. "We should see if we can get some horses. I'm not made for that much foot travel."

Brayan agreed, and we ducked into the horse trader, who was largely selling nags that he probably bought half-dead, fed for three days, and sold for a disgusting profit. Brayan pointed to two horses. "How much?" he asked, in Thereni.

In Thereni.

And I understood him.

That was interesting. I turned to the marketplace streets, listening. Mostly, I heard a garble of sharp sounds I didn't understand. But here and there, when people were speaking slowly enough, I could make out a few phrases.

I grasped a sliver of memory—the rise and fall of a voice, a melody of Thereni saying something I couldn't make out before it slipped through my fingers.

"Max!" Brayan barked, impatient. He gestured to the horse to his left—a grey, lumbering thing who already looked equally irritated with me. "Let's go. We can make it out of the city before nightfall."

My horse gave me a disapproving grunt and snapped at me as I swung over its back, barely missing my backside.

"That was uncalled for," I grumbled.

The horse gave me a *harrumph* that said it disagreed.

"Wait." Brayan stopped short, just as we were able to leave. "How much is that?" he asked the shopkeeper, pointing.

I followed his finger to a small, rusty sickle hanging on the wall. The shopkeeper, caught off guard, named some absurd price, and Brayan paid it without complaint.

"Here." He handed it to me as we left the stables. "I'm not

about to risk the attention or the time of seeking out a weapons shop, but you should have something to defend yourself if needed."

I eyed the rusted sickle as it hung off my saddle. It was intended for cutting wheat, not flesh, and I suspected it was probably not very good at that, either.

But Brayan was right. Something pointy was something pointy. I'd take what I could get.

"Don't tell me you can't wield it," Brayan said, sharply. "I spent fifteen years training you. You can wield anything."

Was that a compliment?

"I agree," I said. "I wasn't going to say anything. Thank you."

A fragment of memory—Brayan handing me a weapon, very different from this one. *Happy birthday.*

Gone before I could make sense of it.

"You speak Thereni?" I asked.

"I lived out here for a few years," he said. "When I was with the company."

It came back to me after a moment—the Roseteeth Company, a prestigious private army. Right. I did remember, vaguely, Brayan's time with them. He returned because... was it because the Ryvenai War broke out?

"You fought in..."

"Essaria, mostly. They secured us to help conquer those little nations—Deralin, and all that. I left before they ran out of money and the Threllians turned on them, too." He shook his head. "I've never seen a stronger military. The Threllians knew how to win a war."

A sour taste filled my mouth.

My old memories brightened with spots of color, as if dust was being swept away. The Roseteeth Company was considered prestigious, and Brayan's position there was a source of great pride for my father, the sort of thing that earned impressed eyebrow-raises from other lords and military leaders. But I remembered now what I used to call it to get under Brayan's skin —"overpriced mercenaries."

"How much does it cost to hire someone to conquer a nation for you?" I asked.

He shot me a glare. "I'm so glad that your sense of moral superiority has survived, even if you can't remember anything else."

I shrugged. "Just a question."

He scoffed and nudged his horse into a trot. "It's better not to talk about those sorts of topics here."

The sky lit up in brilliant magenta, then violet, and it was all fading into dusk by the time we made it past the outskirts of the city. The main road bent west, following the coast, while a much smaller trail arched north into dense woods.

We halted at the junction.

"Let me guess," I said. "We should go through the woods and battle mosquitos and wild animals all night instead of staying on this lovely, paved road."

"The woods go north. We're going north."

"Fantastic."

My horse let out a grunt that echoed my enthusiasm.

"You're smarter than to complain about going somewhere remote right now," Brayan said, nudging his horse forward.

I paused a moment longer, looking at the dark trail.

My grumbling aside, I knew Brayan was right—it was in our best interest to stay out of sight right now, and to get out of Threll as quickly as possible. But when I blinked, visions from Ilyzath lingered behind my eyelids—visions of dark forests and the monsters that lurked within them, of reaching hands that looked like they belonged to corpses. Of someone calling me.

I extended my hand and rubbed my fingertips together, calling to magic—calling to flame.

Once I didn't even have to try. It was another part of me, like a limb. But now, even that tiny request of my magic was met with an impassable wall.

I gave up and reached for the lantern dangling from the saddle instead, pushing my horse forward.

"Oh, please," I muttered, when my horse released another

loud, frustrated groan. "It isn't that ominous, is it?"

It was indeed that ominous. I think the horse knew it, too.

———————

THE DARKNESS ENVELOPED US. The road here was not completely deserted, but close to it. There were a few small buildings nestled in the forest—stores, perhaps, or hunting outposts, and a few supply shops closer to the main road—but soon those grew fewer and farther in-between. Our lanterns cast garish shadows and bloody-red streaks over the palms and leaves. Brayan rode ahead, his sword close to his grasp, shoulders squared.

We were half an hour past the last dregs of civilization when I heard the sounds.

I pulled my horse to a stop.

I didn't need to say a word to Brayan. He did the same. We sat in the silence, listening. I heard distant sounds from the last outpost in the distance—a mill. Rustling from creatures in the wood. The wind caressing the leaves.

No. I'd heard something else. I knew I did.

Brayan and I exchanged a look. No words, but effortless communication. Silently, he drew his sword. I unhooked my ridiculous sickle from my saddle.

The voice seemed to come from everywhere and nowhere at once, echoing through the trees:

"Maxantarius Farlione and Brayan Farlione, you are wanted by order of the Queen of Ara. Surrender, and you will not be harmed."

That, obviously, was out of the question. I gripped the handle of my weapon, turning slowly.

Nothing but shadow.

Wielders. I couldn't judge how many. It would only take one to disguise them in the trees and obfuscate the direction of their voices, but it was a guarantee that there were more ready to apprehend us.

It was the unknown factor sitting between "more than one" and "a small army" that concerned me.

My horse snorted, uneasy. Brayan and I circled, falling into formation to cover each other's blind spots.

"This is your final warning." This time the voice came from a single direction. The underbrush to our left rustled, shadows moving between the tree trunks. Brayan turned to face it, sword ready.

No. Too easy. Too obvious, for magic users capable of stealth and misdirection.

I faced the opposite way, watching the still silence of the forest.

"Careful, Brayan," I muttered. "These are Wielders—"

I didn't have time to finish. The figure came at us so fast that it was a smear of shadow and glinting steel, lunging for Brayan.

I moved faster.

Our bodies collided, my horse letting out a screaming whinny. Pain nicked my knuckles as I threw up my sickle to divert a sword, barely succeeding.

Behind me, I heard the clatter of steel.

They descended upon us all at once, from every direction. I had no time to do anything but react.

To my left, a flash of white—a Valtain, silver hair glinting in the darkness. A stab of pain in the back of my head, a burst of wind so strong I had to fight to stay on my horse.

Shadows deeper than the darkness of night surrounded us, moving too quickly for my eyes to track. I blocked and dodged blows as they were fractured seconds away from my flesh.

A wound opened on my shoulder. I retaliated, bending around the blow. My sickle sank into something hard. A voice let out a wheezing cry.

I couldn't see. Couldn't rely on sight. Ascended fucking above, what I would do to get my magic back right now.

My horse let out a shriek and suddenly, I was going down.

I threw myself from the saddle, hit the ground hard. Rolled and immediately scrambled for my weapon's handle.

Just in time to block a blow above me.

Blood rained over my face.

I found myself looking up at Brayan from atop his horse, his sword skewering my attacker's throat.

"Take the axe," he rasped, before his horse, too, went down.

I grabbed my attacker's axe from his death-stiff hands, abandoning my sickle. I didn't like axes—they didn't move as fast as I did—but at least the thing was sharp.

I whirled around just in time to catch the shoulder of a man swinging for Brayan. He screamed. The force of the blow nearly took off his arm.

Yes, this would do.

I bought Brayan seconds to get to his feet, barely avoiding the thrashing hooves of his panicking horse.

"Get over here," I panted. The two of us naturally fell into position—easier, now, with us both on foot. We couldn't rely on sight, not with Wielders in play. So we had no choice but to make sure we left no slivers of vulnerability anywhere.

Fifteen years, Brayan had trained me.

My broken mind had understood this in a distant sort of way, but it was only here, in action, that I realized exactly what it meant. It meant that his fighting style and strategies were tattooed as deep into me as the Stratagrams all over my skin—deeper, even, because while there was no doubt in my mind that I would have been utterly screwed if I had been magic-less by myself, Brayan and I fit together so well that we became a machine of pure, efficient death.

Our fighting styles complemented each other perfectly—Brayan's movements powerful and definitive, all sheer strength, while mine were lighter, faster, more precise, even with my ill-suited weapon. We found a rhythm, three of my strikes to one of his, protecting each other in our vulnerable seconds.

We began to move, pushing our way forward through the forest, still maintaining our formation and staving off our attackers.

One final swing from Brayan's sword, and block from mine,

and another body fell to the ground, joining the growing pile of corpses around our feet.

I finally allowed myself to think, *We're actually going to make it out of this.*

Then, the ground trembled.

Brayan and I, as we ran, exchanged a glance—one that mutually asked each other, *Did you feel that, too?*

It came again, this time harder. My eyes scanned the darkness. There was nothing out there.

Until, suddenly, there was.

A flash of light arced across the sky, blinding me. My back slammed against something hard—a tree, then underbrush, then the ground.

For a moment, everything was hazy. I was somewhere else, in a field of flowers, nostrils burning with the smell of citrus.

Get up, May-oocks.

My back was definitely fucking broken. I couldn't move. My chest rattled when I inhaled.

GET UP GET UP GET UP—

My eyes snapped open.

For one second, I saw a person—*creature? Thing?*—so horrifying that I thought I had to be hallucinating.

And then I forced myself to leap out of the way just in time to avoid a streak of lightning.

I fell back into the shadow of the trees, looking for Brayan. The creature turned, and my stomach roiled.

Holy fucking hell.

The first thing I noticed was the legs. It had four of them, long, spindly appendages of vein-covered, bone-white flesh. Those legs alone were taller than any man, even by a margin of several feet, and had several joints that bent the wrong way back.

They all culminated at a single point. A… person. Or maybe something that had once been one. Because it looked more like a corpse than a living being, dangling there as if hanging from its flesh-colored stilts. It was naked. One arm was missing, torn off at the elbow, as were its feet. A massive, singed wound tore from the base of its throat all the way down to its pelvis, like an incision that had not been allowed to heal. Within it was simmering white light, lightning cracking at its edges.

But it was the face that paralyzed me as the thing staggered, turning back towards me.

It had once been a face, at least. I could make out the shape of a humanoid skull, a brow bone, streaks of long dirty red hair, and—were those pointed ears?

But the eyes were nothing but pits of torn flesh, crackling with the same light as the wound down its abdomen. And the entire lower part of its face, mouth and jaw, were missing, as if hacked away and discarded.

Its face snapped towards me.

I dove, and a split second later I felt it land behind me.

Where was my axe? I'd dropped it somewhere when I lost consciousness, but Ascended knew where.

I caught a glimpse of gleaming metal and dove for it.

…only for a sudden pain to light up across my back.

I stumbled. Lurched around. Another soldier was there, sword drawn and bloodied. Fuck, how many of these people were there?

Out of the corner of my eye, I saw the creature lurch. It moved strangely, like a puppet controlled by too-long strings.

A flash of steel. Movement in the woods. Brayan, diving at the creature.

That's a terrible fucking idea, you idiot, I wanted to yell at him. Brayan was never good at knowing when he was outmatched.

I kicked my attacker down, buying enough time to grab my axe.

A second more and I would have been dead. Instead, I was just fast enough that it was my weapon buried in the man's neck rather than the other way around.

But I was injured. When I tried to get back to my feet, I stumbled, and the world tilted. Blurred.

A garden. A stone house. A single green eye.

Get up.

I did, somehow.

That creature was not looking at me. No, it was facing away —and that somehow managed to be twice as terrifying, because if it wasn't coming for me, it was going for Brayan.

I forced myself into a run.

That thing—that monster—would kill him.

It was standing still. White magic snapped in unnatural fissures in the air around it. It was looking down.

I ran faster.

I raised my palms. I was close enough to smell the stench of rotting flesh.

It was going to kill my brother.

Get up, Max.

Do something. Act.

I opened my palms and released a wall of flames.

The creature let out a terrible, human-sounding scream of agony. Its too-long legs tangled as it tried to face me.

At first, I didn't notice the pain. But I looked down and saw my skin bubbling, the ink of the Stratagram tattoos burning into me like acid.

My legs gave out.

The creature pinned me. The tips of its limbs were exposed bone, bloody. One went straight through my forearm.

Slowly, it lowered. It was making sounds. Speaking? If so, in a language I had never heard, though the cadence of it sounded like a plea.

The fire was running wild, now. I should have been able to control it. But when I reached for my magic, once again, it evaded me.

The creature drew closer. I realized that it was decomposing in real time—one ear now falling off, skin rotting, burning eyes drooping.

My vision faded just as I heard voices in the distance, approaching fast: "Call that thing off before it kills him!"

That was all.

CHAPTER TWENTY-TWO

TISAANAH

"This is a trap."

I knew it was a trap.

I was careful to appear calm, but the paper in my hands trembled like a leaf in the breeze, betraying me.

We had been traveling for nearly a week. Ishqa, Sammerin and I stayed away from civilization, instead choosing to journey through the plains and forests. This was the first time we had stepped foot in a town in days—and this settlement barely qualified, more resembling a ramshackle collection of buildings put here by people who had stopped to rest along the road and simply never left. A cluster of homes, a single inn, a single pub, and a smattering of stores. We would get some supplies, we had decided. We would not stay the night—too risky, with such a recognizable group. In and out.

Everything had changed when I saw the news bulletin nailed to the post of the pub: "War criminal Maxantarius Farlione has been apprehended in Saroksa."

Apprehended.

He was out of Ilyzath? *How*?

I was holding the paper so tightly that it crumpled around my fingertips.

"How did he get out?" Sammerin murmured, as if to himself.

I couldn't even speak.

"This is a trap," Ishqa said again, as if we hadn't heard him the first time.

I'd heard him just fine, and I also knew he was right.

It wasn't even a good trap. It was woefully transparent. This was not the sort of news that would be pumped out so far into the reaches of Ara's Threllian colonies. Nura wouldn't be eager to advertise the fact that she had let a prisoner, let alone one so high profile, slip from Ilyzath's grasp at all. Not unless she had a good reason for doing so.

I was that reason. Even when she was distracted by the war with the Fey, Nura had never stopped hunting me. And here was her chance to lure me right to her.

"She's making good use of her bad luck," Sammerin said.

"If he ever escaped at all," Ishqa said. "The entire thing could be a fabrication."

I read the headline over and over again. There was a little line drawing accompanying the article—supposedly portraying Max, though the resemblance was questionable. Still. I found myself tracing the scratchy ink lines.

"We cannot go after him," Ishqa said.

Sammerin let out a slight scoff, as if to say, *That's a ridiculous statement.*

It was. Ridiculous.

I didn't dignify it with a response, instead examining the article.

Saroksa.

It wasn't that far from here, perhaps two days travel southwest. It was firmly in the heart of Ara's Threllian colonies, which meant that it wasn't far from the former Mikov estate.

"I am sorry, Tisaanah," Ishqa said, gently.

"Why?"

"Even if we cannot rescue him now, we will find him in the future. After we have found the Lejaras."

"Oh, we are going after him now," I said, simply.

Ishqa blinked at me, the closest I had ever seen him look to stunned.

"But it is a—"

"Trap. I know. But I am still going."

"He might not even be there," Ishqa said. "It could be a trick, to draw you out."

"I'll verify it before we make ourselves too vulnerable."

"That is not enough."

At last, Sammerin spoke. "It will have to be enough. Obviously, we are going to go after him. Trap or no trap."

Gods, I could have kissed him.

Ishqa looked at us, his jaw tight. "That would be foolish. This goes beyond simple self-sacrifice. Risking the Queen of Ara coming into possession of that, or even learning that it exists…" He gestured to my hand and the gold spreading across it. "That is very, very unwise."

Internally, I knew it to be true.

Outwardly, I said, "We won't allow her to take it."

"I respect your confidence," Ishqa said, in a flat tone that told me he did not respect it at all. "This is exactly the sort of rash action that Caduan fears that you will take. Make no mistake, he will hear of this. And when he does, the fact that you are bringing the wayfinder so close to Nura's grasp will only make him more motivated to find you and take it back. It will validate all of his worst fears."

True, again, but I was getting tired of being confronted with immovable truths that would change nothing.

"Do you expect me to leave him?" I snapped. "Truly? What if it was your son's face on this poster? I understand everything that you're saying, but it doesn't change anything. It just is what it is. Either you help us, or you stay here and wait for us to return. Those are the only options I can offer you."

Ishqa's lips went thin with disapproval, but he did not argue.

I turned to Sammerin, who gave me a small nod, affirming his support. "What's next?"

That was the question, wasn't it?

Nura would have nearly unlimited visibility of the area. No doubt the prison would be well-guarded and under close surveillance, especially if this was a trap designed to lure me.

I had only myself, Sammerin, and Ishqa. We were good, but not good enough to fight our way in on sheer strength alone.

What did I have that Nura didn't?

Yes, she had manpower, but where did that manpower come from? Would it be Arans brought here from the mainland? The war was not going well in Ara. She would need her soldiers there.

So… perhaps these were Threllian slaves, overseen by Aran captains.

An idea took root. I had to suppress a smile. *There* it was.

My fingertip brushed the angle of the drawing's jaw.

I am coming for you.

"We do not have time to waste," I said. "We'll talk as we move."

CHAPTER TWENTY-THREE

AEFE

Caduan did not want humans anywhere near Ela'Dar, so we were the ones to travel to Threll. We used magic to get there, Caduan slipping us through nothingness in several leaps. Strange, how much had changed in five hundred years. In my first life, such magic was not used by the Fey. Not everyone had the ability to travel this way, although Fey who couldn't were able to with the help of some supplemental potions. Fey magic now, I had noticed, relied heavily on the use of potions and enhancements.

We leapt through Ela'Dar, then Besrith, then parts of Threll, until we arrived at the designated meeting place.

Before our sight even returned to us, there was the smell, so intense it made my eyes water. Smoke and flesh and decaying bodies.

I identified it right away. I had been on many battlefields.

The Threllians had requested that we meet at the estate of one of their high-ranking Lords. But this place was nothing now but a burnt-out shell. Shattered white stone, bright and stark, nestled in nests of ash, surrounded us. The house before us had once been majestic, but was now nothing more than a gutted frame. The smoke was thick enough to choke the sun. Fires still burned in the distance. There was little movement.

Meajqa muttered a disgusted curse when we arrived. Luia's lip curled. Caduan barely reacted, save for a single wrinkle over the bridge of his nose.

I did not tell them that a part of me sighed in relief at the familiarity of this sight. I had missed this. It was so much simpler, easier to understand, than Caduan's court.

The humans were waiting for us, as was Iajqa, who had come to meet us here from her post in southern Threll. A human man and a woman approached us, both wearing flowing white clothes, spotless despite the carnage. The man was tall and thin with dark hair, the woman young and petite with golden curls and large blue eyes. Lord and Lady Zorokov.

Immediately, I hated them. Their clothing reminded me of a room of white and white and white—reminded me of the angry, sad memories in Tisaanah's mind.

"King Caduan. It is an honor to meet you in person at last," Lord Zorokov said. He spoke in Thereni. I understood it, perhaps because of my history living in other bodies. They both bowed, though only with the top of their heads. "Thank you for meeting us."

Caduan surveyed the wreckage.

"What happened here?"

Lord Zorokov looked somewhat offended by his abruptness, but Lady Zorokov laughed. "I've heard that you have no patience for pleasantries. I appreciate that. Better to get business done."

"It must be important business," Meajqa grumbled, shooting a disdainful glance at a corpse to his left, "to ask our king to come stand among your dead."

"Oh, not *all* of the dead are ours. But too many, sadly, are." Her smile faded, and I recognized the look that replaced it— anger, hidden beneath the smooth skin of her pretty face. "We have told you many times of our... escalating challenges with the rebels."

"Your rebelling slaves?" Caduan said, coldly.

Lord Zorokov, once again, looked insulted at Caduan's tone. Lady Zorokov's mouth tightened.

"The extremists who seek to collapse the nation of Threll and slaughter our children," she said. "The ones that you have refused to help us put down."

"We sent one of our highest-ranking generals to hunt down the leadership of your rebel groups," Meajqa said.

"With all respect, we both know that the only reason you sent her was because Tisaanah Vytezic stole from you," Lord Zorokov said. "Not out of any sense of loyalty to us."

"And their leadership slipped away regardless. The consequences of which are... dire." Lady Zorokov spread her arms, gesturing to the city wreckage. "Behold, the consequence of inaction, King Caduan."

"Your slaves did this?" Meajqa said, his voice going sour at the word "*slaves.*"

My ears pricked.

Tisaanah—did Tisaanah do this?

"The extremists did this, yes. Over the last six months, they have been successfully capturing and turning small outposts and villages. Of course, we were concerned, but those followings were nothing compared to the might and strength of Threllian leadership. But four days ago, they launched an attack on this estate. Their violent and underhanded tactics, dishonorable by Threllian law, gave them a temporary advantage."

Lady Zorokov beckoned. She led us up cracked marble steps, into the swaying shell of what must have once been the estate's central home. Only the tile floor was still intact—a sun design of silver and piercing sapphire blue.

At the center of the circle lay six human corpses. A wrinkled old woman and an equally old man beside her. A woman with dark hair and a man with greying temples. A young woman. A child. All were somewhat green, their bodies bloated and misshapen. They wore white, stained red.

"The Asmiroffs were kind people and respected Threllian nobility," Lady Zorokov said. "They did not deserve such horrible deaths. They were tortured for hours by their own beloved slaves, while they listened to the rebels take control of their city from outside their walls, helpless." She knelt beside the bodies, stroking the young woman's blonde hair. Her voice was brittle when she spoke again. "My sister was found in a room alone, ripped to pieces. I imagine what it must have been like for her, to wonder if her children were being subjected to the same torture that she was."

"I am sorry for your loss," Caduan said. "And I sympathize with your grief."

"Thank you." Lady Zorokov remained kneeling at her sister's corpse.

I looked out over the horizon. The decimation extended in all directions. Meajqa did the same. I wondered if we were thinking the same thing.

"How did this happen?" he asked.

Lord Zorokov's face hardened. "We burned the city," he said. "Fire and Aran lightning dust."

"You burned it instead of retaking it?"

I could see how Meajqa would be a talented diplomat. He carefully layered the judgement in his voice, coating it with enough honey to mask the bitterness, however pungent.

"Retaking it would have been... costly," Lord Zorokov replied. "Better for it to burn than to remain in the hands of the extremists."

Meajqa and Luia exchanged a glance of shocked disgust. But I was not surprised. This was what humans did. They destroyed what they could not have. So many times, they used me to do it.

I rubbed my palm, where the flower had sat mere hours ago.

"Why have you brought us here?" Caduan said.

Lady Zorokov rose, her grief replaced with a rueful smile. "We have been accommodating with your requests. As we should! We are honored, after all. For your people to come out of centuries of hiding and immediately ally with Threll... well, power attracts power. Our peoples have many differences, but I see many similarities, too."

Luia looked a bit sickened by this comparison.

"However, I'm afraid we have a problem. We have given you tens of thousands of soldiers, sent them to Ara's reaches—"

"You had equal interest in staving off Ara's advancement in Threll," Meajqa pointed out. "We discussed this at length."

"That is partly true, but we also would not have earned Ara's ire if we hadn't allied with the Fey. Now tens of thousands of our most skilled soldiers are fighting a war on your behalf, while our most respected Lords are being murdered in their own homes by sewer rats."

Lord Zorokov leveled a hard stare at Caduan. "We have fought your war for you, all while you send barely a handful of Fey soldiers and some of your... creations to the south. This cannot continue. We need to divert focus from Ara and deal with the rebels once and for all."

He said it like his word was law. He flicked a cold glance to me, and I almost snarled at him.

"Besides, this too would be mutually beneficial," Lady Zorokov added. "Seeing as the rebels have stolen the mysterious item that holds such high importance to you... even if, sadly, you haven't trusted us with its significance."

Such sweet, poisoned words.

"What do you propose?" Meajqa asked, tightly.

"The rebels are weak," Lord Zorokov said. "They're slaves, after all. Poorly educated, and physically inferior. But one of their greatest weaknesses is also their greatest strength—their decentralization. There are many of them, and they move quickly, finding new strongholds like vermin moving to a new nest. There is no single head for us to sever. If we strike in one place, they will retreat and regroup before we can flush them out, and soon there will be another attack in another district of Threll. But we can wipe them out all at once with one powerful attack. We strike all four of their key strongholds at the exact same time. They'll have no time to run, regroup, or warn." His gaze swept over the four of us. "But to do this, we need power."

"Pull your forces from the south, then," Iajqa said.

"We need more than that. We need *magic*. Give us ten thousand Fey soldiers. At least half of them skilled in magic use. That number is a mere fraction of the Threllian soldiers who have assisted you against Ara."

"I can offer shades," Caduan replied, without hesitation.

"The shades are not enough. They lack intelligence. We need warriors. Magic Wielders. There are few Wielders in Threll, and too many of those that are here are among the rebels. This is non-negotiable."

Iajqa's jaw went tight. "Watch your tone," she said, in a low voice.

"We mean no disrespect." Again, Lady Zorokov smiled. "We only intend to set out a clear request."

"I appreciate your honesty," Caduan said, "but, sadly, I must deny it."

The Zorokovs did not look pleased with this response.

"You came to us asking for Threll's alliance with the promise of all the power of the Fey kingdom," Lord Zorokov said. "Yet you have barely shown us such power. Your shades are weaker than they once were. You speak of a skilled army of warriors, but we've barely seen them."

Caduan's facial expression did not change. "I promised that I would bring your enemies to their knees, and I intend to uphold that vow."

"We've never doubted that, but we have given thousands of Threllian lives and property to your cause while you have given us... what, exactly?"

"You wish to build an empire that stands for an age," Meajqa said, sweetly. "We have already done it. Trust that our friendship is very valuable to you. We will offer you more support in the future."

"Look around. We don't have that much time. Our empire is falling *now*." Lady Zorokov gestured to the wreckage.

"I urge you to take some time to consider it, King Caduan," Lord Zorokov said. "If you cannot uphold your end of our alliance, I cannot promise that we can uphold ours."

"SNAKES," Meajqa spat, the moment the Zorokovs were out of earshot. "All of them. They burned *their own people* in that city. And then for them to make those kinds of disrespectful demands of you—"

"We can't afford to be hotheaded, nephew," Iajqa said. She looked to Caduan. "We may be forced to consider granting their request. Even if we give them half of what they asked for, they might be assuaged."

"Are you willing to lay thousands of your warriors at their feet?" Caduan shook his head—the answer was already clear to him.

It was clear to me, too.

"A few rebel slaves will not cause significant loss of life," Iajqa said. "It will earn us their goodwill. Raiding the rebel strongholds may also help us locate the wayfinder."

"Tisaanah Vytezic isn't with the rebels anymore. If she isn't there, we will not find the wayfinder there."

"Then are you any closer to locating it?" Iajqa sounded slightly irritated, and Caduan winced.

"Not yet. But I can."

His eyes flicked to me for a moment before moving away.

"My King—" Iajqa let out a breath through her teeth. "I have been out here for six months. I'm as repulsed by the Threllians as you are, but I also see every day how much we rely on their numbers. We can't lose their support. Worse, they are not the type to amicably part ways. If they stop being our ally, they will quickly start being our enemies, and unlike Ara, they are not an ocean away. Either we act against them, or we need to keep the

Threllians content. I do not think we are ready to do the former. Not yet."

"I understand. Trust that I know the consequences of this decision. And trust that if I'm making it, I know our options." I tried not to notice how his gaze slipped to me, even though I felt his stare like hands on my flesh. "We have options."

CHAPTER TWENTY-FOUR

MAX

I awoke in a room of solid stone, with no openings save for a single slat in the iron door. There was no furniture. When I opened my eyes, I was on the ground. I was alone. No Brayan.

I pushed myself to my feet—my body was not happy about that—and tried to find a way to orient myself. The slat in the door was covered with iron, which I presumed would open at some point when someone decided they wanted me. The only light spilled from beneath the door. No lanterns I could use, torches I could manipulate. Not that I could, anymore.

Just to be sure, I tried to use my magic and was rewarded by searing pain and not so much as a spark. In the darkness, I could make out severe blistering on my forearms, along the lines of the Stratagram tattoos.

Any naive hope that I had somehow managed to cure myself fell away.

Brayan. Where was he?

Was he dead?

I pushed that thought, and the ensuing stab of fear, as far into the back of my mind as it would go. I needed to think.

Evaluate.

Where was I? How long had I been out? Long enough to take me back to Ara? The ground was still. This was not a boat. I rubbed a finger on the stone wall. Smooth stone, not rough-hewn brick. No hint of sulfur in the smell of it. No dampness.

Judge.

This wasn't Ara.

So I was still in Threll, then. That was good news.

I pounded on the door, bellowing a string of expletive-laden demands. Then pressed my ear to the iron and listened.

Faint footsteps in the distance. Hints of garbled Thereni. A few words of Aran.

"...awake."

"Give it...hours. Wait...be here."

Hours until what? Until I was transported back to Ara?

That would be good, at least. If they opened the door, I could fight my way out. They'd be ready for that. Without my magic, I probably wouldn't even have a chance. But I'd rather die fighting than go back to Nura's table willingly.

Besides, there were other benefits to fighting, even in a fight that would end in guaranteed defeat.

Act.

I pressed my back to the wall behind the door, and waited.

I'D EXPECTED them to be eager to get me back to Ara. No doubt Nura would feel much more comfortable the minute I was safely encased in Ilyzath's walls.

But hours passed. No one came. I pressed my ear to the door, trying to steal any shards of information that I could glean through thick iron.

The only clue as to why came in one of the few clear strings of words I managed to hear:

"...she'll come...they're...sure."

She?

Eventually, the door opened.

187

I was ready. The soldier, a young man, hit the ground in seconds. I struck the next before he had time to see his friend fall —before he had time to call for help. Through the open door, I glimpsed freedom. A stone hallway. Dead end to the left. Exit to the right.

I seared the layout into my memory.

I managed to take down four of them. But by the time I turned on the fifth, four more men had joined them, overwhelming me. I hit the floor in a heap, wind knocked out of me by the largest of my assailants.

"'Scended, I didn't think he'd get through so many without magic," one of the guards muttered.

"I'm flattered," I wheezed.

"You think we're stupid, captain? Think we wouldn't be prepared for you?"

No, not really. But it was worth a shot.

Besides, I didn't need to win. I just needed to see.

Two of the guards yanked me to my feet. One, a woman, was a Valtain. The other, a young man, wore a sun sigil on his jacket. The Order of Daybreak. They had more Wielders here than I might have expected.

A middle-aged man wearing a captain's uniform leaned against the doorframe. He eyed the wall, newly drenched in light from outside. He nodded towards it. "What's that?"

I turned to see a messy drawing etched into the dark stone, faintly, as if with a fingernail—three familiar shapes, in a familiar arrangement. I didn't even remember drawing it, but then again, my hands so often just idled in that pattern.

"Your guess is as good as mine," I grumbled.

"It's clearly a map," one of the other guards said. "Some sort of islands."

"None that I recognize," another added.

"Copy it down before it rubs away," the captain said, turning to leave. "And take him for a walk. Edges of the compound."

A walk?

My first thought was that this must be some sort of metaphor.

A walk to an executioner's block, perhaps. But no. The walk was just a walk. My ankles and wrists were shackled, and I was brought outside into blinding late-afternoon sunshine.

It was immediately obvious that we were, as I suspected, still in Threll. The compound was made of polished cream-colored stone, surrounded by fern-dense forests. There were only a handful of small buildings here, encircled by high stone walls. My captor took me along the edges of the grounds.

It took me awhile to realize that we were walking in circles.

"What the hell is this for?" I asked my companion. "My mental health?"

He shot me a look that bordered on apologetic.

"I'm sorry," he said, quietly. "I fought with you in the civil war. Best captain I've ever had."

I did not remember this man at all.

"Thanks," I said. I wasn't sure what else to say. I knew it wasn't his fault. He was a soldier, and orders were orders. "I can't convince you to free me, can I?"

He gave me a half-smile, half-grimace, and I sighed. "I figured not."

By the third lap, I came to a conclusion.

She'll come, I'd heard the guards say. I was being used as bait. But for whom?

Time blurred. We walked and walked and walked. It was kind of them, at least, to give me such a comprehensive view of the layout of the compound.

Halfway through this never-ending journey, I felt a strange prickling beneath my skin, as if there was some invisible force in the air that called to me.

I stopped short, looking into the forest, seeing nothing but the wall and the greenery beyond it.

"Come on," the guard muttered, and nudged me along.

Half an hour later, my guard was relieved. The person who replaced him was a middle-aged man who wore a different uniform, black instead of Order of Daybreak green. A Threllian.

He said nothing until our second lap, when we crossed the

quiet side of the compound. Then, just as we passed behind a building, he leaned closer and whispered in Aran so heavily accented that I barely understood him.

"We have too few guards. West part empty at night. Your brother in southern building. Door will be open."

Then he grabbed my hand, and the movement was so abrupt that I didn't realize what he had given me until he had pulled us along, walking again as if nothing had happened. I closed my hand around that piece of metal, and then carefully slipped it up my sleeve.

A key.

The guard didn't speak another word to me. I didn't have the faintest clue why a Threllian guard would help me escape, but I was in no position to start questioning gifts.

I was taken back to my cell after the sun set, after hours of walking around the outside of the compound. I sat there in the darkness, staring at the door. The key, I quickly realized, was not for this door, which didn't open at all from the inside. Was it for Brayan's, then? For the gate?

Hours later, as I was sitting in pitch darkness, a faint click sounded. The door creaked open into an empty hallway.

Ascended above. This definitely had to be some sort of trap. This was too fucking easy.

I crept from my cell, sliding along the walls, allowing myself to fall back into the shadows. The guard was right—I could see now that they were indeed woefully understaffed here. Maybe they needed to send soldiers to other locations at night in order to distribute forces. Earlier today, it would have been nearly impossible to sneak from one building to another—too many soldiers and too little cover. But now? I could hide in the shadows easily, and there were rarely more than two guards on a single path. I managed to slip past the soldiers monitoring the one from my cell to the southmost building. The door was locked, and my key didn't open it, but a cracked window offered me a way in, even if scraping my blistered skin along the sill made me wince.

Inside, six prison cells—more open and less secure than mine. Five were empty. And the sixth—

Brayan leapt to his feet. "I thought they executed you."

"Sh," I hissed, scrambling to open his cell, though my first impulse was to say, *I'm very glad you're alive, too.*

"These people are idiots," he said as I unlocked his door. "They don't watch what they say in front of me. You're being used as bait."

"I know." I pushed his door open. "I don't think we have much—"

He added, frowning, "Does the name Tisaanah Vytezic mean anything to you?"

I stopped short. "What?"

"It's familiar, but I can't place it. It sounds like that's the person they're—"

Bang!

We both whirled around. A sudden commotion rang out in the north end of the compound, a cacophony of crashes and voices.

I couldn't move. I felt a strange sensation that reminded me of the one that had nagged at me during the walk earlier—but now it was stronger, overwhelming. I felt it down to my bones. Something *familiar.*

Brayan was already halfway down the hall. "Why are you just standing there? Let's go."

I didn't know how I'd answer that question—even if I'd had time to before the door to the compound flew open.

CHAPTER TWENTY-FIVE

TISAANAH

Nura had many advantages over me. She had managed to build an impressive presence in Threll over these last months, branching out from the land the Orders had obtained after the fall of the Mikov family. And she had the slaves that she had purchased, a thought that still made my stomach turn.

I'd seen the reaches of her influence here over these last months. But it never got less strange to see this—soldiers in Orders' uniforms swarming Threllian compounds.

I was so close.

When I had seen Max, chained and guarded at the edges of the compound, I'd almost wept. I couldn't make out his face. Yet I immediately knew that it was him, the recognition hitting me like a punch to my gut.

"Are you *sure* it is him?" Ishqa had pressed, over and over again, making no secret of his skepticism.

I was sure.

Her people, of course, were waiting for me.

The explosion, a gift from Ishqa's Fey potions, rocked the gates, leaving the massive stone doors hanging from the hinges. The smoke was thick, purple from the Fey magic mingling with the blue of Lightning Dust—we'd only managed to get a little of it, but it was plenty to make the blast powerful enough to break through stone.

The smoke burned my lungs, my eyes. I charged straight through it. Let them think that I was Wielding it. Let them believe that I still had the power they'd heard whispered about during the Aran civil war.

I'd memorized the formation of the guards. Memory, combined with my weak vestiges of magic, filled in what sight could not.

At first, I was so focused on my fight that I didn't feel it—but as I crossed the threshold of the compound, what had been a punch to my gut earlier became a yearning hunger pang. I could feel Max's presence as if every trace of magic inside of me reached for him.

The soldiers were on me in seconds. I fought on instinct alone, blocking weapon after weapon, hitting bone.

Pain exploded in the back of my skull. White light flashed. Magic.

I countered too slowly. Another blow landed. My knees hit the ground.

Too many sets of hands swarmed me, holding me down. I reached for my sword, but it was yanked from my grasp.

I let out a snarl. Bit an arm that reached over me. Fought back like the animal they thought I was. But soon I found myself pinned, soldiers wrestling shackles onto my wrists. I had made it ten feet beyond the compound gates.

I blinked the blood from my eyes. A man in a captain's uniform stood over me.

"After all I had heard about you, I have to say, I expected this to be harder," he said.

I spat at him. He rewarded me with a crack across the back of my head, hard enough to make my vision blur.

"Threllian bitch," he muttered, wiping the spittle from his face in disgust. "Lock her up. The Queen wants her alive. Keep her far away from him."

I fought them the whole way. Tears streamed from my eyes—from the smoke of the explosion. I let them believe it was because I was caught.

I pretended that I hadn't planned for this to happen exactly as it did.

They dragged me to the eastern side of the compound. There, one of the guards—one of the Threllian guards—came just close enough to me to mutter in my ear.

"The west side. He's been freed," he whispered in Thereni. The other guards weren't close enough to hear, and couldn't understand us if they did, anyway.

It wasn't the Threllian guards that we had to worry about. I saw the moment I was taken into captivity that they recognized me.

This was the factor Nura didn't consider.

She had the land, the manpower, the magic, the prisons. She set a trap with iron teeth. Tallied on paper, it was laughable to think that one person could pose any threat to these things. But she was thinking of me, a single slave—not the hundreds that oiled the gears of her burgeoning Threllian empire. She prioritized earning the steadfast loyalty of her Threllian subjects, but she didn't know this place, didn't know *them*. I'd learned a long time ago that there was nothing you couldn't do if you knew what people truly wanted.

I knew what this man wanted.

His name was Viktor. He had come into Nura's possession because he had been a slave on Esmaris Mikov's estate and had chosen to stay after the Orders had taken it over. I didn't know him personally, at least not well, but when I had seen his name on the list of soldiers stationed at this base, it had sparked familiarity. His sister and his nephew were among those Serel, Filias, and I had freed from a neighboring estate several months ago. They had joined the rebellion. Viktor wouldn't know that they had been freed, or where they were now—but I did.

So, hours earlier, when Viktor had been making his daily early-morning patrols of the ground, it hadn't even been difficult to find him alone in a base this understaffed. He knew who I was immediately. When I told him of his family, I watched his eyes widen. I'd seen that look so many times. Before he even opened his mouth, I knew he would help us. People will do anything for hope.

Now, Viktor took my arm, pulling us out of sight from the rest of the base. We had seconds. Even though the base was woefully short-staffed at night, I had attracted attention and riled up the guards here—just as I had intended to.

Viktor shoved a sheathed dagger into my hands, which I slipped into the waistband of my trousers. My heart was beating so fast.

"I saw him go," Viktor said. "He and his brother are leaving now."

Brother?

I barely cared about that moment of confusion. I was minutes away from seeing Max again. The hope was so intense that it terrified me.

"Go to the east side," I said. "My friends will be waiting for you. They will get you out."

His eyes gleamed beneath the lantern light. He slipped me a small metal key, and as he did, he paused to squeeze his calloused hand around mine. "Thank you, Tisaanah. Thank you."

I nodded, my own throat tight. "You're the one who deserves the thanks."

He gave me a small smile, then looked over his shoulder. "We should wait no more than a half hour before freeing you. They'll be sending the rest of the Aran soldiers back now that they know you've been captured. It will only get harder to get you out later, and if they realize he's gone—"

The high-pitched screech cut through me like a scalpel, sharp enough that it shattered the air. It lasted for several long seconds, and by the time I managed to regain my senses, I realized the ground was shaking. Panicked shouts erupted outside. "Get that thing under control! Stop it! Kill it! *Kill it!*" someone was shrieking, before going silent.

Viktor's eyes went round. Happiness fell away in favor of sheer terror.

"What is that?" I asked.

"We need to go right—" Viktor started, just as the most horrifying creature I had ever seen tore through the wall of the base.

CHAPTER TWENTY-SIX

MAX

A well-dressed man stood in the doorway, a small, knowing smile on his lips.

"Good to see you, Max," he said, and held a spear out to me.

He looked so frustratingly familiar. I took the spear. My mind sifted through scattered, incomplete memories.

"Um... thanks," I said, and the man's smile faded slightly, as if something was confusing about my response.

"Imat?" Brayan's voice came from behind me.

Imat. Sammerin Imat.

It clicked. I *did* know him. We'd both served in the Orders division of the military at the same time, though I'd only met him a handful of times—at least as far as I could remember.

I had no idea why he would now be showing up to help me from captivity. I'd been getting a lot of confusing help today. Not that I was about to question it.

"Brayan. Why are..." Sammerin shook away his questions. "Never mind. We only have a few minutes." He grabbed another sword from the wall and tossed it to Brayan, who caught it midair.

"What was all that?" I asked, as Sammerin led us through the open door. A remarkably empty path led from the back of the building out to the wall, through an ajar gate, and into the forest beyond.

Too easy. All too easy.

And yet, as Sammerin and Brayan set off down the path, I found myself hesitating for a reason I couldn't explain. Like I had forgotten something crucial.

Sammerin glanced over his shoulder.

"She's coming," he said. "She'll meet us out there."

She?

Does the name Tisaanah Vytezic mean anything to you?

"Quickly," Sammerin hissed, pointing to the opening in the wall. We slipped through the night, hugging crates and walls until we reached the gate. The commotion had calmed, but guards still flocked to the other end of the compound.

What *was* all that?

We hit the wall, slipped through the gate, then stepped into the lush undergrowth of the forest.

You forgot something, a voice in the back of my mind still nagged. *You forgot something very, very important.*

We made it two steps into the forest when the shriek made me double over, knocking the breath from my lungs. It was a terrible sound, like agony distilled into a single tone.

I recognized it immediately.

I forced myself upright to see that the base had devolved into chaos. Just out of view, blue and white light flickered in the air, reflecting in puffs of smoke. Screams in Aran and Thereni mixed into a mangled blur.

I gripped my weapon. Without my permission, my feet brought me two steps closer to the gate.

"What *is* that?" Sammerin joined me, his eyes darting around the base.

"If that thing is back, we'd better go," Brayan said.

"What thing?" Sammerin asked.

I didn't move. A particularly loud screech split the air. A crash, and the roar of crumbling stone. A building on the other side of the base collapsed as a blast of blinding white light burst through brick.

The monster came roaring out of it.

Even when I was expecting it, the sight of it stunned me all over again. It looked even worse than it had when Brayan and I encountered it. Now, its face was almost entirely gone, the empty, light-drenched eye sockets melding with its missing jaw.

The creature stumbled from the wreckage wailing, inhuman limbs thrashing.

Sammerin drew in a sharp gasp of horror.

The smoke dissipated to reveal that the monster was *chasing* someone.

The figure glanced over their shoulder at us. It was a young woman. She had strange, dual-tone skin, Valtain-pale with a swatch of color over one side of her face. White hair streaked with black whipped in the wind. Through it, one green eye fell to me.

That stare skewered me through the chest. I couldn't look away.

The moment broke. The woman had to turn, blocking with her sword, bracing herself for impact. That idiot was *fighting* this thing.

I didn't hear Brayan shout my name. I was already running back into the carnage.

CHAPTER TWENTY-SEVEN

AEFE

The vision was a crack of lightning that split my world in two. One moment, I was in my chambers, practicing my magic—and the next, the sensations buried me in an onslaught.

I saw iron bars and steel blades.

A night sky over an emerald forest.

A horrible face, half decomposed, covered with stringy red hair.

The flood of magic. The scorch of fire.

And *pain pain pain.*

I couldn't catch my breath. I had fallen to the ground. I pressed my palms to the cold tile of the floor until I felt it steady beneath me.

The connection still burned in my chest, unmistakable. The particular strain of magic we shared, the kind that reached deeper than the soul, pulled me like a thread tied around my throat. Just as it had when I showed it to Caduan.

Tisaanah and Maxantarius were far from where they had been before.

And they were together. *Together.*

I forced myself to my feet and stumbled out of my room. I

didn't stop running until I had reached Caduan's chamber. I snarled something wordless at the guards and threw open his door. "We need to go," I panted.

Caduan had been sitting at his desk. He sat up, blinking at me blearily, looking exhausted. "Go...where?"

Words. Such infuriatingly clumsy tools to communicate such important things.

"We need to go. *Now.*" When Caduan stood and approached, I grabbed his arms hard enough to leave marks in his skin. "*I feel them. Now. Right now.*"

All remnants of Caduan's weariness disappeared. He threw his jacket on and didn't bother buttoning it.

"Stay calm," he said, sharply. "Maintain the connection."

Holding onto that thread required increasingly more concentration; it grew thinner and more slippery by the second.

He stood behind me and put his hand over mine. Our fingers intertwined. His skin felt so hot. I leaned into the sensation of his warmth.

Life. Heartbeat.

"What we're about to do is dangerous. We're traveling fast, and I am going to ask you to steer where we go. We could lose control—"

"Go!" I choked out. We didn't have time to waste on Caduan's explanations. Already, I could feel the thread leading me to Tisaanah and Maxantarius beginning to wane, threatening to snap.

Caduan's mouth closed. Without another word, he pulled me close, one arm locked tight around my waist, the other reaching around me to cradle my hand. "Let it pull you," he murmured in my ear. "Just feel the direction we need to go, and I will do the rest."

That wasn't difficult. I was so focused on it that I barely felt the world dissolve around us.

———————

CADUAN'S BEDCHAMBER BECAME A FOREST. We were waist-deep in water. Caduan's body was still braced around mine.

The thread of connection felt tighter, stronger.

Closer.

A broken image flashed through my mind—fear, as a horrifying face leaned over me.

"Again!" I commanded, and Caduan obeyed.

With every landing, every clumsy arrival in another nowhere, the presence crept closer.

The familiarity was intoxicating. I had been dropped into an unfamiliar world and an unfamiliar body, but in this moment, in this single shred of connection, my fingertips brushed the soul-deep bond we had once shared.

I had not realized how much I craved it until now.

"Again!" I would gasp with every arrival, and Caduan would take us away again. I lost track of how many times we had leapt when my knees came crashing down on a riverbank.

Perhaps I should have been concerned that this time, Caduan had arrived several feet away from me, wrenched away in transit—but I was not.

"This is getting dangerous, Aefe," he said, as he crawled back to me.

"Dangerous?" I laughed, a strange, high-pitched noise. How dangerous could it be to go home? Especially now, when I felt so connected to everything—myself, and them. Euphoria devoured any twinges of discomfort. I was Aefe, I was powerful, I had control of my own magic and breath and heartbeat, and I felt all their souls *right there*, so close I could taste them.

"No. We are close." I grabbed Caduan's hand, forced his arm around me again.

Perhaps I should have been concerned by the labor in his breath—but I was not.

"I can get her. I can bring her to you." I had never been so certain of anything. This was what it was to have *purpose*.

Perhaps I should have been concerned that Caduan hesitated—but I was not.

I clung to the thread of connection and let it catapult us through the earth.

We landed.

The world was cold and dark.

Everything that had not concerned me collided at once as I sank into the water, Caduan nowhere to be found.

CHAPTER TWENTY-EIGHT

TISAANAH

Thinking was a living nightmare, and it was going to kill me.

As its horrific half-rotted face loomed over me, I thought it might be fitting to go this way, because this was what the face of death must look like. Cold light leaked from beneath torn, paper-thin skin, blinding behind those gaping eyes.

The soldiers had tried and failed to control it. Now they just ran.

Those sightless eyes looked only at me, as if it could smell something in me that it desired. I could feel it, too—sour, curdled, tainting the rhythm of magic that ran beneath this world.

When I'd looked over my shoulder to see Max—gods, *Max*—standing at the gate, I'd thought, *At least I got one last look. At least he is free.*

But then the world crashed down around me, and I had no time to think about anything, anymore.

It attacked, and I was barely fast enough to evade. I plunged my sword into too-soft flesh, revealing another tear of light. If this creature felt anything, it didn't show it.

I barely glimpsed a smear of gold behind the creature — Ishqa, injured, trying and failing to get to his feet. He met my eyes just as I rolled.

A fragment of lightning scalded my shoulder.

I cringed for another incoming blow, too fast to dodge —

But the creature let out a sickening screech.

I felt Max before I saw him. I knew it was him before I got to my feet.

He had buried his spear in the monster's opened abdomen, just one quick strike before we evaded. Our eyes met barely for a moment, just long enough for a silent agreement.

I'd never felt less alone than I did when we fought together. Our rhythm resumed like a heartbeat. He knew my every move before I made it, covering me when I needed it, offering me openings for my own strikes.

The creature didn't know where to look first, where to attack. It was wild, directionless.

At one point, I miscalculated, veering left when I should have gone right. Max saw it before I did, grabbing for me too late.

The monster lunged — then lurched to an abrupt, unnatural stop.

Behind me, Sammerin stood with his arms lifted, face twisted with exertion. "*Go!*" he grunted.

I wasn't sure if he was prompting me to attack or to run, but I knew in my bones that this thing would not stop chasing us. So instead of fleeing, I charged, even though I knew it was hopeless.

I couldn't defeat this with a little piece of steel. Did it have magic I could use? Did I even *want* whatever putrid, rotten magic this thing would give me?

No time to be picky.

The monster was low enough for me to reach its flesh. Max attacked it from the right. Another blur of movement came from behind it — the stranger, with the long dark hair, striking from behind.

I opened just one nick in its flesh, sliced my hand, pressed the wounds together.

That was a mistake. The pain was ice-hot and instant. Decay withered across where we touched. Immediately, I yanked my hand away, letting out a gasp of pain. The agony ran up my spine, through my veins. I couldn't move.

A wordless voice filled my head:

Let me go. Make them let me go. Let me go. Make them let me go.

Distantly, I heard Sammerin curse. The monster broke from the grip of his magic and came for me.

A familiar body slid in front of mine, pushing me back.

The wall of flames drowned out everything else. I rolled to see Max's silhouette enveloped in fire. Something snapped in the air, like someone yanked hard on a thread inside of me, waking up magic that had been dormant. It was like another sense flickered to life. I reached out for the creature's mind—felt its struggle between the animal fight for survival and a chilling desire for death.

Ishqa had managed to rally himself, but he was weakened, too slow. The creature moved faster, grabbing him like he was a rag doll in one clawed hand. Ishqa let out a grunt of pain.

I grabbed Max's abandoned spear and plunged it into the white light seeping from the monster's abdomen.

It let out a piercing wail. Its long, backwards-bent leg dropped Ishqa, who collapsed in a heap.

In its mind, I sensed the yearning for merciful death disappear beneath feral wrath.

It pounced, not for me or Max or Sammerin but for one of the soldiers behind it, tearing him to fiery pieces. Then another, crushed beneath a speared foot.

Moments of distraction. Seconds of opportunity.

"Run," Sammerin panted. "I can't control it. Its flesh won't listen to me."

I helped Ishqa get to his knees. He was barely conscious.

"Can you walk?" I grunted.

If he couldn't, I didn't know what we were going to do.

Another shriek cut through the air. I looked up and let out a gasp of horror. The creature had discarded another soldier, and now held Viktor in its grasp.

I was leaping after him before I could even think. But just as quickly, a familiar wall of warmth surrounded me. Max's arm gripped me around my shoulders, pulling me against him.

"You can't." His voice was low in my ear. "I'm sorry. You can't."

By the time the words were out of Max's lips, Viktor was in pieces.

"Let's go!" A cart rumbled beside us. The long-haired man — Max's brother? — was in the driver's seat. He could barely control the panicking horse. "Now. Fast."

Seconds, while that thing was distracted by the guards. The cart didn't even come to a stop. We leapt into it. Ishqa barely managed to lift himself onto the incline, and Max had to drag him onto the deck.

The base rushed past us as the cart rumbled over uneven paths, rattling after the increasingly frantic horse. We weren't staying on the road.

Crack! The cart jolted as a wheel began to give out, caught on the uneven terrain. Ahead, the forest loomed. We would never make it. Even if we did, the cart couldn't go there.

"We need to Stratagram out of here," I said, voice raised. "Now!"

"I can't," Max said, looking down, and I followed his gaze to the blistering black Stratagram tattoos peeking from under his sleeve. My stomach fell. I couldn't either. Not reliably. I still didn't understand what determined when my magic worked or didn't.

Across the base, the creature dropped the final dead soldier. Turned to us.

Max's brother hissed a curse. He notched a bow, let an arrow fly.

It did nothing. The monster was now running.

CRACK!

The cart floor fell several inches as our frantic horse tried and failed to drag it over root-riddled dirt.

I peered over my shoulder. "*Sammerin?*"

He cringed. "I can't take five people."

"I can fly." Ishqa could barely speak. He pushed himself slowly to his feet.

"No, you can't—"

"I can," he said, firmly. Then, to Sammerin. "Four people."

Sammerin muttered a curse. He withdrew parchment.

The monster barreled towards us, shrieking, light collecting in its abdomen.

"Quickly, Sammerin," I murmured.

"*I know,*" he snapped.

I grabbed Sammerin's arm in one hand, Max's in the other. Max hurled his spear from the back of the cart, a streak of fire at its tip, then he gripped his brother's wrist, linking all of us together.

Sammerin drew the last line of his Stratagram.

The spear found its target, right in the gaping wound of the creature's stomach. It let out a scream and tumbled to the ground. Its cry echoed in my thoughts.

Ishqa pumped his wings one, two, three times, and launched into the sky.

And the world dissolved.

CHAPTER TWENTY-NINE

AEFE

My limbs flailed in frantic, fruitless search for solid ground. I drew in a gasp, only to choke on a lungful of water. It was dark. I could feel nothing, see nothing. Which way was up? Down?

Water. You are in water. Swim, Aefe.

I did not know if my body knew how to swim, but in a disoriented panic I kicked until my face broke the surface. I had never been so grateful for air.

I clumsily swam to shore, dragging myself through thick mud on my hands and knees. I coughed until my ribs ached, mouthfuls of putrid water dribbling past my lips. My head pounded and limbs shook.

For one horrible moment I thought perhaps I had lost my connection to Tisaanah and Maxantarius. I took several deep breaths, stilled my rising worry. As my heartbeat slowed, I found it again—*there*.

A smile twisted my lips.

Close. They were *so* close.

It was only then that I realized that Caduan wasn't.

I forced myself to my feet and looked around. Nothing but forest, trees looming over me like shadowy guardians.

"Caduan?" I called out.

My eyes fell to the river. I had pulled myself from a deep but relatively calm section of it, but downstream, multiple tributaries combined into churning rapids dotted with jagged rocks.

What if he had landed in the water, too? What if he had been smashed upon those stones before he even had time to react?

"*Caduan?*" I called again, more frantically.

I heard voices behind me. Human voices, speaking Aran—a language I recognized immediately.

I spun around. Four humans emerged from the brush. They wore double-breasted jackets bearing a sun sigil.

My heart beat faster.

They spoke to each other—or to me?—in Aran. I knew this language, but it took several long seconds before I could make my mind translate their words.

The oldest of them, a man with a greying beard, was speaking.

"...alright, sweetheart?"

Do not panic.

You are Aefe, not Reshaye. They cannot hurt you. You have your own heart, your own breath.

I counted them in the darkness. Five. I had fought so many more than that.

"You're not far from a military base," the man said. "Best you not wander out here alone at night so close to the wall. Folks have been a bit twitchy lately."

"What the hell is wrong with her?" another soldier muttered.

Don't come closer to me! I wanted to shout, but the Aran words twisted on my tongue.

My hand closed around the hilt of my dagger at my hip.

One of the soldiers lurched to a sudden stop, eyes going wide. "Fucking hell, look at her ears. She's one of *them*."

In that moment, I went from being a young woman in need of rescue to a dangerous animal to be contained.

I had been in enough battles to understand what was to happen next.

I grounded myself in my quickening heartbeat, and the magic that lurked beneath it. Gripped the cold steel of my black dagger.

You are not nothing, Aefe, I reminded myself.

And as soon as they took another step closer, I lunged.

I plunged my dagger into the youngest man's neck, his blood spurting all over my face. He grabbed at me as he fell, sword spasming and knocking my leg from under me.

His companions were on me at once. They were Wielders. Light flashed, scalding my back. Stone leapt from the ground, locking around my feet.

So quickly, my composure unraveled.

I thrashed, stabbing with my blade. I struck flesh multiple times, moving too fast to know who. I kicked against the rock. My ankle cracked, sending my body collapsing.

Still, I struck out with my teeth, my fingernails. I tasted nothing but iron. But even just the three remaining were too many. I was on the ground. Weight fell over my chest.

The man with the grey beard was leaning over me, his forearm over my throat. He was so close that I could smell his breath. Blood covered his face. It dripped into my eyes.

Through the crimson, I could see only his hatred and nothing else.

I could not move.

I was helpless as horrific pain speared through me, the blade slowly, so slowly, sliding through my abdomen.

I cried out. The man did not release me. I could not move.

Suddenly I was Reshaye again, trapped in a useless body in a room of white and white. Suddenly I was on a stone floor, being dragged away by humans just like these ones, watching Ishqa walk away.

I was helpless.

I tried to scream, but air evaded me. I tried to lash out, but all my limbs were pinned.

Who were you to think that you could do this? To think that you were something? You have always been nothing.

What good is a heartbeat, anyway?

They would hurt me, they would kill me, and I would be helpless and *I was helpless* and I was nothing and nothing and—

A hot spray of blood spattered over me.

The man on top of me was suddenly gone, his face replaced by the point of a branch that now plunged through his skull.

The other woman tried to turn, sparks of magic at her hands. Before she could, vines wrapped around her throat, her wrists, her waist, crawled over her face as they yanked her off the ground. The vines grew thicker, tauter, then abruptly pulled apart, leaving her in pieces.

I tried to move, but my muscles would not cooperate. Tried to breathe, but each gasp left me even more desperate for air, like I was drowning with each one.

The fight was only shadowy, formless figures. Brief flashes of crimson and light danced across my fading vision. Screams cut through the air for split seconds before becoming garbled moans.

My hands came to my abdomen and felt a ragged, slick puncture.

I was back in a stone room, paralyzed. I would be tortured. I would be dismantled and everything would be taken away and I could do nothing.

I could do nothing.

I no longer felt my heartbeat.

Someone touched me and I let out a weak attempt at a scream, lashing with my fading strength. A human. A human was touching me and they would rip me apart and I could do nothing and—

"It's me. It's me, Aefe. *Stop.*"

Someone pulled me close, holding my shoulders. Took my blood-soaked hand and pressed it to smooth skin. Beneath it was the faint thrum of a heartbeat.

"It's me, Aefe," Caduan murmured, his forehead against mine. "Keep breathing."

Fear. I heard fear in that voice.

"You are safe," he whispered.

I thought, *You can not lie to me.*

I realized I was sobbing. I realized I couldn't breathe.

But he held my hand against his chest, and it was the last thing I felt as I faded.

"Keep breathing, Aefe."

CHAPTER THIRTY

TISAANAH

My eyelids fluttered open. Blades of grass tickled my nose. The air was silent. Peaceful, even.

It took a few long seconds for the events of the night to return to me.

I shot upright. I was in a field beneath a starry sky. I'd been holding onto both Sammerin and Max when Sammerin executed his Stratagram, but neither were beside me now.

I struggled to my feet, frantic.

"Sammerin? Max?"

My voice was weak, at first.

"*Max?*"

I couldn't have lost him again. Not again.

Then there was movement in the grass. To my left, the long-haired man — Max's brother, gods, *that* was a story I needed to hear — rolled over and pushed himself up.

To my right, Sammerin sat up from behind a pile of rocks, rubbing his temple.

"I cannot *believe* I just did that," he muttered, as if to himself. "A Stratagram with four people. Ascended."

And then, at last, Max emerged from a cluster of trees.

He moved with a slight limp. His clothes were torn and burnt, his dark hair much shaggier and longer than it had been before, one cheek smeared with blood. He was leaner. And it was only now, when I had the time to get a proper look at him, that I realized the tattoos covered every inch of him but his face — Stratagrams on top of Stratagrams.

His eyes — those beautiful, milky blue eyes — lifted to meet mine, and it was those eyes that were my undoing.

I ran to him, threw my arms around his neck and buried my face against his shoulder. Though he had lost weight, he felt the same, every angle and curve and swell of his body falling against mine in a way that felt like home — my *home*, and gods, I was never leaving, I was never letting go, I would live here, in the scent of him, in the feel of his breath against my chest, forever.

My breath was ragged. I probably looked like a blubbering mess. I didn't care. I was too happy.

How long did it take me to realize he wasn't hugging me back?

CHAPTER THIRTY-ONE

MAX

The woman hugged me, and I just stood there, not sure what to do.

I bowed my head and was struck with the overwhelming scent of citrus. With that scent came the ghost of a thousand other memories. It smelled like home. I wanted to fold my arms around her, bury my face in her hair, hold it in my lungs like smoke from fine tobacco. This stranger.

Instead I settled for that single hand laid gently between her shoulder blades.

My eyes flicked up and landed on Sammerin's face. He was looking at me like something was wrong.

Eventually, the woman went stiff and still, as if the same realization had fallen over her. When she stepped away, I resisted the sudden urge to pull her back again.

She looked up at me.

Ascended fucking above, she was stunning. Her eyes were mismatched, one silver and one amber-green. Moonlight pooled in the silver iris.

"Max?"

The way she said my name made me stop breathing for a moment. Two syllables, spoken like a melody.

"I don't..."

I don't remember you.

No. That wasn't right. Not really. I didn't know this woman's name, or how I met her. I held no memories of her. But *I knew her.* I knew her somewhere intrinsic, deeper than flesh. That part of my past called to me, and fuck, I *wanted* to reach for it—but even that instinctual drive for my past was met with a wall and a sudden spike of pain through the back of my skull.

I was bad with words at the best of times, let alone now, as I struggled to explain something I didn't even understand myself.

"There's a lot that I don't remember," I said, at last.

A wrinkle deepened between the woman's eyebrows. "Like... what?"

"I remember my childhood, mostly. But anything after seventeen or so... it's just... gone."

Even that didn't describe all of it. The way I felt the imprint of the past but couldn't recall the details that made it that way.

"Gone?" she repeated. "I don't understand."

I opened my mouth, then closed it, increasingly frustrated with everything I couldn't put into words. "What's your name?"

For a split second, the woman's face just collapsed—first in shock, and then in devastation. She took two steps backwards, and I closed the distance again without thinking.

"You are not asking me that," she choked out.

She quickly forced her face back into neutrality, but I could still see her heart breaking, and the sight of it made mine ache, too.

I stepped closer again. I wanted her to say something more, but her mouth was now tightly closed, like she feared whatever might slip out.

"But before, he remembered nothing at all," Brayan added. "This is an improvement already."

Sammerin let out a small breath. "So your memory is coming back."

"Maybe." I didn't think that was necessarily true, even if I hoped it was. I still couldn't take my eyes off that woman, who now stood with her arms crossed tight over her chest, as if shielding herself.

"I have so many questions." Sammerin rubbed his temple. "How did you get out of Ilyzath? We've been trying to break you out for months."

They had?

If explaining my memory loss was difficult, explaining the bizarre circumstances of my escape seemed downright impossible. "That answer is... complicated."

A wrinkle deepened between his brow. "Did Nura do that to you? The memory loss?"

He was a friend, I thought. A good friend. I could feel the imprint of that too, even though the details, again, remained locked behind a wall I couldn't breach. Even if I hadn't felt the echo of that relationship, then the slight, restrained anger in his voice at Nura's name would have betrayed it.

The winged Fey came closer. His stare made me uncomfortable—that ageless bright gold seemed to pick me apart. My gaze lingered on the points of his ears. He was clearly an ally to these two, but I knew Fey only as the creatures that I watched tear Ara to shreds over the last months.

"May I?" he asked and took my wrist before I had the chance to answer, pushing my sleeve up my arm.

"Excuse you," I muttered.

He ignored me as he examined the tattoos. The ones on my wrists and hands blistered fiercely.

"What are these?" the Fey asked. "Human magic?"

"Stratagrams," Sammerin offered. "Visual manifestations of magic to help Wielders execute complex spells." His eyes flicked to me. "Did she put these here to bind your magic? I've never seen so many on one person."

I nodded as I pulled my arm away, oddly self-conscious.

The Fey looked dissatisfied with this answer. "But you used your magic in the battle."

"I can, sometimes. Only for a few minutes at most. Seemingly at random. I don't know how or why."

What I didn't say is that when I came here, when I fought beside this stranger, my magic felt more alive than it had in months. I still paid for it, and it was still unpredictable, but it wasn't even that hard for me to slip Nura's chains.

"Interesting," the Fey murmured.

Sammerin's fingers lingered at his chin, deep in thought. "And your mind… the Stratagrams did that?"

"I don't think so. That came—"

"Before."

The woman looked at me with wide eyes, then broke my stare and went silent.

I cleared my throat, awkwardly. "Maybe. I don't—it's hard for me to say."

"But your magic… it's not gone. Only locked." Sammerin surveyed the tattoos.

"Yes."

"You drew from a deeper level tonight," the Fey said. "That is why you were able to use it. You drew from it before, and that magic does not obey the rules of your human—"

"Wait." I held up my hand. "I could draw from it before? What does that mean?"

The Fey went silent. He looked to Sammerin, then the girl. "You and Tisaanah are capable of drawing from these streams of magic."

Tisaanah.

The sound of her name just… fit. I glanced up at her. She was silent, her arms crossed around herself.

"Why?" I asked.

A tiny whisper in the back of my head:

Do not ask questions you do not want to answer.

Sammerin and Tisaanah exchanged a heavy glance.

"That is a very long story," Sammerin said, at last.

"I don't care," I said, but that sharp pain was building in my skull, like a knife held with steadily increasing pressure. I blinked and saw a burning girl, saw a closed set of gates with a lion at their arch.

There is a door you cannot open. A place you do not wish to return.

I gritted my teeth and tried to ignore it. "And what, then, are the three of you doing? What does it have to do with me?"

Tisaanah made a small, breathless noise, a sort of strangled laugh.

"You are familiar with the war," Ishqa said.

"Of course," I said. "I spent enough time on Nura's table because of it."

A wince flitted across Tisaanah's face, and she turned away again, as if she couldn't stand to look at me. That made my chest ache for reasons I didn't understand.

"We have an opportunity to stop this war before it results in the genocide of either of our peoples," Ishqa said. "But the only chance we have of doing that is with the magic that you, Tisaanah, and precious few others have access to."

Ascended above.

Of their own accord, my fingers pressed to my temple. The pain had gotten so intense that it had become difficult to focus on anything else, let alone anything as unbelievable as what these people were telling me.

"Before we go anywhere else, we must help him." Tisaanah looked pointedly at Ishqa. "Do you know anyone who could do that?"

Ishqa looked hesitant.

"You want me to find and harness the Lejaras?" She thrust out her palm, and in a ray of moonlight I caught a glimpse of gold splashed across it, like metal etched into her skin. My eyebrows arched, my fingers going to the strange symbol on my own hand—the one Ilyzath had given me. "I cannot do it without him. So if we are to do this, then we need to help him first."

"I have only one idea," Ishqa said, after a long moment. "I know of someone who may be able to help in Zagos."

"*Zagos?*" Brayan let out a scoff.

"You know it?" Ishqa said.

"It doesn't exist."

"It very much does exist."

"Then I can't imagine we're going to find anything good there."

"What is Zagos?" Tisaanah asked.

"It's a mythical fugitive city," Brayan said. "I can't count how many times I'd been hired to go apprehend some criminal or another that was claimed to be in *Zagos*."

Ah, now I understood Brayan's attitude. He was just bitter that if the place existed, he hadn't been able to find it.

"It is… an interesting place. But it is on our route north anyway. Besides…" A wry smile tugged at Ishqa's mouth. "Where does one go to find forgotten things? The place where people go to be forgotten."

A distant commotion rang out, echoing through the forest. The sound was loud enough to jar us from the depths of our conversation. We all looked around and seemed to simultaneously remember that we were standing in the middle of a field, Ascended-knew-where, and that no doubt there was a small army—potentially, soon to become a large army—searching for us.

"We shouldn't linger." Tisaanah was the first to turn, pointing north. "If we will find help in Zagos, then we will go to Zagos."

She was soft spoken, but every sentence had an air of finality to it—enough finality to send Sammerin and Ishqa following.

As the rest of the group departed, Brayan held me back.

"We can just go to Besrith on our own," he said, voice low. "Just like we planned. There is nothing forcing us to stay with them."

I almost laughed in his face. Perhaps I didn't remember these people, but something stronger, deeper, than memory tied me to them. Leaving seemed incomprehensible.

"Of course I'm going."

"Nura will never stop hunting you if you stay with them."

"Nura will never stop hunting me anyway," I said.

My eyes fell to Tisaanah. She was at the head of the group. Moonlight dripped down her white hair, tracing her silhouette. Once I found her, I couldn't look away.

It didn't even feel like a decision. Just a simple fact.

"We're going," I said.

CHAPTER THIRTY-TWO

AEFE

Keep breathing.

I fell into a river of dreams.

My consciousness swung in and out of my grasp like the pendulum of a clock. I opened my eyes to the cradle of night or the warmth of sunrise, only for seconds at a time.

Pain.

I was not in my chambers. I was in a circular stone room. The bed was hard. Everything hurt, outside my skin and within it. Orange markings glowed upon the walls, the floor. They cast a harsh glow over the hard lines of Caduan's face. I reached out to touch him.

I needed a heartbeat.

He took my hand, gently pressed it to the sheets.

Not yet.

Keep breathing.

Blink, and death caressed me. Its touch was just as I imagined it would be, warm and inviting and familiar. Already a part of me.

Come home, my love, it whispered in my ear. I reached for it. Our fingers barely brushed.

Blink, and it was sunrise.

Caduan looked exhausted. The markings glowed brighter. I tried to speak and could not. I looked down at my own body as if I was a separate entity.

He turned to me and stroked my hair.

Keep breathing.

Blink, and an age had passed.

A thousand different moments collided in me as nightmares and reality blended. I would lash out at the women who came to move me from my table—at the humans who would bind me to the table—at Nura, who would torture me—at Caduan, who would heal me.

I would lean into the whispers of Tisaanah, in a mind we shared, *You are safe.*

Into the whispers of Caduan as he murmured into my hair, *You are safe.*

I would lose myself in the steady beat of a heart, my own, Maxantarius's, Tisaanah's—Caduan's.

Caduan's was real.

A palm pressed against warm skin, held tight, as if holding me to this world.

Keep breathing.

Keep breathing, Aefe.

But the pain got worse before it got better. One day I dreamed of a door. Before me stood death. *Come home, come home.* I pressed my hand to death's chest. There was no heartbeat there.

Then, another voice behind me. *Come home.*

I turned to see Caduan's hand outstretched. I touched it and felt the thrum of his pulse beneath his skin.

A warm glow, and the choice was taken from me. Caduan's reaching hand found me, pulling me into orange light. Living was more difficult than death. The pain ate me from the inside out.

But I leaned into that heartbeat. Leaned into it and let myself fall.

I waved to death, but it refused to say goodbye.
I will see you again, it whispered.
The door grew farther away.
Keep breathing, Caduan whispered.
Keep breathing.

CHAPTER THIRTY-THREE

TISAANAH

I *did this. I did this. I did this.*

I despised Nura for what she had done to Max. She tortured him, imprisoned him, crippled his power. When he had so casually mentioned being "on Nura's table," I had bitten my tongue so hard I tasted blood.

But the destruction of that perfect mind... that was not Nura's fault. That was all me.

How many times had I played out the moment in my head? The Fey king had been using Max as a conduit, leveraging his connection to the deepest levels of magic to assert his presence in Ara. My mind had reached into Max's, and I'd seen it—all those threads wrapped around his thoughts, like a raging infection spreading. *Cut it out,* Max had told me.

And I had known, then, that it would be dangerous—that I could kill him. I'd felt his mind, all those precious memories, shatter like glass.

I did this.

I handled this the only way I knew how to: I turned pain into a plan into action. We would go to Zagos. We would remove the Stratagrams from Max's skin—*gods, when I saw those tattoos, the rage that I felt*—and get him back his magic. And we would find a way to reclaim mine, too. I would be able to reassemble his mind. I would be able to fix what I had broken. Then I would turn my attention to Nura, and killing her as slowly and painfully as I possibly could.

I cemented these steps into certainty.

We traveled all day, and then into the night. I was eager to get to Zagos as quickly as possible, and the others seemed to share my impatience, all for our own reasons. I knew Ishqa's priorities—the sooner we arrived at the city, the sooner we could start using the wayfinder. Selfishly, I struggled to care about the wayfinder as long as Max's mind was in pieces.

Sammerin and Ishqa were able to use magic to take us parts of the way, though we had to do some traveling on foot. Max's brother—Brayan, I had learned—clearly detested magic travel, quietly excusing himself afterwards and returning to the group looking slightly green.

As we traveled, Max peppered us with questions. We told him of the war and the Fey. Ishqa told him of King Caduan and his bloodthirsty vendetta against humankind, which had Brayan cursing quietly to himself. In return, he told us of the strange circumstances of his release from Ilyzath, which none of us, not even Ishqa, knew what to make of.

Max took everything we told him shockingly in stride, but as the questions went on, they would also get slower and farther between. He would touch his temple and wince, and his teeth would grind, and soon after that, they would cease completely.

I was secretly grateful when that happened. Sammerin was, too. Certain questions simply hit on topics we did not know how to discuss. We told him about Reshaye, in the vaguest possible terms. But whenever we encroached deeper on that topic, Sammerin and I would shoot each other helpless looks of uncertainty.

Max's truth was so hard. So complicated. Even if we did tell Max the full story—the *full* story—about Reshaye, we certainly couldn't do it in front of Brayan. This excuse allowed us some precious borrowed time while we grappled with this unspoken dilemma.

It hurt to think that Max did not remember what we had built together. But it hurt even more to think about what it would feel like for him to learn the truth of Reshaye, and what it —he—had done to his family.

Maybe some part of his subconscious still knew that, too.

I watched him constantly. I drank him in like rain in the desert. I wanted to learn every part of him again, every angle of his current, leaner body, the shape and placement of every blade of hair on his chin. I was quietly obsessed with him.

And yet, when he would approach me—and he would, *always*, approach me—and ask me little, searching questions that were far more personal than the ones he asked Sammerin, I suddenly found it difficult to breathe.

One night, near the beginning of our journey, Max rolled over to face me in the darkness. The way the moonlight settled into the angles and hollows of his face reminded me too much of the nights we had sat together in the garden, both too haunted by our pasts to sleep.

"What were we?" he asked.

"I was your apprentice. We told you that."

So much had changed in our relationship, and yet, even with our history erased, he still gave me that same piercing stare, and it still dismantled my carefully constructed defenses the same way.

"Beyond that," he said.

I swallowed, my throat suddenly thick. "We were friends." A pause, and then, "Lovers."

I didn't know why that word was so hard to say. Maybe it was because in that question, it really hit me: I looked at Max and saw the love of my life, but the person who traveled with me now was a stranger. He was close enough to touch and yet farther away than he had ever been.

Even Max seemed like he didn't quite know how to respond

MOTHER OF DEATH AND DAWN

to this—as if my answer had confirmed something he already suspected, but still left him lost.

He wasn't alone in that, at least. It left both of us lost.

My relationship with Max had been built slowly. Over the course of a million little moments, I learned how to trust him. To love so deeply was terrifying, even then—now, with the foundations of the safety we had built together torn to pieces, the thought of opening my heart again overwhelmed me.

I wanted him so much I couldn't breathe whenever I looked at him. I wanted to bridge that gap between us. I wanted him back.

And yet, with each passing day, another thought crept into the back of my mind—one that hurt even more.

I often lay awake and watched Max sleep at night. I knew him so well that I know what he looked like even in rest. I knew how often his dreams would wake him. Now, I watched how long he went without waking.

For some reason, Zeryth's voice would float through my mind then, from what felt like a lifetime ago. I had negotiated for Max's freedom when I signed my life away, and Zeryth had simply laughed at me. *A clean slate*, he had said, with a wry smirk. *Wouldn't we all like one of those.*

Zeryth, of course, had not gotten a clean slate. He died covered in the consequences of all his past mistakes.

But perhaps Max had gotten that gift.

Perhaps his broken mind, and all the horrible things it left shrouded in the dark, was the only thing that saved him in Ilyzath. Perhaps forgetting everything—and in doing so, forgetting me—was the only thing that saved him, even now.

That thought haunted me night, after night, after night, until we at last reached Zagos.

CHAPTER THIRTY-FOUR

MAX

To say that it's strange to be constantly surrounded by people who know more about you than you yourself do is an understatement. It was one thing when it was Brayan, who I apparently hadn't seen in more than a decade before I got myself thrown in Ilyzath. Another thing altogether to be surrounded by people who *only* knew me the way that I was, entire relationships crafted from memories that I just... didn't have. The ghosts of that past were still there, and I could feel them every time I looked at Tisaanah or Sammerin—a faint shadow of intimacy, but everything that had created that bond was gone, stuck behind a door I didn't know how to open.

The rest of it, of course, was fairly outrageous, too—the Fey, the war, the Lejaras. With every explanation Tisaanah, Sammerin, and Ishqa gave to my near-constant questions, Brayan seemed to increasingly lose the will to live. Even when we were children, he had never been very good at dealing with unknowns.

I, on the other hand, found them comparably easy to swallow. It was only once I tried to unravel my role in all of this—or the bonds that had put me there—that things got... difficult.

The door was closed. The voice would whisper in the back of my head, *You don't want to go here anymore.*

Yes, I fucking do, I told it, frustrated. But the headaches decided otherwise. I could only make it through a few minutes of questions at a time before the stabbing pain brought me to surrender. Tisaanah and Sammerin seemed secretly grateful for it. I knew there was something they weren't telling me. I didn't like feeling that I was being lied to, even if by omission.

It had been a week of this when, at last, we landed from another Stratagram leap and Ishqa turned to the west. It was sunset, the sky bright magenta.

A rare smile broke over Ishqa's face. "We have arrived."

He pushed aside some ferns, revealing a shoreline of gritty grey sand. Several hundred yards out into the still tidewater was an island, marked by a smattering of orange lights glinting in the distance. The island was visible only in silhouette, but its shape was taller than I might have expected, like all of the structures on it built up to a point. If so, it appeared to be mostly uninhabited, as the lights clustered only around the shore.

Tisaanah pushed through the ferns to stand beside me, and my skin prickled. The scent of citrus swept by with a breeze and briefly took with it my capability for intelligent thought.

I glanced at her and had to remind myself to look away.

At every moment, my entire body was acutely aware of her proximity. If I didn't pay attention to where I was walking, I often found myself wandering closer without noticing until I'd stop and realize that I was close enough to trace the shape of the brown-and-white skin on the back of her neck, and count the strands of hair that fell over it. Every one of these minute features felt like a reminder of something important.

One evening, she tilted her head back to tie up her hair, revealing a crescent-shaped patch of tan skin on the underside of her chin. The sight of that little patch of skin brought with it another image, her leaning over me, body bare, hair wild and unkempt, her head thrown back. It was so vivid that I had to step away and take a few deep breaths.

And yet, despite this overwhelming—disconcerting, even— sense of intimacy, Tisaanah was the one who avoided me the most.

Now, she took in Zagos with a skeptical stare. "So this is the place that will solve all of our problems."

"It looks barely inhabited," Brayan said. "If this qualifies as a city, it's a tiny one. This is supposed to be some hub of magical knowledge?"

Ishqa gave Brayan a disapproving look. "The size of it is irrelevant—"

Tisaanah's mouth went thin, an odd expression passing over her face.

"—and has no bearing on what it can do for us."

Tisaanah's cheeks got red. Her eyes flicked to me, and my expression must have pushed her to the breaking point, because an ungraceful laugh burst from her clamped lips.

Meanwhile, I stared at her in slight bewilderment.

Ishqa gave her an odd look. "Why are you laughing?"

"Right, why *are* you laughing?" I narrowed my eyes at her.

It wasn't even funny. Unless you were a twelve-year-old boy. Even then, some had moved on to more sophisticated humor.

Still, a stubborn smile tugged at the left side of my mouth.

"It's... nothing." Tisaanah collected herself with only partial success.

Brayan looked like he was ready to throw himself into the lake. Sammerin looked affectionately unamused. Ishqa just looked unamused.

"We do not have time for... whatever this is." Ishqa waved a dismissive hand at her, as if to wordlessly berate us for being unsophisticated humans. "We have places to be."

He pointed to the left, down the beach. A long wooden bridge extended from the shore all the way out to the island.

"Does everyone here know how to swim?" I remarked.

"It is perfectly safe."

"Says the one who can fly. It looks like it's being held together purely by the vengeful drowned spirits beneath it."

Tisaanah now once again was very serious as she set off down the beach. "I think we all know how to handle vengeful spirits. Or at least we should by now, yes?"

———

ONCE WE ARRIVED IN ZAGOS, I realized why the island had looked so odd from the shore. The entire city was built into ruins. Streets weren't so much planned roads as they were paths between crumbling, ancient buildings. Collapsed marble columns cradled businesses, shops, and pubs, creating a strange blend of architectural styles. Strings of lanterns, some filled with fire and some with floating orbs of magic light, dangled between the violent peaks of shattered rock. Above us, in the distance, a decaying palace loomed over the city. It must have once been something to behold, but now it was a shrouded, misty shadow.

There was flora everywhere—crimson flowers perched on ivy that consumed expanses of stone, peeking up from between cracked cobblestones, flourishing over entire hundred-foot spans of sheer cliffs above. I had to stop at one point and admire a particularly stunning bright red blossom, with seven pointed tips. I couldn't bring myself to pick it—it seemed a bit sacrilegious—but I picked up one that had fallen to the cobblestones, smoothed out a crinkle on its petal, and handed it to Tisaanah.

"It would be a waste to let it sit on the ground," I said, by way of explanation.

Sammerin gave me a look that silently said, *Really? That's what you're going with?*

But Tisaanah smiled faintly and took the flower, tucking it behind her ear. Red suited her.

As we continued into the heart of the city, the streets quickly grew more crowded. Everything was dimly lit, still—those who lived here apparently didn't mind residing in darkness. But then again, that seemed appropriate. I had never seen a place that so loudly announced itself as a seedy underbelly of society. Suspicious eyes peered at us from the shadows. With every step, the haze of drug-sweetened smoke grew thicker.

Sammerin's eyebrows shot up as a tall woman with long black hair walked by. At first I thought it was because of her beauty—fair enough—but then he said, "Was that a *Fey*?"

Fey?!

I looked at the people around us more closely. Sure enough, I realized to my shock that there were indeed some Fey here. Most of the people in the streets were human, or appeared to be. But perhaps a third of them had pointed ears, either a long point like Ishqa's or subtle ones that were more easily mistaken for human.

Brayan lurched to a stop, shooting Ishqa a suspicious glare. "You brought us to Fey lands?" The question was all accusation.

"No," Ishqa said. "This is Zagos. Just as I said."

Tisaanah looked around, confused. "Then how—"

"Zagos has only been known by this name for the last hundred years or so. Long ago, it was known as Niraja. For a time, both Fey and humans lived there together. It was hidden from human society, and exiled by the other Fey Houses. What is today known as Zagos is just a small part of what was once Niraja."

Sammerin looked somewhat awed. "Is the idea of this as inconceivable to Fey as it is to us?"

"The world was very different half a millennia ago."

"So what happened to it?" I asked.

Ishqa was quiet for a moment. "It fell," he said. "To the Fey laws of old, interbreeding with humans was considered nearly beastiality."

"How flattering," I muttered.

"They were allowed to exist in exile for a century or two, but..."

He stopped short, his gaze locking on something in the distance.

"But?" Tisaanah prodded.

He didn't answer. Instead, after another moment, he looked to Tisaanah and I.

MOTHER OF DEATH AND DAWN

"Please excuse me. The place that can help you, or try, is just ahead if you follow the fork to the left. The door has a lily on it."

"Where are you going?" Tisaanah called after him, but he was already slipping away into the crowd.

"I will find you again later," he said, not even bothering to turn.

Sammerin let out an exasperated exhale. Tisaanah shook her head.

"Does he do that often?" I asked.

"Always." Tisaanah sighed and started walking. "But he always comes back."

I matched her pace. I caught a whiff of citrus and resisted the urge to crowd closer.

"Is it smart?" I asked, voice low. "Trusting him?"

"Trust." Tisaanah let out a small scoff. "I don't know if I *trust* Ishqa, exactly. But we have—ah, what would be the right way to put it—a mutually beneficial relationship. The rebels have managed to capture four key Threllian cities, and we wouldn't have managed to make it so far without Ishqa's help. Do I think he's loyal to us? No. But I do believe he's loyal to his cause."

"His cause."

"I think there is nothing he wouldn't do to halt the war between humans and Fey."

Nothing he wouldn't do. I didn't love the sound of that desperation.

Tisaanah looked as if she read my mind. "It is possible there will come a time when his goals do not align with ours. But right now, they do. I'm not in a position to turn away help." One eyebrow twitched. "Why? You don't trust him?"

"I just recognize a man with secrets."

Tisaanah chuckled. "If I didn't trust anyone with secrets, I would trust no one."

Well... yes. Exactly.

"*Farlione!*"

The booming voice cut through the buzz of the crowd. I

slowed, turning, but Brayan caught up to me and pulled me forward.

"Don't acknowledge."

"What—?"

"*BRAYAN FUCKING FARLIONE!*"

Brayan cringed and walked faster.

A second later, a massive man with cropped brown hair and a scar over the back of his skull grabbed Brayan's shoulder, forcing him to turn.

"Well, fuck me. It *is* you."

"It's impolite to grab other people," I said, before I could help myself, and Brayan glared at me.

"Well, it's impolite to ignore an old friend," the man said.

Brayan donned a refined smile. It was funny how similar it was to the one he used to wear at our parents' parties. Always far more convincing than mine. "How nice to see you, Atriv—"

"*How nice to fucking see me? That's* how you greet me?"

Brayan scoffed and turned away, only for the man to yank him back.

"You fucked me!" he snarled.

And Brayan—*Brayan*, the elegant golden child of the Ryvenai upper class—slowly flicked his eyes over his assailant and said, calmly, "You aren't my type."

I huffed a laugh, just because it was so unexpected.

The man's face contorted with outrage, his shoulders heaving. Now he seemed to notice the rest of us, gaze turning to me, Sammerin, and finally lingering on Tisaanah. His stare was one part lecherous, one part curious.

My teeth ground. I did not like that. I did not like it at all.

I pushed past the man, putting myself, conveniently, between him and Tisaanah. "We don't have time for this. Kindly excuse us."

The minute I decided to do it, I knew what his reaction would be. I was ready for the blow. Big men like him threw their weight around carelessly. Oftentimes it served them well. This time, it made it easy to use his size against him. He was on the ground, arm twisted in my grasp, before the strike could land.

"That's enough of that, don't you think?" I said.

Tisaanah watched, arms crossed, looking annoyed. We had started to attract some attention.

Brayan's friend slipped my grip and lunged. But midway through the movement, he jerked to a sudden stop, muscles straining before his limbs folded in on each other in an unnatural tangle.

Sammerin stepped over the man's paralyzed form, now a heap on the street, and simply said, "Enough."

We left him twitching behind us, very slowly pulling himself out of the knot Sammerin had tied him in. We'd be long lost by the time he was up again.

"That was unnecessary," Tisaanah muttered as we pushed through the crowd. "Too many people were looking at us."

She wasn't wrong to worry. We were an unusual group, and Tisaanah's skin tone made her especially recognizable. I certainly would have preferred that we made it through Zagos without being recognized.

Brayan's face was completely still, which I knew meant he was furious.

"Who was that?" Sammerin asked.

"And did you really fuck him?" I added. "Literally or otherwise."

That earned an actual scowl.

"No one important," he said. "An old colleague from the Roseteeth Company. We collaborated for a time when we both went independent. I got some assignments he didn't, and he never got over it."

So not only had we been recognized, we'd been recognized by a mercenary. Terrific.

Tisaanah's steps faltered. "You were in the Roseteeth Company?"

"A long time ago. Perhaps a decade." Brayan said it with the tone of one humbly downplaying an obvious accomplishment.

He didn't realize that Tisaanah wasn't exactly fawning over his accomplishments.

"Where did you fight?" she asked.

"Essaria, mostly. Why? Do you know someone who fought with them?"

"No. They just helped conquer my country."

She didn't miss a beat. Just kept walking.

My eyebrows twitched.

Brayan looked a bit like he had been struck. "I…" He cleared his throat. "It was an assignment. I didn't get to choose."

"I know."

I refrained from pointing out that he *did* choose, actually. He chose to join the Company.

"What happened to the Essarians was unfortunate," Brayan said. "We all wished it hadn't gone that way. But commissions are business. It wasn't… personal."

She gave him a calm, cold stare. "It never is."

Brayan shut up after that.

BY THE TIME Tisaanah and I made it to the door with the lily, it was just the two of us. Ishqa never returned from his detour. Brayan had slipped into a weapons shop, declaring something about stocking up on supplies, though I suspected he just wanted to get away from Tisaanah. Sammerin's neck had nearly snapped when he spotted a beautiful blond woman drinking alone at a pub table, so soon enough he was gone too. Secretly, I was relieved. I didn't know what we were going to find here. And if Ishqa's contacts were able to restore my magic, and my mind… I didn't know what breaking open that door would look like. I would be lying if I said that vulnerability didn't make my palms sweat. Maybe he knew that.

The building was unassuming. It was built beneath collapsed ancient stone, the doorway constructed under two tipped-over columns. There was no sign, only a lily burnt into a plain wooden door.

I raised my hand to knock and hesitated.

"Good luck, Max," Tisaanah said, with a small smile that I instantly returned.

"Good luck, Tisaanah."

I knocked. The door swung open right away. A white-haired man with faint points on his ears greeted us with a wide smile.

"Welcome, welcome. Tisaanah Vytezic and Maxantarius Farlione, we are so very excited to meet you."

CHAPTER THIRTY-FIVE

AEFE

I opened my eyes slowly. I was greeted with no racing heart, no panicked start, no dramatic fight for breath—only the sight of a familiar bronze tiled ceiling.

I rolled over. My room came into focus. Piles of books buried every flat surface. Mid-morning light flooded through the windows, bright enough to make my head ache. Everything ached, actually. My mouth was so dry that I thought I might choke on my own swollen tongue.

I stretched my fingers, and my left hand brushed something soft—hair?

The head jerked up. Caduan blinked away sleep, rubbing his eyes. The moment his gaze fell to me, though, all vestiges of exhaustion fell away. A faint smile twisted his mouth.

"At long last, welcome back, Aefe."

He helped me sit up, and gave me water. My bones, muscles, and head screamed at me, but the wounds in my gut and my throat had been healed.

"You're fortunate to be alive," Caduan told me. "You were nearly dead by the time I got to you. Your recovery has been... difficult."

The memory of it all came back slowly. The humans who had attacked me. The blood. The way life felt draining from me. And the shadowy image of Caduan, tearing my attackers apart.

The sour taste in my mouth now had nothing to do with my thirst.

"Did you find them?" I asked.

"Who?"

"Tisaanah. Maxantarius. Your wayfinder."

Caduan placed the cup in my hands. "No."

My heart crashed to the ground.

I looked down at the water and my faint reflection within it— a face I still barely recognized. Once I had destroyed entire armies. Now, five humans had nearly killed me.

My knuckles were white around the glass, clenched tight. "I was stronger than them. It should not have happened that way."

"It shouldn't have. But not for the reasons you mean." I could feel Caduan's stare on me, but I could not bring myself to meet it. His voice softened. "I knew you weren't ready. I was selfish and impatient, and you paid for that. That was a mistake."

"I felt them. I could have fought through, I could have—"

"It was too soon."

A surge of frustration. I slammed the cup down on the night-stand. "I was using magic. I am powerful enough to—"

"Yes, you are powerful. More powerful than you know, and yet weaker than you've ever been. I was so caught up with the potential of the former that I forgot…" His eyes fell to my throat. "I forgot that flesh is flesh. You are just as fragile as anyone else. Perhaps even more so, because you have been given a new body and so little time to understand its workings and limitations."

"I understand my limitations."

"Do you know how difficult your recovery was? How close you were to death?" He spoke sharply, then abruptly paused. When he resumed, he was once again carefully calm. "I thought for a time that… maybe I wouldn't be able to save you, and my own hubris would be to blame for that. I owe you an apology. I put too much on your shoulders."

Those piercing eyes flicked back to mine, paralyzing me. They reminded me of images from my fever dreams—bracketed by darkness, peering from shadow, surrounded by strange orange light in a room that was not this one.

A knock on the door pulled me from the memory.

Caduan rose to his feet as Iajqa entered. When she saw me, she smiled. "Ah, some good news at last. It's wonderful to see you awake after so long, Aefe." Then, to Caduan, "I apologize for interrupting, my King. The caravan has arrived. We are ready."

It was only then that I realized he was wearing unusually formal clothing—a long black jacket lined with gold thread, and the copper crown perched upon his head.

"Yes. Thank you. I'm ready." He turned to me. "I wish I did not have to leave, but I'll be back in a week. In the meantime, Meajqa has agreed to—"

"Where are you going?"

I was getting better at reading faces. I knew he did not want to tell me.

"Threll," he replied. "I have decided to grant the Zorokovs' request and support them in their attack on the rebels."

Shock nearly stole my words.

"Why?" I demanded. "Why would you offer your help to those creatures?"

"Their time for reckoning will come, but we can't afford to lose the Threllians' manpower. Not yet."

Caduan's tone was so careful, so calm. But the truth crashed over me all at once, bringing with it a tide of shame. I remembered the way that he had looked at me after our meeting with the Threllians. *We have options.*

I was the option. And I had failed. Now, he had no choice but to cede to the Zorokovs' demands.

"I can still do it," I said. "I can find Tisaanah, and the wayfinder—I can still find them."

I pushed myself upright, and Caduan jerked forward a little, as if preparing to steady me. "I think…I think they were nearby,"

I went on. "The soldiers mentioned a military base. Perhaps they are still there. Let me go back and search."

Caduan's face shifted. "There was a military base, but they aren't there."

"How do you know that?"

"Because nothing is there anymore."

It took me a long moment to understand.

There *was* a military base.

Caduan's expression was always so calm that, at first, I did not notice the intensity of the hatred lurking beneath it, sharp enough to cut the breath from my lungs. I realized this was exactly what he must have looked like when he killed the humans that attacked me.

This was what he must have looked like when he went back to that military base and wiped it off the earth.

The vengeance is for you.

Caduan turned away. "Rest, recover, and we'll discuss what comes next when I return."

I wanted to say something more, but I didn't know what. Caduan offered me one final smile as he left with Iajqa.

The room was now very silent. I sat in bed alone, feeling foolish. I tethered myself to my heartbeat and whispered to my magic. A tiny black rose sprouted in my palm. I stared at it.

How had I been so pleased with this? How had this little flower earned Caduan's proud smile?

This was a war. I needed to kill, and you could not kill anything with a flower.

CHAPTER THIRTY-SIX

TISAANAH

"I didn't know it was possible for a half-Fey to be a Valtain."

The man laughed as he set down cups of steaming green liquid before me and Max. "I'm not half Fey, darling. Just have some blood from some distant great great grandmother or such. But the ears do make me look exotic, no?"

He looked expectantly at me, as if he was waiting for an answer, so I nodded. "Oh yes. Very."

The man's name was Klasto. He introduced us with equally bubbly enthusiasm to his partner, Blif, a middle-aged woman who sat in the back of the shop with a book perched in her hands and did not bother to get up as we arrived. She peered at us from beneath a blunt black fringe, gave a little wave, and let Klasto do all the talking.

That, it turned out, was not difficult, as Klasto apparently *never* stopped talking. Even as he and Blif excused themselves to go gather some supplies, his voice still rose and fell down the hallway.

Max lifted the tea to his nose and frowned. When I went to take a sip of mine, he stopped me.

"I think this is wyarwood root. It's a hallucinogen. Look at their pupils. These people are high out of their minds."

Sure enough, when Blif and Klasto returned, I realized Max was right—their pupils were so dilated that they nearly consumed their irises.

Max and I exchanged a glance. I was almost certain we were thinking the same thing: *I don't know about this.*

But we had come this far, and I didn't have any better ideas.

So, when Klasto asked us to explain our predicament, I gave him the details, careful to omit things that we needed to keep closely guarded. Ishqa, apparently, had already given them some background. While I talked, Klasto circled, *hmm*-ing as he examined us like we were sick livestock. He squinted at the scars on my arms, pursed his lips at Max's tattoos, and paused for a long time to stare at the gold on my palm.

"What is this?" he asked.

Blif said, without looking up from her book, "It's a wayfinder."

Klasto's white eyebrows arched. "A wayfinder? How fun. Ishqa told me that he was looking for the Lejaras, but I didn't realize you managed to get your hands on a wayfinder." He smirked and added, "If you forgive my pun."

Ishqa told him about the Lejaras? I was torn between being surprised and being annoyed. Ishqa had hesitated to tell Max about the pools of magic, but had apparently seen fit to inform a couple of drug addict Wielders about our mission.

My surprise must have shown on my face, because Klasto laughed and gave my shoulder an affectionate squeeze. "Oh, sweetheart. Don't look so concerned. Yes, of course we know about them. They're legend, and we live in legends. The Lejaras, the three pools. One that embodies change, one that embodies life, and one that embodies death."

Max and I exchanged another glance. That part was new information to me.

"*That's* what they do?" I said.

Klasto shrugged. "Who knows? That's what the whispers say.

But whispers have been wrong before. In fact, one might say there's plenty of evidence that the whispers are wrong about the Lejaras existing at all."

"If they existed," Blif said, not looking up from her book, "someone would have found them by now."

Klasto rolled his eyes. "So sayeth the non-believers. You are no fun at all."

"So what… are they, exactly?" Max asked.

"They're raw, powerful sources of magic that draw deeper than—"

"No, I know that part. But what *are* they? Are they things? Are they places? Are they literal pools of magic, like a lake?"

"Yes."

"Yes, to which part?"

"Do dragons have green eyes or yellow?"

"What?"

"Exactly. You can't tell me if dragons have green or yellow eyes, because they don't exist. Or at least, no one has seen one. So, as long as that remains the case, then yes. They have green eyes *and* they have yellow eyes. Therefore, the answer to your question, too, is *yes*. The Lejaras are all of those things, and none of those things, because no one has seen them. They are whatever your beautiful heart wishes for them to be."

"Because they do not exist," Blif said, and Klasto rolled his eyes.

"It's nice to dream, though, isn't it? But alas, we don't have all night. So let's begin." He reached towards me. "May I?"

I wasn't sure what he was asking.

"I won't touch your memories, I promise," he added. "That isn't quite the nature of my gift, anyway. Your privacy will remain intact."

Ah.

For all the times that I'd reached for the minds of others, it was rare that someone reached into mine. I wasn't enthusiastic about the idea… but if there was even a chance it would help restore my magic, it was worth it.

I nodded. Klasto laid his fingers gently on my temple. I felt a strange pressure on my thoughts—not painful or even uncomfortable, but odd. It lasted for a few seconds, then he withdrew his hand.

"Hm." He frowned, then turned to Max and reached out.

Max caught his wrist. "No."

"Just like I said to her, no memories. Totally painless."

"No."

Klasto looked annoyed. "You expect me to fix all of this"—he gestured to the tattoos on Max's exposed forearm—"*and* all of this"—he gestured to Max's face, presumably his head—"all without any visibility into what the problem could possibly be? I won't force you to do anything, darling, but it will certainly limit my options."

Max's teeth ground. I understood that look. He knew Klasto was right, even if he wished he wasn't. I was the only one Max had ever willingly let into his mind. And look at where that had gotten him.

I laid my hand over his in wordless encouragement. His flesh was warm and smooth. His fingers rearranged to accommodate mine right away—so fast it surprised me, as if some intuitive response still remained even if his memories of me did not.

Max glanced at me, looking a bit startled, then back at Klasto.

"Fine," he muttered.

Klasto, pleased, placed his hand at Max's temple, eyes closing in concentration. Max's eyes closed too, but more like someone bracing for impact.

A few moments later, Klasto's eyes opened again.

"Will you stop?" he snapped.

Max looked confused. "Stop what?"

"If you're going to let me work, then let me work."

"I *am* letting you work."

"You're putting walls up against me. I don't appreciate being strung along and I—"

"I'm not putting up any Ascended-damned walls!"

Blif had looked up from her reading with mild interest. Klasto's face slowly shifted as he realized Max was serious.

"That's... oh, my."

"What?" Max demanded.

"It's just... interesting."

Gods, I hoped that when this was all over, no one described us as "interesting" ever again.

"You have..." Klasto cleared his throat. "Many, many walls, my friend."

"What does that mean, exactly?"

Klasto stood, his thoughtfulness disappearing beneath a bright smile. "It means we'll save that bit for later, then. First, let's tackle the obvious." He gestured to Max's Stratagram tattoos. "Kindly remove your clothes, please."

"Remove my clothes?" Max repeated.

"Well, you may keep your undergarments. Provided there are no tattoos in that region."

I choked a little at that thought.

Max looked away. "There are no tattoos in that region," he grumbled.

"Well, I'm relieved to hear that on your behalf. Come come. Don't be shy."

The awkwardness on Max's face was a stark reminder of the difference between what I remembered and what he did. I mourned his hand as it slid from my grasp. He stood and pulled his shirt over his head.

I had to stifle my gasp.

I hadn't seen Max's body since he returned. Once, I had memorized the shape of his form, knew the topography of every muscle and scar. All those things were still there, yes. But now Stratagram tattoos covered every inch of his skin, layered on top of each other in a grotesque mosaic. Some were large—one spanned nearly the width of his pectoral, and when he turned he revealed another on his back that reached blade-to-blade across his spine. Most were small, trailing in interlocked sequences across the lines of his body—a string of them running along the muscle line from his hip all the way up beneath his armpit, clusters beneath the undersides of his arms, over his stomach, his throat, his back, his hands. He dropped his trousers, revealing the same over his legs and ankles. As he removed his boots, I briefly saw two large ones tattooed on the soles of his feet.

He had new scars, too, so easily distinguishable from the old not only because they looked fresher, but because they were surgical in placement and precision. A streak of mottled red from his navel to his sternum. Two semi-circles over the backs of his shoulders. Three perfectly straight parallel lines across his left forearm.

My breath had gotten fast and ragged.

Max had not spoken much about his imprisonment. But here before me was horrific evidence of what they had done to him—evidence of everything I thought about each night, everything I feared when I was dragged away from another failed rescue attempt.

Six months.

Six months, they had done this to him.

I no longer just wanted to kill Nura. I wanted to dismantle her.

Klasto's face had gotten uncharacteristically somber.

Max turned to him. "Well?"

"Oh, dear." Klasto's voice was small. "This—this all must have been quite painful."

Max looked as if he might say something, then thought better of it, and just asked, gruffly, "What now?"

Klasto gestured to a sheet-covered table at the center of the room. "Lie down."

Max obeyed. Blif had stood, taking her place beside the table. Klasto joined her. I went to the table, too—I couldn't help myself.

"We are going to start by freeing you from these chains," Klasto said.

"These tattoos are magic-scorched," Blif said. "We can't remove them, not completely, but we can break them."

"I apologize in advance for the fact that this will be unpleasant, darling."

"I do so love unpleasant things." But despite the joke, I could hear the tension in Max's voice. I felt it in my own bones, too. I never wanted Max to endure even a single unpleasant thing ever again.

I stepped across the room and took his hand, without thinking.

Klasto nodded to Blif, and they began their work.

CHAPTER THIRTY-SEVEN

MAX

I had figured that when Klasto told me that "this would be unpleasant," what he really meant was, "This is going to be outrageously agonizing." So I was prepared, to some extent. I knew how to survive pain by now.

Still, this tested me. It was just as bad, if not worse, than getting the Stratagrams tattooed onto me. The lanterns flared, then dimmed. A cold white light suffused the room, building with each second. The air seemed to curdle, my body rebelling against it at every level. I clutched Tisaanah's hand so hard that it trembled.

CRACK!

The sound was so loud and the agony so intense that I thought, *That must be my bones snapping.*

But the blinding white light faded. The roaring in my ears subsided. The pain faded to a tolerable ache.

I opened my eyes to a cracked stone ceiling strung with lanterns. My eyesight was blurry. Somewhat reluctantly, I released Tisaanah's hand.

"Don't sit up right away," Klasto said. "You're going to be —"

I sat up and looked down at myself.

Ascended fucking above.

I was still covered in tattoos, but what had once been endless circles were now fragments of black. The Stratagrams had been shattered, as if someone had reached into my flesh and taken a hammer to each one, leaving the ink lines in broken shards rather than closed circles.

"We couldn't remove the ink," Blif said. "But the Stratagrams, and the magic beneath them, are now severed."

"How do you feel?" Tisaanah asked.

Like I've been run over by a horse, I wanted to say, until I took a moment to actually think about the answer to that question. I was dizzy and sore, but as the pain and shock continued to subside, I realized that something was just... gone, too. A certain weight I hadn't known I was carrying had disappeared.

I allowed myself to hope.

"It will take some time before—" Klasto started.

I extended my hand. A flame unfurled in my palm.

My face broke into a smile. Beside me, Tisaanah drew in a sharp breath.

I whispered to my magic, and for the first time in so long, it listened to me. I made the fire larger, reaching it up to the ceiling in twirling dances, then pulled it back to me in a perfect sphere between my palms.

I hadn't realized how much I'd missed this—how deep a part of me it was. I felt like a bird who had been restored flight.

My gaze flicked to Tisaanah. She was grinning. The sight made my chest clench. The flame intensified, casting a stronger orange light across her face.

I was capable of more than this—so much more. I reached for every lantern in the room, spoke to those flames—

For a moment, they brightened, and—

Fuck.

Control slipped from my grasp. The thread of connection between me and my magic snapped. I tried to grab for it again, only to be met with an impassable wall.

The lanterns fizzled back to normal. The flame in my palm

disappeared into a puff of smoke. My glimmer of freedom snuffed out.

"It's alright," Tisaanah murmured. "Try again."

I did. The flame in my palm was smaller this time. When I tried to push it, once again control evaded me.

I tried again, again, and again, my frustration rising with each failed attempt.

I'd been so fucking close, and now I was being shoved back into that room of stone.

"Something is wrong here," I bit out. "You missed something. I could do so much more than this."

Klasto and Blif looked at each other, as if having a silent conversation.

"I told you," Blif said.

Klasto rolled his eyes before turning back to me. "The Strata-grams were only part of the problem."

Only part of the problem? I'd had every inch of my Ascended-damned skin covered in my own imprisonment and that was *only part of the problem?*

"You are having similar challenges, darling, yes?" Klasto said to Tisaanah.

"It is inconsistent. Sometimes, I can use it, a little bit. Other times, nothing. There are no rules to it. No consistency."

Blif scoffed. "*Rules.* Ridiculous."

"I think what my partner expresses so rudely is that you two have pushed yourselves far past the point where rules make sense." Klasto turned, retrieving paper and a pen from the book-case. "You two have shared magic, yes?"

I didn't know how to answer that. I glanced to Tisaanah.

Klasto, misreading my hesitation, laughed. "No need to be shy about your sex life, darling. In fact I applaud your taste. It's delightful."

That conjured an extraordinarily vivid image.

"I—We have. Yes." Tisaanah glanced at me before quickly looking away. "But it wasn't... sex."

I'm ashamed to admit that just hearing Tisaanah say the word sex did something to me.

"Well, that's an oversight on your part, but no matter. So that means you were actually using your magic together, yes? Drawing from each other?"

Tisaanah nodded.

"Were you, by any chance, connected in that way when the connection to your magics collapsed?"

A pause. Tisaanah nodded again, slower this time.

I had tried so many times to remember what had happened that day. It was gone.

"Well, that explains it," Klasto said. He drew several parallel lines across the parchment before him. "The levels of magic. Valtain, Solarie, Fey, et cetera et cetera. And, of course, this chaotic mess."

He added a bunch of squiggling lines at the very bottom.

"Deep magic, which no one seems to know all that much about. Under normal circumstances, everyone stays in their designated stream, and we go on our way. But, sometimes, people make things complicated."

He added two figures at the top of the page, above the streams of magic—hilariously crooked, with massive swollen heads and stick bodies.

"You two," Klasto went on, "started complicating your relationship to the streams. First, you started drawing from deep magic." He drew lines from the figures to the chaotic scribbles at the bottom of the page. "And then you started drawing from each other, even though you both Wielded different types of magic. *And* if you were actually making use of that magic together, then you were accessing deep magic *through* each other." He drew lines between the two figures, and more that ran from each figure, to each other, to each of the streams, to the scribbles, and back. It quickly devolved into a tangled mess.

"It may look messy, but this actually would have worked fine for you if you'd managed to avoid getting A'Maril and dying. But..." He drew a slash across the page, cutting through all the lines. "If something were to disrupt those connections, especially if, as you say, you were together when it happened, then it's much more likely to affect both of you."

This all seemed, frankly, ridiculous.

"So what does this mean, exactly?" I asked. "You're saying that if we're going to fix this, we need to do it together?"

"You don't *need* to, but it would be the easiest path."

"What do we do?" Tisaanah already looked prepared to face down the world. It was a little charming.

Klasto smiled. "We're going to be a bit unconventional, darlings. I hope you forgive me."

HE PUT us in a fucking closet.

It was pitch black. I sat cross-legged on the ground, at the center of a Stratagram, per Klasto and Blif's instruction. Tisaanah sat directly in front of me, facing me. I couldn't see her in the darkness, but it would be impossible not to sense her. I could practically feel her warmth. And of course, there was that scent.

"They locked us up," Tisaanah chuckled quietly. She was whispering—the darkness and silence made it seem like we should.

"Well, naturally," I replied. "It's the obvious solution."

"Perhaps he got so annoyed with us that he will just lock us away forever."

Her voice was closer, highlighting the mere inches between our faces. I thought about how easy it would be to close the gap. Wondered if she tasted like citrus, the way she smelled of it.

Klasto's voice floated through the air, everywhere and nowhere at once. "You think so little of us, after we've built such a friendship."

"We are simply removing sensory distractions," Blif's voice said.

I still had many sensory distractions.

"And we will be assisting," Klasto added. "From out here."

"I won't lie to you, this can be dangerous," Blif said. "The walls that are blocking you from your magic are strong, especially yours, Maxantarius. But neither of us, not even Klasto, can break those down for you. You have to dismantle them yourselves. If things get... difficult... we'll be here to pull you out."

A drop of blood rolled off my palm and soaked through my trousers. I'd barely felt the cut, not when the rest of me was still a web of aches. Before throwing us in the closet, Klasto and Blif had slit both of our hands and explained to us that by sharing our magic again, opening our minds to each other, we could potentially break down the barriers between us and our magic.

Did I have any better ideas? No. It was worth a shot.

This... box, closet, whatever... was clearly soundproofed with magic. I heard only my own heartbeat and Tisaanah's breath.

I leaned slightly closer. "You ready?"

Our hands found each other's easily, even in the darkness. Her blood was hot and slick.

"Yes," she whispered.

I nudged open the door to my magic and my mind. Let her draw from me.

The rush came all at once.

I didn't expect this to be so easy. It was like burning up and loving every fucking second of it. I felt her everywhere. Her heartbeat matching mine. Her breath growing rapid. That scent of citrus surrounded me, and with it I disappeared into *her*—her presence. Strong and determined. Sheer force of will.

Images fluttered by like butterfly wings. A starry night sky over the plains. A stern, beautiful woman's face. A sneer, a whip, blood on a marble floor. Barely hidden—for a moment she didn't want me to see it—but fear, and fear that still lingered. Her fear in the past as she thought, *He's going to kill me.* Her fear in the present as she thought, *What if this doesn't work?*

She resisted this vulnerability at first. It was my impulse, too, as she pressed against the darkest crevices of my mind. I didn't know this woman. I didn't want to show her all my secrets.

Is that what it is? Or do you not want to see them yourself?

But when I began to cede to her—when we began to cede to each other—something between us began to swell to life.

Warmth suffused my face. Distantly, in the physical world, I heard the snap of flames. Tisaanah's hand tightened around mine. But that was a million miles away. Here, we were falling, deeper, deeper, through a flaming sky. I looked up and saw glowing threads rearranging, like scars healing.

But so quickly, it fell out of control.

A grinding halt. We hit a wall. Tisaanah tried to push past it, but that sent pain spearing through me, enough to disrupt my focus.

Focus.

It's not a wall. It's a door. Open it, Max.

Before me was a door with a lion's head at its center.

You don't want to go here anymore, a voice whispered.

I placed my hand on the door.

Don't be a fucking coward, I told myself. *Open it.*

Everything was spiraling, dancing the line between power and chaos. The fire in the sky was breaking, falling like shooting stars. Beside me, Tisaanah was still trying to push through, charging at the walls that boxed our magic in with everything she had.

My hand was still on that door. *Open it.*

But the door would not give.

The force that had formerly seemed so invigorating now threatened to consume us, with nowhere else to go.

Agony ripped up my spine, yanking me back into the real world. Tisaanah's hand shook violently. Erratic sparks of unnatural white light snapped in the air like fragments of lightning, briefly illuminating split seconds of Tisaanah's head lolling.

Fuck. Stop, stop, stop—

"Klasto, open the fucking door!" I demanded.

Tisaanah slumped back. The splinters of light became

streaks. One struck my shoulder and left a streak of burns. I struggled to control the stream of magic we had opened, so it now rushed between us with nowhere else to go.

"*KLASTO!*" I bellowed.

The door flew open. Klasto cursed and threw up his arm to shield him from the fire, while Blif tried to fight them back with her magic.

Klasto grabbed Tisaanah and pulled her away from me. Her hand clung to mine with such ferocity that he had to pry it away. He seized each of our hands and I didn't have time to protest his invasion when I felt his magic press against my mind. The connection between us was immediately severed.

Everything seemed like it got very quiet very suddenly. The flames and white light were gone. Tisaanah was a heap on the ground, still.

I couldn't breathe. I crawled over her, taking her listless face in my hands. "Tisaanah."

Klasto and Blif both leaned beside her.

"She should have stopped," Klasto muttered. "It was stupid of her not to stop."

Of course she wasn't going to stop. Even I, someone who had known Tisaanah for all of a week, found it so glaringly obvious that she would never have stopped if there was even a shred of a chance of success, not even if it meant burning her own Ascended-damned hands off.

Her eyes slowly opened. I let out a ragged breath of relief.

"You are an idiot," I muttered. "That was such a stupid thing to do."

"He's right," Blif said. She took Tisaanah's hands and flipped them over, revealing a blistering burn over her opened palm.

"I'm fine," she insisted, even though she clearly had to fight for consciousness.

"None of that was fine," I shot back.

Klasto leaned over Tisaanah, tilting her chin up to look into her face, eyes narrowed in concentration. "He's right. You pushed forward when —"

"And *you*." My glare snapped to Klasto. "What are you scolding *her* for? What the fuck was that?"

"It was the best way to give you both the opportunity to—"

"You locked her in a fucking box with—" *With me.* I choked on the words. "You locked her in a fucking box. Where the hell were you? Why did you let this go so far?"

"Would you rather I have pulled you out when you might have righted it?"

"No," Tisaanah said, firmly. "I could have fixed it."

"No, you couldn't have." I stood and extended my hand to Tisaanah. "Let's go."

Blif's eyebrow arched. "One attempt isn't enough."

Tisaanah gave me a disapproving glance, but as she rose, she faltered slightly. That one little sign of pain, no matter how much she tried to hide it, was enough for me.

"We should try again," she said.

"I'm not doing it. Absolutely not."

That was all I had to say about it.

CHAPTER THIRTY-EIGHT

TISAANAH

The injuries were worse than I had let on to Klasto, Blif, and Max. The truth was, when we returned to the others, I could barely move. At least Sammerin healed the burns easily. He didn't bother to scold me, though he did give me that disapproving *"Don't-think-I-don't-see-you"* look that he gave all his uncooperative patients.

Ishqa was not pleased that we had left. He proposed that we go back tomorrow with Sammerin present to make things, as Ishqa put it, "safer." I was more than willing, but Max was steadfast.

"Absolutely fucking not," he'd say, every time the topic was broached. "She could have died."

These days, I regularly confronted my own mortality. So what?

A part of me was secretly glad, though, that we didn't return to Klasto and Blif right away. A knot in my stomach persisted through the rest of the day at the thought of what I had witnessed. Max's body. His mind. Yes, the tattoos had been rendered useless, but the ink would cover him forever. I knew how it felt for someone else's will to alter your body without permission. He would have to think about Nura, and what she did to him, every time he looked at his own skin.

And even that, as horrible as it was, was nothing compared to what I had seen in his mind. It was a patchwork of scars and walls, either markings of a vicious wound or the defensive measures raised to prevent another one. I was so close to the man I loved, close enough to cradle the precious pieces of every-thing that made him *him*.

And yet, that also meant that I was also close enough to see how badly he had been hurt—been hurt by me, intentionally or not.

I was quiet for the rest of the evening. I didn't want to open my mouth for fear of what might come pouring out. We got rooms in a dilapidated inn—if it could even be called that—and went our separate ways early. Sammerin was the first to go. Zagos was a strange place, but it was a real city, and not one that was in the midst of a war. Sammerin was eager to disappear into a dark room full of beautiful strangers.

"This place is dangerous," I said to him, as he slipped off into the streets. "Don't get yourself killed."

He gave me a tiny smirk over his shoulder that scolded me for not knowing him at all.

Ishqa, of course, disappeared again and declined to tell us where to. Brayan retreated to his room, and Max to his shortly after. But I had no interest in sleep.

A few doors down the street, I found a pub that seemed like it had once been a library—books lined the walls, stuffed into the crevices between cracks and crumbled stone. Most were written in languages I didn't recognize, let alone understand, and time or water had long ago destroyed their legibility even if I did.

Still, the place was quiet, occupied only by an old man with a scarred face who looked like he was halfway to the grave. He spoke neither Aran nor Thereni, so I gesticulated through a request for…something. What I got was a cracked wine glass full of clear, hot liquid. One sip burned all the way down to my stomach. It was, by a significant margin, the strongest alcohol I had ever tasted.

Right now, I wasn't sure that I minded all that much.

The pub-slash-library was divided into many little rooms—by nature of its placement in ruins that forced it to accommodate their shape—and I kept walking until I found a tiny, secluded spot in the back. There, I drank and practiced. For hours, I watched white butterflies of light sputter to life and wither away in my palms.

Useless, yes, but at least it was *something*. That was more than I had before. Whatever Max and I had done had been partially successful.

But those walls...

Butterflies lived and died in my hands, over and over and over again.

My drink was three-quarters finished when I heard footsteps. I looked up to see Max leaning against the doorframe, watching me.

I started. "How long have you been here?"

Confusion briefly crossed his face, and I realized that in my drunkenness, I'd spoken in Thereni without thinking.

"Short minute," he replied, in heavily accented Thereni.

My throat bobbed. I hadn't been expecting that—for him to remember Thereni.

"I'm sorry," he said in Aran, as he sat beside me. "That's more or less all I can say. Yes, no. Big, small. The colors. That sort of thing. I don't know why I know it."

I did.

"What about the curse words?" I said. "Thereni has very good curse words."

"Enlighten me."

I did, and Max repeated the phrase with hilariously intense concentration.

"Beautiful," I declared.

His pronunciation was terrible, actually, but it still brought me great joy to hear Max saying "dick-sucking asshole" with all the focused deliberation of someone learning ancient prayers.

He chuckled, and I watched the path his smile tread over his face. It disappeared when he looked at my drink. He picked it up, sniffed it, and made a face. "You're going to be very unhappy tomorrow."

"I am perfectly sober."

"Ah yes. You've convinced me. You're *puffechtly soober.*" He smeared the words into an exaggerated slur.

In all seriousness, I hadn't realized how drunk I was until this moment.

"How did you find me here?" I asked.

"I don't know. Luck. But…" He cleared his throat. "I'm glad that I did. I owe you an apology. For today."

"You have nothing to apologize for."

He scoffed. "That isn't true."

"It is true."

You don't even understand how much.

I leaned against the table. My head was foggy, emotions close to the surface. When I opened my mouth, I had intended to say something innocuous. Instead, I said, "Tell me about Ilyzath."

Max's face changed. I cursed myself immediately, wishing I could take the words back.

"It was more or less what you'd expect an ancient magical prison designed for torture to be."

"I tried to get you out," I said. I couldn't stop talking. Gods, I was drunk. I was never, ever doing this again. "Many times. I hope you didn't think we had forgotten you. That I had—had let you go. Even when you were in there, you were not alone."

A wrinkle formed between Max's brows. He gave me a weak smile. "The truth is, I didn't think much of anything, in there. It strips you of everything that tethers you to reality. Takes away any connection to the physical world. Surrounds you with things that look real and smell real and feel real, but are figments pulled from your own head. It's terrible, but at least it's just one long dream."

"When you saw things, did you…"

"Did I understand what I was seeing? No. Not really." He gazed into the dark. I wondered what he saw within it. "They were horrible images."

I remembered visiting Ilyzath with Max. It had shown me my mother, dying, begging me to save her—so real that even though I knew it was an illusion, I found myself questioning every rule I knew of reality.

"But they were like shadows," Max said. "I knew they must be related to my life in some way, but not how. Maybe that was a sick sort of gift."

A gift. Perhaps. Perhaps the walls that had so horrified me today had been the only thing shielding his sanity.

"I'm so happy you're free," I murmured.

His eyes flicked back to me, abandoning the past for the present. "Me too."

"I missed you."

"I—"

"I still miss you."

My voice cracked.

Don't cry, you idiot. Don't make such a fool of yourself.

I had gotten so skilled at locking away every shred of vulnerability inside of me. Until Max. Until I allowed him to see those weaknesses and unspoken fears. I hadn't known until then how much I needed it, how much strength came from the act of sharing weakness. I was so tired of being strong.

And the man in front of me, so close that I could feel the heat of his body and smell that agonizingly familiar scent of ash and lilac, barely knew who I was. He was not my lover. But gods, he looked just like him. And right now, I wanted to pretend.

The way he was looking at me sent a shiver up my spine. "I'm right here, Tisaanah," he murmured.

"Not all of you."

A wry smile. "Maybe I'm better off without the parts I'm missing."

But those were the parts I loved.

"You know..." He shifted closer—such a small movement, but every part of me reacted to the closing of the distance between us. "I'm not... good with words. But I do feel something. Maybe the memories are gone, but when I saw you, you weren't a stranger."

I was so desperate for him, even this admission seemed like so much.

I stood and stepped closer, closer, until Max was inches away, his gaze locked to me. Slowly, I parted my legs and climbed over him, my knees on either side of his hips. The hard warmth of his body suffused mine, my breasts barely brushing his chest with each breath. Something sharpened in his stare. His hands fell to my hips, grasping me a little tighter than I expected, as if he was holding himself back from pulling me closer.

I didn't want him to hold himself back. Self-control made a soul tired. I was sick of it.

I traced the lean muscle of his shoulders, then his neck, swirling my fingertip over the ink fragments of the broken Stratagrams—brushing his jawline as his throat bobbed, then his temple, then the tense line of his brow. Down the slope of his nose. And finally, over his lips, which parted slightly at my touch.

One of his hands slid around my back, grasping tighter. The other moved up my body, caressing the curve of my waist, barely brushing the underside of my breast—lingering for a split second, and if he thought I didn't notice, I did, because every muscle in my body wanted to arc into that touch—before leaving and settling at my cheek.

Not pulling me to him, but wanting to.

I knew he wanted to.

I wondered if he would taste the same. If he would move the same way as he filled me. If he would still reach for me when he came, as if he wanted me as close as possible in that moment, with all barriers between us erased.

If he did, would that change anything? Because there would still be a barrier, even if it was a different kind, the kind that lived between me and every memory he had of us.

That thought chilled me even in my drunken loneliness. It whispered in my ear, *This could hurt you.*

Worse, it could hurt *him.*

I hesitated.

It wasn't so much as a movement, but Max saw it anyway. I watched his own uncertainty flicker across his face.

"You're drunk," he murmured. "You don't know if you want this."

What I wanted was not the problem.

I moved closer, so close my nose brushed his. "What do you want?"

He huffed a laugh. "What a question. You haven't taught me the Thereni words for that yet."

The hand at my back tightened, grasping a handful of my thin dress. A wave of heat surged between us, and my hips rolled of their own accord, drawing a hiss from Max and a small, wordless groan from me.

Max whispered, "We—"

It was so easy. I was already so close. It took just the slightest turn of my head to kiss him.

It was not a kiss between strangers.

It was a kiss that gave, and took, a thousand unspoken words. Slow—not frantic and messy, but languishing, desperate. My lips parted for him immediately and his tongue slipped against mine, exploring my mouth with deliberate, thorough care. Everything he had been resisting snapped, and he pulled me so close that I thought he might crush me, and I would welcome it. I put my arms around his neck, clung to him, pulled myself closer with every kiss.

Heat built at the apex of my thighs, just from our closeness, even with our clothing between us. When he shifted, drawing me closer, sparks of pleasure spiraled up my spine. Pleasure and want—no, more than want, *need.*

Our mouths broke out of sheer necessity for breath and I released a tiny whimper. Max's hands clenched around me.

"That's the most beautiful sound I've ever heard," he murmured, the words rumbling through me.

I kissed him again. Again, again. My hands slid over his head, his hair, his neck, his shoulders. I memorized him all over again.

Something was building between us, a growing fissure. Every sense was connected to him. Every breath. A haze fell over me that had nothing to do with the alcohol.

He pulled away. "You're drunk."

He kissed me one more time, gently. His hand slowly released my hair, at the same time as he let out three heaving breaths, visibly struggling to collect himself. His eyes searched mine.

"Not like this," he murmured, voice rough.

He was going to ruin this moment of suspension. I didn't want to let it go, because I feared that we would never reclaim it if we let it slip away.

I leaned in closer again, but he withdrew. He looked down, brows furrowed.

"Tisaanah—"

"What?" I whispered.

And then I realized something odd—that warm light now fell over Max's face. I followed his stare, where Max cradled my right hand, palm up.

The gold mark was glowing.

I gasped.

"You have been difficult to find."

My head snapped up to see Ishqa standing in the doorway.

I was about to show him the wayfinder. But something about the look on his face that made even those important words fall from my lips.

"What happened?" I scrambled off Max's lap, too worried to be embarrassed. "What's wrong?"

Ishqa said, "Come. We need to talk."

CHAPTER THIRTY-NINE

AEFE

Two days later, Meajqa arrived at my room bearing a book, a lopsided smirk, and an obnoxiously chipper attitude.

"Good afternoon, my ill-tempered friend. Apparently, we will be spending plenty of time together. How do you feel about romances?"

I had been crawling the walls. Even my magic had grown frenetic and unpredictable. When I heard the knock on the door, I thought it would be Caduan. When I saw Meajqa's face instead, I failed to hide my scowl.

His brows lurched. "Well, that's always the expression I like to see when I enter a room."

"Where is Caduan?"

"He isn't here."

"Why?"

"Because he is in Threll."

I was confused. "You went to Threll also, did you not? The attack must have launched by now."

"It has. The king is overseeing it."

Words escaped me. I had imagined that Caduan was managing the diplomatic agreements, like Meajqa, and then returning. Not that he personally was charging into a battlefield on Threll's behalf. Memories careened through me of seas of bodies and how easily they broke.

"He is the king," I bit out. "He should not be out there."

"He would never ask his warriors to do something he wasn't willing to do himself. You couldn't have talked him out of that. Everyone has tried at one point or another." Meajqa opened his book. "I thought we might read. This one is new to me. The plot sounds a touch cloying, but—"

"Why aren't you out there, then?"

Tension swept across Meajqa's face, then he smiled at me. "I have never been a particularly strong warrior, much to my father's disappointment. Even worse now, considering my, we'll say, handicaps." He twitched the stump of his wing. "Besides, as Caduan's second, I need to remain here to keep Ela'Dar running smoothly. That, and, of *course*, even more importantly, keep you from going insane." He lifted the book and arched his eyebrows. "Though you do not appear to have much interest in my stories."

I could not believe that Caduan was on a battlefield with humans, of all things, and Meajqa was trying to talk to me about stories.

"What use are those in times like this?" I snarled—even though a distant version of myself remembered a time when I used to so love stories, loved them enough to cover my skin with them. That fondness was the only part of me that remained when I became nothing.

"Stories are always useful. Life is more than a series of acts of violence. And while I respect our king and his commitment to teaching you practical skills, he is not always the most emotionally intelligent person." Meajqa flashed another smile. "Perhaps because he doesn't read enough romances."

I hissed my disapproval, but Meajqa simply flipped open the book, cleared his throat, and began to read.

———

DAYS PASSED. With each one, the tension in my chest grew tighter. Caduan did not return.

Meajqa was my company, returning each day to read to me for an hour. Instead of listening, I practiced my magic, though without Caduan's presence I felt like I could only accomplish a fraction of what I was capable of. It was impossible to concentrate, anyway, with Meajqa droning on in the background about two insufferable people and their seemingly endless longing. At least he was an enthusiastic reader, his smooth voice rising and falling with the rhythm of the words and spinning distinct, if at times ridiculous, voices for each character.

Still, I reluctantly began to admit to myself that I looked forward to Meajqa's visits. Few people in Ela'Dar treated me like a real person, and Meajqa not only treated me like a person, but like he actually enjoyed my company. On the surface, he and I were nothing alike. But beneath, perhaps we both recognized something of ourselves in each other. I had gotten better at presenting a more palatable version of myself to the world, and as a result, the servants no longer scurried around me like mice evading a cat. But with Meajqa, I didn't need to.

One day, more than a week after Caduan had departed, Meajqa was much later than usual. When he did arrive, he sat down without his typical smile.

"Shall we pick up where we left off?" he said, foregoing a greeting.

I must have gotten better at reading the thoughts of others by their faces, because I knew immediately that something was not right.

"You are different," I said, regarding Meajqa warily.

He flicked his eyes to me. "What?"

"You are different. Something is wrong."

His mouth thinned. He did not deny it.

I stood.

"Tell me," I demanded.

He was quiet.

"Where is he?"

Meajqa let out a sigh through his teeth, rubbing his brow. "I don't know."

"He is the king. How can you *not know?*"

"We have lost contact with him. No word from him or from the other generals on that front."

No hesitation. "Take me there."

He scoffed. "Of course not."

"You are going, are you not?" I looked pointedly to his clothing—not the casual robes he had worn before, but a heavier, more formal coat, as if he was preparing for travel.

"Yes," he said.

"Then take me with you."

"He would kill me." He said this very seriously, as if it was the literal truth.

"By any account I am unstable," I shot back. "Who knows what I will do if left all alone by myself? The king would be more upset if something awful were to happen, would he not?"

Despite his grim expression, one corner of Meajqa's mouth tightened in something vaguely resembling a smile.

"Emotional intelligence. I am almost proud. Almost." Then he let out a sigh. "Fine. But *not* because you tried to threaten me, just to be clear. Because you are a Fey who deserves the same grace given to her as any other, and I don't believe you deserve to be locked up in this castle."

I darted across the room to grab my coat, not even allowing myself the time to respond.

"It's likely that everything is fine," Meajqa said, as we went to the door. "Communication lines are often disrupted on a battle front. It hasn't been so long that we need to worry."

But he did not sound particularly convinced.

CHAPTER FORTY

MAX

Tisaanah clutched the letter so hard that it crinkled in her hands. She didn't read it aloud, but her form communicated enough. She was nearly doubled over on the bench, reading it over and over again in silence, while Ishqa told us that the Fey had allied with the Threllian Lords on a massive assault against all four of the rebel strongholds.

"I did not expect Caduan to send such extensive Fey support to the Threllians," Ishqa said quietly. "The fact that he did so shows that he is getting desperate. Which is why I know we have an opportunity." His gaze fell to her hand—still glowing. "We can follow the wayfinder—"

Tisaanah cut him off. "Did any other messages make it through to the rendezvous point?"

"No."

"You need to fly over Malakahn when we can."

"I will."

Tisaanah muttered a curse under her breath and read the letter again.

Ishqa knelt down before her. "I know this is a great deal to process. But the wayfinder—"

I was offended on her behalf. "Give her a minute," I snapped. "Let her think, for fuck's sake."

Sammerin leaned against the window frame, watching the moonlight-drenched Zagos streets. I joined him.

Brayan had not returned to the inn. He was probably attending to business of some kind, but I'd feel more comfortable if he wasn't wandering around in Zagos in the middle of the night. The city never slept. It was just as active now, past midnight, as it had been when we arrived.

Sammerin muttered, "That man has walked by four times."

"Which one?"

"Leather hat."

I found the man he was referring to—middle-aged, but tall and broad, wearing a brown hat and his hands buried in the pockets of a long jacket. He looked like any other of the ten-million seedy individuals around here.

That is, until he passed the door, and his eyes flicked to us, quickly but intentionally. A split second that set my teeth on edge.

I thought of Brayan's very public confrontation earlier today, and the way that man had yelled out Brayan's name—and thus, *my* name—in the middle of a crowd of Ascended-damned mercenaries.

Fuck.

"I think we should be going sooner than later," Sammerin said, keeping his voice low. "Where's Brayan?"

"That's the question of the fucking day."

Behind me, Tisaanah stood, sliding the letter into her pocket. The gold streaks that ran over it still glowed, as if light pulsed between cracks in her flesh. I hadn't noticed it before, but it was dark enough in here that it was clear that the light was moving, too—the center point of the glow subtly shifting from her palm to the tip of her finger.

Ishqa could barely look away from it.

"It's leading me somewhere," Tisaanah murmured.

"Where?" he asked.

"I'm not sure. Somewhere… close, I think."

"We need to follow it."

Tisaanah's eyebrows shot up.

"I need to go to my people," she said. "I'm holding a letter covered in my best friend's blood. They need my help."

"And that is exactly why we must get that power first. You would be useless to them now. But if we had the power that wayfinder leads to, you would be able to help them." He stepped closer. "If Caduan gets to it before we do, they will be in greater danger than ever. Think of what would have happened if he had it when he attacked Malakahn. None of them would have survived, and likely, neither would we."

Tisaanah's jaw clenched. She cradled her glowing hand, silent.

Ishqa's voice softened. "I will fly to them. We—"

A crash cut off the rest of his words, coming from the back of the apartment. I grabbed my sword and ran towards it, only to nearly take Brayan's head off as he pushed past me and stumbled into the living room.

"We need to go," he ground out. "Right now."

"Ascended above, what the hell happened to you?"

He was dripping wet. Rivulets of watered-down blood ran down the side of his face, and crimson soaked the midsection of his shirt.

Tisaanah rose. "You're hurt."

"It's nothing. I—is your hand… glowing?" He shook his head. "Never mind. Later. As we're leaving. We have to go through the back. I got—"

Sammerin, still stationed by the front window, let out a curse. I peered out beside him. Up the street, a cluster of men were headed towards our door—and heading them up was Brayan's friend from earlier.

I whirled to my brother. "Brayan, what did you do?"

"I didn't *do* anything, except nearly get myself killed trying to get back here to warn you in time."

So much for lying low.

I grabbed the swords from the wall and tossed one to Sammerin, then one to Tisaanah. Ishqa was already plenty well-armed.

"Do we have another one?" Brayan asked.

"Why would we have another one? Where's yours?"

"I don't want to get into it."

Ascended fucking above. We had what, thirty seconds before a pack of bounty hunters were at our door? I snapped my fingers and conjured flame to my fingertips. It was weak compared to what I knew I was capable of, but it would need to be enough.

I held the weapon out to Brayan. "Here. I can—"

"Don't be a self-sacrificing fool." Sammerin gave his sword to Brayan instead, before shooting me a disapproving glance. "I have magic that's *actually* useful. I'll be fine without."

Ouch. I might have been offended, if he hadn't been right.

We slipped out through the broken window in the back of the inn, landing directly in a puddle of rancid water in a back alley. Tisaanah went last. Just as I was helping her down, another crash carried from within the inn, followed by the sound of splintering wood.

Brayan swore, and urged us on.

By the time our pursuers found our escape route, we were already on the streets. At first, we tried to blend in, walking fast with our heads bowed down. That lasted for only a minute or two before shadowy figures began to close in on us from all directions.

The opportunity for stealth had passed.

We had just broken out into a run when someone first tried to grab Tisaanah—perhaps thinking, foolishly, that she was the easiest target. She'd half-gutted the man before I could even turn. But that sudden movement tipped us over the blade's edge. It seemed like every shark circling us decided to take their shot at once.

In seconds, our stealthy escape became an outright brawl. There was no time to think, only to act and react. I cut through four people—or maybe five, I didn't care to count—only to yank my sword from the last one and nearly collide face-first into a blade. Tisaanah saw it coming before I did and leapt in front of me to drive her own sword through his stomach.

"Thanks," I panted, and she nodded, too out of breath to answer.

There is no graceful way to fight and run at the same time. We moved in fits and starts, devolving into bloody tangles of fighting when we were attacked, and bolting as fast as we could the moment an opening presented itself. This cycle repeated over and over again until, at last, we reached the bridge.

A bottleneck. Either the best thing that could happen to us or the worst.

The idea of *running* over that rotted wood to get across such an ominous body of water would have been highly off-putting in any other scenario. Now, I welcomed it, because it stood between us and safety. If we made it to the forest, we could lose our assailants.

I whirled around at the head of the bridge. Figures stepped from the shadows in every direction—from the streets ahead, from the tall reeds at our left, the dense trees to our right.

"Go." Sammerin didn't take his eyes off them. "Go right now. I have an idea."

We didn't have time to argue, not with all those hunters closing in on us. One by one, we ventured out onto the bridge as fast as we could bring ourselves to travel. With every footfall, wood creaked nauseatingly beneath my boots.

Tisaanah had made it three-quarters across, Brayan right behind her. Ishqa had taken to the air instead, and Sammerin had insisted upon going last. We were nearly halfway to the other side when I glanced over my shoulder to see our pursuers taking their first steps onto the bridge.

"Whatever this idea is, Sammerin, we should—"

"Can you burn it?"

I wished the answer was an easy yes. Once, it would have been. Now I nodded, even though I wasn't sure.

"Do it when I tell you to," Sammerin said.

He stopped short, whirled around, lifted his hands, and all of our attackers fell to their knees, limbs going rigid and twisted. He let out a wordless grunt of exertion, and their stiff bodies were dragged several feet forward onto the planks, tumbling over each other in a mass of arms and legs.

"Now!" he grunted.

I was ready, pooling as much of my pathetic magic that I could muster. I thrust my palms to the rotting wooden railings on either side of me and pushed fire down the paths of wood with everything I had.

I was as surprised as anyone when it actually worked. Two streaks of flame shot from my fingertips, igniting into crackling bursts when they reached the end of the bridge. It wasn't a lot, but it was enough to send the planks up in flames. I silently thanked Klasto. A partial cure, this time, had been enough.

The hunters screamed. Sammerin released his hold over them with a ragged exhale.

"Now we *run* before this bridge collapses."

277

CHAPTER FORTY-ONE

TISAANAH

We were deep into the woods by the time we were able to stop. The impending sun stained the dim sky. My sides screamed in exhaustion. When Ishqa landed and told us that we'd successfully lost our pursuers, I collapsed to my knees in the mud. Max, Brayan, and Sammerin all let out grunts of relief and sank down to the ground. Max flopped over onto his back, sprawled out like a corpse.

Several minutes passed in silence as we caught our breath. My hand slipped into my pocket, finding the letter that Ishqa brought me from Serel. It was still damp with my friend's blood when I received it. Now it was damp with my sweat, too.

I pulled it out and read it again, even though I had practically memorized it by now. Every time I opened it, I hoped I would see something different in it this time.

I did not.

Tisaanah, the letter opened. *I'm praying to any and every god that this is not how I say goodbye to you.*

Serel's handwriting was neat and delicate, nearly a work of art, but here all of those sweeping loops and even lines morphed into frantic parodies of themselves. He wrote to me from a bunker at the center of Malakahn, hiding from an onslaught of fire from the Threllian Lords and the Fey. He described Fey magic Wielders breaking down stronghold walls and doors, tearing apart houses.

They're killing everyone they see, he wrote. *Even the Threllian citizens of Malakahn. The goal is clearly to destroy, not recapture.*

Then, after a long stretch of paper:

They will succeed.

Serel was a practical person. He spent most of the page describing in detail the formations of magic users and the types of power they Wielded. He listed the Threllian houses that he could identify, so I would know who had exhausted their resources. He told me that they burned all tactical plans in the west building, but the east had been infiltrated before they had time to burn them. He warned me that any information we recorded there had likely been taken by the Threllians.

As he wrote, the writing grew sloppier. Drops of red now blotted out entire words. And it was this second part of the letter that clenched in my chest, the words I couldn't shake from my head:

Don't worry about me. We are going to try to get to Orasiev. We'll get this letter out before we go. Hopefully it will reach you. I should say that I want it to reach you because the information above is important. That's true, but the real reason you need to get this letter is because I want to make sure you know that I love you.

I'm so sorry about Max.

The lines here grew shorter, choppier, the writing outright scrawls.

I should have helped you find him. I know how much how much you loved him. I should have known thats a thing you don't let go of, ever tell filias I love him if you see him

If you dont then I suppose i will wherever I go
thank you for the wild ride.

serel.

I stared at that scratched signature. The letter would have
been written somewhere between days and weeks ago. Ishqa had
not been able to retrieve letters from the rendezvous point, and
even if he had, who knew how long this one had taken to make it
out of a war zone. It was a miracle we had gotten it at all.

Was Serel still alive, somewhere? Had he made it to Orasiev?
Or was he still in Malakahn, dying slowly in the ruins of our
greatest success?

My head spun. The alcohol I had consumed earlier that night
churned in my stomach.

I stood, leaned over, and vomited into the sand.

Sammerin held my hair back as gags wracked my body in
waves. Between bouts, I moaned, "I feel awful."

"I don't doubt it."

"Can you —?"

"I'm afraid not. A Valtain healer would be able to help, but
my gifts are relatively useless against nausea."

Terrific, I thought, and vomited some more.

Finally, when I had exhausted myself, I slumped back against
a fallen log. I felt like all the blood had left my limbs. Alcohol was
poison. I was never drinking it ever again.

Max handed me a canteen of water. "Drink. As much as you
can keep down."

I did, but my mouth was still sour and ashy.

His fingers brushed my shoulder — the touch was so small,
and yet so affectionate. "Are you alright?" he said quietly. The
way he was looking at me now was so similar to the way he used
to look at me then. He knew I was not alright, and his voice said
as much. Still, I nodded.

His lips thinned. He turned to Brayan. "What the fuck was
that?"

Brayan scowled. "Don't talk to me like someone else jumping us was my fault."

"It was *absolutely* your fault."

"There's a price on your head—and hers—that could make these people rich for life. The minute we were recognized, our time in that city was limited." Brayan's lip twitched. "That prick came after me first, still angry about that contract he lost. He'd followed me from our inn. I let him think he killed me. He and his friends dumped me in the river."

"Well, clearly they know you're not dead now."

"Unfortunately," Sammerin muttered. "We need to keep moving."

My stomach churned. I must have looked horrible, because Ishqa seemed genuinely sympathetic as he said, "You keep traveling north. I will fly over Malakahn and get more information."

I was desperate to find out what happened to Serel. And yet, a part of me didn't want to learn the truth, because I so feared it would crush me.

I only nodded and thanked him.

"I'll return quickly," he said, and launched into the sky.

CHAPTER FORTY-TWO

AEFE

The city stank of flesh. When we arrived in Malakahn, I had to press my hand over my mouth to stop my stomach from emptying. The smoke was so thick and unnaturally acrid that it made my eyes drip. Shouts and screams in a cacophony of languages echoed in the distance.

Meajqa muttered a curse.

Everything smelled like death—the air even tasted of it. Destruction stretched in every direction. Once this had been a majestic city of white marble, but now it was crumbling and ash-stained, painted with blood. To our left, a building still stood, walls only partially collapsing, and hordes of soldiers pushed against it, magic slowly but methodically ripping the stone to shreds while those within scurried and shouted like mice trapped upon a sinking ship. Banners marked with Threllian house sigils burned. In the distance, we spotted gold flags—the banners of Ela'Dar, barely standing.

Meajqa turned to the others. He had brought a small group of ten soldiers and commanded that everyone split up in groups of two to locate our Fey battalions.

I looked down to my feet. I stood on a slab of stone. A pale, ash-covered hand reached out from beneath the rubble.

"What if they are buried?" one of the soldiers asked, following my gaze.

Meajqa glared at her and told her not to ask unhelpful questions.

I remained with Meajqa. I thought he would go to the Threllian leaders clustered at the far end of the city, but he sent soldiers to do that instead and we walked alone through the rubble.

It was incredible. The city was just… *gone*.

It reminded me of the level of destruction that the Zorokovs had showed us when they called us to Lady Zorokov's sister's estate—a place where humans had lived their lives, now nothing but a graveyard. But this was worse, because while that city had been a ghost of itself, this one was still writhing through its death throes. The glorious euphoria of battle had passed, but the slow drip of death had not.

We walked in awkward zigzags to sidestep the bodies strewn over the ground. I kept my gaze drawn down to the corpses, not only to avoid stepping on them but to inspect each of their faces. Just in case.

We were nearly to those broken banners when I tripped. I looked down to see long fingers wrapped around my ankle, gripping with surprising strength.

It was a human woman, trapped beneath a slab of stone. When I turned to look down at her, her expression changed, spasms of pain running over it.

I could have pulled away easily and kept walking. She was weak. Instead I found myself kneeling down beside her. I watched her with fascination. The muscles in her face twitched. Her breaths were long and rattling. One eye was obscured by bloody gore, but the other locked to me. It was green, a shade that reminded me of someone that I knew in another life.

Blood poured from her abdomen onto the dusty ground. I removed my cloak, folded it in half, and pressed it to her wound.

She writhed and let out a gargle. The fabric was soaked in seconds.

Meajqa grabbed my arm and yanked me away.

"What are you doing? She would've killed you if she had the strength for it. That isn't how war works. You don't try to save the other side."

He dragged me to my feet, and we continued towards the banners. When I glanced over my shoulder, the woman was no longer moving.

BY THE TIME we reached the Fey banners, the smoke was thick enough to blot out the sky. There was little movement. I feared the worst, and Meajqa did too, based on his tense silence.

We crested a hill and saw a cluster of soldiers, silhouetted in the mist. My heart leapt. At a flash of copper, I began to walk faster. When we approached, one of them turned around—to my utter relief, Caduan.

His face changed immediately when he saw us. "What are you doing here?" he asked, as soon as we were close enough.

"Five days with no word," Meajqa shot back. He didn't bother to hide his annoyance, though with it came a visible breath of relief. "Of course we would send reinforcements."

"We had no time to write letters. This is the longest we've gone without a clash in a week."

Meajqa's gaze flicked across the field, and the soldiers that surrounded Caduan. "My aunt? Is she—"

"She needed to fly south to handle another conflict, before this one began. She is safe."

Caduan took several steps through the wreckage towards us. Though he ducked his head, I noticed the wince, and though he moved slowly, I saw the pain in his movements.

"You're injured," I said.

"No. Just tired." He looked to the horizon line, and it was only then that I saw beyond our encampment to what was happening in the valley below. Threllian and Fey soldiers clustered together. Before them, uniformed humans stood in straight lines, hands bound behind them.

Someone shouted. The humans knelt. And then, before I had time to react to what I was seeing, the Threllians and the Fey walked up and down the lines of rebels, executing them. The bodies flopped into the dirt one by one like discarded rag dolls.

Further in the distance, our soldiers yanked humans out of houses, door to door. It was all very methodical, systematic.

Once, nothing had been more comforting to me than to be surrounded by death. I could hide my powerlessness beneath my wrath and make the entire world just as stagnant and empty as I was. Even now, shameful as it may be, it felt like slipping back into clothing that had once fit me perfectly.

But this? This cold, mechanical taking of life? It seemed wrong.

Caduan had moved closer to me. "I did not—"

"To the east!" One of our soldier's shouts cut through his voice. We turned to see him pointing up.

I looked up and saw a flash of gold in the sky.

My breath hitched. I recognized Ishqa right away, even from this distance. You memorize everything about your nightmares.

Meajqa cocked his bow.

"What the hell is he doing here?" one of the soldiers muttered.

"Shoot him down!" Caduan commanded.

Meajqa let his arrow fly before the words were out of Caduan's mouth.

Ishqa's graceful movements lurched. The arrow missed, but only barely, nicking his left wing. He ventured lower, coming closer to us.

Caduan's lip twitched. "I am surprised he has the nerve to approach us." Then he glanced at me. "Are you alright?"

I understood all he was asking with those three words.

"Yes."

"You can leave."

"I want to see him."

In five hundred years, I had not confronted my fears. I knew Ishqa's face, or at least I thought I did. In my dreams he was as still as marble, his gold eyes unnervingly bright, his mouth frozen in perpetual disinterest. It was the face of someone who had not even cared—had not even thought twice—about betraying me.

The man who stood before me now looked exactly as I remembered him, and yet, so very different. His face was not so still, his eyes not so bright. When his gaze fell to Caduan, it was not emotionless detachment that lingered in it, but genuine pain.

He remained far away, beyond the reach of hands or weapons. Meajqa's aim held.

"Are you pleased with yourself?" Ishqa said, voice stretching across the rubble. "Does all this death bring you the satisfaction of a job well done?"

"It was stupid of you to come here," Caduan replied.

Meajqa's only response was to let forth another arrow, which Ishqa dodged easily.

Meajqa had said he was no warrior, but he truly was a terrible marksman.

Ishqa's lips thinned. "Iajqa. Where is she? I know she was a general here. I have not seen her."

"You lost the right to ask after your family."

"Don't be ridiculous, Caduan. You forgot that we were friends for four hundred years." Ishqa's gaze fell to Meajqa, who still aimed at his father. "I will never stop asking after my family. You know it as well as I. And I hope they know it, too."

Meajqa's jaw tightened. He let another arrow fly. This one didn't even come close to hitting, burying itself uselessly in the ground several feet to Ishqa's left.

No, this wasn't right. I didn't like any of this.

Ishqa was pretending to be someone kind, someone who looked at his son with such open affection, someone who chided Caduan—*Caduan!*—about the morality of this battle.

I did not like to be lied to. And this version of Ishqa was a lie. I knew it because the real version, the true version, had destroyed me without a second thought. I wanted to peel all the skin off his beautiful face until it exposed the rotting darkness underneath.

Without intending to, I took several steps closer, just enough to reveal myself from behind the line of Caduan's soldiers.

Ishqa's eyes met mine and went wide.

I was not expecting his stare to strike me as it did, yanking me back to a terrible day five hundred years ago without even a touch.

His lips fell open, as if words escaped him.

"What is this?" he choked out, after a moment. He whirled to Caduan. "What did you do?"

Caduan stepped in front of me.

"How did you do this?" Ishqa staggered closer, and I tensed —and that was enough to break the thread of Caduan's restraint.

"Leave before we kill you," Caduan said, calmly. "Now."

Meajqa let an arrow fly just as Ishqa launched himself into the air. He hit his mark this time, though only enough to make Ishqa stagger as he arced gracefully through the sky. He flew fast. Seconds, and he was gone beneath the cloud cover.

But my pounding heart and shaking hands lingered long after he left.

———

THE EXECUTIONS LASTED LATE into the night. There were many humans to kill. Caduan told us that the battle had been lengthy and hard-fought, and that he hadn't been able to send word back to Ela'Dar because there simply hadn't been time—we had arrived only hours after the tides had turned, leading to Threllian victory. Even he had underestimated the strength of sheer numbers the rebels commanded.

We piled bodies over bodies. The pyres burned so high and hot that often they threatened to spiral out of control, requiring groups of frantic Threllians to rush in with pails of water and Fey magic users to force flames back with whispered spells. I was certain my clothes and hair would never stop smelling of burning human flesh.

The piles of burning bodies were reserved only for the rebels and those killed within their territory. The Threllians burned their dead separately, in neat, individual pyres by the shore presided over by priestesses. Their dead slave warriors were burned separate from the rebels, too—the Threllians believed that even their loyal slaves deserved to be separated from the rebel traitors.

As for the Fey—by Caduan's order, the dead were treated with the utmost care and respect. We collected all the Fey bodies, painstakingly combing through rubble to make sure we recovered all of them, even those that were in such terrible condition that they were unrecognizable. We wrapped the corpses in ivory silk shrouds and laid them side by side, far away from the burning humans. Soon, rows and rows of pristine white punctuated the charred remains of the city.

Caduan barely spoke to me—barely spoke to anyone—the entire time. Days passed of this. Eating, sleeping. Collecting the dead.

On the third day, Caduan at last sank down beside me. The hours were between midnight and dawn. I had not seen him rest once.

"Why did you come here?"

I struggled to verbalize the answer to that question. "You were gone for too long."

"And that mattered to you?"

It did matter to me. Only now did I realize how different that was from the way I had been when I had first returned to this body—that the word I had really been looking for was "concern."

The sensation of caring for someone else was, oddly, frightening.

Caduan seemed as if he made this connection, too.

"I did not want you to see this," he said.

"I have seen plenty of death, in all of my lives."

"It isn't the violence I wanted to shield you from. It was…" His stare was glassy as they stared out into the destruction—at those rows of neat, white-wrapped bodies. "The day humans came for the House of Reeds, they killed and destroyed and burned and slaughtered as if it was simply a matter of duty. So many of us tried to reason with them, but the humans had decided that we were inconsistent with their own survival. With that decision, we became animals to them. Pests to be eliminated."

The memory was buried somewhere deep, far beneath centuries of my time as Reshaye. But lately, these thoughts had been closer to the surface. The image of Caduan's blood-soaked body lying in the swamps came to me easily.

"Do you know what I thought that day, as I dragged myself away from my home? I thought, *what a waste*. Thousands of years of knowledge and history obliterated with one stupid, selfish human decision. Full lives destroyed as if they were worth nothing. *Wasteful*." He spat the word, a curl of disgust at his lip. It did not disappear as he turned to gaze out at the charred remains of a once-great city. "Humans don't care. They are willing to destroy and discard with abandon. And here, I helped them do it. I sacrificed Fey lives for this. The way those people fought. The way they screamed—"

He seemed to remember that he was speaking aloud, straightened, and looked away. "I have no illusions about the realities of what my task will entail. But this… it reminded me too much of things I would rather forget."

And it aligned him with the monsters he swore to destroy.

Was he looking for me to validate his choice? I didn't want to. Perhaps one of his advisors might have said something soft and comforting, something like "there was no good decision" or "you had no choice" or "you did the best thing for Ela'Dar." Perhaps all those justifications were true, but true things did not have to be acceptable.

I was just as angry as Caduan was. Hated these humans, and what they made him do, just as much.

"I know what it is like," I said, softly, "to become the thing you hate the most."

"I won't let us become them."

"No. We will be better."

Caduan's gaze snapped to me fast, as if this was an unexpected response. I felt like he was seeing me, truly seeing me, for the first time since I had gotten here.

Pleasure shivered over me at that stare.

He put his hand out to help me stand. I took it, but only so I could slide my fingers over the soft skin on the inside of his wrist, where his pulse thrummed. I let my hand remain there even after I stood.

"We will be better," he agreed.

On Caduan's lips, it was a promise.

———————————

WE RETURNED TO ELA'DAR EXHAUSTED. I traveled with Meajqa, and Caduan, along with our other troops, would follow soon after. When we arrived at the palace, I went to my chambers and immediately collapsed onto my bed. *Now* I understood why mortals liked these things so much. When you feel like your muscles have all been peeled out from beneath your skin, the softness doesn't seem so overwhelming.

I did not even feel myself dozing off, until I blinked through my bleary half-sleep to see a silhouette in the door.

I sat up. Caduan did not look as if he had stopped anywhere before coming to me, his clothes still bloodstained and face still dirty.

"I see you have come to appreciate beds," he said.

"It is... not horrible."

"Enjoy it while you can. We start training again at dawn."

"Good," I replied.

"Good," he echoed, nodded stiffly, and said nothing more.

After he left, I lay back into my nest of pillows, stared at the copper ceiling, and smiled.

CHAPTER FORTY-THREE

TISAANAH

Ishqa returned many hours later. He landed and was still for such a long moment, gaze to the ground. Immediately, my stomach was in knots.

I stood. "What did you see?"

He was silent, his hands curled at his sides. Unusually, he didn't magic away his wings immediately, leaving the shimming golden feathers out and trembling beneath the sunrise breeze.

"What did you see, Ishqa?"

He turned, and I was so taken aback by the fire in his eyes that I stepped backwards.

"This war will destroy all of us. My people. Yours. Yours." He gestured broadly to everyone here—Fey, Threllian, Aran, and people who were none of those things.

I had never seen Ishqa like this. Max, Sammerin, and I glanced at each other uneasily. Dread coiled in my stomach.

"*What did you see?*"

I was really asking, *Are all my people dead?*

The sadness etched into his face told me too much. He shook his head.

"Malakahn fell. Nothing remains."

Everything went numb.

Gods, we had fought and bled and wept for those cities. Months of strategizing, of operating in the shadows, of taking over from the inside. My friends had died for this.

Gone.

"Serel," I choked out.

"I could not see individual bodies. He may have escaped."

I rubbed my temples.

I needed to believe that Serel had gotten out alive, just as I had needed to believe it a year ago, when I was desperate to return to Threll to save him. I needed to believe that he had escaped with the rest of our leadership—that they had made it to Orasiev, and that Orasiev had held. The alternative was to believe that in a single strike, the movement that hundreds of thousands of people had fought and bled for had been killed.

I could not allow myself to believe that.

"There is more," Ishqa said, gravely. "Aefe was there."

My brows contorted in confusion. "What do you mean, she was *there*?"

Aefe was dead. Aefe had become Reshaye. We knew that Caduan had Reshaye in his possession—but Reshaye was a very different being than the Fey woman it used to be.

"I mean what I say," Ishqa said. "Aefe was there. Aefe, just as she looked five hundred years ago."

"In a… body?"

"Not just *a* body. *Her* body."

"That's impossible," Sammerin said. "No one can be brought back from the dead."

"She was never truly dead," Ishqa said. "A part of her lived as Reshaye."

Perhaps more of her was in Reshaye than I ever realized.

I relived those terrible moments again—the moments when my mind, Max's, and the Fey king's were interlocked. I had felt Reshaye inside of me then, being dragged back into this world. I knew it was possible he had taken it successfully. Ishqa and I had discussed this at length. But I had never considered the possibility that the Fey king would want it for something more than to be a weapon in his own mind, as it had been a weapon in mine.

"Still. It's still impossible." Sammerin shook his head, looking offended that something so outlandish had even been brought up. "Do you have any idea how much a human—or Fey—body consists of? The sheer intricacy of tissues and bones and nerves? No one can create a living thing from nothing, let alone one that complex."

"But he *has* been creating things from nothing," Max said. "He's created those monsters, hasn't he? The ones he keeps hurling at Ara."

"He can't be creating those from nothing, either."

"And they are very different from… a body," I added. "A *normal* body."

"There is nothing normal about her," Ishqa said, harshly. "I have never been so certain of anything as I am of that. If he created a body for her, then that body is capable of monstrous things. And the fact that he was able to do such a thing at all means that we're in greater danger than we realized. The fact that he hasn't moved yet, at least not with all the power at his disposal, means nothing. Today I saw what he is capable of with only a fraction of the power at his fingertips. And now a city no longer exists." Ishqa turned to me, his eyes fire. "We cannot waste time. We need to follow the wayfinder immediately and claim the Lejara it leads us to now."

A chill ran up my spine. I looked down at my palm and the light still emanating from it. I could feel it tugging me northeast, like a song sung in a frequency no human ears could hear, calling to my deepest soul.

My heart ached to go to my people—fight with them if not mourn with them. If Serel was indeed dead, and, gods forbid, if Filias and Riasha had met the same fate in Orasiev, then the rebellion had no leadership.

They needed me.

But I would be no use to them unless I had enough power to help them.

"I know," I said.

"You have another problem." Brayan's deep voice rang out from the back of the group. He winced as he rose to his feet, pressing a cloth to his abdomen. "In the time we were in Zagos, the price on all our heads has been rising by the hour. No doubt that trend continued. We may be thousands of miles away from Ara, but when someone is willing to pay *that* much for someone, news travels fast and far."

"We have been wanted this entire time," I said.

"Not like this. Nura must be getting more... motivated."

"Then it was unwise of her to use us as bait," Max muttered, which was very true.

"It's probably not much of an exaggeration to say that every bounty hunter or mercenary on four continents is now looking for you."

I cringed and muttered a curse. Inconvenient.

"It makes things considerably more difficult for you. But Max and I are going to Besrith anyway, and that's a hub of mercenary operations. At the very least, it's where the Roseteeth are based, and I don't doubt that many of the most skilled people coming after you are Roseteeth affiliated in some way. Max and I can draw their attention east. Maybe I still have enough pull these days to broker some sort of deal with them."

Max and I are going to Besrith.

That sentence made my heart lurch.

"I'm not going to Besrith," Max said, without missing a beat.

Brayan looked like this was news to him. "What? Why?"

"Because... I have other things to do."

"Things like providing double the attack surface to this group of people and centralizing all of Nura's targets in one place?" Brayan retorted, irritated.

"That is a risk," Ishqa said. "If we remain together and get captured, then we have just handed the Aran queen—or the Fey king—every option we have. Perhaps he is right. It might be safer to separate."

No. I wanted to scream. *No, no, no. I just got him back. You can't ask me to give him up again.*

And that was why I even surprised myself when the words slipped from my lips.

Max said. "I'm staying with you," at the same moment that I said, "You should go to Besrith."

His eyebrows lurched. The hurt that split across his face gutted me. "I—what?"

"What?" Sammerin repeated.

"Ishqa was right," I said, carefully. "It is dangerous for us to stay together. Not only does it mean that we are a single target, it also means that if we were to get captured, Nura would have too much at her disposal. She will have a greater reach in Threll than in Besrith. It will be safer for you. And you, as Brayan said, can help deal with the mercenaries."

All of these very logical reasons tasted like ash on my tongue.

He shook his head. "No."

"Tisaanah…" Sammerin murmured.

"There is no arguing with it," I snapped. "It's the right thing to do."

Max looked stunned, then angry. "What if I refuse?"

"That would be foolish," Ishqa said.

"It would be foolish to run away," Max shot back. "I'm not running away."

"No, you aren't," I said. "We need you there."

"I—"

"Don't sacrifice yourself for me. You don't even know who I am." I spoke more harshly than I had intended. The words felt like razors coming up my throat.

They stopped Max in his tracks. He opened his mouth, then closed it.

The expression on his face reminded me of a memory that I held, and he did not—the memory of the day I stood on the steps of the Towers and told him I would not leave with him. The same hurt. The same shock.

It killed me. Gods, it killed me.

"I do," he said. "I know you."

My chest ached. I shook my head. "When the road splits, we need to separate."

Muffled voices rang out far, far in the distance. We all shut up and looked back towards Zagos. Dawn was still hours away. Brayan's warning took on a new urgency.

A muscle twitched in Brayan's eyebrow, as if to say, *See? Didn't I tell you?*

"We're going to have two dozen hunters on us in an hour," he said. "We need to move."

———————

SAMMERIN PULLED me aside the moment he had the chance. "Why did you do that?" He didn't raise his voice, but I could hear the hidden undercurrent in it—a shrouded tone that said, *What the hell is wrong with you?*

I wouldn't look at him. "It's the best thing for him."

"That's not for you to decide. Tisaanah—stop walking."

He grabbed my wrist, gently but hard enough to turn me to face him. I expected to see anger and frustration in his stare, but it held only sadness.

I couldn't have this conversation. This was too difficult.

"I know you by now," he said, quietly. "I know exactly why you're doing this. You told me once that Max told you he wanted to spend his life with you, and you didn't give him an answer. Why?"

I squeezed my eyes shut and looked away.

"Because it is easier for you," he said. "You're willing to sacrifice everything you have for your people. But fighting for their future won't be any easier for you if you don't give yourself a future to fight for."

The words struck me like an arrow sliding between plates of

steel armor. I hadn't realized how much Sammerin saw. And yet, in this, he was still wrong. He wasn't wrong about what he saw in me, but he was wrong about the conclusion.

"In all likelihood, I'll die doing this," I said. "This war will kill me."

"That's isn't—"

"It is true."

I had come so close to death, so many times. I wasn't stupid. I knew a high probability when I saw one. "I can only escape it for so long. And then Max will have another person to mourn."

Sammerin looked pained. "That's a sad way to approach relationships, Tisaanah."

"Think about it. What are his choices? Come with us, remember a horrible past, fight a terrible war? Lose more people he loves? You talk about my future, but think about his. If we let him go, we are giving him an actual *future*, Sammerin. He has a chance at"—I choked on my words—"at a clean slate. Isn't that kinder than remembering all the things he spent decades trying to forget?" Tears stung my eyes. "Don't accuse me of not loving him."

I didn't even mean to say the last part aloud. But the idea of it, the idea that maybe someone might view my actions as indifference and not love... the thought devastated me.

Sammerin's gaze softened. "I would never think that."

"He has a chance most people never get. He spent so long trying to escape his past."

"His past is all over him, Tisaanah. Memories or not."

"Perhaps traces of it. But don't tell me this isn't the only reason he survived Ilyzath. It could not torment him with a past he didn't remember. You were there during the worst days of his life. Would you really want him to live through that again?"

Sammerin was silent. I saw it in his face the moment he realized I was right.

I had spent every single day for the last six months obsessed with Max's freedom. I'd been willing to sacrifice my body, my soul, my life. I didn't realize then it would be so much harder to sacrifice my heart.

Sammerin looked at me with such sadness. I was lucky to have a friend who looked at me that way—who saw so much more than I ever gave him credit for. But there was inherent weakness in leaning on someone else, and if I allowed even a wisp of that weakness to slip through my armor, I would collapse. I couldn't afford to do that. Not now.

I pulled away and kept walking.

CHAPTER FORTY-FOUR

MAX

"I'm not going to Besrith."

The split in the road wasn't far ahead. As we continued the last leg of our journey, Brayan and I intentionally lagged behind.

Brayan shook his head. "Don't do that to me. It was always our plan."

"It was our plan a lifetime ago."

"And what changed? If anything, it's a better idea than ever. Besides, was I the only one listening to that conversation? They want you to go. Let them deal with their war."

"*Their* war?" I spat, disgusted.

"If you allow it to become our war, it will never let you go. I know that much. And right now, it isn't our war. Not yet."

"Why? Because they're not paying you?"

I actually thought that Brayan would strike me. He pushed closer, face hard. "Do you want to end up right back in Ilyzath? Staying here—with them—is how you are going to end up back in Ilyzath. And you're going to get her locked up there, too. You would make them more of a target than they already are. Bring them more trouble than they already have coming. If that's what you want to do, little brother, I won't stop you. But I want you to recognize that you'd be thinking with your dick, not your head, and you won't be doing it for them."

"Meaningful words on loyalty from the man who won't even acknowledge his own daughter."

Brayan was an excellent fighter. The blow came so fast that I barely had time to react before it sent me to the ground. I spat a mouthful of blood onto the dirt.

"Everything alright?" Sammerin's voice called from ahead.

"Peachy," I replied, wiping the wound on my lip.

Brayan sighed, then offered me his hand. That was the closest I would get to an apology. Just the same as when he used to beat the shit out of me every day in the name of training when I was thirteen years old.

I pushed myself to my feet without taking it, and he rolled his eyes.

"You're the same as you were as a child," he muttered.

"Right, you too."

"I've never understood what you were so angry at me for. Whatever I did, you're in your right to feel it, I suppose." We tramped through the underbrush. I shoved my hands into my pockets. He pushed ahead of me, not looking back. "I won't stop you if you want to stay with them. But I'm going to Besrith. You can be emotional and short-sighted and remain here. Or you can think about it, recognize that I'm right, and come with me. Your choice."

———

THIS DIDN'T FEEL RIGHT. None of this felt right, no matter how many times Brayan or Ishqa or Tisaanah—especially Tisaanah—insisted upon it.

You don't even know who I am.

She was wrong. I was missing something—some critical piece of my past that was preventing me from understanding this. It was like a splinter under my nail, nagging but inaccessible. It was the only thing I could think about when we reached the split in the road.

"The wayfinder is pulling me this way," Tisaanah said, pointing in one direction.

"This road leads north, to Besrith," Brayan said, nodding down the other path.

We all looked at each other, the unspoken weight of our separation hanging between us.

Brayan uttered a stiff, tight-lipped goodbye and migrated down the road, leaving me alone with them. I said goodbye to Ishqa first, which was easy because we didn't especially like each other. Tisaanah wandered into the woods, her back to us, as if she didn't want to allow herself to be seen before she was ready. So I turned to Sammerin.

He was an enigma to me in many ways, always calm and quiet. But I knew that we'd been close friends once. Some imprint of that familiarity still nagged at me when I looked at him.

Even now, a part of me considered telling him that I was going to stay with them.

Yet, as we traveled, Brayan's words had echoed incessantly in my head. *You're going to get her locked up there, too. You make them more of a target.*

They were louder than ever, now.

"So," Sammerin said. "You're going."

Despite myself, I couldn't bring myself to confirm it aloud. Sammerin seemed like he heard the internal struggle I didn't voice.

"We've been friends for a long time," he said. "Twelve years. When we first met, you were an egotistical, prematurely promoted Captain, and I despised you."

He said it so matter-of-factly. I scoffed a laugh.

I wanted to ask—no, *demand*—that he tell me about those years. Really tell me, including all the things that I knew he and Tisaanah were holding back. But the moment my lips parted, the pain that skewered my skull took my words away.

"The thing is, Max," he went on, "they were not all good years. I have been doing a lot of thinking about those times. The good days. The bad days. And some of the bad days were very, very bad."

The hair prickled at the back of my neck. That image—the image of Sammerin saying, "*That was a very bad day.*"—brought with it the ghost of a memory, gone before I could grasp it.

"I want to know," I said.

But the moment the words left my mouth, the fire poker lodged in my brain twisted, and white-hot agony pulsed through my head. I nearly doubled over, my hand at my temple. Sammerin gripped my shoulder.

"You alright?"

"Fine."

I forced myself upright. Sammerin's expressions were always subtle, but I could see the concern in this one as stark as if it had been painted across his forehead.

"Is this the right thing?" I said. "I trust you, not that I even really understand why. Do you think it's actually for the best, if I go?"

Sammerin was silent for a long moment.

"Yes," he said, at last. "I don't think it's a perfect thing, but I think it's the right thing. And in times like this, perhaps that's the most we can hope for."

WHEN I SAID goodbye to Tisaanah, the others moved away. She and I stood face-to-face in silence as they fell back into the woods, finding sudden overwhelming interest in the flora and fauna just out of earshot.

A breeze rustled the trees, and the scent of citrus washed over me, and it was almost all over right there and then.

I shouldn't have stopped her that night in the pub. I wished I had gotten the opportunity to know all of her, even just once.

Before I could stop myself, my hand reached for hers and

enveloped her fingers in mine. Her eyes met mine, spearing me straight through my soul.

"One word," I said, my voice rough. "One word and I stay."

Even if it was the selfish thing, like Brayan had said. Even if it put her further at risk. I wanted any stupid, self-indulgent excuse to stay.

I asked for one word, and she gave it to me.

"Go," she said, softly.

Fuck, I didn't expect that to hurt the way that it did.

"It was a gift, Max," she murmured. "A gift to have known you. I hope that you have the most incredible, happy life. I hope you find a future worth forgetting your past. Make it worth it. Find joy. Do you understand?"

In this moment, nothing seemed worth this. I was going to argue with her, but then her hands gripped either side of my face, and our mouths crashed together. The kiss devoured our unspoken words. My arms wrapped around her like the shape of her body was already a homeland I knew by heart.

We parted too soon.

"I love you," she murmured.

I didn't like that. Those words sounded like a goodbye.

"Ask me to stay, Tisaanah," I rasped.

But she pulled away too abruptly for me to stop her, the air between us suddenly cold and empty. She didn't say another word. Didn't even look back at me again. I watched her walk down the path to Ishqa and Sammerin.

I could not shake the sensation that I had done this before — stood still and watched her leave. I imagined her walking up white stairs, pausing at a set of silver double doors. I imagined desperately praying that she wouldn't open them.

This is a mistake. You can still do something. You can still go with them.

"Max." Brayan nodded down the path in the opposite direction. "We have to move."

You can still change your mind.

I turned away.

CHAPTER FORTY-FIVE

AEFE

The human knelt before Caduan's throne, his head lowered. He seemed highly out of place in this room, the jewel of Ela'Dar's palace—vast and stately, with walls of glass and a copper-cradled ceiling many stories high. Unlike most guests who bowed here, this man was not swathed in silks and furs but in dirty, torn rags of many contrasting styles, as if each piece had been stolen off a different corpse. His hands and ankles were bound, though this did not seem to bother him.

"I am certain, your majesty."

He looked up at Caduan, revealing a lined, scarred face, a bald head, and a generous grey beard.

Caduan leaned forward. "And how did you hear of this?"

"I didn't need to hear of it. I *saw* it." He tapped the corner of one drooping eye. "Wasn't hard to find them. They stood out. Fragmented Valtain girl. The two Farliones. And their winged friend—like you." He jerked his chin to Meajqa. "Tall. Hair prettier than any woman's."

Caduan and Meajqa exchanged a glance. Ishqa.

"Very well." Caduan rose. He swayed slightly in the movement. He had not been well since the battle at Malakahn, and

though I knew he tried to hide it, I saw his pain in every movement. I watched him so closely, after all, during our many long
hours of training. These days, I likely spent more time with him
than anyone else did, even Meajqa or Luia.

Caduan had, it seemed, taken my words from the battlefield
to heart—*we will be better.* He threw that promise at me hour after
hour as we trained. Caduan taught like he sparred, the graceful
strikes of a rapier replaced with calm, sharp words. *You must be
better, Aefe.*

It did not feel like an admonishment under Caduan's tutelage.
It felt like encouragement. Once, I had told Caduan that no one
had ever given me the opportunity to be better. Now I strove for
it with every passing hour.

Caduan stood before the human and eyed him warily. "I trust
that your information is correct."

I let out a breath without meaning to.

I had listened to this man with my eyes slowly growing wider.
At night, I had been waking up with odd dreams, dreams of
forests and, later, of ruins, still grey water and broken walls of
stone.

Now it all made sense.

This man was telling us that Tisaanah and Maxantarius had
been barely south of here as little as two days ago. Perhaps they
were even closer now. In fact, I was almost certain they were.
The dreams had been growing more vivid. Hours ago, I had
awoken from a dream of a forest breaking into a lake, the silhouette of a crumbling palace, and the bitter pang of heartbreak.

This was on the tip of my tongue as Caduan stepped past me
to stand before the human.

I had to give the man credit. It took a brave human to stare
down the king of the Fey.

"You look as if you have something more to say," Caduan
said.

"Many are paying generously for this information," the
human replied. "The Aran queen, too."

"And you believe yourself to be doing a favor to the Fey by

bringing it to us instead." Caduan cocked his head. "Speaking of which, tell me, how did you find your way here to Ela'Dar?"

"I have half-breed friends in Zagos."

"And why are your *half-breed friends*—" Caduan diced the term into pointed syllables. "—not here with you?"

The human shrugged. "Didn't want to come."

Lies. Humans always lie. They lie like they breathe. This man's "half-breed friends" were at the bottom of the Zagos river somewhere, throats slashed and limbs weighed down with stones. I was certain of it.

Caduan glanced at me, then back to the human. "What were you expecting from us for this?"

The human smiled. "A token of appreciation."

"You come to us with this information. Sneak into our palace. See the inner workings of our city. And you expect me to hand you a pile of gold and send you on your way?"

The human's smile withered. The realization fell over his face slowly. He had made a crucial miscalculation. He thought that coming to the Fey would allow him to instigate a bidding war for this information. Why sell it to the Fey when he could sell it to the Arans, the Threllians, *and* the Fey?

"You lie." I stood. The words slipped from my lips without my permission.

Fear had now settled over the human's face.

"Tell us where they went," Caduan said.

"F-For a—"

"For what? For a gift? No. You do not get any gifts."

Caduan beckoned, and with that movement alone, the man began to choke, as if Caduan was yanking the air from his breath.

"Speak. Tell us where they went."

"North," he choked. "They went north. Two days."

Caduan nodded. Dropped his hand. He approached the man and, for a moment, smiled down at him, stroking his face.

"Thank you," he said.

The man let out a ragged sigh of relief.

Then a sickening *SNAP* echoed through the room. The human collapsed to the ground, his neck twisted backwards at an unnatural angle.

Caduan stepped over the body to me, taking my hand in his. He didn't need to say a word. I knew what he was asking.

"The dreams match," I said. "He is right."

Caduan squeezed my fingers before releasing them and turning to Meajqa.

"Meajqa, go to Luia. We need to prepare the army."

"The army? For four people?"

"We can't be under prepared. It has long been suspected that Niraja has access points to the pools of deep magic within it. I was never able to find it… but…" He trailed off, then looked at me. "If something is there, we will need you to find it. Potentially even to harness it."

Months ago, I would have railed against this statement. I would have thrown it in his face like a dagger, ripped him apart with claims that he was using me, that I was nothing but his weapon.

But this was different. The world fell away but for this and the way he looked at me.

I understood now.

This was not him wielding me. This was him handing me the means to be something more. This was him trusting me with power. Putting himself at my feet, even though he was the king, even though I owed him my life.

It was not a command. It was an offer.

I nodded. "I am ready."

CHAPTER FORTY-SIX

TISAANAH

When I returned to the group, I was breaking. I tried not to let it show, but I knew it was obvious, anyway. Even Ishqa looked sympathetic.

"It was the best thing," he said.

Was that how the Fey said, *I'm sorry?*

I bit my tongue and didn't say a single word save for muttered directions at splits in the path. That, at least, was a welcome relief. I could handle putting one step in front of another.

The wayfinder's call grew stronger as we walked. Eventually it got so loud that I couldn't imagine how I never noticed it before—surely, this song had always been playing in the back of my mind. Surely, this thing that was inside of me must have always been whispering.

Hours had passed when Ishqa suddenly stopped short.

"It led you here?"

I looked around, seeing only the same trees we'd been walking through all day. "Why? Do you know this place?"

He pushed past us, parting the ferns until the forest broke. Sammerin and I followed. The glowing in my hand intensified.

I felt foolish for not realizing it sooner: we had been following the edge of the lake this entire time, though we had done some bobbing and weaving through the woods on the way. Now, we stood at the shore, cracked slabs of stone at our feet. Before us, a dark, broken palace loomed over us from the island ahead. Curved bridges extended from its peaks out above us, and a crystal dome rose from the shores like a gruesome entryway from the grey, motionless water.

"This is Niraja," Ishqa said. "The *true* Niraja."

He sounded rattled.

"The part of the island that was inaccessible through Zagos," Sammerin murmured, taking in the scene. "It's..."

"Beautiful."

That was the word that came to mind, but even as it left my lips, it didn't seem like quite the right one. Yes, the ghost of a kingdom before us was beautiful, in the way that ancient gravestones were beautiful. But with that beauty came something darker, something that made the hairs raise on my arms.

Ishqa swallowed thickly. "It was, once. Long ago."

I stepped into the swampy water, then onto one of the stone slabs. Maybe once they had formed a bridge, but now they were large, broken pieces.

"It calls me in," I said. "We can get across on these. At least we will not have to make you carry us, Ishqa."

Sammerin climbed up on the slab, but Ishqa did not move.

"Is there a problem?" I asked him.

He shook his head after a long silence. "No. No problem."

———————◆———————

No place should be as quiet as this. I could hear nothing but ghosts here.

Perhaps Zagos had been partially built over the remains of the dead kingdom, but this—this really was Niraja. The swamp was still and murky, the water smooth as black glass. Mist reduced ruins to dark, formless shapes. Sometimes a breeze would rustle our hair, but it moved soundlessly through the leaves, leaving no whispers.

We walked along the stone bridge, careful not to slip into the depths between the broken blocks of stone. A faint glow outlined the debris to the south—the distant lights of Zagos, but the city felt as if it was a million miles away from this tomb. There, we had been able to see small traces of what Niraja had once been long ago. But here, the lost kingdom's past was suspended in amber—the beauty and the tragedy alike. The bridges arched overhead, vines and flowers tickling our hair. I paused to admire a sheet of stained glass reaching up several stories to the second and third tiers of the bridge above us. Faded colors composed a portrait of two people, a man with shoulder-length fair hair and a woman with dark waves, crowns atop both of their heads. A number of the glass panels had shattered, but the image was still striking. The glow from my hand, now so bright it hurt to look at it, cast a mournful flicker from below.

"This place must have been stunning," I murmured.

"It was." Ishqa paused before the stained glass. "That is Ezra, the king of Niraja, and his human queen, Athalena."

Sammerin's brows rose. "Human?"

"Yes. Full-blooded human. I never understood…" Ishqa's brow furrowed. "Surely he knew that the kingdom he built would wither long before he did. Why would anyone want to do that? Put themselves in a position to watch their wife and children and grandchildren die?" He looked over his shoulder, and I was taken aback by how utterly confused he seemed, like he was genuinely seeking an answer from us.

I couldn't give him one. I wanted to say something about the preciousness of love, however fleeting it may be. But I had just sent Max away because I could not stand the prospect of losing him. If I were Ezra, would I have taken a human wife knowing I would lose her?

Sammerin said simply, "Because it was worth it. Does that seem so unbelievable?"

Ishqa shook his head and kept walking. "I witnessed this

palace burn with their children trapped inside. Nothing was worth that."

———————

WE TRAVELED DOWN, down, down, through seemingly endless, intricate staircases of rusted metal and cracked marble. Eventually, we reached the bottom of the final set of stairs, which hugged the curvature of the castle. Brackish water lapped at our toes. Silver arches curved above us, creating a half-collapsed entryway that seemed to lead to nothing. The ruins overhead closed in on it, making the route ahead a dark tunnel into the swamps. My hand glowed so brightly that it painted garish shadows over the walls.

I stepped into the swamp after a moment of hesitation. I expected the ground to be muddy and the water to be cold. Instead, the ground was hard, as if tiled, and the water, despite its unnatural darkness, was oddly warm.

"It's leading me in there," I said.

Sammerin looked wary. "That's ominous."

None of us could disagree with that. Even Ishqa looked a bit disconcerted.

"I… what am I looking for?" I turned to him. "What—"

A crash shivered through the air. The black water around my ankles trembled.

We all whirled to the left at the same time.

"What was that?" I whispered, after several seconds.

Ishqa didn't answer, instead stretching out his wings and launching himself into the sky. When he returned, the frantic look on his face made my stomach drop.

"We are not alone here. The Ela'Dar army approaches from the south—"

Sammerin swore.

"—and an Aran army approaches from the west."

This time I swore, louder.

"Both of them?" I gasped. "How did we miss this?"

"Half of the people in Zagos are bounty hunters," Sammerin muttered. "Everyone knows where we went."

I cringed. He was right—and worse, we had ended up barely a few miles from where we had started. Nura had battalions throughout Threll. With the help of magic, she would have been able to mobilize them very quickly.

Brayan had been serious. The bounty hunters and spies and mercenary networks worked *fast*.

"My fear is that they are not after us," Ishqa said grimly, "but the power that we came here to get."

A horrible thought occurred to me.

"Aefe," I said. "Was she with them?"

"I could not get close enough to tell." Ishqa had the thought a moment after I did. "Do you think she could find it, too?"

I looked down at my hand. How much of this pull would I feel if I didn't have the wayfinder? How much was the artifact, and how much of it was me? "I don't know."

I thought of my strange dreams, the ones that seemed so vivid—dreams in which I felt I was being watched. How much of this magic did Aefe have? Did she feel what I did?

The Arans were probably coming for me, and that was frightening on its own. But the Fey? The Fey were likely coming for *this*, and that was utterly terrifying.

Another crash, this one closer. We didn't have time to stand around and worry about it. "Then we should hurry."

I stepped into the swamp and Sammerin began to follow, but Ishqa didn't move.

"Sammerin and I should stay," he said.

"What?" Sammerin and I said in unison.

"They are coming fast. If they rip this place apart, you could be trapped or cornered inside. Someone needs to defend you."

"You'll defend me against an entire army? *Two* entire armies?"

"We do not have a choice, I'm afraid." Ishqa's eyes flicked past me, to the swamp. "And... I do not know whether either of us will be able to withstand contact with such deep magic, without your inherent tolerance."

I blanched. This concern seemed like something Ishqa should have mentioned earlier.

"You're saying that just touching this thing could kill us?" Sammerin said. He sounded like he did not like that fact at all.

"Kill, perhaps not. Harm? Maybe. Could it take our sanity?" Ishqa made a gesture that could only be described as a strong version of a shrug, which seemed odd coming from an elegant, 600-year-old Fey.

I wanted to dismiss his fears out of hand, but I'd watched Zeryth unravel at the hands of magic too deep for him firsthand. There was nothing outlandish about the idea of powerful magic destroying one's sanity.

The crashes had now turned into a rolling, distant roar.

"We don't have time," I barked. "Fine. I will go alone. But—"

"You aren't going alone," Sammerin cut in.

"Yes, I am. If this thing can injure me or take my sanity, then you two can… respond accordingly." Briefly, I was struck by an image of myself as one of Nura's horrific creations, crazed and deformed. I shook it away. "This is not a negotiation."

I gave Sammerin no time to argue with me, instead turning to Ishqa.

"Tell me what I am looking for. An object? A… a place?"

The question was so broad it sounded ridiculous. Fine, I could wander into a swamp in search of anything that felt like a "source of world-ending-powerful magic." Then what?

Ishqa looked a little hopeless.

I let out an exasperated sigh. "You do not know."

"I do not know."

At least he admitted it, even when doing so clearly pained him.

"Fine." I turned to the tunnel of darkness ahead.

Despite myself, I was afraid. This place felt… strange, wrong. My body protested entering, the way our animal instincts protested sticking our hand into flame.

But then again, I had learned to love fire, too.

"Be careful," Ishqa said.

"Stay safe, Tisaanah." A crease of worry separated Sammerin's brow. "Come back if it's too much. If you're alive, we can always try again. But if you're dead, that's it."

I nodded, but we both knew I'd die there before giving up.

"I'll see you soon," I said, and ventured forth into the darkness.

CHAPTER FORTY-SEVEN

MAX

Brayan and I walked in silence. My head hurt so much that I probably wouldn't have been able to hear anything that he had to say, anyway—the sounds of our footsteps were drowned out by the throbbing of my own blood in my skull.

The only thought it let through was, *I made a mistake.*

We had only made it a couple of miles down the road when the strap on Brayan's pack got caught on a hanging tree branch and snapped in two. Brayan muttered a string of expletives and sat on an overturned tree to try to mend it. I sat beside him, silent. I had a stick in my hand, which I'd been absentmindedly peeling bark from. Now I used it to draw in the dirt. I drew, of course, the same thing I always did—the three shapes, always in the same arrangement.

Brayan glanced at me. "Your lip is bleeding again."

I touched my face. "So it is."

"I—It won't scar."

Ascended forbid Brayan apologize.

"Is that Brayan-Farlione-speak for 'I shouldn't have hit you?'"

"You deserved it," he said, though he sounded unconvinced.

I sighed. I didn't actually care whether Brayan was sorry or not.

"We can do more good this way," he said—gently, which was strange to hear. "For Ara. We can do more in Besrith."

I wasn't sure if I gave a flying fuck about Ara anymore. I said nothing and drew the shapes again.

Brayan nodded at my drawing. "We should figure out where that is. Maybe we can go there, if Besrith isn't to your liking."

"It's not a place."

I shocked myself with the statement. It slipped from my lips without my permission, and immediately, I sat upright.

What did I mean, *it isn't a place?* It looked like a place—like a map, a cluster of islands.

"You know what it is?" Brayan sounded confused.

"I—"

I do.

I fucking do.

Ascended fucking above.

I picked up the stick with a trembling hand. Slowly, I drew a line—long, curved, encompassing all the frames, with a delicate point at the bottom. Then one in the middle, slightly upturned at the edges.

And at last, I drew two more shapes near the top.

Eyes.

One green, in the center of the shape on the left. The other silver.

The shapes weren't a map, or an island, or a code. They were the boundaries where tan skin met white. They were a *face.*

Tisaanah's face.

I was such a fucking idiot.

Brayan looked over my shoulder. "Shit. You're right. It's not islands."

I stood. "I'm going."

"What?"

"I'm going back."

I was already walking down the path. With every step, my

headache grew more intense. I felt like something was clawing at that door in the back of my mind, slowly chipping away at the metal.

You don't want to go there —

Shut the hell up.

"Max!"

"You can come, or you can go to Besrith," I called back.

Silence for a few footsteps. A muttered curse.

And he followed.

CHAPTER FORTY-EIGHT

AEFE

E la'Dar's army was ready to fight. A shiver of anticipation
rippled through the soldiers, lined up in their armor, weapons
ready—it was obvious even in Meajqa, who rode with the warriors,
too. In the wake of the losses we had sustained on behalf of the
humans, we were eager to shed some blood for our own people.

We rode to Niraja through Zagos, our soldiers pouring
through the streets like a rising flood. Still, the death we
distributed in the city was efficient, not vicious. Caduan was
clear: our objective was not to destroy Zagos—not yet—only to
get to Niraja as quickly as possible.

Zagos was a strange city, and it overwhelmed me—too many
lights, too much movement, too many people. But we cut
through it fast, moving north swiftly as our horses trampled over
those congested streets. Soon, we reached the northernmost
boundary of the district. Above us, the peaks of a grimly silent
palace loomed in the distance.

The hairs rose on the back of my neck. I knew this place.
Just as my broken home had, it made me feel like a walking
ghost.

Before us, piles upon piles of shattered stone blocked any further advancement. Caduan raised a fist, and with that single movement, an entire army halted in silence behind him.

He examined the obstruction before us. I often wondered how Caduan's mind worked—now, it seemed to be carefully dismantling the barrier, piece by piece, and putting it back together in a thousand different variations. Then he extended a hand to me. "Help me."

I was confused. "Help you…?"

"Help me."

I took his hand. I had learned to recognize so much in the sensation of Caduan's skin—one touch, and I felt so connected to him.

"What do I do?" I whispered. I was oddly conscious of those behind us, watching.

"We practiced this."

We had practiced, yes, but nothing like this. I'd practiced creating flowers and leaves and vines in my hands, manipulating the warmth of light to the beat of my heart. None of those things were powerful enough to destroy a wall of stone.

I looked at it hopelessly.

"I am not strong enough," I muttered, bowing my head close to him so no one else would hear. "This is not like… like making a flower."

"What makes you think you are not strong enough? You created life from nothing with those flowers and manipulated it to make them grow. Such life is everywhere here. In the plants. In the soil. In the stone itself. In me. And within you." His warm fingers slid up my hand, pressing on the thrum of blood beneath the tender skin on my inner wrist. "I will help you."

Somehow, those four words made things seem so much more manageable.

We will be better, I told myself.

I closed my eyes. Caduan's magic reached for mine, an open question waiting for an answer. He was right, I realized. We *had* practiced this, with every exercise, every late night, every word-less communication we had forged together.

This magic was everywhere, waiting for me to draw upon it. I opened myself to it and wielded it.

Caduan raised his free hand, and with a single sweeping motion, the stone shattered.

The soldiers behind us let out gasps and stepped back. Even I nearly leapt backwards in shock of what I'd just done—that is, until Caduan glanced at me and smiled, as if it was the most natural thing in the world.

The army was utterly soundless as we rode into the ruins. We traveled through what had once been city streets, elegant town-homes now crumbling into dust. Above us, the shell of a castle stood as a mournful monument. I looked up to a balcony on that castle and drew in a sharp breath.

The memories struck me in jagged pieces. I remembered standing on that balcony and watching soldiers in black overtake this kingdom like ants to a carcass. I remembered the enraged face of a grieving mother and waiting for death at her hands.

I remembered Caduan falling over that railing, a crossbow bolt in his gut.

I remembered screaming.

I tore my gaze away, trying to shut out the images. "You died here."

"Almost. Or perhaps I was born." Caduan lifted his chin towards a rocky ravine near the foot of the palace. "That is where Ishqa found me and told me that you were dead."

The anger hit me in a breathtaking wave.

If Caduan had known that I lived, what would he have done? Would he have been able to rescue me? Instead, Ishqa told a single lie, and Caduan grieved while my soul was slowly ripped away from me, bit by bit, over five hundred years.

We reached the foot of the palace. "What do you sense?" Caduan asked.

I felt... something. A strange sensation, like a buzzing in the air that skittered over my skin. I could barely grasp it.

Caduan watched my uncertainty, then took my hand and pressed it to my own chest.

"Just listen," he murmured.

I closed my eyes.

At first, nothing. But I fell deeper—into my own heartbeat. Deeper still, into what lay beneath, into the parts of me that were scarred remnants of what I once was.

There. I grasped a faint thread, tugging me forward. I knew that connection. Of course I would recognize those I had once shared a soul with.

When I opened my eyes, I knew exactly where we needed to go.

I pointed ahead—to the series of arches that led down, down, down, beneath the palace. "This way."

"My king!" We turned to see Luia frantically urging her horse through the wall of soldiers. Her next words came between panting breaths. "Human troops are approaching from the west side of the city."

"Human troops?" Caduan pressed.

"*Aran* troops."

I stopped breathing.

"That human bastard," Meajqa muttered. "He sold the information to the Arans before he even came to us."

"It makes no difference." Caduan regarded the soldiers. "We came here ready to fight, did we not?"

A ripple of agreement shivered through the crowd.

That was all Caduan had to say to them—there were no battle cries, no rallying calls, no screams of bloodlust. Yet, the desire for warfare grew so thick I could taste it in the air—taste it on my own tongue, because I too was ready for blood.

Caduan turned and nudged his horse ahead.

"Lead us," he said to me.

I reached deep into my mind, closed my fingers around that thread of connection to the magic beneath, and complied.

CHAPTER FORTY-NINE

TISAANAH

Had this place been a shrine once? A church? The water grew deeper, to my knees and then to my thighs, warm as bathwater. There were no fish, no algae, no bugs. The water was smooth and dark as black glass.

I ventured deeper. The palace had partially collapsed over these swamps, creating a crumbling ceiling of beautiful marble and silver ahead from the remnants of those fallen walls, braced upright by the arches that marked my path.

My hand felt as if it was on fire. It shone just as brightly, too —bright enough to light my route. My head pounded, my vision blurry.

Distantly, far above, the sound of fighting echoed, growing louder with each passing moment. But so much stronger than the sounds was the *feeling*. I could *feel* the deaths above, just like I could feel the emotions of others when my magic was at its strongest, as if every sensation was amplified down here.

Suddenly, the trickle of magic that I had been following became a gushing stream, threatening to drown me.

The light in my hand went out. Darkness swallowed me whole.

I tried to steady my shaking breaths. Fear fell over me.

{Hello, little butterfly.}

The voice came from everywhere and nowhere.

My breath caught. No. This wasn't real. That voice didn't exist anymore. Reshaye, at least as it had once existed, was gone.

{Is anything ever really gone?}

"Yes." I said it out loud because I wanted to hear my own voice. It sounded flat and empty.

A low laugh. A different voice. *What a naïve response, coming from someone who bears so many marks of her past.*

I felt hands on my back, my scars. I drew in a gasp and lurched away, my eyes searching desperately and finding nothing but endless black. I heard no movement in the surrounding water.

I questioned my sanity.

"Who are you?"

You don't recognize me?

Now, the voice of a young girl, perhaps of ten or twelve, speaking Thereni so close to my ear that I should have been able to feel her breath.

Despite myself, panic was building.

Do not be afraid.

Esmaris. That was Esmaris's voice, unfurling through the darkness like smoke. The sound of it paralyzed me with fear against my will. I was thirteen years old again.

Why are you frightened? he whispered, and the most terrifying thing is that he sounded so genuinely tender—I had forgotten that he had sounded that way, sometimes. *I am the one that used to rock you back to sleep at night. I gave you so many of your best days.*

It was the truth. Esmaris had been my oppressor, but he had also been my lover, my father. All roles that should never have been so sickeningly combined.

"You're dead," I whispered.

I'm dead? Esmaris laughed, the way that he often did when I had done something silly and charming. *So innocent. I can never die. By marking you, I will live forever.*

His hands caressed my back—after all this time, I still knew exactly what they felt like, right down to the placement of their callouses.

Think, Tisaanah, I told myself. *This is not real. Where are you? You are standing in water, in Niraja. You are going to find the Lejara here. This is deep, powerful, nonsensical magic. You are half in another world.*

"Stop," I commanded.

The hands disappeared.

Silence. I steadied myself in the beat of my pounding heart. I touched my own face to remind myself of my physical presence.

My name is Tisaanah Vytezic. I am in the city of Niraja. I am here to reach the Lejara. I am here because my people need me.

I rooted myself in this purpose.

I looked up. Above me, two realities blended together. One was the ruins, the arches and marble soaring above me—the physical world. But superimposed over it was what looked like a starry night sky, violet streaks slashing across it.

I was in two places. My body, in the ruins. And my mind, which had been pulled far into the fathomless layers of magic.

I had to be close to the Lejara, to have been pulled in this deeply without realizing it. But I still didn't know what I was looking for, let alone how to use it. Was it… a consciousness, as Reshaye had been?

"What are you?" I asked.

You don't know yet? Max's breath was warm against the shell of my ear. The ghost of his embrace enveloped me, only to disintegrate into the stagnant air.

Not real, I told myself.

"I've come here to wield you," I said. "Help me understand how."

A laugh in many voices. The stars—not-stars—above me lit up in ripples with the sound.

You are welcome to try, a voice said—the voice of a young girl.

And then a young boy. *But you are only one half of a whole. You cannot fly with only one wing.* A giggle. *Or, maybe you can! You want to try, anyway?*

The dark had become all-consuming. I wanted to flail my hands out to steady myself.

Hey. The whisper was so close that lips brushed my ear. *Did you know that caterpillars become nothing before they become butterflies? Gross, right?*

I knew that voice. Kira. I turned, expecting to see Max's sister as I remembered her in his memories.

Instead, my mother stood before me.

The sight of her knocked the breath from my lungs. Ten years had been greedy, eating away my memory of her face. Her dark hair was wild and unkempt around her shoulders, but I no longer recalled the distinct shape of her eyes or the line of her chin, her features reduced to vague guesses.

You wish to wield this? Her voice was a hundred variations at once. Every time I looked at her, her face was slightly different. *Then wield it, my love.*

She extended her hand, palm up.

It's a trap, I told myself. *This is not real. It's not her. This is some pit of magic that is trying to consume me.*

But my thoughts were sticky, like a moth caught in a web. I found myself moving before I could stop myself.

I took her hand.

Immediately, the magic overwhelmed me.

CHAPTER FIFTY

MAX

I ran until every part of my body burned. In the beginning, Brayan was following me, not that I slowed enough to let him catch up. I left him behind when, on nothing more than impulse, I tried drawing a Stratagram—and this time, it *worked*. I was too grateful to care why. I made one jump, then another. The ground beneath my feet shifted from the damp earth of the forest to the swamp of the shore to the stone of long-abandoned streets.

I was already drawing my next Stratagram when I landed between two soldiers, right in the path of swords mid-swing. I cursed and rolled out of the way seconds before their blades clashed. The movement nearly flung me right into another skirmish, clawing the dirt to stop myself.

I was in the middle of a fucking battle zone, surrounded by a tangled mass of flesh and steel and magic—horses screaming, humans screaming, Fey screaming. The uniforms were all so bloodstained, in red or violet, that I couldn't even make out who was fighting who. Chilling shadow creatures that I recognized as the Fey's monsters tore through handfuls of soldiers as if they were rag dolls. Mangled beasts on stilted legs—Nura's creatures

—roared through the battlefield, gutting whoever crossed their path no matter what uniform they wore.

Fuck. I groped around the bloody cobblestones for my sword.

I didn't have time to ruminate on how this mess had happened. I just needed to find—

BANG!

The ground shook. The sound rattled my skull. Ruins that had been stable for hundreds of years groaned warnings of imminent collapse.

The fighting paused only momentarily. Those who stopped too long to look around in confusion were cut down.

But none of these things earned my full attention. It was what lay under it—a sudden chasm that had opened in a world that I sensed deep beneath this one, a disruption that was just as tangible, just as real, as all of this.

I knew where I needed to go.

I grabbed my sword and drew one more Stratagram.

<hr />

I LANDED in an inch of black water. The sudden quiet was jarring. I could hear the battle happening not far from here— coming closer, as both armies tore through the ruins, alerted by the explosion—but it was oddly dampened, like my ears were stuffed with cotton. I struggled to see. Even the scent of the swamp seemed muted.

But where these senses had dulled, others were painfully sharp.

Something pulled me deep into the darkness, where collapsing arches of silver led into the dark water. Every shred of my body was allured and repelled by it at the same time. This, I thought, was what flies must feel like in the face of a carnivorous plant. I wondered if they, too, heard the voice that warned, *This is dangerous. Turn away. Never come back.*

That voice was screaming at me now: *You don't want to go there, Max. You don't want to open that door again.*

But like the fly, I ignored it.

I ran into the tunnel and made it four steps before everything went dark.

CHAPTER FIFTY-ONE

AEFE

We made it only partway through the ruins before the Aran military was upon us. I thought I was braced for it. But when the humans spilled from every hidden crevice or road in Niraja, it was so much more than I thought it would be.

How had I forgotten it was like this? How had I forgotten how much I *loved* it? All this time, I was so desperate to feel alive. And it was right here! Here, balancing on the edge of death!

I threw myself into it with unfettered glee, barking directions at Caduan every time he looked to me for guidance. The thread of magic guided me towards the far end of the city—towards power.

The past blended with the present. The last time invaders had flooded into this place, it was my fault, and I had failed. Not today.

When I killed, it was like returning home. A human lunged at me as I turned a corner. He was young, inexperienced. A single stroke of my sword and his head dangled by a few threads of flesh.

I could not think of anything but this moment, and I was grateful for that reprieve.

Caduan threw himself into it just as easily. I remembered that once he had fought gracefully, as if performing the steps to a dance. That had changed after all these years. Now, he fought like someone out for revenge, killing with abandon. His magic and his rapier were equally vicious, dismantling body after body as we worked through the city.

Another flood of power shook the world far beneath me, the farthest reaches of my magic trembling with its force.

"That way!" I pointed. We were so close.

But I turned to see that Caduan was no longer behind me. In my frenzy, I had lost track of him.

That sobered me quickly. I whirled around, striking down two humans who got in my way.

Caduan had fallen behind, trying and failing to quell an enormous tide of human soldiers rushing through the streets. His eyes met mine through the chaos.

My glee withered to fear.

The thin line between life and death had invigorated me. But now, watching Caduan be swallowed up by a flood of enemy bodies, I realized all at once that the thread was just as tenuous for him, just as easily cut. That thought terrified me.

I fought my way back to him. The Aran soldiers were not highly skilled, but they were numerous. This was the problem with humans. They bred like mice.

"We're overwhelmed," Caduan shouted. "Go after them. Go alone!"

No. I wasn't leaving him behind.

He grabbed my arm and pulled me closer, our foreheads pressed together. "Go, Aefe. Go to them and claim the power you deserve."

Them—Tisaanah and Maxantarius. I knew they were close. I always felt it.

I wondered if they knew I was here, too? Did they feel me the way I so easily felt them?

I longed to be reunited with them. So I could claim the power that Caduan wanted, yes. But I also could not shake this strange fascination with them—obsession. I had lived inside of them. Once I had wanted their love more than anything.

I hesitated, but Caduan took that opening to push me away. "*Go,* Aefe!"

I went.

CHAPTER FIFTY-TWO

MAX

Y ou cannot go any farther.
My eyelids fluttered.

It was foolish of you to come here, lost child.

Darkness. My head felt like knives were plunging into my skull. Tepid, shallow water soaked my back. The sound of the distant fighting had grown very dull. I sat up.

Before me was a set of double doors. They were dark wood, punctuated by gold hinges and copper filigree decorations. A golden lion loomed above it, surrounded by swirling metalwork flowers.

And with that sight, as it always did, came the thought: *You don't want to go here anymore.*

You can retreat, the voice said. It took a few minutes for me to assign markers of recognition to it—gender, age. A woman. My mother, I realized. *Perhaps it will let you leave if you turn around now.*

Turning back suddenly seemed like a very smart idea. Why wouldn't I? For a moment, I couldn't remember why I had come here to begin with.

Funny thing, memories, the voice said. *Losing them is the ultimate absolution, right?*

And isn't that what you've always wanted, Maxantarius? Another voice—deeper. Familiar. Brayan's?

I looked up, above the door. A night sky spread out above me, somehow superimposed over the ruins—endless, like I could see all of it at once without even turning my head. Streaks of light crossed between violet stars. Sometimes those streaks would explode in tiny sparks, the stars fizzling out in their wake.

I frowned, struggling to cut through the fuzziness in my brain.

No, these weren't stars. That wasn't the physical world—it was the layers of magic above me. My body was in one place, my consciousness in another. I could feel each one of those little explosions, like ripples on a pond, barely tapping into the depths beneath. And there, beyond the door, a massive pillar of light pierced the darkness. If every explosion of stars above was a tiny splash in the sea, this was a tidal wave.

Tisaanah. Her presence was as unmistakable as the sight of her face.

But even from here, I could tell that the magic she wielded was unstable—weighted on only one side of a delicate scale. It was out of control, just as the magic we had shared in Klasto's home had been, but magnified thousands of times over.

I leapt to my feet and went to the door. *This fucking door* had separated me from my memories, from my magic, and now from Tisaanah.

No more.

The pain in my head grew unbearable as I grabbed the handle.

You don't want to go here.

Yes I do, I said, and threw it open.

TELL ME, my ashen son, do you know how much a million memories weigh?

How about one?

It weighs enough to break a spine. It weighs enough to break a soul.

I knew this voice. How?

My mind was filled with a thousand walls. Ahead, the tear grew wilder, more out of control.

I pushed forward, and the first of many memories assaults me.

CRACK.

You stand in the parlor of a beautiful house you once called home. A dark-haired woman and a dark-eyed man huddle close, whispering, tense. Brayan stands beside you.

War.

War. The word rippled through a hundred memories, cascading through my home, Korvius, the Orders, as a series of walls shatter.

Crack.

Your sister, a shy girl with curls in her hair, sits on a window sill with a knife in her hand. You take the knife from her. "Go to sleep," you tell her. "I promise I'll take over your watch."

Remember now how she looked at you? Like the possibility of danger under your watch was simply impossible.

I took another step towards that tear of light.

Crack.

You are at the top of the Towers, talking to a man you once admired deeply. He offers you a contract. You are angry at your brother. You are desperate to prove yourself.

"Don't," I call into the void, but the younger version of myself draws the knife across his flesh, anyway.

I had to stop out of sheer exhaustion. My head hurt so much I thought it couldn't possibly be anything but death.

Turn back, a voice pleaded. I knew it right away, this time. My younger sister, Marisca. *Turn back before you see it.*

But that wasn't an option. Tisaanah was still ahead. I knew where I had to go.

I continued on.

———————

334

WITH EVERY STEP, I pushed through another wall. Claimed another memory.

You open your eyes and hear a voice in your head that is not your own.

Crack.

You strike down opponent after opponent in sparring. Then your own captains. You feel nothing but pride.

Crack.

You are in your first battle since your bargain—since Reshaye. You turn yourself over to it, delirious with your own power.

Reshaye tells you, {This is everything you have ever wanted.}

Here is the thing that will later make you seethe with anger at yourself: it is right. You are an incredible killer, and it is everything you ever wanted.

Here, I hesitated. Dread loomed over me like a long shadow. I knew something worse was coming.

But I needed to reach that light ahead, and I couldn't do that without pushing forward. So I kept walking, and the walls kept breaking.

Crack.

Your youngest sister looks just like you. She is your favorite, and you are hers. She strives for your attention and respect just as you strive for your elder brother's, but you love her more—you are determined not to squander this. When you are home on leave, she snaps her fingers and shows you the nearly invisible fragment of lightning. You are overjoyed. She will be your apprentice. You will teach her like your brother taught you, but you will be a better teacher in every way. You were thrilled that day. And so was she.

Crack.

The city is called Sarlazai—

I almost stopped right there. Right at the recollection of the name.

But I couldn't.

—and so many of your friends are dying here. The death has begun to weigh on you. You do not wish to hurt these people.

But you remember the rest, don't you? The silver gaze of someone you thought loved you. How easily she betrayed you. The blood of thousands on your hands.

So easy. A single moment and so much changes.

I SAW TISAANAH NOW. I was close enough to make out her silhouette, kneeling in the water. The wild stream of magic tore from between her cupped hands. It was so out of control that it stretched the stitches of the world that surrounded us. If she didn't have help, and fast, it would burn her up.

I approached her, wincing as several more memories flooded my mind. She looked up at me. Her face was burned, the skin blistering at the tip of her nose and the curve of her cheeks.

I fell to my knees before her.

Crack.

You are at home. Drunk. You are gardening. You find it satisfying to clip away dead petals the way that you wish you could clip away the dead parts of yourself.

An old friend, lover, enemy arrives. She has brought someone with her. You turn around and see for the first time a young woman with spotted skin and mismatched eyes, wearing a ridiculous nightgown. You do not know it yet, but your whole life has now changed.

And changed again, with every secret you tell her.

And changed again, with every day that you fall a bit more in love with her.

We had tried to do this, or a much smaller version of it, at Klasto's shop. Even that had hurt her. What if I did the same thing here? What if I couldn't control what I offered her, and the force of it killed her?

It's possible, a bodiless voice said, and I recognized it immediately as Kira. *It would not be the first time you destroyed what you loved most.*

But I looked up to the sky, and the tear in magic that stretched its length. If we didn't control this, the resulting eruption of power would kill everyone here. And yet, I still hesitated.

Why are you afraid, Maxantarius? the voice asked, and this one… this one, for the first time, was myself. *Do you hope that you might never see the moment when everything changed, the moment before meets after?*

Perhaps such a moment is in the Arch Commandant's office, with your blood on a contract.

Perhaps it is in the ashes of Sarlazai, with your lover in your arms.

Perhaps it is in the moment when you let yourself believe in a foreign stranger's dream.

Or perhaps it is here, right now, in the choice that you make today.

A realization came to me, one that I had been grappling with for the last ten years. There was no single moment when everything changed. No single before and after. There was just… life. A million decisions and a million consequences.

All this time, I had thought I had been erased of my past. But I had been wearing it all over me, as permanent as the tattoos on my skin.

One final door remained in the back of my mind. One final barrier I could not break.

How much does a memory weigh?

Too much to carry alone.

Tisaanah looked into my eyes and took my hands.

CHAPTER FIFTY-THREE

AEFE

The condition of the ruins grew worse the further I fought. By the time I cut through the northern part of the city, I had to slow down just to make it through the broken stone. I was soaked in human blood and my own. None of my wounds, though, compared to the headache. My skull felt like it was shattering. I knew I was close.

It was quieter here, though the rest of the fighting would reach me soon. A few stairs led down into several inches of water, beneath melancholy arches of white.

I stepped into the water, and an involuntary gasp ripped through me.

For two seconds, I felt as if I was falling, even though my physical body had not moved. I looked up and saw stars glowing bright violet above me. I was so deeply attuned to every sensation for miles. A powerful force called to me. Ahead, a streak of blinding light, growing more intense by the second, reached for the sky.

It was the Lejara, and more importantly, it was *them*. I knew it. I shared their souls. I would recognize them anywhere, even by spirit alone.

I stepped forward —

I was suddenly yanked backwards. My head smashed something hard. The world was cold.

I was no longer with them. I was back here, in the ruins of Niraja, my body cracking against marble stone.

I barely managed to turn my head, just in time to see a flash of blond hair and a sword swinging at my face.

I rolled out of the way and grabbed my weapon. By sheer luck, I managed to recover fast enough to block Ishqa's strike.

Ishqa.

For several seconds, I just needed to take him in. He was so much closer than when I had seen him last, his face mere inches from mine.

All thoughts of Maxantarius and Tisaanah withered away.

No. I wanted blood. I wanted justice. I wanted vengeance.

"You," I snarled. "You did this to me."

I drew my second blade and plunged it into his side.

He staggered back. I was after him just as fast. He recovered quickly, even as blood gushed from the wound in his side. Ishqa was a powerful warrior. He was stronger — but I was faster.

I threw myself at him, strike after strike after strike.

"Do you know what they did to me because of you? Do you know what they took from me?"

I didn't even realize I was speaking aloud until my throat began to hurt. Didn't realize I was crying until the tears blurred my vision.

"Five hundred years. So many days. Nothing but white and white and *pain.*"

He barely managed to evade the knife I aimed at his face. Blood smeared the side of his cheek. I'd sliced off one of his ears, or part of it.

Taking an ear wasn't enough. The people he had given me to had cut off every part of me until there was nothing left. And then they had cut away my soul.

I pushed him against the wall. He was badly wounded — I could feel it in his struggling breaths.

"Do you know everything they took from me?" I snarled.

"I do," he said.

I do? No. I wanted more. I wanted him to beg for my forgiveness as I emptied his entrails.

"Why?" I heaved. "*Why?*"

I was getting better at reading the expressions, but I could not understand this one.

"I have regretted it every day since, Aefe."

This answer enraged me. He winced as I drove the tip of my knife a little further into his throat.

"Do you think your regret is equal to my suffering?"

"No."

"Then what good is your regret to me?"

Now, I understood this expression—sadness. "None," he said. "My regret is worthless."

This sentence was such an injustice. He was right. His regret was worthless. But he had carried it for five hundred years, and I had sustained my pain for just as long. Now what? What could come of all those years of suffering?

Kill him, a voice whispered in the back of my head. *His death will make you feel whole again.*

Yes. Maybe blood could fill what apologies could not. I drew back my blades, a snarl on my lips.

Ishqa was ready to meet death—until his gaze flicked over my shoulder, and his eyes widened.

He threw his weight against me, sending both of us falling to the dirt. I clumsily rolled to free myself from beneath his weight. When I looked up, I strangled a gasp of horror.

It was the creature from my nightmares.

It was almost Fey—tall, as if walking on stilts, its body stitched together in ways that did not seem to quite make sense. The open wound in its stomach glowed white. The one I had seen in my visions had stringy red hair. But this thing had a different face, one that looked as if it might have been beautiful before it was cut apart and stitched back together again, framed by long, fair hair. A single gold thread dangled around its neck.

Ishqa crouched on all fours, looking up at it in horror. When he spoke, it was a choked sob. *"Iajqa."*

No.

Was that truly her? Could it be?

It seemed impossible to think that this… this *thing*… could be the dignified general. And yet…when its eyes settled on me, their gold hue, even surrounded by bloodshot veins, was unmistakable.

Iajqa had traveled south. Had traveled closer to the Aran queen's territory. And she must have been —

It lunged.

The creature nearly tore Ishqa in two. He didn't even fight back at first, still gaping at this thing that used to be his sister. He was saved by chance — the creature grabbed another one of the Fey soldiers instead, stringing him between razored fingers and ripping him apart. The blue light that poured from the open wound in its abdomen sputtered in small explosions that left those around it rolling away in agony.

In the next ten seconds, I watched, paralyzed, as it killed a dozen Fey without seeming to even try.

Iajqa was nothing if not loyal. She never would have raised a hand against her own people, let alone so indiscriminately. If this thing had been Iajqa, there was nothing left of her within it now. She had been pulled apart and put back together again as something that would live a short, painful life, designed only to kill.

Ishqa kept screaming her name, over and over again, dodging her frantic blows but never striking.

The creature turned her eyes on me, and her frantic flailing stopped. The light beneath her skin shivered.

I readied my blades —

She was on me before I could move, her hands on my shoulders. One of those gold eyes was a little lower than the other, far from the perfect symmetry of her previous face. Her nose had been cut off. A wound opened from the side of her mouth, extending almost to her ear.

The overwhelming smell of death nearly emptied my stomach. And that revulsion spread, too, to the magical senses beneath this world. It was wrong on every level, physical, spiritual, magical. This creature was made from magic its maker should not have been trying to wield.

It made a noise that almost sounded like words—almost sounded like, *Stop me*—and then tried to rip me to pieces.

My blades seemed pitiful against this kind of strength. It barely reacted to wounds that would maim or kill another. When Ishqa finally snapped himself out of his trance and levied a devastating blow with his broadsword, she hardly faltered.

She grabbed me instead, claws squeezing, squeezing. I opened my mouth and blood dribbled out. My hands flailed in panic for my weapons, but they had fallen to the ground in my brief seconds of distraction. I was helpless. Just as I always had been for so many years, fighting and fighting against a force I couldn't meet.

Time slowed.

I heard Caduan's voice. *You are not nothing.*

I became acutely aware of my heartbeat, rapid in panic. My breath, ragged and gurgling.

The line between life and death blurred, like twilight on the horizon line. I could reach out and touch death, it was so close. *I have longed for you*, it whispered, *for an age.*

But in this moment of clarity, something else came to me, too. A power was churning and roiling in the world below this one, my thread of connection to that deepest well slowly igniting to a screaming rope of fire.

In that magic, I had strength.

I could let myself die here. I could finally let my lost lover take me away, as I had prayed for it to do for hundreds of years.

Or... I could live.

With blurring vision, I looked up over Iajqa's sinewy shoulder to the battle beyond. What had been chaotic minutes ago had now devolved into nightmarish slaughter. Ela'Dar's warriors were overwhelmed. The Aran queen's creatures were too numerous for them, combined with the sheer number of human soldiers. They needed me.

I thought of Caduan's reaching hand. He had offered me a choice—offered me power, and with that power came the desire to act on behalf of something more.

I turned away from death. I grasped power.

I looked deep within myself, reached into the magic that now seemed so close to the surface, and I unleashed it. Iajqa let out a shrill shriek, her skull suddenly spilling with light, the gold eyes melting from her face. She dropped me as her ruined body began to dissolve.

I was already running.

CHAPTER FIFTY-FOUR

TISAANAH

The magic was too fast, too much, to control by myself. The realization that this would kill me didn't come in a single moment, but in a slow solidification of truth.

When I saw Max, I wanted to weep, wanted to tell him, *What are you doing here, you fool, you're supposed to be free and safe somewhere far away from here?*

And yet, my traitorous heart was happy.

When Max took my hands, he didn't need to say a word. I knew exactly what we were doing. I opened my mind and my body to his magic, and he yielded to mine. I almost gasped when he let me into his mind. It was so different from before—walls replaced with claw-gouged passages, as if he had ripped them out with sheer force. They were tender and bleeding, like wounds.

Well… they were wounds, weren't they?

Only one wall remained. It was the thickest, the most imposing. His fingers squeezed mine. His fear shivered through me as if it was my own.

We would dismantle this one together.

—————————

I STAND BEFORE THE DOOR. Max is beside me. He takes my hand. It trembles slightly.

He cannot bring himself to open this door. He has torn out all the rest. But this one he cannot face alone.

I open it for him.

We step through it together. I stand beside him as the memory floods through it. We watch as a younger version of himself falls victim to terrible power he cannot control. We watch him, one by one, slaughter his family.

We end in the cottage in the woods, over the burning body of a twelve-year-old girl.

We end with Max on his hands and knees, weeping.

Max clutches my hand and does not let go.

—————————

I OPENED my eyes to meet his. They were looking at me the way they always had—it was the gaze of someone who knew every word of our story.

Tears streaked his cheeks. I wiped them away with my thumb.

"I love you," I whispered—because what else could I offer him? I could not erase his past. I could not take away his grief. But I could love him, no matter what, always. Was that enough?

Everything was dissolving into streaks of color and light. I now held onto this power by only a single fraying thread of control. My power was a single wing, one half of a scale. I needed him.

"I love you," Max murmured, and opened his second eyelids.

I had forgotten how powerful he was. With the barriers between him and his magic removed, it now met mine with equal strength. The boundaries between us erased, my Valtain magic and his Solarie magic combining into a single symphony.

Together, we reached down, down, down, into the lowest

levels of magic—reached for this power that called to us and repelled us in equal measure.

And it was only with our combined powers, the passage between us opened, that it was distilled into balanced, raw force. Time and place and space disappeared. We were a river stretching out in all directions. We were the bodies and breaths of the soldiers above. We were the sky and the ruins and the city of Niraja in the past and the present. We were ourselves as we were ten years ago, lost, alone, and as we were now—found, together.

We Wielded the core of power like snatching a burning star from the sky.

CHAPTER FIFTY-FIVE

AEFE

Caduan was right. Life existed everywhere, and I spoke to that magic — Wielded it — like it was a language I was born with. The earth shivered beneath my every step. Vines and leaves flourished around me even without my command. Light collected at my fingertips, a purer form of life, of power, that clung to the edge of my blade.

The Arans' monsters had surrounded us, ripping through Fey soldiers and their own alike. Most were in horrible condition, their bodies actively falling apart at the seams. Every one of these beasts had once been a Fey.

The humans had turned our own people against us.

I tore through the humans, one after another after another. Before long, they didn't even try to fight me, instead scrambling away in frenzied — unsuccessful — attempts to escape. I loved their fear. It made me strong.

Was I a monster to them? Good. They had created me.

I found Caduan fighting with Meajqa in the heart of the battle. They were overwhelmed, hordes of soldiers closing in. I relished in Caduan's expression when he saw me — unfettered awe, like the sight of me made him forget that everything else existed.

That look alone told me I had made the right decision.

I whispered to my magic, and bodies fell. I was so drunk on my own power that I didn't count them, didn't watch them die.

I stepped over their corpses to Meajqa and Caduan. Meajqa was wide-eyed and speechless. Caduan barely breathed. He reached out to touch my cheek. "You are—"

A terrible crash rang out. The ground shook. We stumbled, but while Meajqa and Caduan righted themselves quickly, I remained doubled over, my fingers pressed to my forehead.

I could not breathe. Suddenly I was in three places at once— here and somewhere infinitely deeper, connected to two other souls who had once shared mine. An overpowering force swelled there, like a wave preparing to break. Fear cut through my euphoria.

I found myself leaning against Caduan, gripping him so hard my fingernails dug into his shoulders. "Retreat," I gasped.

His brow furrowed.

"Caduan—they *have* it. *Run.*"

His face changed immediately. He whirled to the soldiers, lifted his hand to shoot a flare of magic into the air, and screamed the command. Across the battlefield, Luia followed his lead, and soon Ela'Dar's army fell back in full retreat.

The wave rose, rose. The power of it took my breath away. My heartbeat, my one constant, raced faster and faster.

I turned back, pushing against the tide of soldiers. Caduan grabbed my arm. "Where are you going?"

"I will join you soon."

"No, Aefe. You need to come with—"

"I need to *help* you!" I didn't have time to explain. We were still surrounded by Aran soldiers, Aran soldiers who had no idea what was coming. And the wave that would wipe us out in seconds could be powerful enough to destroy my people if they did not get more time.

Caduan's jaw set. He released my shoulder.

"Come back to me soon," he said, quietly.

I was almost grateful that I had no time to think about all the shades in his voice.

I pulled away from him and ran deeper into Niraja. Aran soldiers surrounded me while the Fey had fallen back.

The wave crested. Magic swelled in the air, thick enough to taste.

I seized upon it. No time to think. Only to act.

I opened my hands. A burst of light enveloped me. The ground shook. Vines and trees shivered and roared. When it faded, bodies piled the ruins. I barely saw them. My ears rang, vision blurring.

The wave broke.

I looked up to see a wall of magic rolling over the ruins, a shimmering sheet of translucent light, nearly invisible, and yet so beautiful I couldn't look away.

The work of a Lejara. It had to be. This kind of power could be nothing else.

How far had Caduan made it? Were they out of the city?

I braced myself and pushed back against that magic with everything I had. I had the ability to reach just as deep. I had a tether that reached just as far. I rooted myself in that weakening connection and pushed back with everything I had, slowing it, stifling it.

I was a single rock standing against rushing rapids—the force merely parted and flowed around me. Pain erupted beneath my skin. I only realized I was screaming when my throat began to hurt.

One second. Two. Three.

Seven.

Ten.

Fifteen.

Thirty.

Were they out yet? Were they free?

I had no choice. When I reached sixty seconds, the wave had begun to calm. I released my hold upon it. For a moment I wavered, my knees feeble. I looked down at the rocks, which danced in my doubling vision.

I needed to run. I needed to go after my people. But I couldn't make myself move. My muscles did not cooperate. I fell—

—Only to be caught by a strong grip.

I thought Caduan's face was a dream.

"That was incredible," he murmured.

"You left." My words slurred. "You are gone."

"No. I sent them away and came back for you."

I struggled to focus my vision. Blue-black streaked his cheek, mottled with violet. I frowned and tried to touch the wounds, but my hand flopped uselessly instead.

"Let's take you home," Caduan said.

Home. Yes. It is nice to have a home.

That was my last thought as I let him carry me away.

CHAPTER FIFTY-SIX

TISAANAH

Shadow and silence surrounded us like a blanket, save for the distant sounds of the soldiers above. The water around our waists was cold.

Max's eyelids slid closed. He was pale and shaking. Water dripped from his hair, mingling with the tears rolling down his cheeks. I tasted salt and realized they streaked mine, too.

"You're back," I choked out, as we collapsed together. Our hands clutched something hard between us—I couldn't look away from him long enough to even see what it was.

He smiled through his tears, and as the rest of my vision faded I thought, *If I die here, what a perfect last sight.*

"I'm back," he said.

CHAPTER FIFTY-SEVEN

MAX

How much does a memory weigh?

A lifetime's worth weighed enough to make my consciousness dull and fuzzy. Tisaanah and I fell together in the swamps of Niraja's ruins. I awoke briefly to Sammerin and Brayan dragging us out of the water.

"What *is* this?" Brayan muttered, reaching for the thing grasped tightly in my hands.

I summoned my nearly non-existent strength to pull it back. Even half-conscious, I knew this thing was important—dangerous. I wouldn't let anyone take it from us.

"Max?" Sammerin leaned over me. The sight of my friend's face summoned an overwhelming onslaught of memories.

"Sammerin," I choked out.

I wasn't sure what I was trying to tell him. But Sammerin's brows lurched, and I knew that even in all the words I left unsaid, he understood that something had changed.

"They're retreating," Sammerin said. "We have a window to go—"

I couldn't keep my eyes open anymore. I let the darkness take me.

PART TWO:
FOUND

CHAPTER FIFTY-EIGHT

MAX

When I woke again—really woke—I was in a bed. That alone was almost enough to convince me that I was dreaming. I sat up to see Sammerin's back, hunched over a desk. Tisaanah was already up, and she gave me a grin that made my heart stop when I rolled over.

Sammerin rose and turned to me, the corner of his mouth lifting in a pleased smirk. "At long last. Welcome back, Max."

Brayan and Sammerin had brought us to a nearby city on the outskirts of Threllian control. They said that the Fey and Aran armies had both retreated once things started to get wild—and, apparently, things did get *very* wild. To hear them tell it, Niraja, even in ruins, no longer existed at all.

"I have never seen anything like it," Sammerin said, when we gathered around the table to regroup. "It was like… the landscape was moving beneath our feet. People were getting caught in rocks and plants that just *moved* of their own accord."

"It was one of the Fey," Brayan said, stiffly, clearly uncomfortable with everything we had witnessed. "She was doing things that no one should be able to do."

"She?" Tisaanah said.

"Reshaye," Sammerin murmured.

The thought made me sick. With the fresh context of my newly restored past, I understood better than ever exactly how bad it was that *thing* not only still existed, but existed *in its own body.*

We needed to change that, and fast.

"It was…" Sammerin frowned. "If I hadn't seen it firsthand, I don't know that I would have believed it. We are in uncharted territory, even by our standards."

As if on cue, we all looked at the table, and the mysterious item that sat at its center.

By the time Tisaanah and I were pulled from the swamps, we barely clung to consciousness. We had hardly looked at the thing we'd dragged back with us. Now, in the harsh light of day, I could appreciate just how unnerving it was.

It was a heart—an anatomical heart that looked as if it had been carved from white marble. Sammerin had examined it thoroughly and told us, with some unease, that it was incredibly accurate, to the point where he suspected it was an actual human heart that had been… preserved? Petrified?

Certainly, it was no normal object. It spoke to some deep power within me, deeper than my flames and even deeper than Reshaye had once drawn from, strange and volatile and… inhuman.

"So is this it?" Sammerin asked, quietly. "Is this what Ishqa had sent us to go find?"

I didn't have an answer to that question that I liked.

Tisaanah looked at her hand—the mark no longer glowed quite as brightly, but it had spread, now crossing the boundary of her wrist. "It's what the wayfinder led me to," she said.

Ishqa had spoken of magic that would spell the life or death of nations. Could this thing do that? It seemed, at once, equal parts impossible and inevitable.

"Ishqa had better get back here," Sammerin muttered.

We all shifted uncomfortably at that. No one had seen Ishqa since Niraja. Sammerin said they had gotten separated when the chaos erupted. While Brayan had found Sammerin, neither of them had been able to locate Ishqa before they were forced to drag Tisaanah and me away.

"He'll find us," Tisaanah said. "He's like a cat. He always makes his way back."

She had a bit more faith in Ishqa's trustworthiness—and durability—than I did. Still, I hoped she was right. I didn't know how we would learn anything at all about this thing without his help.

After a long, awkward silence, Brayan rose, cracking his back.

"We should be safe here for a while," he said. "We give Ishqa three days. After that, we assume he's dead."

Harsh, but fair. We had few other choices in wartime.

"In the meantime," he went on, "I suggest we all get some rest. We aren't in any condition to do anything useful now."

Sammerin nodded. He looked exhausted.

"Good," Brayan said. That was as much of a goodbye as we were going to get. He left without another word.

I glanced at Tisaanah. She was still looking at the heart with an intense concentration etched into her face, a tiny wrinkle between her eyebrows. A dizzy flood of affection fell over me at the sight of it—because it was such a familiar expression, and I loved that it was suddenly so familiar.

Yes, a lifetime of memories was a heavy weight. When they returned, I had thought some of them might break me.

But then, some of them were this.

I brushed my hand over the small of her back. I hadn't been able to help myself. Those little touches had been sprinkled throughout this conversation, like I needed to remind myself that she was here. She looked over her shoulder and smiled, and that made all this other ridiculousness seem inconsequential.

Sammerin stood. "This is disgusting."

"What?"

He gave me a deadpan stare. "Wait until I'm out of the room before you rip each other's clothes off."

"You should be so lucky."

He scoffed as the door slammed behind him.

And finally—finally, finally, finally—we were alone.

Tisaanah stood up and stretched, then gasped sharply. "There has been a terrible mistake."

I leapt to my feet, alarmed. "What?"

She gestured to the room. "There is only one bed in here!"

I exhaled a rough laugh. There was indeed only one bed in here. One wonderful, luxurious bed.

Fine, it was in actuality a tiny, rickety bed that seemed to slant slightly to the left. I didn't care. It was still the best bed I had ever seen.

"Ah. You're right," I said. "That's a problem."

Tisaanah turned to me, her wide eyes sparkling with amusement at her own hilarity. "*Huge* problem." She flailed her arms out, then placed them around my neck. Her accent broke the word up into several sing-song syllables—*hu-u-uge!*

Fuck. I was gone. Even when I didn't know who she was, I was gone.

My hands settled at her waist, our bodies aligning. Her smile faded, the ever-present wrinkle of thought returning as she examined my face.

I pressed my thumb against it. "We don't need this right now."

"Don't we?"

We would, of course. There was so much to talk about, think about, worry about that it made my freshly demolished head spin. But I didn't want to do any of that right now.

Instead, I wanted to re-familiarize myself with her—every part of her. I wanted to trace every scar, the outlines of every shade of her skin, the curve of every muscle or swell of flesh. I wanted to lose myself in her in every sense. I wanted it so much that it overwhelmed me, like a starving man before a feast.

She pressed her hand to mine. Blue-white light shivered at her fingertips. My magic answered that call as if it was second nature. My flames mingled with her cool, smooth light, tickling both of our hands but never burning.

"It's so easy," she said.

"It is," I agreed. The flames intensified, spiraling around my forearm. The lanterns in the room brightened, then dimmed.

"Show off," she said, even as she grinned and let silver butterflies unfurl from her free hand.

"Me? Look at yourself."

"I will not deny it. It's good to finally feel strong again."

I could not imagine Tisaanah ever being anything but strong. Still... I knew what she meant. For six months, I'd been a prisoner of my own body. I'd forgotten how wonderful it was to speak to magic so effortlessly. I vowed to never take it for granted again.

Tisaanah's magic reached out for me, and mine met it with ease—a far cry from the walls that had barred us the last time we tried this. I let her reach into my mind. Let her see everything that evaded words. Let all the boundaries between us fall away.

The lanterns in the room flared again.

I couldn't wait anymore.

I kissed her, hard, and she fell into it immediately, lips parting. She wrapped her arms around my neck and I pulled her closer—still not close enough. She tasted like home. Like everything good about reclaiming where I had been.

We stumbled to the bed, our kisses growing more frantic, my grip around her tightening as my grip on everything else fell away. I didn't give a damn about Ilyzath or my memories or the Fey or the end of the world. All those things became utterly inconsequential compared to the almost-sound that Tisaanah made when my hand slid over her breast, and the slight parting of her thighs as we collided gracelessly with the edge of the mattress.

No. None of those serious, important things would matter again, I decided, for a very long time.

My hand slipped between us, my fingertips barely brushing

the apex of her thighs over the too-thick fabric of her trousers, and Tisaanah drew in a desperate gasp against my mouth.

If I was a stronger man, I could be patient. I could take my time to re-familiarize myself with her slowly, inch by inch, over the course of hours.

Her hips lurched, and she fell back onto the bed, pulling me with her. Our kisses never broke. I reached for her shirt, closed my fingers lightly around the seam.

I decided that I was fucking weak.

The fabric was thin. The buttons tore off easily. Tisaanah wore no undergarments, her beautiful breasts exposed to the chill of the air, peaked by the cold. I abandoned her lips to taste each one, a louder, so much more satisfying moan escaping her as I swirled my tongue around each peak.

Even her *skin* tasted like citrus.

"Max," she breathed—a request, a plea—and I had so missed the way she said my name. I had to pause, look down at her splayed out messily on the bed beneath me, lips swollen, skin bared, hair fanned out in tangles around her.

"Max…" she murmured again.

"I know."

Fuck, did I know.

She started to unbutton my shirt, and I ripped it off over my head. She unbuttoned her pants and before she had even finished the motion, my hand was sliding down between her legs.

She whimpered, her hips bucking against me, and I groaned a curse. My trousers were painful.

She freed me from them, and I hissed another, more creative expletive as her grasp settled around my length.

I kissed her deeply, cupping her tipped-back chin as my tongue explored her mouth. "I need you now," I growled into her lips. "I can't wait."

She breathed in Thereni, "Yes."

We weren't even completely on the bed, her backside barely resting against it, me still kneeling on the ground and leaning over her. She kicked down her trousers just enough to open her legs. She was so wet that even the first stroke was hard, deep, her hips rising to meet mine with equal force.

She said again, in Thereni, "Yes," and I decided it was my new favorite word—decided it over and over as she moaned it again, as I drove into her again, again, again. One hand clutched a fistful of her hair—the other gripped the curve where her waist met her hip, bracing her.

I could fucking die here.

Like I said, I was weak.

This wasn't sweet, slow lovemaking. Wasn't a languid reunion. This was frantic, desperate, feral.

Her thighs tightened around me. Her teeth closed on my lip, hard enough to draw forth a spike of pain and the taste of iron. I felt her coiling, felt her muscles tightening.

I was greedy. I gripped her wrists above her head, stretching her beneath me so I could take her whole body, push myself deeper.

I'd almost forgotten how fucking beautiful she was when she climaxed. I had to stop kissing her just so I could watch her, control fully relinquished, her head thrown back, lips parted and muscles trembling as she contracted around me.

The sight pushed me to the edge. I thrust deeper into her and threw myself over it, burying my face against her neck, tasting her skin, teeth marking her as I groaned her name.

The intensity of it washed me away.

When the wave crashed and faded, I was face down in her hair. Her chest heaved under mine as she struggled to catch her breath.

Everything in the world was a little fuzzier and softer. I felt content. Not sated—yet—but content.

We lay in silence, not moving, the room soundless save for our serrated breaths.

Then I pushed myself to my elbows and turned to her.

"I'm fucking *furious* with you."

CHAPTER FIFTY-NINE

TISAANAH

I'm fucking furious with you.

That cut through the post-sex contented haze. My eyes snapped open to see him leaning over me, lips thinned, stare sharp with anger.

"Do you know how close I came to not being here right now because of you, Tisaanah?"

Oh.

I had been dreading this conversation.

Max rolled off of me and straightened his trousers as we both shifted fully onto the bed.

"It is a waste of time to put those back on," I said.

"Don't try to distract me with your wiles."

"My wiles?"

Wy-uls. It was a little exciting to find a new Aran word after so long.

"You told me to fucking leave."

I bit my lip and looked away. I didn't have anything to say for myself. With one finger, he steered my chin back to him. "It was luck that I decided to come back, you know that? Pure luck."

"Why did you?"

The corners of his mouth tightened. "Because I realized that, even though I didn't remember you, I *knew* you. That sort of thing was bigger than a few memories." He shook his head, looking slightly embarrassed. "It sounds ridiculous, but it's the best way I can describe it."

"It doesn't sound ridiculous at all."

His words, clumsy as they were, touched me deeper than I could express. I meant it—it was not ridiculous. Once I'd thought that love was the sum of its parts, the result of a collection of traits and experiences, like a structure steadily built from bricks layered over bricks. If you collect enough of them, there is love. But that had been a child's view of the world. The bricks were important, but what they created was more than just a pile of stones. It was the difference between a house and a home. If the building burns down, something is still there that makes it home.

If the memories are gone, something is still there that makes it love.

"Are you glad you came back?" I asked, quietly.

Max glanced pointedly at my naked body and said, "Yes," as if it was a very stupid question.

"No jokes. You know what I am asking."

Was it worth it?

Was I worth remembering?

His face softened. His fingertips traced the curve of my cheek. "You want the truth? The memories are hard, yes. But none of that scared me as much as the prospect of exactly how close I came to never seeing you again. *That's* what fucking terrifies me."

"I'm sorry," I said, my voice rougher than I intended. "I just… your past held so many horrible things. Most people never get the opportunity for a second chance without it. I thought that if anyone deserved that freedom, it would be you. I thought you would *want* that."

"I was still the result of all those things, even if there was a wall keeping me from them. I would have had to confront them sooner or later."

He was trying very hard to sound blasé about it, but I knew him well enough to see that it was ever-so-slightly forced.

"I'm glad that you were with me when I did," he said. "Even though you were infuriatingly determined to make that not be the case."

"I was —"

"You were trying to do what's right. I know, you insufferable, stubborn creature." He gripped my chin, his eyes searching my face. "Listen," he said, after a long pause. "I'm not much for words, so I'll only say this once. If you ever have to guess what I want, or what is best for me, *it is you*. Alright? I have made that decision already. I do not make it lightly. Don't disrespect that by claiming that you know better for me than I do. I have made bad decisions before. But you are not, never have been, and never will be one of them. It is *always* you."

I didn't know what to say to that. If I opened my mouth, I was certain that whatever sounds would come out would be pathetically weepy.

Perhaps a stranger might have looked at my life and seen a series of misfortunes. But here, in this moment, I could not imagine being more blessed — more gluttonous — with luck.

I didn't have any other response but to kiss him. The kiss quickly deepened, until I found myself half draped over him on the bed, my bare breasts pressed to his chest. Desire stirred in my core, simmering but never satisfied from our earlier tryst. The night was young. We had our whole lives, and almost certainly an early death, to sleep.

"I need verbal confirmation of your understanding, Vytezic," Max murmured between kisses.

"I understand, captain."

His lips curled into a sly smile. "General. I was promoted, remember."

"Don't get too full of yourself, mysterious snake man."

He laughed — a beautiful sound — and grabbed my waist to

pull me on top of him, my thighs straddling his hips. The hardness pressing against my core was enough to make my own laugh die on my lips.

"So demanding," he said, as his hands slowly ran up my sides. "Put me in my place, then."

I reached down and pulled down his trousers, lifting my eyebrow at him. "I told you not to put these on."

"You were right."

"I always am."

"Not *always*."

I discarded his trousers with the rest of our clothes on the floor. I crawled back over him, trailing kisses up his body—his knee, his thigh, his hip—and at last at his cock, which I kissed too, then ran my tongue up in languid, slow strokes.

Max groaned, his hand falling to the back of my head, and the sound became a hiss as I took him in my mouth.

He said my name like a prayer. Gods, I loved that—not only the sound of his pleasure but, selfishly, the control it gave me. I loved the way he tasted, the way his muscles tensed as I worked. I pressed my palm to his abdomen and his other hand, the one not clutching my hair, covered it in a gesture that was surprisingly tender compared to the force of his grip.

I pushed deeper, and Max let out a louder curse.

"Stop, Tisaanah. This isn't how I want to go."

I lifted my head enough to bat my eyelashes at him.

"Really?"

"Not this time."

I wanted to challenge him just because I could, but the desire at the apex of my thighs—a yawning emptiness that demanded more—told me otherwise. Before we had taken each other fast and hard, but I wanted to relish how he felt inside me.

I let him pull me back to him, into a long kiss. That, too, was different from before. Slower exploration, carefully marking each other's mouths. His hands ran up my back, tracing the shape of my scars.

His hardness nudged my entrance. I was ready. All it took

was one shift in my hips to lower myself over him. Slowly, this time, savoring every inch that stretched me—savoring what it felt like to be together again.

We both groaned into our shared serrated breaths. His hands moved to my thighs, gripping them hard enough to no-doubt leave marks in the pale patches of my flesh, but he didn't try to move. We were perfectly still and yet acutely aware of each other, and how every expanse of skin felt against the other.

Slowly, I sat up, breath hitching as the movement made him press deeper inside of me. It was almost enough to give in to what I wanted so badly—wanted more friction, more movement, wanted to forego patience in favor of our earlier frantic pace.

But instead I just looked at him.

When I was touching him, I knew his body so well that even the parts of him that had changed were inconsequential. But visually? Visually, he looked so different. The sheer amount of alchemical ink that now marked him still shocked me. The marks were even more jarring now that the Stratagrams had been broken, so the tattoos were not circles but sharp lines layered over each other. I traced one of them with my fingertip over his stomach, making his abs twitch and an almost-laugh escape from between his teeth.

"Don't do that to me now," he said. "I'm begging you."

"I hate them."

"The tattoos?" When I nodded, he said, "I think they make me look mysterious and dangerous." His hips shifted, his hands running up and down my waist—pausing at the top to press his thumb over my breast. "Don't you want a mysterious and dangerous lover?"

The spark of pleasure almost distracted me. Almost.

"I don't hate… *them*. But I hate that you have them."

"I don't hate anything right now." His hips shifted again, and this time I couldn't help but meet the movement with my own, drawing moans from both of us. His touch migrated to my back, fingers playing at the raised skin of my scars, and for a moment his eyes darkened. "Well. Some things."

366

At least we understood each other: *I love your scars and hate the person who gave them to you.*

"Come here," he said. "I miss you. Thank you for giving me such a lovely view. But too much talking. Not enough fucking."

He pulled me down to him, gave me a long kiss that made me forget my own name—made me forget everything except delirious agreement with him—*yes, too much talking, not enough fucking.* Without my permission, my hips began to move, rolling over him again, again, again, in a slow, building rhythm. The pleasure built like the sound of an orchestra, round and full, overtaking all my senses. I kissed his lips, his cheeks, his forehead, his throat.

More. I wanted so much more.

My movements became more demanding, and he met them with equal fervor. My climax was rushing towards me, and I was eager to fall over the edge with him. But just as I was about to crest, he lifted me off of him and pushed me to the bed.

I let out a wordless whimper of frustration.

"Patience." His smug smirk was warm in his voice.

I cussed at him in Thereni, and he laughed. "You actually taught me that one."

I hurled another, even more offensive expletive at him—one that I definitely had not taught him—and he laughed again as he gently turned me so I was on my side and positioned himself behind me. We were both lying on the bed, one of his arms around my shoulders, the warmth of his body curled around mine. Then he slid his free hand down over my body—pausing at my breasts, which made me moan and move impatiently against him, then my stomach, and finally, ending at the ache in my core. His fingers moved agonizingly lightly there, barely touching me. Against my permission, my body pushed towards him, begging for more, but his grip on my shoulders kept me still.

"I want to be able to see you *and* feel you when you come for me this time," he murmured in my ear, closing his teeth around the shell of it in a gentle bite as he opened my thighs and slid back into me.

Stars erupted over my vision. The position and angle left me at his mercy, but even his willpower was only so strong. He pumped in and out of me as I spread wider for him, my body now nearly draped over his. His hand stroked the length of my body as if he wanted to feel all of me, trace every muscle and inch of flesh, the movements more frantic as our pace quickened.

"I missed you," I moaned, almost a sob—gods, it could have been a sob, I could barely feel my own body anymore, could barely form words. "I missed you so much."

I turned my face back towards him, blindly, not sure what I wanted but knowing I wanted something, anything, everything. He kissed my mouth. Kissed the tear rolling down my cheek. Then kissed my ear as he said, "I missed you, too. I missed you so fucking much, Tisaanah."

He pushed into me in one powerful thrust, in the same moment that his fingers found my core, strumming me like my pleasure was an instrument completely at his mercy.

I shattered into a million pieces. I was nothing but this, but him, and the oblivion we shared. I didn't even care if I was ever put back together.

THE HOURS PASSED in a euphoric blur. We drew the curtains and let the outside world cease to exist. It took a few minutes to collect myself after that. We didn't say another word to each other. He just got up, got me a glass of water, and then settled back behind me so I was nestled against him, sheltered in his embrace, and the two of us dozed off into the quiet twilight of sleep. I had no idea how many hours it had been when I rolled back over him, still half-asleep, and our bodies melted together again in sleepy, languid strokes.

Each time we woke, it was like we rediscovered each other and were overcome yet again with blissful relief.

Eventually, we dragged ourselves to the washroom and washed ourselves off—after, of course, crawling all over each other in the steaming water and washing ourselves off again. We climbed out of the tub, only to make it about three steps and fall together on the floor.

That time, Max pulled away from me long enough to look around with faux horror.

"I feel bad for whoever has this room after we do."

"I don't," I said. "I'm sure we are not the first to—"

"Stop." He put his finger over my lips. "Don't say it. It will ruin everything if I have to think of any other human being doing the disgusting acts on this floor that I want to do to you right now."

I made a show of pressing my lips closed. "I am silent." Then I opened my arms. "Now debase me."

He leaned down to kiss me over the still-pointedly-closed seam of my lips. "If you insist."

———————————

ALL GOOD THINGS, of course, must end—and those two days, exhausted and euphoric and sex-drenched, were the best of good things.

Max and I were asleep when there was a pounding on the door. We lay in bed face-to-face. Our eyes both opened at the same time, and neither of us moved at all, just looking at each other. In that moment, we shared a grim, silent acknowledge-ment of what was about to happen—that we were about to open that door and return to the real world of terrible, complicated things, and people who needed us.

Whoever was at the door banged on it again, louder.

Max's thumb brushed my cheek. "I had a lovely time with you."

I kissed his palm. "Me too."

Then I got up, threw on a shirt and my trousers—gods, I was a bit sore—and opened the door.

Ishqa looked unhappy enough that I decided not to point out

that it was the second time that he had interrupted my nice moment with his grim tidings.

"You made it back," I said, relieved.

Ishqa said, "We need to talk."

"Sounds like bad news," Max said, leaning against the door-frame as he shook out his own crumpled-up shirt.

Ishqa looked genuinely perplexed by this comment. "Is there any other type?"

CHAPTER SIXTY

AEFE

I stared at myself in the mirror.

For months, I had avoided doing that. I didn't like to look at myself and see a stranger who was nothing but a mimicry of a person I used to be many years ago. Now, for the first time in a long time, I realized that perhaps there was more to see in myself.

Or perhaps I only felt it because I was dressed... well, like this.

My gown was long enough to brush the ground, sparkling ebony chiffon pooling at my feet. The fabric was dark as the night sky, woven with tiny threads of silver, so as the dress hugged the swells or dips of my body, the light did too. It was tight across my breasts, my waist, and my hips, before flaring out into loose layers of black over my legs, with a high slit that allowed me to walk somewhat easily. The neckline plunged in a sharp V that ended at my sternum, held up by silver straps over my shoulders. Two long strips fell down my back like a cape.

My face had been painstakingly painted, my lips colored with a tiny brush dipped in crimson, my eyes lined and powdered and lined again with shades of purple and brown and black. My hair piled atop my head, several strands of deep red dangling around my cheeks.

When the maid finally allowed me to look in the mirror, the shock of it stunned me into silence. In the week since we had returned from Niraja, I'd felt like an exhausted, walking corpse. Now, though my injuries had not fully healed, I looked like an entirely different person.

"Beautiful," the maid said. She sounded a bit surprised.

At first, it seemed strange to adorn this body. Like decorating a prison cell. But...

I drew my eyes over my form. I had grown more muscular, my posture stronger. I no longer looked like someone inhabiting a vessel that did not fit me. This was a powerful body. I had used it to do incredible things.

Perhaps that was worth adorning.

Still, something here didn't seem quite right.

The maid let out a strangled gasp of horror as I drew the back of my hand across my eyes, smearing the sharp perfection of my eyeliner, and then my lips, blotting down the bright red.

"Oh no, why would you—"

At last, I smiled at myself. My lips were stained as if by berries. Darkness now smudged my eyes, enhancing their size and downturned shape.

There. This was me.

"Much better," I said.

The maid looked like she was about to cry.

The door opened, and Meajqa and Luia entered. Meajqa's eyes ran up my body, brows arching. "I suspected you'd clean up nicely, but I have to say, this exceeds my expectations."

He looked magnificent himself. He wore black trousers that followed the shape of his legs and a long jacket made from threads of many shades of gold. A long swath of metallic bronze draped from his hip over one shoulder, hanging down his back between his wings. I'd seen many of his kind wear similar clothing, but I wondered if this style was chosen for reasons beyond fashion—the fabric partially covered the stump of his missing wing.

Luia was just as impressively dressed, donning embroidered trousers in deep emerald green and a long white jacket that flared out behind her with every step. Still, she looked unhappy. "We should be working," she grumbled. "Not wasting time on festivals."

Meajqa scoffed. "So negative. We have dead to send off. We have a victory to celebrate and a war to survive. It sounds like a perfect time to get uproariously drunk to me."

What he did not say aloud still came to me clearly: *Because we might not have the chance to again.*

Tonight was the Eve of Occassus, the largest celebration in Ela'Dar all year. Meajqa described it to me as a festival of death and rebirth, intended to celebrate the cycle of life and bring forth a new year. The night would begin with a ceremony to send off the dead and end with a feast to bring in new life.

"Along with all the other fun that entails!" Meajqa had said, with a sly smile and a pointed look. I did not understand what he meant and did not ask.

In some ways, it seemed strange to celebrate now. The casualties from Niraja had barely been laid to rest. The wounded were only just starting to heal. Even the shallowest of my own injuries had hardly begun to scab over.

And of course, we all knew it was only the beginning. I had tasted blood and I wanted more, and I knew I was not the only one who did. I had watched humans kill my people. We had allowed a terrible and powerful magic to slip from our grasp.

But with that defeat had also come victory. We had dealt a devastating blow to Ara's forces. And we had reclaimed our own power—*I* had reclaimed my own power.

So perhaps I understood when Meajqa had said, "The dead should be mourned properly, and there is no greater collective mourning than the Eve of Occassus. And our victory should be celebrated properly, and there is no greater night of celebration, either."

So even with our society in shambles, the festival went on.

"I, for one, expect this to be the best of our celebrations," Meajqa continued. "Death is a powerful aphrodisiac, and it came closer than ever this week. Besides, if this war kills us, at least we will have had our fun before we go." His smile stiffened in that way I could always recognize—when it shifted from something genuine to something forced. "During Occassus last year, I was locked up in that Aran bitch's dungeon, getting my wing hacked off. I plan to enjoy this one to the fullest."

He lifted his glass and took a long drink.

Luia eyed him, disapproval warring with concern. "You should slow down. You have scriptures to read."

"I am perfectly fit for reading scriptures, thank you."

I looked past Luia and Meajqa, to the empty hallway beyond them.

"Where is Caduan?" I had barely seen him since our return to Ela'Dar, save for a few brief appearances during which he seemed tired and disengaged.

"He has many required duties ahead of the festival," Luia said, as we went to the door. "You'll see him there."

Meajqa again looked me up and down. "He'll certainly be happy to see you," he said, draining his glass.

———————————

THE FUNERAL WAS HELD beneath the moonlight at the edge of the palace grounds, where the rocks of the mountains met the forest. The entire area—grounds and city streets alike—had been cleared and meticulously decorated for the event, every inch of the walls covered in flowers and greeneries, bundled with silver fabric and filigreed decor.

Caduan and Meajqa stood by a stone platform, empty save for a small table at its center with a ceramic bowl upon it. The rest of us gathered around the stage, the crowd so thick that it sprawled out far into the streets of the city.

I stood close to the front with Luia and watched Caduan and

Meajqa. Caduan's clothing was comparatively simple compared to the elaborate outfits I had seen many wearing, and yet he managed to look more striking than any of them. He wore deep green and gold, his coat flawlessly fitted to the shape of his body, and a cape of bronze falling down his back. It matched the shade of his stag-horn crown, which he rarely wore but now sat upon waves of auburn hair looking as if it belonged nowhere else.

I wanted him to look at me — *why did I want him to look at me?* — but he didn't acknowledge the crowd at all. He simply ascended the steps with Meajqa and turned his back to us, facing the forested hills and distant moon.

Meajqa held a large, leather-bound book in his hands, from which he began to read. He told a story about death, and all the things that death fueled in this world. I listened in fascination. But only a few lines into the speech, Meajqa's voice faltered. The words blended together like running paint. He needed to stop, then start, then stop, then start again.

Warmth crawled up my neck as I watched him, ashamed on his behalf.

He glanced up at the crowd just once, for a split second, and he looked like an embarrassed child.

But there was not a hint of judgement in Caduan's form as he calmly turned to Meajqa, laid a hand on his shoulder, took the book, and began to read.

Meajqa turned his back and faced the sky, hands clasped before him, and Caduan took up the verses. His voice was smooth and melodic, like the sound of the wind through the trees —a part of nature, speaking of natural things.

"Is he speaking to the gods?" I whispered to Luia.

She gave me a strange look. "The gods?"

"Is it prayer?"

"There are no gods, Aefe." She said this as if it was obvious. "He is speaking to *us.*"

Caduan's deep voice rang out with solemn reverence, speaking of the cycle of death and life the way one would address a power so much greater than themselves.

He is speaking to us.

Without thinking, I pressed my hand to my chest, feeling my own heartbeat.

A power greater than ourselves.

Perhaps we didn't need gods to find our place in something larger. Perhaps it already existed in us.

When the verses ended, Caduan turned the book to its final page and withdrew a piece of parchment. He unfolded it as he and Meajqa gathered around the ceramic bowl, both looking out to the forest.

And then Caduan began to read names. The first one was Iajqa Sai'Ess. It was, I realized, a list of the dead.

With each name, Meajqa threw a handful of ash into the sky. The ashes swirled against the stars for a moment, as if carried on an unnatural current of wind, dancing before the moon before falling into the trees below.

Caduan just kept reading, and reading, and reading.

The crowd grew so silent it was like we had all stopped breathing.

"Normally this is only a few names long," Luia whispered, her voice slightly rough.

But Caduan read name after name after name. The floor of the forest must have been covered with ash.

CHAPTER SIXTY-ONE

MAX

We settled in Sammerin's room, which was the only one large enough to have a sitting area. I was actually surprised to see the blinding sunlight streaming through the curtains. I had lost all perception of time. I wandered about the room, looking for a calendar that I could casually glance at in a way that would tell no one that I'd been so busy sleeping and fucking that I literally didn't know what day it was anymore.

Not that my subtlety fooled Sammerin, who gave us one look up-and-down and remarked, drily, "I'm glad I had the foresight to make sure my room wasn't next to yours."

"So superior. As if you've been sitting here all alone like a priest." I picked up a discarded hair clip from the end table and arched an eyebrow at Sammerin, who shrugged as if to say, *Fair enough.*

Despite myself, I smiled.

It was strange. I had been traveling with Sammerin for weeks, and yet, the restoration of my memory gave me a new appreciation for my friend. I'd missed him.

Ishqa sat down, unamused. He looked tired.

"Where have you been?" I asked, trying to keep the accusation from my voice and not quite succeeding.

I wasn't sure why I didn't trust Ishqa. Was it just because I knew he had betrayed his friend, and that sort of thing, even five hundred years later, bore a mark on his character that I couldn't shake?

I was self-aware enough to recognize the hypocrisy of that, if so.

"Here." Ishqa produced a letter and slid it to Tisaanah. "For you."

Tisaanah's throat bobbed. She opened it and read silently — and a grin broke out across her face. "Orasiev held."

"They withstood weeks of onslaught from the Threllian military."

Tisaanah sagged against the table in relief. "Thank the gods."

I eyed Ishqa. "So why do you look so unhappy?"

He stared at me just long enough to be unnerving. "Something is different about you."

"Something is the same again, actually." I tapped my temple.

His brows rose slightly. "How?"

"He broke down the barriers separating him from his magic, just as Klasto and Blif said," Tisaanah said. "When we retrieved this."

She placed the petrified heart on the table.

Ishqa blinked at it, utterly stunned. "This is it?" he murmured.

"Apparently so," I said. "Not that we have any clue what it is, or does, or how we use it. That, actually, is what we were hoping you could tell us."

"If it is an object, then it must be a conduit. An object that calls and channels the magic beneath."

"And who made this conduit?" I asked. "Why is it a heart?"

"And whose heart is it?" Sammerin added, a little too quickly, like he'd been thinking about this question for the last two days.

"I do not think that is relevant," Ishqa replied.

"I think it's very relevant," I said. "I'd like to know who is going to come haunt me because I've been carting around his heart."

"It could be a her," Tisaanah pointed out.

"Fair. His or her heart."

"If it *is* a person's heart, it would be from many thousands of years ago," Ishqa said. "Likely from long before the initial fall and re-opening of magic a millennium ago. Whoever forged these channels did it so long ago that even my ancestors have forgotten these facets of history." The corner of his mouth rose in a rueful, humorless smile. "Humans and Fey alike have been hungry for power they should not have for as long as we have existed. Whoever created it very well may have ended up destroying themselves with it."

"Lovely," I muttered.

"Which is why, however we decide to use it, we must be very careful with it," Ishqa said.

"Maybe we shouldn't be using it at all." I knew too well the negative consequences of playing around with that kind of power. I had no desire to unleash another Reshaye upon the world—at least, not any more than we already had.

"If we are able to make that choice," Tisaanah muttered.

"The important thing is that we obtained it before Caduan or Nura did. I think that is clearer than ever, after seeing what it is capable of. Little remains of what was once Niraja, and what is left is… different."

"Different?" I asked.

"I do not know how else to describe it. I went back to the ruins after the soldiers fled, when it was quiet. The stone is… different. The marble is as clean and white as it must have been a thousand years ago. But it is uncut, as it would be when it was harvested, no longer forged into pillars and bricks but lying over the island like mountains."

Well. That was… strange.

Tisaanah and I exchanged a glance. We'd barely been conscious down there, with no way to really know what we were doing. The whole thing felt more like a fever dream than an intentional Wielding of magic.

"I have never heard of anyone doing anything like that," I said. "Let alone at that scale. A thing can't just be changed into another thing."

Tisaanah jolted, like a thought just hit her hard. "Klasto told us that there were rumored to be three types of deep magic," she said. "One creates life, one destroys life, and one changes life."

We all looked at the heart in the middle of the table with fresh eyes. Ishqa let out a strangled chuckle. "A mortal heart. The most fickle of things for a fickle, changing magic."

Ascended fucking above.

"So if this magic gives us the power to... change life... what does that mean, exactly?" I said. "Could we stroll over to Cadu-an's army and change them all into frogs?"

"And why stone?" Tisaanah mused, deep in thought.

"Was 'change' a direct translation?" Sammerin said.

Tisaanah seemed to understand immediately what Sammerin was asking. "In Old Besrithian, the word for 'change' only refers to... the way things change over time. Like..." She struggled to find the Aran translation.

"Evolution," I finished.

"The city was built of stone, and once those stones were mountains, so they became mountains," Sammerin said.

"This is all *ridiculous*." Brayan looked like he wanted to peel off his own skin.

"I think we must let go of the notion that any magic this old and volatile will ever bend fully to the bounds of mortal logic," Ishqa said, remarkably calmly. "None of it will make sense the way we want it to make sense."

The rest of us gave him a flat stare and took a long moment to mourn our sanity.

"Well." Tisaanah rubbed her temples. "At least now we have ammunition. Until we know where the other magics are, we should go to Orasiev and work with the rebellion against the Threllians."

Ishqa's face changed immediately. "The Threllians? No. We go after the Aran queen."

"The closest thing we have to an army is the rebellion, and they cannot help us when they are fighting for their survival. If we defeat the Threllians, we rip out the teeth of Caduan's army, give ourselves more resources, and free the rebels to help us against Nura and Caduan."

She was right. The only resources we had were tied up in a war against the Threllian Lords.

"There's a factor we aren't considering," Sammerin said. "Perhaps we can work on both fronts. Nura has never been very popular, even before all this. And while she managed to build a legal claim to her power, I don't doubt that most understand exactly how tenuous it is. Perhaps our allies there could lay groundwork before we arrive."

The name came to me immediately. Tisaanah glanced at me, like she was having the same thought.

"Iya," we both said.

The most reasonable person who sat in Orders leadership — and the Councilor who had backed me in my attempted bid for Arch Commandant.

Sammerin's brow knitted. "I'm surprised she allowed him to stay in his role."

"She needed the support of the Council," I said. "The rules she built her claim on would collapse beneath her if she openly executed Orders leadership."

"*Openly*," Tisaanah muttered. "I hope he has someone testing his food."

Ascended above, I hoped so, too.

"Fine. Iya," I said. "I trust him. So how do we communicate with him? Communications to and from the Towers are being monitored closely, I'm sure."

"I can handle it," Brayan said. "Roseteeth Company whisper networks reach everywhere, Ara included."

I scoffed. "We were just run out of town by mercenaries, and you want us to trust the Roseteeth with something this sensitive?"

Brayan looked offended. "The Roseteeth are not *mercenaries*, they're—"

"A 'private army.' Sure. And the man who tried to kill you in the streets of Zagos? Was he a 'private soldier' too?"

Brayan's lip twitched. "I trust these men and women with my life. But if you don't, fine. What is your alternative?"

At the ensuing silence, his lips curled into a smug smirk that looked exactly the same as it did when he was an obnoxious know-it-all eighteen-year-old.

Tisaanah rose, pressing her palms to the table. "Fine. Then it is decided. We will go to Orasiev first, move against the Threllians, and, by extension, the Fey. We will keep our fingers on the pulse of Ara through Iya."

I nodded. "And when the time is right, we strike. Hopefully, by then, with the force of the rebels behind us, too."

We looked around for confirmation. Sammerin nodded, and Brayan let out a grunt of agreement.

I sighed. "It seems as good a plan as any." It was the most enthusiasm I could muster.

Ishqa was silent, his jaw so tight it trembled.

"Ishqa?" Tisaanah pressed.

"It does not seem like enough."

"It—?"

He stood so abruptly that he nearly knocked over his chair, eyes bright and furious. The change in him was startling. "Your human queen tortured my son, and she did the same to my sister. She turned her into a monster. I fought *my own sister* in Niraja. The Aran queen deserves death for what she has done."

Gone was the elegant, calm Fey who seemed like he might as well be made from marble. This was the face of someone out for blood.

I almost said, *You sound like your king.*

A wrinkle of pity deepened between Tisaanah's brows. "I'm so sorry, Ishqa," she murmured. "I didn't know…"

Ishqa drew in a deep breath, then let it out again as he struggled to collect himself.

"I understand you," Brayan said quietly. "Trust me, when I confronted the people who killed my sisters…" He shook his head, once, a sharp movement that said more than words could. I had to look away, suddenly nauseous.

"You are not the only one who wants her gone," Tisaanah added. "And she will be. I promise you."

Ishqa sank back into his chair. "I know. I—I apologize." He folded his hands carefully over the table, his eyes downcast. Then he let out a rough, humorless laugh, a sound so odd it struck me off guard. I had never heard him laugh before.

Sammerin, Brayan, Tisaanah, and I exchanged awkward glances.

"It is just… sometimes, I understand him," Ishqa said, shaking his head. "Caduan. I despise what he is doing in the name of his vengeance. I despise what he is doing to the world, to all of us. But I understand him. At times, that seems like cruelest part of this of all. We all feel the same things, and we will still die trying to kill each other for it."

CHAPTER SIXTY-TWO

AEFE

In the aftermath of death, everyone was only more eager to celebrate life.

When the feast began, wine glasses were emptied in seconds. The music was so loud it vibrated in our bones, great cacophonous sounds that seemed at first like they didn't belong together, but soon became inseparable. Long tables were brought out, so many that they were forced wherever they would fit—not only on the stone patio of the palace, where Caduan sat at the head of a massive table that must have dined fifty, but also throughout the streets, wobbling legs on uneven cobblestones steadied with whatever people had on hand.

There was food everywhere, and more platters brought out before the current ones even began to be exhausted. The table became a painting of colors—the deep bronze of roasted meat, the bright red of berries, the purples of root vegetables, the white of cream cakes, the cream of great bowls of sauces or soups.

Meajqa and Luia quickly entertained themselves with others. I sat between them, close enough that their elbows jabbed me with every one of their gesticulations, but feeling very alone.

I glanced up to the head of the table at Caduan, who looked

deeply engaged in whatever Vythian was talking to him about. He met my stare and gave me the faintest ghost of a smile before looking away.

The night quickly turned to joyful euphoria. The music grew louder, more frenetic—the guests grew more drunk and affectionate. Plates of food were abandoned for dance floors, where Fey reveled in the movements of each other's bodies. All those impeccable outfits devolved into sloppy streaks of color. Couples, or more than couples, fell all over each other, delighting in unraveling each other's clothing.

I watched this in fascination. This sort of pleasure was oddly foreign to me, like a mathematical equation I had yet to decode.

Meajqa was suddenly beside me, caressing the bare skin of my shoulders. If his misstep at the ceremony still bothered him, he hadn't shown it—he had joined the festivities with seemingly carefree enthusiasm.

"Dance with me, Aefe," he purred in my ear, words slightly slurred. "We both look too good not to."

"I do not know how."

"It's alright. I'll teach you." His fingers trailed my arm, making goosebumps rise to the surface. "Or we could skip the dancing part."

I frowned, confused. I did not know what that meant.

He took a seat beside me. "Would you like to be alone, Aefe? Find a little pleasure together?" he said quietly. He smiled, but this time, it struck me as a sad expression. "Maybe us broken things need to stay together."

The realization hit me—*sex*. He was talking about sex.

I considered it. Meajqa was a handsome man. And perhaps he was right. We were both broken. Perhaps there would be no better person to show all my ragged edges to.

But it didn't seem… right. So I shook my head and said, "No, Meajqa."

Meajqa gave me a wry shrug. "I had to ask." He stood, kissed me on the cheek—so unexpected it made me jump—and was off again to the dance floor, a bright smile lighting up his face as if our solemn moment had never happened.

———————

I SAT ALONE for some time longer. Luia had long ago abandoned her seat in favor of dancing, leaving me to be the only one on this side of the table, elbows leaning in the only patch of clear space among discarded plates and half-empty wine glasses.

I became aware of Caduan before he spoke, in a way that hit my every sense at once.

"Did you like the ceremony?" he asked, behind me.

I turned. I realized that something had indeed changed in how I perceived this world. I now understood how to truly admire beauty. And when I looked at Caduan now, I thought, *Beautiful.*

He sat in Luia's empty chair, waiting for my answer.

"It was…" I paused, and then said the only word that my mind would now produce. "Beautiful." I looked around at all the celebrating. "It is strange that no one seems sad."

"Why would they be sad?"

"There was so much death."

"Death is not a reason to be sad."

I thought of what Caduan had said to the Fey lying on the table, rescued from the Aran queen, what seemed like a lifetime ago.

Death is not an end. Death is a door.

"Do you truly believe that?" I asked.

"I do."

You can not lie to me, I thought.

And it was a lie. I knew this because he had gone to such lengths to return me from death. Perhaps death was a door, but if it was, he had torn it open to drag me back.

This realization made me uncomfortable. I did not like to think of Caduan as a hypocrite.

"But, I think there is certainly plenty to love about life, too, and it should be saved whenever possible." Caduan looked at my plate, then at the dance floor. "You aren't eating or dancing. Why not?"

"I just… I don't feel the way that they do about these things."

His smile softened. "You looked a bit lonely over here."

Not anymore, I thought.

"I confess that I often feel like an outsider, too," he said. "I was watching you and thought, 'She looks just like I feel.'"

"But you looked so—"

"Attentive?" He let out a short laugh. "Do you remember how I used to be? I used to think there was no value in pretending for pleasantries like this. But when I built Ela'Dar, I realized that people sometimes need you to be a different version of yourself. Sometimes, it being important to them"—he nodded out to the dancing crowd—"is enough to make it important to me. So I pretend."

"You lie."

"It isn't a lie. I respect my people and what matters to them. And besides…" He took in the surrounding celebration. "This has grown to mean a lot to me, too. It is important to remember the joy in being alive."

The joy in being alive.

Was that what it was when I felt Caduan's heartbeat?

Caduan watched me like I was a puzzle he was trying to put together. "You should eat. The food is delicious. The best of the year."

The overflowing plates overwhelmed me. I didn't know where I would start. And—"delicious." What did "delicious" even mean?

I must have looked lost, because Caduan reached for a cream-covered pastry and held it out to me. "Here. Try this."

The piece of cake between his fingers was yellow, with white frosting and bright raspberries over its top.

I took a long drink of wine. Then I leaned forward and ate the pastry from Caduan's fingers.

Caduan's eyebrows arched, an almost-laugh of surprise

escaping him. Not that I was paying attention. An explosion of
sweetness rolled over my tongue, the texture of the cream cool
and smooth compared to the soft warmth of the cake, all cut by a
sharp punctuation of berry.

A wordless sound escaped my throat.

Pleasure. *This* was pleasure.

I looked at Caduan, eyes round, and he chuckled.

"Good?"

"It's... It's..."

"Your body is capable of powerful things, but it is capable of
pleasure, too."

I felt foolish for not realizing this sooner. First, I thought my
body was a prison. Then I realized that it could be a tool. And
now I realized that it could allow me to experience things —
useless, wonderful things — that I had long ago forgotten.

I took another drink of wine, savoring the way the bitterness
mingled with the sweetness still left on my tongue — savoring,
too, in the soft blur it draped over my senses, making everything
stronger and softer at once.

Then I pointed to a plate near Caduan. "That one. I want to
try that one."

"As you wish." It was a strange looking food, some sort of
flaky pastry designed in a shallow cup, filled with glistening gold.
He handed it to me. "Be careful, it's —"

Sweet, sticky custard filled my mouth,

" — Messy," Caduan finished.

I didn't care how messy it was. It was too wonderful. It was
only after I swallowed that I thought to be conscious of how
ridiculous I must have looked.

Caduan was giving me a strange look that I could not decipher. Heat rose to my cheeks.

"You have..." He reached out and pressed his thumb to the
curve of my lip, gently tracing its shape. A bit of cream still sat
on his fingers, left over from when I had unceremoniously
snatched the pastry from his hands.

Without thinking, I brushed my lips over his thumb, my

tongue darting out just enough to lick the cream from his skin. The sweetness mingled with the clean, salty taste of his flesh.

Time seemed to hover for a long, suspended moment. The amused smile faded from Caduan's face. Something I could not identify drew tight in the space between us, a strange fissure of tension that skittered across my skin.

Then he pulled his hand away and chuckled. "Better than letting it go to waste," he muttered.

I took another drink of wine.

Suddenly, I felt very aware of my own body. Every sense seemed fuller than it had been, every feeling stronger and more intense—no longer overwhelming, but joyful. How had I found this music too loud and ugly? Now the beat of it thrummed through my skin like my heartbeat. I wanted to drown in it. I wanted to see how far this would go.

I jumped to my feet, without fully meaning to.

A bemused smile curled Caduan's mouth. "Do you want to dance?"

"It seems… silly. There is no purpose in it." I looked out into the mass of dancing bodies. It was…an oddly appealing move-ment, and now that I could feel the music washing over me, I could understand the desire to move with it.

"There isn't," Caduan agreed. "But for them, that's the plea-sure in it."

"I will try it," I said, and again I thought of the way sugar tasted as I watched the smile roll across his lips.

———

CADUAN and I danced for a long time. He was right—there was something pleasurable in useless movement, especially with Caduan's scent surrounding me and his forehead pressed against mine. I felt like my understanding of the world, and this life, had changed dramatically—like a mysterious equation had, at last, been solved, and I reveled in the answer.

Eventually, though, I grew tired. The blur of wine combined

with the sheer overwhelming volume of sights and sounds and sensations began to wear on me. Caduan must have seen this, because he pulled me closer and murmured in my ear, "We can go somewhere else."

I was relieved to escape.

We walked away from the party, tracing the paths that wound behind the palace where the stone met the forest. We'd gone this way once before, I remembered, when Caduan took me to the training house at the edge of the grounds. Then I didn't notice such things, but now I found myself transfixed by the wild, untamed elegance of the gardens back here. Flowers of clashing colors, wildly overgrown, crept over the trails.

I watched Caduan carefully as we walked.

"You are tired," I said.

"Hm?"

"You are frequently tired."

He smiled wanly. "I'm getting old."

This statement startled me. It had not occurred to me to think of Caduan as old. As Reshaye, age did not exist. Time was a flat line stretching out in all directions. Humans changed, but I remained the same.

I remembered Caduan in another life, as a young man with a crown too heavy for him. But five hundred years had passed between then and now. Caduan had borne the weight of every one of those years.

Caduan would die, one day.

I did not like this thought.

"Do you fear death?" I said.

He did not react to this question, as if he did not find it at all surprising. He was silent for a long moment before answering. "I fear only what it could take from me."

I realized that I feared Caduan's death.

"I wanted to die," I said.

His expression changed slightly. "I know you did."

"You do not understand how painful endless existence is. Existence that should not be." I shook my head. "It's torturous."

Caduan said, softly, "I do understand."

"I wanted to rest." I swallowed. My time as Reshaye felt like a whole other life, just as my time as Aefe before that did. I answered to both names now, but neither of them felt like me. I carried both sets of memories, but they were like windows into other lives. "I thought I was dead already, before you brought me back. I gave up my life to save Tisaanah's."

"I didn't know that."

"A curse demanded payment. A life. And there were two of us, in her. My life as Reshaye was nothing but rage and desire, and that was my sole reason for living. Even then, a part of me was afraid of death. I knew only want, and death is the end of wanting."

"Why did you do it, then?"

My brow furrowed. It felt so long ago. Deciphering my past intentions seemed impossible. "I had made many marks on the world," I said. "But all of them were scars. I wanted to leave ink instead, like the stories I used to wear. Tisaanah sometimes made me feel that… that there was more in me. I had committed centuries of violence. But in that moment, I felt…" I swallowed. Pressed my hand to my heart, without thinking, like I did every time I needed to remind myself that I was no longer Reshaye. "I felt for the first time that I had a choice in what I wanted to be. Centuries of violence, and just one act of sacrifice. One act of generosity." I gave him a weak smile. "That and… I wanted to rest. I was ready to rest."

He looked at me solemnly. "You wanted control over who you were, because you never had it before."

"Of course I had control. I defeated entire armies by taking control."

"No. That was destruction," Caduan said. "But that is not the same as control. You were still at their mercy. The real claim of power was letting it go."

I stopped walking.

This realization shook me. As Reshaye, I had craved power.

But there was no true control in that. It was wild and greedy, and that desire had dominated me.

But it also took my pain away.

There was no shame in those things. Perhaps that desire for blood was just as invigorating as the taste of sugar on my lips.

"Perhaps," I said. "But I am learning to find joy in hunger. And I had never been hungrier than that."

We rounded a corner. We were now far behind the palace. I saw movement ahead, where the gardens gave way to the trees of the forest. In the darkness, it took me a moment to decipher what I was looking at: two forms, tangled up so that they were an indecipherable mass of limbs, fabric bunched around bare skin. Golden hair, cooler than usual beneath the moonlight. A single silver-gold wing.

It was Meajqa, I realized, entangled with a woman. He pressed her against a tree. Her legs wrapped around his waist. His lips were against her throat, and her face, covered by her dark hair, was thrown back in pleasure. Their discarded clothes sat in a pile of fine fabric in the dirt.

Caduan let out a huff of a laugh and tugged my arm. "I suppose we'll go another way."

We took the opposite path, now walking through the western gardens.

I was silent.

Despite myself, I replayed the image of them in my mind. They looked strange, ungraceful, nothing but a tangle of bodies and movements too hungry to be elegant. And yet there was a beauty to the hunger of it—or fulfillment of it.

When I was Aefe, long ago, I knew the pleasure of sex. But as Reshaye, I didn't understand it, not even when I experienced those desires as Tisaanah or Maxantarius had felt them. I had looked at the carnal uselessness of it and been confused. What was the purpose of such feelings?

But...

I pictured the pleasure on that woman's face, brazen and impassioned.

"Aefe?"

"Hm?"

I hadn't realized he was talking to me.

Caduan seemed amused. "You look like you're thinking very hard."

I said, without hesitation, "Meajqa asked me if I wanted to have sex with him."

Caduan choked, lurching to a stop. "He what?"

"He didn't use those words. But that was what he was asking."

Caduan looked straight ahead, blinking twice, not moving. I had never seen him behave this way.

He cleared his throat and continued walking. "What did you say?"

"I said no."

The muscles of Caduan's jaw flexed.

Realization dawned on me.

Could that be jealousy? Possession? When I had been Reshaye, I had wanted nothing but to consume and be consumed by the person I was with. It was a desire so deep and so all-encompassing that it took over all of me. That was love, and it was awash with jealousy.

If Caduan felt jealousy, did that mean that he loved me?

Because jealousy meant love, yes?

This string of epiphanies hit me one after the other, knocking me somewhat off kilter.

"You could have said yes," he said. "If you had wanted to."

For some reason, I was a bit hurt by that.

"I didn't want to." We walked in silence that had become suddenly awkward. "When I was Reshaye, I did not understand it."

"Understand—?"

"Sex. What does it feel like?"

Caduan made a strange, wordless sound, something between a laugh and a strangled clearing of the throat. "It feels... good."

"Like it feels to taste honey?"

The corner of his mouth curled. "Perhaps in select scenarios."

I had to admit, I was a bit intrigued by this. That was a very, very good feeling.

"If you're curious about it," he asked, very casually, "why did you reject Meajqa's generous offer?"

"I don't know. Perhaps I should not have."

The first part was true. The second, less so.

But I took gruesome delight at Caduan's reaction to this. Again he stopped short, turning to me, and for a split second, he looked... was it angry? More intense than I had ever seen him.

I enjoyed it when he looked at me like that.

He stepped closer once, and then again. My back pressed against the stone of the palace wall, cold against the bare expanse of my skin. And then he was leaning over me, the contrasting warmth overwhelming, the scent of pine surrounding me.

"You're that curious?" he said. His voice was soft and hard at once. Full of promise.

It was an invitation.

I met his stare and said, "Yes."

I was delirious with all the pleasures I had experienced tonight, but instead of feeling sated, I wanted more.

His hand pressed to the wall over my left shoulder, his head bowed close to mine.

"When it is right, it feels like ruination." He spoke quietly, voice low and rough. His fingertips trailed down my waist, then my hip, and then slipped between the layered slit of my dress. I drew in a breath as he touched the tender skin of my upper thigh —hot and cold at once.

My blood felt so hot in my veins, and my heartbeat pounded, skin reddening with the rush.

"And?" I breathed.

His fingertips trailed further, landing between my thighs, sliding over the silk of my undergarments in a feather-light touch.

Such a small movement, but my gasp shook my whole body.

A spark of pleasure shot up my spine. Everything in the world fell away but his eyes, and that single touch.

"Should I stop?" he asked, quietly.

"No."

No, no. We had barely started. My hunger was now something uncontrollable. My thighs parted slightly, without me even meaning to, and Caduan's forehead pressed against mine as he let out a slight breath.

His eyes were fire.

His fingers moved again, in small, gentle circles.

My world began to unravel. I released a sound I didn't even realize that I had made—my knees went weak. I was nothing but mindless desire. Pleasure consumed me and yet it only started to fill the yearning inside me—I needed more.

"It feels like the stars," Caduan murmured. "It feels like touching everything about another person's body. Like devouring them and letting them do the same to you."

Everything, he promised. But this was not everything, this was just one touch and the desire for more—for so much more— even as that single touch reduced me to nothing.

I wanted to tell him this, demand more from him, but I opened my lips and only managed to produce a single strangled whimper.

He was leaning heavily against the wall now, closer to me. His body, and the stone against my back, were all that kept me standing.

The circles grew faster, harder. The additional pressure drew a moan to my throat, made me press against him.

"It feels like the basest hunger," he said. "It is selfish... and giving."

His fingers pushed aside my undergarments, and two slid inside me.

I swore.

Everything disappeared except for the sensation of him within me—still not enough, not enough, not enough—and yet so much that my body didn't know how to react, that I forgot how to breathe and see and speak and move. The pain was brief, gone quickly beneath a wild, impatient pleasure slick with my desire.

I didn't know what was happening to me. I didn't know what I wanted, except that it was everything—faster, slower, deeper, gentler, harder, I didn't know, I only knew that I was coming undone and I wanted more of him everywhere.

He bowed his head, brushed his lips to my throat. He pressed against me, and the pressure of his body, even clothed, was too much.

It was too much.

"Let go, Aefe," Caduan murmured against my skin, his voice rough and demanding—like he was begging me, like he needed this just as much as I did—and I didn't even know what he was asking me to do but suddenly I was doing it, I was falling, I was exploding, I was stars and earth, I was everything, and I was relinquishing all of it to him.

It was only once I started coming back to myself that I realized I had been saying his name, over and over again, in desperate moans. I was boneless, barely managing to stay upright. I felt messy and undone and... and exposed, like I had just shown him something raw and vulnerable.

He breathed heavily, too, looking as shattered as I did.

He, too, looked afraid.

My lips parted, though I didn't know what to say. But his hand swept over my cheek in a small caress and tipped my chin towards him.

I did not know how to kiss someone. But this kiss was easy. The touch of his lips was gentle over mine. Slow. Almost shy— perhaps it should have seemed strange to share such a timid kiss in this moment, something so tentative, but it felt right. He tasted like honey.

He pulled away, and for a moment, neither of us breathed. I leaned in again.

But then Caduan's face changed abruptly. He jerked away from me, leaving me scrambling to push myself upright.

"I—This—" He ran his fingers through his hair. "This isn't —" He glanced at me and snapped his jaw shut, then turned away. "I shouldn't have—I should go. Goodnight, Aefe."

I didn't know what was happening. One moment, his presence surrounded me, and the next he was halfway down the path. The world was cold without him.

"Caduan!" I called after him.

But he was already gone.

CHAPTER SIXTY-THREE

MAX

We set off in the morning. It wouldn't take us too long to get to Orasiev, at least not with the help of Stratagram travel—we were lucky to now have multiple functional Wielders, which made life so much easier. We stayed away from main roads, choosing to move along side paths and camp at night instead of finding inns. Getting run out of town by bounty hunters once was more than enough for me.

Ishqa, as we had come to expect, came and went as he pleased. He traveled with us for the first day, then said he had business to attend to and abruptly flew off into the sunset, leaving us a few feathers to contact him.

What "business," I wondered?

I kept waiting for the moment when Brayan, too, would announce his departure, but it never came. At the end of the first day, as he was putting together his tent, I approached him.

"You're staying?"

"Of course I'm staying."

"I clearly remember a conversation or two where your attitude was more along the lines of, *'I'm going to Besrith and you can come or not,'* et cetera et cetera."

"I don't appreciate being mocked, Max." He gave me a flat stare over his shoulder. "Do you *want* me to go to Besrith?"

That was a complicated question. My new memories—the darkest ones—weighed heavily on me. Heavier than ever, every time I looked at my brother's face.

"No," I said. "I'm just saying, there's nothing 'of course' about it."

"I changed my mind. Are we done?"

"We are done, General." I gave him a sarcastic salute and turned away.

I made it three steps when Brayan's voice said behind me, "I thought you would end up back in Ilyzath if you stayed with them. I was trying to..." A pause, then a grumbled, "Never mind."

I didn't turn. I couldn't decide if I was angry that Brayan was essentially confessing that he manufactured the urgency of going to Besrith, or touched that he had done it because he was trying to protect me.

I settled on both. I tucked my hands into my pockets and kept walking without another word. It was always easier for Brayan and me to just not talk about things, anyway.

ON THE THIRD night on the road, I dreamed of my family.

I had forgotten how bad the dreams could be. Before, the ghost of grief was there, yes, but the absence of the memory eased the pain of it in so many ways. Ilyzath had shown me their faces every day, but the walls in my mind had protected me from the truth behind that torture.

Now, the wounds were as raw as they were the day it happened. When I dreamed of their faces this time, it skewered me. When I watched them die, it tore me to pieces.

I woke up covered in sweat. Tisaanah's body curled around mine.

"Wake up," she murmured in my ear. "You're dreaming."

I was, and I wasn't.

I blinked in the early morning sun streaming through the tent. I kissed Tisaanah's forehead and then silently extracted myself from her embrace. My whole body was tense, as if cringing for an incoming blow.

"Max…" Tisaanah's voice behind me was an unspoken question — *what's wrong with you?*

I put on my clothes. "It's just a hard day."

I didn't even have to look at a calendar. When there is a day in your past that's *that* bad, you just know.

Tisaanah understood immediately, because of course she did.

THE SILENCE at breakfast was suffocating. Sammerin knew what day it was, too, and if there was any doubt, the way Brayan almost took his head off over something totally innocuous acted as an apt reminder.

I could barely look at Brayan.

I hadn't allowed myself to think too hard about the lie I was telling him just by being here. Compartmentalization was a beautiful thing. But it was broken, today. Today, everything was just too big, too loud, too painful to sit inside those neat boxes.

Brayan looked like he hadn't slept at all.

"We need supplies," he grunted, in the first words anyone spoke over breakfast.

"There's a market nearby," Tisaanah said. "We can go today."

Her fingers traced mine. She had hardly let go of me all day, like she felt like she was the only thing tethering me to the earth. She may not have been far off.

"I can hunt," Brayan said.

"We can buy meat, I am sure."

"I —" His jaw ground. "I think Max and I should go hunt."

I could feel both Tisaanah and Sammerin's stares drilling into the side of my face.

The absolute last thing I wanted to do today was go

anywhere with Brayan, let alone somewhere secluded with weapons. My feelings towards him were so complicated they didn't even make sense anymore—a massive tangle of grief and guilt and anger that I couldn't pull apart even if I wanted to, which I most certainly did not.

I forced myself to meet his eyes, and I was taken aback by how abjectly sad he looked.

"It's good to get out," he said, a little hoarsely. "Go somewhere alone. Spend time in nature. On… days like today."

"Maybe we should all stay together," Sammerin suggested, in a noble attempt to give me a way out.

But Brayan had just sounded so… desperate.

"Fine," I said, surprising even myself. "Let's go hunt."

TOGETHER, we moved through the underbrush. The forests in Threll were odd, not as green or dense as the ones in Ara, and full of tall, ivory-barked trees with few branches. It made it easier to spot animals, but harder not to be spotted by them. We moved silently. It was a good excuse not to talk.

It was Brayan who finally said it. "You know what day it is today?"

What kind of question was that? Of course I knew what day it was today. "Yes."

"Do you usually… do… anything?"

"Drink myself into a stupor," I said.

"Do you want to—?"

I scoffed. "No." I'd come to realize that alcohol usually caused more problems than it solved.

"I usually… do this. Go hunting somewhere. By myself."

If I hadn't been trying so hard to keep myself together, I might have found it a little funny that Brayan's tactic for dealing with unwelcome emotion was running off to go stab things in the woods. Farlione men. Sensitive to the very end.

"I shouldn't have said what I did to you," he said, after a long, uncomfortable silence. "Before. Back in Sarilla."

I didn't want to talk about this. I wanted to be by myself and not talk to anyone about anything that felt this terrible, ever, let alone with Brayan. Doing this had been a mistake.

I thought, *You have every right to scream at me for whatever the fuck you want. You don't even know how much you have that right.*

I said, "It's fine."

"The truth is," Brayan said—and Ascended fucking above, I despised his sudden desire to talk through his feelings—"I didn't want to find you, back then. I was grateful you weren't there when I got home." He stopped and turned to me, and even though I knew better, I did the same, meeting his stare. It was oddly childlike, despite the fact that he looked every bit the hardened warrior he was. "I didn't want to have to look at anyone who looked like me."

A pang of sharp, familiar pain rang out in my chest. I hated how much I knew how that felt. I spent ten years alone, hating myself, and I was both obsessed with the thought of Brayan and utterly repulsed by the idea of seeing him again. Some of it was guilt, of course. But just as powerful was the physicality of it, the sheer gut punch of seeing eyes so similar to the ones that looked back at me from the flames that day.

How strongly he resembled our father.

I didn't want to look at anyone who looked like me.

The image of Sella's daughter, a little girl who looked so much like Brayan, flashed through my mind, and a reluctant understanding clicked into place.

"It was just—a lot to do alone." Brayan turned back to the brush.

Brayan—Brayan, the man who had held me to such impossible standards that I signed my life away to the Orders just because I wanted to prove myself to him—had needed me. Strange how this realization so stunned me.

"I should have been there," I said, quietly.

Even knowing all that I knew now, I meant it.

He shook his head. "It's... it is what it is."

I turned back to our task. I thought we were done. But after another few minutes, Brayan said, "They let me do it, you know."

"What?"

"The Ryvenai extremists. The murderers. The military let me be the one to execute them."

Fuck. I didn't know that people had died for this—for my crime. I'd never asked, never wanted to know. I still wished I did not know.

"Did it make you feel better?" I asked.

"Yes." A pause. "No."

Sounded about right.

I was desperate to end this conversation, but Brayan kept talking. We were barely even pretending to hunt anymore. "It's... strange. There's something I can't stop thinking about. They weren't what I was expecting."

"What?"

"The murderers. The ones who did it. They were just so... they were so *weak*. There were ten of them, but more than half were scrawny, drug-addicted teenagers. How did that happen? How did our father let that happen? He was one of the most effective warriors in Ara, and yet these—these *rats* managed to kill them, with him in the house?"

I couldn't move, couldn't breathe.

I knew the answer, of course. Remembered the way my father's face had changed when he saw mine. How he'd been ready to fight but had paused just long enough to temper his shot, make it non-fatal. Even as he watched me do the most horrific things, he was not willing to kill his son.

I spent a lot of time thinking about our father, too. Thinking about that moment.

"I couldn't get my head around it," Brayan went on. "And I came to a conclusion. I think that they must have taken hostages. I think they probably would have gone after the girls first. Maybe Kira, maybe Shailia, but I think Marisca would have fought them and—"

I couldn't take it anymore. I threw down my bow and whirled to him. "*Stop*. I don't want to listen to this."

A flicker of—fuck, was that *hurt?*—crossed Brayan's face. His jaw tightened.

"You don't want to know what happened?" he said. "You haven't spent the last decade agonizing about that?"

Suddenly, I understood why Tisaanah and Sammerin viewed sending me away and never seeing me again as a mercy compared to the truth.

"You want it to make sense," I said. "It's never going to make sense."

"It could make more sense than it does."

"And what fucking good would that do? Why do you want to know how they suffered before they died? Is that how you want to remember them?"

"It is the only way I remember them now," he said, between his teeth. "I remember them a million different ways in a million different seconds in the same two-hour span. I imagine them in the unknown of all of those questions. Did our mother have to watch them die?"

"Brayan, stop."

"Did those pieces of shit *rape* our sisters —"

Fuck, I absolutely *could not listen* to this. "*STOP.*"

"I can't," he ground out. "*I can't stop.* This is what I'm telling you. I imagine them in infinite horrors. *It never stops.* You don't feel that way?"

It was almost darkly funny. He'd spent ten years trying to find one horror. I spent ten years trying to forget all of them.

"Besides," he said, "don't they deserve that? Don't they deserve to have their last moments known, instead of lost like that? Even soldiers on the battlefield get to have their final words witnessed."

"You know better than —"

"*I should be able to do this for them.*" It was practically a snarl. He turned around abruptly, his back to me, his shoulders rising and falling.

I don't know why it had never occurred to me that he was suffering as much as I was. The realization struck me dully, now. It was hard for it to change anything when I was struggling to hold myself together, too.

"I'm sorry," I said.

The words were a little choked. I didn't expect them to hit as hard as they did—just two words that encapsulated so much more than Brayan knew.

He let out a long, long breath and turned around. He no longer looked angry, only tired. "I—It's not your fault."

I bit my tongue so hard it bled.

He sighed. "It's just a hard day."

"It's a hard day," I agreed, quietly.

Maybe I could have said more to him. Maybe I should have said more. Instead, I swallowed the truth as far away from the surface as I possibly could, and the two of us worked in silence for the rest of the morning. We barely spoke again.

CHAPTER SIXTY-FOUR

TISAANAH

I was careful when we went into town. Without Ishqa, I couldn't glamor myself—nor would I waste one on this—but I could still take care to make my appearance less obvious. I put on a jacket and buttoned my shirt up to my throat to hide as much of my unusual skin as possible, then wrapped my hair up beneath a hood. It wasn't uncommon for people in Threll to cover up like this—protection from the sun in the middle of the day—so I blended in well enough as Sammerin and I went to the marketplace together.

In any other circumstance, I might have enjoyed the trip. The marketplace reminded me of the ones my mother would take me to when I was young—rows and rows of open-air stalls set up along twisting pathways, peddling anything and everything that one might think to want, some of it useful, and most of it junk. Where else in the world could you go if you wanted to pick up paintings, toys, scarves, shoes, weapons, seventeen different types of fruit, and questionable meat from an unidentified source?

Sammerin and I wandered the stalls, collecting ingredients

for dinner tonight and enough supplies to keep us going for the rest of the journey to Orasiev.

"Should we get meat, too?" Sammerin asked, carefully.

I thought of Max and Brayan, and sighed. "Yes. Probably." I suspected hunting would not happen today.

My chest ached at the thought. I should have found a way to get Max out of going with his brother. I couldn't imagine how agonizing that must be for him.

Sammerin read my face. "He'll be alright."

"I know he will be."

It wasn't the future I was worried about. It was the past, and no one could do anything about that.

"I think it's a good sign that he went," Sammerin said. "For years I watched him avoid so much as acknowledging Brayan's existence. Even in the early years, when Brayan was trying hardest to find him." He lifted a shoulder in a faint shrug. "Perhaps this is… growth?"

Surely it was, by some measure. But what was the cost of that?

"I think their grief is bad for each other," I said, quietly.

Sammerin was silent for a long moment before responding. "Maybe. Fire and oil."

We moved on to the next booth — beautiful skirts that, despite myself and the direness of our situation, I found myself a little transfixed by. I had a crimson shade of red between my fingers when I heard a sound that stopped my heart.

I froze. Suddenly, I was thirteen years old again.

"What's wrong?" Sammerin asked.

I abandoned the skirt and pushed through the market streets. There, up ahead, I saw them: wide-brimmed black hats. Long black leather jackets. Behind them, bars. Behind those bars, people.

Sammerin let out a low curse under his breath.

The slave marketplace was small, much smaller than the one that Esmaris had plucked me out of when I was fourteen years old, but all these places looked the same in the ways that mattered. The cages—the pen, really—were as large as a full block of the merchant stalls, the people within chained to the bars so that potential buyers could easily inspect them. They were divided by sex, age, specialty. The unskilled women here. The children there. The skilled workers and artisans at the end. The beautiful women over there. The only exception was the young, strong men, who were separated, to prevent the possibility that they might be able to physically overpower their captors if kept close enough to work together.

I remembered all these things from my time in a place like this, too. I remember that they debated whether to put me with the women or the children. *Look at those breasts,* one of them had said. *She goes with the women. That's what they'll want her for. An interesting, exotic fuck.*

"Someone you'd like to see, lovely?" a rough voice said, far too close to me, and I glanced over my shoulder and then looked away.

The man in the wide-brimmed black hat smiled at me like a person, not a product, which was more than they ever did back then.

"No," I said. "Thank you."

I almost choked on that *"Thank you."*

I walked up and down the bars, around the edges. Many of these people were clearly ill, some potentially drugged. They barely acknowledged me. Only one of them did, a little girl that couldn't have been older than eight, who leapt to her feet with a gasp.

"You," she breathed. "I heard of you!"

Her face split into an enormous grin, the kind that children make when presented with an incredible surprise gift, and my heart snapped in two.

Sammerin put a hand on my shoulder. "Tisaanah—"

"I can do something."

He looked at me hopelessly. I pulled away from his grasp and walked the length of the enclosure again, this time down the next row this time to avoid suspicion, though I could feel that little girl's eyes boring into me the entire time. Surely there had to be something. A weakness in the gate I could exploit with a bit of magic. A poorly guarded exit that I could open with a single, quietly killed guard.

"We can't," Sammerin whispered in my ear.

"We *can*," I hissed back.

I'd just turned a gods-damned city to rubble. It seemed ridiculous to think I couldn't save this one little girl.

Yet all my fantasies dissolved with every lap I took around the block. The cage was sturdy. The slavers were everywhere. If it was them, and them alone, I would burn this place to the ground. But the marketplace was crowded. It was broad daylight. We were wanted.

No, no, no, a part of me still protested. *You cannot just leave them.*

Sammerin put his arm around me and abruptly steered me away from the cages.

"That slaver has been staring at you all the way down this street," he muttered. "We need to go, right now. I'm sorry, Tisaanah. Truly."

I glanced over my shoulder. Three of the men in black hats huddled together, whispering. At the same time, all of them looked at me.

I turned away fast, my heart sinking. Sammerin was right. It had been a mistake to come here at all. I was too easily recognized.

"Fine." Gods, the word physically hurt.

We walked quickly through the streets. The marketplace was massive, nearly the size of a small village all on its own. I glanced to my left and saw a man in black keeping pace beside us in the next row over. Glanced over my shoulder to see another behind us, walking fast.

"They are definitely following us," I muttered.

We needed to go left, but another slaver nearly collided with us that way, so we quickly changed route, heading in the opposite direction.

Ahead, the stone walls loomed. We were being cornered.

We needed to get out of the marketplace. The minute we were free from the throng of people, I could rip these animals apart.

As if in preparation, without my even needing to tell it to, magic tingled at the surface of my skin. My awareness spread out around me—I could taste the simmering emotions of the crowd, a buzz of thoughts and interest. I didn't want to hurt these people, let alone the slaves so close by.

All we had to do was lead the slavers out of the market.

We turned a corner, into a secluded alley—

The hair lifted at the back of my neck.

I sensed the blow coming a split second before it did. I managed to slip the man's grip and dodge the full force of his strike, though the club still hit the side of my head with enough force to send the world spinning. My magic was ready. When the next one grabbed me, it was only briefly before he howled in pain and yanked his hands away, black with rot.

Sammerin and I fought like animals. Sammerin's magic made him an incredible killer. He forced men to lurch to awkward stops, twisted their limbs, collapsed their lungs with the flick of his fingers.

Soon, bodies littered the ground around us. The shoppers at the marketplace gasped and reeled away, a wide-eyed crowd gathering to watch at a safe distance.

I whirled to kill another attacker, only to force myself to stop, too late, when I realized who my opponent actually was. There was no black jacket here, no wide-brimmed hat. The man who came after me next bore a standard-issue spear and a wolf sigil on his armband, matching the one tattooed on his throat.

A slave. He was a slave, performing the task he had been *forced* to do.

Sammerin's magic snaked out for him, but I shouted, "Stop!" and Sammerin pulled away at the last minute, shooting me a confused look. *What's wrong?* it asked, though the words did not have time to leave his lips.

A horrific *crack* rang out as Sammerin went careening to the ground. Blood gushed from the wound at the back of his head, making crimson rivers through the cobblestones.

He didn't move.

I fought back panic, barely managing to evade another blow. I was surrounded now. Not a single one of the men looked at Sammerin's limp body, stepping over it as if it were nothing on their way to me.

My magic glowed at my hands, at the ready. It would be easy for me to kill them. I could fight my way out of this. But more than half of these men were slaves. One twist of fate and Serel would have become one of them.

I would not hurt these people.

So I let them grab me, let them force me to my knees. My eyes found Sammerin's limp form, terror in my throat.

Don't be dead. Please don't be dead.

My magic reached for his mind. He was in pain, but he was alive.

I fought myself free long enough to throw myself over his body in what would have looked like a desperate show of concern. Grasped tight in my hand was a wad of fabric—an armband that I had ripped from one of the slaves during our fight. I stuffed it into his jacket pocket just before the slaves dragged me off of him.

I recognized the sigil on that armband. It was the same as the one that had been tattooed onto the hands left at my doorstop months ago. The Zorokovs.

There were worse things, I decided, than planting myself within the walls of my greatest enemy. I prayed my friends would understand that, too.

One of the men in the black hats approached me—the others seemed too nervous—and tilted my face towards him. My hood had long ago fallen, my hair free around my face.

He smiled. "What a prize. Do you have any idea how much Zorokov will pay for her?"

A blow to my head sent my world spinning. "Careful!" one of the slavers barked. "Don't fucking *damage* her, you idiot!"

They dragged me away. Distantly, through flashes of darkening, blurry vision, I felt myself being loaded up into a cart. Heard the clatter of iron snap closed. Chained bodies surrounded me.

My consciousness was gone before I felt the cart begin to move.

CHAPTER SIXTY-FIVE

AEFE

Days came and went. Caduan refused to see me.

He would meet with Meajqa, Luia, and Vythian for court related matters, privately. I was not invited.

He would rarely appear to the public. If he did, he left before anyone, including me, could speak to him.

He did not come to my room. When I tried to go to his, guards turned me away.

After several days of this, Meajqa asked me, "What happened between the two of you, anyway?"

After a long pause—I truly was thinking about the question —I answered, helplessly, "I don't know!"

Meajqa gave me a curious sidelong look and took a long drink of wine.

At first, I was confused. Surely this must be a mistake. Surely something was wrong. Had I done something insulting? Had there been something about what happened between us that had been offensive or repulsive? At night, I would run over those moments again and again, searching for clues. Was that really desire in his voice, or was it anger? What had I missed?

Then, I was hurt.

I had not realized how much I relied on Caduan until he wasn't there. I didn't *need* him anymore—not the way I had in the beginning, when I probably would have withered away if he hadn't been supervising me to make sure I ate and slept and didn't throw myself off the balcony. But I liked him, and that almost felt worse. I had learned what it was to experience pleasure in someone else's company, and now I missed it.

I missed him.

The days passed.

And then I grew angry.

Who was he to do this to me? What right did he have to make me feel like this? I had shown him vulnerability that I didn't even know I was capable of, and he left me trembling alone in the garden. He made me feel something for him and then abandoned me.

He abandoned me just like so many others had. Like every human host that held me, like Maxantarius, like Tisaanah.

This thought infuriated me.

A week later, Meajqa asked me again, "I mean it, I'm now desperately curious—what happened?"

This time, there was no hesitation. "He is a coward," I snarled.

Meajqa's eyebrows rose. "Hmm. Sounds as if perhaps he should have read more romance novels," he said, and took another long drink of wine.

Coward. That was what I told myself when I craved his attention at night. When I missed the sound of his voice.

He is a coward.

You don't need him anyway.

You don't want him.

But the worst part was, coward or not, I did.

CHAPTER SIXTY-SIX

MAX

I didn't like that Tisaanah and Sammerin had not returned.

All my nerves felt very close to the surface of my skin today, frantic energy clenching my hands and leading my feet to pace back, forth, back, forth around the camp. Brayan and I hadn't said a word to each other on our walk back from the woods, and we didn't say a word to each other at camp, either.

And then, when Sammerin and Tisaanah did not return, I thought, *What a day for the worst kind of scenarios.* It was easy for me to invent terrible things today.

Eventually, I turned to Brayan and announced, "I'm going to look for them."

"You'll just make it harder for them to find you when they come back."

"I don't care. Something—"

Something isn't right, I was about to say, when a blood-soaked Sammerin appeared at the camp.

He landed on his feet for a moment and immediately fell to his knees. He was covered in blood. One hand clutched a wet piece of parchment, his Stratagram so messily scrawled on it that I had no idea how it had managed to get him here.

My heart stopped beating.

I leapt to his side. He doubled over, his hand hovering over his head, face contorted in pain. The flesh of his scalp moved very slowly, not enough to close the wound, but enough to lessen the bleeding. It was nearly impossible for a healer to heal themselves. The fact that Sammerin was even able to do this much spoke to his extensive skill.

"Bandages," I barked to Brayan. "Right now."

He obeyed, and I pressed handfuls of rags to Sammerin's wound. His dark eyes flicked to me, and the look was enough to confirm all my worst fears.

"Where?" I bit out. "Where is she?"

Sammerin shoved a shaking hand into his jacket and produced a wad of fabric. I took it from him and uncrumpled it. A bloody sigil of a wolf snarled back at me.

"That's a Threllian Lord's sigil," Brayan said.

"Slavers," Sammerin wheezed, with great effort. He had now moved to his throat, where he painstakingly attempted to close the gaping cut, stitch by stitch.

"Which one?" I thrust the armband in Brayan's face. "Who does this belong to?"

"I knew so many back then." His brow furrowed. "It's been a long time."

"You have to remember."

All I could think, over and over again, was, *I can't lose her. I can't lose her ever, but not today of all days.*

I didn't go with her because I had been too busy drowning in the past. How was that for poetic justice?

I racked my brain. Tisaanah had so many enemies, especially among the Threllians. But who would have special use for her?

"The Zorokovs," I said. "Is it theirs?"

Brayan's eyebrows lurched in realization. "The wolves. Yes. That's them."

Sammerin, still unable to speak, nodded.

Blood rushed in my ears, fear and anger rising until it overtook me. There were practically sparks at my fingertips already. I was ready to burn those fucking people to the ground.

Sammerin grabbed my wrist. A silent conversation passed between us.

My jaw tightened until it ached. My knuckles trembled around the armband, the fabric at its edges scorching as my magic responded to my anger.

"I know." I took a deep breath and let it out, slowly. "I know."

I couldn't go after her alone. Not this time, not like I had when she had been locked up in Aviness's dungeons.

I loved Tisaanah enough to want to tear anyone who threatened her into pieces. But I understood her enough to see what she couldn't tell me herself.

Tisaanah had her magic back. She was a strong fighter and a stronger Wielder. I knew it because I had taught her, and I had watched her get just as good, if not better, than me. She'd told me of all the time she spent hiding in plain sight in Threllian Lords' homes. She knew how to do this.

And she was sending us a message. Yes, I could chase after her caravan right now, murder everyone in sight, and bring her home before the cart even reached the gates of the Zorokov estate.

If I did that, she would be furious with me—because that would be a rescue for *her*. It wouldn't be a victory for *everyone*.

This arm band didn't say, *Here I am. Come rescue me.*

It said, *Here I am. Bring me an army.*

"If we go now," Brayan said, voice gruff, "We can stop the caravan before she even reaches the Zorokovs' district."

He was already reaching for his sword. In any other context, I would have paused to be more surprised that he was so eager to leap into battle to save Tisaanah.

I said, "No. We have to go to Orasiev."

Brayan looked at me like I was insane. "Tisaanah is in chains right now, and you *don't* want to go after her?"

Oh, I *wanted* to. I wanted to so much it physically hurt.

"We *are* going after her." My fist closed around the fabric, and I looked down at Sammerin. "But she doesn't want a rescue. She wants to fucking end them. So that's what we'll do. We get to Orasiev as fast as we humanly can. We gather the rebels, and then we destroy those bastards. *That's* what she wants."

I felt the pulse of magic from the artifact I carried, strange and powerful enough to rearrange realities.

Brayan looked unconvinced. "I don't understand how —"

"I wasn't asking for your opinion," I snapped. Sammerin slowly pushed to his feet, removing his hand from his throat. The wound still looked horrible, but he'd managed to stop the bleeding. I looked him up and down. "You're alright?"

His voice was a hoarse whisper. "Good enough to topple an empire."

I choked out an almost-laugh. "Glad to hear it, my friend."

CHAPTER SIXTY-SEVEN

TISAANAH

The Zorokov estate was just as beautiful as the Mikov estate had been, if not more-so. It was certainly grander, with more obvious signals of wealth. Esmaris had so much power that he had little to prove, and his taste in decor had reflected that. Everything had been crafted immaculately out of white marble, the kind that needed no decoration to announce that it was wildly expensive—you just felt it.

The Zorokovs' taste was a bit louder. Silver and gold edged the roofs of their buildings, which rose above us in blocks like an ivory mountain. We were all silent as the cart rumbled through the gates. More than a dozen of us were packed into this cart, all chained, though I was the only one to have multiple sets of restraints around both my wrists and my legs. They bound me to the bars, the bench, myself... like my captors were afraid I would fly away.

I would not fly away, of course. I was very good at being the perfect slave, the perfect prisoner.

I'd stood under many of these entry arches by now. Still, every time the shadow of another Lord's sigil passed over me, I stiffened. I had always been standing at a different entrance, going back to a different master, back when I was just a child.

I swallowed this fear. I was no longer a child.

I watched the city as we rolled through, memorizing the layout. There were two walls, one around the broader city and another around the home itself. The streets were wide, I noted, and very straight. Convenient.

The little girl that had recognized me in the cage was here, too. She sat across from me, her neck craned to watch me the entire journey. Now she leaned closer and said, quietly, "Did you really kill Esmaris Mikov?"

I shook my head at her—not saying no, but saying, *shush!*

Too late. "Don't talk to her," one of the slavers snarled, and whacked her so hard across the face that her small body was flung against the woman next to her.

"Don't do that!" I bit out, before I could stop myself. "She—"

WHACK.

Pain cracked across the back of my head.

Everything faded.

I woke up still in chains. My head was pounding. My stomach churned. I was half unconscious when I found myself on all fours, vomiting.

All my senses seemed dulled. By the time they started to return to me, the first thing I heard was a wordless sound of disgust.

"You wretched thing," a rough, female voice muttered. "Now I have to clean that mess up."

With great effort, I lifted my head, then sank back against the wall.

My wrists and ankles were all bound with iron and chained to the corner, where the wall met the floor. The floor was marble, like, no doubt, everything else in this house. A small bed sat to my left, just far enough that surely my chains were too short to lie on it. The room was tiny. A single desk. A single dusty mirror. No windows.

A thin woman with wiry grey hair and a stress-pinched face regarded me with open revulsion.

"I expected you to be bigger," she said. "After all the trouble you've caused."

I blinked at her blearily as my vision cleared. She wore fine clothes—slaves' clothes, yes, but they were well-made, which meant she was a house slave. People of this class liked to be surrounded by visually appealing things.

She held a mop, which she slapped to the ground beside me to clean up my mess, hard enough to send flecks of it over my face.

"They're thrilled to have *you*, let me tell you that."

"Where is this?" My voice was hoarse.

"Surely you aren't stupid, after all you've done."

"The Zorokov house."

The woman rolled her eyes in a way that I chose to interpret as agreement.

"The *main* house?" I asked. This was a house slave's quarters that had been outfitted to keep me in. Not a dungeon, which would be in a separate building on the estate grounds.

"They want to keep you close. Hence why I'm here scooping up a prisoner's vomit. Not usually my gods-damned job."

A forceful scrub of the mob sent a small wave of watered-down vomit soaking through the hem of my tunic.

I scooted away from it. "And who are—"

"My daughter's dead because of you, you know," the woman cut out, without looking at me. "They took her hands first. I hear they sent 'em to you."

My mouth closed, a pang of hurt in my chest. I thought of those hands every day.

"I'm sorry."

The woman shrugged. "Doesn't do much for me now."

I tried to reach for her with my magic, only to realize why my head was so fuzzy—it was only because I was so disoriented that I hadn't recognized the sensation earlier. I had been dosed with Chryxalis. By the feel of it, massive amounts.

"You'll be gone soon," the woman said, slapping the mop down on the tile again. "I think that'll be better for all of us. Just let everything go back to how it was. Back when you only got your hands cut off for stealing, not because some uppity Nyzre-nese bitch decided to start a gods-damned civil war."

I could tell her that she was too late. Even if I died today, the fire had grown too big to be stomped out. Too many people were too angry to ever go back to the way things were.

"What was your daughter's name?" I said, instead, and her movements paused for a split second.

"Salen," she said.

"That's a beautiful name."

Her eyes shot to me, as if I had said something horribly offensive. She looked quietly furious. Then she turned back to her work, running the mop over the floor one more time and dropping it with a loud *SPLASH* into her bucket.

"She was a stupid, hotheaded girl. She thought what you were doing was just wonderful. Just loved it. Right up until the end."

Rusty wheels screamed as she yanked her bucket of water to the door.

"Wait," I said. "What's your name?"

She threw open the door. "Laron," she said, and slammed it behind her.

———————————

I TRACKED the time by the warmth of the light that spilled beneath the door. I watched it grow colder, and then warmer again, due to the setting sun and the glow of lanterns in the hall.

That was when Lady Zorokov came to see me.

It had become obvious to me by then that they had pumped me full of a truly massive amount of drugs, made even more potent by the concussion I was clearly suffering. When Lady Zorokov entered the room, I couldn't get my head to turn until she had been standing there for several full seconds. Once I did, my vision was so fuzzy that she seemed like an apparition, her long white dress pooling at the floor, golden curls falling nearly to her waist.

Two guards stood on either side of her, dressed in black, silent.

"It is lovely to see you again, Tisaanah," she said, with a sweet smile and a voice that sounded like music.

"Likewise." My voice, on the other hand, did not sound like music.

Lady Zorokov laughed.

"Forgive me if I skip the pleasantries," she said. "Today has been a very busy day, so let's get down to it, shall we?"

And what, exactly, I wanted to ask, *are we getting down to?*

I didn't have time. Because it only took seconds—less—for Lady Zorokov to nod to one of the guards, who then crossed the room in two long strides, grasped my right hand, and bent my small finger back until it snapped.

The pain exploded through me. I let out a strangled cry. I tried to yank my hand away, but the guard gripped my wrist too tightly to allow me to move.

"Again," Lady Zorokov said, in a world that sounded very far away.

"No—" I choked.

The guard grabbed my ring finger. Bent it back.

SNAP.

Oh gods oh gods oh gods oh gods—

My limbs thrashed on instinct, every part of me reaching out to strike him, to get away.

"Again."

Perhaps if I had been able to think through the pain, I might have paid more attention to the way the guard cringed slightly before he obeyed, like he was stabbing some sort of vicious animal and bracing for inevitable retaliation.

He grabbed my two broken fingers and twisted.

I didn't realize I was screaming.

My restraints cut into my skin as I thrashed. Ages passed. Civilizations rose and fell. None of those things were as constant as this agony.

Lady Zorokov said something I couldn't even hear over my own screams. The guard released my hand. I was shaking and covered in sweat.

The reprieve was only enough to let me catch my breath. Then the guard moved behind me and pushed me to the ground, pain spearing my dangling fingers as I used my hands to stop my fall.

RIP.

My shirt tore. My back was cold and bare, my shirt in tatters around my waist. The guard pushed me roughly to the ground, my chin nearly smacking the marble.

Lady Zorokov's eyes flicked over me. She would have a full view of my back.

"Look at those scars," she murmured. "What a shame. You had such a lovely body."

I heard a sound I couldn't identify behind me.

My heart was racing. I was so afraid. I'd forgotten what it was like to be at the mercy of another.

"Stop." The word came out as a whimper.

"We'll see whether you can make me." She smiled. "Just like you made Esmaris Mikov stop. Do you know what his problem was? He loved you too much. The rest of us used to whisper about it when we went to those parties of his. The way he *doted* upon you." She clicked her tongue and nodded to my scars. "Those? Those are passion. But I promise you, darling, there is no passion in this. I take no joy in it."

The knife moved slowly over my back, slicing a slow, straight line over my skin.

Oh gods. Oh gods. I couldn't breathe. Couldn't think.

The knife dug deeper. I could feel the resistance of my skin, the sinew beneath it, parting. The knife moved down. Again.

An explosion of pain. Resistance.

They were peeling off parts of my skin.

My self-control gave out. I screamed.

"Stop, stop, stop—" The word rolled from my lips without my permission. My muscles shook violently; my stomach lurched, and I would have been vomiting if there was anything left in me.

I felt him tear off another chunk of skin. It dropped in front of me, nearly grazing my nose. A bloody chunk of white-and-tan flesh against the marble.

Oh gods. I would die. This would kill me. I wouldn't survive.

"Can you make me stop, Tisaanah?" Lady Zorokov asked, calmly.

I railed against the restraints. Her bodyguard stepped a little closer to her, as if preparing to protect her. But I flopped uselessly against the chains, and that knife kept on cutting.

An age later, Lady Zorokov said, "I think we've seen enough. She's sufficiently clipped."

Six neat squares of skin now seeped on the tile before me.

The guard released me, and I collapsed half-naked onto the floor, tears streaming my cheeks.

"Poor thing. Look at that little broken bird," Lady Zorokov cooed. I forced myself to look up at her. Pain and the drugs made my vision blurry, but she leaned in close enough to be the only sharp thing in this world.

"Your rebellion has no teeth, Tisaanah," she said, and only now was there emotion on her face, a little sneer at her lip. "Look at all of you, stumbling around trying to be fierce, like kittens learning to hunt." She scoffed. "No. A lion knows a lamb when they see one. Too bad I can't hang your skin up to let the rest of them know they're wandering into the slaughterhouse."

AFTER SHE WAS GONE, I forced myself to my hands and knees. A gasp escaped my throat when I moved—everything hurt so badly I wanted to curl up and die.

But I knew that I would not die. The Zorokovs needed me for something. The torture was painful, but it wasn't fatal. They wouldn't allow me the mercy of death.

Their goal wasn't to kill me. Their goal wasn't even to punish me. No, that had been a test, and a shockingly obvious one. They'd heard all about what happened at the Mikov estate. They wanted to make sure they clipped my wings.

It had taken all my self-control not to break, not to lash out with the dregs of magic I still did have at my disposal. But a few chunks of my flesh were a small sacrifice to hide my flight.

My head swam as I crawled across the floor. I had been drugged more, though, apparently, I had been unconscious when they'd been administered. Perhaps it was in the water I'd chugged down earlier. Every part of my body ached to go to sleep, but I forced my mind to sharpen.

The drugs made it difficult to tell how much time had passed since I had arrived here, but surely by now Max knew what had happened. The fact that he hadn't yet come for me meant that he understood what I wanted him to do, which meant—I hoped— that he was on his way to Orasiev.

If I was going to be ready for what happened next, I still had work to do.

Unpleasant, unpleasant work.

I dragged myself to the wall and looped my chains around my good hand. With the other—using my two functional remaining fingers—I picked up the tatters of my old shirt and stuffed the fabric between my teeth.

I set the chain over my shoulder. It was rusty. Just the touch of the cold, rough metal to my still-bleeding skin made my vision blur.

Gods, the things that I do.

I clamped my jaw down hard on the fabric.

And then I pulled at the chain as hard as I could, sawing my wounded back against it, feeling my flesh rip deeper and deeper and deeper.

I counted the first few strokes before I lost track. Blood pooled around my knees, then hands.

I stopped when I lost consciousness.

CHAPTER SIXTY-EIGHT

AEFE

F inally, I was called to court. Meajqa summoned me to the library to meet with the rest of the court. He came to get me personally, which was unusual.

"I'm here myself because I need to confirm that you will not attack the king if I bring you to see him."

He was dead serious.

I did not know if I wanted to make that promise. I said, "I'll try."

"I don't know that I can accept that answer, my vicious, mysterious friend."

"You have no choice but to accept it," I snapped.

Meajqa cringed and, reluctantly, beckoned me to follow.

As we walked down the halls, I counted all the things I would scream in Caduan's face. I imagined what it would look like to get him on the ground. When I was Reshaye I would have simply killed anyone who made me feel so powerless.

But when I finally saw Caduan's face, I didn't want to kill him. Because when I walked into the room, his eyes immediately found mine, as if he had been waiting for me. He looked... relieved.

Like he was happy to see me. Like he had missed me.

Our gazes met and lingered for a long moment before he cleared his throat and turned to the rest of the table. Luia and Vythian were there as well, and I wondered if I imagined the fact that they were watching the two of us with just as much abject curiosity as Meajqa was.

That went away as soon as Caduan spoke.

"Vythian's spies have come back with important information," he said.

Everyone was now all business. Vythian nodded gravely. "The Zorokovs and other leading Threllian Lords have been communicating with Ara."

Meajqa's face went as cold and still as stone. He set his wine glass down.

"They *what?*"

"They have been sending letters to Ara." Vythian gave us a pointed stare. "To the Aran palace."

The Aran palace. The Aran queen. Nura.

Meajqa said, sweetly, "Well, why would they be doing a silly thing like that?"

"Do you want what I know or what I think?"

"Both," said Caduan.

"I know only that the letters are being passed through Threll to get to Ara. I know that at least three of them—likely more— have been passed to the Aran crown. I do not know the contents of these letters. I do not know exactly how many there are. They are being carefully hidden, and extreme measures have been taken to make sure they remain that way."

"Encouraging behavior from an ally," Meajqa said.

"Indeed. There are a variety of reasons why Threll might be in contact with Ara. But that brings us to what I think." His face went colder. "I think they are betraying us."

Meajqa scoffed. "After we ceded to their demands. After so many of our own and one of our greatest generals died on their battlefield. They turn and stab us in the back."

"Is anyone truly surprised?" muttered Luia.

"I admit that I thought they would see more value in our alliance than to treat it this way," Vythian said.

I was not surprised. I still held Tisaanah's memories within me, as vivid as my own. I could feel that whip upon my own back, marks placed there by the betrayal of someone she had thought loved her.

Humans betrayed. They lied. It was in their souls.

Caduan's lips thinned. "And our options?"

"We could give them the opportunity to explain themselves," Vythian said. "Knowing, of course, that they could lie. But it would give us the chance to find out what information they know while preserving the alliance."

Meajqa scoffed again and took another long drink of wine.

"*Or,*" Caduan said, coldly.

"Or we destroy them." Anger made my words quick and sharp—they left my lips without my permission. My anger was everywhere at once, bubbling over at Caduan for abandoning me, at the Arans for centuries of torture, at the Threllians for their betrayal now.

But I did not have to accept such things. I knew how good vengeance felt. How much pain could be soothed with the iron taste of blood.

I stood, my fingernails biting my palms.

"We are more powerful than we were before," I snarled. "I alone killed hundreds of human men at Niraja. We are beyond needing the Threllians' pathetic resources. It's time to stop being *cowardly.*" I spat the word across the table like an arrow. "We are stronger than them. You set out to make a strong move against the humans. None of them are more disgusting, less worthy of life, than the society the Threllians have built. We have spent too long being cautious. We've spent too long hiding because we are afraid of what we are capable of."

"If we do this," Caduan said, calmly, "there is no coming back." He did not look at anyone but me. He barely blinked.

"You claimed that you would destroy human civilization because it brought nothing but pain and death. You claimed that we would put an end to them. Your country has rallied behind you in that. Last week you read three hundred names of Fey dead by human hands. What does it matter whose color they bore? The Threllians would have killed them just as willingly as the Arans. Let us avenge them."

I was not talking about the three hundred dead Fey.

The vengeance, Meajqa had said, *is for you.*

And as I spoke, I saw that fire, that hunger, seep into Caduan's eyes.

"Are we ready?" he said.

I knew what he was really asking. If we were to do this—wage our war in earnest, rely on our own power instead of the numbers provided by the Threllians—he needed me. Needed my power. Needed my rage.

"I am ready," I said, without hesitation.

Something like pride flickered across Caduan's face. He rose and turned to the map on the wall. "Then we destroy Threll," he said.

He pressed his hand to Threll then swept it away, leaving behind a smear of crimson over the parchment—human blood.

"We are done being cowards."

CHAPTER SIXTY-NINE

MAX

We moved fast. It took only two days to get to Orasiev, and I had spent every second of them thinking of Tisaanah and what she was going through in captivity. At times, my worry was so overwhelming that I was ready to throw away this entire stupid idea in favor of storming the gates myself and bringing her home with me, even if it meant getting myself killed, war be damned. I wanted her—needed her—safe with me. The faster we got to Orasiev, the faster that came to being a reality.

When we arrived, I could have fucking wept for it.

It was strange to think that Orasiev was once a Threllian Lord's estate, the sort of city that would look exactly like all the other white stone cities built by the Threllians. The rebels had done so much to separate it from that legacy. The ivory had been splashed with paint, creating a cacophony of colors that reminded me of my garden. Strips of colorful fabric hung from the city walls—flags, I realized as we approached. Many, many different flags. When the breeze blew, they flew into the air like wings, revealing deep cracks beneath them, jarring scars from the siege that the rebels had only just managed to survive.

Once you noticed those cracks, you started to notice all the other signs of war, too. The haphazard spears stuck to the tops of the walls — some broken, some bloody. The boarded-over doors. The guards that milled about at the gates, though they barely even looked like soldiers so much as random collections of half-starved, battle-scarred people who happened to wear the same scarves around their necks: red.

Still…

When we Stratagrammed into the area, and I saw that city for the first time, my throat got suddenly tight. All that color rising up from the smooth gold of the plains, refusing to be silent, refusing to become invisible. It had held against two of the most powerful militaries in the world. Against all odds, it still stood.

This was what Tisaanah had fought so hard for. This was what she had dreamed of when she crawled to the Orders' steps, half-dead.

"I can't believe it's still here," Sammerin muttered, amazed.

"They withstood the Threllians *and* the Fey here?" Brayan sounded downright awed.

I could have stood there longer just to take it in. But I was acutely aware, in every horrible way, of what Tisaanah was suffering right now. I found myself recalling what Brayan had said about unknowns. A million terrible scenarios looped through my mind, constantly.

"Come on," I said. "No time to waste."

The moment we approached, five soldiers at the top of the wall trained arrows on us, shouting down Thereni too fast for me to decipher.

We put our hands up. I glanced at Sammerin and Brayan. "Did either of you get that?"

Nothing.

I sighed and turned back to the guards.

"My name is Maxantarius Farlione," I called up, in Thereni. "I come to speaking with Filias. He is where?"

I almost certainly butchered that.

The guards glanced at each other warily. The youngest man glowered down at me.

"You're Aran," he sneered. "An Aran spy."

I didn't have time for this. I probably held one of the most infamous names on this continent or Ara's. If I was a spy, that made me a fucking terrible one. I would've said that, too, if I could speak the language well enough. Instead, I settled for, "Why should I say lies?"

"There are lots of reasons to lie, actually," Sammerin muttered.

My teeth ground.

"It is for Tisaanah Vytezic," I shouted, frustrated. *"Please."*

It was Tisaanah's name that made the man's face change. He was about to say something when he was interrupted by some commotion behind him that I couldn't see, and he disappeared.

I cursed in frustration.

But then a moment later, a blond head of hair poked up from the wall. A bruised and bandaged Serel leaned over the railing, an enormous grin on his face. "Max! It is you!"

I heaved a sigh of relief. Despite the circumstances, I found myself smiling. That grin of his really was infectious.

"It is indeed. Let me in. We need to talk." My smile faded to a scowl as the guards scrambled to raise the gates. "By the way, I hear you wanted to leave me to rot in prison?"

———————

AT FIRST, Serel was thrilled, speaking so fast in Thereni that none of us understood a word of it. But when he met us at the gates, I saw the exact moment he realized Tisaanah was not here. He had been ready to take us on a grand tour of the jewel of the rebellion, but when the realization hit him, his face fell and steps faltered, and all of that was abandoned in favor of a single room at the top of Orasiev's tallest building.

Once, this must have been the study of the Lord that ruled over this estate. The furniture was disgustingly ornate, perched upon luxurious furs and decadent tile mosaics, all framing an expansive view of Orasiev's skyline. But whereas this room had likely once been all white, now splashes of color had been painted over the walls—the same seven colors that adorned the banners at the wall—and maps and notes and diagrams had been pinned over every surface.

Filias, Riasha, and Serel gathered with us, and in a broken mix of Thereni and Aran I stumbled through telling them what had happened to Tisaanah. Serel barely let me finish before he leapt to his feet.

He and Filias exchanged a knowing look. "The meeting," Serel muttered, and Filias nodded.

I glanced between them. "Meeting?"

"We got some interesting intelligence recently," Filias said. "From slaves working in Nura's Threllian territory. She had traveled to Threll, but she's keeping it very quiet. Apparently, she has some secretive meetings set up with Threllian Lords. No one is supposed to know." He gave a half-smile. "Slaves are good at not existing, though. Hear all sorts of things we aren't supposed to."

My brow knitted. Nura? Nura, in Threll? She had been getting hit from all directions by the Threllians, on behalf of their alliance with the Fey. Perhaps the Threllian Lords, enterprising as they were, were beginning to consider reshuffling their loyalties.

The thought of Nura having the manpower and brutality of the Lords on her side made me uneasy. But the idea that Tisaanah might be turned over to Nura—that Tisaanah might get locked up in Ilyzath's torturous walls or strapped to Nura's laboratory tables—downright *terrified* me.

"All the more reason to get her out right away," Serel said. "We can leave immediately. Me, Filias, some of our best fighters —we can get her out of there *fast*."

"No," I said. "We do more than that."

Serel had already made it halfway to the door. Now all three of them looked at me like I had lost my mind.

"I don't understand," Riasha said. "Isn't that why you're here? For backup?"

"Yes. I…" Ascended above, I had a whole new appreciation

for how Tisaanah must have felt, trying to stumble through such important conversations with a language barrier this wide. "We can stop them. Stop the Zorokovs for *always*."

Filias said, understandably, "I don't know what that means."

Brayan stepped in. "We have an opening to make a big move against Threllian Lords." He opened his hands up, as if to demonstrate the scale. "A big move that will make a big victory. The Zorokovs are a strong house, and small many remain after the Mikovs fell. If we end them now, we can end the Threllian empire."

His Threni was marginally better than mine, and judging by the shocked expressions on their faces, it got the point across. Of the three of them, Serel paled the most. He turned to Filias and spoke in low, very fast Threni, then turned back to us.

"How can we possibly win in an all-out offensive against the Zorokovs? I barely survived Malakhan. I saw what they can do, especially with the help of the Fey. Nothing can stop me from getting Tisaanah out of there, but going against *all* of them? I don't know if we can survive that."

Pity twinged in my chest for Serel. I recognized the undercurrent in his voice. A part of him was still in Malakahn, thinking he would die there. I would not wish a siege on anyone. They did something to a person, and those kinds of marks don't fade fast.

I wouldn't tell him he was wrong—he wasn't. I wouldn't try to push him, because no one should be pushed onto a battlefield.

Instead I only told him the truth.

"I want promise you," I said. "I want promise for a win. I cannot. But we have…" I touched the pouch at my hip and struggled to find a Threni word that could describe this. "…strength. *Magic.*" I used the Aran word. "We have a chance right now. Maybe we do not get one again."

Serel looked uneasy and sank back down into his seat. Filias rose and stood behind him, his hands resting on Serel's shoulders, one thumb circling in a barely-there caress.

"I won't ask you for promises," he said to me, "but do you really think we can do this?"

What a difficult question. I had a couple of decade's worth of finely curated pessimism to cut through before I answered.

"Yes," I said, at last. "I do."

Even if it made me an idiot.

"And more important," I added, "is Tisaanah believes it. You know she does."

The corners of Filias's mouth tightened in a wry smirk. "Oh, I know."

He and Serel exchanged a long look, one that seemed like it was having an unspoken conversation.

"Fuck it," Filias said. "I think we should do it. We didn't get this far by being cautious. If we were measuring ourselves by the odds, I would still be lugging Esmaris Mikov's grain around all day. We have exceeded their expectations again and again. Let's do it one more time."

Serel still looked nervous. Filias peered down at him, gently tipping Serel's chin back to meet his eyes.

"Don't you want to make those bastards bleed, Serel?"

He said it quietly, meant only for one, yet the words hung thick in the air. Serel's throat bobbed. He rose and turned to me.

"Fine," he said, at last. "Let's do it."

CHAPTER SEVENTY

TISAANAH

It was nearly a full day before someone came to see me, and by then I was deliriously feverish. I could do nothing but lie on the floor, listless, moans dripping from my throat.

I was barely conscious when Laron came into my room and swore to herself. She flipped me over to look at my face—which, of course, pressed my decimated back to the floor, making me cry out. She held her hand to my forehead and swore again.

Darkness took me.

When it parted again, someone else leaned over me—a man, middle-aged, with dark salt-and-pepper hair.

"She's burning," Laron muttered, sounding a little panicked. "Look at her back! Idiot girl. That's worse than what they did to her. I don't know how she made it so much worse."

The man was silent as he felt my face, my pulse, and gently turned me to examine my seeping back. As he leaned over me, I caught a glimpse of the tattoo on his wrist—a sigil. He was a slave.

Just as I thought. Good.

His hands ran over my back, and I let out a whimper as his magic fluttered across my skin.

"I'm trying to help," he muttered, sounding tired but kind.

I made a sound halfway between a moan and a sob.

"She can't die, Merick," Laron hissed. "They'll have my gods-damned head. Do you know how the Lady would react—"

The man had a bag with him, which he pulled closer. Inside, I glimpsed many little glass vials. He grabbed two, then mixed them. A flash of magic radiated through the liquid.

"Hold her head back."

Laron obeyed. Pain shook me as she pushed me upright.

"Sorry…" She sounded as if she meant it.

The potion that Merick poured down my throat burned the whole way through me, and it was so potent that I would have thrown it up were it not for his hand clamped hard over my mouth. Eventually my body accepted it, and they released me, allowing me to fall to the ground.

A call rang out in the distance. Laron leapt to her feet and swore.

"Go," Merick said, softly. "I'll stay with her."

Laron thanked him before rushing out of the room, leaving Merick and I alone. With great effort, I forced my head up to look at him.

Days of constant drugging, combined with the infection, had taken their toll. But this, now, was my chance.

No one, not even Threllian Lords, could have that much Chryxalis on-hand without a Wielder available who knew how to make it. And that Wielder likely would have been a healer—someone who knew how to manipulate bodies.

The potions in Merick's bag only confirmed my theory.

And this moment, now, the next step in my plan, was worth my self-inflicted injury, was worth the fever.

"Hello," I rasped, my voice dull and scratchy. "I need to ask you something."

I DIDN'T KNOW how many days passed. My fever faded as a result of Merick's care, but they kept me so drugged that I was nearly incoherent, dreams and reality and pain blending together. I continued to meet with Merick, the gears of my plan continued to turn, and time passed.

One day, I felt a little clearer. I was able to actually get up. I ate the bread and soup I was given, and still had an appetite after. My fingers had been set, and while they ached, it was manageable. My back was painful, but no longer nursed a raging infection.

After I ate, the door flew open and three maids, Laron included, entered. One bore a wheeled rack of fine clothing, another carried a box of shoes, and Laron was armed with hair and face brushes.

"What is this?" I asked.

"The day we get rid of you," Laron said coldly. But her expression held a hint of something I might call concern.

They lengthened my restraints enough to give me a range of movement about the room. I discarded my dirty, bloody, urine-stained clothing. Water was dumped over me, and the grime scrubbed away.

I was given a white silk dress to wear. It slid smoothly over my clean skin as if an hour ago I hadn't been covered in my own filth.

My jaw was tight, my nerves close to the surface.

I thought of Max, Sammerin, Serel. *Where are you?*

I wasn't surprised by the showmanship. The Threllians prized beauty—even in their enemies. I knew by now that I was a gift for someone, and a gift from the Threllians would always be presented with a flourish, even if it simply meant swaddling death in velvet and silk.

I had come to the conclusion that I was most likely going to be given to the Fey. It made the most sense. The Threllians and the Fey were allies; both wanted me dead. By turning me over to King Caduan, the Threllians proved their usefulness to the Fey and made a dramatic gesture of goodwill.

Only now did real fear settle in my stomach.

I had been so certain that if my friends came for me, I would know it. But what if I had been overconfident? What if my careful measures were not careful enough?

A chillingly vivid image of Max, bloody and limp, pinned to the Zorokovs' pristine walls flashed through my mind, and I had to fight to keep the bile down.

I imagined my mother, as she had wiped my terrified tears when I was a child. *None of that.*

None of that, Tisaanah.

I was not afraid.

The other maids left the room, leaving Laron and I alone. I sat in front of the mirror. I looked, despite everything, beautiful, or at least beautiful the way that the Threllians liked it—colorless and clean. My lips were pink and shiny, my eyes wide and framed with brown and pink kohl, my cheeks flushed with powder. Laron stood behind me and worked the final tangles from my hair.

I watched her in the mirror. The lines that etched her features were not the marks of cruelty, but of worry. In some ways, she looked familiar. I had seen the beginnings of those lines on my own mother's face, even all those years ago.

I wondered if my mother had lived long after she was sold.

I wondered if she, too, had been bitter at the world that had taken her child from her, and at the hope that was too painful to even acknowledge.

"Your daughter should still be here," I said.

Laron stopped brushing my hair but did not look up. Then she resumed.

"Should be."

"I know she deserved more. She deserved the life that she dreamed about. I wish I had been able to give that to her."

Laron's features had grown hard. "Me too," she said.

"Laron."

At last, her gaze flicked up to meet mine in the mirror.

"Give me one chance," I said.

441

A slow wave of anger passed over Laron's face, and I thought for a minute that she would scream at me.

"They killed her for nothing," she spat, between clenched teeth.

Now I understood. Her anger was not for me. Her anger was for *them*.

"What if it doesn't have to be for nothing?" I whispered.

Laron trembled with rage. Her eyes were bright and shining. She set the brush down.

I HEARD THE FEAST BEGIN — THE horns gave it away, their tinny melody echoing down the hall. I sat politely with my hands folded in my lap until guards arrived and took me by each arm. They led me down immaculate hallways, that music growing louder and louder, until at last we arrived at a banquet hall. Just as they had when I was a slave at Esmaris's estate, dozens of white-clad bodies turned to me when I entered. I was entertainment, after all—then as the dancer, now as the gruesome, sacrificial gift.

I did not acknowledge the slow confusion roll over Lady Zorokov's face as she took in my outfit. Not the white of a slaughtering lamb, as she had selected, but bright, bloody red. I kept my face very, very still.

And yet, I could not stop a single, shocked intake of breath when I was brought down the center of the ballroom to be presented to the guest of honor.

I had been prepared for so much.

But I had not been prepared for Nura to be the one sitting beside Lady and Lord Zorokov, smiling back at me.

CHAPTER SEVENTY-ONE

TISAANAH

I was led to the center of the room and forced to my knees. Nura rose from her chair at the head table. I had to fight to keep my expression neutral. I hated her more than I had ever hated anyone.

"A gift for you," Lady Zorokov said. "A gesture of goodwill, celebrating the birth of a beautiful alliance."

The corner of Nura's mouth curled. She looked at me the way a cat looked at a songbird.

"If I recall correctly," she said, "you made some very unpleasant threats not very long ago because we would not send you her head."

Nura's Thereni was heavily accented, but still elegant and icy.

Lady Zorokov laughed, while Lord Zorokov merely smirked.

"Forgive us for the harsh words we had for your predecessor," he said. "I understand that we both have similar attitudes towards our enemies. I'm sure that her head will end up on a stick either way, but our gift to you is the pleasure of being the one to do it."

"How kind." Nura walked around the table and leaned down before me, so we were nearly at eye level.

"It's good to see you," she said, in Aran. "It's been awhile."

"You're a long way from home," I said, in Thereni. "We speak my language here."

Her smirk soured, but when she spoke again, it was in Thereni. "Where is Max?"

I gave her a serene smile, one that made confusion ripple across her face.

"I know that you know where he is," she said, lower. She struggled now to keep up her facade of cold indifference. All that tension—all that desperation—was so much closer to the surface. Even drugged, my magic fluttered with it.

Something had changed about her, in these last months. As if hour by hour, she had been pushing herself closer to the edge of a cliff, chipping away at her own carefully maintained restraint.

I looked around. This room was not very different from the ballrooms that I used to dance in, night after night, offering myself up for consumption to people who saw me as nothing but an interesting novelty. *Look at me*, I'd commanded, then, and I'd survived by showing them exactly what they wanted to see.

Now I said, *Look at me.*

And when I rose from my knees, they did, drawing in gasps of shock. Casually, I walked to the head table.

"Guards!" Lady Zorokov cried.

The guards did not move.

"*Guards!*" she shrieked again.

I leaned over the table. The Zorokovs had taken inspiration, it seemed, from Lord Farimov's dinner menu. Every nation that Threll had conquered was represented here. I touched a bowl of Nyzrenese blood apricots, and they turned to rot.

"You are just so easy to trick," I said to her. "It's like you want nothing more than to underestimate us."

I pushed deeper into my magic and relished the way it felt flowing through me. The bountiful feast slowly withered, the sour-sweet stench of death replacing the mouth-watering aromas.

It felt good to finally release the magic I had been hiding all this time. Merick had made sure that my dose of Chryxalis was, today, as mild as he could get away with under the watchful overseer's eye.

But even drugged, I felt like a phoenix.

At first, they all stared at me, too shocked to move. Nura struck first. I heard her steps behind me, whirled out of her grip and caught her slender wrist.

She didn't break eye contact, barely wincing as decay ate at her skin.

Over her shoulder, I glanced at the entrance to the great room. Bright gold streaks of sunset splashed over white tile. Laron stood beside the door, hands clasped before her. She lifted her chin to me in confirmation of what I already knew.

"You're looking for Max?" I said. "No need. He'll be here soon."

Nura's brow knitted. "What?"

I could not have planned it better than the way it unfolded. At that moment, a foreman rushed into the room, half-stumbling over the guests in a way that earned a glare from the Zorokovs.

"I couldn't stop them," he panted. "I couldn't—no one would fight, and—"

The guests whispered uneasily. Lord Zorokov rose. "Full sentences," he snapped.

The foreman swallowed, trying and failing to catch his breath. "The west," he said. "An army."

The whispers became murmurs.

"—and the east," the foreman spit out. "And they're here, they're *in the house*."

East?

That part I didn't know about.

Lady Zorokov asked, "Who?"

As if on cue, the double doors opened, and we all looked to the entrance of the great hall.

I expected Max to be standing there.

But it wasn't Max. It was the King of the Fey.

CHAPTER SEVENTY-TWO

MAX

I couldn't believe how good she was.

We marched into the city through the west side, crossing over a series of bridges across the canals. The guards just let us pass. The ones that were slaves knew we were coming. The ones that weren't were so lethargic they were nearly unconscious, half-slumped over at their posts, in no shape to stop us. Sammerin paused to examine one of these men, forcing open his eyes to look at his pupils.

"This was magic," he said. "By a Solarie flesh-worker who specializes in potions. Solid work. It won't wear off for days."

How did Tisaanah do that? Arrange the drugging of so many guards? It's a strange thing, to be proud of your lover as you walk past piles of slumped-over bodies, but I felt it, nonetheless. Even Ishqa was somewhat awed. When he had arrived in Orasiev, he hadn't bothered to hide his annoyance at our sudden acceleration of plans. It seemed like he was growing a bit more convinced now, as we saw the measures Tisaanah had taken, even from captivity, to make this a success.

As we advanced through the city, though, dread supplanted that pride. Many of the slaves that allowed us to pass were disfigured—hands gesturing us forward with missing fingers, hair barely hiding burnt-off ears, faces marked with streaks of scar tissue. The Zorokovs had sent Tisaanah the deaths of hundreds of innocents for nothing more than petty revenge. What could they have done to her during her time here?

This is too easy, I thought. *It cannot possibly be this simple.*

I reached into the leather pouch at my hip—secured by *multiple* buckles—and touched the petrified heart. Magic pulsed at my fingertips, stirred merely by having it close by. Actually, my magic was unusually active today, like a boat on top of a churning sea.

"You'd better guard that thing with your life," Sammerin said.

I planned on it. I prayed I wouldn't have to use it.

I stopped walking and frowned. Something was strange. Something felt… odd, deep beneath the surface of my senses and my magic.

A flash of gold hurtled through the air and landed gracefully before us.

I knew immediately that something was wrong. Ishqa looked slightly panicked.

"The king is here," he said, the way someone would warn that the ground was about to open up beneath their feet.

I looked to the east, and my heart stopped beating.

The king is here, Ishqa said, as if it was one person.

No. At the gates was an Ascended-damned *army* of Fey—hundreds, perhaps even thousands, rolling in a wave down the hillside.

Cold fear settled over me. We had not been expecting this.

Frightened whispers already rippled through our rebel ranks. They'd been prepared to inflict vengeance on their former abusers—but most of them, save for those who had been at Malakahn, had never encountered so many Fey before. Killing a bunch of out-of-shape slave owners was one thing. Going up against thousands of Fey was another.

Serel already paced up and down the lines, trying to talk them down.

"Go." Filias grabbed my shoulder and pushed me forward. "We'll lead. Go find her."

I didn't need to be told twice. I ran.

CHAPTER SEVENTY-THREE

AEFE

I t felt good to be looked at with this much fear. These people —these selfish, pathetic humans—looked at us like we were gods.

I wanted to laugh. I felt more powerful than I ever had since returning to this body. I was a little drunk, too. Meajqa had slipped me a flask before we entered the city, and I had not cared to turn it down. I wanted to feel unstoppable.

Meajqa had given me a nod and a wink then, practically playful. Now, his face was stone as he stood next to me. I followed his stare—followed it to the Aran queen, who stood near the table. Beside her was Tisaanah. The sight of her, even from a distance, made my heartbeat quicken.

Caduan entered the ballroom first. He observed the party with a frigid stare.

"What is this?" he said, in Thereni. "We were not invited?"

For a long moment, all the humans were still. At last, Lord Zorokov rose. "Get out of my home."

Caduan's laugh was the edge of a blade. "You call this a home? This is not a home. This is a prison." Guests scrambled away from him as he crossed the room, one portly woman trip-

449

ping backwards over a chair. He regarded her with cool disgust. Then his gaze settled on Nura, and the disgust turned to outright hatred. "But I suppose lack of respect for life is a common trait among your kind."

"We aren't—" Lord Zorokov started.

"No need. Save your words. I know what is happening here, and I am not even surprised by it."

One of the noblewomen let out a strangled cry and dove for the door. Luia caught her arm, yanked her back, and in one smooth movement, gutted her with her blade.

"She would not have made it far," Caduan said calmly. "The doors are barred."

Lord Zorokov advanced, fury settling into the lines of his face. "You don't know who you're threatening. You can't do this to us."

"I am not threatening. I am warning. And certainly, I *can* do this to you. I don't need you anymore."

Perhaps once, Lord Zorokov had been considered a great warrior by his people. Perhaps that was how he'd gained his power—by speaking the only language humans knew. Perhaps by those standards, the lunge he made for Caduan was a skilled one.

But for us? It was nothing.

I smoothly stepped in front of Caduan. My magic had been itching at my skin this entire time, desperate to be released. The bright light cut through the air like lightning. My blade struck him just as my magic did. His blood spattered me in a hot spray.

I hated this man.

When he fell to the ground, throat opened, burns on his face and black flowers growing from his eyes, I turned myself over to the glorious euphoria of battle.

In an instant, chaos broke loose. The humans screamed, climbing over each other in wild attempts to either escape or attack us.

But I looked only at the Aran queen across the room, and I let the anger sweep me away.

CHAPTER SEVENTY-FOUR

MAX

I opened my second eyelids. I needed to move faster than my limbs could carry me—as magic, I moved like the air, racing through hallways in a stream of flame.

Inside, I was greeted by a tableau of death. It was a blood-bath. The floor was slick with violet and crimson, mixing together like running paint. The Fey, apparently, wasted no time. There were already bodies everywhere, mostly Threllians clad in white. As I ran, I threw open doors and smashed windows to give people avenues of evacuation. Most of the slaves knew that we were coming and had found a way to get out if they could, but those who hadn't been able to now clustered huddled up in bedrooms or closets.

With every room I searched, I grew more panicked.

Where are you, Tisaanah? Where are you?

I reached down, down, down, like a coin falling into a well, searching for her in the dregs of the magic we both drew from.

And...

There.

There she was. A wordless answer to my call: *Here I am. Come to me.*

I obeyed.

CHAPTER SEVENTY-FIVE

TISAANAH

When all hell broke loose, I didn't give myself time to consider what was happening. I just *ran*.

The sword I'd grabbed from a fallen guard was too heavy for me, and it had no channels to accommodate my magic. I often missed Il'Sahaj, but never so fiercely as I did now, hacking through body after body as I pushed myself down crimson-bathed hallways.

West. I needed to get to the west side of the city. I could feel Max's presence somewhere close in the deepest layers of the magic we shared, though I struggled to remain attuned to it. My senses were dulled by the effects of Chryxalis and by my exhaustion. My body was weak from the torture I'd endured.

The scale of destruction was greater than I ever could have anticipated. This was not a battle. It was a systemic slaughter. The Fey had no goal but to kill everyone here.

I rounded a corner to see a one-winged Fey gutting a Threllian woman from her navel all the way to her throat, so focused on his task that I was able to slip by him and keep running.

Where are you, Max. Where are you.

I reached down into the magic and felt a returning tug. Relief flooded through me.

But it only lasted for a moment. Because then I sensed another presence there, too. One that I knew as well as my own.

Eventually, I found myself at a dead end—a circular gallery at the end of the hall, with no doors out save for a wide, curved balcony and a long drop beneath it. I lurched to a stop, panting. Generations of Threllian conquerors stared back at me disapprovingly through oil-painted glares.

The hairs rose on the back of my neck in a way that told me I was not alone.

I turned. A Fey woman stood in the entrance to the room. She was tall and slender, bloody strands of dark-red hair hanging around a gaunt face. She had the most entrancing eyes, large and downturned, and a striking color of rusty violet.

I had never seen this face before... and yet, I knew this person.

Suddenly I was very, very afraid.

"It's you," I whispered. "Reshaye."

CHAPTER SEVENTY-SIX

AEFE

S he was so close. I had never seen Tisaanah's face anywhere but in the mirror. She was the same, and yet, so very different. I could see so much more of her this way, and so much less. When I stepped forward, I half expected her to move with me.

I had not realized, then, exactly how unusual she looked to the rest of the world. I loved her mind for all the crevices her broken pieces gave me—how easily we fit together. But even her face was composed of many fragments, those patches of tan and white making her look like a cracked porcelain doll.

She looked like home.

For the last few weeks, I had at last begun to feel right in this body. But the sight of her released sharp pangs of grief in all the empty parts of me that she would have occupied. It shook me down to my core.

A part of me still wanted to crawl inside of her skin. A part of me still wanted her.

"It's you," she whispered, sounding as if she hadn't intended to speak. "Reshaye."

I approached her until I was close enough to feel the warmth of her body. Our noses nearly brushed. I could have kissed her.

455

"That is not my name."

"Aefe."

Why did it feel so strange to hear her voice saying that?

"Maybe that is not my name, either."

The sight of her shook loose the fragile grip upon my new sense of self. I had started to feel like Aefe, but now I found myself questioning it. Maybe I was still Reshaye. Or maybe I was half of each, and all of neither.

Her brow furrowed, and I struggled to decipher her expression. "Why are you here?"

I nearly laughed. Did she think I did not know what she was asking? The same thing Tisaanah always asked in her subtle ways—*what do you want?*

"Justice," I said. "Retribution."

It was only now, as the words left my lips, that I realized the full extent of their meaning. That I realized how much of that justice today was for *her.* Perhaps it was because I still felt her memories burning in my heart. Perhaps it was because I still felt her scars upon my own back.

"It won't stop after this," she murmured. "What your king wants to do."

"I know." And that was the joy of it. It was only the beginning.

"It does not have to be this way, Aefe."

I smiled, nearly breaking into a laugh. "You can not lie to me. I know what your mind feels like. I know you yearn for your vengeance just as much as I yearn for mine."

Her eyes were hypnotic, large and mismatched. They refused to relinquish my gaze. "Not like this. Not what will come after it. You do not have to be this, anymore. No one can make you."

I was confused. Make me do this? I *wanted* this. For the first time, I was choosing my path. I was fighting for *my own people,* not someone else's.

"I want this," I bit out. "You are the one that taught me what it was to leave a mark upon the world, and I will leave it." I pressed closer, my eyes bearing into hers. "The Lejara. We know that you have one. Where—"

Instead of answering, she said, "You sacrificed yourself for me. I saw you, Reshaye. Aefe. I *saw* you."

Those three words made me stop short.

I saw you.

It was the truth. As Reshaye, no one saw me. I was a living being trapped in a world where no one acknowledged me, except for a single soul. What choice did I have but to become obsessed with them? Tisaanah had become everything to me then. My lover, my enemy, my captor, my slave. All these things, bound inextricably to what I had once been.

I reached out with a trembling hand and stroked her cheek. She was so soft. So fragile. And so unremarkably human.

She tried to hide it, but could not. She could not hide her flinch. She could not hide the tensing of her muscles. She could not hide the slight buzz in the air between us as I felt her magic simmer to life, ready to act.

She was afraid of me. We were no longer the same. She was *human.*

Once I had thought what we shared was love. But even then, she had abandoned me, just as all the other humans had. She would not hesitate to murder me now, rip me away from my newfound purpose, drag my corpse to a room of white and white. Just as Maxantarius had cast me out and left me to hundreds and hundreds of days of torture. Just as my father had turned on me, in another life.

It was Reshaye who had craved Tisaanah. Not the new version of myself, who had a new home and a new purpose. And Aefe could not live until Reshaye was dead.

Once, I had loved her. But now, she was the enemy.

"No," I said, quietly. "I am exactly who I wish to be."

My hand trailed down past her jaw, resting at her throat.

Tightened. Tightened.

Tisaanah was smaller than I, her neck slender compared to the length of my fingers. Her eyes bulged as I lifted her off the ground. She clawed at my hand, leaving wounds of rot and pus that I barely felt.

My anger flared, demanding release. Black flowers sprouted at my fingertips, their vines crawling over her skin.

Tisaanah had become powerful through the gifts I—*I!*—had given her. She had used me and discarded me, just as her own captors had done to her.

She was like the rest of them, I told myself. Now, I had my own people who loved me, who trusted me. Tisaanah could not live if they were to survive. If she did not destroy us, then she would be captured and exploited by people who would.

Still, something made me pause as her head began to loll— just long enough that I was caught off guard when fire surrounded me.

CHAPTER SEVENTY-SEVEN

MAX

I knew what she was. She looked at me like I'd known her for a hundred years. One look at those eyes, wild with fury, and I knew.

Aefe—Reshaye—hit the ground hard. She dropped Tisaanah, who rolled and gasped for breath. I had only seconds to kneel beside her, touch her shoulder in a wordless *"Tell me you're alright."*

She nodded, rubbing her throat. Then her eyes widened, and she pushed me out of the way.

Aefe lunged for us. Her magic was unlike anything I'd ever seen, light and—fuck, were those *flowers?*—flaring at her finger-tips. I was a little too slow. A glancing blow from her magic at my shoulder nearly immobilized me with unnatural, intense pain.

He needs her power, Ishqa had told us. *He needs her to win this war.*

It didn't matter what face it wore. This thing should not exist.

I opened my second eyelids and met Aefe's attack head-on. Blinding light erupted through the room, white and red clashing. She was strong—stronger than a human, maybe even stronger than a typical Fey. When fire licked her flesh, she barely reacted.

I slipped her grasp one, two, three times. Struck at her legs to make her fall. I crawled over her, pinning her. My magic burned up in my veins. I had been using too much of it. Something was unstable in the layers of magic beneath. My power was growing harder to control.

But then again, maybe I didn't need control now.

My worst nightmares had been given a human face, but there was nothing human about this thing. Nothing real, just a power that should never have been allowed to exist. A tragic person who had been distorted long past a time when she should have been alive, turned into something grotesque.

I had called Reshaye a monster the day it ruined my life. And as I leaned over this thing that had nearly killed Tisaanah, this creature that looked so deceptively alive, the word floated through my head again:

Monster.

With my free arm, I lifted my blade —

—Only for a crippling force to rip me away. I slammed into a wall, a painting frame shattering beneath the impact. My vision blurred. My connection to my magic stuttered. An arm pressed to my throat, pinning me.

Looking at me with something akin to curiosity was an auburn-haired Fey man with a copper crown on his head.

"Maxantarius Farlione," he said, quietly. "I have heard so much about you."

The Fey king.

The Fey king was *right here*, inches away from me.

I took my shot. Flames roared around us both. The king winced, but did not release me, his interest souring to fury. Vines wound over my arms, crawling to my throat like snakes. Tightening, tightening —

Tisaanah struck him, sending him collapsing to the tile floor. In an instant, Aefe was at his side.

I seized upon the opening. I reached deep, deep, sucking up any dregs of my remaining magic, and then released everything I had.

Just as they rose, the blast hit them with enough force to

send them falling together in a tangle of limbs over the balcony's edge.

It would stop them only for seconds. Tisaanah dove for me. Our hands intertwined. I was already reaching for the petrified heart. When I touched it, it seemed to call to us so much louder than before. *Come with me*, it sang. *Let us tear the world apart.*

Dizzying. Intoxicating. Seductive.

"Are they out?" Tisaanah panted. "Did everyone get out?"

"I—I think so."

Tisaanah looked pained, and I probably did too. *I think so.* So many uncertainties in "*I think so.*"

The plan had always been to get the slaves out as quickly as possible. We knew there was a possibility we would need to use this magic. Knew we needed to get everyone far away if we did.

Did they have enough time?

The thrum of magic from the heart shivered over us. Tisaanah looked to the balcony, which overlooked the east side of the city. Waves upon waves of Fey warriors poured through the gates.

The sight of it overwhelmed me. A horrible thought solidified into certainty:

Thousands would die if we did nothing.

"We push them out," Tisaanah said, voice frantic. "Focus on the east side, where the Fey and Threllians are concentrated. We change the terrain, not the people. Block them with stone, just like we did in Niraja."

Ascended above, I didn't like the sound of this at all. We had no idea how to use this thing. Could we even direct that magic that way?

BANG, as more doors in the distance collapsed.

Over Tisaanah's shoulder, I saw more Fey warriors rounding the corner. In the window beyond her, the streets were awash in red and purple blood.

No time.

I slit my hand and reached for Tisaanah's. We held the heart between us. Its power flowed through us so quickly, more potent than any drug I'd ever taken, more powerful than any magic I'd ever Wielded.

Let us rewrite the world, the heart sang.

The last thing I saw was Tisaanah's nod, as the world went white.

CHAPTER SEVENTY-EIGHT

AEFE

W e hit the ground hard, Caduan and I on top of each other. I felt a shift happen immediately, felt the sudden tear in the magic below, like sand falling away beneath my feet.

I rolled over. Caduan was not moving. Panic crawled up my throat.

"Caduan."

He did not move.

My senses screamed as the tear grew wider.

The Lejara. They were using the Lejara.

"CADUAN!"

His eyes snapped open just as the rip burst, as light began to bubble around the house, similar to what we had witnessed in Niraja.

It all happened at once.

Caduan rolled over me, pushing me to the ground beneath him. I felt him struggling with his magic as he tried to carry us away. But he was weak, injured. His own power resisted him.

Blinding light surrounded us.

He wouldn't be fast enough. I needed to act.

I lifted my hands, summoned every scrap of magic inside of me. *Protect us protect us protect us* —

"Don't let go," Caduan ground out, as his magic gave one final, powerful push.

White light consumed everything.

———————

WHEN I OPENED MY EYES, everything was different.

Caduan and I lay together in a tangle. We were not in the house any longer. Somehow, he had managed to complete his spell. We lay beyond the walls of the main building.

I pushed myself to my knees and looked around. The aftermath of the Lejara's power surrounded us. Walls had been rearranged without being broken, buildings now spotlessly half-buried in the ground.

The house was ahead of us. It was barely recognizable, a leveled pile of white rubble. Before it, the ground had cracked and shattered, rough stones jutting up into the air like the rocks at the bottom of a waterfall, rising so tall that they blotted out the late-afternoon sun. At first glance, it reminded me of a white version of the Obsidian cliffs.

No part of the terrain had been untouched. It was as if the hand of a god had reached down and simply rearranged the earth itself.

I looked down. Caduan was on the ground, not moving.

Panic. I forced myself to my knees, shaking him. *Wake up, wake up,* I shouted, or thought I did, because I could not hear myself.

My hearing returned with a loud *POP,* and my own screaming rang clear in my ears.

Now I heard what I couldn't before: *"AEFE!"* Meajqa skidded to a stop beside us, covered in human blood, his sword in his hand.

And with his shout came a hundred, or a thousand, other screams, here and in the distance. Wails of pain or shouts of soldiers trying to find their comrades. Cries of sheer shock at what they had just witnessed.

At last, Caduan's eyes opened.

Hours ago, I had been telling myself how much I hated Caduan. Now the sight of those eyes, open, piercing through me, was the most beautiful thing I'd ever seen.

Meajqa helped us to our feet. Caduan was weak, barely able to stand. When Meajqa released his arm, he nearly fell back to the ground.

"Are you hurt?" Meajqa asked, brow knitted.

"No," Caduan said, in an obvious lie that Meajqa did not challenge. "Are you?"

"I'll survive."

Caduan turned to the scene around us. Ahead of us, the landscape had been irreparably changed. Blood-streaked white stone blocked us from the Zorokov's main estate. But behind us, a different kind of carnage unfolded. Ela'Dar's soldiers had poured into the eastern end of the city, and while they had stopped to gape in confusion at whatever had just happened, it was clear that they were making quick work of the Threllian leadership—the streets were strewn with white-clad Threllian bodies.

Meajqa turned back to the strange wall of stone and let out a long, shaky breath. "What in the seven skies *was* that? I was seconds away from being caught in it."

"That," Caduan said, "was the work of a Lejara."

Meajqa swore.

"We go after them." My voice was raspy. "Right now. We go get it from them." Despite myself, I teetered on my feet. Blood soaked my midsection.

I saw Caduan take careful stock of these things, and not answer.

"We cannot just *leave* them," I spat. "We are so close."

Caduan's lips thinned, the wrinkle between his brows deepening. He leaned heavily against a pile of stone, though he seemed like he was trying to disguise his weakness. A button of his shirt had fallen open, revealing a glimpse of strange purple bruising before his hand quickly moved to close it.

"We were not without victory," Meajqa said. "Between the humans and us, there's not a single one of those Threllian bastards left alive." He cast a glance down the hill, where Fey opened throat after throat. "Or won't be, soon. Let the rebels keep what remains. Luia and her men can cut our way north. Leave the south… for now."

Caduan looked like he did not love this plan either. "And just leave Vytezic?"

"Temporarily. Besides… we have found something else that will lift your spirits, I'm sure." Meajqa's eyes glinted with hungry pleasure. He led us down the path and signaled to a soldier.

"What a gift," he drawled, and motioned to the stones below —and the listless, half-conscious body of the Queen of Ara. Her white jacket was now almost completely crimson, a rod of gold protruding from her stomach. She was alive, but barely. Two of Luia's soldiers knelt beside her, carefully binding her hands and ankles as she moaned.

Meajqa was right. Seeing her like this, powerless, was almost enough to make me forget that Tisaanah and Maxantarius had slipped away from us.

Meajqa dropped to his knees before her. "My," he crooned, "we are lucky, aren't we?" He reached out and stroked her face, like a lover would, as her head rolled back. His touch lingered at her throat. "Let me kill her. Don't I deserve to be the one to do that?"

I was drunk on death. I wanted him to take her apart the way she had done to him, and I wanted to help.

But Caduan said, "No. We let her live."

Meajqa whirled around. "Let her *live*?" Even I recognized the hurt in his voice.

"For now," Caduan said. "She has our people in captivity. We need to find out where they are and how to reverse whatever she has done to them. Then we can kill her."

"But—"

"Are you telling me that your vengeance is more important than saving our people?"

Meajqa's jaw was tight, as if forcibly keeping his words to himself. "I apologize," he said, eventually. "As you command, my king."

Caduan laid a hand on his shoulder. "Your time will come."

Meajqa gave a silent nod.

"Tell Luia to keep pushing through," Caduan said. "Head north. Take down the Threllian cities that you pass. It should be easy now. Their leadership is gone." He looked to the Queen. "We have more important battles."

CHAPTER SEVENTY-NINE

TISAANAH

W hen I first came back to myself, I thought something was wrong with my eyes—and then I realized that the house just *looked* like this now, the walls rough-hewn stone, the floors broken and slanted.

I stood up. The house had been rearranged like a dollhouse that had been assembled incorrectly. The bodies that remained here were so broken that I couldn't even identify what they had once looked like—bodies crushed between walls, bodies pinned to the floor, bodies missing arms, legs, heads. Some were rearranged bloodlessly, like someone had jumbled up limbs and glued them back together.

All of them were clad in what had once been white—all Threllians. I noted this numbly, like I was watching another version of myself make this observation. My blood rushed in my ears, dulling my senses. A strange power still thrummed through me. The heart was still clutched in my hands.

Max staggered to his feet beside me, taking the heart and tucking it back away in his pack, but I still felt its power even when it was no longer in my grasp.

We looked to the east. Beyond the balcony, the Fey moved away from the city in neat lines of green. Retreating.

We walked up what remained of the stairs. The top of the building had once been a dining room that showed off a view of the city below. Now, it was just a slab of stone, open to the elements, with the rest of the house collapsed around it.

The blond hair stood out in the carnage. Lady Zorokov cowered beneath a pile of ruin, curled up like a frightened child. When I approached her, she let out a sob and put up her hands, which were so badly ruined that they were just a mass of bloody fingers jutting out in all directions.

"Please, no. *Please, no.*"

I looked at this terrified, pitiful, injured woman, and I felt nothing but hate.

I grabbed her and dragged her out into the waning sun. "Please," she wept, over and over again.

"Is that what they said?" I could barely hear myself—could barely hear anything but the roar of my own power. It was painful and intoxicating, thicker even than Reshaye's rage. "Did they beg for their lives when you cut off their hands? All those innocent people? All those babies?"

Tears streamed down Lady Zorokov's cheeks. "I can give you anything. I can give you money, influence. You want my title? It is yours."

"I don't want your title." My hand fell to her throat. It was so fragile beneath my grasp, the lingering magic lending me strength. "I could say that this is for them. For every one of the people you murdered. But the thing is, that's a terrible trade. What good does your life do for theirs? It's worth so much less."

Her face crumbled. I forced her to her knees, her back to me, my arm tight across her chest. Max stood silently beside me, his hand sliding into mine on the opposite side.

"Look," I snarled in her ear. "Look at the country that you worked so hard to steal. When I kill you, this country will fall. And I want that to be the last thing you see, Lady Zorokov. I want you to watch your empire die."

469

"Please—" she wept.

It was so easy. I was so connected to this power that Max and I shared, the boundary between our magics erased. The flames understood me like they were the air in my lungs. Lady Zorokov ignited easily. I held her there as she screamed. I wanted to let her burn, wanted to let the heat consume her slowly.

"Tisaanah..." Max's hand tightened. I knew what he was saying, even though I didn't want to hear it.

I squeezed my eyes shut, pushing against the seductive draw of my own rage.

"This isn't you," he murmured.

Burning was a slow, terrible way to die. But she had inflicted such painful deaths on so many innocents. I wanted her to suffer. I *hated* how much I wanted it.

But Max was right. It wasn't who I was.

I reached through the flames, gripped her face, and snapped her neck in one powerful movement.

Still, I let her body burn there, high up at the top of her fallen empire.

A beacon across all of Threll, signaling the end of an age.

BY NIGHTFALL, the city had gone quiet. There was no one left to kill. Threll had fallen. The Fey had retreated, for now. They would return. That would be tomorrow's problem.

Today, though, the rebels celebrated. What had been a field of carnage by day turned into a blood-drunk celebration by midnight. Maybe to some they would have looked like they'd lost their minds, laughing to the moon while still covered in battle-drenched clothing. But freedom was a drug these people had been denied their entire lives. It hit a heart hard.

I felt strange, like I was walking through a dream world. I was injured, but didn't hurt. I smiled at my countrymen, but it didn't reach my eyes.

Serel.

I staggered through the chaos and debris looking for him. After hours, I found him sheltered beside one of the remaining houses, crouching on the ground, his blood-matted head bowed.

Cradled in his arms was Filias's ruined body.

He looked up at me, and his face crumpled.

"It's what he would have wanted," he choked out, barely able to speak through his tears. "He would have been proud to die this way, Tisaanah. He—"

Suddenly, the bloodthirsty rage, the strange numbness, the intoxicating power was gone. All of it disappeared under the devastating wave of Serel's grief.

I collapsed next to my friend and wrapped my arms around him, and he abandoned words in favor of heaving sobs.

"It's what he would have wanted," Serel kept saying, over and over again, as if it made anything better.

But Filias's was not some grand cosmic trade. Yes, we had won our country back. But sometime today, a million deadly combinations of a million deadly acts converged in exactly the right way, and just like that, my best friend lost the love of his life.

That would never be a fair exchange.

The night wore on in wild celebration. But I stayed there with Serel and held him as he wept.

———————

IT WAS dawn by the time Max ushered me away. Filias's body was taken by Riasha for the funeral pyre. Serel now cried quietly and no longer spoke. Max and I brought him into one of the remaining houses. I laid him down and watched Sammerin heal his wounds. I kissed him on his forehead as one of Sammerin's medicines sent him to a merciful, dreamless sleep.

Sammerin healed Max and I the best he could, then pointed to another uninhabited cabin and said we should get some rest.

Max led me there. I was silent as he ran a bath, helped me

from my clothes, lowered me into the warm water like I was a child.

"Thank you." My voice sounded strange. "Thank you for coming for me."

"Always, Tisaanah."

He kissed my forehead. My nose. My cheeks, left then right. "What did they do to you?"

"Nothing I couldn't survive."

His touch lingered on my crooked fingers, on the new marks on my back, on the welts at my neck, but he asked no more questions.

"When this is all over," he said, softly, "maybe it won't be about surviving anymore."

For some reason, I found it difficult to speak past the lump in my throat. "Do you ever worry that you don't know how to do anything else?"

He arranged himself behind me in the water, so his arms formed a warm embrace around me. "I know how to do some other things," he murmured, and pulled my hair aside to kiss the back of my neck.

It was such a heartbreakingly tender gesture.

Before I knew what was happening, the tears were coming so hard I couldn't breathe. My body shook with rough, painful sobs.

Max did not ask why I was crying. He did not tell me everything was going to be alright.

He just took a cloth and washed the blood from my back, stroke by stroke, gentle as a lullaby, and let me cry.

CHAPTER EIGHTY

MAX

I t took many hours for Tisaanah to fall into a restless sleep. I
lay there with her, not tired, curled around her naked body.
As she slept, I took inventory of her injuries—the crooked
fingers, the wounds, the new scars across the top of her shoulder
blades. Six neat squares.

They had fucking *flayed* her.

When I saw that, I regretted giving Lady Zorokov a quick
death. Fuck morality. She should have burned.

I peered at Tisaanah's face. She had cried so much that even
in sleep, her eyes were red rimmed. I kissed her on the cheek and
was careful not to wake her when I got out of bed. If she woke, I
knew that she would immediately fling herself back outside to
work, and it had been difficult enough just to get her to rest for a
few hours.

Riasha and Tisaanah had spearheaded the initial recovery
efforts, and though everything was still a mess of rubble, it was
beginning to look more like a settlement and less like a battlefield. The recovered bodies burned beyond the edges of the city.
The rebels had secured wine from the inside of the Zorokovs'
palace, and though it was midday, the streets were full of

drunken partying—one part funeral reception, one part freedom celebration, one part exhausted release.

I found Sammerin in a house not far from the one that Tisaanah and I were staying in, which he and another healer had formed into a makeshift hospital. He sat on a bench outside, head tipped back to rest against the outer wall, smoking.

"You look horrific," I said.

"Thank you. So do you." He let out a long puff of smoke and regarded me up and down. "Though fairly unremarkable looking for someone who has now ended three different wars under strange and mysterious circumstances."

I gave him a smile and a very polite, "Fuck you." I took a seat on the bench beside him, and he offered me his pipe, which I declined.

"That's terrible for your health, you know," I said.

"Oh? Is it?" Sammerin gave me a deadpan glare and took another defiant puff.

I nodded to the door. "How're things in there?"

"About what one would expect." He glanced at a group of people nearby who wielded half-broken instruments to make joyously horrible music. "Big contrast between out here and in there."

"Victory is expensive."

Sammerin let out a scuff of a laugh, like this was a cruelly funny joke—and it was, wasn't it?

For so many, today was the happiest day of their lives. For others, the most tragic.

I looked down at my hands. They hadn't stopped shaking since the battle. The pads of my fingertips tingled, like they still felt the remnants of the heart's magic.

I swallowed past a lump in my throat and shook away the image of those rearranged bodies.

"How's Tisaanah?" Sammerin asked.

I didn't know how to answer that. "She's... alive."

"Oof."

"Right." I rubbed my temple. "She's resting."

"She'll be furious when she realizes that you didn't wake her up."

"She'll get over it."

He gave me a look that said, *Really? Will she?*

I shrugged. "Someone's got to keep her from working herself to death."

"Maybe that's how she wants to go."

He only sounded like he was half-joking, and the image of Serel curled up in his grief flashed through my mind and refused to leave. I felt a little sick, because it was too close to being true. I knew what it was like to place no value in your own life. I knew it well enough to see that in Tisaanah—the fact that she'd be willing to sacrifice everything, anything, for her cause.

I couldn't make those kinds of jokes today.

"You might want to go see Brayan," Sammerin said, mercifully changing the topic. "He seems a little lost."

An unsupervised Brayan was never a good thing.

I found him helping to clear some rubble in the back of the city. He, like everyone else, looked tired.

"Congratulations," he said, when he saw me. "You're a hero. Again."

My stomach turned. *Hero.* Sure. How come that word was only applied to me when a bunch of people were dead? I wanted to say, *Are we looking at the same city?*

He said, "Now I understand."

"What?"

"How you could do it." At my confused stare, he touched the corner of his eye. "This. I noticed your eyes were different. I didn't realize why."

"I... it's..." One would think by now I'd have a better way of describing it. "The Orders did it to me, during the Ryvenai War."

"Hm." He awkwardly looked away. Brayan had never been comfortable with the existence of my magic, and this only made it more difficult for him to understand. He preferred a straight-forward world.

He cleared his throat and changed the subject. "Has Nura been found?"

"No. She's either dead and buried somewhere beneath wreckage, or she escaped, or..."

Or captured. I hoped she was dead. If she wasn't, what was coming next would be worse.

Brayan continued to pick through the broken planks of wood. "I went after her," he said. "During the invasion. She asked me to join her, again."

I stopped moving and turned back to him. "And?"

Brayan looked at me like I was stupid. "Obviously, I didn't. But she said something... strange." He furrowed his brow and turned back to his work. "She said something about that day. She said that I didn't know what they had died for." The wrinkle deepened. "What do you think that means? It's such an odd thing to say. Do you think we missed something?"

He sounded hopeful. Fucking hopeful.

"Nura would say anything, if she thought it would help Ara," I said, carefully. "She's desperate."

Brayan's face hardened, but then he sighed. "You're right."

It was probably the only time in thirty years that Brayan had uttered those words to me, and it was... because of this.

I couldn't bring myself to even look at him for a long moment. When I finally did, he was staring into the distance in deep, serious thought.

"You know..." He frowned. "I've never fought with anyone like this before."

"Like this?"

"People who are... well, really fighting for something." He jabbed his thumb to a cluster of dancers further down the street, and his mouth quirked in an almost-smile. "I never saw *that* after one of my Roseteeth victories."

Despite myself, I chuckled. "The great Brayan Farlione, discovering the heart beneath the warfare. Who would have thought?"

That fleeting smirk disappeared, replaced with a disapproving shake of the head. He turned back to his work, and I decided to quit while I was ahead.

———————

LATER, I checked back in on Serel in Tisaanah's stead. He was no longer asleep, now perched on the edge of his bed. His arm was in a sling—Sammerin had had to heal it in phases since it was a complex break. He simply sat in the dark, in silence, completely still.

When I opened the door to see this, I apologized and backed away.

"No," he said, giving me a weak smile. "Come." He spoke in poor Aran.

"Just seeing how you are," I said, in Thereni, and his smile grew slightly.

"Your Thereni is better, you know. I meant to say that earlier."

I scoffed. "Only a small bit."

"Tisaanah probably only taught you the bad words."

This was true. I tried my best Thereni approximation of, "Fuck yes she did," which earned a hoarse chuckle from Serel.

"I don't think that particular curse means what you think it does."

I was willing to be the butt of the joke, if that's what it took to earn that raspy laugh.

"Do you need anything?" I asked him.

"No, thank you. I'm fine."

"You do not need to be."

"There are things more important than my grief right now."

For a moment, I had to marvel at him. All I could think was that if it was Tisaanah, I would have been crawling my way to the top of the nearest tower to hurl myself off of it. Absolutely nothing in this world or any other would be more important than my grief.

"The hurt will still stay," I said, in choppy Thereni. "Even if you hide it."

A wave of sadness passed over Serel's face, and he went to the window.

"I know." He looked down at the celebrations below. "But at least they have a future."

"You do, too," I said, and Serel was silent.

"It's strange," he murmured. "It doesn't feel that way. I don't know what a future without him looks like."

I was at a loss for words. I had to switch to Aran. "It will take time, but you'll build another version of that future, Serel."

He looked at me over his shoulder and gave me a wry, sad smile. "Would you?"

No. Of course the answer was no. If Tisaanah was gone, my future would be too. A simple truth.

I was quiet. I had no more platitudes to offer Serel. No more comfort.

"It's alright," he said, quietly, turning back to the window. "The dream was worth it."

CHAPTER EIGHTY-ONE

AEFE

The Aran queen seemed so small. In my memories, she loomed larger than that, inflated by Maxantarius's hatred —and love—for her, and by my own fear of her when she would come for me night after night all those years ago. But I'd forgotten. She was just a human. She was so slender and weak. Tall, but not as tall as me now. Without her magic, she was just a little pale waif, sagging against her restraints.

Caduan almost had refused to let me into this room. I had to fight with him for it. I had spent too long haunted by her actions. I deserved to see her face-to-face.

Caduan conceded reluctantly, but he stressed that I needed to be there as an observer only. I agreed to that, with equal reluctance.

It was worth it.

We waited patiently for her to regain consciousness. When she did, she blinked blearily at us, then her silver eyes went round when she realized who we were.

"Good morning," Caduan said. "Would you like some water?"

It took a moment for the steel in her stare to return, like she had to remind herself to hoist up those walls. Her chin lifted and eyes narrowed.

A smile quirked at one corner of my mouth. She could not lie to me. I knew she was terrified. Something was different about her now—a darkness closer to the surface, even if she was adept at hiding it.

"If you want water," he said, "I recommend that you have some now. We have a long night ahead of us."

Nura just glared at him.

"Fine. I am not much for pleasantries, either." Caduan stepped closer, and Nura cringed, but he made no move against her. "You have twenty of our people. Tell me where they are."

Nura said nothing.

I glanced at Meajqa, whose arms were crossed tightly across his chest, as if he wasn't sure what he would do with his hands if he freed them. It looked like remaining uninvolved physically pained him.

"It is in your best interest to just give us this information," Caduan said calmly. "Because we are going to get it, and the only thing up for debate is how much you suffer before we do."

When she still was silent, Caduan beckoned to Meajqa.

Meajqa frequently smiled, though they often seemed shallow. Not this. This was a smile of genuine delight.

He perched on the stool before Nura, bearing that beautiful grin. He asked, in heavily accented Aran, "Do you remember me?"

Nura's shield cracked, a single fissure of fear falling across her face.

"I hope you are flattered. I learned this language only so I could speak to you one day. So I could hear what you say. Because I remember *everything*." The stump of his missing wing twitched. "I remember when you took this. Do you?"

At last, she spoke. "You came onto my land. You threatened my people."

Meajqa's smile withered to a sneer. "I was injured. I never meant to enter your land. I did not even know it was yours."

"*I saw you,*" she spat. "I saw visions of what would come to us by your hands. I have no regrets about what I've done."

Caduan said, coldly, "Tell us where our people are."

Nura answered, just as coldly, "No."

Caduan cast the faintest glance in Meajqa's direction. I hadn't even seen the knife until he was bringing it down, hard, on Nura's hand.

She let out a shocked, wordless cry. But Meajqa wouldn't let her pull her hand away, grabbing her wrist as he brought the blade down again to finish the cut. Blood spurted over his face.

He smiled down at Nura's small finger, which remained on the table after he released her. Her whole body trembled as she cradled her hand, glaring at us.

"Do you know how much it hurts to lose a wing?" Meajqa said. "One finger is nothing in trade."

"Fine," Nura snarled. "Take it. You're right. A finger is nothing. You have no idea what I've already sacrificed to stop you."

She lifted her chin as she said this, like a marble statue, and I couldn't stop myself from laughing. She made her actions sound so selfless. The torture of innocents. The murder of children. All wrapped up in her noble causes.

My laugh made Nura look to me for the first time. A petty part of me so enjoyed her attention. I stepped out from the shadows.

"Aefe," Caduan hissed, but I ignored him.

As the light fell across my face, her brows lowered in confusion, which delighted me. She would not recognize my face. But some part of her, some intangible sense, knew what I was.

"What are you?" she whispered.

"You don't recognize me?" I chuckled. "I recognize you, Nura. You may claim that your desires are selfless. But you can not lie to me about that jagged steel mind of yours."

"Who—"

I leaned close to her, giving her a good look at me.

"Aefe," Caduan whispered again, more sharply, and again I ignored him.

"I saw so much of you," I whispered, a soft snarl, "those nights when you tried to force me into you, night after night."

The realization shattered Nura's composure. "*Reshaye.*"

No. I wasn't no one. Not anymore. "My name is Aefe. My body and my mind belong only to me, now."

I loved that it was the sight of me—*only me*—that made the terror overtake her expression completely.

"How?" she breathed, face snapping towards Caduan. "How did you do that? No one can create life. I've tried so—"

"The questions are not for you," Meajqa said, and again, so quick, that blade was out, and her hand was on the table, and another finger was gone.

This time she let out a muffled scream of pain through a clenched jaw, doubling over across the table. It was a messy cut. Hot, crimson blood spattered across all three of us. It landed in streaks across my face.

Meajqa did not smile this time. He looked utterly furious, lustful for something more than fingers.

I felt it, too. As I watched Nura wither, I could only think of two words:

Not enough.

"That's enough." Caduan stepped in front of me, putting his body between mine and Nura's. "We need our answers, human queen, and we need them soon. Many Fey are eager to take pieces from you."

He went to the door and motioned for us to follow. For a moment, neither of us moved.

"Aefe," Caduan said, sharply. "Meajqa."

Reluctantly, we followed. With the door closed firmly behind us, Meajqa snapped, "I could have gotten that information out of her."

"You disobeyed my orders. We talked about this, Meajqa. It was a mistake to let you in there."

Meajqa practically snarled. I had never seen him like this before. "I told you I could find what we needed, and I can. *You* made me *stop* before I could get it."

"You were looking for revenge," Caduan shot back, "and that would not fill the hole you pretend doesn't exist, Meajqa."

Meajqa let out an ugly, vicious laugh. "And what about you? Why is it unacceptable to feed my vengeance some human bitch's fingers, but yours can devour an entire race?"

It was as if all the air left the room at once. Caduan's face went so still that it sent a shiver up my spine. His gaze flicked to me, just for a split second, as if he didn't intend to allow himself to do it.

Then he stalked towards Meajqa and said, very calmly, "You are dismissed for the rest of the day. Do not go back into that room until I tell you to."

Meajqa was drawn so tight that every muscle trembled. He did not move as Caduan kept walking past him, disappearing down the hall without another word to either of us.

Eventually, after a few tense minutes of silence, Meajqa stalked away in the opposite direction, and did not so much as look at me.

I wouldn't have noticed even if he had. I remained there alone, swaying beneath the weight of a sudden realization—the shift where a suspicion became a certainty.

The vengeance is for you.

I licked my lips and tasted a stray drop of the Aran queen's blood.

And then I went to Caduan's room.

CHAPTER EIGHTY-TWO

TISAANAH

I scanned the crowd and hundreds of eager faces stared back at me. Many were still visibly injured, bruised or bandaged, marked with stitched-up wounds or missing eyes. The last time I stood before all of them like this, I had been mourning with them. The time before that, I had been promising them vengeance. Now, we gathered to determine what came after it.

Earlier that morning, we had received a letter signed by the few remaining Threllian Lords. Their slaves, inspired by the stories of our victory against the Zorokovs, had turned against them. Those who were not killed and had managed to hold on to their estates surrendered in a bid to keep their lives. Now their bloodstained parchment was pinned to the wall behind us, a dagger through its center.

It shouldn't have surprised me that the conversation immediately turned to retribution.

"Fuck them and their surrender," one of the rebel captains spat. "Our first order of business is to execute the Threllian bastards. Every last one of them."

A chill ran up my spine as this earned a ripple of approval.

"The Lords can, and should, stand trial," I said. "They should face their execution. But the rest of the Threllians? Many of them are middle-class or poor families who had nearly as little control over their oligarchical government as we did. What will we do, sweep through the country and execute every Threllian man, woman, and child like dogs?"

A smattering of *"yes"*es rang out in the audience. My magic sensed their simmering anger, still fresh from the exhausted adrenaline of battle.

"I burned Lady Zorokov alive," I snapped. "I understand how important justice is, and make no mistake, we'll have our justice against our conquerors. But if we do that, then in twenty years we'll have their orphaned children at our doorstep, ready to destroy us."

"We might not even make it twenty years," Riasha said. "We just toppled one of the most powerful empires in the world. We need to focus on making sure this country doesn't fall apart, not digging mass graves."

I shot Riasha a grateful look and nodded. The two of us knew this all too well. I'd spent the last three days holed up in my room, trying to piece together the logistical records of the Zorokov estate. We knew how to farm, how to hunt, how to keep the gears of a country turning—we had carried those inner workings on our backs for decades.

But we didn't know what a "new Threll" looked like. Threll's economy had been built upon free labor that they viewed as disposable and unlimited. Once we dug our way out of the euphoria of victory and the cloud of grief, it became clear to me that we might not survive this. Not because the Fey would conquer us, but because we might not be able to continue producing enough food for our population, or because the trade routes might fall apart, or because our economy might just... collapse.

In some ways, these things scared me even more than the prospect of impending war. What if we lost our nation—*again*—not because someone came to take it from us, but simply because we couldn't manage it?

But today, no one wanted to talk about trade routes and currency and farming. They wanted to talk about blood.

A man in the back of the room rose from his seat. "Then let the nations decide! Each country can decide how they handle the Threllians occupying their territory."

"Yes," another member of the committee agreed. "If Nyzerene wants to offer the Threllians mercy, they are welcome to. But Deralin will be doing no such thing, I assure you."

Each country.

Those words stopped me short. I felt stupid for not having considered that this would happen. It stood to reason that some would want to return to the way our continent looked twenty years ago, before the rise of the Threllian Lords—seven different nations that all eventually were consumed by Threll's conquering warpath.

I had been so busy trying to make sure that we survived the next few months that I didn't think about what it might be like to have Nyzerene back—the home I remembered in only ghosts of sweet smells and warm embraces and a distant concept of a place that once, long ago, had been somewhere I truly belonged.

The whispers in the crowd had gotten louder, more excited, as people allowed themselves to think of the possibility of reclaiming the homes they had watched crumble.

I exchanged a glance with Serel, unease stirring in my stomach.

I said, loud enough to speak over the din, "Wait."

A hush fell over the spectators. I was a little satisfied that finally, after years of effort, I'd earned that kind of respect.

"I propose that we do not separate," I said. "Perhaps it's wiser to remain unified."

Riasha looked shocked. "And continue to call ourselves Threll? Fly their banners and discard our own?"

A part of me hated the words coming out of my lips—a part of me wondered if my mother, who had so loved her country, would be ashamed of me for even saying it. At least I was a child when Nyzerene fell. But many of the people here, Riasha included, had been well into adulthood when they lost their mother lands.

"This country would never be the Threll that the Lords created ever again," I said. "We will keep that from happening. But think of how it got that way. The Threllian Lords were able to conquer this continent because our disparate countries were so easily turned against each other. And in turn, the Threllians fell because their Lords were constantly hungry for individual power. If we stay together, we become stronger than that."

Riasha seemed saddened by this thought. "And remain forever defined by what Threll did to us?"

"We will always be defined by what they did to us. We can't erase that past, no matter what we do to our borders." I shifted, suddenly very conscious of my scars. "But we survived by taking their abuse and making it our strength. We can embrace that, now! What better way to claim our independence than to take the unity they forced upon us, and use it to build a nation stronger than they ever were?" I thrust my finger at the top of the Zorokovs' palace, where Lady Zorokov's charred body had hung. "Can you think of anything *she* would hate more?"

This earned tentative murmurs of thought.

"I agree," Serel said. "We could still keep the seven original nations as districts. Elect... elect a senate." His face lit up, and my chest tightened to see my friend show even that small glimmer of enthusiasm. "We could do this. It would work."

I glanced at Max, who leaned against the doorframe, watching. He lowered his chin in a silent nod of encouragement.

The rebels were still uncertain. I understood it—we'd had so much taken away from us already. They feared losing those pieces of themselves forever. I feared that, too. But even more, I feared that we would not survive at all.

"Six months," I said. "Let us spend six months as one nation while we decide our next steps. The Fey have claimed the northern territories of Threll. Soon they'll be coming for us. We need to stay together if we're going to survive this."

The crowd whispered, discussing this amongst themselves.

Just six months, they murmured. *We can do that.* Aside from a few grumbling detractors, most seemed to agree that now—standing in the ruins of a broken nation and facing yet another war—was not a good time to start drawing borders.

"I still refuse to call this country Threll," Riasha said. "Even for six months."

"We're the Rebellion!" one enthusiastic woman called from the crowd.

"Not anymore, really," another grumbled, eyeing the ruins of the Zorokovs' house.

"No, we aren't," I agreed. "A rebellion is united *against* something. I like to think that now, we're united *for* something." Despite myself, I couldn't stop the smile from spreading across my face. "I think we're an alliance, now. The Alliance of Seven Banners."

It was the first thing said all day that no one disagreed with.

———

"I DO NOT KNOW why they are celebrating." Ishqa looked out the window and crossed his arms in disapproval as he watched the festivities below—they had been going on for more than a week straight, at this point.

"Perhaps because not being in slavery after twenty years of it is, by most standards, celebration worthy?" Max offered.

"That is short sighted. They, and we, are in more danger than ever." Ishqa turned to us, and it struck me exactly how old he looked. When I had first met him, I marveled at his eerie ageless-ness despite his centuries of life. Now it seemed like every time I saw him, the years weighed heavier.

As he so often did, Ishqa had disappeared for several days after the fall of the Zorokovs. We returned to the little house we had claimed as our temporary home to find him sitting on the stoop like a lost pet.

"See?" I whispered to Max, after we let him in. "I told you. Just like a cat."

Now Ishqa paced the floors of the living room. He seemed agitated. "I flew up north," he said. "Caduan's armies have slaughtered entire townships on their path back to Ela'Dar. Lest you forget their ultimate purpose."

It was impossible to forget their ultimate purpose after seeing how they had behaved at the Zorokovs' estate. They had locked the doors of that place not with the intention of conquering, but with the intention of slaughtering. It was pure luck that they hadn't killed more of our own.

"Of course we haven't," I muttered. My head hurt fiercely. It was exhausting to be flung from one disaster to another.

"Caduan would not have disposed of the Threllians unless he knew that he had other, more powerful weapons within his reach," he went on.

"Reshaye," Max said.

"Yes. Aefe. And…" Ishqa's mouth opened, then closed as he trailed off.

"What?" I pressed, and he was silent for a long moment before sighing and shaking his head.

"I do not know. It's only… a sense. There is something else. I do not know what. But I was close friends with Caduan for half a millennium. I know him well enough to see when there is something he is not showing the world. The power he holds now is bad enough, but I am even more afraid of what he keeps hidden."

I exchanged a glance with Max, who shrugged, as if to say, *Mysterious signs of impending doom. What else did we expect?*

We were interrupted by a firm knock on the door. Brayan and Sammerin entered. Brayan gripped a crumpled-up letter, which he held out to Max.

"The Roseteeth secured a letter from Ara," he said, "for you."

CHAPTER EIGHTY-THREE

MAX

I read the letter four times, and I still couldn't wrap my head around whether it meant what I thought it meant, and whether it was a good thing if it did.

"Well?" Brayan pressed, impatient. "What do you think?"

I held up a finger and read it again. Passed it to Tisaanah, who read it twice, then passed it to Sammerin.

"It means that there's a power gap in Ara," Brayan said, urgently, "and that means opportunity."

When he talked like that, I could see him as the man who led a bunch of mercenaries to overthrow foreign countries. He wasn't wrong, but it seemed distasteful to be so excited about it.

The letter was from Iya, one of the sparse communications that we were able to acquire thanks to Brayan's Roseteeth connections. The letter informed us that Nura had not returned to Ara after leaving to forge her alliance with the Threllian Lords. The Syrizen and the council had not been able to locate or contact her for weeks.

My running theory had been that Nura had managed to escape during the fall of the Lords. But she would have made it back to Ara by now, unless something had else gone wrong—and even then, she certainly would have communicated with the rest of Ara's leadership. If the Council hadn't heard from her at all, that meant she'd either escaped and met some sort of tragedy in Threll, or she had been captured by the Fey.

But Iya's letter was far less concerned with Nura's whereabouts than it was for the impacts in Ara. Iya wrote:

Nura has been gone long enough that many people are starting to murmur about how they might fill the gap she left behind. But there are few powerful names left in Ara, and fewer still that have a claim, even tenuously, to either the throne or the title of Arch Commandant. In fact —I can only think of one.

I write this knowing that if it is found, my head will be rolling down the Palace steps.

But, Maxantarius Farlione, I strongly recommend that you return to Ara as soon as possible.

Your time in Ilyzath has only martyred you in the eyes of most Aran citizens.

Your relationship with Tisaanah brings with you foreign allies and wins the hearts of our more romantic people.

Your military background appeases the militaristic.

Your Wielder background appeases the Orders.

Your noble blood appeases the traditionalists.

Come now. As fast as your magic can carry you.

The Council will support you.

I could tell when Sammerin finished reading the letter because he let out a long, slow breath that ended in a muttered curse.

I looked to Tisaanah, whose expression was oddly unreadable.

"The Roseteeth would fight for you," Brayan said. "If you made a play for that throne, you would not only have a strong claim for all the reasons Iya listed, but also because you'd have the most powerful private army in the world at your back."

"Is the Roseteeth Company willing to participate in coups?"

Ishqa said. He spoke of it like we were debating what to have for dinner, and the casual use of the word "coup" made me feel physically ill.

Brayan shrugged. "They're an army, and they do what armies do."

"No," I said. "Absolutely fucking not. This is an idiotic idea."

Ishqa said, infuriatingly calmly, "Why not?"

"*Why not?* You're asking me to steal the Ascended-damned throne of Ara. You just used the word 'coup' to describe what this would be."

"And what word would we use to describe what Nura did?" Brayan said. "Would we call that a legitimate succession? Hell, would we call what *Aldris* did a legitimate succession?"

"That's your argument? Everyone is usurping left and right, so we might as well jump in on it?"

I leveled a glare at Brayan, my jaw grinding. He met my stare combatively.

Did he think I didn't know why he so wanted me to do this? He wanted a Farlione on the throne, with all the status that implied. Brayan had always put so much weight in this sort of thing.

"He's right," Sammerin said, quietly. "You are just as legitimate a ruler as Nura is. Probably more. And if you were to do this, it would give you the ability to end this war."

"It would force me to finish a war that has already started."

I couldn't think of anything worse than that. Overseeing a million unavoidable deaths.

"Besides," I said, "I can't end a war by myself. I could show up, promise to be better, very publicly decry all future sadistic magical torture, and the Fey could still—rightfully, I might say—decide to wipe Ara off the face of the earth."

For the first time, Tisaanah spoke. "And this is all so far ahead of where we stand today. How do we know we would not just be sending him to his death? What if Nura returns to Ara before he does?"

Ishqa paced the room, his hands clasped in front of him, looking deep in thought. At last, he turned to us.

"There is something else you should consider," he said. "Something that I have been working on that may make things... easier."

"Something you have been working on?" Tisaanah echoed.

I didn't like the sound of that—Ishqa having secret machinations.

He inclined his chin. "Let us take a trip."

───────────

ISHQA BROUGHT Tisaanah and I with him as he used magic to leap us to the outskirts of the city, then a forest, then three more times until we found ourselves standing before a stone house surrounded by trees. The house was small, but grand, clearly made for someone with an appreciation for the finer things in life. In design, it looked as if it could be part of a great estate, perhaps as a large guest house for high-ranking visitors, but there was no estate here, only forest. There was little in the way of landscaping, not even a gate, just a single brick path that led to a huge set of dark-stained wood doors.

The woman who opened the door was inhumanly beautiful— it was obvious that she was Fey long before I saw the points of her ears. She had a delicate face and sleek dark hair. She did not seem particularly happy to see us.

"Ishqa," she said.

"Sareid." Ishqa bowed his head. "We're here to see your brother-in-law."

"I don't know if that is a good—"

"Please, Sareid. It is important."

Her eyes flicked over Ishqa's shoulder, to Tisaanah and I.

"They are safe," Ishqa said. "Friends."

A wrinkle of concern deepened between her brows, and she looked unconvinced, but she opened the door and stepped aside.

The home was dimly lit, the door leading directly into a

narrow hallway with a curved ceiling, decorated with dusty paintings. We were led into a large sitting room that, funnily enough, reminded me of my old cottage. The furniture was mismatched, scattered about the room in an awkward semi-circle, and every individual piece seemed like a relic from a different age. Two large windows spilled tree-dappled light over fur rugs, but a fire still roared in the hearth anyway. A man sat before it, his back to us.

"Ezra," Sareid said. "Ishqa is here to see you again."

"Thank you for meeting me, as always." Ishqa bowed. He shot me and Tisaanah a pointed look, and we hastily followed suit, though we didn't know why we were bowing or to whom.

Sareid backed out of the room and closed the door. The figure before the fire stood and turned to us. He was tall and slender, with a smooth, ageless face. He was fair, with bright blue eyes and silver-gold hair cropped close to his skull, which emphasized the size and point of his ears.

"Maxantarius, Tisaanah, this is Ezra," Ishqa said. "Ezra is one of the last remaining old kings of the Fey. He once ruled over the Kingdom of Niraja."

Despite myself, my eyebrows lurched.

Niraja, as in, the city of ruins that we recently destroyed? And Ishqa still calls this man a king?

"Ezra, allow me to introduce you to Tisaanah Vytezic, leader of the seven Threllian nations, and Maxantarius Farlione, rightful Arch Commandant of the Aran Order of Midnight and Order of Daybreak."

I almost choked. He introduced us like we were *royalty*. I glanced at Tisaanah, who looked like she was trying very hard to control her facial expressions.

Ezra looked us up and down. "Hm."

Tisaanah recovered from her shock quickly. A split second later it was replaced by a gentle smile and another, deeper bow. "It is an honor to meet you, King Ezra."

"Yes." I cleared my throat. "An honor."

It would have been an even greater honor if Ishqa had both-ered to give us some background on this mess.

Ishqa said, "I bring them to meet with you, Ezra, because I think it is finally time."

Ezra looked confused. "Time for what?"

"Time to reclaim your throne."

Ezra made a choking sound that was almost a laugh. "My throne? My throne is gone."

Ishqa almost cringed. He stepped closed to Ezra. "We have discussed this, Ezra. Ela'Dar."

"Ela'Dar is not my home. Niraja was my home."

I shot Tisaanah a look that said, *What the hell are we doing here?*

This man—this supposed king—seemed like he didn't even know how to string a conversation together.

"We talked about this, Ezra." A hint of exasperation seeped into Ishqa's voice. "Do you remember our previous meetings?"

"I don't..." Ezra went to the window and looked out into the forest. "I struggle to remember things, these days. We did meet, I suppose."

"We did. I do not want you to miss this opportunity. In ruling Ela'Dar, you could bring back the spirit of Niraja. You could make Fey society everything you had hoped for your kingdom."

Ezra let out a bitter laugh, rough as torn paper.

"I remember little of the last five hundred years," he said. "I won't pretend otherwise. But the last thing I do remember is that Fey society destroyed my kingdom."

"Things can be different—"

Ezra turned in one sudden lurch, and I found myself stepping in front of Tisaanah on instinct.

"What does it matter to any of you who sits on Ela'Dar's throne?" he spat.

"You had a dream," Ishqa said. "A unified world in which Fey and humans lived together in peace. King Caduan is not amenable to such a dream."

"Caduan?" Ezra's brow creased. "I think I have met him."

"Ela'Dar's king is actively hostile to such a future. But...

the whispers that I have discussed with you still ring louder. There are many Fey in Ela'Dar who remember you. And many of Caduan Iero's people do not forget his lack of old royal blood."

"Caduan Iero," Ezra repeated, his stare glassy. "Yes, I *do* remember him. He was a kind man. What difference does it make if he has old royal blood?"

"It matters to some of his people." Ishqa's voice was a little strained, like someone who was struggling to keep their patience while talking to a child. "It certainly matters to those who would back you. You have a rightful claim to any Fey crown, Ezra. Five hundred years ago, you had a vision, and you built a beautiful kingdom with it. The Fey need that vision, now. A vision of creation instead of destruction. A vision of unity." He gestured to us. "And you would have the support of the leaders of the humans."

Excuse me?

Tisaanah and I exchanged another alarmed look.

Ezra turned and regarded us all in silence, a cacophony of subtle emotions passing over his ageless face.

"You are asking me to be a king again," he said.

"Yes, Ezra. I am."

"The last time I was a king, I lost everything. Thanks in no small part to the actions of your people."

"I know," Ishqa said, softly. "And I will spend the rest of my days trying to correct the mistakes I made then."

Ezra turned away, arms crossed over his body. I noticed for the first time how thin he was—the knobs of his spine pronounced beneath the skin of the back of his neck, his shoulder blades visible even through the fabric of his shirt.

"My kingdom was beautiful once." He peered over his shoulder at Tisaanah and I. "You cannot possibly understand, without having seen it, what it was like there. A place that thrived against every injustice." His gaze slipped back to the forest—slipped back to the past. "But what would the point be in creating such a thing again? I built it for my family."

Ishqa said, quietly, "Athalena would have wanted you to do this."

"I buried my wife in her last dream. Why would I grant her ghost another?"

"Because your life is not over yet, Ezra."

Ezra was silent for a long, long moment. I was certain this conversation was over.

But then, so quietly we almost didn't hear him, he said, "Fine. I will do it."

———

"WHAT THE HELL WAS THAT?" I snapped at Ishqa, the moment we left Ezra's grounds.

"You should have discussed that with us before we went," Tisaanah said.

"My opportunities to meet with Ezra have been limited," Ishqa said, calmly. "I had no time to waste on explanations."

"How long have you been meeting him?" Tisaanah asked.

"Perhaps half a dozen times since the war began. The first two times he tried to kill me."

"Wait." I pinched the bridge of my nose. "You're telling me that was, in fact, the latest of *many* meetings with him? He seemed like he barely even knew who you were."

"Did he even know about the war?" Tisaanah murmured, as if to herself.

"I've told him about the war," Ishqa said.

I threw my hands up. "Well, he doesn't seem to remember much of anything you talked about with him, so yes, sure, he seems like an excellent candidate to lead a coup."

"I do not need your permission for anything," Ishqa snapped. "I am trying to save my people *and* yours. How I do that is between me and Ezra. It is a courtesy that I involved you in that discussion."

"You involved us because you wanted him to think he had the full backing of the humans," Tisaanah said, quietly.

"It would be true," he said. "If Maxantarius takes the throne of Ara. And you, Tisaanah—you have control over the Threllian alliance."

"Limited control. *Very* limited control. I am not their queen."

"Perhaps you could be. Have you considered that?"

I threw my hands up. "Because we are all stealing thrones today, aren't we?"

"We need to do something. Caduan and Nura are rapidly driving towards destroying each other's countries and taking the rest of us with them. If you take Ara's throne, Tisaanah influences the alliance, and Ezra unseats Caduan as the King of Ela'-Dar, that is the only path I see of limited bloodshed. Ezra was a great ruler, once."

"When? Five hundred years ago?"

Ishqa's jaw clenched. "Life has been unkind to him."

"Well, he can join all the fucking rest of us in that. But that doesn't mean we should put a man with diminished mental faculties in charge of the Fey nations."

"Could we, even if we wanted to?" Tisaanah asked. "Even unpopular rulers become better liked in wartime, and you described Caduan as a king who was already beloved by his people. How could Ezra challenge him?"

Ishqa let out a breath, conflict settling in the tense lines of his face.

"Not all of the Fey would support him. Perhaps not even most of them. But some, mostly those who are too young to remember the old Houses, romanticize royal blood. They are nostalgic for days before their time. There likely are not enough of them to exceed Caduan's support, but they may cause enough divisiveness to topple him."

My brows lurched. "You're talking about collapsing your own country."

Ishqa whirled to me, fire in his eyes. For a split second, I was struck by how intimidating Ishqa could be. I was so used to seeing him as an odd, ethereal advisor that I had never really seen him as a warrior, but he must have been a formidable one, once.

"I do not do *any of this* lightly. I am watching my people run towards a path of extinction, and I am powerless to stop it. I don't know what to do. Is that what you wish for me to tell you? The truth? That I am doing the best that I can under impossible circumstances? That I do not know how to save my own son?"

He snapped his jaw shut and abruptly turned away, his shoulders heaving as he let out a long breath. "That is the truth. I am desperate. But I see the end coming, Maxantarius. I see it coming fast." He peered at us over his shoulder. "Go to your country and take your throne. I will handle mine. And maybe— maybe, if we are very, *very* lucky—we can save this pathetic world from extinction."

CHAPTER EIGHTY-FOUR

AEFE

Caduan's guards tried to turn me away, but I refused to leave. I pushed past them, went to his chambers, and pounded on the door until he answered it himself.

He hadn't washed Nura's blood off him, either. It dotted his cheeks.

"What is it, Aefe?" he said, clearly in a sour mood.

"Do not ignore me."

His expression was indecipherable. "I am not ignoring you."

No. I was sick of this. He gave me affection, and then he pushed me away. He took my body, and then he abandoned it. He saved my life, and then refused to speak to me.

All while he waged the greatest war the world had even seen in *my name*.

He was already shutting the door in my face when I spat, "I thought we were done being cowards."

He froze mid movement. The door swung open again, sharply.

"Don't you dare call me a coward."

"Then stop deserving it," I snarled, and then my mouth crashed against his.

The kiss was nothing like before. It wasn't gentle or shy. We threw ourselves at each other like we were in combat. The door slammed closed, and he pinned me against it, his tongue claiming my mouth, the warmth of his body surrounding me. I didn't know how to do this—I didn't know what I wanted to touch, only that I wanted to touch everything. My arms wrapped around his neck, my fingers tangling in the waves of his hair.

The need from that night had never gone away, only lowered to a simmering heat that now roared back to life. Desire swept up the insides of my thighs, tightening at my core.

I didn't want him to touch me the way he had before. I wanted more than that. I wanted to become intertwined with him. I wanted him to mark me.

The taste of blood mingled on our tongues. I yanked him closer, kissed him harder, closed my teeth around his flesh until it earned a hiss from him and a returning bite that sent a spark of pain through my lip.

I liked it. I liked feeling so many things at once.

We parted just enough for his eyes to look into mine. I must have had more of Nura's blood on me than I realized. Crimson smeared his cheek, his throat, his hair where my hands had trailed through it.

"You asked me if you frightened me," he breathed, then kissed me again, harder. "The answer is yes. You terrify me."

His lips moved to my jaw. One of his hands slid down my body, making the need that rose to the surface of my skin nearly unbearable. My knees parted, offering him room—his hips aligned with mine, and the hardness there made my breath hitch.

I didn't have the language to describe what I wanted, only that I wanted it, needed it, desperately.

His mouth brushed the soft skin where my jaw met my throat. "You terrify me because you make me want what I cannot have."

Take it, I thought. *Take all of it.*

My hands were shaking. Even my fingertips ached for him —ached for his skin, his breath, his heartbeat. But I forced them away from him, to the straps of my shirt. I slipped one from my shoulder, and then the other. Then my trousers, loose enough to fall easily to the ground. I wore nothing beneath any of it.

Caduan's nostrils flared.

"There is nothing you can not have," I said, my voice weak, breathy. For all my boldness, for everything that blood and vengeance and power and death had instilled in me, I now felt almost... shy.

Time slowed. He leaned closer again, his lips ghosting over my skin—barely brushing me when I wanted them to seize me. His knuckles skimmed the curve of my waist, running up my ribs and pausing at my breast, where his breath shuddered slightly, his thumb lingering at the hardened peak of my nipple.

"This is not true," he whispered, voice rough against my cheek.

"It is tonight." My hand covered his, gently trailing it down all the places I wanted him to touch me—down past my waist, my hip, my stomach, and finally, guiding him between my thighs, to that yearning emptiness that begged for him.

He groaned, pressing against me harder, his mouth again moving to mine but stopping just short of meeting it.

"We take what we want tonight," I said, and kissed him—the kind of kiss that did not ask but demanded.

Caduan wanted.

His fingers tightened at my hips with enough force to leave marks on my bare flesh. His teeth marked my lip, my throat, my shoulder. The hardness of his length between us grew unbearable.

I wanted to feel his skin against me. My hands went to the buttons on his shirt, ready to tear them apart if I needed to, but his hand caught mine and wrenched it to the wall, pinning me there.

A wordless sound of protest escaped my lips, muffled by his kiss.

But so easily, it was forgotten. Because his other hand slipped between us instead, circling one too-gentle touch at my core—*not enough, not enough*—before working at the buttons of his trousers.

Seconds later, the rough press of clothing against me was replaced by the hard, smooth silk of skin.

I tore away from his kiss for just a split second, casting a brief glance down—at my parted thighs and him nestled against the place between them.

I felt drunk, the world fuzzy. The desire was overwhelming. I tilted my hips, my movement limited by our position, but it was enough to make both of us release ragged moans.

Caduan grabbed my face, hard, and turned it to him. Both of us were covered in blood. I distantly became aware that we must have looked ridiculous—smeared with human blood, me naked, him half undressed, both of us utterly undone.

"If you want me to stop, then tell me now," he said. "I need you now. Right now, before I think better of it."

I kissed him and opened my thighs wider, angling myself so his tip prodded at my entrance.

"Yes," I murmured.

It was all that he needed. He kissed me, his tongue plunging into my mouth, just as his hands grabbed my backside, lifted me, spread me, and then he impaled me.

The world dissolved. First, there was pain—this body was new, and his size stretched it in ways that were unfamiliar and painful and, yet, the greatest pleasure I had ever known, like he was searing himself into every inner crevice of me.

Everything disappeared. It took several long seconds before I returned to my body, as he groaned into my hair, "Aefe, you feel... you..."

His muscles trembled. Was he holding himself back?

"Are you alright?" he asked.

I kissed him, my teeth nipping at the wound I had opened there, making him flinch. My legs closed around his waist, and his fingernails dug harder into my backside.

"More," I moaned.

He let out a long, shaky breath.

Tension snapped.

He obeyed.

His hips shifted in one abrupt thrust, spearing the rest of his length into me. Pain and pleasure claimed me in an overwhelming burst, but I didn't have time to catch my breath, didn't have time to do anything but cling to him. His thrusts were fast, rough, wild, like he wanted to claim every angle of me.

But I still wanted more. I wanted to fall apart until I didn't know my own name anymore.

My fingernails dug into the hard muscle of his back, earning a hiss and brush of teeth against my ear, as I whispered against his skin a demand: *More.*

This time, there was no hesitation. Caduan's movements were smooth and calculated. He withdrew from me, and barely gave me time to mourn the loss of him before he spun me around and bent over me, pressing his hand over mine against the wall. When he pushed back into me from behind, I no longer had the presence of mind to clamp down the strangled cry that escaped my throat.

Whatever final dregs of self-control I had were now gone.

I no longer cared who I was, or the fact that I didn't know. I no longer felt alone in this body—how could I when he was reshaping it so thoroughly around him? How could any body feel empty and dead when it was being filled this way, touched this way, loved this way?

"Caduan." I hadn't meant to say his name, but my lips needed to form something, and the only thing I could think—would ever think again—was him.

Pressure was building, building, within me—like what I had experienced the night of the festival, but so much more. With every stroke, he filled me deeper, his movements growing more vicious.

I moaned his name again, asking for something, and at the sound of it he let out a ragged groan and slammed into me hard enough to push me flat against the wall, his body braced behind me, the warmth of him trapping me there.

It was too much. I couldn't breathe. Couldn't think. I needed release.

"Yes," he murmured, the need in his voice sending a shiver up my spine. His hand slid between my body and the wall, wrapped around my waist, pulled me closer to him as he thrust into me at the same moment his teeth closed on the skin of my ear.

"Now, Aefe," he murmured, and as he commanded, I fell apart.

Every muscle went taut, the world shattering into annihilation except for him and the place we were connected. He drove deep, holding there, and I felt myself fill with him—distantly, in what little coherent thought I had left, I thought of how much I liked being full of another person.

An age seemed to pass with us like that, our muscles straining together, lost in our shared ecstasy.

When it faded, the first thing I became aware of was his lips softly kissing my neck. The second thing I became aware of was our heaving, trembling breaths. I had no strength. His arm around my waist, firm, was the only thing keeping me standing.

He kissed me one last time and gently, so gently, released me. I collapsed slowly to the floor, panting. I was covered in sweat and smudged flecks of human blood.

When he withdrew from me, when the warmth of his embrace was gone, I suddenly felt so empty.

"Aefe."

I loved how he said my name.

I looked up to see his hand outstretched. I was naked and trembling—he was standing, and still fully clothed. He took my hand and drew in a sharp breath.

"You're shaking."

I nodded.

I didn't know why.

"Come to the bed."

I obeyed. My legs barely carried me. After two steps, Caduan scooped me up and brought me there, laying me down tenderly over silken emerald-green sheets.

"Do you need anything? Water? Food?"

I shook my head.

"Are you cold?"

I shook my head again.

His brow lowered over those magnificent eyes. "Did I hurt you?"

Again, I shook my head.

His expression was indecipherable. He brushed his lips over my sweat-slicked forehead and began to stand. "I'll go get—"

Panic spiked in my chest. I grabbed his wrist, hard.

"Don't go."

He looked down at me, the wrinkle on his brow deepening.

And I could not even bring myself to be self-conscious as I said—as I *begged*—"Don't leave me. Stay."

My body felt as if I had been turned inside out and emptied. My mind felt fuzzy and overwhelmed, as if the closeness we had just experienced together had thrown my entire brain into shock. And my heart—my heart simply felt suddenly terrified for reasons I could not understand.

Caduan's expression softened. Still, he did not move for a moment.

"Please," I begged.

Everyone had always left me.

When I was Aefe, each body I shared my soul with was gone by morning. As Reshaye, each soul I shared a body with was ripped away from me.

I had the sudden, horrible feeling that Caduan was going to leave me, and at the same time, the sudden, horrible realization that I could not survive it if he did.

"I'm not." He closed his hand over my grasp in gentle affection, then got into the bed beside me, clothes and all. I sank so easily into the warmth of his form, my head lying on his chest, ear pressed to his heartbeat, my bare legs twining around his clothed ones. His arms encircled me, holding me firmly—one hand stroked my hair, and the other laid over mine. My fist closed around the fabric of his shirt, tight, not to allow him to escape.

"I am not going anywhere," he said again, his lips passing over the top of my head.

We had lain there for several minutes, when he finally murmured, "I'm sorry. For how I behaved after... the festival. I was..." A long, shaky breath. "I was afraid."

I did not need to ask, *afraid of what?* Because I knew, here as I melted into his pulse, exactly what was so frightening about this.

"I don't care," I said, and I meant it. He was here now. His flesh had become a part of mine. And I was here, intertwined with him, as intimate as sharing a body with another soul.

We did not speak again. I just listened to his heartbeat all night long, and for the first time since I had opened my eyes into this strange body, I did not feel lonely at all.

CHAPTER EIGHTY-FIVE

MAX

"So? What do you think?"

When we returned to our temporary home, Tisaanah sagged over her desk, rubbing her temples.

"I don't know," Tisaanah said. "I don't think it will be simple to separate Caduan from his throne. And I do not like the sound of what Ishqa proposes, smashing his country to pieces to weaken its foundation. I have seen that story before. But..." She let out a long breath through her teeth. "*But*. He's also right. What other choice does he have?"

"I don't trust that man. I don't think he can do this."

"He doesn't seem capable of it," Tisaanah admitted. "But Ishqa seems to believe it would work, and his judgment has helped us many times before."

I thought of the look on Ishqa's face earlier. The desperation. The regret. "I think there are a lot of reasons why Ishqa would want to believe a broken person can change."

The corner of her mouth quirked. "You did."

I didn't know what to say to that, so instead I grumbled something wordless.

"We have so little control over the Fey," she went on. "We barely understand them. Even if we disagree with Ishqa's plans, I do not think we could stop him. But Ara…"

Just the sound of the name made me nauseous.

"Right," I said. "Ara."

Tisaanah at last abandoned her papers. She stood, giving me that look—the kind that cut right through me, seeing all sorts of things I didn't want her to see.

"I do think you would make a wonderful king," she said, quietly, a tiny smile at one side of her mouth.

I scoffed. "You don't need to flatter me to get me into bed. We're long past that."

"I am serious."

"So am I! Please, Tisaanah. Let's think about this. Can you think of anyone *less* well-suited to prancing around with an Ascended-damned crown on his head than me?"

Her expression soured. "I can think of at least one other person."

Fair. I walked into that one.

She stepped closer, taking my hand loosely in hers. "Perhaps you have never seen yourself as a king. But you have always been a leader, crown or no. The people you led during the war still remember and support you. That did not go away because of Nura's lies."

"What about the other lies, though? That admiration is built on things like Sarlazai and wild rumors about whatever I did during the war. None of that was *me*."

"Perhaps some of it. Just as it is for me. My people see a version of me that is bigger than reality, too."

"That's different."

"Why?"

"Because you're…"

Words evaded me. What I was thinking was, *Better.*

She gave me a bemused smile. "Did your name become a legend because of stories and exaggerations? Yes, perhaps partly, but there is no legend that is anything but. And they are not fighting for Maxantarius Farlione, the legend. The thing they actually fight for is respect—respect you earned, by standing beside them. It wasn't the legend that did that. It was the man."

She looked at me like she actually believed all of these things. Sometimes, that alone was almost enough to make me believe them, too. Almost.

"Does it even matter?" I said. "Do I deserve that trust?"

The corner of her mouth tightened. "I always ask myself that question."

I almost laughed at that one. I understood why the rebels trusted Tisaanah. She had given them everything. She fought for them. She listened to them. She built them up. Of course they respected her. They would be fucking idiots not to.

The one upside, perhaps, to being a king would be the ability to make Tisaanah a queen.

"Here is what I think," she said, quietly. "I think it is a risk. I think it might not work. But I also think—no, *know*—that you will be a good leader for Ara in a time of few good things. You don't have to do it forever, just until this war is over. Until Nura is dealt with."

I sighed and leaned my forehead against hers. I wanted to say, *Absolutely fucking not. This is a terrible idea.*

Instead I said, "Why do you do this to me?"

"What?"

"Make me do things. You're always making me *do* things."

She laughed. "As soon as the war is done, I will never make you do a single thing ever again."

My chest clenched a little. It was rare that I ever heard Tisaanah talk about the future. Hearing her mention it, for some reason, made all of this seem a bit lighter.

Her enormous mismatched eyes looked up to meet mine. I was close enough to see every thread of color within them.

"Come with me," I said. "If I do this, I need you."

She chuckled. "You don't *need* me."

Oh no, you don't understand, I thought. *I very, very much do.*

But before I could say anything, her mouth pressed against mine in a long, deep kiss.

"Yes," she said, against my lips, when we parted. "I'll go with you."

CHAPTER EIGHTY-SIX

TISAANAH

I couldn't say no. It scared me, exactly how much I couldn't say no.

The truth was that until Max asked me to go to Ara with him, it never even occurred to me that I wouldn't. I had fought so hard to have him back at my side. There was no way I was about to let him walk away from it—no way I would ever allow him to walk back into Ara, his traitorous home, alone.

It wasn't until later that night, when I began to get arrangements together for my departure, that the knot grew in my stomach. I was leaving my people when they were especially vulnerable, our new society on wobbly legs like a baby fawn. We needed to leave as quickly as possible—Max, Sammerin, Brayan and I would be departing Threll first thing in the morning, giving me only twelve hours to make sure that my newborn nation would not collapse in my absence.

I visited Serel, wild-eyed and clutching armfuls of disorganized papers, and told him everything. As I listened to all of it come out of my mouth, shame bubbled up in my chest.

The moment I finished, I paused, and then said, "I should stay. I need to stay."

Serel frowned. "Why?"

"The Alliance needs me."

"We do. But we can survive for a few weeks without you. Besides, it's smart for you to go to Ara. It shows the Arans that Max has foreign support."

"I agreed to go so quickly. I didn't even think about it." I said this the way one would make a terrible confession. "I should have—"

"Stop." Serel stood and came closer to me, and as the lantern light fell across his face, I found myself examining him. He looked a little better, but darkness still shadowed his eyes. He'd resumed his leadership duties almost immediately, and smiled frequently, but those smiles were fleeting. I often saw the lights on in his house long after sunset and before dawn. It pained me to see the sadness in him, even though I knew better than to expect anything else. Grief was not a virus to be cured and expelled. It was a chronic condition that would shadow him forever.

Another reason why you shouldn't be leaving, a cruel voice whispered in the back of my mind.

The words slipped from my lips without my permission. "I'm sorry."

"Why are you apologizing?" Serel laid a hand over mine and gave me a soft smile. "Don't apologize for that. You haven't done anything."

"I shouldn't be prioritizing—"

"Prioritizing what? Him? You *love* him, Tisaanah."

I did. Gods, I did. But it wasn't the love itself that scared me. It was the sheer power of it. It made me selfish. It made me want so many things that hurt to even think about.

"I'm saying this to you not as a colleague, but as your friend." He elbowed my arm. "Your brother. As… someone who loved someone I lost. Do you know what kept me alive when I was inches from death in Malakahn? I thought about Filias and imagined the future we would have when I got out." The grief that rocked across his expression broke my heart. "What are we even doing any of this for, if not for a future with the people we love?"

I squeezed Serel's hand. "I didn't have room to love anything more than I love this country. And look at how far it's gotten us."

"Our people love you, too, but they love you as a figurehead. It's different to be loved as a person. More valuable than anything. I love you that way, Tisaanah. Not as a leader or a savior, but as a person. The friend who laughed at stupid jokes with me at midnight and held me through heartbreaks…" Here, he flinched. "Even this one. I know you, and I know that nothing scares you more than the thought that you might fail the people who rely on you because you're too selfish."

He gave me a weak smile. "As a friend, I want you to have that future with someone who loves you. And as a member of the Alliance, I know that you will not fail us, especially not because you're too happy."

My chest was so tight that I barely trusted myself to open my mouth.

"It feels… gluttonous," I choked out. "To love someone so much."

Serel laughed. "Yes. It does. But it's not a weakness. It's a strength."

I looked at my friend, at the silver lining his eyes and the grief over his face, and I felt gluttonous for all the love I had for him in this moment, too.

"You'll be okay?" I asked, quietly.

Serel kissed me on the cheek. "I'll be okay."

I SPENT the rest of the evening going over plans with Serel, and then, when I finally left him, I went to Riasha and ran her through them as well. I gave her all the documents she needed. I told her to write to me anytime, about anything at all, and that I would return as soon as I could. She nodded through all of it.

And then I got to the final item on my list, one that made me pause.

"There is one more thing," I said. "We hope to be able to take the Aran throne without bloodshed, especially with the backing of the Roseteeth."

Riasha's expression soured at the mention of the name, which I wholly agreed with.

"But I may need you," I said. "Would you come, if we needed you to fight?"

Riasha let out a long breath. "I would need to bring it to the others."

"Of course. But your informal thoughts."

She gave me a wry smile. "Child, I think these people would follow you anywhere. As would I."

I swallowed thickly. I understood how Max had felt—the weight of that kind of trust was suffocating, and yet I treasured it beyond words.

"And Serel," I added. "You'll watch over him for me?"

Her face softened. "I love that boy as much as I loved Filias. Always."

The weight on my shoulders lifted, ever slightly. "Thank you."

"Of course." Then she patted my hand, took the papers I had brought her, and stood. "Good luck, Tisaanah. Go make this world a little less broken."

I DIDN'T EXPECT it to hurt so much to leave. But when I stood at the rail of the ship, looking out into the distance at rolling golden fields, my throat was tight.

It would be the third time I had made this journey.

The first time as a refugee, a half-dead slave searching for someone to save her.

The second time as a weapon, a slave to a new master ready to go fight someone else's war.

And now, at last, as a liberator.

Max stood beside me, his hand over mine, fingers fitting so easily between my own.

We watched the Threllian shoreline drift away, and as the distant outline of Orasiev's silhouette drew smaller, I had to push back the beginnings of tears.

Max kissed my temple.

"Thank you," he murmured, in Thereni. "It means very much to have you with me."

I closed my eyes, falling into the sound of Max's voice rendering Thereni words. Always so comforting in ways I couldn't express.

"We will come back," he said.

"I know."

CHAPTER EIGHTY-SEVEN

MAX

Many Wielders assisted us on our journey—including Tisaanah—which allowed us to move very quickly across the sea, making a weeks-long trip in mere days. I spent most of it hanging over the rail, vomiting. Three trips over this very ocean, and one would think it wouldn't be so bad anymore, but alas, no such luck.

Sammerin was clearly pleased to return to Ara—he had been homesick for months. Even Brayan seemed uncharacteristically chipper, though maybe that was because he was just very passionate about this "throne stealing" idea. I still wasn't sure how I felt about it. Ishqa would remain in Threll for the next several days, but would be joining us in Ara when it was time to make our move.

It was a foggy afternoon, the sky grey and soupy, when we arrived in Ara. The Towers came into view first. When Tisaanah called Sammerin and I over, shouting that the Towers were visible, I expected to see those two imposing streaks of silver and gold looming over us.

What I saw instead made the words die in my throat.

The Towers were shattered. They still stood, and still

managed to look defiantly majestic, as if gouging their form into the sky. But where they had once been unbreakable columns tall enough to disappear into the clouds, now they ended in jagged spears, fraying like torn fabric.

Somberness fell over all of us. Sammerin's obvious pleasure at the thought of returning to Ara became quiet concern. Brayan's boastful confidence dampened to solemn sadness. All of us had known, logically, that we were headed to another war zone. But the shattered Towers served as an unexpectedly vivid reminder that things here had been even worse than we had imagined.

When we docked, Iya was waiting. The docks were quiet, too —yes, fishing boats and transport ships and military vessels all went about their business, but people were hushed and focused. No one even cast a second glance at Iya, standing there like a monument in the mist, his white hair and white skin and white robes cutting through the dusk. He lifted a hand to us in greeting as we left the ship.

"Maxantarius. Tisaanah. Sammerin." His accent plucked at our names like strings. "And... *my*, is that Brayan Farlione? Welcome home. I hope you've all had a safe and blissfully uneventful journey."

The idea of describing anything that was happening now as "blissfully uneventful" was incomprehensible. Instead, I grasped Iya's outstretched hand, gave him a smile that felt manic but I hoped looked reasonably calm, and said, "Thank you, councilor. Now, where's the coup?"

"*WHERE'S THE COUP?*" Tisaanah hissed in my ear, barely holding back her laughter.

I shrugged defensively. "What else was I supposed to say? Don't answer that," I added, when her lips opened. "We all already knew I have poor social graces. If that's disqualifying for this entire thing, then we're in trouble from the start."

Tisaanah rolled her eyes, and Sammerin let out a scoff that sounded a bit too much like agreement for my tastes.

Still, I clung to that one little sound of almost-amusement, because we needed it as Iya led us through the streets of the Capital.

I had never thought of myself as a particularly patriotic person — I had witnessed too many times what such attitudes cost — but seeing Ara in this state left me nauseous. I had seen some of the damage when Nura would pull me out of Ilyzath, but what had been hairline fractures then had now become massive rifts. Entire districts of the city were dark — Iya told us it was because certain areas were hit hard by attacks from the Fey's creatures, and residents were afraid to return — and we passed many buildings with shattered windows or crumbling walls, claw marks gouging them like curtains shredded by a house cat. Mourning flowers were pinned on most doors, intended to mark households that lost soldier relatives — sometimes the red of a lost husband or father, the white of a lost friend, and too many of them, the black of a lost child.

We were solemn as we walked through the streets. Iya glanced back at us. Our expressions must have said what our silence didn't.

"It has been a long few months," he said.

"I want a briefing on this," I said, gesturing to — well, all of it. "I need to know the context of everything that's happening."

"Already arranged."

Iya, to my surprise, led us to the foot of the Towers. Up close, their state was much better than it had appeared from a distance. The entrance and the first twenty floors or so seemed to be perfectly intact, albeit far quieter than I was used to seeing them. The few people who were present in the Towers' lobby stopped and looked at me as soon as we entered, which, on instinct, made me seize up.

"What?" Iya sounded amused. "Do you expect to be apprehended?"

I had to admit that a part of me did.

"This is the Orders," he said, quietly. "These are *your* people."

Now that was a sentence that, two years ago, would have made me burst out laughing. The idea that the Orders would ever be "*my*" people again had been incomprehensible.

"Surely at least some of them are Nura's people."

Iya's expression hardened. "Not many. Not anymore." He led us through the familiar hallways of the Tower of Midnight, bringing us to the platform and bringing us down, to the archives and libraries below the lobby.

My body tensed as the platform lowered. The last time I had been here, it was to be subjected to hours of torture that nearly killed me. I was stiff as we walked through the halls. I didn't quite expect the bolt of irrational panic that shot through me as Iya started to open the door.

"Wait." I grabbed his shoulder, too abruptly. "Vardir. Is he here?"

Iya's mouth thinned in disapproval. "No, thankfully. Nura started to get more paranoid over these last months. She moved her more... controversial projects outside of the Towers."

"Where?"

"Even the Council doesn't know. I suspect no one does, except her and Vardir."

"And the people she has locked up there," Tisaanah murmured.

I felt ill at the thought of it.

"We'll take care of that," I muttered, and Tisaanah nodded and squeezed my hand.

The door that Iya opened had never been one of Nura's labs, anyway. This one I had been in before, long ago, when I was competing for Arch Commandant the first time—it was an archive room, one of the largest, with hundreds or perhaps even thousands of shelves of books and records lining the walls and packed into narrow aisles.

Iya gestured to the closest bookcase, and the only one that was partially empty.

"Records," he said. "Detailing military operations, casualties, forms of attack, preparations, results… anything and everything that was considered worth writing around the conflicts with the Fey. If you wanted to read before the briefing tomorrow."

I felt dizzy just looking at it. "Thank you. That will be helpful."

Brayan looked up and down the rows. "This is like the military archives."

"Yes," Iya said. "It's the same concept."

"So why are these records here, instead of there?"

"If the subject has strong Orders participation or impact, the records go here. The military archives are largely centered upon non-Wielder experiences."

"Hm." Brayan looked around the room, intrigued.

"I'll go through these," I said. "Thank you."

"And after that?" Tisaanah asked Iya. She already had that look in her eye—that *"Let's-make-a-plan"* look. "What happens next? We have limited time."

"I have already called the Council together. They are arriving in the morning. At which point… we'll make the formal bid for Maxantarius to supplant Nura as Arch Commandant, and all the power that entails at this strange time in history."

I let out a long breath that trembled a little despite by best efforts. "Alright."

Iya gave me an encouraging smile. "Get some rest until then. Read. Think. Go see the city. Just be careful after nightfall."

CHAPTER EIGHTY-EIGHT

AEFE

Caduan and I spent a long, long time in bed. I had never realized how wonderful sleep could be when it was not plagued by unwelcome dreams, and instead was cradled by a warm embrace. I woke to Caduan kissing me, not with hungry kisses but small, tender ones. I took him into my body again, this time with him on top of me, moving slower, so I could appreciate all these different sensations. I wanted to touch him more, feel more of his bare skin against mine, but when I tried to undress him, he pinned me down and kissed me hard enough to make me forget that mission.

Afterwards, Caduan left to the washroom and I, now alone, rolled out of bed. My whole body was soft and languid, suffused with a new awareness.

Was this how living beings felt all the time? With this much pleasure built into their form? I was almost offended that I had missed out on it for so long. I spent months hating my body and the life it locked me into, when I could have been eating honey and listening to music and riding crests of carnal bliss.

Caduan's chamber was grand and beautiful, like everything in Ela'Dar's palace. Glass decorated with swirls of bronze stood floor-to-ceiling on one side of the room, with a large, sliding door that now sat partially open, leading to the balcony. I rose, not bothering to cover myself, and went outside.

It was raining. Within seconds, I was soaked, but the water was warm and pleasant.

I leaned against the railing and looked out to the mountains below. The city of Ela'Dar spread out before me, glistening in the silver rain and the misty embrace of the clouds. It seemed like a lifetime ago that Caduan had brought me here to show me this view, when I had first awoken in this new body.

I had thought I could never appreciate the beauty of it. But I did now.

"What are you doing?"

I turned to see Caduan walking out onto the balcony, seemingly undeterred by the rain, which quickly plastered his dark shirt to his skin and hair to his forehead in auburn swirls.

"I was thinking of the House of Obsidian," I said. "I used to feel so small when I stood before the Pales, and all the stories carved into their surface. I never thought I could feel that way again. But…"

I turned and looked again out over Ela'Dar.

"There are stories written across Ela'Dar's landscape, too," Caduan said. He sat in one of the chairs and observed the view. "In a different way."

"How?"

"The topography of Ela'Dar is always changing. Every time I look at it, something is different. Sometimes it's the landscape itself. That ravine, for example, opened three hundred years ago, after an earthquake—it revealed some of the most useful scientific breakthroughs I've ever had. But most of it is in the lives of the people themselves. Families move and evolve, greeting new members or mourning those who have departed. Businesses open or shutter. People paint their walls or change their homes. All of those things are visible from up here. As much as I disagreed with your father, I had always appreciated that about your people. That stories, even those of everyday people, were held in such high regard."

I looked down at the single mark on my wrist. Once I'd had tattoos covering my body that told my story. Now such a tale was far too complicated to tell in a line of symbols. It spanned hearts and minds and ages and the boundary of death itself.

"What about yours?" I asked. "Where is your story?"

"My hope is that the parts that matter are written into Ela'Dar itself. What else matters?"

I stared at him, stunned that he would even say such a thing. Ela'Dar was magnificent, but this landscape said nothing of the way Caduan's eyes looked when he was deep in thought.

"You do not feel that way," I said.

"What way?"

"That nothing else matters but Ela'Dar."

His face, still, had been tilted out to the horizon, but now his eyes slipped to me. I could not decipher the emotion that shadowed them as he rose and approached me.

"Some things, perhaps," he said, his voice rising slightly over the intensifying sound of the rain.

I was going to ask him what he meant, but then he kissed me hard enough that it didn't matter anymore, anyway.

———

MEAJQA, quite literally, interrupted our days of strange, suspended peace.

Caduan and I barely left his chambers, though he often disappeared for short stretches of time to deal with some business or another. The hours passed in either deep planning, thoughtful conversation, or, of course, physical pleasure. A strange balance of activity by some standards, perhaps, and yet it seemed oddly fitting for these times. I understood now what Meajqa had said the night of the Feast of Occassus. When the line between life and death was thinnest, everything felt more... intense.

"Caduan, there is—*oh*."

We were on the balcony when Meajqa arrived, Caduan lost in research and me looking out over Ela'Dar. I was naked—I realized it was very comfortable, and Caduan certainly did not seem to mind it, though he always remained clothed himself.

At the sound of the new voice, I whirled around to see Meajqa hastily turning his back, leaning against the frame of the open balcony door.

I crossed my arms over my naked body.

"Consider knocking, Meajqa," Caduan muttered, putting aside his parchments.

"I *did* knock. I see why there was no answer now, but I did not expect to find everyone frolicking naked."

Caduan retrieved a robe for me, which I wrapped around myself before we returned inside. "It is safe," I said, and Meajqa turned around again. He glanced between me and Caduan with a strange expression on his face.

"So this is why both of you have been so mysteriously absent."

"I have still attended every meeting, Meajqa," Caduan said. "It is wartime. I have work to do."

He spoke very sternly, and yet, did I imagine that he seemed, perhaps, a bit pleased with the way Meajqa was looking at us? Like he wanted Meajqa to know what had changed between us. When Caduan crossed behind me and brushed his hand across my back, in full view of Meajqa, my suspicion became certainty.

I liked this.

Meajqa cleared his throat.

"Well?" Caduan asked. "What was so important?"

"Two things. First, interesting rumors that our spies have heard whispered in the south. Some say that Maxantarius Farlione and Tisaanah Vytezic are currently traveling to Ara, with the intention of taking advantage of our... *guest's* absence."

My ears perked.

Caduan's brow twitched. "Hm. And second?"

"As long as we're speaking of attempted coups," Meajqa said, coolly, "I am pleased to report that we now have Ezra in custody. It was so very difficult to find him, stumbling around Ela'Dar's streets like a drunkard, trying to meet with all of our highest-ranking generals."

"Ezra?" I asked. The name sounded familiar.

"A madman who used to be a king, a very long time ago," Meajqa replied. "Somehow, he seems to think that means he has a right to Ela'Dar's throne, which is ridiculous for all the obvious reasons and more."

A wince flitted across Caduan's face. "You have him now?"

"Yes. Luia can have him taken away, or —"

"No," Caduan said, firmly. "I want to speak with him."

———————

THE MAN WAS NOT KEPT as a prisoner. This was not a dungeon, just one of the many sitting rooms in the castle. He sat at a small table in the center of the room.

"Ezra," Caduan said, and the man looked up.

Recognition speared through me.

I'd met this man once... long ago. The memories were fuzzy and half-formed. I had reclaimed so much of my former self, and yet so many individual experiences still lingered just out of reach.

Caduan turned to the servant who had followed us in, took a glass of water and a plate of bread from them, and then dismissed them. He joined Ezra at the table, sliding the food across to him.

Ezra pushed the plate away. "I suppose you will execute me."

"I will do no such thing." Caduan gave him a steady stare — the kind that methodically pulled its subject apart, as if he wanted to examine all the pieces that made someone whir to life. "You have been busy."

Ezra was silent.

"It's not poisoned, I promise you."

"We hear that you have been working on raising an army," Meajqa said. "Poorly."

Ezra's gaze flicked up to Meajqa. "You strongly resemble your father."

Meajqa's face hardened at the mere mention.

"You must have something to say," Caduan said.

"I have nothing to say to those who helped my kingdom fall."

Luia let out a short laugh, but Caduan remained utterly serious.

"I almost died the night Niraja fell," he said. "I never supported what happened to your kingdom."

"But you support an even greater slaughter."

"I support a world that is safe for our people."

"For *your* people. Would my wife have been safe in the world you are trying to build?" Ezra's face crumbled as he shook his head. "No. No, he was right. No, she would not. She would not."

He was right.

Meajqa and Caduan exchanged a pointed glance.

"He?" Caduan questioned.

But Ezra seemed as if he hadn't even heard him. He sagged over the table as if all his energy had left him at once. "I cannot do this. I can't. I cannot be a king. What was I thinking?"

Luia scoffed in disgust, but I felt a knot of pity in my chest.

"This wasn't your idea," Caduan said. A statement, not a question.

Ezra just kept mumbling, "I can't do this, I can't, I... I..."

Caduan remained there, but every question after that was met with only Ezra's mumbled, nonsensical responses. Eventually, Caduan sighed and rose.

"Take him to the prisons," he told the guards. "Don't harm him."

The guards obeyed, ushering Ezra from the room while Caduan joined the rest of us.

"What was he thinking?" Luia muttered. "Trying to mount an insurrection? He could barely string a sentence together."

"It wasn't his idea," Meajqa said, coldly. He looked out the window to the clear blue sky. "Someone has been putting this thought in his head. Whoever could it *possibly* be?"

Luia swore. "That traitorous bastard."

"I'm almost disappointed by what a horrible idea it was," Meajqa said. "Though, not that much. It could have been catastrophic if Ezra had been even a touch more coherent." He cast Caduan a dark glance. "We need to address it. Forcefully."

A wrinkle of thought deepened between Caduan's brows. "The Aran queen. Have we gotten anything from her?"

Luia sneered. "No. She will not talk. No matter what we do to her."

"Try once more. If you get nothing from her by tonight, kill her. She is too dangerous to keep alive."

Luia inclined her chin, but said nothing, an awkward silence falling over her and Meajqa. They shot each other a glance, then looked back to Caduan.

Luia seemed to choose her words very carefully as she asked, "And who should execute this order?"

I watched Meajqa, who was failing to fully control his expression. I could practically feel his bloodlust.

Caduan's eyes slipped to Meajqa. "You wish to do it."

"I deserve to," Meajqa replied, quietly but too quickly, like he had been holding himself back from saying it before. "I—I need to."

Caduan was silent. I wondered if perhaps Meajqa's words from before were echoing in his head as they echoed in mine:

Why is it unacceptable to feed my vengeance some human bitch's fingers, but yours can devour an entire race?

I thought of Ishqa's face, and how I would feel if he was the one locked up in that cell. I knew what it was to have a hole in yourself that could only be filled with the blood of the one that hurt you. Perhaps Caduan did, too.

"Fine," Caduan said, at last. "Do it."

A vicious smile spread across Meajqa's mouth. "As you wish, my King."

"Be careful with her, Meajqa. Do not underestimate her. And Luia, take care of Ezra. Keep him somewhere comfortable. His life has been difficult enough, and he is harmless."

"Where are you going?" Luia asked, as Caduan moved to the door.

"I'm going to wait for an old friend."

———————

CADUAN DID NOT COME BACK. Meajqa poured himself a glass of wine, clearly overwhelmed with anticipation for the moment he would at last get his final revenge. I was happy for him. Perhaps this would bring him the peace he so clearly needed.

"If you wish to say a final goodbye to your old friend," he said, casually, "perhaps you should do so now."

He gave me a knowing look out of the corner of his eye. He and I, after all, always understood each other.

Nura looked even more pitiful than she had when I last saw her. Bruises bloomed like flowers over her skin, severe enough to be visible even beneath her burn scars. They marred her shoulders, her arms, the entire left side of her face. She was listless, barely able to hold her head up. Her hand with the missing fingers had been bandaged and treated, if only because Caduan had wanted to make sure she did not die before he was ready for her to do so.

I crouched down before her, and finally, she stirred from her half-conscious state. She jerked her chin up, as if scraping together the last scraps of her strength for a single glare. I saw through that act.

"It is strange to see you this way," I said, "when for so long you were so much more than that to me. It makes me think of how so much is different now."

"How long will your king keep me here like this?"

I smiled. "Not much longer. Unless you give him what he wants."

"He wants to destroy my country. I won't let him have that."

"You act as if it isn't deserved."

A sharp, bitter laugh. "*Deserved*. You want to start throwing those stones, Reshaye?"

"My name is not—"

"You're the same. I watched your king order the doors locked in the Zorokov estate and slaughter those people."

"Slavers. They did not deserve to live, even by human standards."

"What about the Farliones? Did they deserve to live?" She lurched forward, yanking against her restraints. "You killed the only people that ever mattered to me. Children. What had they done? If you had wanted to kill us, the ones who had sinned, fine. I can understand that. But you—what you did—"

The memory rocked through me—the sheer, overwhelming scale of my hurt when Maxantarius had pushed me away in the wake of the greatest gift I'd ever given him. I had been so, so angry, and I had wanted him to have nothing but me, so that finally, for once, someone would see me, and I—

No. No, not *I*.

Not *me*.

"That was not me," I said.

"It was you," Nura snarled. "It is *still* you."

I launched myself at her, my hand coming to her throat, and I had to hold myself back from killing her. "*It was not me*. When I was Reshaye, I was not even a person anymore, because *you*, because *humans like you*, took everything from me over centuries of torture. Your human mind cannot possibly even understand it. It was not me."

For a split second, there was pure, satisfying fear in her eyes. But then a smile rolled over her lips, and she laughed.

"You believe that, don't you?" The smile soured like rotting fruit. "I have spent nearly a year trying to lead a country that your king is trying to destroy. I've lost count of how many little bodies I've pulled out of the wreckage after another attack, and another, and another. If I'm lucky, they're already dead. If I'm not, they're mortally wounded and screaming. On the worst days, I get to see one of those shadow creatures of his rip them apart alive while they cry for their mothers. So no, do not tell me that you're the good ones, Reshaye."

"Look at what you have done to the Fey you kidnapped. No creature that deserves life could do such things. Even your own people hate you. Maxantarius and Tisaanah are going to Ara to take your throne from you, did you know that? Your own sickened country is ready to be rid of you. And we are ready to be rid of you, too."

My fingernails dug into her pale flesh. Shock, then hurt, then anger twitched across her face, and I drank up each split-second of emotion with sadistic glee. It felt almost as good as her throat did beneath my grasp.

I realized that Nura had changed since I had last seen the inside of her mind. Then, she had erected so many steel walls to keep such feelings far, far from the surface. But something had eroded those walls over these last months. I was so close to her that I could see every muscle in her expression and how they all warred with each other to fight her emotions back—but all of it was still there, lingering just beyond her restraint, ready to explode.

Perhaps she had driven herself mad in her desperate pursuit of power, like her predecessor before her.

Good. She should know what it was for her mind to escape her own control.

My fingers tightened.

She struggled to remain conscious, her left eyelid twitching ever so slightly as she glared at me—like it took all of her will to hold that silver-edged stare.

She had no remorse for what she had done. She was a broken creature who weaponized her shattered edges and used them to draw blood over blood over blood. Caduan was right. He had always been right.

But... she was not mine to kill. Meajqa needed that more than I.

I released her. She slumped against the back of her chair, wheezing in a hollow gasp.

"Only one thing will stop this," I muttered as I straightened. "Until your kind is gone, it will always continue."

I turned away, but behind me, Nura spat, "You shouldn't even exist. I felt it the moment you walked into the room. I feel it even now, pulsing from somewhere in this wretched city. Whatever magic your precious king used to create you, it is just as dark as mine. He and I are the same. The only difference is that he succeeded in creating what I haven't been able to."

I stopped.

She lies. She always lies.

I did not give her the satisfaction of seeing my reaction. I gritted my teeth and opened the door—just as she let out an ugly laugh, high and manic, like her final shards of control at last collapsed.

"I know what you are. I took you into my mind, too. You're nothing but rage and pain. When this war is over, you'll find another thing to burn. It's all you know how to do."

CHAPTER EIGHTY-NINE

TISAANAH

It was strange to be back in this place, especially under such circumstances. Despite myself, I was nervous. The archives that Iya had showed us were extensive. Max, Sammerin, Brayan, and I brought boxes of records back up the Towers.

Iya had, graciously, given us his private apartment in the upper floors of the Tower of Midnight. The apartment was spacious and immaculately elegant, like most rooms in the Towers. When we arrived, two long, fabric-wrapped items were waiting for us on the table. There was a note with them.

Maxantarius and Tisaanah —

I believe these are yours. They have spent six months locked up in the Orders armory, but I thought you might like them back. Unfortunately, I suspect the time for needing them has not yet passed.

Iya.

When I unwrapped Il'Sahaj, I grinned. It really did feel like being reunited with an old friend. I suspected Max felt the same way, though perhaps a bit more reluctantly, as he held his spear once more.

"One day, I won't have to pick this thing up again," he muttered.

One day, hopefully. But not today.

We spent hours combing through pages upon pages of documentation in silence. Perhaps we were all grateful to have something to focus on.

We made it through only one of six boxes in three hours. After Max turned the final page, he glanced at the others and sighed heavily.

"We aren't sleeping tonight."

"You weren't going to be sleeping tonight, anyway," Sammerin pointed out.

"That is likely true."

I flipped through the scattered folders before me and paused at one leather-bound stack of papers. A smile spread over my lips.

"I have an idea." Max, Sammerin, and Brayan all looked to me. I held up the papers—a roster. "Maybe we can take a small detour. Just for a few minutes."

———

I WASN'T USED to the cold anymore. I tugged my cloak tighter around my body and adjusted my hood. It was dark now. Max, Sammerin and I—Brayan had chosen to stay behind—stood in the shadows, watching groups of uniformed men and women leave the mess hall. Dinner had just ended. Their attitudes were more subdued than one might expect. None looked our way, which was probably for the best.

I grinned. "There he is."

Even at a distance, I recognized him right away. He was a little taller, a little broader, but that messy halo of curls was the same.

Sammerin called out, "Moth!"

The boy lurched to a stop. The light from the mess hall silhouetted him as he turned to us, utterly still.

Sammerin lifted a hand.

For a long moment Moth did not move. Then he approached us, slowly.

"Sammerin?"

Even that one word made my eyebrows leap. Gods, his voice sounded different.

"Hello, Moth," Sammerin said, smoothly. "Have you been practicing?"

Moth drew close enough that we, finally, could see his face. In six months, he had gone from a child to a teenager. A scar nicked his lip, running down nearly to his chin. And yet, he still had that innocent roundness to his face.

Max gave him a wave and a bemused smirk. "Good to see you again."

Moth just stood there, like he didn't know what to do with himself.

I couldn't help myself—I ran to him and drew him into an embrace. He was almost as tall as I was, and broad enough that running into him felt like colliding with a wall of bricks. But when he said, "Hi, Tisaanah," with his words slightly wavering, he seemed just like the child I used to practice magic in the garden with every week.

I released him, and his eyes, shining and bright, darted between the three of us.

Max looked amused. "Happy to see us?"

After a long pause, Moth spoke. "I thought you were all dead," he said, and broke down into tears.

＊

WE COULD STEAL ONLY a few minutes with Moth—he was due back at the barracks, and we didn't want to be seen by everyone else yet. But that was more than enough for him to tell us what these last few months had been like, especially because the most meaningful information came not from what he did say but what he didn't. Moth's emotions were loud and his face expressive, and though the military had dampened some of that in him—which, honestly, made me a little sad—it was still obvious how difficult it had been.

"Why are you here?" he asked, eventually. "Are you—are you staying?" He cleared his throat and added, "It would be best for Ara if you did."

My heart warmed at that, because I knew that the reason Moth was asking had nothing to do with the noble greater good of Ara.

"I hope so," said Sammerin.

"You hope so?" Moth repeated. "What does that mean?"

A bell rang in the distance, and he glanced nervously over his shoulder. "I should go."

But he didn't move—like he was half afraid that if he let us out of his sight, he'd never see us again.

"Everyone still talks about you, you know," he said, haltingly. "They all remember you. That didn't go away."

Moth addressed all of us, but he looked only at Max.

Max tried to be stoic, but I knew him well enough to see how deeply this hit him.

"Are you... really back?" Moth asked. "Back for good?"

"That's a complicated question."

Gods forbid that Max ever said anything that could be interpreted as a promise he might not be able to fulfill.

"How about this," Sammerin said. "We came back here to do whatever we can to make this better. Can we promise we will succeed? No, because no one can make those kinds of promises. But we aren't leaving until we try. If this doesn't work, we will try something else."

He spoke in the same steady tone he would use to comfort a patient through uncertain odds. Somehow, it made even the unknowns seem manageable.

Moth seemed slightly more satisfied by this answer. The bell rang again, and he jumped. "Fuck, I'm late."

Sammerin's eyebrows leapt. "Such language, Moth."

Max looked a bit proud.

Moth let out a tiny laugh, bid us an awkward goodbye, and started to run back to the barracks.

"Moth," Max called.

Moth stopped and turned.

"Show us your magic."

He grinned and cupped his hands. Yellow-white light bloomed between them, illuminating his grin, zipping through the air in sparking rivulets. His hair rustled with the force of it. The sparks flew to the sky and made it past the tops of the trees before fading like embers.

"I haven't broken anything in a month and a half!" he added, somewhat proudly, and Sammerin laughed as he gave us a wave and hurried away.

———————

AFTER SEVERAL MORE HOURS OF preparations, we returned to the bedroom Iya had loaned us. Brayan retired to the other one in the apartment, and Sammerin, understandably, had chosen to stay in the city for the night rather than sharing a bed with Brayan—an image that made me snort laughter despite myself.

Though it was very late, Max and I hadn't even tried to sleep. Now Max leaned against the wall beside the balcony doors. The windows overlooked the boundary between the shore and the land—a ragged edge, as if the city was clawing its way back inch-by-inch from the ocean.

"I still cannot fucking believe that I'm doing this," he muttered.

"You said that last time, too," I said.

"And look at how that turned out."

I winced. He had a point there.

I watched him, silhouetted against the moonlight. He was shirtless, the broken tattoos and patchwork of scars over his back in full view, one hand tucked into his pocket and the other braced against the glass.

"What if we aren't any better at doing this than she is?" he said, quietly.

"You will be."

Certainties were rare and precious in times like these, but one I held in firm regard was the fact that Max would be a wonderful leader.

I rose to join him, and together we looked out at the empty, star-dusted sky.

"Where is Ishqa?" Max muttered. "He was supposed to be here by now."

"He will come."

"He'd better."

We were both having the same thought.

I glanced at Max.

"I have a question," I said.

"Hm?"

"Let us imagine that everything goes well."

"Let's."

"Let's imagine that you take the title of Arch Commandant tomorrow, and Nura never returns, and we are able to make peace with the Fey, and the war ends, and the seven Alliance nations remain peaceful, and everyone is happy."

Max let out a wry chuckle. "I'm imagining, but your story-telling is getting increasingly lax on believability."

"Then what?"

A pause. "Then what?"

"Will you keep the title?"

"No," he said, like the thought was ridiculous.

"Arch Commandant, or king?"

"Either. First of all, it was a ludicrous fraud that combined the two titles to begin with. Arch Commandants have historically done a terrible job of just ruling the Orders, let alone running a whole Ascended-damned country."

Agreed.

"But even then, even if the titles were split again, I don't think I'd keep the title of Arch Commandant, either." He scoffed. "If my twenty-year-old self could hear me say that, he'd fucking kill me."

"Why not?"

"Because…" His brow furrowed. "I don't know. I don't believe in it."

"Perhaps you could make the Orders something worth admiring again."

"Me? No. You though? You could."

He said this so earnestly, so simply, that it knocked me a little off kilter.

I swallowed past a sudden lump in my throat.

"Max," I said. "There's something that I want to—"

BANG!

The door flew open hard enough to slam against the wall. My hand was already closing around the hilt of my sword as I turned.

Brayan stood in the doorway, every inch of his body tensed. A piece of parchment was crumpled in a fist in one hand.

"You fucking *lied* to me."

CHAPTER NINETY

AEFE

Caduan was gone for hours. It was strange how difficult it had gotten for me to be without him, especially now, with something inside of me unmoored. I went to my room and sat alone, feeling like I had when I first opened my eyes in this empty body—trapped with nothing but the sound of Nura's voice telling me that I did not know how to do anything but destroy.

Eventually, I couldn't take it anymore. I knew I shouldn't—I knew he would not want me to. But I crept upstairs to Caduan's chambers. I had spent enough time there recently that no one gave me a second glance. He demanded privacy, so once I slipped through the main door, there were few guards or servants to worry about. I moved through the halls until I reached Caduan's bedchamber, which I peered into. The room was empty, the covers on the bed crumpled as they had been this morning.

Even without Caduan, I felt better here—less alone, comforted by even the ghost of his presence. If I drew in a deep breath, I could smell him, the crispness of the forest mingling with the warmth of candle flames.

I wandered through his room, debating crawling into the bed

to let him find me when he returned. I paused at the bureau, which was open, a drawer half-ajar. Where I might have expected to see clothing or undergarments, instead it was filled with small bottles, nearly half of which were empty. As I approached, I felt the air waver—like something radiated from them in a sense beneath all the others, reminding me of the way I had felt when we fought at Niraja.

I frowned and reached out for them.

A sudden *whoosh* of air behind me pulled me away. I realized that Caduan was here—I'd simply missed him. He sat out on the balcony, at a small table set with a board, his back to me.

And Ishqa had just landed before him.

In several long, silent strides, I crossed the room and pressed my back to the doorframe. My blade was out, and I was ready to strike if I needed to. I half expected Caduan to already be making a move of his own. But instead, he simply gestured to the empty chair across from him.

"Sit. Join me for a game."

I could barely see Ishqa, only a sliver of his profile. A wry smile flitted across his mouth. "I am out of practice."

"So am I. I have no good opponents. Meajqa is terrible. You failed in that part of his education."

"I failed Meajqa in many ways." Ishqa sat, and I scooted further behind the doorframe so he wouldn't see me.

You should kill him, a voice whispered in the back of my mind. *He is not expecting you. He should die. Make sure your face is the last thing he sees.*

But I didn't move.

I heard the clack of marble pieces moving against the wooden board.

"You're here because of Ezra," Caduan said, mildly.

"Is he dead?"

"No. Why should I punish him for an act that was clearly not his idea?"

Clack.

541

"That was you," Caduan stated. "Uncommonly stupid. Surely you must have known that he couldn't do this."

"Desperate times," Ishqa said.

Clack clack, as one piece claimed another.

"Do you really hate Ela'Dar so much?"

"I love Ela'Dar. I helped you build this empire."

"You were ready to shatter it. And don't try to tell me that was not what you were doing. You have many faults, Ishqa, but you are not stupid. You knew that positioning Ezra as a king would break us, whether he succeeded or didn't."

A long silence.

Clack.

"I will take one fractured country over a devastated world," Ishqa said, at last. "Even if it pains me."

"A devastated world," Caduan repeated slowly. "Would you say that what the humans did to my House was devastation? Or what they did to Aefe, because of your betrayal? Is that an example of your inclination for the greater good?"

Clack clack clack—each movement harder.

"What I did to Aefe is the greatest regret of my life. I valued my loyalty to my House over my loyalty to a friend. I valued my Queen's desire for power over the greater balance of life. I will not make that mistake again."

"And your son? *That* is devastation, Ishqa. What they did to him. It destroyed him. You left before you could see the extent of it. Or maybe you left because you didn't want to."

Ishqa's voice shifted so suddenly, cold and lethal like a drawn blade. "Watch your tongue, Caduan."

"Too close to the truth?"

"Meajqa is the only good thing I have ever brought into this world. I am doing this for him, and I hope he sees that one day."

"He is ashamed of you and will be until the day he dies."

Clack clack CLACK. Two pieces claimed by Caduan, but Ishqa did not even move to respond.

I barely breathed, edging closer to the glass. I could close the distance between myself and Ishqa in a heartbeat. He would not have time to react if I lunged.

"Let's discard the double talk, Caduan," Ishqa said. "I came here to ask you, one last time, to stop this. No—to beg you."

"I have no intention of stopping before I have finished my task."

"I helped the humans recover after the fall of the Zorokovs. I saw the consequences of a war between the humans and the Fey."

"You are the one leading the humans on a chase for the Lejaras."

"Only to keep you from using them. End this, and I will help destroy them."

Clack.

Caduan chuckled. "When I first met you, I never would have thought you would be so foolishly trusting."

"You know the consequences of the powers we tamper with. It could destroy this world."

"Then advise them to surrender."

Clack, as Caduan calmly placed another piece.

CRASH, as Ishqa sent the board smashing to the floor and leapt to his feet.

I tensed.

"This is ridiculous, Caduan," Ishqa spat. "What will you do when this is over? What will you do when you stand upon a pile of corpses and ash? Will that make you feel better? Will it help Aefe? I warned you once about the intersection of vengeance and victory. You are not looking for victory, you're looking for vengeance, and nothing you do will ever be—"

"If you want someone to blame, blame *yourself*." Caduan rose, too. "None of my people will ever suffer the way that Meajqa did, the way that Aefe. *Never again.* Someone needs to be willing to—"

Caduan's body lurched.

He doubled over, his hands pressed flat to the table. And in the same moment, Ishqa leaned closer.

I didn't wait. I was already coiled. I was already moving.

I lunged onto the balcony. Ishqa gripped Caduan's shoulder. I caught only a glimpse of his face, his brows furrowed deep, before my body slammed into his. We landed together in a tangle against the railing, my blade already poised at his throat, my magic pulsing at my fingertips. Tiny sprouts of vines grew slowly across his skin.

"Aefe, *stop*!" Caduan commanded, before I could land my strike.

"Let me kill him," I snarled. "He was moving for you."

But Caduan was not even looking at me. He was looking only at Ishqa—and in turn, Ishqa looked only at him, wide-eyed, even as I pinned him.

"Now, I understand," Ishqa said, almost sadly. "After all this, now I understand."

For a moment, the whole world balanced on a knife's edge.

Ishqa murmured, "Does she—?"

"Enough." A shadow passed over Caduan's expression. He turned away. "Kill him, Aefe."

You have waited for this for five hundred years, a voice inside me whispered—and it was only now that I realized that voice was myself, as Reshaye.

I leaned over Ishqa, and at last, his gaze turned to me. His face was the final, dying sight of my old life. And now, mine would be his.

I *hated* him.

And yet, he looked at me with only resigned sorrow. "I am so—"

His blood sprayed over me. I cut his throat with such force that the blade hit bone. Leaves and flowers grew over his skin, consuming his mouth, his nostrils, piercing those beautiful eyes and smiting them from his face.

My heart was racing, my blood rushing in my ears, my muscles shaking.

I hated him.

I hated him I hated him I hated—

I let out a ragged, wordless cry and pushed Ishqa's body from the balcony. This person who had dominated my dreams and nightmares was nothing but a limp sack of flesh as he fell to the rocks below.

I rose slowly, shaking with rage and grief and hatred and anguish and, and, and—

Caduan reached for me wordlessly, and I let him pull me into his arms as I wept.

———

I THOUGHT I would feel release of some kind, once it was done. Thought I would feel satisfied, or triumphant, or relieved. Thought his blood would fill the hole within me.

But instead, numbness strangled the emotions that built and built beneath my skin with nowhere to go. The hole gaped as wide and painful as ever.

I had thought my life would begin once Ishqa was dead.

Instead, my life was the same.

CHAPTER NINETY-ONE

MAX

You fucking lied to me.

I didn't say anything. I couldn't. I'd only ever lied to Brayan once, and it was the kind of lie that devoured everything else.

Brayan stepped into the room and closed the door, hard. I half expected it to crack the walls.

"You were there," he breathed. "You were there the day that it happened."

I wasn't prepared for this. I wasn't ready. The topic always hit me like a sudden strike, the kind that knocked all the wind out of me.

So I did nothing but stand there as he thrust the crumpled papers into my hands.

Numbly, I unfolded them. They were discharge records from the Orders. Many soldiers had been sent home in the time immediately after Sarlazai, mostly due to injuries, so the paper was packed with many, many rows of names and locations.

Still, I easily found mine, right there in the middle of the page. *Maxantarius Farlione. Temporary discharge. Korvius.*

I just stared at it.

The Orders had spun me such a perfect, intricate cover story. But it was the fucking bureaucracy, this stupid slip of paper buried in the archives, that destroyed it all. It was almost fucking funny.

"Max," Brayan snapped. "What is this?"

"I—"

I could say it was a mistake. I could say that I lied to the Orders about my destination because I was going to go party in Meriata. I could say that I left before the attack happened.

I could tell so many lies.

But I had been cursed with a face that painted every thought that crossed my mind for the world to see, and all those fake explanations sat rancid, unspoken, at the back of my throat.

"I want the truth," Brayan demanded.

And I—being so, so stupid—said, "You don't. It won't help."

I'd never seen Brayan like this. I'd seen him angry, but this was like his body ceased to function, overwhelmed by rage. "I swear to the fucking Ascended, Max, *I need the truth.*"

If I'd been able to look at anything but him, I might have acknowledged Tisaanah edging closer to me, shaking her head. But my lips were already opening.

This is a mistake, Max. Big mistake. Nothing good will come out of this.

"Reshaye," I choked out. "Reshaye was more than you know."

Brayan seemed confused. "Reshaye? You mean, the power that the Orders gave you. The… eyes."

"No. More than that. It was… sentient."

"Sentient?" Brayan's brow furrowed. "As in it, what, talked?"

It sounded so fucking ridiculous out loud. "What I did in Sarlazai wasn't me. Reshaye did that."

He scoffed. "I knew you had some guilt, but—"

"Believe me or don't," I snapped. "You wanted the truth and I'm giving it to you. It wasn't me. It acted with my body. But it wasn't me. Before, I'd always managed to control it. But that day, when we were overrun in the city..."

Suddenly I was there again, soaked with blood and melted snow, my consciousness waning, Reshaye thrashing in my mind, and Nura—Nura looking at me like she had back then, her fingers caressing my temple seconds before she betrayed me.

And I didn't even realize that I was talking anymore, but the words were pouring out of me.

"I never wanted to do that. I wanted to retreat. But when Reshaye took over, I lost control. I was conscious for every second of what it did to those people. With my magic. My hands. And then... then it was over and everyone was around me calling me a fucking war hero. Celebrating that. *You* were celebrating that."

I drew in a breath and when I let it out, it trembled.

"That was why they discharged me. Because I'd killed thousands of Ascended-damned people, many of whom were my own. They discharged me because I was a fucking mess and I, being the—the *idiot* that I was, just wanted to go home. I just wanted to hide and pretend that none of it had happened."

A mistake. Such a mistake.

How many times had I thought about that in the years since? There were so many moments to regret, but I'd pinned most of them on that decision—the decision to return home, when I *knew*, when I should have known—

I opened my mouth, but the rest of it, now, strangled me.

Brayan said, "And?"

So much came after that word.

And.

I barely felt Tisaanah's hand clutching my arm, barely heard her murmur, "Max, you don't need to—"

"I was so fucking angry at it. And it was possessive. I should have known that I wouldn't be able to control it this time. My mind was—everything was rearranged. I couldn't lie to it. I couldn't lock it away."

I was ten years in the past, staring at the bedspread, arguing with Reshaye in my head.

You're a monster, I called it.

{If I am a monster, what does that make you?}

{You make me do this.}

"I was *so stupid*. I made such a stupid mistake. But once I realized, it was too late. I couldn't control it. It was angry at me and it wanted to—I don't know what it wanted."

{Now you have no one but me,} it had whispered to me, while Kira's body burned.

Tisaanah held my arm so tightly that her fingers shook.

But I only looked at Brayan, not breathing. He didn't move. His expression didn't change.

"Clarify," he said, the way he would command a soldier for a debrief.

"I—"

I had never once actually said the words out loud before. "It wasn't rebels." My voice was strangely choked. "It was me. It was me."

"Reshaye," Tisaanah said, quickly. "It was Reshaye. It was not you."

But neither Brayan nor I seemed to hear her.

People like to say that there's catharsis in speaking the truth out loud, as if some weight is lifted in the act of discarding a lie for an ugly reality.

That, I decided in this moment, was not true at all.

I watched a muscle twitch in Brayan's throat.

"You are telling me," he said, quietly, "that the last thing they saw was *you*?"

He stalked closer, slowly.

"You are telling me that you *murdered our family?*"

His voice rose, step by step, with each word.

"No," Tisaanah said. "Reshaye did. He had no control over it."

True or not, it seemed like such a pathetic excuse. I'd examined all the angles of my guilt countless times, and there were many. Maybe there was nothing I could have done to stop Reshaye in those moments, but there was plenty I could have done to keep myself away from that situation entirely.

My back slammed against the wall. Brayan pinned me, his arm against my throat. He was always so carefully controlled. When his emotions spiraled out of control, it wasn't a slow rise, it was an explosion.

"You let me believe a lie for ten years," he snarled. "You let me believe that I killed those bastards, when really, it was you — it was you that—"

"There's nothing you can say to me that I haven't said to myself, a million times over." My voice was slightly raspy, and I had to force it out through the pressure of Brayan's forearm. "I would have done anything to erase that moment. Anything."

"You let me believe that there had been *justice* for this."

Justice. I'd wanted that too, for so long. I thought if I died in the slums of Meriata, maybe something would be set right in the universe. Maybe some debt would be repaid.

Brayan's eyes shone, and I realized he was close to tears.

"There was never going to be justice, Brayan," I said, quietly. "No matter who you killed for it. I meant everything I said when I told you that nothing was ever going to make it make sense."

"You—You—" He discarded words and abruptly left me, leaving me catching my breath. He went to the door, and when he turned again, his sword was drawn.

"Get your weapon."

He looked every inch the renowned warrior of Ara, the golden son. And yet, I pitied him. His whole life had been built around a set of unquestionable truths, and chief among them was that there was no problem that could not be solved with a firm hand or a sharp blade.

"I'm not going to fight you."

Brayan lunged anyway.

Tisaanah was in front of me immediately, her hands up and magic ready, prepared to shield me before I could stop her.

Brayan didn't hesitate before he readjusted, dodged her blow, grabbed her arm, and wrenched her out of the way.

That was it.

Fire roared to life at my hands, and then I had Brayan flung against the wall. The red light of the fire flickered across his face, emphasizing every line of hatred.

"Don't you *dare* touch her."

"Or what? What will you do? Kill your last brother?"

We all had the same eyes, my siblings and I, so dark they were almost black. Mine had looked just like theirs before Reshaye had altered them. Now, the darkness of his acted as a mirror to the flames, begging me to take the challenge.

He wanted me to fight him, because that was all he knew how to do. It was the only way he knew how to deal with pain.

I let my magic fall away and stepped back.

"I made so many mistakes, Brayan." My voice cracked. "So many mistakes. Reshaye was so far outside my control, but I won't pretend that I'm not at fault. That there weren't a hundred different decisions I could have made that wouldn't have put me in that room that day. You know what I wished more than anything?" I let out a rough laugh. "I spent years wishing that you had been there. Because I was certain you would have killed me before I could finish it."

My father had hesitated when he saw it was me. Softened his blow to avoid killing his son.

Brayan would have done no such thing. I knew it then, and I knew it now.

"I made mistakes," I said. "I'll spend the rest of my life trying to atone for that, and I'll fail, because there's nothing I could ever do that would be worth their lives."

Brayan was trembling, the muscle in his jaw feathering rapidly. He jerked his chin up, but despite himself, a tear rolled down his cheek.

"That isn't enough."

"No," I agreed. "It isn't. Nothing ever will be."

He was still, his shoulders heaving, knuckles white around

the hilt of his sword. I tensed, preparing for him to lunge at me again.

I wouldn't even blame him if he did.

Instead he said, "You're right. I would have killed you," and slammed the door behind him.

CHAPTER NINETY-TWO

AEFE

Time passed in a blur. I curled up in the dark in the corner of Caduan's bed. He lay beside me, his hand on my waist, and neither of us said anything at all. I did not realize we had fallen asleep until I was being jerked awake again.

"My King! *My King!*"

Luia sounded frantic. And yet, my consciousness returned so, so slowly. I questioned at first whether this was real, or a dream—everything seemed too soft and too sharp at once, my skin covered in goosebumps, the air acrid.

I forced my eyes open to see Luia on the bed, crouched over Caduan, shaking him.

My panic was sharp enough to cut through the unnatural haze in my mind. I jerked upright. Caduan's head lolled back, limp even as Luia practically picked him up by his collar.

I did the only thing I could think to do. I slapped him across the face as hard as I could.

Luia, shocked, dropped him. He fell in a heap to the pillow. For several harrowing seconds, he still did not move.

"Caduan?" My voice shook. It came out softer than I expected, or maybe it just sounded that way, because my ears were ringing—why were my ears ringing? Why did everything feel so strange?

And then, at last, he opened his eyes. Awareness came to him slowly. And then, moments after it, came panic. His hand shot to his chest, clutching it.

Luia let out a shaky breath of relief. "Thank the gods. My King—Caduan, it's—"

"What happened?" The words were ragged. His breathing was uneven. He pushed himself upright in an ungraceful lurch, hand still at his chest. "I—Something has—"

"Meajqa," Luia choked out. She was near tears. "That drunk fool, he tried to do it alone—the prisoner—"

A terrible wave of dread crashed over me.

Before Luia could finish, Caduan staggered from the bed. "Stay here," he commanded, but I was already standing too— only to find myself nearly tipping over, as if the whole world had been tilted sideways on its axis.

Luia caught my arm, her brow knotted. "What is wrong with you? *Caduan*—!"

She tried to stop Caduan, too, but he was already throwing open the door, half-running, half-stumbling down the hall. I followed him, catching up quickly enough to catch his arm and stabilize him—I felt dizzy and off-kilter, but at least I had my strength, while Caduan looked like his body was actively failing him. We swept through the halls, and I couldn't even think to ask where we were going, until Caduan fell to his knees.

Nura's cell was open. Meajqa, limp and bloody, was crumpled in a heap just within the door, surrounded by guards attempting to revive him.

The cell was empty.

A cold fear fell over me. Caduan stared at it in horror.

Upstairs, I heard someone scream, a single shout that soon became a cacophony.

Caduan stood and started limping down the hall.

"Wait—"

He ignored me. We ran up the stairs, to the front entrance,

the one that opened up closer to the city. The palace was in chaos, soldiers and guards and servants running in all directions.

He threw open the door and half-fell down the steps.

Below us, the city of Ela'Dar burned. People, from here little more than ants, ran frenzied through the streets. Screams rose from the city walls.

Everything went numb.

I heard shouts behind me and turned. A group of guards backed against the wall, eyes round, facing off against this...

This...

Was it a person? A Fey? They wore the uniform of Ela'Dar's military. They had pointed ears and black hair. But their movements... no, their movements were wrong, just as their proportions were, every part of their body a little ill-fitted to the others. When it turned to us, its eyes were a million miles deep, black holes that took me through the center of the earth when I looked at them.

Wrong wrong wrong wrong, every primal instinct within me screamed.

Then I realized: this thing was a *corpse.*

And Ela'Dar was overrun with them.

ELA'DAR HAD BURIED SO, so many dead these last six months. Now those dead flooded the city. Caduan barely allowed himself time to take it in before racing into the madness. His terror seemed to have brought him a wave of frenzied energy, because now he just ran, ignoring all else as he focused on his destination.

The destruction was all-consuming.

Death was everywhere. Fey civilians were being torn apart by their own lost loved ones. Homes collapsed. Walls of stone crumbled as if they were paper. Around us, soldiers poured from the barracks, panicked and ill-prepared. Distantly, Luia's commands drowned beneath the sound of screams of horror or pain.

Caduan did not stop, and so, neither did I. We flew to the edge of the palace grounds. A creature lunged at us, leaving burning marks in my skin with a mere brush of its fingertips. It grabbed Caduan, but I wildly stabbed it until its face—could one even call it a face?—was a disfigured mess seeping black. It released him and slumped to the ground long enough for us to slip its grasp. Out of the corner of my eye I saw it rise again seconds later, but by then, we were gone.

A circular stone building came into view through the trees.

I recognized this place. I had come here that night so many months ago, awakened by the strange force that seemed to shift in the air—the night I had found Caduan slumped against the wall, surrounded by the shades he had created, and we had walked back together in the night.

There were no shades here now. Not anymore.

Instead there was merely an open door and an empty room. The table at its center, a round slab of iron, was empty. The light that had once burned through the patterns in the floor had now dimmed. The glow in its center was gone.

Caduan collapsed over the table. For a moment, he just leaned there, breath heaving.

"I don't understand," I managed. "What is—"

And it was only then that I noticed his body. The monster had torn his shirt to shreds, leaving half his chest and most of his abdomen exposed—revealing streaks of darkness, overtaking his flesh like roots.

"I'm so sorry, Aefe."

He looked up at me, and the pure devastation on his face was so much more terrifying than anything we had just witnessed. More terrifying than looking into the eyes of living death itself.

"I'm so sorry."

CHAPTER NINETY-THREE

AEFE

I did not get to ask any more questions of Caduan before he ran back out into the wreckage. When I tried, he only barked that we had no time to talk, only to fight. And in this, he was right. Ela'Dar had been ravaged. The beasts were nearly impossible to kill. The sheer number of them, and the fact that we had not been expecting them, brought the city to its knees in hours. Our dead turned on us so fast that we had no choice but to fight for our lives. Some tried to burn the bodies, only to send flaming corpses running through the city, spreading wildfires as they tore through houses and crashed through forests.

How many hours did the nightmare last? I did not know. Time became a distant concept as survival narrowed my thoughts.

It was long past nightfall by the time the city was under control enough for me to follow Caduan back to his rooms. He had spent part of the evening with Luia and Vythian, then Meajqa from his healer's bed after he regained consciousness, whispering frantically about things I was forbidden from hearing.

When the door closed, I watched Caduan come undone, like

sails collapsing on an abandoned ship. He sank down onto his desk chair, his head in his hands, while I remained at the door, breath still heaving and heart still racing.

"What was that?" I choked out. "What were those things?"

Caduan did not answer. Instead, he stood and went to his closet. He had thrown on an ill-fitting jacket, which covered his shredded shirt and... and all it revealed. He stepped behind a divider and tossed the jacket out from behind it, and then the tattered shirt.

"Tell me," I demanded. "Tell me what just happened. Tell me *how* that just happened."

"That," Caduan said, far too calmly, "was the work of a Lejara. Creation magic, to be specific."

A Lejara? That didn't make sense. "But you have spent the last six months searching for the Lejaras."

"Searching for the other two. Yes."

"But if you already had one—"

"No one knew it was here. No one but me."

My mouth closed. I could not see Caduan behind the divider, which made me angry.

"Why would you hide it?"

There was a long silence, so long I was ready to tear down the wall between us so I could force him to answer. "What were those things, Caduan?"

"The Aran queen took the Lejara. She must have used it. She would have known—I should have known she would feel its presence, considering how obsessively she has been studying such forces."

"But how—"

"Creation is just as dangerous as death. More dangerous, perhaps. There is nothing more dangerous than life that should not exist."

I felt so sick. "Why didn't you tell anyone that you had it?"

"Because..." At last, he stepped out from behind the divider. He had a fresh shirt on, too white against his blood-and-sweat caked skin. He left the buttons open, revealing his body beneath.

I had not imagined what I had seen in the circular room. The lines of black covered his entire torso. They started at the center of his stomach and fanned out, spreading like rotten roots up his chest, collecting at his sternum and ending shy of his throat.

"What is that?" I asked, quietly.

I had never seen Caduan ashamed before.

"I did not tell anyone, not even Meajqa, about the magic I had, because I wanted to be able to use it as I saw fit without justifying that decision to anyone."

"You used it to create the shades."

Pain cracked every line of Caduan's features. "Not just the shades."

I looked down at my hands. My soft, mortal, living hands.

So many moments roared through me at once.

The shock and horror on Ishqa's face the first time he saw me. *How? How did you do this?*

Meajqa's voice, that night in the pub. *I don't ask those types of questions.*

Nura. *Whatever magic your precious king used to create you, it is just as dark as mine.*

And then, immediately after, came the image of the corpses attacking my kingdom.

There is nothing more dangerous than life that should not exist, Caduan had said.

You knew from the beginning that you should not be alive, the voice jeered at the back of my mind.

Me. He used it to make me.

"So no one knows," I choked out. "No one knows how you made me."

Caduan took two steps forward, as if he couldn't stop himself. "I didn't make you. You were already there. I simply made you whole again."

"I—"

Whole? Is that what you are?

I approached him, so I could look at his body up close. The darkness looked like veins, or spiderwebs. They pulsed slightly beneath his skin as if in time with his heartbeat. Merely being close to them felt sour and wrong, just as I had felt when standing in the presence of the living dead.

It hurt to think of something as beautiful as Caduan's heartbeat marred by this... this... corruption.

I touched it with my fingertips, and Caduan flinched.

Do not ask, the voice whispered. *You do not want to know.*

But I said, "What is this?"

The seconds before Caduan's answer were excruciating.

"Mortals were not intended to do such things," he said, quietly. "Not intended to channel such forces, especially not those powerful enough to..."

His voice faded, and his knuckles brushed my cheek — such a light, tender touch. My eyes flicked up to meet his.

Look away.

"I don't understand."

You do understand.

"I did not bring you back to be a weapon, Aefe. I brought you back to be everything you could have been, if you had lived. To be everything I should have been, once I run out of time."

No.

"I do not understand," I said again, almost a snarl.

"I am dying, Aefe."

How weak a mortal heart is. The words cut deeper than any battle wound.

"No." I shook my head, hard. "No, that is not true."

Caduan's eyes shone. "I have always known the dangers. I knew what I was doing. But that night... the night I needed to make more shades. I pushed too hard. I knew that night, it was going to be the end."

That night. The night the earth seemed to tear apart, when I found Caduan in that circular room, when he could barely stand, and I walked with him through the forest —

"No," I choked out.

Don't leave me, I had begged him.

"I knew from the beginning the side effects of handling magic

this potent. Doing it for so long. And I was always willing to—"
He reached for me, but I batted his hand away.

How quickly, the pain turned to rage.

"How could you do this?"

"Aefe—"

I hated the way he said my name.

"You brought me here just to abandon me. You—you brought me here and gave me this empty body and this empty heartbeat and you—and all the while you—"

He stood a step closer, and I wanted him to say something, I wanted him to scream at me, I wanted him to hurt me, because every piece of warmth within me had now become this horrible, blistering fire that I only knew how to feed.

Don't leave me, I had begged, and he had told me, *I am not going anywhere.*

"You—You *lied* to me," I spat. My vision was blurry—why was my vision blurry? "You betrayed me. You betrayed your entire kingdom."

He stepped closer again. "I never wanted—"

Lie. He did want. He had been nothing but want that night.

"You *made me love you.*" My words were jagged and raspy with sobs.

He reached out for me, such a gentle, tender touch. "Aefe, please. We need you."

I backed away.

He said, more desperately, "*I* need you."

Once he had said that to me and I had hated those words because I thought he needed me the way one needed a weapon. But now I knew a different sort of need—the way he needed me the night I let him into my body. The way he needed me when we held each other at the sunrise.

I knew, no matter how angry I was, that when he said, *I need you,* this was what he meant.

And that, that genuine affection, hurt deeper than all of it.

"*I hate you.*" I hurled the lie at him like a throwing knife, and I did not let him say a single tender word to me again.

CHAPTER NINETY-FOUR

TISAANAH

Max looked like a ghost.

When Brayan left, he turned to me and asked, too calmly, "Did he hurt you?"

As if one enraged non-Wielder man could hurt me. Even if he had, whatever scratch he'd given me was laughably inconsequential to whatever Max was going through.

"No. Are you alright?"

Of course he was not alright. He was so far from alright, and all of it was written all over his face.

He pinched the bridge of his nose, let out a long breath, paced the length of the wall. "Fuck, we—we won't have the Roseteeth anymore."

"We do not need to worry about that this second," I said, quietly. "That isn't what I asked. Are *you* alright?"

"I'm alright."

A lie. I wrapped both my hands around his, squeezed tight. "It wasn't your fault. You know that. No matter what Brayan says."

He scoffed, and I repeated, "*It was not your fault.*"

Despite my best efforts, fear seeped into my voice. I was

suddenly terrified. Not because of our abrupt reduction in forces. Not because of how Max's mental state might impact his ability to gain support tomorrow. Not because of the war, or the crown, or the Orders, or the council.

But because the idea of Max, the best person I knew, in this kind of pain was agonizing to me.

"Tell me what you need," I murmured. "Tell me how I can help you."

He pulled me into an embrace, and I held him tightly as I felt his body shudder slightly against mine. He kissed me on the forehead, then the mouth.

"I'll be fine. We can't do anything but focus on tomorrow," he said.

Max was not fine.

But he was right. There was only one thing we could do. Wait.

So we waited. Hours passed. Ishqa still had not arrived. Sunrise approached, and Max and I spoke less as our collective anxiety rose. Eventually, we collapsed into bed, falling into a restless, fitful sleep against each other, not acknowledging the fact that we were waking every few minutes.

Movement outside stirred us sometime near dawn. The sky was stained with misty pink from the impending sunrise. I opened bleary eyes to see a golden, feathered blur sweep through the sky.

I quickly rose and went to the balcony, Max right beside me.

"Where the hell have you been?" Max hissed, rubbing away sleep, as Ishqa landed on the balcony. He was silhouetted, his back to us, the early morning sun painting his outline in gold.

He didn't turn. He just stood there, swaying slightly in a way that seemed… odd.

"Ishqa?" I whispered.

I reached out for him—

He turned in one lurching movement. A strangled cry of horror leapt from my throat.

He had no eyes, the gold replaced by rotting black pits. His throat was slashed, a waterfall of putrid violet blood painting the front of his body. His limbs were too long and off-balanced, the arrangement of them grotesque compared to his usual grace.

The next thing I knew, he was against me, his claw-tipped hands clutching my shoulder hard enough to pierce my skin.

"I tried—I tried—"

A horrible, twisted version of Ishqa's voice, desperate and pleading.

Max was trying to get him off me, but his grip was so tight, all his muscles contracting at once.

"I can't, I can't—" Ishqa begged.

I looked down.

And that was when I saw the parchment nailed to his chest, violet soaked:

THEY ARE COMING FOR YOU.
  AND SO AM I.

LOVE,
  NURA.

I looked up into Ishqa's face and saw a despair deeper than centuries.

"*Go,*" he choked out.

Blue powder spilled from his rotting mouth.

I realized too late. Saw the light start within him too late.

Horror fell over Max's face. "That's—"

Lightning dust.

We didn't have time to say it.

Because then Ishqa, or the thing that was once Ishqa, exploded into a smear of fire and light. The floor fell out from beneath us, and a shattering sound filled the air, and the last thing I saw was broken glass scattered through the sun-stained sky like stars.

And then we were falling.

Do something, Tisaanah. Magic. Protection. Now, now, now!
And then there was nothing.

CHAPTER NINETY-FIVE

TISAANAH

I opened my eyes in a bed of glass.

For a moment I thought I had to be dreaming. The sky was tinted red, like the bloodiest of sunsets. A numb buzz rang in my ears. My skin was pebbled with goosebumps. The pain came slowly, and with it the realization that I was not dreaming. The buzzing faded as the sounds of horrified screams rose.

I had fallen from the Towers.

I sat up and was immediately rewarded with stabbing pain where glass bit into my palms. Sharp rods of silver and gold jutted from the wreckage like spears. I looked down and saw a book lying beside me, pristine, bearing a sun and a moon symbol intertwined.

Beside it was a single, perfect hand, attached to nothing.

I had not fallen from the Towers. I had fallen *with* the Towers.

The panic hit just as my senses careened back to me in full, overwhelming force.

I ignored the pain as I forced myself to my feet. A perfect circle of debris surrounded me—I had succeeded in my final, half-conscious attempt at protection.

But Max was not beside me. "Max?" I said, quietly.

And then, more frantically, "Max!" I turned to see him behind me, near the edge of the circle, splayed out and motionless.

I didn't remember running to him, just leaning over him and shaking him, saying his name over and over again. When his eyes opened, I could have wept.

"Tell me you're alright," I choked out.

He didn't answer, but I watched his eyes grow larger and larger as the memories came back to him.

"Ascended fucking above." He jerked upright. He surveyed the landscape and with every second, the panic on his face grew sharper.

I did the same, and suddenly lost the ability to breathe. The fear consumed me so completely that I could think of nothing else.

The Capital city had been destroyed. The Towers were gone. The surrounding area had been decimated, buildings ripped apart as if they were crushed dollhouses. A strange, red mist coated my vision—I couldn't figure out what I was looking at, until I realized that it was coming from beneath us, like steam rising from a crack in the earth. It made my skin tingle and my heart race.

I looked down to see that my palm was burning. The gold mark on my hand had spread all the way to my forearm, and it had grown redder, as if irritated.

The realization left me in a panic.

"The heart," I gasped.

It wasn't hard to find it. We were both drawn to it, and the fabric of magic itself seemed to pull towards it, like finding a tear in a piece of clothing. We dug through the glass until we found it.

The Lejara glowed red, as if surrounded by odd, heatless flames. One glance, and I knew that something about it had changed irreparably. The magic that surrounded it was now chaotic and volatile.

Because the heart had been shattered into many, many pieces.

CHAPTER NINETY-SIX

AEFE

I couldn't do anything but run. My mind was somewhere a million miles away, and my body was just running—running through the halls of Ela'Dar, down endless stairs to the ground floor. I stumbled through the city, my eyes burning and blurry, reducing the world to indistinct shapes of ruin.

Nobody so much as glanced my way. Just another broken soul, they would think, in a kingdom now full of ghosts.

I kept running until my legs burned too badly, and then I walked as far as they could carry me. I didn't know where I was going. When the cool embrace of the Pales' shadows enveloped me, I was dimly surprised.

I climbed through the ruined Pales, scaling stories upon stories of black stone while tears rolled down my cheeks. It was sunset, the searing light setting fire to black stone in jagged gashes. The lights that were built into the stone still burned, however softly, and when the sun disappeared beneath the horizon, they simmered to life like a sky full of stars. I climbed through the corpse of my home until I got to the throne room. I pressed my palm to the violet stain on the floor.

Orscheid had died here. Her life had spilled here. And I

thought, perhaps, I might have been able to feel some part of her here.

I need you, my sister. I need you.

But there was nothing of my sweet, kind sister here. There was only the mark of a life ripped violently from this world, too soon, like so many were.

Like Caduan would be.

I wept there for a long, long time, curled up on the cold floor.

Eventually I rose. I had no more tears. Everything inside of me had gone numb. I walked a familiar path through the halls of the Pales, avoiding chasms in the floors and piles of shattered stone, until I reached a little door to a little room.

I opened it.

The familiarity was like a dagger wrenched through my chest. And yet, this room didn't even feel like it was mine. It had belonged to some other girl named Aefe, centuries ago, before she knew exactly how much she would lose.

A crack ran across the center of the room, but otherwise, everything else was untouched—all the way down to the moth-eaten bedsheets piled, forever unmade, on the bed. Mechanically, I got into the bed and wrapped those rotting blankets around my shoulders. They did little against the chill.

In another life, a lost Fey princess felt safe here.

I pressed my palm to the wall, just as that girl did every night. She took such comfort in the Pales, in the knowledge that she was connected to a thousand others in a home carved from the same piece of rock. She would press her skin to this wall and feel all of their souls here with her.

But tonight the walls did not feel like a connection to a thousand other souls. They just felt like stone.

I DID NOT KNOW how long I remained there. I watched the sunlight paint jagged streaks over the wall through the cracks in the Pale, moving across the rock in a rhythmic pattern day after day. There was water here—the systems built into the Pales to funnel rainwater into aqueducts and pipes were still intact, so the faucet in my room still worked. I had little food other than what was already stuffed in my pockets, but I didn't mind. I was not hungry. When my abdomen ached, I ate a couple of nuts. When my tongue was so dry it hurt, I drank a sip of water.

Then I returned to the bed.

Eventually, I heard my name ringing out through the hallways. No—not my name, *a* name, just one that I was known by before. It was silly of me to think I could ever claim that name again.

The voice was so distant at first that I thought it might be Caduan, a thought that sent a shock of pain through me—pain, and then dread, because I could not bear to see him.

But no, it wasn't Caduan. I listened to the shouts grow closer and did not answer, not even when they were in my room, and grew suddenly silent.

"Aefe?"

Fear in his voice when I did not move.

Get up, Aefe. This is your friend.

I managed only to roll over, slowly.

Meajqa looked like the light within him had gone out. Even the false smile that permanently graced his lips had disappeared. And yet, at the same time, something seemed sharper about him, like a haze had been stripped away.

"Aefe," he breathed, and sank to his knees beside the bed. "Are you alright? Are you hurt?"

I shook my head, and Meajqa's face changed slightly in confusion.

"Why didn't you answer me? I have been looking for you everywhere. Caduan thought you might be here, and I thought that seemed farfetched, but…"

His voice trailed off as he noticed how I was staring at him. A stare that went straight through him.

I was looking at Meajqa and thinking of his father.

"I killed him."

It was barely a whisper, hoarse and graceless.

A cacophony of emotion twitched across Meajqa's expression. "I know." And then, a moment later, "Good."

I do not believe you, I thought.

Meajqa had so wanted revenge—against his father, against Nura, against the humans. I considered telling him that it changes nothing, that everything hurts just the same even after you pull that knife from your enemy's flesh. But I did not.

Perhaps he already knew.

"I could not kill her," he said, quietly. "I tried. I was—I had been drinking. Too much. I went alone. I wanted to watch her die. I thought it would fix... me." His throat bobbed. "But you know what her magic is. Manipulation of fear, of minds. Even here, I..."

I realized what had changed about him. I realized that perhaps for the first time, I was seeing Meajqa utterly sober. No alcohol dulled his shame or his sorrow.

"I made a foolish, stupid decision, and now Ela'Dar suffers."

I placed my hand over his, and the corner of his mouth rose in a weak smile, even though his eyes were still so sad.

"Come back to Ela'Dar with me," he said, gently. "Caduan is—"

It hurt just to hear his name. My compassion for Meajqa disappeared under my own grief. I pulled my hand away. "I do not care."

"It is bad, Aefe. He would not like how I'm describing this, but—it's—I'm questioning—" He let out a breath, like the words were damaged. "It is *bad*. Please, come back with me."

"Why didn't he come?"

"He doesn't want you to feel forced. He wants you to return of your own choice. Or at least, that's what he..." Meajqa shook his head. "He doesn't know that I'm here."

I wanted Caduan to be here. I wanted him to fight for me. And at the same time, I didn't, because if he did, it would only make it harder to watch him die.

The heartache was suddenly so intense that it took my breath away.

"No," I said.

Frustration decimated Meajqa's features. "He loves you. He is terrified for you. He will never say it that way, not in those words, because it's him and he is so... because it's him. But anyone who knows him can see it."

No, he did not.

To love someone is to want to keep them forever. To love someone is to curl up with their bloodstain on the floor. But it is not love to leave someone voluntarily. It is not love to cradle someone's heart and take it with you to the grave.

"You love him too," Meajqa said, quietly. "And you can —"

"I do not," I snapped.

"Liar."

I did love Caduan. This realization hit me only now. I knew I loved him because I would do anything to keep him with me.

"He is dying," I ground out.

Meajqa's mouth closed, eyes going serious. "Yes. He is."

"Did you know?"

Please say no.

"Only now. I suspected something was wrong before, but I wasn't certain."

Words tangled in my throat. They were such clumsy instruments for this. I began to roll back towards the wall, but Meajqa's hand grabbed my shoulder, stopping me mid-movement.

"He is desperate, Aefe. He is ready to storm Ara no matter what it costs. He feels he doesn't have time for a measured response, for anything less than everything. I cannot describe how — how — He is just so *calm*. But the calm is what terrifies me. He is breaking. Please come back with me. Help me fix this."

My whole body hurt, deep within, somewhere deeper than my bones. I hurt when I thought of the prospect of seeing Caduan's face again. I hurt when I saw Meajqa's suffering, right before me.

No one had told me this. That caring for others hurt so much.

I cannot help you, Meajqa. I want to, but I can't. I am not strong enough for this.

I wasn't even strong enough to say the words aloud. So instead, I said nothing.

Meajqa stood abruptly, his sadness replaced with anger.

"Do you think I don't want to do this, too?" he snapped. "Hide somewhere where no one will find me? Cut away everything that would bring me pain? I still dream of the humans' laboratory every night. I even still grieve my father. I shed tears for that traitor. Even now, I feel it." His lip curled into a sneer. "And I would give anything to carve all that away. But I can't, Aefe. I know because I've tried. I have tried to drown it in wine and smother it beneath warm bodies and strangle it with vengeance. But it persists. Only now have I finally realized that it always will. And our king... for the first time... I am afraid of him. Afraid of what he will do to kill his own fear, and what will die alongside it."

So much. I knew it, too. Still, I said nothing.

Meajqa's voice was hard with anger and rough with desperation.

"If not for him, then for me. We are friends, aren't we? The two most broken things in Ela'Dar's palace? I'm asking you not as a noble, not as Caduan's lover, but as *my* friend. Come back with me. Please."

Go with him. He is your friend. You care for him, too. He needs you. Be what he needs you to be.

But I couldn't make my voice work. Could not make my body move. The weight of hopelessness and grief smothered me like a pillow made of lead.

When Meajqa looked down at me with disgust, a part of me reveled in it. It was easier to be hated than loved.

"Fine," he muttered.

I rolled back to the wall and listened to his footsteps fade.

CHAPTER NINETY-SEVEN

MAX

I had not seen this level of absolute destruction since Sarlazai. Tisaanah and I set to work immediately, trying to dig survivors from the rubble of the fallen Towers. A few Wielders had been able to summon their own spheres of protection in the seconds before the collapse, like Tisaanah had for us.

Most were not so lucky.

Many of the surrounding houses simply ceased to exist, now reduced to scorch marks on the cobblestones that outlined the former footprint of someone's home. Tisaanah took charge immediately, putting spectators to work with a firm, steady leadership and comforting words, a balance that she managed to strike as if it was second nature. I, meanwhile, rallied the military to help with search and rescue.

Sammerin was one of the first to run to the Towers. When he saw us, he just collapsed onto the block of broken brick, his head sagging, like his relief had left him deflated.

"Staying in the city was an excellent call." The joke fell flat. My voice was wan and strained.

He nodded, speechless, and we stood there together for a few stolen seconds before he rose, picked up his healer's bag, and got to work. He and Willa set up a makeshift hospital in the wreck-age. So, so many people needed help.

Iya arrived shortly after the explosion, summoned by the commotion. His decision to relinquish his apartment to us, it turned out, had saved his life. When he saw what had become of the Towers, he covered his mouth and was still as a statue for a long, long time. "How?" he said.

Tisaanah and I explained what we saw. It still seemed strange to recount it. That face, like the living dead. That note.

How could Nura have done this? I was no longer under any illusions about the goodness of her heart, but I had truly believed that in her own, strange way, she loved Ara.

Now, I wasn't sure what I believed anymore. I didn't see how this could possibly be love, even to a mind as twisted as hers.

Iya's Valtain-pale face still managed to grow even more wan. "Then we have very little time. The other members of the Coun-cil…" He cleared his throat. "The surviving members of the Council should reach the Capital by nightfall."

The thought paralyzed me. I didn't even know if I wanted to go ahead with this now. It seemed ridiculous to think about something as arbitrary as a title under these circumstances.

I said as much to Tisaanah after Iya left.

"It is more important than ever now," she replied. "Your people have never been more in need of someone to believe in."

"The mere idea of that someone being me makes me a little ill."

"It may seem unkind to say this, Max, but the way it makes you *feel* is perhaps the least important thing right now."

A petulant part of me wanted to argue with her. But she gave me a deadpan stare that cut off my unspoken retort with, *I escaped slavery, killed my master, forced a foreign country to take me seriously, traded away my autonomy, led a revolution, overthrew an empire, and then followed you back to your stupid broken country to support you only for you to whine about how you don't "feel" like you can do this?*

So I swallowed my protests and instead said, "Don't give me that look."

575

"What look?"

"*That* look."

The corner of her mouth quirked. "Do you want to know a secret?"

"What?"

"I wish the world held itself to the standards that you do."

———————————

THE COUNCIL HAD WEAKENED over the years. It was now just a handful of aging Wielders. They called me into the Palace in the obvious absence of the Towers. I hadn't been here since it had been inhabited by Zeryth—since, in fact, we killed him there. It seemed odd to conduct yet another assassination here.

This half of the city hadn't been damaged by the explosion at the Towers, but it was still chaotic. The streets swarmed with displaced people escaping the wreckage, hastily raised healing stations, soldiers milling about certain that *something* important needed doing but unsure exactly what it was. The interior of the Palace was, by contrast, eerily quiet.

We gathered in the throne room, just beyond the balcony that looked out over the city. When I looked at the five robed figures before me, each donning their crimson sash, it seemed almost laughable that this handful of people would decide the fate of an entire country—and that such a fate might rest on me. I was covered in blood and dirt. When I was a stupid, idealistic teenager dreaming of being handed this title, I thought I would do it in spotless regalia, not in bloody rags. This, somehow, seemed so much more fitting.

I sat in a chair before the five of them. Tisaanah watched from the doorway, staying out of the way. Selfishly, I was glad to have her in the room, even as a silent observer. I didn't expect to be so nervous.

"Let us begin," Iya said. He turned to the four other councilors. "We gather, councilors, in a state of emergency. The unexpected absence of Nura Qan, Arch Commandant of the Orders and Queen of Ara, is already cause for deep concern. But I think we can all agree the situation has now become… much more dire."

A murmur of agreement across the Council.

"We have learned of darker news," he went on. "Nura has lodged an attack on her own people. She is responsible for the destruction of the Towers."

The councilors gasped.

"*What*?"

"Surely you can't be implying —"

"I don't *imply* anything. It is fact. It seems that she did not take kindly to Maxantarius's return to Ara. The Lightning Dust that destroyed the Towers was sent by her."

The councilors gaped, speechless.

I didn't blame them. It was a lot to process.

Iya, still, remained shockingly calm. "In light of this, I hope we all can agree that Nura Qan cannot remain Arch Commandant. Only one viable candidate from the sixteenth cycle of candidates remains."

He nodded to me, and four sets of eyes turned to me as I rose.

"And so, I have summoned us together today to call upon Maxantarius Farlione. Councilors, how do you rule?"

The first councilor stood. His name was Waine, and he looked like he had aged a decade since he granted this title to Nura mere months ago. "Under these dire circumstances, I accept this nomination. I bestow the title of Arch Commandant to you, Maxantarius Farlione."

I wasn't expecting those words to hit me as hard as they did.

The second councilor rose and repeated her approval. And then the third.

At last, the fourth stood—a woman by the name of Helena. Of the five remaining councilors, Helena was the one I was the most concerned about. She had been one of the councilors who nominated Nura for her original candidacy a decade ago. She was a pragmatist, who ruled according to the law interpreted as strictly as possible.

"Do we have evidence of Nura's involvement in the attack?" she asked. "That is a serious accusation."

Iya glanced at me, and I shook my head. "Unfortunately not, Councilor. It was destroyed in the explosion."

Nura's little love note would have been the first thing to go up in the burst of Lightning Dust.

Helena looked pained. "I worry, Iya, about taking rash action before we understand our situation."

Iya chose his words carefully. "Nura has already been willing to bend the laws of the Orders. She has been dabbling in magics that have been known to strip one's sanity. Surely we all saw what happened to Zeryth Aldris. What's more, if she had been captured by the Fey, she likely suffered torture at their hands. I've never known that to make someone more *moderate*. Have you?"

"If we are looking for moderate, then why should we hand the title to a convicted war criminal?"

Waine scoffed, and Helena added, pointedly, "Regardless of what we *personally* may think of the legitimacy of the conviction, it stands, nonetheless."

"Most Arans view what happened in Sarlazai as a victory, not—"

"They shouldn't," I cut in. "Sarlazai never should have been allowed to happen. If you want to disqualify me on that basis, I won't object. Perhaps I would do the same thing in your position."

"You are familiar with the circumstances behind that, Helena," Iya said, quietly. "The responsibility of Sarlazai doesn't lie with him. We bear as much of it as he does. More, even."

"We do," Helena admitted. "In wartime, things seem more desperate. We become more willing to take... extreme measures, when presented to us." Her eyes slipped to me, apologetic and pitying. "Reshaye was an extreme measure, Maxantarius. We should not have allowed it."

"I understand the weight of what you're entrusting me with," I said. "Not just for the Orders, but for Ara. As long as I hold that power, I will make sure that nothing like that ever happens again. I can't promise that I will be a perfect ruler. But I can promise that I will do everything that I can to lead us out of this mess with our country and our souls intact."

I was almost surprised to hear such strong words come out of my mouth. And yet, as I said it, I fully meant it.

What was the point of having this power if I didn't use it to improve this world?

It is a privilege to do nothing, Tisaanah had once told me.

Helena let out a long breath. "I had such hopes for her," she muttered, as if to herself. Then she turned to me. "I bestow the title of Arch Commandant to you, Maxantarius Farlione. Wear it well."

CHAPTER NINETY-EIGHT

TISAANAH

There was no celebration among the Council once Max was formally given the title. Everyone understood how solemn of an event this was. Congratulations and well wishes were murmured like condolences at a funeral. I gave Max a long, firm embrace, and he did not say a word.

Iya insisted that Max address the crowd that gathered outside the Palace. "They need to hear from you," he said. "They need leadership."

I thought Max might protest. But he drew himself up, looked out over the balcony to the people gathering beneath, and said, quietly, "Alright," as if to himself.

Iya opened the glass doors leading to the balcony. Max approached them, but did not go through. He cast me an uncertain glance. "Should I be embarrassed by..." He gestured to himself, and his disheveled appearance. "All of this?"

"No," I said. "Never. You got that way because you've been out there helping them."

"Not alone." His knuckles brushed my cheek. "Come out there with me."

I started to shake my head, but he said, "You are my partner. I don't care about traditions."

I wanted to argue with him—this wasn't my country, it wasn't my place—but how could I, when he was looking at me like that?

We walked out onto the balcony hand-in-hand, and as we crossed through the doors I stole a single look at him—just one glance. He was a mess, dirty, sweaty, bloody. I could feel his hand shaking around mine, which he clutched the way one clutched a life raft out at sea. But the sun outlined his profile, and his chin was lifted, and his gaze strong and clear. He was beautiful. So different than the man I had discovered drunk in his garden so long ago. And yet…

He glanced at me and gave me a little, nervous smile. Left side first.

…And yet the same. In all the best ways.

He went to the rail and a hush fell over those below. He still did not relinquish my hand, so we stood side by side, equal before a sea of people who were not mine—before Ara. This country had saved me and damned me. Used me and freed me. When I first came here, I thought everything about it seemed so different from my homeland. But the way those below us looked at Max was the same way my people looked at me.

Perhaps people everywhere, in some ways, were the same.

"I don't know what to say," Max said, beneath his breath.

It's nothing, I could have said. *You just have to sound strong but also relatable, proud but also humble, aggrandizing but also honest, hopeful but also realistic, and all without sounding rehearsed. Easy!*

Instead I said, "Just tell them the truth. What would you say to soldiers under your care who needed your encouragement?"

He swallowed. I released his hand, and he stepped forward.

"I'm not good with words," he said.

Of course that was how he started.

"And maybe right now that's a good thing. We all, after all, have bigger things to do than this. By now I'm sure that you are all acutely aware of what we face in the days ahead: an onslaught from an enemy that isn't even human. I could tell you something encouraging. I could make you promises of victory. But I don't like to make promises unless I know, beyond a doubt, that I can keep them. The only one I feel comfortable making now is that I will never lie to you.

"I know how greedy tragedy is. It consumes everything. It consumes hope; it consumes faith. And in the absence of hope, the only thing that seems worth doing is nothing. The only perfect action. The only path forward. But I met someone who once told me that it is a privilege to do nothing. Many people never get that choice."

His eyes flicked to me, just for a moment. "She was right. And it pains me to say this to you, but we have lost our ability to do nothing. We are facing a power that can rip apart everything that we know.

"I have fought in many wars by now, and—maybe I'm supposed to tell you about the glory of it. Maybe I'm supposed to tell you that there's something sacred or patriotic about it. But the truth is that I have hated all of them. Nothing will ever convince me that the world would not be better off without the bloodshed. And that's why…"

He drew in a deep breath and let it out.

"That's why I do not say it lightly when I ask you to fight with me. Not to destroy something, but to protect what we love. I'm asking you to fight for tomorrow. For those we lost yesterday and those we will lose in the morning. For those we lost in every war past. For those who deserved more."

His voice had risen, his words growing stronger. He believed in this, in every word of it. And that fact alone meant more to me than any poetry ever could.

My eyes stung.

"I might be a fool for saying it," he said. "But I believe we can be better than where we have been. I believe we can survive this, and survive it better, and give ourselves and our children a better version of ourselves. And that's what we are fighting for, today.

For a better, imperfect dawn after a long, imperfect night. I want to see that sunrise with you. Meet me there."

Maybe in another life, one might have expected this speech to be met with a roar of applause. But instead, there was utter silence.

Uncertainty clenched in my chest as the seconds passed.

But then, in the crowd below, something sparked. The setting sun bounced off something shiny, bright enough that it took me a moment to discern what I was looking at. A group of young soldiers, gathered near the front of the pack, had raised their swords up above their heads.

Even from this distance, I could have sworn that Moth grinned as we met his eyes.

The others followed suit, a wave of glinting light cresting as the spectators raised their weapons—swords, axes, daggers. People raised brooms and hoes. They raised scarves and hats. Eyeglasses. And those who had nothing simply raised clenched fists to the sky.

No one cheered. No one shouted. But this—this swelling wave of silent, mournful solidarity—seemed more meaningful than any applause ever would.

I met Max's eyes and raised Il'Sahaj, crimson butterflies unfurling from its blade and rising to the horizon.

And Max was the last to move. He looked out over the crowd, his throat bobbing. He raised his spear. The flames at its length matched the red of the sky, bright and true as a promise.

CHAPTER NINETY-NINE

AEFE

I did not know how long I remained there, in the corpse of my old life. The sun cast its pattern across the room too many times to count. Eventually, I heard footsteps. I did not move as they approached. These were lighter even than Meajqa's, as if they belonged to someone who had been trained their entire life to leave as little a mark upon the world as possible.

The footsteps came closer until I heard them behind me. And then I felt someone lower themselves onto the edge of my bed. Felt a gentle, delicate touch on my shoulder.

Orscheid, I thought.

A dream, I thought.

"My poor love."

I rolled over to see my mother's beautiful face looking down at me.

I was not expecting this. It was enough to jerk me from my dreamlike fog.

"You are not real," I blurted out.

She gave me a sad smile. "I am."

She looked so different. She was still lovely, yes, but she had aged, streaks of barely-there silver in her hair, faint pinches at the corners of her features. And her eyes... no longer did they look straight through me, as if to a dreamworld a thousand miles beyond. They were clearer, sharper—and now, filled with sadness.

For the first time in what felt like forever, I sat up.

"Why are you here? How did you find me?"

"Meajqa is worried about you."

I lurched away from her outstretched hand.

I still could not wrap my mind around the fact that she was here. I could not reconcile this woman with the mad, meek creature from my memories.

"When he told me you lived... I..." Her eyes lifted and drifted around the room, as if chasing ghosts. "I would not wish it upon even my greatest enemies. To outlive your children." Her gaze fell back to me, tenderness flooding it. "I cannot describe what seeing you makes me feel. My poor, lost daughter."

This time, I let her touch me. Her hands were warm and soft, as I remembered them. Some primal piece of me craved my mother's love. Even all those years ago, her affection had been barely a memory, lost with the decline of her withering mind.

"You have always had such a tender heart, my love. Even when you were just a child, I feared what the world might do with it."

I let my eyelids flutter closed, let myself sag against her touch. I was so tired. Everything hurt.

I wanted nothing more than I wanted to feel safe. And here, beneath my mother's caress, I was an innocent child again. There was nothing she could not protect me from. The world had not yet hurt me. Five hundred years had yet to sink their teeth into my soul.

I tried to breathe, and the inhale became a jagged sob.

"Oh, my love." How easily I accepted her embrace. I fell against her. "I have failed you," she murmured into my hair. "I am so sorry. I have failed you, Aefe."

You have. You failed me.

"Orscheid," I choked out.

"I think of her every day. Every second. And you—" Her voice broke, and I realized she was crying too, though while my tears were ugly and graceless, hers were silent and delicate.

Then, through the haze of my sadness, reality slipped in. I pulled away from my mother's arms. Relief so quickly changed to fury.

"Meajqa sent you. Why?"

"Because he thought you needed me."

My heart hardened. "I do not need you."

"Everyone needs someone." She reached for me, but I avoided her touch.

"No. Once I did. When I was a child, and I needed my mother to protect me. That was when I needed you." Grief and anger ran together like bloody paint. "*Orscheid* needed you. She fought for me and died for it. But you did not."

Pain wrenched across my mother's face. "You never need to forgive me. He drugged me for decades, and my mind was weakened. He took more from me than I ever gave. But the only thing I'll ever regret is allowing him to do it to my daughters, too."

"And yet you are still here while Orscheid is dead. While *I* died."

My mother was still on the precipice of tears. Again, she reached for me, and again I pulled away.

"Come home with me," she said. "Let us talk somewhere warmer and safer than this."

"I don't want to go anywhere with you," I snapped. "There is nothing for us to talk about."

I turned back to the wall.

Leave. Go away. It is easier without you here.

But she didn't move.

"I am very afraid of what I see happening, my love," she said quietly. "How long has it been since you left this place?"

I did not answer, both because I didn't want to and because I didn't know.

"Caduan is preparing to make an irreversible move, Aefe."

I disliked anyone speaking of Caduan in such a disapproving

tone. I turned abruptly. "He is eradicating the humans, just as he always said he would. Good. They deserve it."

"It is a mistake."

I hurled my scoff at her like a weapon. "Spoken like a stranger. You have no idea what they did to me. I endured five hundred years of torture at their hands."

"Then tell me of it," she pleaded. "Tell me, my love, what they did to you. Let me help you bear that weight."

My fingernails bit into my palm hard enough to draw blood.

I couldn't. I couldn't tell her. The idea of trying to condense all that pain into words… it was too big, too much. If I let those words free, I couldn't control what other ones might come with it.

There was the torture, yes. The room of white and white and white. But there was also the matter of what I became. What I did, as Reshaye. The unwelcome image of a marble floor and the bodies of five children struck me, and I pushed it away, just as I always had.

"Humans and Fey are capable of living together peacefully," she said, gently. "You are evidence of that. Do you remember that?"

I remembered a dark-haired man, so long ago, meeting me in the moonlight in Niraja.

"I went back to him, Aefe. Your father—your true father. He was half human. We lived together, after the wars subsided. Me, him. His brother, Ezra, who too had lost everything." Tears pricked her eyes. "He loved you so deeply. Even if he never had the chance to know you."

I remembered learning a truth I was not ready to hear. And I remembered the father who had raised me trying to kill me for it.

"This body is new," I said. "Lineage does not matter."

"It is still a part of you, no matter what made your flesh. You can't run from your past. You can't run from your blood. Those are things you cannot kill, no matter how many hearts stop beating."

"Caduan is fighting for me," I snarled. "Fighting for all of us. Like *you* should have."

"It will make nothing better, my love. He could destroy everything, and it will make nothing better. I dreamed of revenge, too, in my moments of lucidity. But watching my wretched husband die meant nothing to me when I watched my daughter die beside him. The worst day of my life. And this— this will be the worst day of so many lives."

And why did those lives matter more than my life? Than Meajqa's life? Than the lives of all the Fey who were tortured and kidnapped and murdered by the humans, and that would undoubtedly be in the future?

But then, in the back of my mind, I thought of Ishqa's blood spraying over my face and the shape of his lifeless body falling over the balcony. I thought of how I had felt in the moments after.

Empty.

I pushed the thought away. "Get out. You have come here to manipulate and use me. I feel nothing for you anymore."

Not true, a voice whispered. *You can not lie to me.*

My mother's heartbreak stabbed deeper than I wished it would. She rose and stepped back.

"Meajqa told me the truth of Caduan's... condition. Or at least enough that I could understand what he did not say."

Every muscle in my body went taut, as if bracing for impact against the words. It did nothing. They hurt just the same.

"Your father's human blood diminished his lifespan. By the time I made it back to him, he had only a few short decades remaining. And yet, those fleeting years were no less precious for it." A tear rolled down her cheek. "Do not fear death, my daughter. We all walk with one foot in each world. There is beauty in impermanence. And what sad lives we would live, if we never loved anything we would lose."

My vision was blurry, my chest aching. My mother gently took my wrist in her hands and revealed the smooth, tan skin of my forearm. Once it had been covered in stories from a life I now barely remembered.

"You have a chance to make another story, Aefe. Make it one of creation, of life. Not destruction. I want better for you than to burn alive in your own rage."

You'll find another thing to burn, Nura's voice whispered. *It's all you know how to do.*

"Get out." I yanked my arm away. "*GET OUT!*"

My magic reverberated through the walls, making it shake. Vines crawled over every inch of stone, barely avoiding my mother's feet.

And there it was. Fear. My own mother now feared me.

Good.

She went to the door, and paused.

"I love you, Aefe. I love you imperfectly, but completely."

For centuries, all I wanted was to hear that someone loved me and to feel that they meant it. I did not know what to make of the fact that I knew, somewhere deep and uncomfortable, that my mother meant it.

I turned to the wall and listened to her leave.

How dare she tell me what to do? How dare she tear me open like this, rip open scabbed-over wounds in my heart? How dare she speak of Caduan that way, as if he was a malignant force to be controlled?

The fury finally cut through the blanket of despair that had pressed me to the bed these last few weeks. I simmered in it for hours. And then, at last, I stood.

CHAPTER ONE HUNDRED

AEFE

Ela'Dar was no longer burning, the wounds that I had left behind now replaced with scars. The air stank of tears and death. The grief lingered like fog, thick with every breath. And interwoven with that grief was anger.

Few noticed me as I returned to the castle, wound through the hallways, and went to the uppermost floor. I found Caduan in his chambers. He stood on the balcony, looking down over the city. His room was a mess. Papers and maps and bloodied clothing were strewn over every surface. Spilled bottles of ink ruined books and records. The bed was untouched.

Caduan did not move as I approached him—did not so much as turn. "We leave in the morning. Ten thousand soldiers. Every-one. Everything we have. Every warrior, every Wielder, every shade. You told me to stop being cowardly, so I am."

He spoke so calmly, but it was the sort of calm that balanced on the razor's edge of sanity, promising collapse.

"Look," he said, still not turning from the view.

I did.

When I had walked through the streets of Ela'Dar, the

violence had invaded my lungs like fog. But from up here, you could see it in the streets—see the humming energy in each crevice of the city. Every person was moving. The sun glistened against metal blades, small as stars. It was a city on the precipice of change, the desire for it swelling like a roiling wave.

"It is for you," Caduan said. He spoke so calmly. Still, he would not look at me. "It is all for you. I never said that. But I found myself regretting that I never told you. When I thought you wouldn't come back."

Why didn't you fight for me? I had asked my mother.

I watched his profile, strong and sharp, looking over the city. With a gentle touch, I turned it towards me.

He looked so different even than he had when I left. Darkness sank into every hollow of his face. I now noticed little black veins around his eyes, so faint that they could be mistaken for shadow, visible only because of the fragile pale of his skin.

Still—he was beautiful. My gaze caressed every dip and plane of his features, traversing from his tight brow to his nose, following the curve of his lips.

And the way he looked at me…

He murmured, barely louder than a whisper, "Let me touch you."

A plea.

I nodded.

His hand rose to mine, which still cupped his cheek, and he covered it with his own. His thumb traced each muscle, so gently that goosebumps rose over my arm—tracing one delicate string of bones, and then the next, and then the next.

It was so soft, as if he was afraid that he might break me, that all the breath left my lungs when some thread of restraint snapped, and he pulled me into a desperate embrace. Like he couldn't stop himself. Like he couldn't believe I was real.

I wrapped my arms around him and welcomed it. I didn't know how much it was possible to miss someone.

I pressed my lips to his throat, his jaw, his cheek. He tilted my face towards him and captured my mouth in a kiss, his tongue meeting mine, every part of me melting against him.

This was what I had so wanted when I was pushed into another body, and another, and another. My flesh was my own, but I felt more connected to a separate soul now than I ever had as Reshaye—and yet, so far apart.

Pulling away from him was a struggle. Every impulse within me screamed against it. But I did it anyway, stepping back just enough to look at him. I pushed him back through the door, back into his chambers, and then my hands were at his shirt, fingers working at his buttons.

His hand went to my wrist quickly, as if to stop me on instinct alone.

I gave him a long stare, and he released it.

I unbuttoned his shirt and let it fall open, revealing the expanse of his body. Shadows painted rivers and valleys over the muscles of his torso. The darkness drowned out all of it. Had I forgotten how bad it was, or had it gotten worse since I had left? Now the thinnest capillaries extended all the way to his shoulders, his hips, his sides, so that few parts of his body were left untouched.

I touched the marks and resisted the urge to pull away. They made my own fingertips burn—like they were coming into contact with something noxious, a thousand worlds beneath this one. Something that my own magic recoiled from, and yet... also called to.

I realized what that sensation was. It felt like death.

"How much time?" I asked.

"Enough to right a millennium of wrongs."

No. It was not enough.

I looked up at him and the force of his stare nearly sent me staggering—so intense that it hit me like a strike. There was so much fury in his eyes, burning bright as fire, even as the rest of his face remained perfectly still.

I felt foolish.

How had I not seen this earlier in him? How had I not felt it? I always had thought that Caduan was so much calmer than me. He wasn't. He was just as angry. He had lost just as much.

Now, that fury mingled with desire. His knuckles stroked my cheek.

"Stay with me," he whispered.

Don't leave me, I had begged of him.

He wanted me to stay, but he would abandon me.

"I won't force you," he murmured. "But I ask you. Please. I want… I want to fill my last days with you. I have spent my entire life chasing knowledge, but now the only thing that I want to know is you. Every part of you. I want you to be the last thing I see when death comes for me. And I want you beside me when we build this new world."

I was reminded of the way Caduan spoke during the feast — the way he read the names of the dead with such solemn weight, such reverence. He spoke that way now. Like his love for me was something sacred.

And now, I knew, would be the time. I could ask him for restraint — I could plead for mercy on the humans' behalf, on behalf of my mixed blood, on behalf of the connection I had once shared with Maxantarius and Tisaanah and a thousand other souls.

I knew, in this moment, that he would listen to me.

But the injustice of this world seethed inside of me like a cluster of broken glass. We were surrounded by a city of people who were angry and grieving. *I* was angry and grieving. I wanted to right the wrongs. I wanted vengeance.

And above all, I wanted him.

I could defeat death. I could save him. I refused to lose anything else, least of all something as precious as him. He had brought me back against all impossibilities. I did not care what it meant for the humans. I did not even care what it meant for the Fey.

This, I realized, was love. Love was worth destroying for.

"Yes. I will stay," I said, and kissed him deeply.

How easily magic came to me. The vines wound around us both, encircling our intertwined bodies. Their leaves were red and violet, splashes of human and Fey blood that quickly withered into blackened husks. And yet, they pulled us into such a comforting embrace, the three of us—me, Caduan, and death.

CHAPTER ONE HUNDRED ONE

TISAANAH

W e didn't know how long we had before one, or both, of our enemies would be at our shores. Max commanded that barricades be set up as quickly as possible several miles offshore in all directions, so hopefully we would get some form of warning once Nura or Caduan make their move. The Wielders built Stratagram networks to facilitate the quick movement of forces—imperfect, but we had to take imperfect. We no longer had the numbers of the Roseteeth Company behind us. We needed to make the most of the forces we did have.

I wrote to Serel and Riasha urgently and asked them for the Alliance's help, whatever they could spare in their own shaky state. I did not know how many that would be. Perhaps I could pretend it would be enough to stave off both Nura and the Fey.

We had so little time and so much to do. It seemed like we could prepare for an age for this encounter, and it still wouldn't be enough. Eventually, after the latest hour of endless strategy meetings, Iya set down his pen.

"I think there is little more we can do," he said.

I didn't know how he could even say that. There was always something more that we could do.

He added, as if already seeing my protest rising before I opened my mouth, "Get some rest. None of us will be doing anyone any good if we're walking corpses ourselves."

Every muscle in me screamed against it, but I had to admit he had a point.

So Max and I returned to the room we had been given in the Palace. It was some guest chamber that we had made into a makeshift base of operations—one part study, one part strategy hub, one part military base. When we arrived, it had been neat and elegant. Now it had been hit with a tornado of ink and parchments.

Max sloppily attempted to clear a pile of paper from the bed, mostly failed, and flopped down on it anyway like a marionette with broken strings. He held out a beckoning hand, as if words were simply too much for him.

I approached the bed but didn't lie down with him. He looked so tired that I reconsidered whether this was the right time for this conversation.

But then again, if I let this opportunity pass, we might not have another one.

"I have something I want to give you," I said.

He opened one eye. "I'm amazed you're in a gift-giving mood after all of this."

I went to my bag—the one thing that had been salvaged from the Towers—and rummaged through it. Most of my possessions had been destroyed. But this, the most important one, had made it out mostly intact. It seemed like a miracle.

Max sat up, and I handed him the scorched piece of canvas.

He stared down at it in silence for a long moment. When he finally spoke, his voice was rough. "How—how did you get this?"

"It was not easy. No one should have to work so hard to get something so ugly."

He let out a strangled laugh.

The painting was, indeed, truly awful. It depicted a very rotund, very naked woman with fair hair, reclining awkwardly on a stone bench in a garden of pink and red roses. The artist had not been particularly talented, the figure flat and oddly proportioned, the colors garishly bright.

But Max had been right—ugly as it was, this picture had been rendered with deep, reverent love. I could see it dripping off the paint just as Max could when he wept in that cafe all those years ago.

The night I let myself fall into my feelings for him, Max had sat with me under the moonlight over the Threllian plains and told me of these paintings. How he had been in a dark place when he saw them, and how they had reminded him that even in the most terrible moments, someone, somewhere, was happy. They had reminded him of the existence of hope. Now, in another dark time, I could feel it here, too.

I had only been able to locate this single small painting, and I had only the canvas, not the frame it was once stretched on. It was now somewhat damaged, one side of it burned from the explosion. Still, Max cradled it like a thing of great, precious value.

I sat beside him, close enough that our shoulders touched. "That night in the cottage, the night when we were... before the hands were sent to us. You asked me if I ever thought about what a future together might be like. I—I couldn't answer you then. But every second that you were locked in that horrible place, I thought about that night and what I did not say to you. I regretted it more than I have ever regretted anything."

"Tisaanah, I never thought—"

I took his hand, squeezed tight. "The truth that I couldn't give you then was that I had never wanted anything so much. It was true then, when you asked me. It is true now. It will be true tomorrow."

Max looked at me like nothing else existed. Despite everything that we had been through together, despite all the weaknesses I had let him—and only him—see in me, I had to fight the urge to look away. Nothing had ever terrified me so much as such raw vulnerability.

"You are my home, Max. I never allowed myself to believe I would ever have one. I never allowed myself to think that I could keep one, if I did. But I have realized that there is bravery in hope for the future. And I—"

Max's kiss, sudden and passionate, swallowed the rest of my words. The taste of him, the scent of him, made them seem so much less important—made them seem utterly inconsequential.

When we parted, our foreheads pressed together, he murmured, "You cannot possibly understand how much I love you."

I absolutely do, actually, I wanted to say, but instead I said, "Marry me."

A stunned pause.

"Say that again," he whispered.

"Marry me, mysterious snake man."

His arms wound around me, pulling me onto his lap, and he kissed me again, and again, and again, until finally we untangled ourselves from each other long enough for him to look into my eyes and say, "Well, I *guess* so."

CHAPTER ONE HUNDRED TWO

MAX

I ya agreed to perform the ceremony, even though we'd dragged him away from the scant rest he could steal while he still could. We had no time to go anywhere, no time for any fanciful celebration. So we simply went downstairs to the Palace's courtyard gardens.

We did, however, take the time to grab Sammerin on our way out. I pounded on his door and cut off his irritated greeting with, "I know you're exhausted. But, we're going to go get married before the world goes to shit. Do you want to… come watch, or something?"

I honestly wouldn't have blamed him if he told me to fuck off. Alas, he did not.

Tisaanah and I took no time to prepare—having the ceremony before our attackers arrived was more important to us than looking the part, so we had settled for scrubbing the dirt off our faces and throwing on clean cloaks that we had found in the Palace. As we walked to the gardens, I picked a few red blossoms from the bushes that lined the path and tucked them into Tisaanah's hair. When she grinned at me in response, there were no gowns or makeup or magic in the world that would have made her more beautiful than she was in that moment.

Iya stood before us, a book perched in his hands. Despite our circumstances, he was in remarkably good spirits. Aran weddings were notoriously long and convoluted affairs, so as he opened the book, I was expecting a long, dry reading.

"You can skip all of that," I said. "No one actually listens to any of it anyway, least of all in times like this."

Iya gave me a knowing smirk. "I agree. I thought perhaps you might appreciate something different."

He tipped the book forward to show us its pages—pages written not in Aran, but in Thereni.

Tisaanah drew in a tiny gasp. "You know Nyzrenese weddings?"

"Passably, if you're tolerant of my mistakes."

"I have never even seen one myself. Only when I was very, very small."

"Then I suppose we can be creative and none of us will be any wiser."

He reached into his pocket and withdrew a white ribbon. He instructed us to touch our hands to each other's, palm-to-palm, fingers splayed.

"A Nyzrenese wedding consists of five gifts in the form of promises," Iya said. "Two from the bride, two from the groom, and one from the gods."

He looped the ribbon loosely around our little fingers and looked at Tisaanah expectantly.

Tisaanah reddened slightly. "I am... not prepared."

"That's alright." He gave her a kind smile. "It will simply make your words that much more genuine."

She was silent for a long moment. Then she looked at me and said, "Max. For my first gift, I give you my future. Our future. I promise you that we will build it together. And I promise you that I will always fight for it, as hard as I need to."

My throat felt thick. I was going to have a hard time speaking.

Iya tightened the red ribbon around our little fingers, then looped it around our ring fingers. He turned to me. "Maxantarius?"

It wasn't that I didn't know what to say. It was that I had too much to say, and none of it seemed like enough.

"I give you my partnership," I said, at last. "I promise that whatever road you walk, I will walk it beside you. Whatever challenge you encounter, I will face it with you. You will never fight alone again."

The ribbon tightened around our ring fingers, then looped around our middle fingers.

"I give you my heart," Tisaanah said. The rest of the world had faded away—it was only us, and the flowers, and our words. "Fully and completely. There is no part of myself that I will hide or shield. I promise you my love, in good times and hard times. You will always have an embrace to return to."

Two streaks of silver ran down her cheeks, and I wanted more than anything to stop and kiss them away—happy tears or not.

A knot. A loop. And another silence, as I grappled with my final gift.

"I give you my soul. It's not a perfect one. It's a little messy. You inherit some scars. But… all the good parts are for you. From the minute you showed up at my door, all the good parts were for you."

And even when I hadn't realized it, it was true. Even then, on that first day, she made me want to be a better version of myself. Even when I didn't even know her name.

And every day after, she helped me make it true.

Tisaanah let out a choking laugh. "They are all good parts, Max," she said, cupped my face with her free hand, and kissed me.

It was easy, to fall into that kiss. She tasted like oranges and salt from both of our tears. Distantly, in a world I didn't care very much about anymore, Iya said, "Well, I was supposed to do one more about the gods or some such, but I suppose it's better that we skip it anyway since I'm not sure if I remember it. As far as I'm concerned, the deed is done. You are married."

We parted, and my wife grinned at me, and I had never so badly wanted to capture a single image and preserve it forever.

We shook the ribbon off our hands so Tisaanah could hug Iya, then Sammerin. When Sammerin released her and turned to me, my brows lurched.

"Ascended above, Sammerin, look at you."

There were no tears in Sammerin's eyes—I'd never seen him cry, and to be honest, I'd be a little disappointed if this was where he chose to start—but the raw emotion across his face still stunned me.

"I just... There was a long period there when I really thought we would lose you, and the idea of a thing like this happening was..." He shook his head and pulled me into a rough embrace. "Congratulations, Max."

"Thank you, Sammerin."

I was thanking him, as always, for so much more than the congratulations. I owed my life to him. I owed a life worth living to him even more.

Under normal circumstances, this was when we'd all devolve into debauchery and celebration, gorging ourselves on food and wine and carefree joy.

Instead, a gust of cold wind cut through the gardens, rustling the leaves. It snatched the red flower from Tisaanah's hair, sending it spiraling up into the sky to be consumed by rust-grey clouds. With it came the sound of bells, echoing in a mournful call.

We all went silent. The warning came from the eastern lookout tower. No one had to ask what it meant. It meant the celebration was over.

It meant, *They are here.*

CHAPTER ONE HUNDRED THREE

AEFE

I had never seen the ocean before. When I stepped onto the ship and looked out to see nothing but water stretching to the horizon, I felt just as small and alone in this body as I had when I first opened my eyes.

But… so much had changed since then. Now I knew why I was here. I was small, but I had purpose burning in the center of my chest. That was enough to make my fear turn to admiration after those first few moments.

That fear, instead, remained for Caduan. His health had declined so rapidly that I now felt so foolish for not realizing sooner how bad it was. He skillfully hid his weakness in casual leaning against rails and walls, in tiny coughs concealed by the back of his hand, beneath shirts that were always buttoned up all the way to his throat.

Still, it was bad enough now that others noticed, even if no one had the courage to comment on it aloud. Perhaps that was why Caduan had limited the number of people on this ship. Me, Meajqa, Luia, a handful of Luia's most trusted generals, and scant few others traveled with him. The warriors packed the rest of Ela'Dar's armada. Every single one of our ships had been mobilized.

Caduan told me we did not have time to do this more than once. I knew what he actually meant—that *he* did not have time to do this more than once.

The first night, I did not bother even trying to sleep. Instead, I stood at the rail and looked at the ocean beneath the moonlight. It moved like sheets of dancing silver in the darkness. Eventually, Caduan joined me.

"I have never seen the sea before," I said. "Not in my own body, at least."

"It fascinates me."

I thought that if I did not look at him, I wouldn't see death consuming him. But I flinched as I realized that I could hear it in his voice, now, too.

"There are three great unknowns in this world," he went on. "The sea is one of them. The undersea goes on for miles. Creatures live beneath it that are bigger than this ship. And those are only the ones that Fey have been fortunate enough to see. We know so little about what lurks beneath it." I finally allowed myself to look at him, as he gazed to the sky. "Like what lies beyond the stars."

My chest tightened as I watched him. "Would you have liked to explore it?"

"The sky? The sea?"

"Both."

"Yes. But even five hundred years has not been enough to conquer every unknown, no matter how much I tried."

Five hundred years seemed so long when I spent it languishing in a series of broken human minds. And yet so tragically, unfairly short, when Caduan spoke of everything he still wished to do.

He gave me that dismantling stare, the kind that seemed to peer into my thoughts.

"I have no regrets about how I spent my life, Aefe," he said, softly. "And I still have unknowns to learn as of yet. Perhaps death is the most interesting one of all. There are many worlds beyond this one."

I thought of what he had said to the dying Fey, what felt so long ago.

"Death is a door," I murmured.

He gave me a tired smile. "A lifetime of learning has taught me the only constant is that nothing ever truly ends."

I let out a faint scoff. "Once, that thought would have appalled me. As Reshaye, I was so afraid of endlessness."

"Not anymore?"

A pause. I did not know how to answer that. "Perhaps. I do not know."

"When I first met you," he said, "I thought you were fearless. You were… interesting. Unlike any person I had ever known before."

"I feel like I have spent my entire life afraid."

"You feel everything." He pushed a flying strand of dark red hair away from my eyes. "That is the bravest act in this world. To feel. I am often too afraid to do it myself."

For all the times that I had thrown Caduan's supposed cowardice in his face, it was little more than a sharp word I wielded as a weapon. Now, I cursed myself for it. He was the bravest person I had ever met.

And he was wrong about me.

Because then he ducked his head and coughed—delicately, quietly, as he always did. But when he turned back to me and gave me a small, reassuring smile, I saw the dark violet on his hand and at the corner of his mouth.

In that moment, I imagined Caduan standing in the doorway to another world, and I did not feel brave at all.

———◆———

THE DAYS PASSED, and the Ela'Dar armada cut through the sea like birds treading a path through the sky. The air grew tighter, jokes replaced by quiet tension. Caduan spoke less and less.

After several days, I realized it was because he was finding it more difficult to hide the labor of his breathing.

We sent Wyshraj scouts in bird form ahead to scout the distance between us and Ara. At last, they returned with a new sense of urgency. They had seen Threllian ships ahead—Aran ships. Nura, as we suspected, was crossing the sea as well, ready to retake the throne of her traitorous country.

"She has an army," the scout told us. "She has assembled all of her Threll-based resources. And she has…"

Caduan put up his hand. He didn't need to hear any more.

I had known something was… odd. I could feel it growing in a world beneath this one with each day we were at sea. What I now realized was that I had been sensing the presence of Nura's stolen Lejara—the magic that had created *me*.

"We go faster," Caduan said decisively. "If we reach Ara before, or at the same time, she does, it will be easy to use their own chaotic infighting against them."

Caduan's command left no room for argument. The sails were let out, and the spells that quickened the ships through the water enhanced. Caduan returned to the bow.

We moved so fast now that I struggled to keep my hair bound. Meajqa did not even bother to tie his back, allowing the wind to whip golden streaks about his face.

Uncharacteristically, he had barely spoken during the trip.

"What is wrong?" I asked him, at last.

"I think this is a mistake," he said. "I think we are in floating caskets."

Then he turned away, face to the sky, and said nothing else.

CHAPTER ONE HUNDRED FOUR

TISAANAH

There was an entire navy in the bay. So many ships blotted the horizon that I could see nothing but blood-red sails. I recognized those sails. These ships had once belonged to Esmaris Mikov—one of the grandest fleets in the world, even though his territory was landlocked. To Esmaris, the usefulness or functionality of such a fleet did not matter. He had the money for it, and the power to flaunt it, so it became his.

And then, in a cruel twist of fate, it became Nura's.

When I saw those sails, my first thought was, *Fitting.* Esmaris's final knife to my back from beyond death.

People stood in the streets in shock, mouths open in horror. At the armada, yes—but also at the sky. Red streaks ran across it like cracks through stone or wounds in flesh.

"Fuck," Max whispered. "How did she get so many people?"

I couldn't even speak.

It looked like the end of the world. Even the air was hot and cold, damp and dry, all at the same time. An indescribable toxicity filled my lungs with each breath, something that the deepest reaches of my magic recoiled from. I had felt this sensation before—in the presence of Nura's failed experiments and in the presence of the Lejara. Even now, too, from the shards of the broken heart that sat at my hip, which seemed more volatile than ever.

Max and I looked at each other. He lifted our entwined fingers and kissed the back of my hand.

"Whatever happens now," he said, "I'm very glad that we got to do that."

I gave him a wry smile. "When I promised you I would fight for our future, I knew I would have to do it soon."

"Noble of you." His voice lowered, a shade more serious. "I forbid you from dying on me, Tisaanah. I would make a pathetic widower."

"I won't if you won't."

The corner of his mouth quirked. "Deal."

"Deal."

His smile faded, and I watched his face morph from that of my friend, my lover—my husband—to that of Ara's leader. I wonder if he saw the same transformation in me, too.

Nura sent a falcon to the shore requesting an audience with Max. Iya relayed this information as if it was a ridiculous proposition, but before the words even had left his lips, Max said, "Yes. We'll go."

Sammerin's brows lowered in concern. "There will be no reasoning with her. We all know that. Are we sure we want to do this?"

"There is always something we can learn from a conversation," I said.

Max lowered his chin in agreement. "I don't know how she managed to get an army this big, but judging by this fleet, we are outnumbered. We owe it to the Arans who are about to die for this to take any possible chance, however small, at avoiding more bloodshed."

To call that chance "small" was an overstatement. Nothing short of a miracle would stop Nura. But at least if we faced her, we would have an idea of what we were about to come up against. Maybe we could learn something.

Max extended his hand to me. He did not bother trying to tell me to stay behind.

"Tisaanah and I will go. And give me any Syrizen we have left. I need people who can get out of there fast if we need to."

WE MET Nura on a naval base, a tiny island about half a mile away from the shore. The first thing I noticed when we landed was the smell—it hit me like a wall, so thick I nearly gagged at my first breath. The noxious sensation weighing on my magic was so much stronger here. Max clearly felt it, too, as did the Syrizen to a lesser extent.

Nura was waiting for us. A gangway had been laid from her ship to the docks. When she approached, I had to fight hard to keep the shock from my face.

She looked nearly as bad as Zeryth had when he died. Black veins surrounded her eyes, sickly dark against her Valtain-pale skin. Her irises seemed so light in contrast that they looked like the milky glazed-over eyes of a corpse. She wore white, blood-stained trousers tucked into tall boots, and a sleeveless jacket that she left open to her sternum. She no longer hid her burn scars. Nor did she hide the darkness on her hands, crawling up her burnt flesh to her elbows.

Light fell over the faces of the soldiers that accompanied her —and this time, I couldn't choke down my gasp. One of the Syrizen pressed the back of her hand to her mouth. Max's nose wrinkled with disgust.

Now I understood how she had populated this armada.

The soldiers behind her were not human. They were not Fey. They were not even alive.

No, Nura's soldiers were corpses—living death with empty faces, every part of them a little bit wrong, eerie light emanating from beneath their skin. Unlike the versions of Nura's creatures that I had seen before, these were not decomposing or spiraling out of control. They stood, soullessly and obediently, behind her.

I realized that this was what Nura's success looked like. This was what she had been trying to create all along.

Nura stepped onto the docks and gave us a chilling smile that did not reach her eyes.

Something is wrong with her, I thought. *Like Zeryth. She has lost control.*

"Hello Max. Tisaanah." Her voice was smooth and melodic. "What an *honor*, to be greeted by people of your elevated station."

"Nura… what did you do?" Max could not look away from the corpses.

"I succeeded where you failed. The Fey had something important, and I took it from them." Her smile faded. "And from what I hear, you thank me for this by trying to turn my own country against me."

Max stepped forward—I had to resist the urge to grab him and pull him away from her.

"Look at yourself," he murmured. "Look at what you're doing."

Her lip twitched. "I see you must be your old self again. Back to your moral judgements. *You* look." She gestured behind her. "I'm waging a bloodless war. Just like you and your bleeding heart always wanted."

"You sent Lightning Dust to your own people. You blew up your own country."

"I didn't—"

But then Nura's gaze fell to Ara's burning skyline behind us. Anger and grief warred across her face in erratic twitches.

"There is no room for dissidents in wartime," she spat. "You were beside me when we learned those lessons in the Ryvenai War."

"Stop pretending this is about the greater good. I fucking *see* you, Nura. I know you better than any other living person does. And maybe you're right. Maybe you do have every right to be angry at Ara. But—"

"I love this country," Nura snapped.

"I've seen what you do to the things you claim you love." He thrust his hand out, gesturing to Ara's smoking shoreline. "We can't survive your Ascended-damned love, Nura. And I think you know it, too. Don't tell me you think this is *right*."

For a split second, Nura looked hurt. The lines across her face were like cracks, revealing more of her emotion than she had ever let slip before.

"I watched Tisaanah burn Lady Zorokov alive," she hissed. "What a terrible death. I was there in the rubble as I listened to her scream. What did you have to say about that?"

Movement stirred behind Nura, at the rail of her ship. Crazed eyes and messy white hair poked up from between the soldiers. Vardir drew in a gasp, then hurried down the ramp. He barely looked at Max and I—only gaped past us, at the Aran coastline.

"Get back on the ship, Vardir," Nura barked, without looking at him.

Vardir did not appear to hear her. He lifted a shaking finger to Ara. "Look—*look* at that!"

"Vardir—" Nura snapped.

"*Look at that!*" His round eyes snapped to Max, and then to me, landing there and holding my stare. "Do you feel this? Surely, with the connections you have to deep magics, you must."

I realized what he was pointing to was not the wreckage, but the stream of red, shimmering smoke that rose from the ruins of the Tower—where the heart had been smashed in the explosion. Even after Max and I had gathered the shards, the strange tear of magic still yawned there.

The sheer intensity of Vardir's alarm made me pause. He was mad—but he also knew more about deep magic than nearly anyone else in the world.

"You feel it?" he said. "The cracks?"

The noxious sensation. The sense of instability, like the earth a thousand layers down was shifting. I did feel it.

Vardir seemed to find this silence validating. "You can't," he said to Nura, all the words running together into a single panicked sentence. "It would be a mistake, I miscalculated, it will all collapse. We have been drawing too deep, far too deep, you can't—"

"Get back on the boat."

"But my—"

"*Get back on the boat!*" Swirls of murky shadows flared at her clenched fists, as if her magic momentarily escaped her grasp.

And despite the corpses, despite the Fey, despite the armada, it was *this* moment—Nura's loss of control—that scared me more than anything.

"What is it, Vardir?" Max said, with a note of unease.

"It—" Vardir started, but Nura flung her hand up.

The burst of magic was unnatural, fitful. A flick of her fingers, and Vardir's body was hurled like a rag doll backwards up the ramp, colliding with a wall of corpse soldiers and sending them staggering. They corrected themselves with uncanny precision, too-long limbs bending to balance their weight, faces blank.

When she whirled back to us, her eyes were a little wilder.

"We both want the same thing. The Fey are coming. I stole their greatest weapon, but they are still a force to be reckoned with. They won't listen to reason."

She outstretched her hand. Three fingers were now stumps. The ones that remained had blackened, pulsing blue and violet beneath the intensifying blood-red of the sky.

"I'll ask you one last time to help me. The only way Ara survives this is if we do it together." Her expression changed too fast, as if all her muscles rearranged in the span of a blink. Now she looked like a child, afraid and pleading. "We can still do this together, Max."

Nura believed her own lies, her own false intentions. But I knew what it looked like when someone wanted power. I'd seen it in Esmaris, Ahzeen, Zeryth. Even Reshaye. This was Nura's revenge against a world that had been cruel to her. She was lost, just like so many others, and there was no guiding her back home.

There was a long silence, filled only with a high, soundless buzz that grew louder and louder, somewhere in a world beyond this one.

Max took a step closer.

"Max," I hissed, reaching for him, but he slipped from my grasp.

My heart was in my throat as he placed his hand in Nura's.

"*Max*," I said again.

A wobbly smile spread across Nura's lips. "We always made such a good team."

Max's fingers tightened around her slender hand.

"I shouldn't give a fuck," he said, "but funny how even after everything, it still seems so important to me that you know I never wanted it to end this way."

I'd watched Max fight countless times now, and yet the speed and accuracy of the strike still shocked me. Nura did not have time to react as the knife slid between her ribs the first time. Her body barely jolted.

The second time the knife entered Nura's body, she started to fall.

Seconds, it seemed, became hours. Her army all moved at once, as if in a perfectly synchronized dance.

I had been waiting for this moment. I struck the first soldier, the one closest to Max, before he even had time to move.

Max did not release Nura's hand as she collapsed, blood staining her white clothing. She gripped his shoulders as she fell, a wrinkle of confusion between her brows, as if, still, she did not expect him to do this.

I relished that confusion. I allowed myself to think, *We got her.* Stupid.

Because then, a cruel, pained smile spread over Nura's lips.

"It hurts to be underestimated by you, of all people, Max."

My satisfaction soured to dread. The soldiers began to move for us. I stabbed one, and then the other, rot spreading over already-decaying skin.

We needed to get out. I knew, implicitly, that we needed to get out *now*.

The heat on my face, the light, was not from Max's flames. Nura had something in her hands. A stone—a stone of amber, with something inside. What *was* that?

A stab of pain through my palm. I looked down.

The wayfinder on my flesh glowed bright.

It was a Lejara. *She had a Lejara.*

"No, you stupid child, *no!*" Vardir wailed, from the ship. "You'll doom us!"

But Nura just smiled. The stone in her hands floated from her grasp, its light now blinding. I felt the magic beneath our world slipping like sand through an hourglass.

I grabbed Max, and Stratagrammed away—

—Just as the explosion hit, and the world went white.

CHAPTER ONE HUNDRED FIVE

AEFE

The coastline of Ara looked like an infected scar, clustered with red-sailed ships. Luia scoffed when it came into view. "We didn't even have to come. We could have let them destroy themselves."

I knew, better than any, that she was right. I had seen inside human hearts. I had been the weapon they had wielded to destroy each other.

But none of this was about watching the humans die. It was about the satisfaction of being the ones to do it. The mere sight of Ara's silhouette stung me, and all I wanted was to drown that hurt in the honey-sweet taste of blood.

A gust of wind blew from the Aran coast, bringing with it a lungful of salty sea air, and Meajqa's entire body shuddered.

"That smell," he muttered. "That was how I knew I was far from home when I awoke. I couldn't see anything. But the smell…"

He spoke quietly, as if to himself. I felt a pang of sympathy for him.

Caduan put his hand on Meajqa's shoulder.

"Never again," Caduan said quietly.

Meajqa swallowed and turned back to the shore, silent.

I watched the sea. There was an armada here already. I felt sick, my stomach churning and skin crawling with clamminess. Halfway between us and land, there was a small island with a building perched atop it—perhaps some kind of naval base. It was difficult to see through the clusters of ships dotting Ara's coastline, but for some reason, I struggled to tear my eyes from it.

Caduan turned to the rest of his leadership, who had gathered around us on the deck. He lifted his chin. Despite his illness, he looked like a king.

A part of me just wanted to take him in while I could. But my gaze went back to Ara—back to that island—

"Remember why we are doing this," he said, voice calm but strong. "Remember why—"

Sudden pain speared me. I doubled over, clutching my chest, even though it was coming from somewhere far deeper than bone and flesh. Caduan drew in a jagged breath, jerking back against the rail as the same sensation shook him, too.

I blinked and saw a million images at once—the Aran queen, donning a bloody smile, surrounded by fire. Maxantarius's face, eyes wide with horror and shock. Two perspectives of the same moment.

"Caduan—" I gasped. I staggered towards him.

But he was looking out over the rail, looking to the island.

"Shields up!" Caduan roared. "Go!"

Seconds before everything went white.

CHAPTER ONE HUNDRED SIX

MAX

How insulting for you, of all people, to underestimate me, Max.
I never underestimated Nura. I just thought a chance was a chance.

Tisaanah barely got us out in time. Maybe it was the sloppy, frantic Stratagram or maybe it was the burst of Nura's magic, but we lost seconds or minutes in the transition. We returned beyond the barricades of the Capital coast. When I opened my eyes, Tisaanah was leaning over me. She heaved an exhale of relief that made me wonder how long I'd been out, then helped me stand.

I had been in many disastrous battles, and so many times I'd thought from within their depths, *This is what hell must look like.*

No. Those had been nothing. *This* was hell.

Nura's soldiers had crashed down upon the shore, a rising flood of corpses wielding sickening, unnatural magic. The Fey, too, had made landfall—only a few of their ships now, but more coming. I could barely see the ocean anymore, just a mass of red and violet and smoke and magic and bodies mutilating each other.

"Ascended fucking above," I muttered.

I gave myself ten seconds to panic, ten seconds to think, *We can not win this. We are all going to die here.*

Ten seconds. And then I forced my fear away.

Tisaanah watched me with that hardened determination of hers.

"We prepared for this," she said.

Yes.

Evaluate. Judge. Act.

Evaluate.

We were outnumbered, but we had a plan. We still held the barriers at the coast, at least for now. That was one piece of good news.

Something else nagged at me, a strange sensation beneath the surface of my skin. The red smoke drifting up from the Towers had grown hotter and more intense, now warping the air like fire. And stranger still, another streak of light had formed, this one at the shore—orange, to the Towers' red.

Vardir's warning echoed in my head. When a man as deranged as him was that alarmed... that was a bad sign. That meant something important.

Judge.

The soldiers were panicking. We needed to hold the barrier, but the plan had unraveled with the unexpected arrival of Nura's troops and the unexpected nature of those troops.

As for the magic... we couldn't deal with any of that if our city was being overrun. We needed to get this under control first, or we would all be dead before we could do anything about it.

Act.

I turned to Tisaanah. She already held Il'Sahaj, which glowed faintly with the blue fire of her magic. I picked up my weapon, opened my second eyelids, and let myself rush away.

OUR MEN HAD NOT BEEN ready for this. No one expected to fight literal walking corpses—not even those who had been finely trained in the art of the impossible after months of fighting the Fey king's grotesque shadow beasts. I got on my horse and galloped among them, up and down the line, trying to keep them steady.

Thousands of soldiers waited to pour into the bay, between the Fey and Nura's forces. It was enough bodies to drown us beneath the scale of it if the line broke. But if we managed to keep everyone calm, we could at least delay the inevitable.

We had arranged our forces by capability, layering defenses.

First, the Valtain who were skilled in water Wielding — they rose the surf, swelling it into massive, crashing waves that sent ships smashing against each other.

The Solarie Wielders skilled in speaking to the earth were just behind them, lifting the rock and dirt in jagged barriers that jutted ten, twenty, thirty feet into the air.

Behind them, more Valtain, those who had an affinity for mind-work, ready to cripple thoughts and manipulate the terri-fied emotions of the Fey spilling onto our shores.

Beyond them, the non-Wielders, the archers, the cavalry.

Beyond them the warriors, for when blood just came to blood.

At first, this seemed to work. What slipped through one layer of defenses was stopped by the next. For a time, we held them off.

But here was the problem with fighting the dead: they didn't stop moving once you killed them. They only stopped once you disassembled them. Soon, their numbers and persistence over-whelmed us. Meanwhile, the shapeshifting Fey turned to birds and flew over our barricades, circumventing our defenses layer by layer.

We fought with everything we had. But in all our planning, there was so fucking much we hadn't accounted for. With every fracture in our formation, I sorely felt the absence of the Rose-teeth — thousands of the most well-trained warriors in the world might have been the difference between narrow victory and devastating defeat.

But eventually, we reached a point of no return—a point when the only thing holding our barriers up was the dead bodies of our own soldiers. I shouted commands until my voice gave out. I killed until my hands were slick and my vision red with blood, killed until it was my instinct every time I moved, killed until everything smelled like burnt flesh.

I watched those bodies—the bodies of people who had trusted me—pile higher and higher.

There was only one sight worse than that:

The sight of those bodies beginning to move.

CHAPTER ONE HUNDRED SEVEN

AEFE

W e crashed upon Ara in a frenzied rush. It was easy for me now to turn myself over to that blood-drunk version of who I used to be. I became Reshaye when we clawed our way from the ship and onto the shore.

I stayed beside Caduan. He fought as well as he was able, but his movements were rough, his strikes too slow. His magic failed him often. But I refused to leave his side, and I compensated for every missed strike, every falter. Life and death mingled together at my fingertips.

We had only one goal: to slaughter until Ara no longer existed. As far as I was concerned, that meant finding Nura, ending her, and taking the power back that she had stolen from us.

We could do this, I told myself. Destroy Ara. Banish those who had tortured me from this world and the next.

And save Caduan.

I could save him.

Every kill I made, every strike, every spurt of human blood spilled over the ground was to the beat of that promise.

I could save him.

CHAPTER ONE HUNDRED EIGHT

TISAANAH

The darkness was oppressive, the hours until dawn endless. The only light arose from Max's fires and the torches along the barricades, which illuminated screaming faces in slashes of crimson. When our own dead began to move, it seemed too nightmarish to be real.

Our defenses had nearly fallen apart. The Fey were making strong headway, cutting through the tide of corpses, though they too struggled against the sheer mass of people. Max ran through the lines of Aran soldiers that still held, roaring commands and encouragements, voice increasingly hoarse. The weight of exhaustion pressed down on our shoulders.

Despite our best efforts, our defenses were starting to collapse.

Crack!

The sound made Max and I freeze. We watched in horror as a third wave of Fey warriors crashed over our banks. Worse, these were magic users—they broke down our Solarie walls of earth as if they were nothing.

I let out a strangled sound.

We were done.

Between the corpses and the Fey, there were just too many of them. Max and I looked at each other, and I could see the same horrible realization in his face.

He swallowed and tightened his grip around his weapon. Flames shuddered to life again along its length. In turn, I lifted Il'Sahaj. At least we would go down together—fighting until our last breath.

Then I caught sight of something strange in the distance, approaching through the pass leading into the city—something that looked different from the rest of the decimated landscape. A string of… light? Of gold? It was nearly impossible to see in the darkness.

I blinked blearily at it, then grabbed Max's arm.

"Max. Look!"

His brow furrowed. At first, he didn't seem to know what he was looking at, either. Then he saw what I did:

It wasn't just light. It was a distant row of torches, thousands of them, illuminating gold armor and matching banners that waved a silent greeting. The banners were too distant to read, but I knew what they bore—the insignia of the Roseteeth Company.

Max nearly fell to his knees, letting out a laugh of exhausted, delirious euphoria. "Fucking Brayan. I have never loved that bastard more."

The Roseteeth worked fast. They poured into the city from the north. Brayan had been right—they were incredible warriors. Their arrival split the Fey's focus, pulling our enemies in multiple directions. Did it turn the tides? It was too early to tell—in the thick of something this bloodthirsty, this dark, what did "winning" even look like? But with the addition of these forces, now we were, at least, surviving. I knew that much, and knew it was more than we could have hoped for minutes ago.

Eventually, Max and I fell back behind one of the few remaining fortifications. We were both breathing so heavily we could hardly speak. My muscles screamed. I was injured some-where, but at this point I didn't even know where.

"Until we kill Nura, this will never end," I panted.

Max nodded, unable to speak. He was bleeding, too. How badly had he been—?

"Maxantarius!"

The figure came out of nowhere. My sword was already inches from his throat when a high voice shrieked, "Wait!"

Max conjured flames and Vardir's terrified face flickered into the light, lips trembling, knobby hands raised.

"I came to help! I came to help!"

"And how is that?" Max demanded.

"I—I—I—" He swallowed hard. "I was wrong. I miscalculated. I didn't understand. Not until now! Not until now, I didn't understand, I didn't—"

"Vardir!" Max snapped. "Tell us what you have to say, *fast*, before we decide to stop being so patient."

"*That*! And—and *that*! It is bad, very, very bad."

I followed his pointing finger—to the red smoke rising from the Towers' ruin, and then to the gold smoke emanating where the shore met the surf, near the naval base.

"You know what that is?" I said.

"I didn't, I didn't realize for the longest time, but it's so obvious, actually—" He laughed, high and frantic. "It's *bleeding*."

"Bleeding?" I pressed.

"We've disrupted the natural order," Vardir said. "We pinched and pressed and stabbed and dug—"

"Get to the point, Vardir," Max growled. He had to pause to stab an incoming corpse soldier. Encroaching violence grew louder from behind the barrier. Any second now, we would be overrun. We couldn't just stand here.

"Yes, bleeding! Bleeding! Like flesh!" Vardir pinched his own sagging skin, as if for emphasis. "Magic is made up of layers, you know, more powerful and volatile the deeper you go. But what happens when you puncture so many holes in the flesh of magic? What happens if you tear out what makes it whole? That is what we have been doing, most of all with the Lejaras. We have been tearing and tearing the barrier between the layers of magic, and today, we have pushed it over the edge."

I barely had time to cut down a corpse before it wrapped its hands around Vardir, who was so absorbed in what he was telling us that he didn't so much as flinch.

My head swam. The buzzing beneath my skin, coupled with the chaos, made it difficult to understand what Vardir was saying.

"The underlying structure is *compromised*," Vardir said again, more pressingly. "The structure of magic itself."

"Which means… a collapse?" I said.

Vardir nodded, a grin spreading over his face. "It is fascinating. I didn't know such a thing was possible!" The grin soured. "Terrible, of course. Terrible. It would mean the end of—well, everything, mostly. Unless the wounds are closed."

"Closed?" Max now had to raise his voice. Fighting surrounded us again like a rising tide of blood.

"It is about balance, you see. One would have to wield all three Lejaras at once. Creation, change, death. Balance them to each other again. And then, close the gaps. Cut off the flow of magic between layers—all of it. And in doing so, destroy them. Simple."

Simple, he said. That made me want to laugh.

I thought of how it had felt to Wield just the change magic—how utterly all-consuming it was. The thought of Wielding all three *at the same time*, and using them to do something so… so *intangible*…

Max kicked another body off his spear. "Vardir," he said, between heaving breaths, "that sounds fucking ridiculous."

"Oh, no, it isn't," Vardir said, brightly. "It might kill you, but I assure you, it is very possible. Though…" His brow knitted. "You probably couldn't do it just anywhere. Few locations could withstand and channel the use of all those magics at once."

Max and I exchanged a hopeless look, interrupted when a blade nicked my shoulder from behind and Max, without hesitation, reached past me to skewer the Fey soldier responsible.

Then he said to Vardir, "Why are you telling us this instead of your queen?"

"I did try to tell her. But sadly, I think she is beyond listening."

"So you came to us? Why?"

Vardir looked offended. "Well I'm not a *madman*, Maxantarius. I'm a man of science. I don't want the *world* to end—"

I saw the strike coming before Vardir did—Vardir, shockingly oblivious, didn't even recoil when the axe came for him.

I struck down his attacker, one of Nura's death soldiers, a split second too late. By then, Vardir was twitching on the ground, nearly decapitated, lips moving as if even in death he still had more to say.

Slowly, even those movements ceased, and he became just another corpse.

I thought of the surgical scars that now adorned Max's body and wished that Vardir had suffered more. But there wasn't time to feel satisfaction in his death. Max and I had to fight our way out of the enclave fast, and by the time we cut through enough bodies to stop and catch our breaths, my hand was burning.

We pressed our backs to a wall. I knew we were thinking the same thing. What Vardir had suggested sounded at worst ridiculous, and at best impossible. And yet... the man, as much as I hated him, was undeniably a genius when it came to magic. If he was right—if there *was* a way to simply end the connection of deep magics to this world—

A stab of pain in my palm jerked me from the thought. I looked down to see the wayfinder was glowing again, brighter than it had even before, specks of gold trailing fast from my wrist to my ring finger.

My head snapped up. A new spark of light arced to the sky— further inland, now, than the one that was at the coast.

"Her," I murmured. It was all I had to say.

Nura.

CHAPTER ONE HUNDRED NINE

MAX

Tisaanah and I cut through legions of corpses, her magic and mine coupling to cripple them with flaming decay. The hordes grew denser as we pushed closer to Nura. Soon, in every direction I met a wall of decaying flesh, going on seemingly forever. I no longer could tell where we were. I lost sight of Tisaanah, even though we'd been so careful to stay together.

"Tisaanah?"

I frantically looked around to see nothing but dead faces.

I reached deep for more power, my depleting magic burning brighter.

"Tisaanah, *where the hell are you?!*"

Did I imagine the distant answering cry? I couldn't tell. I cut ferociously through one, two, three more corpses and —

I stumbled into open air, nearly tripping over the debris-laden ground.

The Towers. We had fought our way all the way to the Towers.

Standing in the middle of the ruins, surrounded by red and gold smoke and the familiar shudder of shadow, was Nura. She stared out over the city, her back to me. Darkness and light wrapped her in a ghostly embrace, sputtering around her form.

I let my flames snuff out, giving my magic a temporary reprieve.

Nura did not move. I chanced taking my eyes off her for just a moment, just long enough to glance over my shoulder at the sea of soldiers, searching for any sign of Tisaanah —

Too long.

Unnatural terror skewered me, so sudden and intense that it left me gasping. The image of Tisaanah's throat opened and the country burning and —

Nura. I'd know that fear anywhere.

I opened my second eyelids, and flames engulfed me, just in time for me to block her first move. The world rushed hard around me when I was in this form, my thoughts slippery and difficult to grasp. But I knew how to fight Nura. We fell into an old pattern quickly. There was a time when we could have sparred for hours with no victor, because we just knew each other that well—we could anticipate each other's movements, dodge, adjust, reframe, on and on until we were forced to draw out of sheer exhaustion.

But something was different today. Yes, we threw ourselves into the same relentless rhythm that we had fought a million times before. But her movements were more jagged now, more openly controlled by her anger. All while mine had gotten more decisive, more precise, more powerful. Before, we could have gone forty moves before one of us even nicked skin. Now, we only made it five before my blade skimmed her shoulder. She flinched away, fire reflecting in the whites of her eyes.

I realized, in that split second, exactly how afraid of me Nura was. I didn't know why it still surprised me. She had nearly burned alive in Sarlazai, after all. I wasn't the only one scarred by my past.

She buried that fear fast, but the hesitation was all I needed. I sent fire down the length of my staff. When I pinned her down in the rubble with the blunt edge of my weapon, she snarled.

I let my eyelids slide closed—my magic was growing danger-ously exhausted—and I didn't like how human Nura looked this way. She looked so broken. All I could see was the girl I had dragged out of Sarlazai, begging her to live.

"You tried to kill me," she spat.

"You didn't give me a choice."

"You always have a choice." Something between a smile and a sneer spread over her bloody face. "Didn't you tell me that?"

Nura thought I would never see her for who she really was. But that had changed. Now, I knew where she kept her knives. I waited for her to lunge, gave her just enough opening to leap to her feet with her blade sliding from her sleeve.

Her strike sent her directly into my grasp.

I countered, twisting her arm, reversing our positions so she was locked in front of me, one arm gripping her shoulders and the other clasping her wrist behind her back. Her magic flailed out desperately, trying to drown me in fear, but that did nothing to me. I had spent six months locked up with nothing but my own past. How cruelly ironic that Nura's punishment made me immune to her.

"*Look.*" I forced her gaze to the decimated landscape. Even I hadn't been able to see it well from the thick of the battle, but here, the view was heartbreaking—nothing but miles and miles of death. "Look at the country you claim you love so much. Look at what you've done to it."

An eerie orange glow harshened the lines of Nura's expres-sion. Her body tensed. Something was clutched in her white-knuckled hand. The angle hid it from me, but I knew it was the Lejara.

"It's not what I wanted," she choked out.

And despite everything, I felt a pang of anguish to hear her voice like that—sounding so much like the child I knew once, a long time ago.

"I know, Nura," I said, quietly. "I know you didn't."

"I can't think. I can't—" She squeezed her eyes shut. "It's so hard to think."

I pitied Nura. I pitied her because she had been created. She had been honed like a weapon and thrust into the hands of a military that simultaneously told her that she would never be enough and that the only part of her worth anything was the part that knew how to kill. Her entire life, she had been taught that maybe one day, if she worked hard enough, if she grew cold enough, if she gained enough power, she would have nothing left to be afraid of.

But the version of Nura before me now, tears painting silver streaks down bloody cheeks, was more afraid than I had ever seen her.

She was afraid of herself.

Out of the corner of my eye, I saw a familiar figure emerge from the crowds surrounding the ruins. I didn't allow myself the sigh of relief. I didn't even allow my gaze to move from Nura's at all.

"You have a choice," I said. "Give us the Lejara. It doesn't need to end like this."

Two more silent tears. "They probably hate me. When I see them in the next life. They will hate me."

They. The people Nura had always loved more than anything. I swallowed thickly.

"You were like their sister. They loved you."

"I don't think so. Not anymore." Pain cut across her face, her features momentarily crumbling.

"We can fix this, Nura. Please." My hand crept a little closer to the stone in her grip.

At first, she looked so unsure—looked like she was considering it. The change in her expression was minute, but I saw it because I knew her. Because for decades she had been the most important person in my life. Even now, even at her worst, I couldn't choke back the leap of hope that maybe the parts of her that I knew still lived inside of her, somewhere, might win.

She tilted her head a little more, allowing me to see more of her face. We were so close I could count the threads of silver in her eyes.

She looked so, so young. Just like the grumpy child that hid from parties with me. My only friend. My best friend.

"Let me help you, Nura," I begged. "*Please.*"

I let myself hope.

Then, her expression hardened, a sheet of ice falling over her vulnerabilities. The anger returned.

"No," she said. "No, I can't stop. I can't be weak."

"Nura, please—"

We had been so fucking close. But through my connection to the deepest layers of magic, I felt Nura reaching for her power.

I raised my weapon.

Yet, I was secretly grateful when it was Il'Sahaj, not my own blade, that sliced Nura's throat.

I stepped back from Nura's falling body. I moved quickly this time, replacing her grip around the amber stone the moment it loosened. I buckled under a wave of intoxication as its magic slithered through me.

Nura had already been so badly wounded. Maybe her magic or even just the sheer strength of her will had been keeping her upright at all. The moment the Lejara left her grasp—the moment she lost its magic—she collapsed.

For a few seconds she fought death, erratic sputters of shadow at her hands. Her gaze fell to me one last time, and I couldn't look away.

A ghost of a smile twitched at her mouth.

"I knew you would. Eventually."

I felt no joy as I watched Nura die.

I felt nothing at all.

CHAPTER ONE HUNDRED TEN

MAX

I couldn't help but hope that the corpses would fall as soon as Nura did, like puppets limp from the loss of their master.

Sadly, this was not the case. Seconds after Nura died, Tisaanah had to drag me away from the quickly encroaching hordes of monstrous soldiers. The haze of exhaustion and anger and sadness cleared enough for a single question to surface:

Now what?

Those were the first words out of my lips when Tisaanah and I managed to steal a few seconds of quiet again, behind a half-broken house. My eyes were drawn down to the amber, which I clutched like my life depended on it.

Your life does depend on it, the magic seemed to sing. *Everything depends on me. Come with me and we can create a new world. You and me.*

I hadn't been able to see the details of it before, when it was tightly held in Nura's grasp. The thing inside it resembled a misshapen fetus, white as if carved in ivory, curled up at the center of the amber stone. It was barely a suggestion of a person at this point, no features, no fingers, no toes, but disturbingly humanoid. It was disgusting... and yet, entrancing.

The power of it thrummed beneath my skin. The heart had

felt staggeringly powerful, too, but erratic and ever moving, like a river rushing around us.

This? This was more… enticing. Like a beckoning hand.

Create the world you wish, it seemed to whisper. *Create life. Do you know what does that? A god.*

"What do we do with that thing now?" Tisaanah said. She was breathing hard, her forearm around her body, clearly cradling an injury.

I glanced over my shoulder to see sheer hell unfolding around us. The magic at my hands tingled.

We could use it. The answer was on the tip of my tongue. *We could use it to win this war and every one after it. We could use it to build the world of our dreams.*

I snapped my chin up, blinking hard.

Ascended above. No wonder this thing had driven Nura to a new level of madness.

"We absolutely should *not* use it," I said.

Tisaanah nodded emphatically. Then she lifted her gaze to the night sky. I followed her stare and noticed that the streaks of unnatural light arcing across it had only grown brighter, stronger.

"Do you feel that?" she murmured.

She pressed her hand to her chest, as if trying to steady something untethered.

I did feel it. A disruption, like waves churning in the magic far beneath us. Noxious.

Her brow was furrowed in thought. "What if Vardir was right?"

I hated Vardir. But knowledge was never his problem. He was almost certainly right.

"Then what?" I said. "We have this." I nodded down to the amber. "And that." I nodded to Tisaanah's pockets, where she still held the shards of the heart—what little we could recover, even though it now seemed so volatile that the very thought of using it chilled me. "But there's a third, and if Vardir is right, then we need it in order to stop all of this."

Death magic.

Right. And also, there was that. *It'll probably kill you!* Vardir had said, so fucking cheerfully.

I ran my hand through my hair, letting out a grunt of frustration. "This is all so—"

Tisaanah's eyes went wide. She grabbed my wrist hard enough to make me stumble.

"How did you not notice this?" she gasped.

I looked down. She held my hand out between us, where Ilyzath's mark was burned into my palm—where Ilyzath's mark was now *moving*. The chaotic lines trembled like Ilyzath's carvings in the shadows. Faint puffs of purple shadow quivered around each stroke.

Ascended fucking above. My hand had hurt, but so did the rest of my body, and I'd spent the last several hours with my hands wrapped around my spear's staff.

"I was a little distracted, but that's—that's—"

Tisaanah lifted her own hand. The gold mark now spread several inches up her forearm. Shimmers of glowing light ran from her palm to her fingertips, glowing towards the amber—but when I looked more carefully, I realized those lights moved in a second wave, too, fainter strings of gold moving towards her little finger. She turned, slowly, and the light grew bolder as her hand pointed to the sea.

Pointed in the direction of Ilyzath.

"Fuck, I'm an idiot," I breathed.

All at once, pieces clicked together. Ilyzath's words echoed in my head, now suddenly so much clearer.

Hands reaching into forces that should not be wielded, it had said, *and thinning boundaries that should not be torn.*

I, too, have lost pieces of myself, it had told me.

I stuck on those three words: *Pieces of myself.*

The Lejaras. *That* was what it had been talking about. And this, what was happening now, was exactly what it had warned of. *Mortal hubris.*

Ilyzath was built upon ancient magic that no one understood.

It was semi-sentient, just as the Lejaras seemed to be. And if any location could hold death itself... well, that was it.

The final Lejara was *in* Ilyzath.

Tisaanah and I looked at each other, wide-eyed, the realization hitting us both.

"I can go alone," I said.

"That is a stupid idea," she said, without hesitation, and reached out to take my hand.

I knew better than to argue with her. A few scribbles on a sheet of paper, and we were gone.

CHAPTER ONE HUNDRED ELEVEN

AEFE

The night wore on, and with each passing hour our battle grew more brutal. We fought the way wounded animals did, clawing for our lives as we teetered on the edge of survival.

In the beginning, I had felt powerful—we all did. Luia was a capable commander and led her forces in stunningly orchestrated attacks. We shattered the humans' stone walls and barriers with our magic users. The Wyshraj took to the sky and soared into the thick of their capital city. And my own magic was stronger than it ever had been, responding effortlessly. No one even came close to touching me.

I could feel Nura's stolen magic calling to me, louder with every passing minute—perhaps because it had created me. To reach her, we would have to cut through countless waves of her dead soldiers. I knew I was strong enough to do it.

Yet, the power I had first found in killing faded so quickly. I realized that the more one had to lose, the more terrifying it became. I watched Caduan's movements grow weaker, watched the flickers of pain on his face grow more pronounced, and fear clenched tighter and tighter in my chest.

I was certain that if I left him, he would be killed. No matter how many times he tried to tell me to move ahead, I remained with him.

We had made it past the second barrier into the city when I felt the shift—like something in the deepest magics I drew from tore open. Fractured visions flashed through my mind.

I saw the Aran queen's bloodstained, tear-streaked face.

I saw glowing amber—felt the power that radiated from it.

I saw Maxantarius's confusion and interest as he cradled it in his hands.

I saw white stone rising into the clouds, and doors that opened like gaping jaws.

The images were so violent, so forceful, that I almost fell to my knees. The only thing that steadied me was Caduan's firm grasp on my arm.

"I felt it too," he said, through heaving breaths. "The change. Did you see anything? Did you see where it is?"

My mind was fuzzy. I could barely form words. I mumbled something about a—a prison, an ivory slab nestled in the mist. I knew that place, I had been there, I—

"*Where*, Aefe?" Caduan pressed.

I reached deep within myself and grasped the thread that connected me to them.

I lifted my eyes, and of their own accord, they landed upon a spot in the distance—a pillar of ivory so far away that it was visible only as a single ghostly break in the waves.

Caduan followed my stare.

Something about the look on his face gave me a panicked, sickened feeling.

"No," I said, grabbing his wrist.

But he simply used my own grip to pull me close, tilted my face to him, and kissed me.

It was only half a kiss, because I pulled away fast, just enough to open my mouth to protest, because I knew he was about to leave, that he was going to—

"There can be more than this," he said, softly.

The last time he said this, you lost him. You lost him.

"*No* —" I begged.

But Caduan, despite his exhaustion, spoke to magic as easily as he breathed. He walked between the seams of space and time so smoothly that I didn't even see him disappear.

When I reached out for him, he was simply gone.

CHAPTER ONE HUNDRED TWELVE

TISAANAH

The sea spattered my face as we landed at Ilyzath's entrance. The air was no longer hot and thick with smoke, but salty and cold. The night sky was unnaturally red, cracks running across like chasms through stone. In the distance, Ara's skyline burned. Those three streaks of magic cut all the way up into the clouds, more striking than ever from miles away.

It's bleeding, Vardir had said. Now, it seemed impossible to see those marks as anything other than wounds.

It looked like the end of the world.

Fear balled in my stomach. Max and I were two of Ara's greatest weapons. Had it been stupid to leave them?

"Well." A tired smile tugged at the corner of Max's mouth. "Look who's here."

I followed Max's stare in the opposite direction, and let out a tiny, involuntary sound.

Ships dotted the horizon—dozens of them, or perhaps even hundreds. They had the same spine-like sails of the Threllians' ships, but instead of white or red, these had been splashed with bright paint of clashing colors.

I recognized those makeshift banners immediately—the colors of the Alliance.

"They came."

"Of course they came. You've fought for them. Did you think they wouldn't fight for you?"

Gods, I loved them. Our nation was tiny, broken, confused. But it was ours.

Even across this distance—even if it was my imagination—I could have sworn I saw a familiar figure, with gold hair and watery blue eyes, leading them on.

I reached deep into the dregs of my magic and summoned a red butterfly between my palms, then sent it shooting across the sea.

Go.

That little streak of red light closed the space between Ilyzath and Ara's coast like a shooting star—and then it flew up into the air, growing larger and larger until its wings eclipsed the moon, where it smoldered in the sky before dissipating into dust.

A beacon, and a thank you, to my people.

"Show off," Max muttered, affectionately.

I smirked at him.

But both of our smiles faded quickly when we turned to Ilyzath's entrance. The doors loomed over us like a gaping maw.

I knew them well by now. I half expected to see the bone-white stone still marked with my blood. How many times had I thrown myself against them when Max was imprisoned here?

I clutched Max's hand.

"Are you ready?" I asked.

"Not even remotely. Are you?"

I thought about the fact that I was wounded, exhausted, nearly depleted of both strength and magic. That I didn't even know what we were looking for or what we would do with it.

I shook my head.

"Great," Max said. "About the best we can expect, isn't it?"

The doors ground open at a mere brush of Max's fingers. Perhaps I imagined the wind whisper, *Welcome home.*

The stone was white, but pure darkness enveloped the hallway before us. Max conjured flame, and together, we walked.

Two steps beyond the threshold, the floor fell out from beneath us.

CHAPTER ONE HUNDRED THIRTEEN

AEFE

Panic. Only panic. I could not center myself. Vines and flowers sprouted and died around my every footstep in a rapid, uncontrolled cycle.

No.

No, I did not accept it. I would not allow it.

I would not let him go.

I ran, ran through people and soldiers and swords and axes and magic. I ran even though my lungs didn't work, even though my skin and eyes burned. I couldn't see. I could only feel.

"Aefe!"

I barely heard Meajqa's voice, not even as he chased after me.

"What happened?" he demanded. "Aefe—stop!"

I ignored him. I rushed to the shore until cold water shocked my feet, soaking through my boots.

Meajqa followed. "Where is Caduan?"

"Gone."

"*Gone?*" It was odd to hear Meajqa openly afraid. "Where? How?"

I did not answer. My gaze found the column of white in the

distance. Too far to reach by boat, at least not fast enough.

I wanted to step through the air, like Caduan did. How did he do that? He had never taught me. My magic was out of control. Meajqa needed to keep stepping back to dodge whipping vines that shriveled as quickly as they sprouted from the water.

I could not do this. I did not know how.

I only knew how to—

You'll find another thing to burn. It's all you know how to do.

I squeezed my eyes shut, blocking out Nura's voice.

She was wrong. She was wrong.

"Aefe!" Meajqa gripped my arm. "Is Caduan alive? You need to tell me if he isn't."

He is alive. He is alive. He will stay alive.

I pressed my palm to my chest. But my heartbeat was wild. My breathing was ragged and panicked. I could not ground myself in this.

"Aefe," Meajqa pressed. "If Caduan is dead, then you need to tell me *now*. Because if he has died, then we need to retreat. We need to end this before more of our people are lost."

"He is not dead," I spat.

I closed my eyes again.

No, Caduan was not dead.

I slipped into a memory—into the day he had let me listen to his heartbeat for the first time. The first time I had noticed the way every part of a living body was alive, in movement, in rhythm.

What do you feel, Aefe?

I reached down, down, down, through the magic that I drew from, through the magic that had created me. I reached across seas and stone, across the sky.

I felt a familiar pulse there, so far away.

"He is not dead," I said again, more quietly, even though I did not mean to speak aloud.

How easy it was then, tethered to his heartbeat, to slip away into the air.

CHAPTER ONE HUNDRED FOURTEEN

TISAANAH

The coins falling onto the marble floor sounded like bells. There were so many of them piled on the mahogany desk that they slid down the sides like dirt off the side of a mountain.

One thousand pieces of gold.

I had danced, I had cleaned, I had sung, I had flirted, I had opened my body to strangers. I had given away so much of myself in exchange for those little metal pieces. And in turn, those little metal pieces would give me my freedom.

I wanted him to be proud of me for fulfilling his demand. But instead, Esmaris looked at me like I had betrayed him.

You know this story, don't you, little butterfly?

I knew the way Esmaris's voice sounded as he spat, "I don't need your money."

I knew the way the marble felt beneath my knees when I hit the ground hard.

And yet the whip was worse than I even remembered—sharper, deeper. He would not stop until I was in pieces.

"Look at me," I demanded.

But this time, when I turned around, Esmaris didn't stop.

When he smiled, droplets of my blood smeared in the creases of his expression.

"What if I have been looking?" he said. "What if you have always been exactly what I saw in you? A whore, a killer, a slave?"

I shook my head. But here, locked in this dreamlike reality, it seemed undeniably true. There was no door. No Serel to save me. No magic at my hands.

"I killed you." My voice wavered. It came out more like a question.

"Have I taught you nothing? My flesh has so little to do with my life. I have left my legacy." He caressed my bare back, tugging at the fresh gashes.

"I have marked you," he murmured in my ear, tender as a lover. "I marked your body, and I marked your soul. Do you think I don't know how often you think of me? Do you think I don't feel it, when you fear that I shaped you more than your own mother did?"

The wounds hurt. But those words hurt more, because they were true. I knew every angle of Esmaris's face, but no longer remembered the shape of my mother's eyes.

"I killed you," I said, like a prayer. "I killed you. I killed you."

I wanted to hear his neck snap, see his face rot. But my magic was gone. I was helpless.

I pushed myself to my hands and knees. My gaze settled on the closet. My clothing had hung there once—a twisted sign of Esmaris's ownership and affection. There had been weapons stored there, too.

Behind me, Esmaris laughed as I dragged myself across the room. "You think there is freedom for you there?"

I killed you. I killed you. I killed you.

I could barely move. I struggled to turn the knob. Blood slicked my palms, making it slippery around the metal. When the door at last opened, I let out a horrified cry.

Max hung there, a rope around his throat. His eyes were

wide open, sightless. There was a single cerulean flower in his hands. He smelled not of ash and lilac, but of rot.

I fell backwards onto my decimated back. I was shaking. Esmaris stepped in front of the closet. He looked down at me with such affection—the same way he used to look at me when I would awaken in the middle of the night with nightmares.

He knelt before me, caressing my cheek. "You never had a future, my little butterfly. It was only a dream."

"I killed you," I said, over and over again. "I killed you. I killed you."

"No." He pressed his lips to my forehead. "I am right here."

Wake up, Tisaanah. Wake up. This is not real.

But suddenly it was so difficult to discern what was real and what wasn't. Perhaps I dreamed of a cottage with endless flowers, and a smile that started on the left side first. Perhaps I dreamed of a life of freedom.

"Come back to bed." Esmaris rose, his hand reaching for me. "I forgive you."

Tears ran down my cheeks. I felt ashamed, silly.

All of this, and I had been the lucky one. I lived a life of comfort while so many people like me were disposable labor in the mines or the fields or between gears of machinery. And I had a master who loved me, at least as much as he knew how to love anything.

I placed my hand in Esmaris's.

He gave me the smile reserved for when he was pleased with me.

But something nagged at me. I didn't move. I touched my throat and felt metal. Butterfly wings.

I folded my fingers around the necklace. The pad of my thumb pressed to the flat back of the design—to the ridges of the Stratagram engraved there.

Home.

I had a home.

It hadn't been a dream. This was real. I'd fought for it, bled for it, killed for it.

Esmaris's face had gone cold and hard, as if he could hear my thoughts.

"Who let you believe you could have that?" he hissed. "You are nothing."

Butterflies came from nothing. I wasn't afraid of being nothing—of being pieces of so many incomplete things.

I knew who I was.

I rose to my feet. I no longer felt the wounds on my back.

"*I killed you*," I ground out. "And I destroyed your empire. And I don't need to think about you again. Not even in a nightmare."

He lunged for me.

None of this was real. I pressed my hand to the Stratagram on that necklace, and I shattered the dream.

———————

I OPENED my eyes to an expanse of white stone. It was chillingly silent. The light consumed all shadows, making the ivory seem unnaturally flat. I didn't know if I was imagining the carvings on the ceiling moving, like leaves in the wind.

I sat up.

I was in a long hallway. No doors or windows. No torches, no sound. Only light. Behind me was a dead end. Ahead, a long stretch of nothing, and a turn to the left.

I looked down at my hand. The gold was so bright, and it moved up the length of my palm in fits and starts.

I stood. I clutched Il'Sahaj, even though I knew that it would do me little good against the things I would encounter in here—a place that played tricks on your mind.

I needed to find Max, and quickly. I braced myself and began to walk.

CHAPTER ONE HUNDRED FIFTEEN

MAX

My head was fucking killing me. When I opened my eyes to see familiar white stone dotted with uncanny carvings, I would be lying if I said that I didn't seize up a bit.

Everything about this place reeked of death. As I lay there, staring at the ceiling, I felt a bit stupid for not realizing what lurked within these walls sooner.

I sat up.

"Hello again."

The burning girl smiled at me. Immediately, I looked away.

I stared at the wall, blood rushing in my ears to the beat of my pounding heart. I stood, carefully keeping my gaze on the stone.

"Why won't you look at me?" the girl said.

Breathe, Max. You know what this place does.

When I had been imprisoned here, my broken mind had saved me. The burning girl had been horrible then, too, of course. The image alone, in any context, was horrifying. But now, knowing who she was —

Knowing what I'd done —

I shut my eyes and drew in a long breath.

"Why won't you *look* at me?" the girl said again.

"I'll need to eventually," I muttered.

Kira. The burning girl was Kira. I hadn't been able to place her when I'd seen her back then—a strange sort of mercy.

Since my memories had returned to me, I dreamed often about the way my favorite sister had looked when she died. It would be another thing to confront her here, where everything seemed so much more real.

It is not real. It is a memory.

You can do nothing to change your past. You're here because of the future.

I heard two small, tentative footsteps. The snap and crack of flames grew nearer. She was right behind me.

I would turn, I decided, and go down the hall quickly. I would barely look at her. I'd look straight ahead until I found Tisaanah—the real Tisaanah, not whatever horrifying nightmare version this place would show me.

I let out my breath slowly and turned around.

"Why did you do this to me?" the burning girl asked. She was blinking fast, like she was trying not to cry but was going to anyway. She stood so close to me that I nearly collided with her.

Keep going. Walk right past.

But I froze.

Because this girl was not Kira.

She too had long black hair, but this child's was sleek and wavy instead of pin-straight like Kira's had been. Her features were different, though I saw myself in them still. Her eyes were wider, and green instead of dark brown—amber-green, like the sun shining through leaves.

A familiar green.

And then it hit me: The burning girl was not my sister.

The burning girl was my daughter.

I had prepared myself for my worst memory of the past. I had not prepared myself for my worst nightmare for the future.

I couldn't move, couldn't breathe.

The little girl's lip quivered. "Why—why would you do this?"

Reality shifted, blended with the twisted logic of a dream world. I looked down at my hands. They were covered with ash and blood.

{You think you can have a future?} Reshaye's voice whispered. *{You think you deserve one, after you brought nothing but agony to your past?}*

I closed my eyes. Centered myself. Focused on my breath. In. Out.

This was not real. This was Ilyzath. I had survived this place before.

I opened my eyes.

I allowed myself to actually look at her, even though I wanted more than anything to avert my gaze. I realized that her features changed slightly every time I looked at them, as if compensating for a million different combinations of the future. The only thing about her that did not change were those green eyes.

I reached through the fire and cradled her face, ignoring the pain. My chest tightened. I loved this child. I loved her so much that the very possibility of her existence terrified me.

Wake up, Max.

"You aren't real," I murmured.

The crying stopped. The girl smiled, eerily. "Not yet. But I will be. And then what will you do?"

Protect you. Fight for you. Love you.

But right now, you aren't real.

I stepped away from her.

She lurched towards me, the strange adult calm on her face replaced with the innocent fear of a child—and even now in this dreamworld, that cry awakened some primal instinct in me.

"Don't leave," she wept. "Don't leave me alone. Don't leave me."

"I'm doing this for you," I said.

Wake up.

The dream shattered.

I opened my eyes.

For several long seconds, everything was silent except for the thrum of my blood pounding. I'd forgotten exactly how fucking creepy Ilyzath's silence was. Unrelenting. Unnatural.

Then, words parted the silence, not quite a voice, perhaps not even a real sound.

Welcome back, my ashen son. Ilyzath's whispers surrounded me like mist. *You have brought my missing pieces home to me. I sense them within these walls.*

The Lejaras. My consciousness was still fuzzy. I couldn't make my mouth form the word.

Strange, Ilyzath murmured, in groans of stone. *I thought you would fail. But of course, you have not shattered inevitability yet.*

I cut through the fog of my dream. "Wait," I started to say, but before I could speak—before I could ask the questions I desperately needed answered—its voice faded.

It was replaced, moments later, by the sound of approaching footsteps. Relief flooded me. I sat up.

"Tisaanah, I'm—"

—so fucking glad to see you.

The words died in my throat. Standing before me was the Fey king.

651

CHAPTER ONE HUNDRED SIXTEEN

AEFE

The prison was a dead place. I nearly stumbled when I ran into those open doors. Every terrible memory seared into every crevice and carving of its walls overwhelmed me.

The doors closed behind me as I ran into its open hallways. When I turned around, they were gone.

The panic took me fast. I could not move.

I was here, in a room of white and white and white and white. I was trapped and powerless. I could not fight back. I could not act. There was no warmth here. No heartbeat. No breath. No skin. The hard angles were not the shape of another mind.

I had never been so alone.

The shifting of the walls seemed to speak to me.

Welcome home, my lost soul, it whispered. *You have always belonged here. You have always lived in death.*

No. No.

I pressed my hand to my heart and for a horrible moment, I felt nothing.

No.

I squeezed my eyes shut.

I thought of Caduan's smile and the taste of honey and the feeling of music vibrating in my veins.

I pressed harder.

And — there. *Ba-dum, ba-dum.* So slow, so faint.

I was alive, I reminded myself. Caduan needed me. I opened my eyes, let out my breath, and ran down the halls.

CHAPTER ONE HUNDRED SEVENTEEN

MAX

The Fey king watched me with detached interest as I leapt up, grabbed my weapon, and backed away from him. My muscles screamed at the movement. Exhaustion and the remnants of my dream clouded my mind.

The Lejara. The thought came in a burst of panic. In the midst of my disorientation, I pressed my hand to my lapel, where the amber stone was safely tucked within my jacket.

I yanked my hand away immediately, cursing my own stupidity. But too late. I saw the Fey king's eyes follow that movement.

"It is good to see you again," he said.

He stepped closer. His sword was drawn and ready. Crimson already dripped from its blade to the floor. At the sight of it, I thought of Tisaanah and my heart stopped. I prayed he hadn't found her first.

With every step he took towards me, I took one back. Slowly, we circled each other.

"I need to take that from you," he said, calmly.

"This is a mistake."

Something was not right about this man's face—about his eyes. The darkness that bracketed them went beyond exhaustion.

Maybe I was wasting my breath by trying to reason with him. But Fey were bigger than humans, stronger, faster. I was wounded. My magic was so depleted that even its dregs were out of reach. Even if this man was injured, the odds were against me in a hand-to-hand fight.

I needed to buy time.

"I know you must feel it," I said. "That something is breaking. This magic is too dangerous to use."

The king's lip twitched. "You did not hesitate to use it against my people when you had it in your possession."

"Fair. But we didn't know its true impacts, then. Trust me when I say our intention was not to end the world."

"I have no reason to believe you."

He moved first.

He was incredibly fast, even wounded. Downright graceful— the way he moved seemed better suited to dancing than killing. I had been watching for this, and the speed and grace of it still caught me a little off-guard.

His weapon met mine in a song of metal against metal, each note faster and faster as we flew down the hall, our steps never stopping. I dodged, blocked, slipped through his strikes—and he evaded each of mine, too, until in one wild cacophony of steel we clashed together and then pulled apart, setting several strides of distance between us.

We circled each other again, faster, the spirals larger.

No magic. I knew he was a powerful Wielder. Why wasn't he using it? Was it for the same reason I didn't? Mine still burned with exhaustion. If I only had one shot, I didn't want to waste it.

I watched his movements carefully, lingering on the heavy rise and fall of his shoulders. Violet soaked his shirt beneath his arm, along his ribs. He was hurt badly.

"I know that you want what's best for your people," I said. "But doing this will hurt them just as much as it will hurt mine."

Minutes. Just a few more minutes, maybe, and I would be able to use my magic again.

He scoffed. The sound was jagged and wheezing—

confirming my suspicion that he was injured. "Humans slaughtered my entire House hundreds of years ago in search of this power, and now you expect me to forfeit it based on your word?"

"I am *more* than aware of humanity's many flaws, trust me. But—"

Apparently, he had no interest in what I had to say. He lunged.

Another cascading melody of strikes, as our weapons collided again, again, again. With each one, we both grew slower and sloppier. This time, we only made it halfway down the hall before we pulled apart again. A sheen of sweat slicked his skin. My breath burned in my lungs.

"She told me about you," he panted, revealing the faintest crack in his calm exterior. "How much you craved power. Spare me your hypocrisy."

"And did she tell you how much I paid for it?" I shot back. "You're right. I was young and stupid. I thought my only path to respect was through violence. But I suffered more than enough for those mistakes."

A rough laugh. "More than enough. How old are you? How much justice can be served in thirty years of life? That is *nothing*, and that is why humans can never be trusted. You die, and then your children make the same mistakes. And we are alive for *all of it*, to bear the consequences over and over again."

This time, there was nothing graceful in his attack. Before, I could anticipate his next move because he set up his entire body for his strike—minuscule changes, yes, but I could read them. But this? It was fast, vicious, designed only to kill. The tip of his rapier opened a river of blood across my abdomen before I twisted out of the way. I managed to land a return hit, the breath knocked out of him as I struck his shoulder with one end of my weapon, his knee with the other, sending him momentarily collapsing before righting himself.

And there, at last, was the magic.

He thrust out his palm and released a burst of power, strong enough to send my back slamming against Ilyzath's walls—so hard I thought its carvings must now be etched into my skin.

His magic held me there as he approached me, coming close enough that his face was inches from mine.

"I would never expect your kind to understand justice," he said. "One act of justice to ensure my people's futures. The last one they will ever need. And I will give them that, no matter what lies you tell me. No matter what you do to stop me."

His expression was still calm—or what I'd mistaken as calm. Now I almost laughed at my own naïveté. What, I thought he wasn't angry because he didn't sneer and snarl like an animal? The calm was worse. This was the face of something deeper than anger. This was hate distilled into a single, unquestionable end.

My eyes drifted down to his throat—to the lines of black reaching up over his skin.

Their future, he had said. Not *our* future. *Their* future.

And then I understood. He was dying.

No wonder he was willing to sacrifice everything. There was no reasoning with someone who had nothing more to lose. He would not listen to anything I told him.

My magic was still drained. But he was close enough that I had a single shot, and I took it.

I opened my second eyelids.

Fire exploded across the white of Ilyzath's walls. The Fey king's eyes went wide. One hand went up to shield his face as flames consumed us both.

I struck with my knife, burying the blade in his side. It was a sloppy strike—not fatal, unless he bled out—but it should have been enough to bring him down.

Instead, he set his jaw and lunged. His magic slammed me against the stone.

Move move move—

I wasn't fast enough. His rapier skewered me.

The pain swallowed everything else.

Maybe I blacked out. Because the next thing I knew, seconds

had passed, and the king was right in front of me. A sneer at last bubbled to the surface of his expression.

With a shaking hand, I touched my lapel, and felt nothing.

Fuck. *Fuck.*

The king's magic still pinned me to the wall, his blade still piercing through me. I realized, for the first time, that I would probably die here. At least I'd go down fighting.

I raised my left hand, preparing one final burst of fire against him.

His eyes fell to my palm, and his face changed. He blinked, and the sneer disappeared as he regarded me with renewed interest. He pressed my hand to the wall, leaning close to examine it —and the mark it carried.

No.

"Why did you come to this place?" he asked, quietly. "What is the true nature of it?"

I called the flames with all my remaining strength.

The king jerked away from the heat, his grip slackening. I fell to the floor. I couldn't figure out why I was struggling to rise until I realized I kept slipping on my own blood.

The remainder of my magic burned out quickly. I had nothing left, and I was bleeding heavily. I barely managed to grab my weapon again, though the metal slid beneath my blood-drenched fingers.

The king turned to me—

And was flung across the hallway.

The strike came so quickly that it merely looked like a flash of red and white and tan. He hadn't been anticipating it. He slammed against the wall, doubled over—the hit was bad, especially on top of his previous injuries.

Through my fading vision, I watched him stumble and turn towards Tisaanah, who rushed at him.

I watched him whisper to his magic and disappear before she could strike.

And by the time Tisaanah knelt before me, I could barely see anything at all.

CHAPTER ONE HUNDRED EIGHTEEN

TISAANAH

Max was bleeding so, so much. That was all I could see. The moment my eyes landed on all that blood, I didn't care about the Fey king or the Lejaras or the war or the end of the world. I only cared about him.

I fell to my knees beside him. I could barely see the gash because it was bleeding so much—it looked to span most of his abdomen. When I touched it, he let out a hiss of pain.

"I'm sorry. I'm sorry. I need to—"

I took off my jacket and then the shirt beneath it, leaving me in just a camisole. I tried to wrap the cotton shirt around his waist, tying it tight even as he exhaled and swore.

"He took it," Max said, hoarsely.

No. Gods, no.

I pulled the fabric tight, and Max cursed again. He started moving, trying to stand, even though I stopped him.

"No. Stay still."

He rasped a wheezing laugh. "I don't exactly have a choice, Tisaanah."

"We can go back," I blurted out. "We can get Sammerin, we can—"

Max could barely open his eyes. But they slid to me with a look that said, wordlessly, *You know we can't.*

I shut my mouth, because he was right. I tucked myself beneath Max's arm and let him lean on me. His steps were short and clumsy.

I didn't realize until this moment how badly he had already been wounded, even before we arrived here. Now I cursed myself for not seeing it sooner.

"He saw my hand," Max rasped. "I think he knows what this place is."

Oh, gods. If there was anything worse than him taking the life magic —

"But you still have the heart?" he asked.

I nodded. I touched my pocket, just in case, but I didn't need to feel the shards of alabaster to know I had it with me. The whispers of that magic made itself known in the back of my head every second I carried it, growing increasingly unstable.

"I think they were —" A pause for a long, laborious breath. "I think they were created here, Tisaanah. The Lejaras."

My brow knotted. "Why?"

"Ilyzath said something — something about its missing pieces —"

The word snagged on a gargled cough, and my heart lurched at the sound.

I looked down at my palm. The glowing led us down the hallway — but even without it, I would have been able to feel which way to go. It was like Ilyzath was whispering to us. *This way, little butterfly. This way.*

The markings on the wall moved as we did, shifting eerily to orient themselves towards us. It was so silent that the drip of Max's blood onto the stone floor was deafening.

"Leave me," he murmured. "I'm slowing you down."

"No."

"You can do this."

"*No.* I am not leaving you."

We continued walking, each step labored. We made it down

one hall, and then another. It was now dimmer, the bone walls bathed in dull, rust-colored light that reminded me of the sky before a twilight storm. The markings grew more chaotic, no longer uniform in size but large and small jumbled together. All of them shuddered erratically, as if trembling in fear.

Hurry, Ilyzath whispered. *Hurry, hurry.*

But we couldn't hurry. Max could barely walk. I tracked the increasing labor of his breathing, the quickening pace of the drops of his blood to the floor. Soon, he slipped every few steps. I had gotten strong, but he was larger than me—the weight of him over my shoulders made my back ache.

"Do you need to stop?" I whispered, after a while.

"No." He could barely get the word out. "No, keep going."

One breath after another. One step after another. I seared this mantra into my heartbeat, just as I had once, a lifetime ago, dragging myself across plains and seas to a little island across the ocean that I was certain would save me.

My name is Tisaanah Vytezic.

I am a leader of a broken country and lover of an imperfect soul.

And I will not let him die here. Neither of us will die here.

"Keep talking to me," I demanded, when Max had been silent for too long. "There must be something you can complain about."

He laughed—a wheeze that chilled me to my bones. "Always."

The next step, I practically had to drag him.

"More," I pressed. "You have more to say. You *never* have *nothing* to say."

His breath was coming hard. I felt it against my cheek as his head bowed low, close to me.

"I love you, Tisaanah."

Oh gods. No. Not that. Don't say that.

"That isn't a complaint," I choked out.

"It was worth everything else," he said, barely louder than a whisper. "This time with you."

"Stop. Shut up."

Silence. I was now practically carrying him. I realized that his blood completely soaked my shirt.

Three more steps.

My eyes burned. We stopped walking. The floor seemed like it was tilting.

"I love you, too," I said, at last.

I could not look at him, or I would fall apart.

I drew in a deep breath, pushed away the pain of my aching back and bleeding wounds, and took another step.

"We are just going to keep walking," I said. "Alright?"

"Alright."

"Keep talking to me." Once the tears began, I could not stop them. "Keep talking to me, Max."

But the words never came.

CHAPTER ONE HUNDRED NINETEEN

TISAANAH

The floors had been flat. There had been no stairs. Yet, somehow, we had been traveling down. When we reached the end of the hallway, I knew without doubt that we were underground. It was so dark that the light only came from below, seeping up between the cracks in the floor.

Before us was an arched door—the end of the hallway.

Max's feet slipped, his legs giving out. I was too weak to catch us. We fell to the ground in a pile several feet before the door.

Max was barely conscious. I helped him lean back against the wall, and he had almost no strength to help me. Then I forced myself to my hands and knees, and crawled towards the door. My palm touched something wet, and I looked down to see that shallow, black water lapped up the hallway, slowly encroaching upon us.

I peered through the door.

Stairs led down curved walls into a deep room. The floor was covered in water, black and rippling calmly in a slow, impossible current. At its center was a sapling upon a perfectly circular mound of earth. Black leaves that pulsed with a faint white light sprouted from its young, fragile branches. Something was floating up to those branches from the ground, glowing as if coated in moonlight—more leaves, I realized, after a moment. Dead leaves, rising from the ocean and reattaching themselves to the branches. Withering, falling, rising, blooming, in a surreal, endless cycle.

I never knew death could be so beautiful. And this thing was, indeed, pure death. Even as my magic was drawn to it, every part of my body recoiled from it. The shards of the heart in my pocket hummed their strange, broken song, as if awakened by the presence of their siblings.

Siblings, plural—because the third Lejara was here, too.

There, standing beneath the shade of that tree, was the Fey king. His palm was pressed to the trunk, his head bowed against it as if in prayer. If he saw or heard us, he did not react at all.

I jerked away from the door, heart pounding. I was shaking.

It is so close.

Ilyzath's whisper shuddered through me, deeper than sound, and yet farther away.

The end is so close, little butterfly.

The end of what? The end of the violence, or the end of the world?

Goosebumps rose on my skin with Ilyzath's wordless, gruesome laugh.

Both.

"Help me," I choked out. It was the only thing I could think to do. "Help me understand what I need to do."

The stone creaked and groaned, as if straining under a million years of weight. The markings that surrounded Max's lolling head swirled around him gracelessly. *He has found his missing pieces. I must reclaim mine, to seal away such forces too powerful for mere mortal hands. The wounds must be healed, or else, they will devour you all.*

Just as Vardir had said. "By Wielding all three. Life, death, change."

A shiver of agreement, slowly fading.

"Then—then how? How do I do it?"

But Ilyzath had gone silent once more.

Max's eyelids fluttered, and he let out a groan. Despite my best attempts at packing his wound, the blood still soaked through the fabric and now drip, drip, dripped into the water.

Even that sound felt like death mocking us.

I tilted Max's face towards me and kissed him. He barely even had the strength or awareness to kiss me back—let alone to understand that I was kissing him goodbye.

Then I stood and unsheathed Il'Sahaj. My entire body protested. I was wounded badly, too, and carrying Max's weight this entire time had done little to help my own injuries. But wounded or not, I had no choice but to make my move. Maybe the Fey king would kill me. If he didn't, the magic that I had to wield almost certainly would.

I turned to the door, laying my fingers over the shards of the heart in my pocket. I took a deep breath—

—and hesitated, as goosebumps rose on the back of my neck, as if I was being watched by a familiar presence.

An overwhelming force struck me, sending me careening into the wall. Pain exploded through my abdomen as my wounds ripped open with the force of it.

I knew who I would see even before I opened my eyes. When you have shared a body with someone, you know them by presence alone.

"Aefe," I rasped.

She stood before me with her hands clenched into fists. Red and violet blood covered her. Vines grew and died around her feet in rapid succession, climbing up her limbs in frantic bursts before withering into blackened husks and falling away, over and over again.

"You cannot hurt him," she said, panicked and out of breath. "Do not touch him."

She raised her blade, and I cringed, certain, in that moment, she would kill me.

And yet, she hesitated. When she struck, it was not at my

body but my sword, sending it sliding down the hall. I took those precious seconds to drag myself to Max—positioning myself in front of him, even though I knew I wouldn't be able to protect him. I was barely conscious, myself.

Aefe didn't move for us. She only stood there amidst her churning magic, her shoulders heaving, staring—as if she was trying to understand something about us, and failing. Gods, she seemed so different now than when I last saw her. She had an almost childlike face. Huge, sad eyes. They looked even sadder now.

She peered through the door, and when she saw the king standing there, she went very still.

"What is that?" Her voice was so, so small.

I answered the only way I knew how. "Death."

"I do not—It does not feel—"

Her breathing was rapid. She pressed her hand to her chest, squeezed her eyes shut, then looked to me abruptly.

"It would kill you. Why would you go down there?"

Funny. She was confused about that as Reshaye, too, the day she gave her life for mine.

I clutched my abdomen. *Drip*drip *drip*drip *drip*drip. Now my blood and Max's both drained to the water, tinting the black around us red.

"Because if he does this, it will end so much more, Aefe," I said, softly. "It will end everything."

She turned to the door again. She looked so torn—like she wanted to run there, but something was holding her back. Every expression on her face was so loud, every emotion so vivid. She turned sharply back to me.

"I do not understand," she choked out. "I have never understood."

I didn't know why I did this. Perhaps it was just because there was nothing else I could do. But I reached out my mind towards hers, opened myself to her emotions and thoughts.

I had to brace myself against the force of them. Gods, it was—it was just so *much*. An explosion of hurt and betrayal, five hundred years of it. The rage at everyone who had damaged her. The bitter agony of grief. The terror of power-lessness.

I dug deeper. And there, at the core of it all, was something I did not expect to ever find in Reshaye's heart—love.

She had experienced so much pain. But this love was the greatest torment of all.

My brow furrowed. "You want to save him."

"Do not tell me what I want," she hissed.

"Why aren't you going to him?"

"I—"

The plants around her feet lived and died faster, crumbling before they even had the chance to reach for her flesh.

She did not speak. Yet I felt her reply in my magic, too loud to remain within the boundaries of her mind.

She did not go because she was afraid. She was afraid of the truth.

"Because you know you can't," I whispered. "You know you can't save him."

The blade moved so fast I didn't see it coming until pain bloomed over my cheek. The black knife was buried in the stone right beside my eye, Aefe's face so close to mine that our noses brushed.

"Yes, I can," she said. "Who are you to tell me what I cannot do?"

"Someone who knows you. Someone who knows loss."

"You know *nothing* about me."

Her emotions still rolled over me, complex and layered and yet... and yet so innocent, so simple. Gods, how had I not under-stood her more when she was a part of me? She was just... lost. A poor, lost heart like I had once been, ripped from world after world, belonging to nothing and everything, desperate for connection.

"This is not love, Aefe. Love is selfless. If he does this, he will be doing the same thing that they did to you. Perhaps his inten-tions started well. They always do. But he will destroy everything. The world is cruel, but it does not deserve that. Not mine, and not yours."

"Yes it does," she snarled. "Maybe letting all of it die is the only justice."

But I saw beneath that rage. I knew that she did not believe it.

"What good is justice, if there is nobody left to witness it?"

Her eyes flicked past me, to Max. Anger, then grief, then regret rippled in her emotions. I knew she was thinking of another version of herself—another version that destroyed needlessly out of twisted, misplaced anguish, and left five innocent children dead.

The world hurt her. She hurt the world. The cycle went on, and on, and on.

"I see you, Aefe." My words slowed. My consciousness was fading. "You can do more than destroy. You can be more than death."

This would be either the best or the worst decision I would ever make. I reached into my pocket and closed my fingers around those shards of alabaster.

Change.

People could change.

I pressed them into Aefe's hands.

"End it," I rasped. "Fix what has been broken. Make something more."

Those enormous violet eyes flicked to me, first wide with confusion, then bright with anger. She snatched the shards from me and stood abruptly.

"Stupid child," she hissed. "You have always been an innocent fool."

She let me slump to the ground. Max was no longer moving. And no matter how desperately I tried, I could not crawl after her as Aefe turned away, joining her king beneath the canopy of death itself.

CHAPTER ONE HUNDRED TWENTY

AEFE

S he was wrong. She was wrong about everything. She was
wrong that I could not save him.

She was wrong.

I held the shards so tight that blood pooled in my palm.

Caduan looked up at me as I approached him. In one hand
was the glowing amber of creation. In the other was the withering branch of death. With every step I took towards this magic,
my body recoiled. My eyes stung at the sight of him. The darkness had progressed so rapidly, black lines now extending up his
throat, over his chin, at the corners of his eyes and mouth.

Tisaanah's words echoed in the back of my mind. *You cannot
save him.*

She is wrong, I told myself.

"You should leave," Caduan said. His eyes were strange —
bright like fire, and yet so far away. "I don't want you here."

You can not lie to me.

I reached for him, and he jerked away.

"Let me help you," I said.

"You can't."

I can. I must.

"You do not have to go," I said, voice cracking. "We have all three, now. We can do anything. We can *save* you."

His expression changed. For the briefest moment, he looked like—like himself. "Save—?"

I showed him the shards.

But the broken Lejara was too unstable, too volatile. The moment I opened my fingers, I lost control of it. The power aligned with that of its siblings—creation, change, death, falling into step with each other. The river swept us away in a powerful rush.

I reached out and grabbed Caduan's wrists, where the three Lejaras now hovered between us, only to gasp and resist the urge to yank my hands away.

I could feel how far he had drifted—could feel how much pain he was in, as the magic ate him alive.

We fell deeper, deeper, into the darkest levels of magic.

I knew this place. As Reshaye, I'd been nothing but a ghost here, trapped between worlds. I expected to see a star-scattered black above us. But instead, it was a grotesque cacophony of colors, red and violet bleeding over the sky like infected wounds.

No. This… this was wrong. It was not supposed to look like this.

He will destroy everything, she had said.

Caduan's hand cradled my cheek.

"I want justice," he ground out. "I want justice for you, for Meajqa, for Niraja, for my house, for your sister. I want it to be made right. I want to die knowing that it will never happen again."

He wanted it so badly that he did not see what else was breaking—he did not understand that he was sacrificing more than himself.

Again, Tisaanah's voice:

What good is justice, if there is nobody left to witness it?

She is wrong, I told myself.

But already, my lies had begun to chip and crumble. All those terrible things Caduan spoke of would happen again.

They were happening right now, in this moment.

I put my hands on his face, looked into those eyes that had once been the only thing in this entire wretched existence that felt *real*. Now, they were clouded with his grief and anger.

Caduan so wanted revenge. It was his final hope. Yet, I thought of the way I had felt when Ishqa's body fell from Ela'-Dar's castle. Empty.

All this time, I felt that death circled me like a lost lover. I had longed for it, loved it, lusted after it. Now my lover had become death, and all I craved was life.

You will find another thing to burn, Nura's voice echoed. *It's all you know how to do.*

She is wrong, I decided.

"This is too much." My voice was a broken sob. "This is not what you wanted. Look at what this power is doing. Look at everything it is destroying."

I forced him to see what was happening around us—how the magic he wielded threatened to rip the foundations of our world apart. I forced him to see what he had refused to let himself believe. We looked up, at the tears shredding the boundaries between magics, wide enough to devour the world. A million years spread out before us, time reduced to streaks across the sky. We watched Ela'Dar crumble, and the eternity beyond it fall into dust.

Emotions shuddered across his face in waves, settling on stubborn resolve.

"No. No, I can do this still. I can control it."

"You cannot lie to me, Caduan," I murmured.

For a moment, he looked angry, and I thought he might resist —but then that fury melted away, leaving only regret in its wake.

"It's too late," he rasped.

"You taught me that nothing is impossible," I said. "It is never too late."

"I can't—" His eyes were pained. His knuckles stroked my cheek. "If we shut this magic away, it will take with it…"

Me.

I knew it, even if he could not bring himself to say it. I was brought back to this world by this magic, and when it was gone, I would be too.

A streak of silver rolled down his cheek. "I cannot save you, Aefe."

And that, I realized, was the cruelest truth of all. He could not save me. I could not save him.

"Together," I choked out. "We go together."

"Your story deserved a better end."

I kissed him, and it was there, on the precipice of life and death, I felt the final shift in his resolve.

"Nothing ever truly ends," I whispered.

We looked at the power between us—the means to create, to destroy, to alter, so powerful that no mortal ever should have wielded them. How many wars were fought over this? How many lives lost?

They were the only thing strong enough to heal the tears that they had opened. The only weapon that could be used against itself.

Caduan took my hands. Together, we stitched the world's wounds closed. Together, we gave the life we were about to leave behind one more chance.

CHAPTER ONE HUNDRED TWENTY-ONE

TISAANAH

I felt it all fall apart. I looked up and saw the sky in shreds of light above me.

I had made a horrible mistake. I had failed, and I had handed Aefe—Reshaye—everything she needed to end the world.

I slipped from consciousness with this final thought, draped over Max's unmoving body.

But then—

The stirring in the layers of magic beneath me kept the darkness from taking me fully. A strange magic reached for me—like a healing, beckoning hand, gently shaking me awake. There was no sight here, no sound, no voices, but I knew it was Aefe.

I felt her magic struggling to contain it—struggling to hold everything together.

I could have wept with relief.

"Max," I breathed.

I could barely feel my own body. I shook him. His breaths were weak and shallow.

"Help me," I whispered in his ear. "We're almost done. It's almost over."

Gods, I prayed it would be true.

Faintly, he squeezed my hand.

I opened my palm, and then his, and then I pressed our hands together. I reached into the mind I knew so well, deep into his magic.

Together, we let ourselves fall, fall, fall, to the furthest layers of this power. I offered Aefe everything we had. One final push, to reshape the world, from all three types of magic—Valtain, Solarie, Fey.

The last thing I thought:

This is either how the world ends, or how it begins.

CHAPTER ONE HUNDRED TWENTY-TWO

AEFE

D*eath is a door.*

In the darkness, I watch Caduan's silhouette stand at its threshold. I cannot see what lies beyond it, but I know that there is something there.

As I hover on the edge of nothing and everything, terror clenches me. I think of honey, and music, and the way a million other souls felt connected to me in a home I knew once, long ago.

Caduan turns.

"Are you afraid?" he asks me.

At first I want to tell him that I am. But then I think of the night I asked him if he feared death. I fear only what it may take from me, *he told me.*

I realize that there is nothing that death can take from me, now. The only thing I need is here.

I have left my mark upon the world.

I have written a new story.

And I have him.

Love is worth creating for. Worth dying for.

"No," I answer.

675

Together we turn to the door. Together we will cross it. Together we will conquer the next unknown.

His hand reaches out for me. His lips curl into a sad smile.

"Come home, Aefe," he murmurs.

I love how he says my name.

I take his hand.

CHAPTER ONE HUNDRED TWENTY-THREE

TISAANAH

I was lying in a field of gold, looking up at a star-scattered sky.

I smelled oranges. I smelled dry, salty air, clean and crisp.

My home. I knew it immediately. My home as I had known it when I was young.

"It's time to get up, my love."

There was no question in my mother's voice. It was clear and strong. I didn't move for a long moment, just relishing it. Then I stood and turned to her.

I choked back a sob.

The vividness of her face struck me speechless. Her features were strong and solid, no blurring, no shifting. The memory of her locked into place immediately, reclaiming what time had begun to steal from me.

How had I ever questioned what she looked like? She looked like *me*.

It had never been my mother's way to fuss. Her affection was quiet and firm, the grip of a guiding hand rather than a doting caress. But she lifted her chin and surveyed me, a ghost of a smile rolling across her lips, and I felt that smile stronger than any tearful embrace.

"You grew up beautiful, my love."

I wanted to tell her so much. I wanted to tell her about the Orders, and Reshaye, and Ara. I wanted to tell her about the Alliance and how we had toppled the Threllian empire — *toppled it for her*, I wanted to say, *it was all for you*. I wanted to tell her about Max.

Instead I found myself saying, "I'm sorry I left you."

She gave me a stern stare. "No you are not, nor should you be. You survived."

But I left her. I left her behind to such a terrible death.

She stepped closer, and when she closed the distance between us the scent of her surrounded me — citrus and warmth, like an embrace of childhood safety, when my mother was unbreakable protection.

"You should be going," she said. "You have a new world to see. I only…" Her fingertips brushed my cheeks, and for the first time, a hint of that sentimentality seeped into her expression. "I only wanted to see you."

"No." The word welled up in me before I could stop it. I didn't want to leave her. Not for a second time.

She gave me another stern look. Just as she had that awful night, she flicked my tears away before they could fall.

"None of that," she said. "You have survived, my daughter. Now live."

She was already fading.

"Wait," I called out, frantic. "Wait. Will I see you again?"

She smiled. "One day. A very, very long time from now."

And she gave me one final kiss — the sister to the one she gave me that night, right between my eyebrows.

It burned long after she was gone.

I DIDN'T KNOW how we got through those hallways. When I opened my eyes next, Max and I were on the outer platform of Ilyzath, collapsed on ivory stone that overlooked the sea. The floor beneath us no longer shuddered with unnatural life or ancient magic. Now it was still and quiet. Just one more skeleton left behind.

I felt a hand on mine, and I turned to see Max pushing himself to his elbows, face tilted to Ara's distant silhouette. It was dark, calm. Empty ships, ships that had once held legions of undead soldiers, now floated in desolate silence.

Max turned my palm upright. The gold was gone, as was the mark on his hand. Even my magic felt different, like the most volatile parts of it had been closed away.

He let out a jagged sigh of relief. His eyes met mine, and I realized with a start that they had changed — no longer membranous blue, but the dark brown he was born with.

"It can't be," he rasped. "After all that, it can't be."

It's over.

The words hovered between us, unspoken. I didn't know how to believe them either. But at the same time, we looked to the sky, softly tinted pink. There were no cracks, no smoke. No terrible magic. Clear, save for a smattering of lingering stars and the imminent promise of sunrise.

Max's hand wrapped around mine, squeezed so hard our fingers trembled. I tried to speak but only let out a choked sob, which Max covered with a messy, desperate kiss. He tasted like a second chance.

We stayed like that, drowning in our elation, as the sun at last crested the horizon — bringing an end to a long, dark night.

Bringing dawn.

CHAPTER ONE HUNDRED TWENTY-FOUR

TISAANAH

1 WEEK LATER

Meajqa Sai'Ess looked very much like his father.

I had seen him before, in passing, but never as close as this. He, Max, and I sat in the Palace drawing room for hours. The topic was, of course, the only one anyone was talking about this week:

What now?

That was a complicated question.

When we had sealed away the deep magic, everything created by it had simply… disappeared. Nura's entire army of death, gone. From what Max and I pieced together from Moth and Sammerin's accounts, that seemed to be enough to leave both the Arans and the Fey confused enough to re-evaluate what was happening. Meajqa and Luia, the two highest-ranking Fey leaders in the absence of Caduan, called back their troops into a tentative cease-fire when they realized that their king was missing.

Caduan's body was found in Ilyzath—a place that now, as far as anyone could tell, was nothing but a stone building. The basement, where there had once been a strange sapling and a fragment of the sea, was empty, save for his body. Black veins spiderwebbed his entire body, including his face, though his eyes were closed as if he had simply drifted off to sleep. His hand was outstretched, as if he had been holding something, or someone.

Aefe was never found. Her body was gone.

I knew she had died. I felt that. It was the last whisper from a magic that had since disappeared. Max and I still had our natural Solarie and Valtain magics, respectively, but no longer had access to the strange, deep magic Reshaye had gifted us.

It stood to reason that Aefe's body had disappeared, just as Nura's corpse soldiers had. She, too, was a product of a magic that simply ceased to exist—and so, she ceased as well.

Whenever I thought about it, I couldn't shake a pang of sorrow for reasons I couldn't articulate. Perhaps because I knew what it felt like to be a ghost that left no mark on the world, even in death. And yet… she had left a mark, hadn't she? She had made the hardest, bravest decision, and we all lived because of it.

For several tense days, the Arans and the Fey waited in tense anticipation. Everyone was afraid to even blink. Would the Fey think that we had murdered their king? Would they accept our offer of peace talks?

Finally, days later, Meajqa emerged as the de-facto leader of the Fey and agreed to a discussion.

He looked so different now than he had the first time we saw him—locked up in the basement of the Towers in Nura's laboratory, looking as if he was on the edge of death. When he sat down across the table from us, and I got a good look at the horrific injury that had been inflicted upon his wing, I thought, *Oh, no. We are going to walk out of this room at war all over again. He will never forgive us.*

But, it turned out, I was not giving Meajqa enough credit. He was wary, yes, and distrustful of everything that we said. But he wanted peace.

He made that clear from the moment he sat down in this

room with us. "I think," he said, his accent like a rolling purr, "we have all lost too much already."

Max and I wholeheartedly agreed.

Still, we talked in circles for several hours. What could we offer the Fey to show them that we meant no further harm? What could they offer us to assure us that they were not a threat? It was layers upon layers of double talk and doubt, until finally, I leaned forward and met Meajqa's eyes directly. I allowed my magic to reach out to him—to taste, however briefly, his emotions.

Exhaustion. Grief. Uncertainty. Just the faintest hint of anger.

But there was hope there, too. Hope that he might be able to lead his people out of this.

I knew every one of emotions all too well.

"I am going to be blunt, Meajqa," I said. "I think that all of us want the same thing. But in order to get it, we will all need to learn to trust each other."

The corner of Meajqa's mouth twitched, and he lifted his chin slightly. "Ah, trust. So simple and yet so complex."

The resemblance to his father in that moment was breathtaking. Max and I exchanged a glance, both struck by the same thing.

"You know..." This was a risk. "I knew your father well."

Pain flickered across Meajqa's face, consuming that smirk.

"He was a good person," I said, softly. "I'm in debt to him. And he spoke very highly of you."

I couldn't quite read his expression—perhaps hiding a shard of anger, like he thought I was lying to him.

"I see why now," I said, "having met you myself. The fact that you are even discussing peace with us, after what you went through... that is courage."

He made a sound that was almost a scoff. "I am surprised, myself."

He rubbed his eyes—he was clearly tired. We all were. It had been a long, long week.

Max stood and went to the corner of the room. He returned with a carafe of wine and glasses.

"Do Fey drink?" he said to Meajqa.

For the first time, Meajqa smiled—a sharp, rueful thing. "Oh, we drink."

"Wonderful." He poured three glasses and then distributed them to us. He raised his. "To surviving the week from hell."

I took a sip. Max took a gulp. Meajqa drained half the glass.

Max set down his wine and leveled a steady stare at Meajqa. "Look. I like you, actually. I think you seem like you're trying to do the right thing, and that counts for a lot, from my perspective. We've already told you that we can't speak for all of our people. Tisaanah needs to talk to the rest of the leadership of the Threllian alliance. I don't intend to keep this crown very long, so I need to talk to the rest of Ara's leadership, too. I won't lie and pretend that the two of us have more pull than we do. But, here's what I can say to you. We are fucking tired of war. I am, Tisaanah is, Ara's council is, and this entire Ascended-damned world is. I think you are, too. Is that right?"

Meajqa's eyebrow twitched, and he took another sip of wine with an expression that offered tacit agreement.

"I don't blame you for not trusting us," Max went on. "Not for a second. If I were you, I wouldn't trust us either. Actually, as it stands, I'm not entirely sure that I trust you at all. But… after being surrounded by so much death, I'm willing to take a leap of faith. Are you?"

I reached across the table and offered him my hand. "We are willing to help create that trust with you, Meajqa Sai'Ess. Brick by brick. Day by day. There is nothing I can offer that will change things overnight. There is nothing I can say that will erase what you have already endured. But if you're willing to work with us, we would be honored to build it alongside you."

Meajqa regarded my hand stonily. He took another sip of wine.

"What is the Aran word for this? Hm… *naive*."

But then a slow smile curled his lips.

"We will try it anyway," he said, and took my hand.

———————

THE NEGOTIATIONS WENT SO MUCH SMOOTHER after that. We hammered out a few measures that helped the Fey tentatively accept our good faith, and a few that would make it easier for our people to accept theirs. If everything was agreed among the Arans and the Alliance, then the Fey would be our allies—not close allies, of course, but there would, at least, be no more war.

I could work with that.

Max and I watched the Fey armada depart, leaving behind only a few diplomatic emissaries who remained to continue peace negotiations. Their ships were beautiful, with big, green sails that fluttered in the breeze. From the distance they looked like leaves skittering across the surface of a pond.

"You look terribly proud of yourself," Max said. I glanced over to see my husband watching me with a bemused smirk on his face, and my heart leapt a little.

It did every time I looked at him, this last week. I didn't know if he really realized exactly how close I came to losing him. It seemed like a miracle that he was with me at all.

He had scoffed when I had told him this, but I saw the way his stares lingered on me, too.

"I am proud of myself," I said.

"You can't take credit for all of that."

"The Alliance is seven countries. Ara is only one. Which one of us is more important? Me, clearly."

He rolled his eyes and heaved a long-suffering sigh. I scowled at him dramatically, and the two of us turned back to the hallway. We had, of course, a thousand things to do.

"I'm proud of you, too," Max said, at last, and when his hand brushed the small of my back, I leaned into that touch as if it was the most precious thing in the world.

———————

HOPE POKED through the doubt like flowers sprouting in rubble. Still, the restoration came very, very slowly. The capital city had been almost completely destroyed, especially near the coast. I was thankful that we had managed to evacuate as much of the city as we had, but still, so many were left without homes. Yes, we had managed to save our people, but victory was never free.

The days passed slowly but the weeks went fast. We cleared the remains. We mourned. We rebuilt. An endless cycle, repeated on big and small scales—hopefully, I prayed, for the last time.

A week after the Fey departed, Iya called an assembly of the Council of the Orders. The group gathered at the foot of the Tower ruins at sunrise, before the city had begun to wake. The worst of the debris had been cleared, but the Towers themselves were still merely shattered skeletons of what they once were.

"I called us here this morning to discuss an important topic." Iya motioned to the wreckage surrounding us. "We must decide what will be done to the Towers, and how we will approach rebuilding efforts."

"That's easy," Max said, without hesitation. "We won't."

Most of the councilors looked appalled at this idea. Iya, I noticed, looked significantly calmer.

"But—but the Orders need the Towers," one of the councilors said, somewhat helplessly.

"What Orders?" Max said, gesturing to the pile of rubble.

Two of the councilors' jaws were literally hanging open.

"*What Orders?*" Helena repeated, aghast.

"The Orders have been used to justify some truly reprehensible things. First of all, multiple coups." Max raised a finger. "War crimes." Another finger. "Torture." A third. "Inciting of *several* wars, and—"

"We understand, Maxantarius," a councilor mumbled, rubbing his temples.

"But you're—you're the Arch Commandant," another said, somewhat helplessly.

"For now. Until I can get rid of the title. And in my opinion, the best way to get rid of it would be to throw the entire sorry thing out in the trash."

I winced a little at his, as always, evocatively tactless choice of words.

He had floated this idea to me, several nights ago, as we lay tangled up in bed. Then, he'd been softer and more pensive— more uncertain. He'd been raised his entire life to see the Orders as the pinnacle of what he should aspire to be. It was not as easy as he was making it seem now to wipe all that away.

"But what could it possibly be after this?" he had said that night. "What good could come from it? Look at what it had become even before this. Look at what they did to you, for fuck's sake. And to the Fey Nura imprisoned. Even..."

"Even to you," I said, quietly.

He just shook his head, too angry to keep speaking.

He was right about that. I'd been thinking it too, though I didn't know how to voice it. As long as the Orders continued to exist, it would be difficult, if not impossible, to convince the Fey that we were not endorsing or repeating Nura's actions. Even the Alliance was skeptical—the Orders, under Nura's rule, had owned slaves, after all. The taint was everywhere.

Most of the Council saw our points, but still argued. It was no small thing to disband an institution so fundamental to their way of life.

"Once an organization sanctions that kind of torture," I said, at last, "how can we continue to support it?"

Even the staunchest advocates of the Orders fell silent at that.

Still... I understood the sadness on their faces. When the decision was made, I still found myself returning long after nightfall. What had once been Ara's most majestic landmark was now just a pile of silver, gold, and glass. I stepped through the ruins and picked up a book embossed with the sigil of the Orders —a sun and a moon intertwined. As a slave, I'd had a similar book. I had learned Aran between its pages, memorized in obsessive nightly readings.

I had so believed in the Orders, then.

"The end of an era."

I turned when I heard Iya's voice. He looked like a ghost in the moonlight, and his stare seemed to peer straight through me.

"It is the right thing," I said, quietly. "But it is still sad."

"I'm surprised you think so. You never got to see what the Orders once were."

"I imagined them." I held up the book and gave him a small smile. "When I was a slave, these Towers were my dream."

"I am sorry for that, child. What a disappointment."

Maybe. Maybe not. They failed me in so many ways. And yet, that dream brought me here, to this life.

"When I was a young man in a land very far from this one, I dreamed of the Orders, too," Iya said. "I came to Ara because of them. It was better back then, but even still... they were not what they were promised to be. When Araich and Rosira Shelane founded the Orders, they were explicitly intended to be independent of all nations, even though they stood on Aran soil. I believed in that promise when I came to this country. But I too found that Arans, even within the Orders, were not so welcoming to those who spoke with a different... flavor."

He gave me a small smile, and despite myself, I chuckled. Yes, I knew that well.

"It is honorable of your husband to willingly give up his power by disbanding the Orders," Iya said. "It's the right decision. But... even I cannot help mourning that promise."

He picked up a little piece of rubble. It was a piece of the mural that had adorned the bottom floor of the Towers—Araich and Rosira's hands touching where the Tower of Midnight met the Tower of Daybreak.

A knot formed in my stomach. I was speaking before I could stop myself.

"Maybe the promise does not have to die."

Iya's eyebrow raised. "How so?"

The seed of the idea came to me just seconds ago. But

seconds were all it took for my mind to race through the possibilities, the roots already embedding in my heart.

Despite myself, I started to smile.

"How hard do you think it would be, Councilor," I said, "to create something new? Something that did fulfill that promise?"

CHAPTER ONE HUNDRED TWENTY-FIVE

MAX

The weeks passed slowly, and yet still too damned fast, a haze of effort and exhaustion and confusion and... fragile, young dreams.

I had never minded throwing myself into work. It distracted me from the aches and pains that still plagued me, and distracted me from the worst of the emotions that lingered under the surface, complicated feelings that I knew I'd have to grapple with sooner or later. I wasn't alone in that, at least. I knew all of Ara was waiting for their moment to weep, but at least we would do it in the secure embrace of a better world. I was determined to make that true.

I was totally certain that disbanding the Orders was the right thing to do. But it introduced a mind-boggling number of logistical challenges, the most pressing of which was: *If there's no Orders, then there's no Arch Commandant, and if there's no Arch Commandant, who the hell is going to rule this country?*

This was a difficult question to answer. The simplest solution would be to revert back to Sesri's bloodline, but after Zeryth's war, most of her heirs had been killed, leaving us in the dangerous territory of having multiple second-cousins-twice-removed with some distant claim to the throne. Tisaanah was working with the Alliance to structure various potential forms of representative government, though they were still early in planning stages. Such a system seemed perfect for the Alliance—all the benefits of one unified nation, coupled with the independence of their original homelands—but I couldn't see it working well for Ara.

In between cleanup efforts, I spent days locked up in rooms with the council and crown advisors hashing this out over and over again, to no avail.

Finally, I was approached by a visitor—someone I never thought I would see again. Tare, Sesri's Valtain advisor, had seemingly disappeared after Zeryth's death. That is, until now, when he showed up at the Palace steps and requested to meet with me. I was so curious that I had to accept.

He was late to our meeting, and when he finally arrived, he entered the room so quietly that I didn't realize he was there until he was practically breathing down my throat.

"Ascended fucking above, Tare." I barely managed to catch the book I had almost dropped, then set it down on the table. "Announce yourself next time."

"People often say that to me."

"I'm not at all surprised by that."

He gave me a weak smile, and just stood there, silent.

"I always liked you," he said. "Back in those days, in the Orders. I never told you that."

"I... thank you."

Personally, I always thought Tare was a bit odd. I was reminded of that now, as he spent too long awkwardly wandering about the room, saying nothing.

At last, he sat down—right on the edge of the seat, as if he was ready to fly away if he had to.

"I want to tell you something important." He cleared his throat, and I realized that he was actually nervous. "Sesri was nothing like what they said she was. They were manipulating her —Zeryth and Nura." A wince shuddered over his face. "Through me. Because I allowed them to. But she... she was a child. A frightened child."

I nodded, slowly, swallowing a pang of guilt. Yes, many people had failed Ara's young queen. Zeryth and Nura had been manipulating her to bring themselves closer to the throne, and we'd all fallen into their trap.

I remembered the day that Sesri had ordered a man killed in the Capital square—the first day Tisaanah had seen the city. Afterwards, Tisaanah had said that she felt overwhelming fear from Sesri. Not malice. Not anger. Fear.

I had been all too willing to dismiss Sesri as a power-hungry brat then. All the while she was being used as a puppet, her worst fears exploited by the Orders to orchestrate her downfall.

"She was so young," Tare murmured. "Just a little girl. All she wanted was someone to trust. And she trusted me." A small, sad smile, as he touched his chest. "Only me. The world had hurt her, you see. She needed someone."

He was silent for an uncomfortably long moment, watching me.

"She deserved better," I said, at last, because I wasn't sure what else to say.

I wasn't expecting it at all when his response was, "I didn't kill her."

I questioned whether I'd heard him correctly. "You—what?"

"Zeryth told me to do it, but I couldn't. She was like... a sister. I had betrayed her. But I—I love her. And she is a good person, no matter what the Orders made her do. She had started resisting Zeryth's guidance. She wanted peace, while he was pushing her for war. That was why he wanted me to do it." His eyes were distant, as if he was lost in the memory. "I faked her death. Sent her out of the country instead."

I was dumbstruck. I never thought Tare was especially— well, especially anything. Apparently I had underestimated him.

"*How*?" I asked. "Zeryth wanted to see a body, didn't he?"

"Little blonde girls die all the time. Accidents damage bodies."

He said this strangely matter-of-factly.

"I thought for a long time about whether I wanted to tell you this," he continued. "I thought, maybe it's better for her, to live a simpler life than this. But... she always wanted to rule. She believed she could make this country better." A small, proud smile ghosted his face. "Even so young, she wanted that."

I had to sit down.

This was a lot to digest. But already, the gears were turning. I would have to see what Tisaanah thought. Sesri was, of course, too young to rule now—she never should have been handed the throne in the first place, though of course we knew now that that was very much intentional. But if we were to bring her home... if we were to reintroduce her slowly... if we were to raise a senate to support her, and balance her...

I blinked away the slew of thoughts, looking back at Tare.

"Did it occur to you," I said, "that if I was in any way inclined to steal a throne, I would be the single absolute worst person you could bring this information to?"

Tare smiled at me. "Yes," he said, and left it at that.

THE ROSETEETH COMPANY remained in the city long enough to help us clean up the wreckage. Several weeks later, they eventually departed. I asked every Roseteeth soldier I encountered about Brayan, but none of them knew where he was, only that he had sent them here.

A part of me was grateful. A part of me never wanted to see him again.

And another part of me did.

They departed early on a cold morning, their gold sails disappearing into pre-dawn mist on the horizon. Before the final ship left, a soldier I'd never seen before slipped a letter into my hands and walked away before I could say a word.

I couldn't bring myself to open it until later that night, Tisaanah beside me, the two of us reading it together.

Max -

I hear you won. Good.

I know there are some things I will never understand. But I will also never stop trying. How can I?

I am sorry for all the ways I failed you, and I am sorry for the way I will fail you now, when I write that I cannot see you again.

The house is yours. The title is yours. The paperwork is in order. Do something great.

I

Here there was a scribbled sentence, violently slashed with ink so many times that I couldn't even begin to make out what it had once said. Then:

You are still my brother.
One day, maybe.
Not now. I just can't.
Until then, live well.

Brayan.

I read this several times, my chest tight, unsure of exactly how to feel.

"It is the best he can offer you," Tisaanah murmured, after long minutes of silence. "It's him. Not you."

I knew this was true. Brayan was just not equipped to work through the complexities of what he had learned. And hell... could I blame him for that? Would it be any different, if I were in his place?

"When those soldiers showed up, a small part of me hoped— I thought—"

I tripped over my words—I didn't even know how to finish the sentence.

But Tisaanah took my hand, nodded as if it made perfect sense. "I know." She kissed my shoulder, then laid her head against it. "But we have a family here, too."

We have a family.

Such a simple statement, but it knocked me a little off kilter. It echoed in my head the next morning, when Sammerin, Moth, Tisaanah and I ate breakfast together before another long day of work. We were exhausted, injured, still recovering, but I looked around at these people who had learned to exist in such easy harmony with each other and I realized that she was right.

We have a family.

And I felt like such an idiot for not realizing it before.

Still, I couldn't bring myself to just throw away the letter. Later, as I went to put it away, I flipped it over and for the first time noticed the postmark stamped on the back:

Sarilla.

I looked down at that word for a long moment. Despite myself, I couldn't hold back a brief, bittersweet smile. Then I tucked the letter away and closed the drawer.

———————

THE FEY HAD GONE. The Roseteeth had gone. Only some troops from the Threllian Alliance remained. Slowly, the Capital began to creak back to life. People found ways to resume their lives.

Eventually, Sammerin told us in the morning that he was going to return to his practice. He had healed the wartime injuries. He'd treated the illnesses, the wounds, the broken bones. He'd paid his dues many times over, and he was ready to go home.

Moth would go with him and resume his apprenticeship, a long-overdue fulfillment of the promise Sammerin made him before we left for Threll.

Tisaanah gave him a warm smile and her hearty approval. But the congratulations I choked out were more stilted than I'd intended, and I found myself poking around my food. When it was time to say goodbye, I wished him luck getting his practice back up and running, clapped him on the shoulder, and left little more said.

Tisaanah gave me a strange look after that.

"What?" I said. "He's going two miles away. What should I do, give him a weepy goodbye?"

Tisaanah narrowed her eyes at me in an *I-see-you* look and left it at that.

She, annoyingly, was right.

I almost surprised myself when I found myself showing up at Sammerin's practice the next day. I was too busy to go anywhere, but I told myself I had five minutes to spare.

The building, thankfully, was far enough into the city that it had not been affected by the fighting, though the whole place had fallen into a bit of disrepair. The sign was peeling, the flower boxes overgrown. When I showed up, the door was open, puffs of dust flying into the street as Sammerin beat the living hell out of a cot mattress.

"It's too early to have that much energy," I said.

Sammerin's eyebrows lurched when he saw me. "You miss me already?"

"You left the Palace for this shit hole?"

"Be careful. I've seen how you've lived for the last ten years." He threw the mattress over the railing, then squinted up at the sky. "It is going to be a gorgeous day."

It was almost funny to see him looking so blatantly optimistic. Like at any moment, chirping birds would start following him around.

Sammerin truly loved his home. He loved Ara. He loved his practice. All he wanted was a disgustingly pleasant, uneventful life, fixing broken people and bedding beautiful women.

He seemed to remember I existed after a few seconds of enjoying the sun. "So? Did I forget something?"

I shrugged and slid my hands into my pockets. "I just wanted to escape for a minute."

"Hm," he said, in that tone that said he didn't believe me.

I shifted awkwardly.

"If you're going to confess your unrequited love for me, Max, just hurry up and do it."

"Fuck you."

"You're a married man. That would not be appropriate."

I barked a laugh.

Finally, at Sammerin's pointed silence, I let out a long breath. "I would not have survived without you, Sammerin," I said, at last. "I don't think I've ever actually told you that. Poor social graces, and everything."

He sighed and shook his head. "We don't have to do this."

"I'm not doing anything. I'm just…" I shrugged. "I'm just saying thank you. For everything."

A momentary softness passed over his face, before he waved me away.

"Stop using me as an excuse to avoid your considerable responsibilities," he said. "I have work to do."

"Fine, fine. Enjoy your… cot dust."

As I began to leave, he sat down on a garden chair, crossing his ankles over the seat of another.

I scoffed over my shoulder. "I thought you said you had work to do?"

"I do. In ten minutes. Or until however long it takes Moth to accidentally destroy something." He tilted his head back and closed his eyes. "We have to take what we can get."

I rolled my eyes, gave him a wave, and turned away. But halfway down the street I paused and glanced back, just for a moment. I watched my friend, lounging in the sun in front of the practice that he had dreamed about for so long, in utter contentment.

I smiled and continued walking.

Sometimes it's nice to see good people live a good life. And Sammerin, I knew—better than anyone else—deserved the very best of good things.

———————————

WILLA SEEMED annoyed to see me. She was aflutter in that way she often was, like she had too many things to do and didn't have the faintest idea where to start. The disbandment of the Orders had left her in an administrative nightmare.

"Is there something I can, ah, help you with, dear?" she asked me, giving me a slightly frazzled smile. Her hair was coming half-undone, her glasses crooked.

"Nothing in particular. I was just thinking…" I slumped into the chair across her desk, resting my heel on the corner of the mahogany wood. "You ran the education program of the Orders."

She blinked at me, mildly irritated. "You know that I did, Max."

"Right. And you had been doing that for… a long time?" I gave her a weak smile. "I was a bit out of touch for awhile there, as you know."

"Oh, well, I don't know. It must have been… well, nearly ten years. I took it up shortly after the Ryvenai War ended."

"So would you say you know a lot about the topic?"

Willa was now openly irritated. "I wouldn't go *so* far, but— well, yes. I know a lot about it. Is there a reason you're asking me this, Maxantarius? I really do have a lot to do."

I didn't know why I was nervous.

I hadn't been able to get the idea out of my head since Brayan's letter.

I now was technically Lord Farlione, a title I couldn't give less of a shit about. And the house—the house that had haunted my nightmares for so long—was now in my possession, taken out of the care of my miserable aunt.

Tisaanah and I, certainly, had no interest in living there. But it was a gorgeous house. A large estate. More space than anyone knew what to do with. Even as a child, my mother—who was no pauper herself—had thought the size of it was just excessive. "I don't know what your father's ancestors did to make them think they needed all of this *room*," she would sigh.

Do something great.

What could possibly be great, after all of this?

I had lost faith in so much over the years. The Orders, the

military, my brother, my father. Even the things that I loved, I had complicated feelings towards. So much of what I had taken as a given when I was younger had turned out to be flat out untrue.

I had joined the military because I had thought it was my only route to prominence. I wanted to learn how to be a powerful Wielder, and joining the military was what talented young men and women did when they wanted to fulfill their potential.

Now, I looked back on that path with disgust. How did we ever think that was normal? To teach people—teach *children*—that the only route to greatness was to learn how to kill?

Do something great, Brayan had written.

I swung my legs down and leaned across the table.

"If one wanted to open a school," I said, "how would one, theoretically, go about doing that?"

CHAPTER ONE HUNDRED TWENTY-SIX

TISAANAH

The time came, eventually, that I had been dreading. The final Alliance ships were leaving for Threll, and Serel, of course, would need to be on them.

We had spent a lot of time together over this last month. In the wake of the battle, we'd held each other in sheer euphoric delight that we had both managed to make it out alive. I'd treasured our time together in the days since—early morning teas before the work began, late night drinks of wine when the hard days were done.

I was a bit surprised when he stayed after the first wave of ships left, and then the second. I knew it was because of me, though I didn't want to question it. These were hard days, and I liked having my friend with me through them.

I knew, even though we left it unspoken, that he was giving me as much time as possible to make my own decisions. And I knew he would support me in whatever they turned out to be.

But I still felt like a traitor when I told him that I was going to stay in Ara.

"Only for now," I said. "Until we finish sorting all of this out. Sesri hasn't even arrived, and the senate hasn't finished being installed, and we haven't yet gotten the school ready, and the guild—"

Serel laughed and jokingly rubbed his temples. "Gods, Tisaanah, you're making my head hurt. I know, you are busy. I get the point." Then his smile softened. "I'm not surprised. I knew you were going to stay."

He meant this as a comfort, but instead it made guilt slide between my ribs.

"Nothing is more important to me than the Alliance," I said. "You know that. Don't you?"

"You *created* the Alliance. You have paid your debt to us, Tisaanah. There isn't a soul in the senate that would disagree." He smirked. "Though I suppose I'll have to let them know that you won't be accepting the Nyzrenese seat. They'll be gutted."

The truth was, even if Max and I had decided to return to Threll, I wouldn't have accepted the Nyzrenese leadership seat. I understood, now, how Max had felt when he took the crown of Ara, even knowing it would be temporary. Their admiration for me was built on so many legends. But I couldn't rule them as a figurehead—and I didn't want to speak for only Nyzerene, a country that I barely remembered.

No, I didn't want to work in service to a country. I wanted to work in service to the entire world.

The things that Max and I talked about in the few spare moments we had during the day, though—the school, the guild that I was building with Iya...

These were things that set my soul on fire. The potential seemed limitless.

Still, now I looked into Serel's blue eyes and doubt clenched in my chest.

"You can stay here," I blurted out. "With us. Everyone here loves you. You could build a life here."

He could have laughed at me, and I wouldn't have blamed him. It was an absurd proposition. This was not his home. He was key to the day-to-day leadership of the Alliance, and he was breathtakingly good at it. It was selfish on every level for me to ask him to stay.

But he didn't laugh. Instead he put his hand behind my neck and leaned his forehead against mine.

"Your heart is a part of my heart," he said. "Even with an ocean between us."

My eyes stung so much that I didn't even trust myself to say anything more after that. I barely spoke as I helped him load his meager belongings onto the ship. I stood on the docks as the boat pulled away, his shock of golden hair a beacon beneath the midday sun.

It had all been because of him. Every moment in this life, every freedom we earned, every happiness that I found. It was all because of him and that single sacrifice that he made for me.

At the last moment, I ran to the end of the dock—so fast I nearly sent myself toppling over the edge.

"I love you!" I shouted.

I would wonder if he heard me, or if my words were lost in the wind and the lapping of the sea. I would wonder countless times if my friend—my *brother*—knew everything that he meant to me.

A heartbeat, and then two.

And then I saw that distant figure bring his hands cupped to his face. And so faintly I could barely hear it, there was the returning echo:

I love you.

———

HOME.

We were so busy for so long that the word couldn't even cross our minds. But soon, Max and I were the only ones who remained at the Palace. And soon, with the senate established, with Sesri on her way back, with the clean-up complete and the Fey peace treaties signed, the word began to slip over our tongues again.

Home.

It smelled like him—like ashes and lilac. The cottage was now little more than a pile of rock and ash, barely recognizable as something that had once been a house. But I had learned long ago that it was not the stone that made something a home. Whatever made this one ours still remained, even if the building was gone.

The garden had flourished, even in Max's absence. The flowers reclaimed every inch of the earth, covering the walkways and even winding over the burnt beams and fallen stone.

I assumed Max would be appalled, but I thought it was beautiful.

"No," Max said, when I told him so. "I think it's beautiful, too."

We walked the boundaries of the grounds, hand in hand. There was the stoop where I had sat outside and refused to leave that first night. There was the clearing where he had taught me how to use Stratagrams. There was the path to the river where we swam together on warm days.

Max paused at what had once been the entrance of the cottage.

"It's not *that* bad," he said, after a long moment.

It was indeed that bad.

"I don't see a wreck. I see…" I spread my arms out. "Opportunity."

Max wound his arms around my waist, and my outstretched hands fell to his shoulders. His eyes, despite their darker hue, sparkled.

"I like your new eyes," I said. "Have I told you that?"

"They're my old eyes, actually."

"I like them anyway."

He smiled, and I wondered if it would ever stop being the most magnificent sight I had ever seen.

"I will still address you by the same title, mysterious snake man."

He snorted. "It no longer fits."

"It will always fit."

"If you say so, demanding rot goddess."

The words disappeared in his kiss. Slow, thorough, tender.

We would build a new house, I decided. A little bigger, though not by much. A huge garden. A sizable library. A warm fireplace.

I told Max this, between kisses, and he hummed his approval.

Then he stopped and pulled away, just enough to look into my face, his expression going suddenly pensive. I traced the lines between his features.

I love you did not say enough.

I love you did not say, *thank you for being my home.*

I love you did not say, *thank you for being my future.*

But all at once, I felt those things, so overwhelmingly that I couldn't speak. And the only thing I could think to choke out were those words, "I love you," even though there was so much they left unsaid.

He gave me a long stare, brow knitted, thumb thoughtfully tracing the curve of my lip.

"It's a strange feeling," he said, at last. "To look forward to so much."

It was. So odd, to minds so unpracticed in such things. But now it surrounded us, so bright it couldn't be ignored, and maybe, just maybe, we were healing enough to let it in.

It was hard not to, when Max swept me up in his arms again, when he kissed me and smiled against my mouth, when he laid me down in the garden where two broken souls had met and built a home in each other.

Hope.

EPILOGUE

It ends with two souls who create a future together.

MAX

The years go down easy. Tisaanah and I build a beautiful little house—bigger than a cottage, this time—in the center of a sprawling garden, and within it, we build a life.

At first, every day is long and arduous. We are so busy that we don't even know what to do with ourselves. Transitioning power to the senate and to Sesri is a long and terrifying process. Establishing the school takes longer than I ever would have anticipated—years, even, before we're able to accept our first batch of students. In parallel, Tisaanah throws herself into the work of establishing the guild. It's everything that she had wished the Orders had been, and she is brilliant at it. Our work perfectly complements each other.

We blink, and five years pass. Three classes of students fill the halls of my former family home. The west wing is the school.

The east wing becomes the Aran headquarters of the guild. I spend every day in that house, teaching. It takes a couple of years, but I no longer see bloodstains when I walk down the hall.

The Alliance thrives, and while the road to becoming an established nation is long and challenging, they're determined to succeed — even if, as Tisaanah often says half-jokingly, that determination is driven solely by spite for the Threllian Lords. We spend a lot of time there those first few years so Tisaanah can help weather the storms. It is important to her, too, to establish a strong guild presence in the Threllian continent. The guild, she emphasizes, is not an Aran organization — but a global one.

I love watching her work. I know that she has spent so much of her life feeling as if she was too much and not enough of everything. But I love that every time I look at her, I find something new, like light refracting through a thousand different shades of glass.

We blink, and another year passes. Our daughter is born. Our son comes two years later.

I've fought monsters and faced death and survived imprisonment, and yet, the single most terrifying moment of my life was the day I held my daughter for the first time. I had never loved so deeply nor feared so intensely. She has amber-green eyes, like the sun through the leaves. Every so often she looks at me and I remember a nightmare I had, a long time ago, and I need to count my breaths until the moment passes.

This, you see, is the thing they don't tell you about the happy endings.

And, make no mistake, our ending is very happy. But Tisaanah and I — the past has left its marks on us. The first few years, it was like my body didn't know how to react to peace. I walked around with my muscles perpetually tensed, as if, at any moment, something would jump from the shadows and rip my new life away from me. *Surely*, I had thought, *this feeling is going to pass eventually.*

But then one year goes by, and two, and five, and seven, and still, that lingering fear remains. Once I watched for swords and magic and Lightning Dust—now I watch for trees that are too tall and rocks that are too sharp and dinner knives left unattended. I am forever conscious of all the ways the world can take something precious away.

One day, I have an epiphany.

Tisaanah and I lie in bed with tiny limbs of sleeping children splayed out over us. It had been a long week, one particularly fraught with my anxieties. Tisaanah had barely dozed off, her lashes fluttering slightly. Our son had tucked himself in her arms and our daughter nestled into mine, snoring like a middle-aged farmer—and yet still utterly charming. It's an almost absurdly perfect moment—the kind of life I never thought I would have.

And there, in this perfect moment, I have a grand realization:

This is what it means to have something to lose.

This is what it means to have something to love.

And these days, I have so much to love.

Still, sometimes I lie awake at night, images that I can't shake painted on the darkness of the ceiling. Sometimes I'm so afraid of the *what-if*'s and the *could-be*'s and the shadows of my past that I can't breathe.

In these moments, Tisaanah slides closer to me. Her palm presses to my chest, right over my heart. And she murmurs in my ear, "We will all still be here in the morning."

And for some reason, just like I always have, just like I did that day when she showed up in my garden and told me the world could be better, I believe her.

I close my eyes.

TISAANAH

ONCE, many years ago, I told Max that I would build a better world.

And I have.

The years are so kind to us. Together, Max and I leave our

marks on the world—a country, a school, a guild, and, finally, our children.

Our daughter is so much like Max, even though she has my eyes and my mother's nose. Our son, even at three, is already so pensive and temperamental. He came into the world screaming, like he was already enraged by the injustice in life. *I know,* I wanted to tell him, the first time I held him. *I know it's bright and cold and too much, but we will protect you.*

We fulfill that promise. Max and I build them a home so stable, so secure, so full of love. My children will never know what it's like to run from their home in the middle of the night. They will never need to fight for their lives.

But one night, when our daughter is five years old, something changes. She recently learned how to braid, so I let her sit behind me and play with my hair as I get ready for bed. And in this mundane moment, she asks a question that makes my heart stop:

Mama, she asks, *why do you have these bumpy lines on your back?*

Max is walking in the doorway, having just put our son to sleep, and he too stops short. We look at each other in sheer panic, as if we both suddenly realize what we will eventually need to do.

I do not need to answer this question today, of course. She is so young, and very easily distracted. Instead I kiss her cheek and say, *Do you want to know a secret? Your father is very, very ticklish.*

And that will set off a chaotic game, one that will end with all of us exhausted with laughter on the floor, Max loudly declaring me a traitor and our daughter snoring long before her bedtime. But later that night, Max and I curl up in each other's arms, and I know we are both thinking about that moment.

We do not have to tell our children about our pasts today, or tomorrow, or the next day.

But one day, our past and our future will collide.

For some reason, this thought is terrifying to me. We have done so much to separate our children from the worst parts of our past. And yet, at the same time, everything we do is driven by it. We have taken the hardest parts of our lives and turned them into something great. Max comes alive every day teaching in the halls of the home that once haunted his nightmares, making a place of death a place of growth and learning—what is that, if not healing?

Maybe I built the guild for the version of myself who is thirteen years old, living in a tiny room in a grand house, dreaming of freedom. The guild is my third child—my first child, in some ways, as terrible as that might sound. We establish bases in every state of the Alliance, in Besrith, in the southern isles. One day, I even want to build one in the Fey lands.

Sometimes, though, I'm overwhelmed by all the work that is still left to do. Slavery may not exist in Threll anymore, but it still exists in countless other countries. And even where there isn't slavery, there is poverty, abuse, subjugation. With every new country I visit, I find it hiding in more places. I find more children in tiny rooms. I find more lost hearts.

I see myself in every one of those children. I look at my wonderful life and I wish I could reach through time and space to that little girl, who dreamed of a life just like this one.

But instead, I reach across mountains, I reach across deserts and seas and plains, I reach across the entire world to all those other children sitting in little rooms just like that one, and I whisper, *"Look. Look at all you can have."*

Is it enough? Never.

But maybe it is something, to change a world one life at a time. It is something.

IT IS EARLY. Max and I often rise before the sun for a few precious moments of solitude before the day begins. We have memorized everything about each other over the years. I know him better than I know myself—every rhythm of his body, every minuscule expression, every small kindness or sign of irritation. Every mundane way he tells me that he loves me.

Today it is by a cup of tea on the table outside before I tell him what I want, prepared as he knows I like it. We sip our tea together in silence as we watch the dawn rise over the garden. There really is nothing like the way the sun paints over the petals —a thousand different colors, and yet they all fit so perfectly together.

"That garden is a disaster," Max mutters. "I need to get it under control one of these days."

But I know Max better than I know myself. And I know that he secretly loves when the garden is this way, feral and over-grown and free, left to thrive by a man who has so many other things to do with his life than clip away dead petals.

I reach out and take his hand, and his fingers fit around mine like they were made for it. In this, he tells me he loves me, too.

Later, I will watch Max teach our children how to pull weeds and water roses. I'll pause my pen over my paper to marvel at the sheer overwhelming abundance of luck that needed to happen to bring us to this moment.

I do not believe in gods anymore. But maybe there's something like a miracle, here.

I think of my mother's words in a dream that felt very real.

You have survived, my daughter. Now live.

This memory crosses my mind just as Max looks up and smiles when he meets my eyes, as if on reflex, like he didn't even mean to, and I return it without thinking.

I put down my pen, and I live.

the end.

ASHEN SON: A 4-PART PREQUEL

GET IT FREE!

Maxantarius is a skilled magic Wielder and a military rising star. But in one terrible night, he has learned that glory is bloodier than he ever could have imagined.

War has broken out, thrusting his family into the center of a savage conflict. In its wake, Max is chosen to compete for the title of Arch Commandant.

The title is all he has ever wanted. But the competition is merciless, and victory will mean fighting against his love… all while he must navigate a war that threatens to destroy those he treasures most.

As allies and enemies alike draw blades at his back, Max learns that no victor walks away with clean hands.

It's only a matter of how far he's willing to go.

Sign up to my mailing list to get all four parts of Ashen Son for free! Part 1 is now available:

carissabroadbentbooks.com/ashenson

ACKNOWLEDGMENTS

It is such a mind-bogglingly surreal feeling to be writing this right now. It feels that way every time, but never more-so than this. This story and these characters have quite literally changed my life, and there are so many people I have to thank for that!

First of all, Nathan—no matter how many times I write these pages, your name will always come first on the list. Not a second goes by that I am not acutely aware of how fortunate I have to have you. Thank you for your love, your friendship, your support, your monster facts, your ad-libbed raps, your hugs and kisses, your endless encouragement, and, above all, for just being the all-around wonderful human that you are. Best husband ever. Seriously.

I have so many people to thank for helping me bring Tisaanah and Max and their world and story into being. Chief among them are my Writing on the Wall crew, who listened to me craft Daughter of No Worlds week by week and ever since have been so instrumental to the development of this series. Steve, Michael, Noah, Tom—I know we haven't had our in-person meetings for quite awhile at this point, but please know that I have always considered this series yours.

Noah, I owe you a truly massive thanks for the huge amount of work that you put into this book, and the ones that came before it too. Thank you for your incredible editing work, your advice, and your encouragement. I owe you! So many of the good things in this book—and series—exist because of you.

To my beta readers, Ariella, Deanna, Sophia, Gabi, Elizabeth, and, of course, my dad: Thank you, thank you, thank you.

. was instrumental to bringing this book through
., and I think it is infinitely better for it! Thank you
r bearing with me as I figured out how to formalize
.ss for the first time, and for the time and care you all
your reading and feedback.

chel, thank you for being an amazing ARC reader and for
eternal helpfulness and amazing eagle-eyes!

Thank you to Anthony for your fabulous proofreading skills
.d for generally being awesome to work with (and for all the
puppy pictures).

To my wonderful friend and writer-sister Clare Sager, thank
you so much for your friendship and for your endless guidance
and support throughout this crazy author journey. I don't know
what I did before we were friends! You are amazing.

Huge thank you to the lovely folks at the Pink Bean coffee
shop—my favorite writing haunt ever! I wrote almost all of this
monstrous book while sitting at the exact same high top table
40+ hours a week. Thank you for putting up with me and for
making the best coffee in the world.

Thank you to my fellow romantic fantasy authors—in particular, Miranda Honfleur and JM Butler, but also too many others
to list!—for your support, friendship, advice, and encouragement. I feel so lucky to be a part of such a wonderful community.

Thank you to my parents for your constant support and
encouragement, from age 0 to 29, without which I wouldn't be
here at all!

And at last, above all, thank you to *you*. I am only able to do
this because of you. Your readership, your reviews, your posts
on Instagram and TikTok and Twitter and GoodReads, your fan
art, your kind messages and comments—I built my career on
these things. And that's not an exaggeration! I quite literally owe
my career to your word-of-mouth readership. So, THANK
YOU. I hope you loved this journey just as much as I have.

And I hope you love the next one even more.

(Alright, *now* I'm crying a little. In a good way. I promise.)

ABOUT THE AUTHOR

Carissa Broadbent has been concerning teachers and parents with mercilessly grim tales since she was roughly nine years old. Since then, her stories have gotten (slightly) less depressing and (hopefully a lot?) more readable. Today, she writes fantasy novels with a heaping dose of badass ladies and a big pinch of romance. She lives with her husband, one very well behaved rabbit, one very poorly behaved rabbit, and one perpetually skeptical cat in Rhode Island.

instagram.com/carissabroadbentbooks
tiktok.com/carissabroadbent
facebook.com/carissabroadbentbooks
twitter.com/carissanasyra